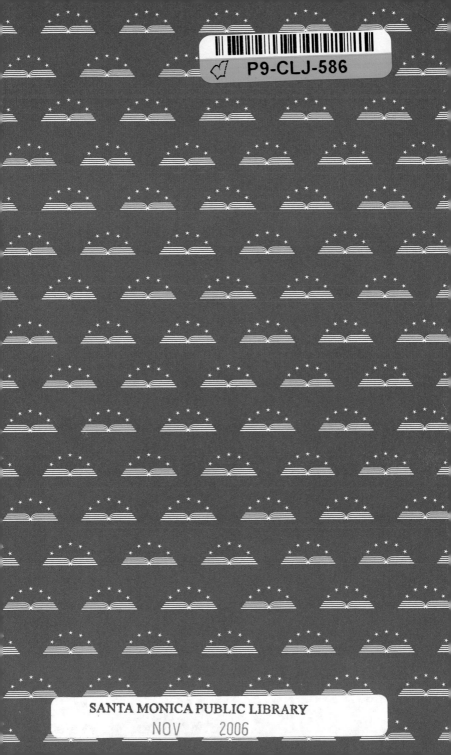

P9-CLJ-586

PHILIP ROTH

# Philip Roth

NOVELS 1973–1977

*The Great American Novel*
*My Life as a Man*
*The Professor of Desire*

THE LIBRARY OF AMERICA

*The Great American Novel* copyright © 1973 by Philip Roth. *The Professor of
Desire* copyright © 1977 by Philip Roth. Reprinted by arrangement with
Farrar, Straus & Giroux. *My Life as a Man* copyright © 1974. Published by
arrangement with the author c/o The Wylie Agency, Inc.

The paper used in this publication meets the
minimum requirements of the American National Standard for
Information Sciences—Permanence of Paper for Printed
Library Materials, ANSI Z39.48—1984.

Distributed to the trade in the United States
by Penguin Putnam Inc.
and in Canada by Penguin Books Canada Ltd.

Library of Congress Catalog Number: 2006041030
For cataloging information, see end of Notes.
ISBN 978–1–931082–96–9
ISBN 1–931082–96–0

First Printing
The Library of America—165

Manufactured in the United States of America

Ross Miller
wrote the Chronology and Notes
for this volume

# Contents

# THE GREAT
# AMERICAN NOVEL

*To Barbara Sproul*

. . . the Great American Novel is not extinct
like the Dodo, but mythical like the Hippogriff . . .

FRANK NORRIS, *The Responsibilities of the Novelist*

# ACKNOWLEDGMENTS

The baseball strategy credited to Isaac Ellis in chapters five, six, and seven is borrowed in large part from *Percentage Baseball* by Earnshaw Cook (M.I.T. Press, 1966).

The curve-ball formula in chapter five was devised by Igor Sikorsky and can be found in "The Hell It Doesn't Curve," by Joseph F. Drury, Sr. (see *Fireside Book of Baseball*, Simon and Schuster, 1956, pp. 98–101).

The tape-recorded recollections of professional baseball players that are deposited at the Library of the Hall of Fame in Cooperstown, New York, and are quoted in Lawrence Ritter's *The Glory of Their Times* (Macmillan, 1966) have been a source of inspiration to me while writing this book, and some of the most appealing locutions of these old-time players have been absorbed into the dialogue.

I also wish to thank Jack Redding, director of the Hall of Fame Library, and Peter Clark, curator of the Hall of Fame Museum, for their kindness to me during my visits to Cooperstown.

P. R.

# CONTENTS

# *Prologue*

CALL me Smitty. That's what everybody else called me—the ballplayers, the bankers, the bareback riders, the baritones, the bartenders, the bastards, the best-selling writers (excepting Hem, who dubbed me Frederico), the bicyclists, the big game hunters (Hem the exception again), the billiards champs, the bishops, the blacklisted (myself included), the black marketeers, the blonds, the bloodsuckers, the bluebloods, the bookies, the Bolsheviks (some of my best friends, Mr. Chairman—what of it!), the bombardiers, the bootblacks, the bootlicks, the bosses, the boxers, the Brahmins, the brass hats, the British (*Sir* Smitty as of '36), the broads, the broadcasters, the bronco-busters, the brunettes, the black bucks down in Barbados (*Meestah* Smitty), the Buddhist monks in Burma, one Bulkington, the bullfighters, the bullthrowers, the burlesque comics and the burlesque stars, the bushmen, the bums, and the butlers. And that's only the letter B, fans, only *one* of the Big Twenty-Six!

Why, I could write a whole book just on the types beginning with X who have called out in anguish to yours truly—make it an encyclopedia, given that mob you come across in one lifetime who like to tell you they are quits with the past. Smitty, I've got to talk to somebody. Smitty, I've got a story for you. Smitty, there is something you ought to know. Smitty, you've got to come right over. Smitty, you won't believe it but. Smitty, you don't know me but. Smitty, I'm doing something I'm ashamed of. Smitty, I'm doing something I'm proud of. Smitty, I'm not doing anything—what should I do, Smit? In transcontinental buses, lowdown bars, high-class brothels (for a change of scenery, let's move on to C), in cabarets, cabanas, cabins, cabooses, cabbage patches, cable cars, cabriolets (you can look it up), Cadillacs, cafés, caissons, calashes (under the moon, a' course), in Calcutta, California, at Calgary, not to be confused with Calvary (where in '38 a voice called "Smitty!"—and Smitty, no fool, kneeled), in campaniles, around campfires, in the Canal Zone, in candlelight (see B for blonds and brunettes), in catacombs, rounding the Cape of Good Hope, in captivity, in caravans, at card games, on cargo ships, in the Caribbean, on carousels, in Casablanca (the place *and* the movie, wherein, to amuse Bogey, I played a walk-on role), in the Casbah, in casinos, castaway off coasts, in castles (some in air, some not), in Catalonia (with Orwell), Catania, catatonia, in catastrophes, in catboats, in cathedrals, in the Catskills (knaidlach and kreplach with Jenny G.—I taste them yet!), in the Caucasus (Comrade Smitty—and proud of it, Mr. Chairman!), in caves, in cellars, in Central America, in Chad, in a chaise longue (see under B burlesque stars), in chalets, in chambers, in chancery, in a charnel house (a disembodied voice again), in Chattanooga (on Johnny's very choo-choo), in checkrooms, in Cherokee country, in Chicago—look, let's call it quits at Christendom, let's say *there*, that's been Smitty's beat! Father confessor, marital adviser, confidant, straight man, Solomon, stooge, psychiatrist, sucker, sage, go-between, medicine man, whipping boy, sob sister, debunker, legal counselor, loan service, all-night eardrum, and sober friend—you name it, pick a guise, any guise, starting with each and every one of the Big Twenty-Six, and rest assured, Smitty's worn that hat on one or two thousand nights in his four score and seven on this billion-year-old planet in this trillion-year-old solar system in this zillion-year-old galaxy that we have the audacity to call "ours"!

O what a race we are, fans! What a radiant, raffish, raggedy, rakish, rambunctious, rampaging, ranting, rapacious, rare, rash, raucous, raunchy, ravaged, ravenous, realistic, reasonable, rebellious, receptive, reckless, redeemable, refined, reflective, refreshing, regal, regimented, regrettable, relentless, reliable, religious, remarkable, remiss, remorseful, repellent, repentant, repetitious (!!!!), reprehensible, repressed, reproductive, reptilian, repugnant, repulsive, reputable, resentful, reserved, resigned, resilient, resistant, resistible, resourceful, respectable, restless, resplendent, responsible, responsive, restrained, retarded, revengeful, reverential, revolting, rhapsodical, rhythmical, ribald, rickety, ridiculous, righteous, rigorous, riotous, risible, ritualistic, robustious (*adj. Archaic or Humorous* [pick 'em], meaning "rough, rude or boisterous," according to N.W.), roguish, rollicking, romantic, rompish, rotten, rough-and-ready, rough-and-tumble, rough-housing, rowdyish, rude, rueful, rugged, ruined, rummy (*chiefly Brit.* don'cha know. *Slang* odd; queer), rundown, runty, ruthless race!

A' course that's just one man's opinion. Fella name a' Smith; first name a' Word.

And just who *is* Word Smith? Fair enough. Short-winded, short-tempered, short-sighted as he may be, stiff-jointed, soft-bellied, weak-bladdered, and so on down to his slippers, anemic, arthritic, diabetic, dyspeptic, sclerotic, in dire need of a laxative, as he will admit to the first doctor or nurse who passes his pillow, *and in perpetual pain* (that's the last you'll hear about that), he's not cracked quite yet: if his life depended on it, the man in the street could not name three presidents beginning with the letter J, or tell you whether the Pope before this one wore glasses or not, so surely he is not about to remember Word Smith, though it so happened old W.S. cracked a new pack of Bicycles with more than one Chief Exec, one night nearly brought down the republic by cleaning out the entire cabinet, so that at morn—pink peeking over the Potomac, you might say—the Secretary of the Treasury had to be restrained by the Secretary of the Interior from dipping his mitt in the national till to save his own shirt at stud, in a manner of speaking.

Then there are the Popes. Of course no poker, stud, straight, *or* draw, with Pontiffs, other than penny ante, but rest assured, Smitty here in his heyday, kneepans down on terra firma, has kissed his share of rings, and if no longer up to the kneeling-down, still has starch enough left in these half-palsied lips for tasting the papal seal and (if there should be any takers) touching somewhat tumescent flesh to the peachier parts of the softer sex, afore he climbs aboard that sleeper bound for Oblivion. Chucklin': "George, what time she due at Pearly Gates?" Shufflin': "Don' you worry none, Mistuh Smitty, I call ya' in time fo' you to shave up and eat a good heffy breakfass' fo' we gets dere." "*If* we gets there, George. Conductor says we may all be on a through train, from what he hears." "Tru'? To where, Mistuh Smitty? De end of de line?" (Chorus behind, ahummin' and astrummin', "Tru' train, tru' train, choo-choo on tru', I wanna choo-choo on home widout delay!") "Seems there isn't any 'end' to this line, George." Scratchin' his woolly head: "Well, suh, day don' say nuttin' 'bout dat in de schedule." "Sure they do, old George, down in the fine print there: 'Stops only to receive passengers.'" "Which tru' train dat, Mistuh Smitty?" "Through train bound for Oblivion, George." "'Oblivion'? Dat don' sound lak no stop—dat de name of a little girl!" ("Tru' train, tru' train, lem-me choo-choo on home!")

Smitty! Prophet to porters, padre to pagans, peacemaker for polygamists, provider for panhandlers, probation officer to pickpockets, pappy to parricides, parent to prostitutes, "Pops" to pinups, Paul to pricks, plaintalker to pretenders, parson to Peeping Toms, protector to pansies, practical nurse to paranoids —pal, you might say, to pariahs and pests of every stripe, spot, stigma, and stain, or maybe just putty in the paws of personae non gratae, patsy in short to pythons. Not a bad title that, for Smitty's autobio.

Or how's about *Poet to Presidents*? For 'twasn't all billiards on the Biggest Boss's baize, sagas of sport and the rarest of rums, capped off with a capricious predawn plunge in the Prez's pool. Oh no. Contract bridge, cribbage, canasta, and casino crony, sure; blackjack bluffer and poker-table personality, a' course, a' course; practiced my pinochle, took 'em on, one and all, at twenty-one; suffered stonily (and snoozed secretly) through six-hour sieges of solitaire, rising to pun when they caught me napping, "Run out of patience, Mr. P.?"; listen, I played lotto on the White House lawn, cut a First Child for Old Maid in the Oval Office on the eve of national disaster . . . but that doesn't explain what I was there for. Guessed yet how I came to be the intimate of four American presidents? Figured me out? Respectful of their piteous portion of privacy, I call them henceforth ABC, DEF, GHI, and JKL, but as their words are public record, who in fact these four were the reader with a little history will quickly surmise. My capital concern? I polished their prose.

GHI, tomb who I was closer than any, would always make a point to have me in especially to meet the foreign dignitaries; and his are the speeches and addresses upon which my influence is most ineradicably inked. "Prime Minister," he would say —or Premier, or Chairman, or Chancellor, or General, or

Generalissimo, or Colonel, or Commodore, or Commander, or Your Excellency, or Your Highness, or Your Majesty—"I want you to meet the outstanding scribbler in America. I do not doubt that you have a great language too, but I want you to hear just what can be done with this wonderful tongue of ours by a fellow with the immortal gift of gab. Smitty, what do you call that stuff where all the words begin with the same letter?" "Alliteration, Mr. President." "Go ahead then. Gimme some alliteration for the Prime Minister." Of course it was not so easy as GHI thought, even for me, to alliterate under pressure, but when GHI said "Gimme" you gam, get me? "The reason they call that 'elimination,' Prime Minister, is on account of you leave out all the other letters but the one. Right, Smit?" "Well, yes, Mr. President, if they did call it that, that would be why." "And how about a list for the Prime Minister, while you're at it?" "A list of what, Mr. President?" "Prime Minister, what is your pleasure? This fella here knows the names of just about everything there is, so take your choice. He is a walking dictionary. Fish, fruits, or flimflam? Well now, I believe I just did some myself, didn't I?" "Yes, you did, Mr. President. Alliteration." "Now you go ahead, Smitty, you give the Prime Minister an example of one of your lists, and then a little balance, why don't you? Why, I think I love that balance more than I love my wife. Neither-nor, Smitty, give him neither-nor, give him we cannot-we shall not-we must not, and then finish him off with perversion." "Perversion, sir, or inversion?" "Let's leave that to the guest of honor. Which is your preference, Your Honor? Smitty here is a specialist in both."

Do not conclude, dear fans, from this or any GHI anecdote that he was buffoon, clown, fool, illiterate, sadist, vulgarian only; he also knew what he was doing. "Smitty," he would say to me when he came in the morning to unlock the door of the safe in the White House basement where I had passed the night in an agony of alphabetizing and alliterating, "Smitty," he would say, studying the State of the Union address whose inverted phrases and balanced clauses seemed at that moment to have cost me my sanity, "I envy you, you know that, locked away down here in blessed solitude behind six feet of sound-proof blast-proof steel, while just over your head the phone is ringing all night long with one international catastrophe after another. Know something, my boy? If I had it to do all over again—and I say this to you in all sincerity, even if I do not have the God-given gift to say it backwards and inside out—if I had it to do all over again, I'd rather be a writer than President."

Waybackwhen, in my heyday (d.), when "One Man's Opinion" counted for something in this country—being syndicated as it was on the sports page of the Finest Family Newspapers (d.)—back when the American and the National Baseball Leagues existed in harmonious competition with the Patriot League (d.) and I traveled around that circuit for the Finest Family, whose *Morning Star* (the whole constellation, d.) was the daily tabloid in the seven Patriot League cities (I see now they are putting Sports Quizzes on cocktail napkins; how about this then, napkineers—*Query:* Which were the seven cities of the old P. League? What drunk has the guts to remember?), back before teams, towns, trusting readership simply vanished without a trace in the wake of the frauds and the madness, back before I was reduced to composing captions for sex-and-slander sheets (not unlike a Jap haiku genius working for the fortune cookie crumbs—in my prime, remember, I was master of that most disparaged of poetic forms, the headline), back before they slandered, jailed, blacklisted, and forgot me, back before the Baseball Writers' Association of America (to name a name, Mr. Chairman!) hired a plainclothesgoon to prevent me from casting my vote for Luke Gofannon at the Hall of Fame elections held every January just one hundred miles from this upstate Home of the D. (sixty-three home runs for the Ruppert Mundys in 1928, and yet Luke "the Loner" is "ineligible," I am told—just as I am archaic in my own century, a humorous relic in my own native land, d. as a doornail while still drawing breath!), back before years became decades and decades centuries, when I was Smitty to America and America was still a home to me, oh, about eleven, twelve thousand days ago, I used to get letters from young admirers around the country, expressing somewhat the same sentiment as the President of the United States, only instead of sardonic, sweet. O *so* sweet!

Dear Smitty, I am ten and want to grow up to be a sports righter two. It is the dream of my life. How can I make my dream come true? Is spelling important as my teacher say? Isn good ideas more important and loving baseball? How did you become so great? Were you born with it? Or did you have good luck? Please send me any pamphlets on being like you as I am making a booklit on you for school.

O sad! Too sad! The sight of my own scratchings makes me weep! How like those schoolchildren who idolized me I now must labor o'er the page! Sometimes I must pause in the midst of a *letter* to permit the pain to subside, in the end producing what looks like something scratched on a cave wall anyway, before the invention of invention. I could not earn passage into the first grade with this second childhood penmanship—how ever will I win the Pulitzer Prize? But then Mount Rushmore was not carved in a day—neither will the Great American Novel be written without suffering. Besides, I think maybe the pain is good for the style: when just setting out on a letter like the lower case w is as tedious and treacherous as any zigzag mountain journey where you must turn on a dime to avoid the abyss, you tend not to waste words with w's in them, fans. And likewise through the alphabet.

The alphabet! That dear old friend! Is there a one of the Big Twenty-Six that does not carry with it a thousand keen memories for an archaic and humorous, outmoded and outdated and oblivion-bound sports-scribe like me? To hell with the waste! Tomorrow's a holiday anyway—Election Day at the Hall of F. Off to Cooperstown to try yet again. My heart may give out by nightfall, but then a' course the fingers will get their rest, won't they? So what do you say, fans, a trip with Smitty down Memory Lane?

aA
bB
cC
dD
eE
fF
gG
hH
iI
jJ
kK

lL
mM
nN
oO
pP
qQ
rR
sS
tT
uU
vV
wW
xX
yY
zZ

O thank God there are only twenty-six! Imagine a hundred! Why, it is already like drowning to go beyond capital F! G as in Gofannon! M as in Mundy! P as in Patriot! And what about I as in I? O for those golden days of mine and yore! O why must there be d for deceased! Deceit, defeat, decay, deterioration, bad enough—but d as in dead? It's too damn tragic, this dying business! I tell you, I'd go without daiquiris, daisies, damsels, Danish, deck chairs, Decoration Day doubleheaders, decorum, delicatessen, Demerol, democratic processes, deodorants, Derbys, desire, desserts, dial telephones, dictionaries, dignity, discounts, disinfectants, distilleries, ditto marks, doubletalk, dreams, drive-ins, dry cleaning, duck au montmorency, a dwelling I could call my own—why, I would go without *daylight*, if only I did not have to die. O fans, it is so horrible just being defunct, imagine, as I do, day in and day out

DEATH

Ten days have elapsed, four in an oxygen tent, where I awoke from unconsciousness believing I was a premature infant again. Not only a whole life ahead of me, but two months thrown in for good measure! I imagined momentarily that it was four score and seven years ago, that I had just been brought forth from my mother; but no—instead of being a premature babe I am practically a posthumous unpublished novelist, ten days of my remaining God only knows how few gone, *and not a word written.*

And worse, our philistine physician has issued an injunction: give up alliteration if you want to live to be four score and eight.

"Smitty, it's as simple as this—you cannot continue to write like a boy and expect to get away with it."

"But it's all I've got left! I refuse!"

"Come now, no tears. It's not the end of the world. You still have your lists, after all, you still have your balance—"

Between sobs I say, "But you don't understand! Alliteration is at the foundation of English literature. Any primer will tell you that much. It goes back to the very beginnings of written language. I've made a study of it—it's true! There would have been no poetry without it! No human speech as we know it!"

"Well, they don't teach us the fundamentals of poetry in medical school, I admit, but they do manage to get something through our heads having to do with the care of the sick and the aged. Alliteration may be very pretty to the ear, and fun to use, I'm sure, but it is simply too much of a stimulant and a strain for an eighty-seven-year-old man, and you are going to have either to control yourself, or take the consequences. Now blow your nose—"

"But I *can't* give it up! No one can! Not even *you*, who is a literary ignoramus by his own admission. 'Stimulant and strain.' 'To control yourself or take the consequences.' Don't you see, if it's in every other sentence even *you* utter, how can I possibly abstain? You've got to take away something else!"

The doctor looks at me as if to say, "Gladly, only what else is left?" Yes, it is my last real pleasure, he is right . . .

"Smitty, it's simply a matter of not being so fancy. Isn't that all really, when you come down to it?"

"My God, *no!* It's just the opposite—it's as natural as breathing. It's the homiest most unaffected thing a language can do. It's the ornamentation of ordinary speech—"

"Now, now."

"Listen to me for once! Use your ears instead of that stethoscope—listen to the English language, damn it! Bed and board, sticks and stones, kith and kin, time and tide, weep and wail, rough and ready, now or—"

"Okay, that's enough, now. You are working yourself into another attack, and one that you may not recover from. If you do not calm down this instant, I am going to order that your fountain pen and dictionary be taken away."

I snarled in response, and let him in on a secret. "I could still alliterate in my head. What do you think I did for four days in the oxygen tent?"

"Well, if so, you are deceiving no one but yourself. Smitty, you must use common sense. Obviously I am not suggesting that you abstain from ever having two neighboring words in a sentence begin with the same sound. That would be absurd. Why, next time I come to visit, I would be overjoyed to hear you tell me, 'Feelin' fit as a fiddle'—if it happens to be true. It is not the ordinary and inevitable accidents of alliteration that occur in conversation that wear down a man of your age, or even the occasional alliterative phrase used intentionally for heightened rhetorical effect. It's overindulgent, intemperate, unrestrained excursions into alliteration that would leave a writer half your age trembling with excitement. Smitty, while you were comatose I took the liberty of reading what you've been writing here—I had no choice, given your condition. My friend, the orgy of alliteration that I find on the very first page of your book is just outright ridiculous in a man of your age— it is tantamount to suicide. Frankly I have to tell you that the feeling I come away with after reading the first few thousand words here is of a man making a spectacle of himself. It strikes me as wildly excessive, Smitty, and just a little desperate. I wish I could tell you otherwise, but there's no sense pulling punches with an eighty-seven-year-old man."

"Well, Doctor, much as I welcome your medical school version of literary criticism, you have to admit that you are not exactly the Pulitzer Prize Committee. Besides, it is only the prologue. I was only opening the tap, to get the waters running."

"Well, it still seems needlessly ostentatious to me. And a terrible drain on the heart. And, my friend, you cannot write a note to the milkman, let alone the Great American Novel, without one of them pumping the blood to your brain." He took my hand as I began to whimper again—he claims to have read "One Man's Opinion" as a boy in Aceldama. "Here, here, it's only for your good I tell you this . . ."

"And—and how's about reading alliteration, if I can't write it?"

"For the time being, I'm going to ask you to stay off it entirely."

"Or?"

"Or you'll be a goner. That'll be the ballgame, Smitty."

"If that's the case, I'd *rather* be dead!" I bawled, the foulest lie ever uttered by man.

> Than longen folk to goon on pilgrimages.

So said Chaucer back in my high school days, and a' course it is as true now as then.

> And specially, from every shires ende
> Of Engelond, to Caunterbury they wende,
> The holy blisful martir for to seke,
> That hem hath holpen, whan that they were seke.

That is copied directly (and laboriously I assure you) from the famous Prologue to his immortal (and as some will always say, immoral) *Canterbury Tales*. I had to copy it only so as to get the old-fashioned spelling correct. I can still recite the forty-odd lines, up to "A Knight ther was," as perfectly as I did in tenth grade. In fact, in the intervening million years—not since Chaucer penned it, but since I memorized it—I have conquered insomnia many a night reciting those dead words to myself, aloud if I happened to be alone, under my breath (as was the better part of wisdom) if some slit was snoring beside me. Only imagine one of them bimbos overhearing Smitty whaning-that-Aprille in the middle of the night! Waking to find herself in the dark with a guy who sounds five hundred years old! Especially if she happened to think of herself as "particular"! Why, say to one of those slits —in the original accent— "The droghte of Marche hath perced to the rote," and she'd kick you right in the keester. "There are some things a girl won't do, Mr. Word Smith, not even for dough! Good*bye*!" On the other hand, to do women justice, there is one I remember, a compassionate femme with knockers to match, who if you said to her, "So priketh hem nature in hir corages," she'd tell you, "Sure I blow guys in garages. They're human too, you know."

But this is not a book about tough cunts. Nat Hawthorne wrote that one long ago. This is a book about what America did to the Ruppert Mundys (and to me). As for *The Canterbury Tales* by Geoffrey Chaucer, I admit that I have by now forgot what it all meant, if ever I knew. I'm not just talking about the parts that were verboten either. I take it from the copy that I have before me, borrowed on my card from the Valhalla Public Library, that those "parts" are still taboo for schoolkids. Must be—they are the only ratty-looking pages in an otherwise untouched book. Reading with the help of magnifying glass and footnotes, I see (at nearly ninety) that it is mostly stuff about farting. Little devils. They have even decorated the margin with symbols of their glee. Appears to be a drawing of a fart. Pretty good one too. Kids love farts, don't they? Even today, with all the drugs and sex and violence you hear about on TV, they still get a kick, such as we used to, out of a fart. Maybe the world hasn't changed so much after all. It would be nice to think there were still a few eternal verities around. I hate to think of the day when you say to an American kid, "Hey, want to smell a great fart?" and he looks at you as though you're crazy. "A great what?" "Fart. Don't you even know what a fart is?" "Sure it's a game—you throw one at a target. You get points." "That's a dart, dope. A *fart*. A bunch of kids sit around in a crowded place and they fart. Break wind. Sure, you can make it into a game and give points. So much for a wet fart, so much for a series, and so on. And penalties if you draw mud, as we called it in those days. But the great thing was, you could do it just for the fun of it. By God, we could fart for hours when we were boys! Somebody's front porch on a warm summer night, in the road, on our way to school. Why, we could sit around a blacksmith's shop on a rainy day doing nothing but farting, and be perfectly content. No movies in those days. No television. No nothin'. I don't believe the whole bunch of us taken together ever had more than a nickel at any time, and yet we were never bored, never had to go around looking for excitement or getting into trouble. Best thing was you could do it yourself too. Yessir, boy knew how to make use of his leisure time in those days."

Surprising, given the impact of the fart on the life of the American boy, how little you still hear about it; from all appearances it is still something they'd rather skip over in *The Canterbury Tales* at Valhalla High. On the other hand, that may be a blessing in disguise; this way at least no moneyman or politician has gotten it into his head yet to cash in on its nostalgic appeal. Because when that happens, you can kiss the fart goodbye. They will cheapen and degrade it until it is on a level with Mom's apple pie and our flag. Mark my words: as soon as some scoundrel discovers there is a profit to be made off of the American kid's love of the fart, they will be selling artificial farts in balloons at the circus. And you can just imagine what they'll smell like too. Like *everything* artificial.

Yes, fans, as the proverb has it, verily there is nothing like a case of fecal impaction to make an old man wax poetic about the fart. Forgive the sentimental meandering.

> And specially, from every shires ende
> Of AMERICA to COOPERSTOWN they wende
> The holy BASEBALL HEROES for to seke,
> That hem hath holpen whan that they were SIX.*

For the ambulatory among my fellow geriatrics here our annual trip to Cooperstown is something very like the kind of pilgrimage Chaucer must have been writing about. I won't go

---

*A "shire" is a county. Thus the word "sheriff"—he is the reeve ("an administrative officer of a town or a district") of a shire. I am using "holpen" to mean "inspired": the baseball players who inspired them when they were six years old. I realize of course from reading the footnotes that it does not mean inspired any more than it means "helped." But it will if you want it to, and I want it to. A writer can take certain liberties. Besides, the word "inspired" appears just twelve lines earlier (line six): "Inspired hath in every holt and heeth." I will not go into what it means there or how it is pronounced— though I do hope you will note hath, holt, and heeth, Doctor!—but the point is I didn't just pull "inspired" out of left field. On the other hand, if you want to understand the line as G. Chaucer (1340–1400) intended, with "holpen" meaning "cured," then change the last word to "sixty." Something like: the baseball players whom they would like to have cure them of being sixty. Not bad. But then you lose the rhyme. And the truth is that these boys are over sixty. Though I suppose you could insert the word "over" in there. I recognize, of course, that "six" does not exactly rhyme with "seke" either, but that is the only word I could think of to get my meaning across. Writing is an art, not a science, and admittedly I am no Chaucer. Though that's only one man's opinion.

into the cast of characters, as he does, except to say that as I
understand it, his "nine and twenty" were not so knowledge-
able in matters of religion as you might at first expect pilgrims
to be who are off to worship at a holy shrine. Well, so too for
the six and ten it was my misfortune to be cooped up with on
the road to Cooperstown, and then all afternoon long at the
Baseball Museum and Hall of Fame. Ninety-nine per cent of
their baseball "memories," ninety-nine per cent of the anecdotes and stories they recollect and repeat are pure hogwash,
tiny morsels of the truth so coated over with discredited legend and senile malarkey, so impacted, you might say, in the
turds of time, as to rival the tales out of ancient mythology.
What the aged can do with the past is enough to make your
hairs stand on end. But then look at the delusions that ordinary people have about the day before yesterday.

Of course, in the way of old men—correction: in the way of
all men—they more or less swallow one another's biggest lies
whole and save their caviling for the tiniest picayune points.
How they love to nitpick over nonsense and cavil over crap all
the while those brains of theirs, resembling nothing so much as
pickles by this time, soak on in their brine of fantasy and fabri-
cation. No wonder Hitler was such a hit. Why, he might still
be at it, if only he'd had the sense to ply his trade in the Land
of Opportunity. These are three homo sapiens, descendants of
Diogenes, seeking the Truth: "I tell you, there was so a Ernie
Cooper, what pitched four innings in one game for the Cincin-
natis in 1905. Give up seven hits. Seen it myself." "Afraid you
are thinking of Jesse Cooper of the White Sox. And the year
was 1911. And he pitched himself something more than four
innings." "You boys are both wrong. Cooper's name was Bock.
And he come from right around these parts too." "Boggs?
Boggs is the feller what pitched one year for the Bees. Lefty
Boggs!" Yes, Boggs was a Bee, all right, but the Cooper they are
talking about happened to be named Baker. Only know what
they say when I tell them as much? "Who asked you? Keep
your brainstorms for your 'book'! We are talking fact not fiction!" "But you're the ones who've got it wrong," I say. "Oh
sure, *we* got it wrong! Ho-ho-ho! That's a good one! Get out
of here, Shakespeare! Go write the Great American Novel, you
crazy old coot!"

Well, fans, I suppose there are those who called Geoffrey Chaucer (*and* William Shakespeare, with whom I share initials) a crazy coot, and immoral, and so on down the line. Tell them what they do not wish to hear, tell them that they have got it wrong, and the first thing out of their mouths, "You're off your nut!" Understanding this as I do should make me calm and philosophical, I know. Wise, sagacious, and so forth. Only it doesn't work that way, especially when they do what they did to me ten days ago at Cooperstown.

First off, as everyone knows, the Baseball Hall of Fame at Cooperstown was founded on a falsehood. No more than little George Washington said to his father, "Dad, it is I, etc.," did Major Abner Doubleday invent the game of baseball on that sacred spot. The only thing Major Doubleday started was the Civil War, when he answered the Confederate Beauregard by firing the first shot from Fort Sumter. Yet, to this day, shout such "heresy" in the bleachers at a Sunday doubleheader, and not only will three out of four patrons call you crazy, but some self-styled authority on the subject (probably a Dad with his Boy—I know the type) will threaten your life for saying something so awful in front of innocent kids.

My quarrel with Cooperstown, however, is over nothing so inconsequential as who invented the game and where. I only draw attention to the longevity of this lie to reveal how without conscience even the highest authorities are when it comes to perpetuating a comforting, mindless myth everyone has grown used to, and how reluctant the ordinary believer, or fan, is to surrender one. When both the rulers and the subjects of the Holy Baseball Empire can sanctify a blatant falsehood with something supposedly so hallowed as a "Hall of Fame," there is no reason to be astonished (I try to tell myself) at the colossal crime against the truth that has been perpetrated by America's powers-that-be ever since 1946. I am speaking of what no one in this country dares even to mention any longer. I am speaking of a chapter of our past that has been torn from the record books without so much as a peep of protest, *except by me*. I am speaking of a rewriting of our history as heinous as any ordered by a tyrant dictator abroad. Not thousand-year-old history either, but something that only came to an end *twenty-odd years ago.* Yes, I am speaking of the annihilation of the Patriot League. Not merely wiped out of business, *but will- fully erased from the national memory.* Ask a Little Leaguer, as I did only this past summer. When I approached, he was swinging a little bat in the on-deck circle, ironically enough, resembling no one so much as Bob Yamm of the Kakoola Reapers (d.). "How many big leagues are there, sonny?" I asked. "Two," he said, "the National and the American." "And how many did there used to be?" "Two." "Are you sure of that now?" "Positive." "What about the Patriot League?" "No such thing." "Oh no? Never heard of the Tri-City Tycoons? Never heard of the Ruppert Mundys?" "Nope." "You never heard of Kakoola, Aceldama, Asylum?" "What are those?" "Cities, boy! Those were big league towns!" "Who played for 'em, Mister?" he asked, stepping away from me and edging toward the bench. "Luke Gofannon played for them. Two thousand two hundred and forty-two games he played for them. Never heard his name?" Here a man took me by the arm, simultaneously saying to the boy, "He means Luke Appling, Billy, who played for the White Sox." "Who are you?" I asked, as if I didn't know. "I'm his Dad." "Well, then, tell him the truth. Raise the boy on the truth! You know it as well as I do. I do not mean Luke Appling and I do not mean Luke 'Hot Potato' Hamlin. I mean Luke Gofannon of the Ruppert Mundys!" And what does the Dad do? He puts a finger to his temple to indicate to this little brainwashed American tyke (one of tens of millions!) that *I* am the one that is cracked. Is it any wonder that I raised my cane?

You can look in vain in the papers of Friday, January 22, 1971, for a mention of the vote I cast the previous day at the annual balloting for baseball's Hall of Fame. But the fact of the matter is that I handed it personally to Mr. Bowie Kuhn, so-called Commissioner of Baseball, and he assured me that it would be tabulated along with the rest by the secretary-treasurer of the Baseball Writers' Association of America. WELL, MR. BOWIE KUHN IS A LIAR AND THE HALL OF FAME SHOULD BE NAMED THE HALL OF SHAME.

Of course, the plainclothesgoon they hire especially to keep an eye on me during these annual election day visits greeted our contingent at the Museum door pretending to want to do no more than make us gentlemen at home. "*Well*, if it isn't the senior citizens from over Valhalla way. Welcome, boys."

Oh yes, we are treated like royalty at Cooperstown! How they love "the elderly" when they behave like *boys*! *Choir*boys. So long as the only questions we ask have to do with Bock Baker and Lefty Boggs, everything is, as they say over there, "hunky-dory."

"Greetings, Smitty. Remember me?"

"I remember everything," I said.

"How you feeling this year?"

"The same."

"Well," he asked of the pilgrims in my party, "who you boys rooting for?"

"Kiner!"

"Keller!"

"Berra!"

"Wynn!"

"How about you, Mr. Smith?"

"Gofannon."

"Uh-huh," said he, without blinking an eye. "What did he bat again lifetime? I seem to have forgotten since you told me last year."

"Batted .372. Five points more than Cobb. You know that as well as I do. Two thousand two hundred and forty-two regular season games and twenty-seven more in the World Series. Three thousand one hundred and eighty hits. Four hundred and ninety home runs. Sixty-three in 1928. Just go down where you have buried the Patriot League records and you can look it up."

"Don't mind Shakespeare," chortled one of my choirboy companions, "he was born that way. Figment lodged in his imagination. Too deep to operate."

Haw-haw all around.

Here the p.c. goon starts to humor me again. He sure does pride himself on his finesse with crackpots. He wonders if perhaps—oh, ain't that considerate, that perhaps—if *peut-être* I am confusing Luke Gofannon of the—what team is that again?

"The Ruppert Mundys."

—Of the Ruppert Mundys with Lou Gehrig of the New York

Yankees. As I can see from the plaque just down the way a hundred feet, the great first-sacker is already a member of the Hall of Fame and has been since his retirement in 1939.

"Look," says I, "we went through this song-and-dance last time round. I know Gofannon from Gehrig, and I know Gofannon from Gehringer, and I know Gofannon from Goose Goslin, too. What I want to know is just why do you people persist in this? Why must you bury the truth about the history of this game—*of this country*? Have you no honor? Have you no conscience? Can you just take the past and flush it away, like so much shit?"

"Is this," asked those two droopy tits known as our nurse, "is this being 'a good boy,' Smitty? Didn't you promise this year you'd mind your manners, if we let you come along? *Didn't you?*" Meanwhile, she and the bus driver had spun me around on my cane, so that I was no longer addressing the goon, but the glove worn by Neal Ball when he made his unassisted triple play in 1909.

"Hands off, you lousy smiling slit."

"Here here, old-timer," said the pimply little genius who drives our bus, "is that any way to talk to a lady?"

"To some ladies it is the *only* way to talk! That is the way half the Hall of Famers whose kissers you see hanging up in bronze here talked to ladies, you upstate ignoramus! Hands off of me!"

"Smitty," said the slit, still smiling, "why don't you act your age?"

"And what the hell does that mean?"

"You know what it means. That you can't always have what you want."

"Suppose what I want is for them to admit THE TRUTH!"

"Well, what may seem like the truth to you," said the seventeen-year-old bus driver and part-time philosopher, "may not, of course, seem like the truth to the other fella, you know."

"THEN THE OTHER FELLOW IS WRONG, IDIOT!"

"Smitty," said the slit, who last year they gave an award and a special dinner for being the best at Valhalla at handling tantrums and rages, "what difference does it make anyway? Suppose they *don't* know it's the truth. Well, they're the ones who are missing out, not you. Actually, you ought to think of yourself as fortunate and take pride in the fact that where others are mistaken, you are correct. If I were you, I wouldn't be angry with them; I would feel *sorry* for them."

"Well, you ain't me! Besides, they know the truth as well as I do. They are only pretending not to."

"But, Smitty, *why?* Now you can be a reasonable and intelligent man, at least when you want to. Why would they want to do a thing like that?"

"Because the truth to them has no meaning! The real human past has no importance! They distort and falsify to suit themselves! They feed the American public fairy tales and lies! Out of arrogance! Out of shame! Out of their terrible guilty conscience!"

"Now, now," says the slit, "you don't really think people are like that, do you? How can you, with your wonderful love of baseball, say such things while standing here in the Hall of Fame?"

I would have told her—and anybody else who wants to know —if I had not at that moment seen coming toward me down the stairway from the Babe Ruth Wing, the Commissioner himself, Mr. Bowie Kuhn, and his entourage. Looking for all the world like the President of General Motors. And she asks me why they feed the people lies. Same reason General Motors does. The profit motive, Mr. Chairman! To fleece the public!

"Commissioner! Commissioner Kuhn!"

"Yes, sir," he replies.

"No, no!" says the slit, but I free myself from her grasp by rapping her one on the bunions.

"How do you do, Commissioner. I would like to introduce myself, in case you have forgotten. I am Word Smith, used to write the 'One Man's Opinion' column for the Finest Family Newspapers back in the days of the Patriot League."

"Smitty!"

"I see," said Kuhn, nodding.

"I used to be a member of the Baseball Writers' Association of America myself, and until 1946 voted annually in these Hall of Fame elections. Then, as you may recall, I was slandered and jailed. Cast my vote in the very first election for Mr. Ty Cobb."

"I see. For Cobb. Good choice."

By now a crowd of geezers, gaffers, and codgers, including the six and ten puerile Methuselahs of my own party, are all pushing close to get a look at the Commissioner and the crackpot.

"And I am here," I tell him, "to cast another vote today." Here I extracted from my vest the small white envelope I had prepared the previous day and handed it to Mr. Bowie Kuhn.

To my astonishment, he not only accepted it, but behind those businessman's spectacles, *his eyes welled up with tears.*

Well, fans, so did mine. So do they now, remembering.

"Thank you, Mr. Smith," he said.

"Why, you're welcome, Commissioner."

I could have burst right through my million wrinkles, I was so happy, and Kuhn, he couldn't tear himself away. "Where are you living these days?" he asked.

I smiled. "State Home for the Aged, the Infirm, the Despondent, the Neglected, the Decrepit, the Incontinent, the Senile, and the Just About Scared to Death. Life creeps in its petty pace, Commissioner."

"Don't mind him, Mr. Kuhn," someone volunteered from the crowd, "he was born that way."

"Bats in the belfry, Commissioner. Too deep to operate."

Haw-haw all around.

"Well," said Kuhn, looking down at my envelope, "have a good day, Mr. Smith."

"You too, Mr. Commissioner."

And that was it. That was how easy it was to trick me into thinking that at long last the lying had come to an end! Shameful! At eighty-seven years of age, to be so gullible, so innocent! I might as well have been back mewling and puking, to think the world was going to right its ways because I got smiled at by the man in charge! And they call me embittered! Why, take me seriously for twenty seconds at a stretch, and I roll over like a puppy, my balls and bellyhairs all yours.

"My, my," said the slit to the plainclothesgoon, "just give in a little to someone's d-e-l-u-s-i-o-n-s o-f g-r-a-n-d-e-u-r, and he's a changed person, isn't he?"

Well, sad to say, the slit spoke the truth. You don't often hear the truth introduced by "my, my" but there it is. Wonders never cease.

Also, in my own behalf, I think it is fair to say that after twenty years of struggling I had come to be something of a victim of exhaustion. When they are ranged against you, *every living soul*, then you might as well be down in the coal mines hacking at the walls with your teeth and your toenails, for all the impression that you make. There is nothing so wearing in all of human life as burning with a truth that everyone else denies. You don't know suffering, fans, until you know that.

Still and all, Kuhn took me in.

What follows is the list of players who, *according to* the BBWAA, received votes that day for the Hall of Fame.

| | | | |
|---|---|---|---|
| Yogi Berra | 242 | Johnny Sain | 11 |
| Early Wynn | 240 | Harvey Haddix | 10 |
| Ralph Kiner | 212 | Richie Ashburn | 10 |
| Gil Hodges | 180 | Ted Kluszewski | 9 |
| Enos Slaughter | 165 | Don Newcombe | 8 |
| Johnny Mize | 157 | Harry Brecheen | 7 |
| Pee Wee Reese | 127 | Walker Cooper | 7 |
| Marty Marion | 123 | Wally Moses | 7 |
| Red Schoendienst | 123 | Billy Pierce | 7 |
| Allie Reynolds | 110 | Carl Furillo | 5 |
| George Kell | 105 | Bobby Shantz | 5 |
| Johnny Vander Meer | 98 | Bobby Thomson | 4 |
| Hal Newhouser | 94 | Roy Sievers | 4 |
| Phil Rizzuto | 92 | Gil McDougald | 4 |
| Bob Lemon | 90 | Ed Lopat | 4 |
| Duke Snider | 89 | Carl Erskine | 3 |
| Phil Cavarretta | 83 | Dutch Leonard | 3 |
| Bobby Doerr | 78 | Preacher Roe | 3 |
| Alvin Dark | 54 | Vic Wertz | 2 |
| Nelson Fox | 39 | Vic Power | 2 |
| Bobo Newsom | 17 | Vic Raschi | 2 |
| Dom DiMaggio | 15 | Wally Moon | 2 |
| Charlie Keller | 14 | Jackie Jensen | 2 |
| Mickey Vernon | 12 | Billy Bruton | 1 |

In that to be elected requires mention on 75 per cent of the ballots, or 271 of the 361 cast (including my own, that is; according to the BBWAA it required only 270 out of 360), the electors issued this statement at about two in the afternoon: "Despite the heaviest vote in the history of the Hall of Fame balloting, the Baseball Writers' Association of America was unable to elect a candidate for enshrinement next summer."

Oh, that set 'em to quacking! You should have heard those fools! How could they keep out Berra when back in '55 they'd let in Gabby Hartnett who was never half the catcher Yogi was! Wasn't half? Why he was twice't! Was! Wasn't! Same for Early Wynn: whoever heard of a three hundred game winner failing to be mentioned by one hundred and twenty electors (excluding me) when right over there is a plaque to Dazzy Vance who in all his career won less than *two* hundred. Next thing you know they will be keeping out Koufax and Spahn when they are eligible! Well, it took Rogers Hornsby six years to make it, didn't it—with a lifetime of .358! And Bill Terry and Harry Heilmann *eleven years apiece*! Meanwhile they are also arguing over Marion and Reese, which was better than the other and whether both weren't a darn sight better than Hall of Famer Rabbit Maranville. Oh what controversy! Tempers raging, statistics flying, and with it all *not a word from anyone about a single player who played for the Patriot League in their fifty years as a major league. Not a mention in the BBWAA's phony tabulations of my vote for Luke Gofannon.*

Billy Bruton! Jackie Jensen! Wally Moon! Outfielders who did not even bat .300 lifetime, who would have had to *pay* their way into Mundy Park in the days of the great Gofannon, and there they are with five votes between them for the Hall of Fame! I was near to insanity.

What was it put me over the top? Why did I hurl my cane and collapse in a heap on the floor? Why had they to hammer on my heart to get it going again? Why have I been bedridden all these days and ordered off alliteration for the remainder of my life? Why wasn't I calm and philosophical as befits a man of my experience with human treachery and deceit? Why did I curse and thunder when I know that writing the Great American Novel requires every last ounce of my strength and my cunning? Tell me something (I am addressing only men of principle): *What would you have done?*

Here's what happened: Commissioner Kuhn appeared, and when reporters, photographers, and cameramen (plus geezers) gathered round to hear his words of wisdom, know what he said? No, not what this sentimental, decomposing, worn-out wishful thinker was pleading with his eyes for Kuhn to say— no, not that the BBWAA was a cheat and a fraud and disgrace for having failed to announce the vote submitted for Luke Gofannon of the extinguished Patriot League. Oh no—wrongs aren't righted that way, fans, except in dreams and daytime serials. "The fact that nobody was elected," said the Commissioner, "points up the integrity of the institution." And if you don't believe me because I'm considered cracked, it's on TV film for all to see. Just look at your newspaper for January 22, 1971—before they destroy that too. *The integrity of the institution*. Next they will be talking about the magnanimity of the Mafia and the blessing of the Bomb. They will use alliteration for anything these days, but most of all for *lies*.

After fighting a sail for forty-five minutes off the Florida coast and finally bringing it in close enough for the fifteen-year-old Cuban kid who was our mate to grab the bill with his gloved hands, pull it in over the rail, and send it off to sailfish heaven with the business end of a sawed-off Hillerich and Bradsby signed "Luke Gofannon," my old friend (and enemy) Ernest Hemingway said to me—the year is 1936, the month is March— "Frederico"—that was the hard-boiled way Hem had of showing his affection, calling me by a name that wasn't my own—"Frederico, you know the son of a bitch who is going to write the Great American Novel?"

"No, Hem. Who?"

"You."

They were running the white pennant up now, number five for Papa in four hours. This was the first morning the boats had been out for a week, and from the look of things everybody was having a good day, though nobody was having as good a day as Papa. When he was having a good day they didn't make them any more generous or sweet-tempered, but when he was having a bad day, well, he could be the biggest prick in all of literature. "You're the biggest prick in all of literature," I remember telling him one morning when we were looking down into the fire pit of Halemaumau, Hawaii's smoldering volcano. "I ought to give you to the goddess for that one,"

said Hem, pointing into the cauldron. "That wouldn't make
you any less of a prick, Hem," I said. "Lay off my prick, Frederico." "I call 'em like I see 'em, Papa." "Just lay off my prick,"
he said.

But that day in March of '36, our cruiser flying five white
pennants, one for each sail Hem had landed, and Hem watching with pleasure the mullet dragging on his line, waiting for
number six, it seemed you could have said anything in the
world you wanted to Papa about his prick, and he would have
got a kick out of it. That's what it's like when a great writer is
having a good day.

It had squalled for a week in Florida. The managers were
bawling to the Chamber of Commerce that next year they
would train in the Southwest and the players were growing fat
on beer and lean on poker and the wives were complaining because they would go North without a sunburn and at night it
got so cold that year that I slept in my famous hound's-tooth
raglan-sleeve overcoat, the one they called "a Smitty" in the
twenties, after a fella name a', I believe. My slit was a waitress
at a Clearwater hotel with a degree in Literatoor from Vassar.
All the waitresses that year had degrees in Literatoor from Vassar. They'd come South to learn about Real Life. "I've never
slept in bed before with a fifty-two-year-old sportswriter in a
hound's-tooth raglan-sleeve overcoat," my Vassar slit informed
me. I said, "That is because you have never been in Florida
before during spring training in a year when the temperature
dropped." "Oh," she said, and wrote it in her diary, I suppose.

Now she was measuring Hem's sail. "It's a big one," she
called over to us. "Seven foot eight inches."

"Throw it back," said Hem and the Vassar slit laughed and
so did the Cuban kid who was our mate that year.

"For a waitress with a degree in Literatoor," Hem said, "she
has a sense of humor. She will be all right."

Then he took up the subject of the Great American Novel
again, joking that it would probably be me of all the sons of
bitches in the world who could spell cat who was going to
write it. "Isn't that what you sportswriters think, Frederico?
That some day you're going to get off into a little cabin somewhere and write the G.A.N.? Could do it now, couldn't you,
Frederico, if only you had the Time."

During that week of squall in March of that year Hem would talk till dawn about which son of a bitch who could spell cat was going to write the G.A.N. By the end of the week he had narrowed it down to a barber in the basement of the Palmer House in Chicago who knew how to shave with the grain.

"No hot towels. No lotion. Just shaves with the grain and washes it off with witch hazel."

"Any man can do that, can write the Great American Novel," I said.

"Yes," said Hem, filling my glass, "he is the one."

"How is he on the light trim?" I asked.

"Not bad for Chicago," Hem said, giving the barber his due.

"Yes," I said, "it is a rough town for a light trim where there are a lot of Polacks."

"In the National League," said Hem, "so is Pittsburgh."

"Yes," I said, "but you cannot beat the dining room in the Schenley Hotel for good eats."

"There is Jimmy Shevlin's in Cincinnati," Hem said.

"What about Ruby Foo's chop suey joint in Boston?"

"Give me Lew Tendler's place in Philadelphia," said Hem.

"The best omelette is the Western," I said.

"The best dressing is the Russian," Hem said.

"Guys who drink Manhattans give me the creeps."

"Liverwurst on a seeded roll with mustard is my favorite sandwich."

"I don't trust a dame who wears those gold sandals."

"Give me a girl who goes in swimming without a bathing cap if a slit has to hold my money."

"I'd rather kill an hour in a newsreel theater than a whore-house."

Yes, over a case of cognac we could manage to touch upon just about every subject that men talk about when they're alone, from homburgs to hookers to Henry Armstrong . . . But always that year the conversation came around to the G.A.N. Hem had it on his brain. One night he would tell me that the hero should be an aviator; the next night an industrialist; then a surgeon; then a cowboy. One time it would be a book about booze, the next broads, the next Mother Nature. "And to think," he said, on the last night of that seven-day squall, "some dago barber sucking on Tums in the basement of the Palmer House is going to write it." I thought he was kidding me again about the barber until he threw his glass into the window that looked onto the bay.

Now he was telling me that I was going to write it. It seemed to me a good compliment to ease out from under.

"Gladly, Hem," I said, thinking to needle him a little in the process, "but I understand that they wrote it already."

"Who is this they, Frederico?"

"The slit says Herman Melville wrote it. And some other guys, besides. It's been done, Papa. Otherwise I'd oblige."

"Hey, Vassar," he called, "get over here."

Of course the slit was very impressed with herself to be out sailfishing with Hem. She liked to hear him calling her "Vassar." She liked me calling her "Slit." It was a change from what they called her at home which was "Muffin." The first time she'd burst into tears but I told her they both meant the same thing anyway, only mine was the more accurate description. The truth is I never knew a girl worth her salt who did not like being called a slit in the end. It's only whores and housewives you have to call "m'lady."

"What's this I heard," said Hem, "that Herman Melville wrote the Great American Novel? Who's Herman Melville?"

The slit turned and twisted on her long storky legs like a little kid who had to go. Finally she got it out. "The author of *Moby Dick*."

"Oh," said Hem, "I read that one. Book about catching a whale."

"Well, it's not *about* that," the slit said, and flushed, pure American Beauty rose.

Hem laughed. "Well, you got the degree in Literatoor, Vassar—tell me, what is it about?"

She told him that it was about Good and Evil. She told him the white whale was not just a white whale, it was a symbol. That amused Hem.

"Vassar, *Moby Dick* is a book about blubber, with a madman thrown in for excitement. Five hundred pages of blubber, one hundred pages of madman, and about twenty pages on how good niggers are with the harpoon."

Here the pole jerked. Hem came off his chair and the little Cuban kid who was our mate that year started in shouting the only English word he knew—"Sail! Sail!"

After the sixth white pennant was raised and the slit had measured Hem's sail at eight feet, he resumed quizzing her about the name of the G.A.N. "And no more blubber, Vassar, you hear?"

"*Huckleberry Finn*," the slit said gamely—and flushing of course, "by Mark Twain."

"Book for boys, Vassar," said Hem. "Book about a boy and a slave trying to run away from home. About the drunks and thieves and lunatics they meet up with. Adventure story for kids."

Oh, no, says the slit, this one is about Good and Evil too.

"Vassar, it is just a book by a fellow who is thinking how nice it would be to be a youngster again. Back when the nuts and lushes and thieves was still the other guy and not you. Kid stuff, Kid. Pretending you're a girl or your own best friend. Sleeping all day and swimming naked at night. Cooking over a fire. Your old wino dad getting rubbed out without having to do the job yourself. The Great American Daydream, Vassar. Drunks don't die so conveniently for the relatives anymore. Right, Frederico?"

Hem had to stop here to catch another sailfish.

According to the slit this one measured only five feet eleven inches. She shouldn't have said "only."

Trying to joke it off, Hem said, "Never be a basketball star, will he?" but it was clear he was not happy with himself. You might even have thought that seventh sail was a symbol of something if you were a professor of Literatoor.

I sat with Hem and we drank, while the Cuban kid fiddled with the fish and the slit wondered what she had said that was wrong. When it was clear the fishing was ruined for the day the kid took in the lines and we started home, the terns and the gulls giving us the business overhead.

"The slit wasn't thinking," I said.

"Oh, the slit was thinking all right. Slits are always thinking in their way."

"She's just a kid, Hem."

"So was Joan of Arc," he said.

"You're taking it too hard," I said. "Try not to think about it."

"Sure. Sure. I'll try not to think about it."

"She didn't mean 'only,' Hem."

"Sure. I know. She meant 'merely.' Hey, Vassar."

"She's a kid, Hem," I warned him.

"So was Clytemnestra when she started out. But once they get going they don't leave you anything. You can count on that. Hey, Vassar."

"What are you going to do, Hem?"

"Sharks like fresh slit as much as the next carnivore, Frederico."

"Don't be a prick, Hem."

"Lay off my prick, Frederico. Or you'll go too. Ever see a shark take after a raglan-sleeve coat with a sportswriter in it? That's the way the Indians used to get them to charge the beach, by waving a swatch of Broadway hound's-tooth at them."

The slit from Vassar who had come South that year to be a waitress and learn about Real Life was showing gooseflesh on her storky legs when she approached the great writer to ask what he wanted. In all that they had taught her about great writers at Vassar they had apparently neglected to mention what pricks they can be.

Hem said, "Tell me some more about the Great American Novel, Vassar. You don't meet a twenty-one-year-old every day who is an authority on fiction and fishing both, especially from your sex."

"But I'm *not*," she said, as pale a slit now as you might ever see.

"You go around judging the size of sailfish, don't you? You have a degree in Literatoor, don't you? Name me another Great American Novel. I want to hear just who us punks are up against."

"I didn't say you were up against—"

"No!" roared Hem. "I did!" And the gulls flew off as though a cannon had been fired.

"*Name me another!*"

But when she stood there mute with terror, Hem reached out with a hand and smacked her face. I thought of Stanley Ketchel when she went down.

She looked up from where Hem had "decked" her. "*The Scarlet Letter*," she whimpered, "by Nathaniel Hawthorne."

"Good one, Vassar. That's the book where the only one who has got any balls on him is the heroine. No wonder you like it so much. Frankly, Vassar, I don't think Mr. Hawthorne even knew where to put it. I believe he thought A stood for arsehole. Maybe that's what all the fuss is about."

"Henry James!" she howled.

"Tell me another, Vassar!"

"*The Ambassadors! The Golden Bowl!*"

"Polychromatic crap, honey! Five hundred words where one would do! Come on, Vassar, name me another!"

"Oh please, Mr. Hemingway, please," she wept, "I don't know anymore, I swear I don't—"

"Sure you do!" he roared. "What about *Red Badge of Courage!* What about *Winesburg, Ohio! The Last of the Mohicans! Sister Carrie! McTeague! My Antonia! The Rise of Silas Lapham! Two Years Before the Mast! Ethan Frome! Barren Ground!* What about Booth Tarkington and Sarah Orne Jewett, while you're at it? What about our minor poet Francis Scott Fitzwhat'shisname? What about Wolfe and Dos and Faulkner? What about *The Sound and the Fury*, Vassar! A tale told by an idiot, signifying nothing—how's that for the Great American Novel!"

"I never read it," she whimpered.

"Of course you haven't! You can't! It's unreadable unless you're some God damn professor! You know why you can't name the Great American Novel, Vassar?"

"No," she moaned.

"Because it hasn't been written yet! Because when it is it'll be Papa who writes it and not some rummy sportswriter in his cute little cottage by the lake in the woods!"

Whereupon a large fierce gull swooped down, its broad wings fluttering, and opened its hungry beak to cry at Ernest Hemingway, "*Nevermore!*"

Or so he claimed afterwards; I myself didn't know what he was carrying on about when he shouted up at the bird, "You can't quoth that to me and get away with it, you sea gull son of a bitch!"

"*Nevermore!*" the gull repeated, to hear Hem tell it later. "*Nevermore!*"

Hem raced down to the cabin but when he returned with his pistol the gull was gone.

"I ought to use it on myself," said Papa. "And if that bastard sea gull is right, I will."

Here he stumbled wildly over the deck, stepping blindly across the slit, and leaned over the side to watch his shadow in the water . . . "Frederico," he called.

"Hem."

"Oh, Frederico; it is a mild, mild wind, and a mild looking sky. On such a day—very much such a sweetness as this—I wrote my first story—a boy-reporter of nineteen! Eighteen—eighteen—eighteen years ago!—ago! Eighteen years of continual writing! eighteen years of privation, and peril, and stormtime! eighteen years on the pitiless sea! for eighteen years has Papa forsaken the peaceful land, for eighteen years to make war on the horrors of the deep! When I think of this life I have led; the desolation of solitude it has been; the masoned, walled-town of a novelist's exclusiveness, which admits but small entrance to any sympathy from the green country without—oh, weariness! heaviness! Guinea-coast slavery of solitary command!—when I think of all this; only half-suspected . . . I feel deadly faint, bowed, and humped, as though I were Adam, staggering beneath the piled centuries since Paradise! God! God! God!—crack my heart—stave my brain!—mockery! mockery! Close! Stand close to me, Frederico; let me look into a human eye. The Great American Novel. Why should Hemingway give chase to the Great American Novel?"

"Good question, Papa. Keep it up and it's going to drive you nuts."

"What is it, Frederico, what nameless, inscrutable, unearthly thing is it; what cozening, hidden lord and master, and cruel, remorseless emperor commands me; that against all natural lovings and longings, I so keep pushing, and crowding, and jamming myself on all the time; recklessly making me ready to do what in my own proper, natural heart, I durst not so much as dare? Is Papa, Papa? Is it I, God, or who, that lifts this writing arm?" he asked, raising the pistol to his head.

"All right, Hem, that's enough now," I said. "You don't even sound like yourself. A book is a book, no more. Who would want to kill himself over a novel?"

"What then?" said Papa, and turned to look at the decked slit. It was to her he said sardonically, "A whale? A woman?"

Only it wasn't the same kid who had boarded with us at dawn that morning who answered him. A few hours with a man like Hem had changed her forever, as it changed us all. That's what a great writer can do to people.

"Wouldn't it be pretty to think so?" snorted the slit.

End of story, nearly. As I did not want to let him out of my sight in that murderous mood, I brought Hem along with me to see the Mundys take their first workout in a week. John Baal, the big bad first-baseman the sentimentalists used to try to dignify by calling him "Rabelaisian"—the first two syllables would have sufficed—was in the cage, lofting long fly balls out toward a flock of pelicans who were cruising in deep center. "I'm going to get me one of them big-mouthed cocksuckers yet," said John, and sure enough, after fifteen minutes of trying, he did. Pelican must have mistaken the baseball for something good to eat, a flying fish I suppose, because he went soaring straight up after one John had hit like a shot and hauled it in while it was still on the rise. When I went to the telegraph office that night to file my story, Papa was still with me, muttering and miserable. The slit had already packed her diary and boarded the first train back to Poughkeepsie. I was not in such good spirits myself.

"Big John Baal of the Mundys," my story began, "was robbed of a four-bagger during batting practice this afternoon in Clearwater. Credit a pelican with the put-out.

"He looked at first glance like any other pelican. He was wearing the grayish-silvery home uniform of his species, with the white velvety neck feathers and the fully webbed toes. The bird was of average size, I am told, weighing in at eight pounds and with a wing spread of seven and a half feet. On close inspection there seemed nothing unusual about the large blackish pouch suspended from the lower half of his bill, except that when they pried the bill open, the pouch was found to contain, along with four sardines and a baby pompano, a baseball bearing the signature of the President of the Patriot League. The pelican was still soaring upwards and to his left when he turned his long graceful neck, opened his bill, and with the nonchalance of a Luke Gofannon, snared Big John's mighty blast.

"We had pigeons when I was a boy. My old man kept them in a chicken-wire coop on the roof. My old man was a pug with a potent right hand who trained in the saloons and bet himself empty on the horses before he evaporated into thin air when I was fifteen. He loved those pigeons so much he fed them just as good as he did us—bread crumbs and a fresh tin of water every day. A boy's illusions about his father are notorious. I thought he was something very like a god when he stood on the roof with a long pole, shaking and waving it in the air to control the pigeons in their flight. And the next thing I knew he had evaporated into the air.

"The press and the players are calling the pelican's catch an 'omen,' but of what they can't agree. As many say a first division finish as a second. That is the range of some people's thinking. Of course there are the jokers, as there always are when the utterly incomprehensible happens. 'Forgive them Father,' begged the suffering man on the cross one Friday long ago, and the smart Roman punk betting even money the shooter wouldn't make an eight in two rolls looked up and said in Latin, 'Listen who's trying to cut the game.'

"The learned Christian gentleman who manages the Mundys is not happy about what Big John Baal is going to do with the dead pelican, but then he has never been overjoyed with Big John's sense of propriety. Mister Fairsmith, a missionary in the off-season, tried to bring baseball to the Africans one winter. They disappointed him too. They learned the principles of the game all right but then one night the two local teams held a ceremony in which they boiled their gloves and ate them. 'The pelican represented as piercing her breast is called "the pelican vulning herself" or "the pelican in her piety,"' Mister Fairsmith reminded Big John. 'She then symbolizes Christ redeeming the world with His blood.' But Big John is still going to have the phenomenal bird stuffed and mounted over the bar of his favorite Port Ruppert saloon.

"I loved my old man and because of that I never understood how he could disappear on me, or play the ponies on me, or train in taverns on me. But he must have had his reasons. I suppose that pelican who made the put-out here in Clearwater today had his reasons too. But I don't pretend to be able to read a bird's brain any more than I could my own dad's. All I know is that if the Mundys plan on breaking even this year somebody better tell Big John Baal to start pulling the ball to right, where the pasture is fenced in.

"But that's only one man's opinion. Fella name a' Smith; first name a' Word."

Nursing Ernest all day, I had been forced to compose the story in bits and half-bits, which accounts for why it is so weak on alliteration. As it says over the door to the Famous Writers School in Connecticut: A Sullen Drunk Packing A Gat Is Not The Best Company For An Artist Finicky About His Style.

I read the story aloud to the telegraph operator, so I could balance up the sentences as I went along, writing the last paragraph right there on my feet in the Western Union office.

Then I turned to see Hem pointing the pistol at my belt.

"You stole that from me."

"Stole what, Hem?"

"First you steal it and then what's worse you fuck it up."

"Fuck what up, Hem?"

"My prose style. You bastards have stolen my prose style. Every shithead sportswriter in America has stolen my style and then gone and fucked it up so bad that I can't even use it anymore without becoming sick to my stomach."

"Put down the pistol, Papa. I've been writing that way all my life and you know it."

"I suppose I stole it from you then, Frederico."

"That isn't what I said."

"Hear that, bright boy?" Hem said to the baby-faced telegraph operator, who had his hands over his head. "That isn't what he said. Tell the bright boy who I steal my ideas from, Frederico."

"Nobody, Hem."

"Don't I steal them from a syndicated sportswriter in a hound's-tooth overcoat? Fella name a' Frederico?"

"No, Hem."

"Maybe I steal them from the slit, Frederico. Maybe I steal them from a Vassar slit with a degree in High Literatoor."

"They're your own, Hem. Your ideas are your own."

"How about my characters. Tell bright boy here who I steal them from. Go ahead. Tell him."

"He doesn't steal them from anybody," I said to the kid. "They're his own."

"Hear that, bright boy?" Hem asked. "My characters are my own."

"Yes, sir," said the telegraph operator.

"Now tell bright boy," Hem said to me, "who is going to write the Great American Novel, Frederico? You? Or Papa?"

"Papa," I said.

"Yes, sir," said the telegraph operator, his hands still up in the air.

"So you think that's right?" Hem asked him.

"Sure," the telegraph operator said.

"You're a pretty bright boy, aren't you?"

"If you say so, sir."

"You know what I say, bright boy? If I have a message, I send it Western Union."

The telegraph operator forced a smile. "Uh-huh," he said.

"Sit down, bright boy."

"Yes, sir." And did as he was told.

Hem walked up and held the pistol to the telegrapher's jaw-bone. "To Messrs. Hawthorne, Melville, Twain, and James, in care of the Department of Literatoor, Vassar College, New York. Dear Illustrious Dead: The Great American Novelist, *c'est moi*. Signed, Papa."

He waited for the last letter to be tapped out, then he turned and went out the door. Through the window I watched him pass under the arc-light and cross the street. Then because I am something of a prick too, I asked how much the telegram would cost, paid, and went on back to my slitless hotel room, never to see Ernest again.

Every once in a while I would get a Christmas card from Hem, sometimes from Africa, sometimes from Switzerland or Idaho, written in his cups obviously, saying more or less the same thing each time: use my style one more time, Frederico, and I'll kill you. But of course in the end the guy Hem killed for using his style was himself.

*

## My Precursors, My Kinsmen

### 1. *The Scarlet Letter*, by Nathaniel Hawthorne

Well, I tend to agree with Hem—having now done my home-work—that the men Miss Hester Prynne got herself mixed up with do not reflect admirably upon the bearded sex. But then make me out a list of a hundred who do? I count it a miracle that the lady didn't latch onto a lushhead as well. And yet, standard stuff as it may seem to a slum kid like myself to hear tell of a sweet young thing throwing away her life on a lout, there is something suspicious about a beautiful, brave, voluptuous, and level-headed slit such as Hester marrying a misshapen dryasdust prof easily three times her age (who undoubtedly had her posing in all sorts of postures in her petticoats in order for him to get it up, if up it would even go) and from him moving on to a "passionate" affair with that puny parson. Ten to one when they saddled up in the woods, it was Hester mounted the minister and not t'other way about. I admire the girl for her guts but have my doubts about any slit who savors sex with sadists and sissies. I only regret that this big black-eyed dish did not reside in the Boston area in the era of the Red Sox and Bees. I might have showed her something.

Students of Literatoor (as Hem was wont to mispronounce it) will have recognized the debt that I owe to Mr. Hawthorne of Massachusetts. Yes, this prologue partly derives from reading that lengthy intro to his novel wherein he tells who he is and how he comes to be writing a great book. Before embarking on my own I thought it wouldn't hurt to study up on the boys Hem took to be the competition—for if they were his then they are mine now. Actually I did not get overly excited about the author's adventures as boss of a deadbeat Salem Custom-House as he ramblingly relates them in that intro, but surely I was struck by the fact that like my own, his novel is based upon real life, the story of Hester Prynne being drawn from records that he discovered in a junk heap in a corner of the Custom-House attic. In that the Prynne-Dimmesdale scandal had broken two hundred years earlier, Hawthorne admits he had to "dress up the tale"—nice pun that, Nat—imagining the setting, the motives and such. "What I contend for," Hawthorne says, "is the authenticity of the outline." Well, what *I* contend for is the authenticity of the whole thing!

Fans, nary a line is spoken in the upcoming epic, that either I heard it myself—was *there*, in dugout, bleachers, clubhouse, barroom, diner, pressbox, bus, and limousine—or had it confided to me by reliable informants, as often as not the parties in pain themselves. Then there are busybodies, blabbermouths, gossips, stoolies, and such to assist in rounding out reality. With all due respect to Hawthorne's "imaginative faculty," as he calls it, I think he could have done with a better pair of ears on him. Only *listen*, Nathaniel, and Americans will write the Great American Novel for you. You cannot imagine all I have heard standing in suspenders in a hotel bathroom, with the water running in the tub so nobody in the next room could tune in with a glass to the wall, and my guest pouring out to Smitty the dark, clammy secrets of the hard-on and the heart. Beats the Custom-House grabbag any day. Oh, I grant you that a fellow in a fix did not speak in Hester's Boston as he did in Shoeless Joe's Chicago—where the heinous hurler Eddie Cicotte said to me of the World Series game he threw, "I did it for my wife and kiddies"—but I wonder if times have changed as much as Nathaniel Hawthorne would lead you to believe.

A more spectacular similarity between Hawthorne's book and my own than the fact that each has a windy autobiographical intro that "seizes the public by the button" is the importance in both of *a scarlet letter* identifying the wearer as an outcast from America. Hawthorne recounts how he found "this rag of scarlet cloth," frayed and moth-eaten, amidst the rubbish heaped up in the Custom-House attic. The mysterious meaning of the scarlet letter is then revealed to him in the old documents he uncovers. "On the breast of her gown," writes Hawthorne of Hester, with admirable alliteration too, "in fine red cloth, surrounded with an elaborate embroidery and fantastic flourishes of gold thread, appeared the letter A." A for "Adulteress," at the outset; by the end of her life, says the author, many came to think it stood for "Able; so strong was Hester Prynne, with a woman's strength."

Well, so too did a red cloth letter, this one of felt, appear on the breast of the off-white woolen warm-up jackets worn by the Mundys of the Patriot League—only their fateful letter was

R. At the outset R for Ruppert, the team's home; in the end, as many would have it, for "Rootless," for "Ridiculous," for "Refugee." Fact is I could not but think of the Mundys, and how they wandered the league after their expulsion from Port Ruppert, when I heard my precursor's description of himself at the conclusion to his intro. "I am," wrote Hawthorne, "a citizen of somewhere else." My precursor, and my kinsman too.

2. *The Adventures of Huckleberry Finn*, by Mark Twain

Listening to Huckleberry Finn ramble on is like listening to nine-tenths of the baseball players who ever lived talk about what they do in the off season down home. The ballplayers are two and three times Huck's age, and contrary to popular belief, most are not sired in the South like Huck, but hail from Pennsylvania—yet none of this means they care any the less for setting up housekeeping in the thick woods first chance they get, cooking their catch for breakfast and dinner, otherwise just being carried with the current in a comfy canoe, their sole female companion Mother N. Boys would be big leaguers, as everybody knows, but so would big leaguers be boys. Why, when a manager walks out to the mound to calm a pitcher in trouble, what do you imagine he tells him? "Give him the old dipsy-do"—? Not if he has any brains he doesn't. If the pitcher could get the old dipsy to do he'd be doing it without being told. Know what the manager says? "How many quail did you say you shot when you were hunting last fall, Al?" And if you think I am making that one up so as to link my tale to Twain's (as I have already shown it to be linked to Hawthorne's) if you think I am—as Huck Finn would have it—telling "stretchers" to falsify my literary credentials and my family tree, then I strongly advise you to read *Pitching in a Pinch* by Christy Mathewson, wherein the great Matty, as truthful in life as he was tricky on the hill, quotes the famous Giant manager and Hall of Famer John Joseph McGraw—as have I. How many quail did you say you shot when you were hunting last fall, Al? Yes, that is the strategy they talk on the mound—same kind they talk on a raft!

And since, admittedly, we are seeking out similitudes of all sorts twixt Twain's microcosm and mine, what about Huck Finn's sidekick, the runaway slave Nigger Jim? Who do you think he grew up to be anyway? Let me tell you if you haven't guessed: none other than the first Negro leaguer (according to today's paper) to be welcomed to the Hall of Fame, albeit in the bleacher section of the venerable, villainous institution: Leroy Robert (Satchel) Paige (see papers 2/11/71). In that Satchel Paige was born in Mobile, Alabama, approximately four years before Sam Clemens died in Hartford, Connecticut, it is doubtful that the eminent humorist ever saw him pitch, except maybe with some barnstorming pickaninny team; what's more to the point, he did not live to hear Satch speechify. If he had it would surely have delighted him (as it does Smitty in Sam's behalf) to discover that the indestructible Negro pitcher who is said to have won two thousand of the two thousand and five hundred games he pitched in twenty-two years in the Negro leagues, is Huck's Jim transmogrified.

Just listen to this, fans, for sheer prophecy: "Jim had a hairball as big as your fist, which had been took out of the fourth stomach of an ox, and he used to do magic with it. He said there was a spirit inside of it, and it knowed everything." And this: "Strange niggers would stand with their mouths open, and look him all over, same as if he was a wonder . . . and he was more looked up to than any nigger in that country." With his hairball Jim could perform magic and tell fortunes—with his fastball, Satch once struck out Rogers Hornsby *five times* in a single exhibition game! But the proof of the pudding is the talking. Listen now to Satch, offering to humankind his six precepts on how to stay young and strong. Students of Literatoor, professors, and small boys who recall Jim's comical lingo will not be fooled just because Satch has dispensed with the thick dialect he used for speaking in Mr. Twain's book. Back then he was a slave and had to talk that way. It was expected of him. Satchel Paige's recipe for eternal youth:

1. Avoid fried meats which angry up the blood.
2. If your stomach disputes you, lie down and pacify it with cool thoughts.
3. Keep the juices flowing by jangling around gently as you move.
4. Go very light on the vices, such as carrying on in society. The social ramble ain't restful.

5. Avoid running at all times.
6. Don't look back. Something might be gaining on you.

Now if this is not the hairball oracle who floated down the Mississippi with Huckleberry Finn, then someone is doing a pretty good imitation.

Colored players started coming into the majors just when Smitty and the P. League were being escorted out the door, so I do not know firsthand how the white boys have managed living alongside them. I suppose there were those like pricky little Tom Sawyer, America's first fraternity boy, who took childish delight in tormenting the colored however they could, and others, like Huck, more or less good-natured kids, who were confused as hell suddenly to be sharing dugout, locker room, and hotel bath with the dusky likes of Nigger Jim. Do you remember, students of L., when Huck tricks Jim into believing the crackup of their raft had occurred only in Jim's dreams? And how heartbroken old Jim was when he discovered otherwise? "It was fifteen minutes," says Huck, "before I could work myself up to go and humble myself to a nigger; but I done it, and I warn't ever sorry for it afterward, neither. I didn't do him no more mean tricks, and I wouldn't done that one if I'd a' knowed it would make him feel that way." It figures that more than a few ballplayers have by this time come around to Huck's way of thinking, as he expresses it so sweetly here. But I expect, given what I know of that lot, that the leagues have still got their share of Tom Sawyers, who even under the guise of doing Jim good had himself the time of his sadistic little small-town life heaping every sort of abuse and punishment he could think of upon that shackled black yearning to be free of Miss Watson. Of course as of 2/11/71 the shackles are off poor Jim and he is not only free but in the Hall of Shame. That just leaves Gofannon in shackles, don't it? The Patriot League, America, those are your niggers now, *for when you are blackballed from baseball, then verily, you are the untouchables in these United States.*

Students of L. and fans, the story I have to tell—prefigured as it is in the wanderings of Huckleberry Finn and Nigger Jim, and the adventures in ostracism of Hester Prynne, the Puritans' pariah—is of the once-mighty Mundys, how they were cast out of their home ball park in Port Ruppert, their year of humiliation on the road, and the shameful catastrophe that destroyed them (and me) forever. Little did the seven other teams in the league realize—little did any of us realize, fella name a' included—that the seemingly comical misfortunes of the last-place Mundys constituted the prelude to oblivion for us all. But that, fans, is the tyrannical law of our lives: today euphoria, tomorrow the whirlwind.

Bringing us to our blood brother.

### 3. *Moby Dick*, by Herman Melville

*Moby Dick* is to the old whaling industry (d.) what the Hall of Fame and Museum was *supposed* to have been to baseball: the ultimate and indisputable authority on the subject—repository of records, storehouse of statisticians, the Louvre of Leviathans. Who is Moby Dick if not the terrifying Ty Cobb of his species? Who is Captain Ahab if not the unappeasable Dodger manager Durocher, or the steadfast Giant John McGraw? Who are Flask, Starbuck, and Stubb, Ahab's trio of first mates, if not the Tinker, Evers, and Chance of the *Pequod*'s crew? Better, call them the d.p. combination of the Ruppert Mundys—d.p. standing here for displaced person as well as double play—say they are Frenchy Astarte, Nickname Damur, and Big John Baal, for where is the infield (and the outfield, the starters and relievers, the coaches, catchers, pinch-runners and pinch-hitters) of that peripatetic Patriot League team today, but down with the bones and the timbers of the Moby Dick–demolished *Pequod*, beneath "the great shroud of the sea." Their remote Nantucket? Ruppert. Their crazed and vengeful Ahab? Manager Gil Gamesh. And their Ishmael? Yes, one did survive the wreck to tell the tale—an indestructible old truth-teller called me!

Gentle fans, if you were to have bound together into a single volume every number ever published of the baseball weekly known as *The Sporting News*, as well as every manual, guide, and handbook important to an understanding of the game; if you were to assemble encyclopedic articles describing the size, weight, consistency, color, texture, resiliency, and liveliness of the baseball itself, from the early days when the modern Moby

Dick–colored ball was not even mandatory and some teams preferred using balls colored red (yes, Mr. Chairman, not white but *red*!), to the days of the "putting-out system" of piece labor, wherein baseballs were hand sewn by women in their homes, then through to the 1910's when A. G. Spalding introduced the first cork-centered baseball (thus ending the "dead-ball" era) and on to 1926, when the three leagues adopted the "cushion cork center" and with it the modern slug-away style of play; if you were to describe the cork forests of Spain, the rubber plantations of Malaysia, and the sheep farms of the American West where the Spalding baseball is born, if you were to differentiate between the three kinds of yarn in which the rubber that encases the cork is wrapped, and remark upon the relative hardness of that wrapping over the decades and how it has determined batting vs. slugging averages; if you were to devote a chapter to "The Tightness of the Stitching," explaining scientifically the aerodynamics of the curveball, or any such breaking pitch, how it is affected by the relative smoothness of the ball's seams and the number of seams that meet the wind as it rotates on its axis; and then if from this discussion of the ball, you were to take a turn, as it were, with the bat, noting first the eccentric nineteenth-century variations such as the flattened bat that Wright designed to facilitate bunting, and the curved-barrel bat in the shape of a question mark invented by Emile Kinst to put a deceptive spin upon the struck ball (enterprising Emile! cunning Kinst!), and thence moved on to describe the manufacture out of hickory logs of the classic bat shaped by Hillerich and Bradsby, the first model of which was turned in his shop by Bud Hillerich himself in 1884—the bat that came to be known to the world of men and boys as "the Louisville Slugger"; if you were by way of a digression to write a chapter on the most famous bats in baseball history, Heinie Groh's "bottle bat," Ed Delehanty's "Big Betsy," Luke Gofannon's "Magic Wand," and those bats of his that Ty Cobb would hone with a steer bone hour upon hour, much as Queequeg, Tashtego, and Dagoo would care lovingly for their harpoons; if then you were to write a chapter on the history of the baseball glove, recounting how the gloves of fielder, first-baseman, and catcher have evolved from the days when the game was played bare-handed, first into something resembling an ordinary dress glove, then into the "heavily-padded mitten," of the 1890's, the small webbed glove of the twenties, and finally in our own era of giantism, into the bushel-basket; if you were to describe the process by which Rawlings manufactures baseball shoes out of kangaroo hide, commencing with the birth of a single fleet-footed kangaroo in the wilds of Western Australia and following it through to its first stolen base in the majors; if you were to recount the evolutionary history of the All-Star game, beanballs, broadcasting, the canvas base, the catcher's mask, chewing tobacco, contracts, doubleheaders, double plays, fans, farm systems, fixes, foul balls, gate receipts, home runs, home plate, ladies day, minor leagues, night games, picture cards, player organizations, salaries, scandals, stadiums, the strike zone, sportscasters, sportswriters, Sunday ball, trading, travel, the World Series, and umpires, you would not in the end have a compendium of American baseball any more thorough than the one that Herman Melville has assembled in *Moby Dick* on the American enterprise of catching the whale. I would not be surprised to learn that his book ran first as a series in *Mechanix Illustrated*, if such existed in Melville's day, so clear and methodical is he in elucidating just what it took in the way of bats, balls, and gloves to set yourself up for chasing the pennant in those leagues. Today some clever publisher would probably bring out *Moby Dick* as one of those "How To Do It" books, providing he left off the catastrophic conclusion, or appended it under the title, "And How Not To."

Only today who cares about how to catch a whale in the old-fashioned, time-honored, and traditional way? Or about anything "traditional" for that matter? Today they just drop bombs down the spouts to blow the blubber out, or haul the leviathans in with a hook, belly-up, those who've been dumb enough to drink from the chamberpot that once was Melville's "wild and distant sea." How's that for a horror, Brother Melville? Not only is your indestructible Moby Dick now an inch from extinction *but so is the vast salt sea itself.* The sea is no longer a fit place for habitation—just ask the tunas in the cans. Two-thirds of the globe, the Mother of us all, and according to today's paper, *the place is poisoned.* Yes, even the *fish* have been given their eviction notice, and must pack up their scales and go fannon—which is just baseball's way of saying get lost. Only there is no elsewhere as far as I can see for these aquatic vertebrates to go fann *or* fin in. The fate that befell the Ruppert Mundys has now befallen the fish, and who, dear dispensable fans, is to follow?

Let me prophesy. What began in '46 with the obliteration of the Patriot League will not end until the planet itself has gone the way of the Tri-City Tycoons, the Tri-City Greenbacks, the Kakoola Reapers, the Terra Incognita Rustlers, the Asylum Keepers, the Aceldama Butchers, the Ruppert Mundys, and me; until each and every one of you is gone like the sperm whale and the great Luke Gofannon, gone without leaving a trace! Only read your daily paper, fans—every day news of another stream, another town, another species biting the dust. Wait, very soon now whole continents will be canceled out like stamps. Whonk, Africa! Whonk, Asia! Whonk, Europa! Whonk, North, whonk, South, America! And, oh, don't try hiding, Antarctica—*whonk* you too! And that will be it, fans, as far as the landmass goes. A brand new ballgame.

*Only where is it going to be played?* Under the lights on the dark side of the Moon? Will Walter O'Malley with his feel for the future really move the Dodgers to Mars? There is no doubt, Mr. O'M., that you cannot beat that planet for parking, but tell me, has your accountant consulted your astrophysicist yet? Are you sure there are curves on Mars? Will pitchers on Venus work in regular rotation in temperatures of five hundred degrees? And fly balls hit into Saturn's rings—ground-rule doubles or cheap home runs? And what of the historic Fall Classic and the pieties thereof—plan to rechristen it the Solar System Series, or do you figure eventually to go intergalactic? Only when you get beyond the Milky Way, sir, do they even *have* October? Better check. And hurry, hurry—there is much scheming and bullshitting and stock-splitting to be done, if you are to be ready in time for the coming cataclysm. For make no mistake, you sharp-eyed, fast-talking, money-making O'Malleys of America, you proprietors, promoters, expropriators, and entrepreneurs: *the coming cataclysm is coming.* The cushy long-term lease has just about run out on this Los Angeles of a franchise called Earth—and yes, like the dinosaur, like the whale, like hundreds upon hundreds of species whose bones and poems we never even knew, you too will be out on your dispossessed ass, Mr. and Mrs. Roaring Success! Henceforth all *your* games will be played away, too. Away! Away! Far far away! So then, farewell, fugitives! Pleasant journey, pilgrims! *Auf Wiedersehen*, evacuees! *A demain*, d.p.s! *Adios*, drifters! So long, scapegoats! *Hasta mañana*, émigrés! *Pax vobiscum*, pariahs! Happy landing, hobos! *Aloha*, outcasts! *Shalom, shalom*, shelterless, shipwrecked, shucked, shunted, and shuttled humankind! Or, as we say so succinctly in America, to the unfit, the failed, the floundering and forgotten, HIT THE ROAD, YA BUMS!

# 1

# HOME SWEET HOME

# 1

*Containing as much of the history of the Patriot League as is necessary to
acquaint the reader with its precarious condition at the beginning of the
Second World War. The character of General Oakhart—soldier, patriot,
and President of the League. His great love for the rules of the game. His
ambitions. By way of a contrast, the character of Gil Gamesh, the most
sensational rookie pitcher of all time. His attitude toward authority and
mankind in general. The wisdom and suffering of Mike "the Mouth"
Masterson, the umpire who is caught in between. The expulsion from baseball of the law-breaker Gamesh. In which Mike the Mouth becomes baseball's Lear and the nation's Fool. A brief history of the Ruppert Mundys,
in which the decline from greatness is traced, including short sketches of
their heroic center-fielder Luke Gofannon, and the esteemed manager
and Christian gentleman Ulysses S. Fairsmith. The chapter is
concluded with a dialogue between General Oakhart
and Mister Fairsmith, containing a few
surprises and disappointments
for the General.*

WHY the Ruppert Mundys had been chosen to become
the homeless team of baseball was explained to the Port
Ruppert fans with that inspirational phrase of yesteryear, "to
help save the world for democracy." Because of the proximity
of beautiful Mundy Park to the Port Ruppert harbor and dock
facilities, the War Department had labeled it an ideal embarka-
tion camp and the government had arranged to lease the site
from the owners for the duration of the struggle. A city of two-
story barracks was to be constructed on the playing field to
house the soldiers in transit, and the ivy-covered brick structure that in the Mundy heyday used to hold a happy Sunday
crowd of thirty-five thousand was to furnish headquarters facilities for those who would be shipping a million American boys
and their weapons across the Atlantic to liberate Europe from
the tyrant Hitler. In the years to come (the local fans were
told), schoolchildren in France, in Belgium, in Holland, in far-
off Denmark and Norway would be asked in their history

classes to find the city of Port Ruppert, New Jersey, on the map of the world and to mark it with a star; and among English-speaking peoples, Port Ruppert would be honored forever after —along with Runnymede in England, where the Magna Charta had been signed by King John, and Philadelphia, Pennsylvania, where John Hancock had affixed his signature to the Declaration of Independence—as a Birth-Place of Freedom . . . Then there was the psychological lift that Mundy Park would afford the young draftees departing the ballfield for the battle-front. To spend their last weeks on American soil as "the home team" in the stadium made famous by the incomparable Mundys of '28, '29, and '30, could not but provide "a shot in the arm" to the morale of these American soldiers, most of whom had been hero-worshipping schoolkids back when the Mundys, powered by the immortal Luke Gofannon, had won three hundred and thirty-five games in three seasons, and three consecutive World Series without losing a single game. Yes, what the hallowed playing fields of Eton had been to the British officers of long, long ago, Mundy Park would be to G.I. Joe of World War Two.

As it turned out, bracing sentiments such as these, passion-ately pronounced from a flag-draped platform in downtown Port Ruppert by notables ranging from Secretary of War Stimson and Governor Edison to the Mayor of Port Ruppert, Boss Stuvwxyz, did work to quash the outcry that the Mundy management and the U.S. government had feared from a citi-zenry renowned for its devotion to "the Rupe-its" (as the team was called in the local patois). Why, feeling for the Mundys ran so high in that town, that according to Bob Hope, one young fellow called up by the Port Ruppert draft board had written "the Mundys" where the questionnaire had asked his religion; as the comedian told the servicemen at the hundreds of Army bases he toured that year, there was another fellow back there, who when asked his occupation by the recruiting sergeant, replied with a straight face, "A Rupe-it roota and a plumma." The soldiers roared—as audiences would if a comic said no more than, "There was this baseball fan in Port Ruppert—" but Hope had only to add, "Seriously now, the whole nation is really indebted to those people out there—" for the soldiers and sailors to be up on their feet, whistling through their teeth in tribute to the East Coast metropolis whose fans and public officials had bid farewell to their beloved ball club in order to make the world safe for democracy.

As if the Mundys' fans had anything to say about it, one way or another! As if Boss Stuvwxyz would object to consigning the ball club to Hell, so long as his pockets had been lined with gold!

The rationale offered "Rupe-it rootas" by the press and the powers-that-be did not begin to answer General Oakhart's objections to the fate that had befallen the Mundys. What infuriated the General wasn't simply that a decision of such magnitude had been reached behind his back—as though he whose division had broken through the Hindenburg Line in the fall of 1918 was in actuality an agent of the Huns!—but that by this extraordinary maneuver, severe damage had been inflicted upon the reputation of the league of which he was president. As it was, having been sullied by scandal in the early thirties and plagued ever since by falling attendance, the Patriot League could no longer safely rely upon its prestigious past in the competition for the better ball players, managers, and umpires. This new inroad into league morale and cohesiveness would only serve to encourage the schemers in the two rival leagues whose fondest wish was to drive the eight Patriot League teams into bankruptcy (or the minors—either would do), and thus leave the American and National the only authorized "big" leagues in the country. The troops laughed uproariously when Bob Hope referred to the P. League—now with seven home teams, instead of eight—as "the short circuit," but General Oakhart found the epithet more ominous than amusing.

Even more ominous was this: by sanctioning an arrangement wherein twenty-three major league teams played at least half of their games at home, while the Mundys alone played all one hundred and fifty-four games on the road, Organized Baseball had compromised the very principles of Fair Play in which the sport was grounded; they had consented to tamper with what was dearer even to General Oakhart than the survival of his league: the Rules and the Regulations.

Now every Massachusetts schoolchild who had ever gone off with his class to visit the General's office at P. League headquarters in Tri-City knew about General Oakhart and his Rules and Regulations. During the school year, busloads of little children were regularly ushered through the hallways painted with murals twelve and fifteen feet high of the great Patriot League heroes of the past—Base Baal, Luke Gofannon, Mike Mazda, Smoky Woden—and into General Oakhart's paneled office to hear him deliver his lecture on the national pastime. In order to bring home to the youngsters the central importance of the Rules and Regulations, he would draw their attention to the model of a baseball diamond on his desk, explaining to them that if the distance between the bases were to be shortened by as little as one inch, you might just as well change the name of the game, for by so doing you would have altered fundamentally the existing relationship between the diamond "as we have always known it" and the physical effort and skill required to play the game upon a field of those dimensions. Into their solemn and awed little faces he would thrust his heavily decorated chest (for he dressed in a soldier's uniform till the day he died) and he would say: "Now I am not telling you that somebody won't come along tomorrow and *try* to change that distance on us. The streets are full of people with harebrained schemes, out to make a dollar, out to make confusion, out to make the world over because it doesn't happen to suit their taste. I am only telling you that ninety feet is how far from one another the bases been for a hundred years now, and as far as I am concerned, how far from one another they shall remain until the end of time. I happen to think that the great man whose picture you see hanging above my desk knew what he was doing when he invented the game of baseball. I happen to think that when it came to the geometry of the diamond, he was a genius on a par with Copernicus and Sir Isaac Newton, who I am sure you have read about in your schoolbooks. I happen to think that ninety feet was *precisely* the length necessary to make this game the hard, exciting, and suspenseful struggle that it is. And that is why I would impress upon your young minds a belief in following to the letter, the Rules and the Regulations, as they have been laid down by thoughtful and serious men before you or I were ever born, and as they have survived in baseball for a hundred years now, and in human life since the dawn of civilization.

Boys and girls, take away the Rules and the Regulations, and you don't *have* civilized life as we know and revere it. If I have any advice for you today, it's this—don't try to shorten the base paths in order to reach home plate faster and score. All you will have accomplished by that technique is to cheapen the value of a run. I hope you will ponder that on the bus ride back to school. Now, go on out and stroll around the corridors all you want. Those great paintings are there for your enjoyment. Good day, and good luck to you."

General Oakhart became President of the Patriot League in 1933, though as early as the winter of 1919–1920, he was being plugged for the commissionership of baseball, along with his friend and colleague General John "Blackjack" Pershing and the former President of the United States William Howard Taft. At that time it had seemed to him an excellent stepping-stone to high political office, and he had been surprised and saddened when the owners had selected a popinjay like Judge Kenesaw Mountain Landis over a man of principle like himself. In his estimation Landis was nothing more than a showboat judge—as could be proved by the fact that every time he made one of his "historic decisions," it was subsequently reversed by a higher court. In 1907 as a federal judge he fined the Standard Oil Company twenty-nine million dollars in a rebate case— headlines all over the place—then, overruled by the U.S. Supreme Court. During the war, the same hollow theatrics: seven socialists up before him for impeding the war effort; scathing denunciations from Judge Landis, hefty jail sentences all around, including one to a Red congressman from Milwaukee, big headlines—and then the verdict thrown out the window by a higher court. That was the man they had chosen over him—the same man who now told General Oakhart that it was "an honor" for the Mundys to have been chosen to make this sacrifice for their country, that actually it would *good* for the game for a major league team to be seen giving their all to the war effort day in and day out. Oh, and did he get on his high horse when the General suggested that the Commissioner might go to Washington to ask President Roosevelt to intervene in the Mundys' behalf. "In this office, General, the Patriot League is just another league, and the Ruppert Mundys are just another ball club, and if either one of them expects preferential treatment from Kenesaw Mountain Landis they have another guess coming. Baseball does not intend to ask for special favors in a time of national crisis. And that's that!"

Back in the summer of 1920, having already lost out to Landis for the commissioner's job, General Oakhart suffered a second stunning setback when the movement to make him Harding's running-mate died in the smoke-filled rooms. No one (went the argument against him) wanted to be reminded of all the boys buried under crosses in France to whom General Oakhart had been "Father, Brother, and Buddy too." Nor —he thought bitterly, when the Teapot Dome scandal broke in '23, when one after another of Harding's cronies was indicted, convicted, and jailed for the most vile sort of political corruption—nor did they want a man of integrity around, either. When Harding died (of shame and humiliation, one would hope) and Coolidge took the oath of office—Coolidge, that hack they had chosen instead of him!—the General came near to weeping for the nation's loss of himself. But, alas, the American people didn't seem to care any more than the politicians did for a man who lived by and for the Rules and Regulations.

Sure enough, when the call went out for General Oakhart, the country was suffering just such panic and despair as he had predicted years ago, if the ship of state were to be steered for long by unprincipled leaders. It was not, however, to the White House or even the State House that the General was summoned, but to Tri-City, Mass., to be President of a baseball league in trouble. With five of its eight teams in hock to the bank, and fear growing among the owners that the Depression had made their players susceptible to the gambling mob, the P. League proprietors had paid a visit to General Oakhart in his quarters at the War College, where he was director of Military Studies, and pleaded with him not to sit sulking in an ivory tower. It was Spenser Trust, the billionaire Tycoon owner, and nobody's fool, who spoke the words that appeared to win the General's heart: he reminded him that it was not just their floundering league that was casting about for a strong man to lead them back to greatness, but the nation as well. An outstanding Republican who rose to national prominence in '33 might well find himself elected the thirty-third President of the United States in '36.

Now as luck would have it—or so it seemed to the General at the outset—the very year he agreed to retire from the military to become President of the P. League, the nineteen-year-old Gil Gamesh came up to pitch for the Tycoons' crosstown rival, the Tri-City Greenbacks. Gamesh, throwing six consecutive shutouts in his first six starts, was an immediate sensation, and with his "I can beat anybody" motto, captured the country's heart as no player had since the Babe began swatting them out of the ballpark in 1920. Only the previous year, in the middle of the most dismal summer of his life, the great Luke Gofannon had called it quits and retired to his farm in the Jersey flats, so that it had looked at the opening of the '33 season as though the Patriot League would be without an Olympian of the Ruth-Cobb variety. Then, from nowhere— or, to be exact, from Babylonia, by way of his mother and father —came the youngster the General aptly labeled "the Talk of the World," and nothing Hubbell did over in the National League or Lefty Grove in the American was remotely comparable. The tall, slim, dark-haired left-hander was just what the doctor had ordered for a nation bewildered and frightened by a ruinous Depression—here was a kid who just would not lose, and he made no bones about it either. Nothing shy, nothing sweet, nothing humble about this young fellow. He could be ten runs on top in the bottom of the ninth, two men out, the bases empty, a count of 0 and 2 on the opposing team's weakest hitter, and if the umpire gave him a bad call he would be down off that mound breathing fire. "You blind robber— it's a strike!" However, if and when the *batter* should dare to put up a beef on a call, Gamesh would laugh like mad and call out to the ump, "Come on now, you can't tell anything by him—he never even seen it. He'd be the last guy in the *world* to know."

And the fans just ate it up: nineteen years old and he had the courage and confidence of a Walter Johnson, and the competitive spirit of the Georgia Peach himself. The stronger the batter the better Gil liked it. Rubbing the ball around in those enormous paws that hung down practically to his knees, he would glare defiantly at the man striding up to the plate (some of them stars when he was still in the cradle) and announce out loud his own personal opinion of the fellow's abilities. "You couldn't lick a stamp. You couldn't beat a drum. Get your belly button in there, bud, you're what I call duck soup." Then, sneering away, he would lean way back, kick that right leg up sky-high like a chorus girl, and that long left arm would start coming around by way of Biloxi—and next thing you knew it was strike one. He would burn them in just as beautiful and nonchalant as that, three in a row, and then exactly like a barber, call out, "Next!" He did not waste a pitch, unless it was to throw a ball at a batter's head, and he did not consider that a waste. He knew a hundred ways to humiliate the opposition, such as late in the game deliberately walking the other pitcher, then setting the ball down on the ground to wave him from first on to second. "Go on, go on, you ain't gonna get there no other way, that's for sure." With the surprised base runner safely ensconced at second, Gil would kick the ball up into his glove with the instep of his shoe—"Okay, just stand there on the bag, bud," he would tell the opposing pitcher, "and watch these fellas try and hit me. You might learn somethin', though I doubt it."

Gamesh was seen to shed a tear only once in his career: when his seventh major league start was rained out. Some reports had it that he even took the Lord's name in vain, blaming Him of all people for the washout. Gil announced afterward that had he been able to work in his regular rotation that afternoon, he would have extended his shutout streak through those nine innings *and on to the very end of the season.* An outrageous claim, on the face of it, and yet there were those in the newsrooms, living rooms, and barrooms around this nation who believed him. As it was, even lacking his "fine edge," as he called it, he gave up only one run the next day, and never more than two in any game that year.

Around the league, at the start of that season, they would invariably begin to boo the headstrong nineteen-year-old when he stepped out of the Greenback dugout, but it did not appear to affect him any. "I never expect they are going to be very happy to see me heading out to the mound," he told reporters. "I wouldn't be, if I was them." Yet once the game was over, it invariably required a police escort to get Gamesh back to the hotel, for the crowd that had hated him nine innings earlier for being so cocksure of himself, was now in the streets calling his name—adults screaming right along with kids—as though it was the Savior about to emerge from the visiting team club-house in a spiffy yellow linen suit and two-toned perforated shoes.

It surely seemed to the General that he could not have turned up in the league president's box back of first at Greenback Stadium at a more felicitous moment. In 1933 just about everybody appeared to have become a Greenback fan, and the Patriot League pennant battle between the two Tri-City teams, the impeccably professional Tycoons, and the rough-and-tumble Greenbacks, made headlines East *and* West, and constituted just about the only news that didn't make you want to slit your throat over the barren dinner table. Men out of work—and there were fifteen million of them across the land, men sick and tired of defeat and dying for a taste of victory, rich men who had become paupers overnight—would some-how scrape two bits together to come out and watch from the bleachers as a big unbeatable boy named Gil Gamesh did his stuff on the mound. And to the little kids of America, whose dads were on the dole, whose uncles were on the booze, and whose older brothers were on the bum, he was a living, breathing example of that hero of American heroes, the he-man, a combination of Lindbergh, Tarzan, and (with his long, girlish lashes and brilliantined black hair) Rudolph Valentino: brave, brutish, and a lady-killer, and in possession of a sidearm fastball that according to Ripley's "Believe It or Not" could pass clear through a batter's chest, come out his back, and still be traveling at "major league speed."

What cooled the General's enthusiasm for the boy wonder was the feud that erupted in the second month of the season between young Gil and Mike Masterson, and that ended in tragedy on the last day of the season. The grand old man of umpiring had been assigned by General Oakhart to follow the Greenbacks around the country, after it became evident that Gamesh was just too much for the other officials in the circuit to handle. The boy could be rough when the call didn't go his way, and games had been held up for five and ten minutes at a time while Gamesh told the ump in question just what he thought of his probity, eyesight, physiognomy, parentage, and place of national origin. Because of the rookie's enormous popularity, because of the records he was breaking in game after game, because many in the crowd had laid out their last quarter to see Gamesh pitch (and because they were just plain intimidated), the umps tended to tolerate from Gamesh what would have been inexcusable in a more mature, or less spectacular, player. This of course was creating a most dangerous precedent vis-à-vis the Rules and the Regulations, and in order to prevent the situation from getting completely out of hand, General Oakhart turned to the finest judge of a fastball in the majors, in his estimate the toughest, fairest official who ever wore blue, the man whose booming voice had earned him the monicker "the Mouth."

"I have been umpiring in the Patriot League since Dewey took Manila," Mike the Mouth liked to tell them on the annual banquet circuit, after the World Series was over. "I have rendered more than a million and a half decisions in that time, and let me tell you, in all those years I have never called one wrong, at least not in my heart. In my apprentice days down in the minors I was bombarded with projectiles from the stands, I was threatened with switchblades by coaches, and once a misguided manager fired upon me with a gun. This three-inch scar here on my forehead was inflicted by the mask of a catcher who believed himself wronged by me, and on my shoulders and my back I bear sixty-four wounds inflicted during those 'years of trial' by bottles of soda pop. I have been mobbed by fans so perturbed that when I arrived in the dressing room I discovered all the buttons had been torn from my clothing, and rotten vegetables had been stuffed into my trousers and my shirt. But harassed and hounded as I have been, I am proud to say that I have never so much as changed the call on a close one out of fear of the consequences to my life, my limbs, or my loved ones."

This last was an allusion to the kidnapping and murder of Mike the Mouth's only child, back in 1898, his first year up with the P. League. The kidnappers had entered Mike's Wisconsin home as he was about to leave for the ball park to umpire a game between the Reapers and the visiting Rustlers, who were battling that season for the flag. Placing a gun to his little girl's blond curls, the intruders told the young umpire that if the Reapers lost that afternoon, Mary Jane would be back in her high chair for dinner, unharmed. If however the Reapers should win for any reason, then Masterson could hold himself responsible for his darling child's fate . . . Well, that game, as everyone knows, went on and on and on, before the Reapers put together two walks and a scratch hit in the bottom of the seventeenth to break the 3–3 tie and win by a run. In subsequent weeks, pieces of little Mary Jane Masterson were found in every park in the Patriot League.

It did not take but one pitch, of course, for Mike the Mouth to become the lifelong enemy of Gil Gamesh. Huge crowd, sunny day, flags snapping in the breeze, Gil winds up, kicks, and here comes that long left arm, America, around by way of the tropical Equator.

"That's a ball," thundered Mike, throwing his own left arm into the air (as if anybody in the ball park needed a sign when the Mouth was back of the plate).

"A ball?" cried Gamesh, hurling his glove twenty-five feet in the air. "Why, I couldn't put a strike more perfect across the plate! That was right in there, you blind robber!"

Mike raised one meaty hand to stop the game and stepped out in front of the plate with his whisk broom. He swept the dust away meticulously, allowing the youth as much time as he required to remember where he was and whom he was talking to. Then he turned to the mound and said—in tones exceeding courteous—"Young fellow, it looks like you'll be in the league for quite a while. That sort of language will get you nothing. Why don't you give it up?" And he stepped back into position behind the catcher. "Play!" he roared.

On the second pitch, Mike's left arm shot up again. "That's two." And Gamesh was rushing him.

"You cheat! You crook! You thief! You overage, overstuffed—"

"Son, don't say any more."

"And what if I do, you pickpocket?"

"I will give you the thumb right now, and we will get on with the game of baseball that these people have paid good money to come out here today to see."

"They didn't come out to see no baseball game, you idiot— they come out to see *me*!"

"I will run you out of here just the same."

"Try it!" laughed Gil, waving toward the stands where the Greenback fans were already on their feet, whooping like a tribe of Red Indians for Mike the Mouth's scalp. And how could it be otherwise? The rookie had a record of fourteen wins and no losses, and it was not yet July. "Go ahead and try it," said Gil. "They'd mob you, Masterson. They'd pull you apart."

"I would as soon be killed on a baseball field," replied Mike the Mouth (who in the end got his wish), "as anywhere else. Now why don't you go out there and pitch. That's what they pay you to do."

Smiling, Gil said, "And why don't you go shit in your shoes."

Mike looked as though his best friend had died; sadly he shook his head. "No, son, no, that won't do, not in the Big Time." And up went the right thumb, an appendage about the size and shape of a nice pickle. Up it went and up it stayed, though for a moment it looked as though Gamesh, whose mouth had fallen open, was considering biting it off—it wasn't but an inch from his teeth.

"Leave the field, son. And leave it now."

"Oh sure," chuckled Gil, recovering his composure, "oh sure, leave the field in the middle of pitchin' to the first batter," and he started back out to the mound, loping nonchalantly like a big boy in an open meadow, while the crowd roared their love right into his face. "Oh sure," he said, laughing like mad.

"Son, either you go," Mike called after him, "or I forfeit this game to the other side."

"And ruin my perfect record?" he asked, his hands on his hips in disbelief. "Oh sure," he laughed. Then he got back to business: sanding down the ball in his big calloused palms, he called to the batsman on whom he had a two ball count, "Okay, get in there, bud, and let's see if you can get that gun off your shoulder."

But the batter had hardly done as Gil had told him to when he was lifted out of the box by Mike the Mouth. Seventy-one years old, and a lifetime of being banged around, and still he just picked him up and set him aside like a paperweight. Then, with his own feet dug in, one on either side of home plate, he made his startling announcement to the sixty thousand fans in

Greenback Stadium—the voice of Enrico Caruso could not have carried any more clearly to the corners of the outfield bleachers.

"Because Greenback pitcher Gilbert Gamesh has failed to obey the order of the umpire-in-chief that he remove himself from the field of play, this game is deemed forfeited by a score of 9 to 0 to the opposing team, under rule 4.15 of the Official Baseball Rules that govern the playing of baseball games by the professional teams of the Patriot League of Professional Baseball Clubs."

And jaw raised, arms folded, and legs astride home plate—according to Smitty's column the next day, very like that Colossus at Rhodes—Mike the Mouth remained planted where he was, even as wave upon wave of wild men washed over the fences and onto the field.

And Gil Gamesh, his lips white with froth and his eagle eyes spinning in his skull, stood a mere sixty feet and six inches away, holding a lethal weapon in his hand.

The next morning. A black-and-white perforated shoe kicks open the door to General Oakhart's office and with a wad of newspapers in his notorious left hand, enter Gil Gamesh, shrieking. "My record is not 14 and 1! It's 14 and 0! Only now they got me down here for a *loss*! Which is impossible! *And you two done it!*"

"You 'done' it, young man," said General Oakhart, while in a double-breasted blue suit the same deep shade as his umpire togs, Mike the Mouth Masterson silently filled a chair by the trophy cabinet.

"Youse!"

"You."

"Youse!"

"You."

"Stop saying 'you' when I say 'youse'—it *was* youse, and the whole country knows it too! You and that thief! Sittin' there free as a bird, when he oughtta be in Sing Sing!"

Now the General's decorations flashed into view as he raised himself from behind the desk. Wearing the ribbons and stars of a courageous lifetime, he was impressive as a ship's figurehead —and of course he was still a powerfully built man, with a chest on him that might have been hooped around like a barrel. Indeed, the three men gathered together in the room looked as though they could have held their own against a team of horses, if they'd had to draw a brewery truck through the streets of Tri-City. No wonder that the day before, the mob that had pressed right up to his chin had fallen back from Mike the Mouth as he stood astride home plate like the Eighth Wonder of the World. Of course, ever since the murder of his child, not even the biggest numskull had dared to throw so much as a peanut shell at him from the stands; but neither did his bulk encourage a man to tread upon his toes.

"Gamesh," said the General, swelling with righteousness, "no umpire in the history of this league has ever been found guilty of a single act of dishonesty or corruption. Or even charged with one. Remember that!"

"But—my perfect record! He ruined it—forever! Now I'll go down in the history books as someone who once *lost*! And I didn't! I couldn't! I can't!"

"And why can't you, may I ask?"

"Because I'm Gil Gamesh! I'm an immortal!"

"I don't care if you are Jesus Christ!" barked the General. "There are Rules and Regulations in this world and you will follow them just like anybody else!"

"And who made the rules?" sneered Gamesh. "You? Or Scarface over there?"

"Neither of us, young man. *But we are here to see that they are carried out.*"

"And suppose I say the hell with you!"

"Then you will be what is known as an outlaw."

"And? So? Jesse James was an outlaw. And he's world-famous."

"True. But he did not pitch in the major leagues."

"He didn't want to," sneered the young star.

"But you do," replied General Oakhart, and, bewildered, Gamesh collapsed into a chair. It wasn't just *what* he wanted to do, it was *all* he wanted to do. It was what he was *made* to do.

"But," he whimpered, "my perfect record."

"The umpire, in case it hasn't occurred to you, has a record too. A record," the General informed him, "that must remain untainted by charges of favoritism or falsification. Otherwise there would not even be major league baseball contests in which young men like yourself could excel."

"But there ain't no young men like myself," Gamesh whined. "There's me, and that's it."

"Gil . . ." It was Mike the Mouth speaking. Off the playing field he had a voice like a songbird's, so gentle and mellifluous that it could soothe a baby to sleep. And alas, it had, years and years ago . . . "Son, listen to me. I don't expect that you are going to love me. I don't expect that anybody in a ball park is going to care if I live or die. Why should they? I'm not the star. You are. The fans don't go out to the ball park to see the Rules and the Regulations upheld, they go out to see the home team win. The whole world loves a winner, you know that better than anybody, but when it comes to an umpire, there's not a soul in the ball park who's for him. He hasn't got a fan in the place. What's more, he cannot sit down, he cannot go to the bathroom, he cannot get a drink of water, unless he visits the dugout, and that is something that any umpire worth his salt does not ever want to do. He cannot have anything to do with the players. He cannot fool with them or kid with them, even though he may be a man who in his heart likes a little horseplay and a joke from time to time. If he so much as sees a ballplayer coming down the street, he will cross over or turn around and walk the other way, so it will not look to passersby that anything is up between them. In strange towns, when the visiting players all buddy up in a hotel lobby and go out to-gether for a meal in a friendly restaurant, he finds a room in a boarding house and eats his evening pork chop in a diner all alone. Oh, it's a lonesome thing, being an umpire. There are men who won't talk to you for the rest of your life. Some will even stoop to vengeance. But that is not your lookout, my boy. Nobody is twisting Masterson's arm, saying, 'Mike, it's a dog's life, but you are stuck with it.' No, it's just this, Gil: somebody in this world has got to run the game. Otherwise, you see, it wouldn't be baseball, it would be chaos. We would be right back where we were in the Ice Ages."

"The Ice Ages?" said Gil, reflectively.

"Exactly," replied Mike the Mouth.

"Back when they was livin' in caves? Back when they carried clubs and ate raw flesh and didn't wear no clothes?"

"Correct!" said General Oakhart.

"Well," cried Gil, "maybe we'd be better off!" And kicking aside the newspapers with which he'd strewn the General's carpet, he made his exit. Whatever it was he said to the General's elderly spinster secretary out in the anteroom—instead of just saying "Good day"—caused her to keel over unconscious.

That very afternoon, refusing to heed the advice of his wise manager to take in a picture show, Gamesh turned up at Greenback Stadium just as the game was getting underway, and still buttoning up his uniform shirt, ran out and yanked the baseball from the hand of the Greenback pitcher who was preparing to pitch to the first Aceldama hitter of the day—and nobody tried to stop him. The regularly scheduled pitcher just walked off the field like a good fellow (cursing under his breath) and the Old Philosopher, as they called the Greenback manager of that era, pulled his tired old bones out of the dugout and ambled over to the umpire back of home plate. In his early years, the Old Philosopher had worn his seat out sliding up and down the bench, but after a lifetime of managing in the majors, he wasn't about to be riled by anything.

"Change in the line-up, Mike. That big apple knocker out there on the mound is batting ninth now on my card."

To which Mike Masterson, master of scruple and decorum, replied, "Name?"

"Boy named Gamesh," he shouted, to make himself heard above the pandemonium rising from the stands.

"Spell it."

"Awww come on now, Michael."

"Spell it."

"G-a-m-e-s-h."

"First name?"

"Gil. G as in Gorgeous. I as in Illustrious. L as in Larger-than-life."

"Thank you, sir," said Mike the Mouth, and donning his mask, called, "Play!"

("In the beginning was the word, and the word was 'Play!'" Thus began the tribute to Mike Masterson, written the day the season ended in tragedy, in the column called "One Man's Opinion.")

The first Aceldama batsman stepped in. Without even taking the time to insult him, to mock him, to tease and to taunt him, without so much as half a snarl or the crooked smile, Gamesh pitched the ball, which was what they paid him to do.

"Strike-ah-one!" roared Mike.

The catcher returned the ball to Gamesh, and again, impersonal as a machine and noiseless as a snake, Gamesh did his chorus girl kick, and in no time at all the second pitch passed through what might have been a tunnel drilled for it by the first.

"Strike-ah-two!"

On the third pitch, the hatter (who appeared to have no more idea where the ball might be than some fellow who wasn't even at the ball park) swung and wound up on his face in the dust. "Musta dropped," he told the worms.

"Strike-ah-three—you're-out!"

"Next!" Gamesh called and the second man in a Butcher uniform stepped up.

"Strike-ah-one!"

"Strike-ah-two!"

"Strike-ah-three—you're-out!"

So life went—cruelly, but swiftly—for the Aceldama hitters for eight full innings. "Next!" called Gamesh, and gave each the fastest shave and haircut on record. Then with a man out on strikes in the top of the ninth, and 0 and 2 on the hitter— and the fans so delirious that after each Aceldama batter left the chair, they gave off an otherworldly, practically celestial sound, as though together they constituted a human harp that had just been plucked—Gamesh threw the ball too low. Or so said the umpire behind the plate, who supposedly was in a position to know.

"That's one!"

Yes, Gil Gamesh was alleged by Mike the Mouth Masterson to have thrown a ball—after seventy-seven consecutive strikes.

"Well," sighed the Old Philosopher, down in the Greenback dugout, "here comes the end of the world." He pulled out his pocket watch, seemingly taking some comfort in its precision. "Yep, at 2:59 P.M. on Wednesday, June 16, 1933. Right on time."

Out on the diamond, Gil Gamesh was fifteen feet forward from the rubber, still in the ape-like crouch with which he completed his big sidearm motion. In their seats the fans surged upwards as though in anticipation of Gil's bounding into the air and landing in one enormous leap on Mike the Mouth's blue back. Instead, he straightened up like a man—a million years of primate evolution passing instantaneously before their eyes—and there was that smile, that famous crooked smile. "Okay," he called down to his catcher, Pineapple Tawhaki, "throw it here."

"But—holy aloha!" cried Pineapple, who hailed from Honolulu, "he call ball, Gilly!"

Gamesh spat high and far and watched the tobacco juice raise the white dust on the first-base foul line. He could hit anything with anything, that boy. "Was a ball."

"*Was?*" Pineapple cried.

"Yep. Low by the hair off a little girl's slit, but low." And spat again, this time raising chalk along third. "Done it on purpose, Pineapple. Done it deliberate."

"Holy aloha!" the mystified catcher groaned—and fired the ball back to Gil. "How-why-ee?"

"So's to make sure," said Gil, his voice rising to a piercing pitch, "so's to make sure the old geezer standin' behind you hadn't fell asleep at the switch! JUST TO KEEP THE OLD SON OF A BITCH HONEST!"

"One and two," Mike roared. "Play!"

"JUST SO AS TO MAKE CLEAR ALL THE REST WAS EARNED!"

"*Play!*"

"BECAUSE I DON'T WANT NOTHIN' FOR NOTHIN' FROM YOUSE! I DON'T NEED IT! I'M GIL GAMESH! I'M AN IMMORTAL, WHETHER YOU LIKE IT OR NOT!"

"PLAY BAWWWWWWWWWW!"

Had he ever been more heroic? More gloriously contemptuous of the powers-that-be? Not to those fans of his he hadn't. They loved him even more for that bad pitch, deliberately thrown a fraction of a fraction of an inch too low, than for the seventy-seven dazzling strikes that had preceded it. The wickedly accurate pitching machine wasn't a machine at all— no, he was a human being, made of piss and vinegar, like other human beings. The arm of a god, but the disposition of the

Common Man: petty, grudging, vengeful, gloating, selfish, narrow, and mean. How could they *not* adore him!

His next pitch was smacked three hundred and sixty-five feet off the wall in left-center field for a double.

Much as he hated to move his rheumatism to and fro like this, the Old Philosopher figured it was in the interest of the United States of America, of which he had been a lifelong citizen, for him to trek out to the mound and offer his condolences to the boy.

"Those things happen, lad; settle down."

"That robber! That thief! That pickpocket!"

"Mike Masterson didn't hit it off you—you just dished up a fat pitch. It could happen to anyone."

"But not to me! It was on account of my rhythm bein' broke! On account of my fine edge bein' off!"

"That wasn't his doin' either, boy. Throwin' that low one was your own smart idea. See this fella comin' up? He can strongback that pelota right outta here. I want for you to put him on."

"No!"

"Now do like I tell you, Gil. Put him on. It'll calm you down, for one, and set up the d.p. for two. Let's get out of this inning the smart way."

But when the Old Philosopher departed the mound, and Pineapple stepped to the side of the plate to give Gamesh a target for the intentional pass, the rookie sensation growled, "Get back where you belong, you Hawaiian hick."

"But," warned the burly catcher, running halfway to the mound, "he say put him on, Gilly!"

"Don't you worry, Oahu, I'll put him on all right."

"*How?*"

Gil grinned.

The first pitch was a fastball aimed right at the batter's mandible. In the stands, a woman screamed—"He's a goner!" but down went the Aceldama player just in the nick of time.

"That's one!" roared Mike.

The second pitch was a second fastball aimed at the occipital. "My God," screamed the woman, "it killed him!" But miracle of miracles, the batter in the dust was seen to move.

"That's two!" roared Mike, and calling time, came around to do some tidying up around home plate. And to chat awhile.

"Ball get away from you?" he asked Gamesh, while sweeping away with his broom.

Gamesh spat high in the air back over his shoulder, a wad that landed smack in the middle of second base, right between the feet of the Aceldama runner standing up on the bag. "Nope."

"Then, if you don't mind my asking, how do you explain nearly taking this man's head off two times in a row?"

"Ain't you never heard of the intentional pass?"

"Oh no. Oh no, not that way, son," said Mike the Mouth. "Not in the Big Time, I'm afraid."

"Play!" screeched Gamesh, mocking the umpire's foghorn, and motioned him back behind the plate where he belonged. "Ump, Masterson, that's what they pay you to do."

"Now listen to me, Gil," said Mike. "If you want to put this man on intentionally, then pitch out to him, in the time-honored manner. But don't make him go down again. We're not barbarians in this league. We're men, trying to get along."

"Speak for yourself, Mouth. I'm me."

The crowd shrieked as at a horror movie when the third pitch left Gil's hand, earmarked for the zygomatic arch. And Mike the Mouth, even before making his call, rushed to kneel beside the man spread across the plate, to touch his wrist and see if he was still alive. Barely, barely.

"That's three!" Mike roared to the stands. And to Gamesh —"And that's it!"

"*What's* it?" howled Gamesh. "He ducked, didn't he? He got out of the way, didn't he? You can't give me the thumb—I didn't even *nick* him!"

"Thanks to his own superhuman effort. His pulse is just about beating. It's a wonder he isn't lying there dead."

"Well," answered Gamesh, with a grin, "that's his look-out."

"No, son, no, it is mine."

"Yeah—and what about line drives back at the pitcher! More pitchers get hit in the head with liners than batters get beaned in the noggin—and do you throw out the guy what hit the line drive? No! Never! And the reason why is because they ain't Gil Gamesh! Because they ain't me!"

"Son," asked Mike the Mouth, grimacing as though in pain, "just what in the world do you think I have against you?"

"I'm too great, that's what!"

Donning his protective mask, Mike the Mouth replied, "We are only human beings, Gamesh, trying to get along. That's the last time I'll remind you."

"Boy, I sure hope so," muttered Gil, and then to the batter, he called, "All right, bud, let's try to stay up on our feet this time. All that fallin' down in there, people gonna think you're pickled."

With such speed did that fourth pitch travel the sixty feet and six inches to the plate, that the batsman, had he been Man o'War himself, could still not have moved from its path in time. He never had a chance . . . Aimed, however, just above the nasal bone, the fastball clipped the bill of his blue and gray Aceldama cap and spun it completely around on his head. Gamesh's idea of a joke, to see the smile he was sporting way down there in that crouch.

"That's no good," thundered Mike, "take your base!"

"If he can," commented Gil, watching the shell-shocked hitter trying to collect himself enough to figure out which way to go, up the third- or the first-base line.

"And you," said Mike softly, "can take off too, son." And here he hiked that gnarled pickle of a thumb into the air, and announced, "You're out of the game!"

The pitcher's glove went skyward; as though Mike had hit his jackpot, the green eyes began spinning in Gil's head. "No!"

"Yes, oh yes. Or I forfeit this one too. I'll give you to the letter C for Chastised, son. A. B. . . ."

"NO!" screamed Gil, but before Mike could bring down the guillotine, he was into the Greenback dugout, headed straight on to the showers, for that he should be credited with a *second* loss was more than the nineteen-year-old immortal could endure.

And thereafter, through that sizzling July and August, and down through the dog days of September, he behaved himself. No improvement in his disposition, of course, but it wasn't to turn him into Little Boy Blue that General Oakhart had put Mike the Mouth on his tail—it was to make him obedient to the Rules and the Regulations, and that Mike did. On his third outing with Mike behind the plate, Gamesh pitched a nineteen-inning three-hitter, and the only time he was anywhere near being ejected from the game, he restrained himself by sinking his prominent incisors into his glove, rather than into Mike's ear, which was actually closer at that moment to his teeth.

The General was in the stands that day, and immediately after the last out went around to the umpires' dressing room to congratulate his iron-willed arbiter. He found him teetering on a bench before his locker, his blue shirt so soaked with perspiration that it looked as though it would have to be removed from his massive torso by a surgeon. He seemed barely to have strength enough to suck his soda pop up through the straw in the bottle.

General Oakhart clapped him on the shoulder—and felt it give beneath him. "Congratulations, Mike. You have done it. You have civilized the boy. Baseball will be eternally grateful."

Mike blinked his eyes to bring the General's face into focus. "No. Not civilized. Never will be. Too great. He's right."

"Speak up, Mike, I can't hear you."

"I said—"

"Sip some soda, Mike. Your voice is a little gone."

He sipped, he sighed, he began to hiccup. "I oop said he's oop too great."

"Meaning what?"

"It's like looking in oop to a steel furnace. It's like being a tiny oop farm oop boy again, when the trans oop con oop tinental train oop goes by. It's like being trampled oop trampled oop under a herd of wild oop oop. Elephants. After an inning the ball doesn't even look like a oop anymore. Sometimes it seems to be coming in end oop over end oop. And thin as an ice oop pick. Or it comes in bent and ee oop long oop ated like a boomerang oop. Or it flattens out like an aspirin oop tab oop let. Even his oop change-up oop hisses. He throws with every muscle in his body, and yet at oop the end of nineteen oop nineteen oop innings like today, he is fresh oop as oop a daisy. General, if he gets any faster, I oop don't know if even the best eyes in the business will be able to determine the close oop ones. And close oop ones are all he throws oop."

"You sound tired, Mike."

"I'll oop survive," he said, closing his eyes and swaying.

But the General had to wonder. He might have been looking at a raw young ump up from the minors, worried sick about making a mistake his first game in the Big Time, instead of Mike the Mouth, on the way to his two millionth major league decision.

He had to rap Mike on the shoulder now to rouse him. "I have every confidence in you, Mike. I always have. I always will. I know you won't let the league down. You won't now, will you, Michael?"

"Oop."

"Good!"

What a year Gil went on to have (and Mike with him)! Coming into the last game of the year, the rookie had not only tied the record for the most wins in a single season (41), but had broken the record for the most strike-outs (349) set by Rube Waddell in 1904, the record for the most shutouts (16) set by Grover Alexander in 1916, and had only to give up less than six runs to come in below the earned run average of 1.01 set by Dutch Leonard the year he was born. As for Patriot League records, he had thrown more complete games than any other pitcher in the league's history, had allowed the fewest walks, the fewest hits, and gotten the most strike-outs per nine innings. Any wonder then, that after the rookie's late September no-hitter against Independence (his fortieth victory as against the one 9–0 loss), Mike the Mouth fell into some sort of insentient fit in the dressing room from which he could not be roused for nearly twenty-four hours. He stared like a blind man, he drooled like a fool. "Stunned," said the doctor, and threw cold water at him. Following the second no-hitter—which came four days after the first—Mike was able to make it just inside the dressing room with his dignity intact, before he began the howling that did not completely subside for the better part of two days and two nights. He did not eat, sleep, or drink: just raised his lips to the ceiling and hourly bayed to the other wolves. "Something definitely the matter here," said the doctor. "When the season's over, you better have him checked."

The Greenbacks went into the final day of the year only half a game out in front of the Tycoons; whichever Tri-City team should win the game, would win the flag. And Gamesh, by winning his forty-second, would have won more games in a season than any other pitcher in history. And of course there was the chance that the nineteen-year-old kid would pitch his third consecutive no-hitter . . .

Well, what happened was more incredible even than that. The first twenty-six Tycoons he faced went down on strikes: seventy-eight strikes in a row. There had not even been a foul tip—either the strike was called, or in desperation they swung at the ozone. Then, two out in the ninth and two strikes on the batter (thus was it ever, with Gilbert Gamesh) the left-hander fired into the catcher's mitt what seemed not only to the sixty-two thousand three hundred and forty-two ecstatic fans packed into Greenback Stadium, but to the helpless batter himself—who turned from the plate without a whimper and started back to his home in Wilkes-Barre, Pa.—the last pitch of the '33 Patriot League season. Strike-out number twenty-seven. Victory number forty-two. Consecutive no-hitter number three. The most perfect game ever pitched in the major leagues, or conceived of by the mind of man. The Greenbacks had won the pennant, and how! Bring on the Senators and the Giants!

Or so it had seemed, until Mike the Mouth Masterson got word through to the two managers that the final out did not count, because at the moment of the pitch, *his back had been turned to the plate.*

In order for the game to be resumed, tens of thousands of spectators who had poured out onto the field when little Joe Iviri, the Tycoon hitter, had turned away in defeat, had now to be forced back up through the gates into the stands; wisely, General Oakhart had arranged beforehand for the Tri-City mounted constabulary to be at the ready, under the stands, in the event of just such an uprising as this, and so it was that a hundred whinnying horses, drawn up like a cavalry company and charging into the manswarm for a full fifteen minutes, drove the enraged fans from the field. But not even policemen with drawn pistols could force them to take their seats. With arms upraised they roared at Mike the Mouth as though he were their Fuehrer, only it was not devotion they were promising him.

General Oakhart himself took the microphone and attempted to address the raging mob. "This is General Douglas D. Oakhart, President of the Patriot League. Due to circumstances beyond his control, umpire-in-chief Mike Masterson was unable to make a call on the last pitch because his back was turned to the plate at that moment."

"KILL THE MOUTH! MURDER THE BUM!"

"According to rule 9.4, section e, of the Official—"

"BANISH THE BLIND BASTARD! CUT OFF HIS WHATSIS!"

"—game shall be resumed prior to that pitch. Thank you."

"BOOOOOOOOOOOOOOOOOOOOOOOOOOOOOO!"

In the end it was necessary for the General to step out onto the field of play (as once he had stepped onto the field of battle), followed behind by the Tri-City Symphony Orchestra; by his order, the musicians (more terrified than any army he had ever seen, French, British, American, or Hun) assembled for the second time that day in center field, and with two down in the ninth, and two strikes on the batter, proceeded to play the National Anthem again.

"'O say can you see,'" sang the General.

Through his teeth, he addressed Mike Masterson, who stood beside him at home plate, with his cap over his chest protector. "What happened?"

Mike said, "I—I saw him."

Agitated as he was, he nonetheless remained at rigid attention, smartly saluting the broad stripes and bright stars. "Who? When?"

"The one," said Mike.

"The one *what*?"

"Who I've been looking for. There! Headed for the exit back of the Tycoon dugout. I recognized him by his ears and the set of his chin," and a sob rose in his throat. "Him. The kidnapper. The masked man who killed my little girl."

"Mike!" snapped the General. "Mike, you were seeing things! You were imagining it!"

"It was *him*!"

"Mike, that was thirty-five years ago. You could not recognize a man after all that time, not by his ears, for God's sake!"

"Why not?" Mike wept. "I've seen him every night, in my sleep, since 12 September 1898."

"'O say does that Star-Spangled Banner yet wave/O'er the land of the free, and the home—'"

"Play ball!" the fans were shouting. "Play the God damn game!"

It had worked. The General had turned sixty-two thousand savages back into baseball fans with the playing of the National Anthem! Now—if only he could step in behind the plate and call the last pitch! Or bring the field umpire in to take Mike's place on balls and strikes! But the first was beyond what he was empowered to do under the Rules and the Regulations; and the second would forever cast doubt upon the twenty-six strike-outs already recorded in the history books by Gamesh, and on the forty-one victories before that. Indeed, the field umpire had wisely pretended that he had not seen the last Gamesh pitch either, so as not to compromise the greatest umpire in the game by rendering the call himself. What could the General do then but depart the field?

On the pitcher's mound, Gil Gamesh had pulled his cap so low on his brow that he was in shadows to his chin. He had not even removed it for "The Star-Spangled Banner"—as thousands began to realize with a deepening sense of uneasiness and alarm. He had been there on the field since the last pitch thrown to Iviri—except for the ten minutes when he had been above it, bobbing on a sea of uplifted arms, rolling in the embrace of ten thousand fans. And when the last pack of celebrants had fled before the flying hooves, they had deposited him back on the mound, from whence they had plucked him —and run for their lives. And so there he stood, immobile, his eyes and mouth invisible to one and all. What was he thinking? What was going through Gil's mind?

Scrappy little Joe Iviri, a little pecking hitter, and the best lead-off man in the country at that time, came up out of the Tycoon dugout, sporting a little grin as though he had just been raised from the dead, and from the stands came an angry Vesuvian roar.

Down in the Greenback dugout, the Old Philosopher considered going out to the mound to peek under the boy's cap and see what was up. But what could he do about anything anyway? "Whatever happens," he philosophized, "it's going to happen anyway, especially with a prima donna like that one."

"Play!"

Iviri stepped in, twitching his little behind.

Gamesh pitched.

It was a curve that would have shamed a ten-year-old boy—
or girl, for that matter. While it hung in the clear September
light, deciding whether to break a little or not, there was time
enough for the catcher to gasp, "Holy aloha!"

And then the baseball was ricocheting around in the tricky
right-field corner, to which it had been dispatched at the same
height at which it had been struck. A stand-up triple for Iviri.

From the silence in Greenback Stadium, you would have
thought that winter had come and the field lay under three feet
of snow. You would have thought that the ballplayers were all
down home watching haircuts at the barber shop, or boasting
over a beer to the boys in the local saloon. And all sixty-two
thousand fans might have been in hibernation with the bears.

Pineapple Tawhaki moved in a daze out to the mound to
hand a new ball to Gamesh. Immediately after the game, at the
investigation conducted in General Oakhart's office, Tawhaki
—weeping profusely—maintained that when he had come out
to the mound after the triple was hit, Gamesh had hissed at
him, "Stay down! Stay low! On your knees, Pineapple, if you
know what's good for you!" "So," said Pineapple in his own
defense, "I do what he say, sir. That all. I figger Gil want to
throw drop-drop. Okay to me. Gil pitch, Pineapple catch. I stay
down. Wait for drop-drop. That all, sir, that all in world!"
Nonetheless, General Oakhart suspended the Hawaiian for two
years—as an "accomplice" to the heinous crime—hoping that
he might disappear for good in the interim. Which he did—
only instead of heading home to pick pineapples, he wound
up a derelict on Tattoo Street, the Skid Row of Tri-City. Well,
better he destroy himself with drink, than by his presence on
a Patriot League diamond keep alive in the nation's memory
what came to be characterized by the General as "the second
deplorable exception to the Patriot League's honorable
record."

It was clear from the moment the ball left Gil's hand that it
wasn't any drop-drop he'd had in mind to throw. Tawhaki
stayed low—even as the pitch took off like something the
Wright Brothers had invented. The batter testified at the
hearing that it was still picking up speed when it passed him,
and scientists interviewed by reporters later that day estimated

that at the moment it struck Mike Masterson in the throat, Gamesh's rising fastball was probably traveling between one hundred and twenty and one hundred and thirty miles per hour. In his vain attempt to turn from the ball, Mike had caught it just between the face mask and the chest protector, a perfect pitch, if you believed, as the General did, that Masterson's blue bow tie was the bull's-eye for which Gamesh had been aiming.

The calamity-sized black headline MOUTH DEAD; GIL BANISHED proved to be premature. To be sure, even before the sun went down, the Patriot League President, with the Commissioner's approval, had expelled the record-breaking rookie sensation from the game of baseball forever. But the indestructible ump rallied from his coma in the early hours of the morning, and though he did not live to tell the tale—he was a mute thereafter—at least he lived.

The fans never forgave the General for banishing their hero. To hear them tell it, a boy destined to be the greatest pitcher of all time had been expelled from the game just for throwing a wild pitch. Rattled by a senile old umpire who had been catching a few Zs back of home plate, the great rookie throws *one bad one*, and that's it, for life! Oh no, it ain't Oakhart's favorite ump who's to blame for standin' in the way of the damn thing—it's Gil!

Nor did the General's favorite ump forgive him either. The very day they had unswathed the bandages and released him from the hospital, Mike Masterson was down at the league office, demanding what he called "justice." Despite the rule forbidding it, he was wearing his blue uniform off the field—in the big pockets once heavy with P. League baseballs, he carried an old rag and a box of chalk; and when he entered the office, there was a blackboard and an easel strapped to his back. Poor Mike had lost not only his voice. He wanted Gamesh to be indicted and tried by the Tri-City D.A.'s office for attempted murder.

"Mike, I must say that it comes as a profound shock to me that a man of your great wisdom should wish to take vengeance in that way."

STUFF MY WISDOM (wrote Mike the Mouth on the blackboard he had set before the General's desk) I WANT THAT BOY BEHIND BARS!

"But this is not like you at all. Besides, the boy has been punished plenty."

SAYS WHO?

"Now use your head, man. He is a brilliant young pitcher—and he will never pitch again."

AND I CAN'T TALK AGAIN! OR EVEN WHISPER! I CAN'T CALL A STRIKE! I CAN'T CALL A BALL! I HAVE BEEN SILENCED FOREVER AT SEVENTY-ONE!

"And will seeing him in jail give you your voice back, at seventy-one?"

NO! NOTHING WILL! IT WON'T BRING MY MARY JANE BACK EITHER! IT WON'T MAKE UP FOR THE SCAR ON MY FOREHEAD OR THE GLASS STILL FLOATING IN MY BACK! IT WON'T MAKE UP (here he had to stop to wipe the board clean with his rag, so that he would have room to proceed) FOR THE ABUSE I HAVE TAKEN DAY IN AND DAY OUT FOR FIFTY YEARS!

"Then what on earth is the use of it?"

JUSTICE!

"Mike, listen to reason—what kind of justice is it that will destroy the reputation of our league?"

STUFF OUR LEAGUE!

"Mike, it would blacken forever the name of baseball."

STUFF BASEBALL!

Here General Oakhart rose in anger—"It is a man who has lost his sense of values entirely, who could write those two words on a blackboard! Put that boy in jail, and, I promise you, you will have another Sacco and Vanzetti on your hands. You will make a martyr of Gamesh, and in the process ruin the very thing we all love."

HATE! wrote Mike, HATE! And on and on, filling the board with the four-letter word, then rubbing it clean with his rag, then filling it to the edges, again and again.

On and on and on.

Fortunately the crazed Masterson got nowhere with the D.A.—General Oakhart saw to that, as did the owners of the Greenbacks and the Tycoons. All they needed was Gil Gamesh tried for attempted murder in Tri-City, for baseball to be killed for good in that town. Sooner or later, Gamesh would be forgotten, and the Patriot League would return to normal . . .

Wishful thinking. Gamesh, behind the wheel of his Packard, and still in his baseball togs, disappeared from sight only minutes after leaving the postgame investigation in the General's office. To the reporters who clung to the running board, begging him to make a statement about his banishment, about Oakhart, about baseball, about anything, he had but five words to say, one of which could not even be printed in the papers: "I'll be back, you ——!" and the Packard roared away. But the next morning, on a back road near Binghamton, New York, the car was found overturned and burned out—and no rookie sensation to be seen anywhere. Either the charred body had been snatched by ghoulish fans, or he had walked away from the wreck intact.

GIL KILLED? the headlines asked, even as the stories came in from people claiming to have seen Gamesh riding the rails in Indiana, selling apples in Oklahoma City, or waiting in a soup line in L.A. A sign appeared in a saloon in Orlando, Florida, that read GIL TENDING BAR HERE, and hanging beside it in the window was a white uniform with a green numeral, 19—purportedly Gil's very own baseball suit. For a day and a night the place did a bang-up business, and then the sallow, sullen, skinny boy who called himself Gil Gamesh took off with the contents of the register. Within the month, every bar in the South had one of those signs printed up and one of those uniforms, with 19 sewed on it, hanging up beside it in the window for a gag. Outside opera houses, kids scrawled, GIL SINGING GRAND OPERA HERE TONIGHT. On trolley cars it was GIL TAKING TICKETS INSIDE. On barn doors, on school buildings, in rest rooms around the nation, the broken-hearted and the raffish wrote, I'LL BE BACK, G.G. His name, his initials, his number were everywhere.

Adolf Hitler, Franklin Roosevelt, Gil Gamesh. In the winter of '33–'34, men and women and even little children, worried for the future of America, were talking about one or another, if not all three. What was the world coming to? What catastrophe would befall our country next?

The second deplorable exception to the honorable record of

the Patriot League was followed by the third in the summer of 1934, when it was discovered that the keystone combination that had played so flawlessly behind Gamesh the year before had been receiving free sex from Tattoo Street prostitutes all season long, in exchange for bobbling grounders, giving up on liners, and throwing wide of the first-base bag. Olaf and Foresti, both married men with children, and one of the smoothest double-play duos in the business, were caught one night in a hotel room performing what at first glance looked like a trapeze act with four floozies—caught by the Old Philosopher himself—and the whole sordid story was there for all to read in the morning papers. They hadn't even taken money from the gamblers, money that at least could have bought shoes for their kiddies; no, they took their payoff in raw sex, which was of use to nobody in the world but their own selfish selves. How low could you get! By comparison the corrupt Black Sox of 1919 fame looked like choirboys. Inevitably the Greenbacks became known as "the Whore House Gang" and fell from third on the Fourth of July to last in the league by Labor Day.

And whom did the fans blame? The whoremongers themselves? Oh no, it was the General's fault. Banishing Gil Gamesh, he had broken the morale of Olaf and Foresti! Apparently he was supposed to go ask their forgiveness, instead of doing as he did, and sending the profligates to the showers for life.

And that wasn't the end of it: panic-stricken, the Greenback owners instantly put the franchise on the market, and sold it for a song to the only buyer they could find—a fat little Jew with an accent you could cut with a knife. And, to hear the fans tell it, that was General Oakhart's fault too!

And Mike the Mouth? He went from bad to worse and eventually took to traveling the league with a blackboard on his back, setting himself up at the entrance to the bleachers to plead his hopeless cause with the fans. Kids either teased him, or looked on in awe at the ghostly ump, powdered white from the dozen sticks of chalk that he would grind to dust in a single day. Most adults ignored him, either fearing or pitying the madman, but those who remembered Gil Gamesh—and they were legion, particularly in the bleachers—told the once-great umpire to go jump in a lake, and worse.

BUT I COULD NOT CALL WHAT I DID NOT SEE!

"You couldn't a-seed it anyway, you blind bat!"

NONSENSE! I WAS TWENTY-TWENTY IN BOTH EYES ALL MY LIFE! I HAD THE BEST VISION IN BASEBALL!

"You had it in for the kid, Masterson—you persecuted him to death right from the start!"

TO THE CONTRARY, HE PERSECUTED ME!

"You desoived it!"

HOW DARE YOU! WHY DID I OF ALL UMPIRES DE-SERVE SUCH INSULT AND ABUSE?

"Because you wuz a lousy ump, Mike. You wuz a busher all your life."

WHERE IS YOUR EVIDENCE FOR THAT SLANDER-OUS REMARK?

"Common knowledge is my evidence. The whole world knows. Even my little boy, who don't know nothin', knows that. Hey, Johnny, come here—who is the worst ump who ever lived? Tell this creep."

"Mike the Mouth! Mike the Mouth!"

NONSENSE! SLANDER! LIES! I DEMAND JUSTICE, ONCE AND FOR ALL!

"Well, you're gettin' it, slow but sure. See ya, Mouth."

When General Oakhart was advised in January of '43 that the Mundy brothers had reached an agreement with the War De-partment to lease their ball park to the government as an em-barkation camp, he knew right off that it was not an overflow of patriotic emotion that had drawn those boys into the deal. They were getting out while the getting was good—while the getting was *phenomenal.* After all, if the fortunes of the Patriot League had been on the wane ever since the expulsion of Gamesh, they surely couldn't be expected to improve with a world war on. In the year since Pearl Harbor, the draft had cut deep into the player rosters, and by the time the '43 season be-gan, the quality of major league baseball was bound to be at its all-time low. With untried youngsters and decrepit old-timers struggling through nine innings on the diamond, attendance would fall even further than it had in the previous decade, with the result that two or even three P. League teams might just have to shut down for the duration. And with that, who was to say whether the whole enterprise might not collapse? . . . So, it was to guard against this disastrous contingency (and convert it into a bonanza) that the Mundy brothers had leased their beautiful old ball park to the federal government to the tune of fifty thousand dollars a month, twelve months a year.

The Mundy brothers had inherited the Port Ruppert franchise from their illustrious dad, the legendary Glorious Mundy, without inheriting any of that titan's profound reverence for the game. Right down to the old man's ninety-second year, sportswriters who in his opinion hadn't sufficient love and loyalty for the sport were wise to keep their distance, for Glorious Mundy was known on occasion to take a swing at a man for treating baseball as less than the national religion. He was a big man, with bushy black eyebrows that the cartoonists adored, and he could just glare you into agreement, if not downright obedience. When he died, they buried him according to his own instructions in deep center field, four hundred eighty-five feet from home plate, beneath a simple headstone whose inscription gave silent testimony to the humility of a man whose eyebrows alone would have earned him the reputation of a giant.

### GLORIOUS MUNDY

1839–1931

He had something to do with
changing Luke Gofannon from
a pitcher into a center-fielder

It was clear from the outset that to his heirs baseball was a business, to be run like the Mundy confectionary plant, the Mundy peanut plantations, the Mundy cattle ranches, and the Mundy citrus farms, all of which had been their domain while Glorious was living and devoting himself entirely in his later years to the baseball team. The very morning after their father had died of old age in his box behind first, the two sons began to sell off, one after another, the great stars of the championship teams of the late twenties—for straight cash, like so many slaves, to the highest bidder. The Depression, don't you know . . . they were feeling the pinch, don't you know . . . between excursions with their socialite wives to Palm Beach and Biarritz!

In 1932, when they took one hundred thousand dollars from the Terra Incognita Rustlers for the greatest Mundy of them all, Luke "the Loner" Gofannon, a tide of anger and resentment swept through Port Ruppert that culminated in a march all the way down Broad Street by thousands of school kids wearing black armbands that had been issued to them at City Hall. The parade was led by Boss Stuvwxyz (and organized by his henchmen), but somewhere around Choco-Chew Street (named for the Mundy candy bar), somebody remembered to give Stuvwxyz his cut, and so he was not present when the police broke up the rally just before it reached the ball park.

Luke the Loner—gone! The iron man who came up in 1916 as a kid pitcher, and then played over two thousand games in center field for the Ruppert club, scored close to fifteen hundred runs for them, and owned a lifetime batting average of .372—the fella who *was* the Mundys to three generations of Rupe-it rootas! Unlike Cobb or Ruth, Luke was a silent, colorless man as far as personality went, but that did not make him less of a hero to his fans. They argued that actually he could beat you more ways than Ruth, because he could run and steal as well as hit the long one; and he could beat you more ways than Cobb, because he could hit the long one as well as drive you crazy on the base paths and race around that center-field pasture as though it weren't any bigger than a shoebox. Oh, he was fast! And what a sight at bat! In his prime, they'd give him a hand just for striking out, that's how beautiful he was, and how revered. Luke kept a book on every pitcher in the business and he studied it religiously at night before putting out his light at 9 P.M. And as he said—on one of the few occasions in his career that he said anything—he loved the game so much, he'd have played without pay. Surprising thing was that the Mundy brothers didn't take him up on that, instead of selling his carcass for a mere hundred grand.

In their defense, the Mundy boys claimed that they were only getting the best possible price for players who hadn't more than another good season or two left in their bones anyway; they were clearing out dead wood, said they, to make way for a new Golden Era. Well, as it turned out, not a single one of the seven former Mundy greats for whom old Glorious's heirs collected a cool half a million ever did amount to much once they left Port Ruppert, but whether it was due to advancing age, as the Mundy brothers maintained, or to the shock of being turned out of the park to which they had brought such fame and glory, is a matter of opinion.

Luke the Loner didn't even make it through one whole season as a Rustler. By August of '32 he already had broken the league record for strike-outs—strike-outs they weren't applauding him for either—and he who was reputed never to have thrown to a wrong base in his life, had the infielders scratching their heads because of his bizarre pegs from center. It seemed that shy, silent Luke, whom everybody had thought didn't need much company outside of his thirty-eight-ounce bat, "the Magic Wand," was just lost out there in the arid southwest, hopelessly homesick for the seaside park where he had played two thousand games in the Ruppert scarlet and white. Inevitably, the fans began to ride him—"Hey, Strike-out King! Hey, Hundred Thousand Dollar Dodo!" As the season wore on they called him just about everything under the sun—and the sun itself is no joke in Wyoming—and though he plugged along like the great iron man that he was, his average finally slipped to an even .100. "A thousand bucks a point, Gofannon —not bad for two hours a day!" He was on his way to the plate—in danger of slipping to a two-figure batting average— when the Rustler manager, believing that enough suffering was enough, and that the time had come to cut everybody's losses, stepped to the foot of the dugout, and called in a voice more compassionate than any Luke had heard all year, "What do you say, old-timer, come on out and take a rest," and a pinch-hitter was sent up in his place.

A week later he was back in New Jersey on his cranberry farm. The legislature of the state, in special session, voted him New Jersey license plate 372 in commemoration of his lifetime batting average. People would look for that license plate coming along the road down there in Jersey, and they'd just applaud when it came by. And Luke would tip his hat. And that's how he died that winter. To acknowledge the cheers from an oncoming school bus—boys and girls hanging from every window, screaming, "It's him! It's Luke!"—the sweetest, shyest ballplayer who ever hit a homer, momentarily took his famous hands from the wheel and his famous eyes from the road, and shot off the slick highway into the Raritan River. That so modest a man should die because of his fame was only one of the dozens of tragic ironies that the sportswriters pointed up in the mishap that took Luke's life at the age of thirty-six.

The Mundys A.G. (after Gofannon) promptly dropped from the first division, and for the remaining prewar years labored to finish as high as fifth. If the fans continued to fill the stands almost as faithfully as they had in happier days, it was because a Rupe-it roota was a Rupe-it roota, and because in the Mundy dugout sat their esteemed manager, Ulysses S. Fairsmith, "Mister Fairsmith" as they called him always, whether "they" roasted in the bleachers, or lorded it over the entire game in the big magistrate's chair of the Commissioner's desk in Chicago. Even the Mundy brothers, who ran the franchise with as much nostalgia as a pair of cobras, were careful to call him Mister (to the world), though they considered him a relic about ready for the junk heap, and when they sold seven of their help for a five-pound bag of thousand dollar bills, kept him on the payroll so as to indicate their reverence for Port Ruppert's Periclean past.

And the cheap, cynical trick worked: seated in his rocking chair ("Fairsmith's throne") in the dugout, wearing his starched white shirt, silk bow tie, white linen suit, Panama hat, and that aristocratic profile off a postage stamp, and moving the defense around with the gold tip of his bamboo cane, the Christian gentleman and scholar of the game was enough to convince the rootas of that rabid baseball town that this heavy-footed, butterfingered nine had something to do with the Ruppert Mundys of a few years back, those clubs now known as "the wondrous teams of yore."

Till the day he died, Mister Fairsmith never set foot inside a ball park on a Sunday. Instead he handed over the reins to one of his trusted coaches so that he might keep the promise he had made to his mother back in 1888, when he went off as a youngster to catch for the Hartford team of the old National League. "Sundays," his mother had said, "were not made for doubleheaders. You may catch six days a week, but on the seventh you shall rest." From his rocking chair in the Mundy dugout, Mister Fairsmith often made pronouncements to the press that one would not have been surprised to hear from the pulpit. "If the Lord ever permitted birth to a natural switch-hitter," he would say, for instance, in a characteristic locution, "it was Luke Gofannon." In his early years as a manager, the pregame prayer was practiced in the Mundy clubhouse before the team took the field for the day. It was eventually discontinued when Mister Fairsmith discovered that the content of the prayers being offered up to God was nothing like what he had in mind when he instituted the ritual: mostly they were squalid little requests for extra-base hits, and pitchers asking the King of Kings to help them keep the fastball down. "Give me my legs, Lord," went the prayer of one aging outfielder, "and the rest'll take care of itself." Still, he was kindly to the players, despite their frailties and follies, and never criticized a man in public for a mistake he had made on the field of play. Rather, he waited a day or two until the wound had healed a little, and then he took the fellow for dinner to a nice hotel, and at a table where they would not be observed, and in that gentle way he was revered for, he would say, "Now what about that play? Do you think you did that right?" If a pitcher had to be removed from the mound, Mister Fairsmith would always have a polite word to say to him, as he headed through the dugout to the showers; it did not matter if the fellow had just given up a grand-slam home run, or walked six men in a row, Mister Fairsmith would call him over to the rocker, and pressing the pitcher's hand in his own strong, manly grip, say to him, "Thank you very much for the effort. I'm deeply grateful to you."

General Oakhart, of course, believed that the Mundy brothers' plan to lease their ball park to the government was just the kind of preposterous innovation that the Ruppert manager could be counted on to oppose wholeheartedly. Vain though his plea had been, Mister Fairsmith had spoken so eloquently five years earlier against the introduction of nighttime baseball into the Patriot League schedule, that at the conclusion of the meeting of league owners to whom the address had been delivered, General Oakhart had released the text to the newspapers. The following day selections appeared on editorial pages all around the country, and the Port Ruppert *Star* ran it in its entirety in the rotogravure section on Sunday, laid out on a page of its own to resemble the Declaration of Independence. What particularly moved people to clip it out and hang it framed over the mantel, was the strength of his belief in "the Almighty Creator, Whose presence," Mister Fairsmith revealed, "I do feel in every park around the league, on those golden days of sweet, cheerful spring, hot plenteous summer, and bountiful and benevolent autumn, when physically strong and morally sound young men do sport in seriousness beneath the sun, as did the two in Eden, before the Serpent and the Fall. Daytime baseball is nothing less than a reminder of Eden in the time of innocence and joy; and too, an intimation of that which is yet to come. For what is a ball park, but that place wherein Americans may gather to worship the beauty of God's earth, the skill and strength of His children, and the holiness of His commandment to order and obedience. For such are the twin rocks upon which all sport is founded. And woe unto him, I say, who would assemble our players and our fans beneath the feeble, artificial light of godless science! For in the end as in the beginning, in the Paradise to come as in the Eden we have lost, it is not by the faint wattage of the electric light bulb that ye shall be judged, but rather in the unblinking eye of the Lord, wherein we are all as bareheaded fans in the open bleachers and tiny players prancing beneath the vault of His Heaven."

Several of the owners present were heard by the General to whisper "Amen," at the conclusion to this speech; among them was the new owner of the Kakoola Reapers, whiskey magnate Frank Mazuma, whose plan to install floodlights in Reaper Field had been the occasion for Mister Fairsmith's address. As it happened, not only did the amen-ing Mazuma go ahead to initiate nighttime baseball that very season in Kakoola—with the result that his club led the league that year in strike-outs, errors, and injuries—but in defiance of an antiradio ban signed by all the Patriot League owners, including Mazuma's predecessor, began to broadcast the Reaper home games on the local station, which he also bought up with his bootleg billions and christened KALE. And, to the surprise of those who had drafted the antiradio ban in great panic some years earlier, Mazuma's broadcasts, rather than cutting further into dwindling gate receipts, seemed, like those bizarre night games, to increase local interest in the Reapers, so that the following season attendance went up a full fifteen per cent, even though the team continued to occupy seventh place one day and eighth the next.

To General Oakhart, needless to say, the idea that people could sit in their living rooms or in their cars listening to an announcer describe a game being played miles and miles away was positively infuriating. Why, the game might just as well not be happening, for all they knew! The whole thing might even be a hoax, a joke, something managed with some clever sound effects and a little imagination and an actor who was good at pretending to be excited. What was there to stop radio stations in towns without ball clubs from making up their own teams, and even their own leagues, and getting people at home all riled up, telling them home runs were being knocked out of the park and records being broken, when all the while there was nothing going on but somebody telling a story? Who was to say it might not come to that, and worse, if there promised to be a profit in it for the Frank Mazumas of this profit-mad world?

Furthermore, you could not begin to communicate through *words*, either printed or spoken, what this game was all about —not even words as poetical and inspirational as those Mister Fairsmith was so good at. As the General said, the beauty and meaning of baseball resided in the fixed geometry of the diamond and the test it provided of agility, strength, and timing. Baseball was a game that looked different from every single seat in the ball park, and consequently could never be represented accurately unless one were able to put together into one picture what every single spectator in the park had seen simultaneously moment by moment throughout an entire afternoon; and that included those moments that in fact accounted for half the playing time if not more, when there was no action whatsoever, those moments of waiting and hesitation, of readiness and recovery, moments in which everything ceased, including the noise of the crowd, but which were as inherent to the appeal of the game as the few climactic seconds when a batted ball sailed over the wall. You might as well put an announcer up in the woods in October and have him do a "live" broadcast of the fall, as describe a baseball game on the radio.

"Well, now, folks, the maples are turning red, and there goes a birch getting yellow," and so on. Can you imagine nature-lovers sitting all huddled around a dial, following that? No, all radio would do would be to reduce the game to what the gamblers cared about: who scored, how much, and when. As for the rest—the playing field with its straight white foul lines and smooth dirt basepaths and wide green band of outfield, the nine uniformed athletes strategically scattered upon it, their muscles strung invisibly together, so that when one moved the rest swung with him into motion . . . well, what *about* all that, which, to the General, was just about everything? Sure you could work up interest even in a bunch of duffers like the Kakoola Reapers by reporting their games "live" over the radio, but it might as well be one team of fleas playing another team of fleas, for all such a broadcast had to do with the poetry of the great game itself.

The General's meeting with Mister Fairsmith reminded him of nothing so much as his tragic interview nearly ten years earlier with Mike the Mouth Masterson, after the great umpire had lost his sense of reality. Where, oh where would it end? The best of the men he knew, the men of principle upon whom he had counted for aid and support—either dead, or gone mad. Would no one of sanity and integrity survive to carry on the great traditions of the league? Would he have to war alone against the vulgarians and profiteers and ignoramuses dedicated to devouring the league, the game, the country—the world? Glorious Mundy, Luke Gofannon, Spenser Trust, all in the grave; and from last report (a news item in a Texas paper) Mike Masterson still traversing the country with a blackboard on his back, hanging around the sidelines at sandlot baseball games demanding "justice." Oh, the times were dark! A Jew the owner of the Greenbacks! Spenser Trust's eccentric widow owner of the Tycoons! A bootlegger gone "straight" the owner of the Reapers! And now Ulysses S. Fairsmith, clear out of his mind!

To be sure, the devout and pious ways of Mister Fairsmith had always struck the General as somewhat excessive (if useful), and frankly he had even considered him somewhat "touched" twenty years back, when he circumnavigated the globe, bringing baseball to the black and yellow people of the world, many of whom had never even worn long pants before, let alone a suit with a number on the back. This excess of zeal (and paucity of common sense) had very nearly cost him his life in the Congo, where he rubbed a tribe of cannibals the wrong way and missed the pot by about an inch. On the other hand, no one could fail to be impressed by the job of conversion he had done in Japan. Single-handedly, he had made that previously backward nation into the second greatest baseball-playing country in the world, and after his 1922 visit to Tokyo, had returned every fall with two teams of American all-stars to play in Japanese cities, large and small, and teach the little yellow youngsters along the way the fine points of the game. They loved him in Japan. The beautiful Hiroshima ball park was called "Fairsmith Stadium"—in Japanese of course—and when he appeared at a major league game in Japan, everyone there, players as well as fans, bowed down and accorded him the respect of a member of the imperial family. Hirohito himself had entertained Mister Fairsmith in his palace as recently as October of 1941—giving no indication, of course, that only two months later, on a quiet Sunday morning, while Christian America was at its prayers, he was going to deal the Mundy manager the most stunning blow of his life by attacking the American fleet anchored at Hawaii. And how could he? For a year now the Mundy manager had suffered an agony of bewilderment and doubt: how could Hirohito do this to Mister Fairsmith, after all he had done for the youngsters of Japan?

"If it is the will of the Lord," said Mister Fairsmith, haggard and wispy from his year of despair, yet with bold blue eyes made radiant by the pure line of malarkey he had sold himself, "if such is the will of the Lord, to send forth the Mundys into the wilderness until the conflagration is ended, who am I to stand opposed?"

"Now, Mister Fairsmith," said the General, suppressing a desire to give the old gent a good shake and tell him to come to his senses, "now, that is of course a very catchy way to put it, Mister F.—'wander in the wilderness.' But if I may take exception, it looks to me more like an endless road trip that is being proposed for these boys. And to my way of thinking, that is far from a good thing for anyone. Such an injustice would test the morale of even the best of teams. And let's face the facts, unpleasant as they may be: despite your managerial expertise"—such as it used to be, said the General, sadly, to himself—"this is no longer a first division club. To speak bluntly, they look to me to be pretty good candidates for the cellar as it is. Wayne Heket, John Baal, Frenchy Astarte, Cholly Tuminikar—they are no longer what they were, and have not been for some time now."

"Which is why the Lord has chosen them."

"How's that? You had better explain the Lord's reasoning to me, sir. On the basis of the logic I studied at the academy forty years back, I can't seem to make head nor tail of it."

"They are to be restored to their former greatness."

"Wayne Heket is? He can't even bend down to tie his shoe-laces as it is. Tell me, how is he going to be made great again?"

"Through trial and tribulation. Through suffering," said Mister Fairsmith, ignoring the General's predictable secularist sarcasm, "they shall find their purpose and their strength."

"And then again maybe not. With all due respect to the Lord and yourself, I think that as President of the league I have to prepare myself for that possibility as well. Sir, in my humble opinion, this is just about the worst thing that has happened to this league since the expulsion of Gil Gamesh. I tell you, Ford Frick and Will Harridge couldn't be happier. They have been eyeing our best players for years—they have been waiting for close to a decade for this league to collapse, so they could just sign up our stars and divide this baseball-loving country between themselves. Nothing could please them more than for the players coming home from the war to have just two major leagues they can play for instead of three. Look, you have got an inside pipeline to the Lord, Mister Fairsmith: maybe you can tell me what it is He has against the Patriot League, if He is the one behind sending the Mundys on the road. Why didn't the Lord choose Boston, and make the Bees or the Red Sox homeless? Why didn't he choose Philadelphia, and send the Phillies or the A's into the wonderful wilderness?"

"Because," replied the venerable Mundy manager, "the Lord is not concerned with the Phillies or the A's."

"Boy, aren't they unlucky! They've just got the Devil looking after them—so they get to stay where they are, poor

bastards! Pardon my Shakespeare, sir, but why Port Ruppert
instead of Brooklyn? They have got a deep water harbor there
too, you know. Almighty God could have cleared the Dodgers
out of Ebbets Field to make way for the Army—why in hell
didn't He! Why were the Mundys chosen!"

"They have been chosen . . ."

"*Yes?*"

"Because they have been chosen."

"They have been chosen because Glorious Mundy is dead
and his heirs are scoundrels! Mammon, Mister Fairsmith, that
is who is behind this move! The love of money! The worship
of money! And what is more disgusting, they cloak their greed
in the stars and stripes! They make a financial killing and call it
a patriotic act! And where is God in all this, Mister Fairsmith?
Where is He when we need Him!"

"He works in mysterious ways, General."

"*Maybe*, sir, *maybe*—*but not this mysterious.* That He should
stoop to the Mundy brothers to do His business for Him is
something even I am reluctant to accept—and I have never
hidden the fact that I am not a particularly devout person.
Frankly I think you do a serious disservice to God's good name
with this kind of irresponsible talk about mysterious ways. And
since I've come this far, I want to go further. I want you to
straighten me out on something, just so we know where we
stand. Are you actually sitting there, without blinking an eye,
and suggesting to me that there is some sort of similarity between the Mundys of Port Ruppert, New Jersey, and the ancient Hebrews of the Bible?"

Mister Fairsmith said, "In the words of our great friend,
Glorious Mundy, 'Baseball is this country's religion.'"

"True, that was Glory's splendid way of putting it. But
surely it is going a little overboard to start comparing a sorry
second division club like yours to the people of Israel. And
yourself, if I am following this analogy correctly, yourself here
to Moses, leading them out of Egypt. Really, Mister Fairsmith,
a proper respect for your own achievement is one thing, but
does this make sense to you? Now I realize all you have been
through in the last year. I have the greatest sympathy with
what you have had to endure over the last decade from the
Mundy brothers. I have the deepest sympathy for the way you

have been treated by the Emperor of Japan. I hate the son of a bitch, and I didn't even know him. But frankly, even taking all of that into consideration, I cannot let you get away with spouting religious hogwash that is going to destroy this league!"

Mister Fairsmith only looked more beatific; the trial and tribulation in which he put so much stock was getting off to an excellent start.

Wearily, the General said, "Look, it's as simple as this, skipper: no good can come of a big league ball club playing one hundred and fifty-four games a year on the road. And I am going to do everything within my power to prevent it."

To which the Mundy manager, hell-bent on deliverance, replied, "General Oakhart, let my players go."

# 2

# THE VISITORS' LINE-UP

# THE '43 MUNDYS

| | |
|---|---|
| SS | Frenchy Astarte |
| 2B | Nickname Damur |
| 1B | John Baal |
| C | Hothead Ptah |
| LF | Mike Rama |
| 3B | Wayne Heket |
| RF | Bud Parusha |
| CF | Roland Agni |
| | |
| P | Jolly Cholly Turminikar |
| P | Deacon Demeter |
| P | Bobo Buchis |
| P | Rocky Volos |
| P | Howie Pollux |
| P | Catfish Mertzeger |
| P | Chico Mecoatl |
| | |
| UT | Specs Skirnir |
| UT | Wally Omara |
| UT | Mule Mokos |
| UT | Applejack Terminus |
| UT | Carl Khovaki |
| UT | Harry Hunaman |
| UT | Joe Garuda |
| UT | Swede Gudmund |
| UT | Ike Tvashtri |
| UT | Red Kronos |

# 2

*A distressing chapter wherein the reader is introduced to each member of the 1943 Mundy starting line-up as he steps up to the plate, and comes thus to understand why Americans have conspired to remove all reminders of such a team from the history books; their records recounted more fully than on the back of the bubble gum cards. Containing much matter to vex the ordinary fan and strain his credulity, which is as it must be, in that real life is always running away with itself, whereas imagination is shackled by innocence, delusion, hope, ignorance, obedience, fear, sweetness, et cetera. Containing that which will move the compassionate to tears, the just to indignation, and the cruel to laughter.*

BATTING first and playing shortstop, No. 1 : FRENCHY ASTARTE. ASTARTE."

Jean-Paul Astarte (TR, BR, 5′10″, 172 lbs.), French-Canadian, acquired in unusual deal late in 1941 from Tokyo team of Japan in association with Imperial Japanese Government—the only player ever traded out of his own hemisphere (and the only player ever traded back). Began career in twenties, down in Georgia, thence to Havana in the Cuban League, Santiago in the Dominican League, finally Caracas. It began to look as though the French-speaking boy out of the freezing North was destined in the end to play for the Equator—but no, misery is never so orderly in its progression; it wouldn't be real misery if it was. Early in the thirties, when baseball boomed in Japan, he was traded to Tokyo by way of the Panama Canal; there he played shortstop for nearly a decade, dreaming day in and day out of his father's dairy farm in the Gaspé. When news reached him in the fall of '41 that he was to be traded once again, he just somehow assumed it would be to Calcutta; he did not understand a word his Japanese owner was telling him (anymore than he had understood his Spanish owner or his American owner when they had called him in to say *au revoir*) and actually started in weeping at the prospect of playing ball next with a bunch of guys talking it up in Hindi and running around the bases in bedsheets. Oh, how he cursed the day he had donned a leather mitt and tried to pretend he was something other, something *more*, than a French-Canadian farmboy! Why wasn't what was good enough for the father good enough for the son? At sixteen years of age, with those powerful wrists of his, he could do a two-gallon milking in five minutes—wasn't that accomplishment enough in one life? Instead he had had dreams (what Canadian doesn't?) of the great stadiums to the south, dreams of American fame and American dollars . . . He boarded the boat with the Japanese ticket in one hand and his bag full of old bats and berets in the other, fully expecting to come ashore in a land of brown men in white dresses, and wound up instead (such was Frenchy's fate) being greeted at the dock by something he could never have expected. "Welcome, *Monsieur*! Welcome to Port Ruppert!" The famous Ulysses S. Fairsmith, the greatest manager in the game! *Mon Dieu!* It was not India he had reached, but America; like Columbus before him, he was a big leaguer at last.

How come? Simple. The Mundy brothers, into whose laps a million tons of scrap metal had dropped, had traded directly with Hirohito, a penny a pound, and (shrewd afterthought) a shortstop to fill the hole that would be left in the Mundy infield when the war started up in December. Yes, there was literally nothing the Mundy brothers didn't have the inside dope on, including the bombing of Pearl Harbor. That's what made them so successful. "Tell you what," they were reported to have said to the eager Emperor of Japan, "throw in the shortstop from the Tokyo club, and you got yourself a deal, Hirohito." Thus did they kill two birds with one stone, and God only knows how many hundreds of American soldiers.

Unfortunately the Most Valuable Player in the Far East found the majors rather different from what he had been imagining during his years of exile. For one thing, he was now thirty-nine, a fact of some consequence when you were hitting against carnivorous two hundred pounders instead of little rice-eaters about the size of your nephew Billy. It was weeks before he got his first Patriot League hit: seven, to be exact. Then there was that throw to first. How come they kept beating out for hits what used to be outs back in Asia? How come the fans booed and hooted when he came to the plate—when they used to cry "*Caramba!*" in Venezuela and "*Banzai!*" in the Land of the Rising Sun? Why, here in the Big American leagues of his dreams, he was even more of a foreigner than he had been in Tokyo, Japan! There he was an all-star shortstop, white as Honus Wagner and Rabbit Maranville—white as them and *great* as them. But here in the P. League he was "Frenchy" the freak.

In '42 he batted .200 for the Mundys, just about half what he'd batted halfway around the globe, and he led the short-stops in the three leagues in errors. His specialty was dropping high infield flies. The higher the ball was hit, the longer it gave him to wait beneath it, thinking about Japan and the day he would return to Tokyo and stardom.

It was Frenchy's error in the last game of the '42 season (and the last game ever played in Mundy Park), that sent two Rustler runners scampering home in the ninth, and knocked the Mundys into last. At the time, finishing half a game out of the cellar or right down in it didn't make much difference to his teammates—by the end of that first wartime season, all those old-timers wanted from life was not to have to push their bones around a baseball field for the next six months. And Frenchy too was able to live with the error by thinking of it as a mere one seventy-fifth of the mistakes he had made out on the field that year—until, that is, word reached him in snow-bound Gaspé (as strange to him now as steamy Havana once had been, for his father was dead, as were all the cows he used to know there as a boy) that the last-place Mundys had been booted out of Mundy Park and henceforth would be homeless.

Unlucky Astarte! Because of my error, he thought, that made us come in last! Because at that moment, his mind hadn't been on Ruppert finishing seventh in the P. League, but Japan fin-ishing first in the war! Yes, Japan victorious über alles . . . Japan conquering America, conquering Yankee Stadium, Wrigley Field, Mundy Park . . . Yes, waiting beneath what was to have been the last fly ball of the '42 season, he had been envisioning opening day of 1943—Hirohito throwing out the first pitch to a Ruppert team of tiny Orientals, with the excep-tion of himself, the Most Valuable Player in an Imperial Japan-ese world . . .

Oh, if ever there was a player without a country, it was the

Mundy lead-off man, who forever afterwards believed himself
and his traitorous thoughts to have caused the expulsion from
Port Ruppert. Was Frenchy the loneliest and unhappiest Mundy
of them all? A matter of debate, fans. In the end, he was their
only suicide, though not the only Mundy regular to meet his
Maker on the road.

"Batting second and playing second base, No. 29: NICK-
NAME DAMUR. DAMUR."

Nickname Damur (TR, BR, 5′, 92 lbs.) could run the ninety
feet from home to first in 3.4 seconds, and that was about it.
At fourteen he was the youngest player in the majors, as well as
the skinniest. The joke was (or was it a joke?) that the Mundy
brothers were paying him by the pound; not that the boy
cared anything about money anyway—no, all he seemed to
think about from the moment he joined the team in spring
training, was making a nickname for himself. "How about
Hank?" he asked his new teammates his very first day in the
scarlet and white, "don't I look like a Hank to you guys?" He
was so green they had to sit him down and *explain* to him that
Hank was the nickname for Henry. "Is that your name, boy—
Henry?" "Nope. It's worse . . . Hey, how about Dutch?
Dutch Damur. It rhymes!" "Dutch is for Dutchmen, knuckle-
head." "Chief?" "For Injuns." "Whitey?" "For blonds." How
about Ohio then, where I'm from?" "That ain't a name."
"Hey—how about Happy? Which I sure am, bein' here with
you all!" "Don't worry, you won't be for long." "Well then,"
he said shyly, "given my incredible speed and all, how about
Twinkletoes? Or Lightning? Or Flash!" "Don't boast, it ain't
becomin'. We wuz all fast once't. So was everybody in the
world. That don't make you special one bit." "Hey! How about
Dusty? That rhymes too!"

But even when he himself had settled upon the nickname he
wouldn't have minded seeing printed beneath his picture on a
bubble gum card, or hearing announced over the loud speaker
when he stepped up to bat, his teammates refused to address
him by it. Mostly, in the beginning, they did not address him
at all if they could help it, but just sort of pushed him aside to
get where they were going, or walked right through him as
though he weren't there. A fourteen-year-old kid weighing

ninety-two pounds playing in their infield! "What next?" they said, spitting on the dugout steps in disgust, "a reindeer or a slit?" In the meantime, Damur began tugging at his cap every two minutes, hoping they would notice and start calling him Cappy; he took to talking as though he had been born on a farm, saying "hoss" for horse and calling the infield "the pea patch," expecting they would shortly start calling him Rube; suddenly he began running out to his position in the oddest damn way—"What the hell you doin', boy?" they asked. "That's just the way I walk," he replied, "like a duck." But no one took the hint and called him Ducky or Goose. Nor when he chattered encouragement to the pitcher did they think to nickname him Gabby. "Shut up with that noise, willya?" cried the pitcher—"You're drivin' me batty," and so that was the end of that. Finally, in desperation, he whined, "Jee-zuz! What about *Kid* at least?" "We already got a Kid on this club. Two's confusin'." "But he's fifty years old and losin' his teeth!" cried Damur. "I'm only fourteen. I *am* a kid." "Tough. He wuz here before you wuz even born."

It was Jolly Cholly Tuminikar, the Mundy peacemaker and Sunday manager, who christened him Nickname. Not that Damur was happy about it, as he surely would have been, dubbed Happy. "'Nickname' isn't a nickname, it's the *name* for a nickname. Hey—how about Nick? *That's* the nickname for nickname! Call me Nick, guys!" "Nick? That's for Greeks. You ain't Greek." "But whoever heard of a baseball player called *Nickname Damur*?" "And whoever heard a' one that weighed ninety-two pounds and could not endorse a razor blade if they even asked him to?"

Indeed, so slight was he, that on the opening day of the '43 season, a base runner barreling into second knocked Nickname so high and so far that the center-fielder, Roland Agni, came charging in to make a sensational diving two-handed catch of the boy. "Out!" roared the field umpire, until he remembered that of course it is the ball not the player that has to be caught, and instantly reversed his decision. The fans, however, got a kick out of seeing Nickname flying this way and that, and when he came to bat would playfully call out to him, "How about Tarzan? How about Gargantua?" and the opposing team had their fun too, needling him from the bench—"How about

Powerhouse? How about Hurricane? How about Hercules, Nickname?" At last the diminutive second-sacker couldn't take any more. "Stop it," he cried, "stop, *please*," and with tears running down his face, pleaded with his tormentors, "My name is Oliver!" But, alas, it was too late for that.

Nickname, obviously, had no business in the majors, not even as a pinch-runner. Oh, he was swift enough, but hardly man enough, and if it was not for the wartime emergency, and the irresponsibility of the Mundy brothers, he would have been home where he belonged, with his long division and his Mom. "How about Homesick?" the sportswriter Smitty whispered into the boy's ear, a month after the '43 season began, and Nickname, black and blue by now and batting less than his own weight, threw himself in a rage upon the famous columnist. But what began with a flurry of fists ended with the boy sobbing in Smitty's lap, in a wing chair in a corner of the lobby of the Grand Kakoola Hotel. The next day, Smitty's column began, "A big league player wept yesterday, cried his heart out like a kid, but only a fool would call him a sissy . . ."

Thereafter the fans left off teasing Nickname about his size and his age and his name, and for a while (until the catastrophe at Kakoola) he became something like a mascot to the crowds. Of course, being babied was the last thing he wanted (so he thought) and so under the professional guidance of Big John Baal, he took to the booze, and, soon enough, to consorting with whores. *They* called him whatever he wanted them to. In sleazy cathouses around the league they called him just about every famous ballplayer's nickname under the sun—all he had to do was ask, and pay. They called him Babe, Nap, Christy, Shoeless, Dizzy, Heinie, Tony, Home Run, Cap, Rip, Kiki, Luke, Pepper, and Irish; they called him Cracker and Country and King Kong and Pie; they even called him Lefty, skinny little fourteen-year-old second baseman that he was. Why not? It only cost an extra buck, and it made him feel like somebody important.

"Batting in third position, the first baseman, No. 11, JOHN BAAL. BAAL."

Big John (TR, BL, 6'4", 230 lbs.), said never to have hit a homer sober in his life, had played for just about every club in

the league, including the Mundys, before returning to them in
'42, paroled into the custody of their benevolent manager.
Baal joined the club after serving two years on a five-year gambling rap—he'd shot craps after the World Series with the
rookie of the year, and wiped the boy out with a pair of loaded
dice. Not the first time John had walked off with somebody
else's World Series earnings, only the first time they caught
him with the shaved ivories. In prison Big John had had the
two best seasons of his life, earning the ironic appellation
(coined, of course, by Smitty) "the Babe Ruth of the Big
House." With Big John in the line-up, Sing Sing beat every
major prison team in the country, including the powerful
Leavenworth club, and went on to capture the criminal baseball championship of America two consecutive seasons after
nearly a decade of losing to the big federal pens stocked with
hard-hitting bootleggers. Inside the prison walls a Johnny Baal
didn't have to put up with the rules and regulations that had
so hampered him throughout his big league career, particularly the commandment against taking the field under the influence of alcohol. If a slugger had a thirst around game time,
then his warden saw that it was satisfied (along with any other
appetite a robust man might develop), because the warden
wanted to *win*. But out in society, you couldn't get past the
dugout steps without some little old biddy in a baseball uniform sniffing you all over for fear that if you blew on their ball
with your sour mash breath, you might pop open the stitching
and unravel the yarn. Consequently, aside from his criminal
record, the only record Big John held outside of prison was for
the longest outs hit in a single season. Christ, he clouted that
ball so high that at its zenith it passed clear out of sight—but
as for distance, he just could not get it to go all the way, unless
he was pickled.

Now, every ballplayer has his weakness, and that was Big
John's. If he didn't drink, if he didn't gamble, if he didn't
whore and cheat and curse, if he wasn't a roughneck, a glutton
and a brawler, why he just wasn't himself, and his whole damn
game went to pot, hitting *and* fielding. But when he had fifteen drinks under his belt, there was nobody like him on first
base. Giant that he was, he could still bounce around that
infield like a kangaroo when he was good and drunk. And

could he hit! "Why, one time in that jail up there," Big John told Smitty upon his release from the prison, "I had me a lunch of a case of beer and a bottle of bourbon and got nine for nine in a doubleheader. Yep, everytime I come up, I just poked her into the outside world. But this rule they got out here—why it's disgustin'! It ain't for men, it's for lollipops and cupcakes! It's a damn joke what they done to this game—and that there Hall of *Fame* they got, why, that's a bigger joke! Why, if they ever asked me to come up there and gave me one of them poems or whatever it is they give, why I'd just laugh in their face! I'd say take your poem and wipe your assholes with it, you bunch a' powder puffs!"

Big John's contempt for the Hall of Fame (and his anti-social conduct generally) seemed to stem from grievances against Organized Baseball that had been implanted in him by his notorious father, who, in turn, had inherited from *his* notorious father a downright Neanderthal attitude toward the game. John's grandfather was, as everyone knows, *the* Baal, the legendary "Base," who is still mistakenly credited with the idea of substituting sand-filled bags, or bases, for the posts used to mark off the infield in baseball's infancy; in actuality he earned the nickname early in his career because of his behavior on the playing field. If we are to believe the stories, Base Baal played on just about every cornfield and meadow in America before the first leagues were organized, before stadiums were built and men earned a living as players. Like many American boys, he learned the fundamentals in the Army camps of the Civil War. The game in that era consisted of several variants, all of which would be as foreign to the American baseball fan of today as jai alai or lacrosse. This was long before pitchers began to throw overhand, back when the bat was a stick that was narrow at both ends, if it was not a fence post or a barrel stave, back when there would be as many as twenty or thirty players on a team, and when the umpire, chosen from the crowd of spectators, might well be punched in the nose and run off the field if his judgment did not accord with everyone else's. The ball was a bit larger, something like today's softball, and "plugging" or "soaking" was the order of the day—to get the runner out, you had only to "plug" him (that is, hit him with the ball while he was between two bases), for him to be retired (as often as not, howling in pain). Frequently a fielder, or "scout" as he was called in some parts of the country, would wait for the runner to come right up to him, before "plugging" him in the ribs, much to the pleasure of the onlookers. And that was Base's stock in trade. In fact, when the old fellow finally broke into the newly formed four-club Patriot League in the eighties —by which time the game had taken on many of its modern, more civilized characteristics—he apparently "forgot" himself one day and "plugged" a runner heading home from third right in that vulnerable part of a man's anatomy for which he always aimed. He was instantly mobbed and nearly beaten to death by the other team—a bearded giant of a man, close to sixty now —all the while crying out, "But that's out where I come from!"

Base's son, and Big John's father, was the infamous pitcher, Spit, who in the years before wetting down the ball was declared illegal, would serve up a pitch so juicy that by the end of an inning the catcher had to shake himself off like a dog come in from romping in the rain. The trouble with Spit's spitball was, simply, that nobody could hit it out of the infield, if they could even follow the erratic path of that dripping sphere so as to get any wood on it at all. Once it left Spit's hand, carrying its cargo of liquid, not even he was sure exactly what turns and twists it would take before it landed with a wet thud in the catcher's glove, or up against his padded body. As opposition mounted to this spitter that Baal had perfected—it was unnatural, unsanitary, uncouth, it was ruining the competitive element in the game—he only shrugged and said, "How am I supposed to do, let 'em hit it out theirselves?" On hot afternoons, when his salivary glands and his strong right arm were really working, Spit used to like to taunt the opposition a little by motioning for his outfielders to sit back on their haunches and take a chew, while he struck out—or, as he put it, "drownded"—the other side. Angry batsmen would snarl at the ump, "Game called on accounta rain!" after the first of Spit's spitters did a somersault out in front of the plate and then sort of curled in for a strike at the knees. But Spit himself would pooh-pooh the whole thing, calling down to them, "Come on now, a little wet ain't gonna hurt you." "It ain't the

wet, Baal, it's the stringy stuff. It turns a white man's stomach."
"Ah, ain't nothin'—just got me a little head cold. Get in there
now, and if you cain't swim, float."

In the beginning, various conservative proposals were
offered to transform the spitter back into what it had been
before Spit came on the scene. The citrus fruit growers of
America suggested that a spitball pitcher should have to suck
on half a lemon in order to inhibit his flow of saliva—fulfilling
his daily nutritional requirement of vitamin C in the process.
They tried to work up public interest in a pitch they called
"the sourball," but when the pitchers themselves balked, as it
were, complaining there was not any room for a lemon what
with teeth, tongue, and chewing tobacco in there already, the
proposal, mercifully, was dropped. A more serious suggestion
had to do with allowing a pitcher to use all the saliva he
wanted, but outlawing mucus and phlegm. The theory was
that what the ballplayers euphemistically called "the stringy
stuff" was precisely what made Baal's pitch dance the way it
did. A committee of managers assigned to study his motion
maintained that Spit was very much like a puppeteer yanking
on a web of strings, and that the rules had only to be rewritten
to forbid a pitcher blowing his nose on the ball, or bringing
anything up from back of the last molar for the problem to be
solved, not only for the batsman, but for those fans who happened to be sitting in its path when it was fouled into the
stands. It might even bring more of the ladies out to see a
game, for as it stood now, you could not even get a suffragette
into the bleachers on a day Baal was pitching, so repugnant
was his technique to the fair sex. Even the heartiest of male
fans showed signs of squeamishness pocketing a foul tip to
bring home as a souvenir to the kiddies. But Spit himself only
chuckled (he was a mild, mild man, until they destroyed him).
"When I go to a tea party, I will be all good manners and
curtsy goodbye at the door, I can assure you of that. But as I
am facin' two hundred pounds of gristle wavin' a stick what
wants to drive the ball back down my gullet, why then, I will
use the wax out of my ears, if I has to."

It was not a remark designed to placate his enemies. In fact,
the discovery that he *had* used earwax on a ball in the 1902
World Series caused the controversy to spread beyond the base-

ball world; owners who had come to consider wetting the ball a part of the game—and Spit a gifted eccentric who would have his day and pass into obscurity soon enough—became alarmed by the outrage of a public that had seemed on the brink of accepting baseball as *the* American sport, now that it had grown away from the brutish game, marked by maiming and fisticuffs, played by Spit's Daddy. The editorialists warned, "If baseball cannot cleanse itself at once of odious and distasteful ways that reek of the barnyard and the back alley, the American people may well look elsewhere—perhaps to the game of tennis, long favored by the French—for a national pastime." From all sides the pressure mounted, until at the winter meeting of the Patriot League owners in Tri-City, following the World Series of 1902 in which Baal, by his own admission, had waxed a few pitches with some stuff he'd hooked out of his head, the following resolution was passed: "No player shall anoint the ball with any bodily secretions for any purpose whatsoever. Inevitable as it is that droplets of perspiration will adhere to a ball in the course of a game, every effort shall be made by the players and the umpire, to keep the ball dry and free of foreign substances at all times." And with these words baseball entered its maturity, and became the game to which an entire people would give its heart and soul.

Spit's career ended abruptly on the opening day of the 1903 season, when he scandalized the country by an act in such flagrant violation of the laws of human decency, let alone the new resolution passed in Tri-City the previous winter, that he became the first player ever to be banished from baseball—the first deplorable exception to the Patriot League's honorable record. What happened was this: throwing nothing but bone dry pitches, Spit was tagged for eight hits and five runs by a jeering, caustic Independence team even before he had anyone out in the first inning. The crowd was booing, his own teammates were moaning, and Spit was in a rage. They had ruined him, those dryball bastards! They had passed a law whose purpose was the destruction of no one in the world but himself! A law against him!

And so before twenty thousand shocked customers—including innocent children—and his own wide-eyed teammates, the once great pitcher, who was washed up anyway, did the unthinkable, the unpardonable, the inexpiable: he dropped the flannel trousers of his uniform to his knees, and proceeded to urinate on the ball, turning it slowly in his hands so as to dampen the entire surface. Then he hitched his trousers back up, and in the way of pitchers, kicked at the ground around the mound with his spikes, churning up, then smoothing down the dirt where he had inadvertently dribbled upon it. To the batter, as frozen in his position as anyone in that ball park, he called, "Here comes the pissball, shithead—get ready!"

For years afterward they talked about the route that ball took before it passed over the plate. Not only did it make the hairpin turns and somersaults expected of a Baal spitter, but legend has it that it shifted gears, *four* times, halving, then doubling its velocity each fifteen feet it traveled. And in the end, the catcher, in his squat, did not even have to move his glove from where it too was frozen as a target. Gagging, he caught the ball with a *squish*, right in the center of the strike zone.

"Stee-*rike!*" Baal called down to the voiceless umpire, and then he turned and walked off the mound and through the dugout and right on out of the park. They banished him only minutes afterward, but (not unlike the great Gamesh thirty years later) he was already on the streetcar by then, still wearing his uniform and spikes, and by nightfall he was asleep in a boxcar headed for the Rio Grande, his old stinking glove his pillow and his only pal. When he finally jumped from the train he was in Central America.

There he founded that aboriginal ancestor of Latin American baseball, the hapless Mosquito Coast League of Nicaragua—if you could call it a league, where the players drifted from one club to another for no reason other than whim, and entire teams were known to disappear from a town between games of a doubleheader, never to be seen again. The Nicaraguan youths that Spit Baal recruited for his league had no local games of their own comparable in complexity and duration, and few were ever really able to maintain concentration through an afternoon of play in that heat. But they accepted without question that you could rub anything you wanted on a ball before pitching it, and in fact took to the spitball much the way American children take to the garden hose in summertime. Down in the Mosquito Coast League, Spit's native boys played just the sort of disgusting, slimy, unhygienic game that his own countrymen had so wholeheartedly rejected by passing the resolution against a wet or a waxed baseball. The few Americans who drifted to Nicaragua to play were sailors who had jumped ship, and assorted nuts and desperadoes in flight from a sane and decent society; occasionally an unemployed spitballer would come crawling out of the jungle swamp and onto the playing field, in search of a home. Carried from village to village on mules, sleeping in filth with the hogs and the chickens, or in hovels with toothless Indians, these men quickly lost whatever dignity they may once have had as ballplayers and human beings; and then, to further compromise themselves and the great game of baseball, they took to drinking a wretched sort of raisin wine between innings, which altered the pace of the game immeasurably. But the water tasted of rats and algae, and center field in the dry season in Guatemala is as hot as center field must be in Hell—catch nine innings in Nicaragua in the summer, and you'll drink anything that isn't out-and-out poison. Which is just what the water was. They used it only to bathe their burning feet. Indian women hung around the foul lines, and for a penny in the local currency could be hired for an afternoon to wash a player's toes and pour a bucketful of the fetid stuff over his head when he stepped up to bat. Eventually these waterwomen came to share the benches with the players, who fondled and squeezed them practically at will, and it was not unusual for such a woman to attach herself to a team, and travel with them for a whole season.

Because the pitchers—whose life was no bed of roses down there—rinsed their mouths with raisin wine even while out on the mound, going to the jug as often as a civilized pitcher goes to the resin bag, in a matter of innings the ball came to look as though it had been dipped in blood; the bat too would turn a deep scarlet from contact with the discolored ball and the sticky, sopping uniforms—numeraled serapes, really—of the players. The clean white stitched ball that is the very emblem of the game as played in our major leagues, was replaced in the Mosquito Coast League with a ball so darkly stained that if you were on the sidelines peering through the shimmering waves of the heat, you might have thought the two teams were playing with a wad of tar or a turd.

Into this life Big John Baal was born, the bastard offspring of the only pitcher ever to dare to throw a pissball in a major league ball park, and a half-breed who earned a few coins from the players in the on-deck circle by pouring Central American water over their ears and their ankles. By the time Juanito was two or three seasons old, his father no longer even remembered which of the dozens of waterwomen around the league had mothered his little son—to him they all looked the same, dirty, dark, and dumb, but at least they were a step up from the livestock with whom his battery-mate found happiness. A major leaguer had to draw the line somewhere, and Spit drew it at goats. When the child asked him "Mamma? Madre?" Spit wouldn't even bother to wrack his brain (in that heat wracking your brain could bring on the vertigo) but pointed to whichever one happened to be rolling in the dust with the reliever down in the bullpen (where, on some days, there was even a young snarling bull). By the age of eighteen months, John was already big and strong enough to hold a green banana in his ten fat fingers and swing at the pebbles that the native-born players liked to throw at the manager's little boy when his father happened not to be around; and when a few years later he was able to swing a regulation bat, the child was taught by his father the secret to hitting the spitter. John shortly became so adept at connecting with the scarlet spitball (or spicball, as the disillusioned and drunken expatriates sneeringly called it among themselves) that by the time he was old enough to leave Nicaragua to go out and take his vengeance on the world, it was like nothing for him to lay into a ball that was both white and dry. Oh, what an immortal he might have been, if only he did not have the morals of someone raised in the primordial slime! Oh, if only he had not come North with a heartful of contempt for the league that had banished his dad, and the republic for which it stood!

"Batting fourth for the Mundys, the catcher, No. 37, HOT PTAH. PTAH."

Hothead, or Hot (for short) Ptah (TR, BR, 5′10″, 180 lbs.), far and away the most irritating player in baseball, and the Mundy most despised by the other teams, despite the physical handicap which might otherwise have enlisted their sympathies. Probably his disposition had to do with his not having one of his legs, though his mother back in Kansas maintained that he had always been crabby, even when he'd had both. To the wartime fans, Hot was more a source of amusement than anything else, and they probably got more of a kick out of his angry outbursts than from the foibles and eccentricities of any other Mundy. However, those who had to stand at the plate and listen to that one-legged chatterbox curse and insult them, didn't take to it too well, try as they might. "Okay, Hot, so you ain't got all your legs, that ain't my fault." But he would just keep buzzing like a fly on a windowpane—until all at once the batter would whirl around to the umpire, his eyes welling with tears. "Do you hear that! Did you hear what he just said! Why don't you do something about it!" "*O*-kay, what'd he say now?" the ump would ask, for Hot had a way of pouring the venom directly into the hitter's ear, leaving the umpire out of it entirely. "What'd he *say*? A lot of unkind words about my mother bein' intimate with niggers down in the south, that's what!" "Now you listen here, Ptah—" But by this time Hot would have ripped off his mask and started in pounding it on the plate, till you expected one or the other to be smashed to smithereens—or else he would just hammer with his hand and his glove on his chest protector, like a gorilla in a baseball suit, howling all the while about his "freedom of speech." Hot could go into the craziest song and dance ever seen on a ball field (or anywhere, including the Supreme Court of the United States) about the Constitution, the Bill of Rights, the Declaration of Independence, the Monroe Doctrine, the Emancipation Proclamation, even the League of Nations, in order to defend his right to say what he did into some poor southern boy's ear. "I know you," Hot would whisper to the batter, starting off low and slow, "and your whole damn family and I know your mother . . ." And then he had the gall to defend himself with the First Amendment. And a hundred more things that most umpires had never even heard of, but that Hot had studied up on in the legal books that he lugged around with him in his suitcase from one hotel to the next. He *slept* with those damn books . . . but then what else could he sleep with, poor gimp that he was? "The Wagner Act! The Sherman Antitrust Act! Carter versus Carter Coal! Gompers versus Buck Stove! The

Federal Reserve Act, damn it! And what about the Dred Scott decision? Don't that count for nothing in this country no more? Gosh *damn*!" And here, having baffled and confused everyone involved, having set the fans to roaring with laughter in the stands (which only burned him up more) he would go hobbling back behind the plate, and the umpire would call for play to be resumed. After all, not being lawyers by profession, the umpires could not be expected to know if what Hot was saying made any sense, and so rather than get into a legal harangue that might end up in the courtroom with a litigious catcher like this son of a bitch, they preferred to respect his so-called freedom of speech, rather than send him to the showers. And besides, if he didn't catch for the Mundys, who would—a guy with *no* legs?

To Hot's credit, it should be said that he had as good a throwing arm as any catcher in the league in '43, and he could drill the ball up against the left-field fence when you needed a run driven in; however, having that leg made out of wood caused him to lurch like something on a pogo stick when he came charging after a bunt, and he was not exactly death on fly balls popped back to the screen behind home plate. His doubles and triples were plentiful, only he was never able to get farther than first on them; and his singles, of course, were outs, the right-fielder, or the center-fielder, or the left-fielder to the first-baseman. (If you're scoring, that's 9 to 3, 8 to 3, or 7 to 3.)

Now obviously, in peacetime a one-legged catcher, like a one-armed outfielder (such as the Mundys had roaming right), would have been at the most a curiosity somewhere down in the dingiest town in the minors—precisely where Hot had played during the many years that the nations of the world lived in harmony. But it is one of life's grisly ironies that what is a catastrophe for most of mankind, invariably works to the advantage of a few who live on the fringes of the human community. On the other hand, it is a grisly irony to live on the fringes of the human community.

"Batting fifth and playing left field, No. 13, MIKE RAMA. RAMA."

Even before the Mundys had to play day in and day out on the other fellow's terrain, Mike "the Ghost" Rama (TL, BL,

6'1", 183 lbs.) had his troubles with the outfield wall. Just so long as there was one of them behind him, whether it was in Mundy Park or on the road, sooner or later the Ghost went crashing up against it in do-or-die pursuit of a well-tagged ball. In '41, his rookie year, he had on five different occasions to be removed on a stretcher from the field in Port Ruppert. The fans, of course, were deeply moved by a brilliant youngster so dedicated to victory as to be utterly heedless of his own welfare. It rent their hearts to hear the *konk* resound throughout the ball park when Mike's head made contact with the stadium wall—was he dead this time? and, damn it, had he dropped the ball? But miraculously neither was the case. The umpire who rushed to the outfield to call the play (before calling the hospital) invariably found the baseball lodged snugly in the pocket of the unconscious left-fielder's glove. "Out!" he would shout, and without irony, for he was describing only the status of the batter. Hurray, cried the fans—whereupon the bullpen catcher and the batboy would come dashing onto the field to lift the crumpled hero from the grass on to the stretcher, and thence to the ambulance that could already be heard wailing across Port Ruppert to the stadium. And how that sound sobered and saddened the crowd . . .

Once the solemnity of the moment had passed the fans did have to wonder if perhaps Mike wasn't a little short on brainpower to be knocking himself out like this every couple of weeks; for it wasn't as though he misjudged the proximity of the wall in his effort to catch the ball, but rather that he seemed completely to forget that such things as walls even existed. He just could not seem to get the idea of a barrier into his head, even after bringing the two into forceful conjunction. Why they came to call him the Ghost was because he appeared to think—if that is the word for it—that what was impenetrable to the rest of us would be as nothing to him: either he did not believe that walls were really walls, or flesh only flesh, or he just was never going to get over having been born and raised in Texas. For down there, where he had been a great high school star, it seemed they did not bother to fence the field in . . . just laid out the bases and let the boys roam like the longhorns.

In Mike's rookie year, Mister Fairsmith would make it his

business to be at the hospital first thing in the morning to fetch the Mundy left-fielder once the doctors had put the pieces back together and proclaimed him ready to have another go at life. They would drive directly from the hospital to Mundy Park, where the two would walk out across the manicured diamond on to the outfield grass. With only the groundskeepers looking up from their rakes to watch the oddly touching scene, Mister Fairsmith would lead the rookie all the way from the left-field corner to Glorious Mundy's headstone in furthest center, and then back again. They might walk to and fro like this for half an hour at a stretch, Mike, under Mister Fairsmith's direction, running the tips of his fingers along the wall so as to prove to himself that it was no figment of anybody's imagination.

"Michael," Mister Fairsmith would say, "can you tell me what is going on in your mind when you act like this? Do you have any idea?"

"Sure. Nothin'. I'm thankin' about catchin' the ball, that's all. I ain't havin' no sex thoughts or nothin', Mister Fairsmith, I swear."

"Michael, I am cognizant of the fact that there were no walls surrounding the ball fields in the part of the world where you grew up, but surely, lad, you had walls in your house when you were a boy down there. Or am I mistaken?"

"Oh sure we had walls. We wuz poor, but we wuzn't that poor."

"And did you, as a child, go running into the walls in your house?"

"Nope, nope. But then a' course I wasn't chasin' nothin' then."

"Son, you are going to be held together by clothesline and baling wire before you are even twenty-one, if you do not change your ways. Keep this up and your next fly ball may be your last."

"Gee, I sure hope not, Mister Fairsmith. I live for baseball. I eat, drink, and sleep baseball. It's just about the only thang I ever thank about, is baseball. I see pop flies in my dreams. I can't even sleep sometimes, imaginin' all the different kinds of line drives there are to catch. Baseball is my whole life, I swear."

"And your death too, lad, if you don't start in this minute thinking about *the reality of the wall.*"

But nothing anyone could say was able to implant in Mike Rama a healthy respect for the immovable and the unyielding. To the contrary, as some men are drawn to wine and some to women, so Mike Rama was drawn to that left-field wall. If he could be said to have had a temptress, that was it. "Why, I'll tell you what I think," said Johnny Baal to Smitty, "if that there wall had titties on it, Mike 'ud marry her."

"Batting sixth and playing third base, No. 2, WAYNE HEKET. HEKET."

Kid Heket (TR, BR, 6', 172 lbs.), the oldest Mundy of them all, the oldest major leaguer of them all, a rookie in 1909 and a utility infielder and pinch-runner thereafter, he had become a regular only after the Mundy brothers had sold everybody of value on the great championship team, and just about everything else that was any good in the dugout "exceptin'," as the Kid told it, "me and the water cooler." Of course he was no longer "so fleet afeet," as he'd been in his pinch-running days, but then, as the aging third-sacker asked, "Who is?" Were his reflexes gone, would he say? "I sure would," replied the Kid. And his eyesight? "Dim durin' the day, practically nil at night. Nope, don't see very good at all no more." His strength? He sighed: "Oh, gone with the wind, Smitty. Call me broken down and I won't argue." Why did he stay on in baseball then? "What else is there? This here is just about all that I am fit to do now, and, as you see, I ain't fit for it."

Fortunately, playing for the wartime Mundys was not really as taxing physically as a job on a farm or a factory might have been for a man of fifty-two. And, during the winter months the Kid could just sit around down home resting up in the barber shop, enjoying the smell of the witch hazel, the warmth of the stove, and the pictures in the old magazines. During the season itself, in order to conserve what little energy he had, he just played as close as he could to the third-base line, hoping in this way to cut down the extra-base hits, but otherwise granting to the opposition whatever they could poke between him and the shortstop. "The way I see it now, if a feller hits it to my left, he got hisself a single and more power to him. If a' course the Frenchman wants to try and get it, well, that's his business and I don't propose to interfere. His ways is his ways and mine is mine. As I gets older I find myself gettin' more philosophical. I got to ask myself, you see, who am I to say what should be a base hit and what shouldn't, a feller with but four years of schoolin' in his whole life. No, some old folks may do otherwise, but I don't propose to set Wayne Heket up as some kind of judge of others at this late stage of the game." By which he meant the game of life, clearly, for even if it was only the bottom of the first, he paid no mind to what was hit between third and short. "At my age you just got to cut down, no question about it. You just got to give up somethin', so I give up goin' to my left. Let's be honest, Smitty, my runnin' days is over, and there ain't no sense in actin' like they ain't."

When the Mundys came to bat, the Kid always made it his business to catch a quick nap—no sooner did his seat hit the bench but he was out like a light. "That's what I credit my long baseball life to, you know. Them naps. So long as I can catch me some shuteye in that dugout there, there is no doubt that I am a better man for it back on the playing field. A' course, as you can imagine, nobody cherishes more than me them times that we get a little rally goin', and I can really slip off into dreamland. There is no doubt about it—and I tole Mister Fairsmith, right out, too—if we was a better hittin' team, I would be gettin' more sleep. The worst for me is when the fellers start swingin' at them first pitches. What in hell's the hurry, I ask 'em, where's the fire anyhoo? Sometimes my stiff ol' bones has barely stopped throbbin' with pain, when they are shakin' my shoulder, tellin' me it's time to go back on out to the field. Best of all was the other day in Aceldama. It was top of the eighth and I was near to droppin', let me tell you. I was up first, struck out lookin'—or not lookin', I suppose—come back to the bench, expectin' that of the old forty winks I'd be gettin' myself maybe four, if I was lucky. Well, what happens, but that whole darn bunch of hitless wonders catches fire and we don't go out until they have batted all the way around to me. What a snooze I had! Like a top! Unfortunately, the Butchers, they come back with seven in their half of the inning to beat us—but if I had not had that good long nap while we was

up, I tell you, I might not have made it all the way through
them seven runs of theirs on my feet. As it was, I dozed off a
couple times in the field, but then I usually does, when we is
changin' pitchers. Tell you the truth, I thought they had scored
only four and we was still ahead by one. I didn't find out till
the next mornin' when I seen it in the paper down in the lobby
that we lost. Must be then that I was out on my feet for three
of them runs—not that it makes much difference. You been
around as long as me, you seen one run, you seen 'em all. That
afternoon, when I run into some of the Butchers on the streetcar goin' out to the ball park, I asked them how come they
didn't wake me up in the eighth yesterday when they was
roundin' third. You don't find that kind of consideration every
day, you know, especially from the other team, which is usually
tryin' to hair-ass you, one way or another. I joked 'em—I said,
'What ever got in to you boys, bein' so quiet and all comin'
round the bag? Don't want to rouse the sleepin' beast or somethin'?' And you know what they tole me? I couldn't believe it.
They tole me they come *whoopin'* round that bag, each and
ever one of 'em, squawkin' their heads off like a bunch of
crows, and I didn't budge one inch. Well, that'll give you a
idea of just how tired a feller can get bein' in baseball all his
life. Maybe that is what it is like bein' in anything all your life,
but I can only speak for myself, you know. And I'm just shot.
Why, if this here terrible war goes on too long, and I keep
playin' in the regular line-up like this, why, I wouldn't be surprised if one afternoon I will just drop off, you know, and
that's that. The other fellers'll come runnin' back in to the
bench when the innin' is over and it's our turn to bat, but not
me. I'll just be left stooped over out there, with my hands on
my knees and a jaw full of tobacco juice, waitin' for the next
pitch, only I'll be dead. Well, I only hope it don't happen while
the game is in progress, 'cause if the other team finds out, they
sure as hell will start droppin' them bunts in down the third-
base line. Now, even alive I ain't hardly the man with a bunt
I was back before the First World War. But with me dead with
rigor mortis, and Hothead havin' only one leg, they could
just about bunt us crazy, don't you think? If they was smart,
that is."

*

"Batting seventh and playing right field, No. 17, BUD PARUSHA. PARUSHA."

Bud Parusha (TR, BR, 6′3″, 215 lbs.) was the youngest of the Parusha brothers, two of whom, Angelo and Tony, were all-star outfielders for the Tri-City Tycoons, and until they entered the service boasted the two strongest throwing arms in the majors. A throwing arm no less powerful and accurate was said to belong to the third brother, who surely would have been a Tycoon outfielder too, if it weren't that the throwing arm was the only arm he'd been born with. It was as though Mother Nature—or, to be realistic about it, Mother Parusha—having lavished such gifts upon Angelo and Tony, had run out of steam by the time she got to Bud, and when it came to finishing him off, could not deliver up anything whatsoever, not even a stump, where the mate to the throwing arm should have been. Consequently, when Angelo and Tony went off to the majors, Bud was left to work as best he could as a waiter in his father's restaurant in Bayonne. Then came the war. Angelo and Tony were commissioned and placed in charge of the hand grenade training program for the entire United States Marine Corps, and Bud found himself elevated to the big leagues, not up to the Tycoons of course—they were the P. League champs after all—but across the Jersey marshes, to the team that seemed rapidly to be becoming a haven for the handicapped. Bud moved in with Hothead Ptah, whose averages in the minors he had followed for years in the back pages of *The Sporting News*, and rumor had it that the two would shortly be joined by a one-eyed pitcher from the Blues, a Jewish fellow called Seymour Clops, nicknamed inevitably, "Sy." "What about a sword-swallower and a tattooed man, while they're at it!" cried Hothead, who did not at all cotton to the idea of being a freak in a freakshow. "And what about dwarfs! There must be some of them around! Oh, I just can't wait to get up some morning and look over and find I am rooming with a left-handed dwarf, all curled up and sleepin' in my mitt. And a Jew on top of it!" The dwarf, of course, when he came, would be right-handed and a Christian, the pitcher O.K. Ockatur.

For those who never saw Bud Parusha in action during the war years—and after him, Pete Gray, the one-armed outfielder who played for the St. Louis Browns—it will be necessary to explain in some little detail, how, and to what degree, he was able to overcome his handicap on the field.

First off, to catch an ordinary fly ball was no more problem for Bud than for any fielder of major league caliber; however, in that he wore his glove on the end of his throwing arm, it did require an unorthodox maneuver for him to return the ball to the infield. Unlike Gray of the Brownies, who had a stump of a left arm under which he could tuck his glove while he extracted the ball from the pocket, Bud (with no left arm at all) had to use his mouth. He was lucky to have a large one—"that old law of compensation," said the sports announcers—and a strong bite which he had further developed over the years by five minutes of chewing on a tennis ball before going to sleep each night. After fielding a ball, he was able instantly to remove it from his glove with his teeth, and hold it clamped between them while he shook the glove from his hand; then he extracted the ball from his mouth with his bare right hand, and hurled it with Parusha-like speed and accuracy to the infield. All this he accomplished in one fluid, unbroken motion and with such efficiency and even grace, that you would have thought that this was the way the outfield was supposed to be played.

In the beginning the fans did not know quite what to make of Bud's singular fielding technique and there were those who laughed at the man in the Mundy outfield who looked from a distance to be giving birth to something through the orifice in his head. There were even those in the bleachers—there always are—who like children popping out of closets would shout "Boo!", hoping in that way to startle Bud and cause him to swallow the baseball. Unfortunately there were occasions when in his anxiety not to drop the ball out of his mouth while flinging off his glove, he would take it too far back between his molars, and find himself unable to extricate it unassisted. It happened infrequently, but always in the same tense situation: with the bases loaded. And each time with the same disastrous result: an inside-the-mouth grand-slam home run. Roland Agni would race over from center and Nickname would tear out from second to try to save the day, but not even those two together, performing the play as they had practiced it—Agni kneeling on Bud's chest, forcing open his jaws like a fellow about to stick his head into the mouth of a crocodile, and young Damur, with those quick hands of his, yanking and jiggling at the ball for all he was worth—were able to prevent the four runs from scoring.

Despite his difficulties—and, in part, because of them—kindly, uncomplaining Bud became popular as Hothead, who had been there first, had never even tried to be. While the sluggers and fancy dans were paid to endorse razor blades and hair oil, Bud's beautifully formed signature soon came to adorn the pages of medical magazines, where he was pictured in his gray road uniform with the scarlet piping and insignia, sitting in a wheelchair, or balancing himself on a crutch. Where it was feasible, he would always test a product before giving it his endorsement—more than most of his colleagues bothered to do for items far less compromising to a ballplayer's prestige than oxygen tents and artificial limbs. And when the Mundys had a free day on the road, he never failed to go off to visit the local veterans hospital, where he would promise one of the amputees to get a base hit for him the next time they threw him anything good. He could not dedicate home runs to them, because big as he was he really could not be expected to hit home runs with only one arm, but every six or seven times at bat, he managed to smack a single, and then from the loud speaker there would be the announcement that Bud's hit had been "for" so-and-so in such-and-such a hospital, and the fans would smile and clap.

Around the league he began to build a real following among the handicapped of all ages; sometimes as many as forty or fifty of them would be out there in the stands along the right-field line when the Mundys and Bud came to town. The public address system had only to announce Bud's number for them to begin banging on the railings with their canes and crutches. "Parusha's Clinic" Smitty dubbed the right-field stands, and in Kakoola and Tri-City they even set up ramps out there to make things easier for the handicapped who turned out to see Bud perform. In their excitement some of his supporters occasionally went too far and would try, for instance, to touch him with the tip of a crutch as he came near the stands to field a foul, endangering his three remaining limbs, not to mention his eyesight. Once a woman in a wheelchair attempted to lean forward to pluck Bud's cap off for a souvenir and tumbled out of the stands onto his back. But mostly they were content to just sit there and take heart from the courage and ingenuity that Bud displayed; in Kakoola, in fact, one fan was so inspired by Bud's example that after ten years in a wheelchair, he found himself up on his feet cheering wildly as Buddy made a diving shoestring catch in the bottom of the ninth. It was in a column about this very fellow that Smitty coined the name "Parusha's Clinic." "I'm walking!" the man suddenly cried out, even as Bud was extracting the ball from his mouth to fire it to first to double off the Reaper runner and end the game.

### CRIPPLE CURED AS RUPPERTS ROMP

the Kakoola evening paper reported to its readers that night— but then could not resist the sardonic subhead—

#### TWO MIRACLES IN ONE DAY

"Batting eighth for the Mundys, and playing center field, No. 6, ROLAND AGNI. AGNI."

Roland Agni (TL, BL, 6′2″, 190 lbs.), in '43 a kid of eighteen tapering like the V for Victory from his broad shoulders and well-muscled arms down to ankles as elegantly turned as Betty Grable's—swift on his feet as Nickname Damur, strong as a Johnny Baal, as mad for baseball as Mike Rama, and in his own baby-blue eyes destined to be the most spectacular rookie since Joltin' Joe. One difference: the Yankee Clipper, aside from being four years older than Agni when he entered the majors, had also played a few seasons down in the minors; what was so amazing about Roland, Roland thought, was that he was leaping right from high school to the big time.

Only there was a catch. Upon his graduation the previous June, Roland had turned down forty athletic scholarships in four sports from colleges all around the nation, and offers from twenty-three major league clubs in order to be signed up by his father with the Ruppert Mundys, the only team in the three leagues that had not even bothered to scout him. It was precisely their indifference that had convinced Mr. Agni that the Mundys were the major league team for his son, if major league team there had to be. Not that Mr. Agni, like some fathers, had any objection to baseball as a career; the problem was Roland's pride, which, in a word, was overweening. The boy had been hearing applause in his ears ever since he had hurled a perfect sandlot game at age six, with the result that over the years he had become, in his father's opinion, contemptuous of everything and everyone around him, above all of his family and the values of humility and self-sacrifice that they had tried, in vain, to instill in him. When his father dared to criticize him for his superior attitudes, Roland would invariably storm away from the dinner table, screaming in his high-pitched adolescent voice that he couldn't help it, he *was* superior. "But," asked his mother, using psychology, "do you want the girls to go around whispering that Roland Agni is stuck on himself?" "They can whisper whatever they want—they'd be stuck on themselves too, if they was me!" "But nobody likes a self-centered person, darling, who thinks only of himself." "Oh don't they? What about the forty colleges begging me to enroll there? What about the twenty-three major league teams pleading with me to play ball for them?" "Oh but they don't want you for your character, Roland, *or* for your mind—they want you only for your body." "Well, they *should*, because that's what's so great about me! That's what makes me so phenomenal!" "Roland!" "But it's true! I got the greatest physique of any boy my age in America! Maybe in the whole world!" "Go to your room, Roland! You are just as conceited as all the girls say! What are we going to do with you to make you realize that you are *not* God's gift to the world?" "But I am—to the baseball world that's just exactly what I am! That's just what the scout said from the St. Louis Cardinals! Them very words!" "Well, shame on him, flattering you that way just so they could sign you up! As if you aren't conceited enough! Oh," cried Mrs. Agni, turning to her husband, "what is going to happen to him out in the real world? How will he ever survive the hardships and cruelty of life with such an attitude? Roland, tell me, whatever made you think you were such a hero at seventeen years of age?" "MY BATTING AVERAGE!" screamed the star, his voice echoing off the dozens of trophies in his room.

Roland's father listened politely to the twenty-three fast-talking major league scouts as each tried to outbid the other for his son's services, and then telephoned the Mundy front office in Port Ruppert to announce that the father of the phenomenal Roland Agni was on the line. "Come again?" said the voice at the other end—"the phenomenal who?" No response could have been more heartening to the boy wonder's dad. He gave the Mundy front office a brief account of Roland's high school career: in four years of varsity play he had batted .732 and regularly hurled shutouts when he wasn't in the outfield robbing the other team of extra-base hits. However, Mr. Agni rushed to say, if hired to play for the Ruppert Mundys, his son was to receive no more than the lowest paid member of the team, was to bat eighth in the line-up in his first year, and to rise no more than one notch in the batting order in each succeeding year. It would be more than enough for a boy as self-centered as Roland to leap from high school directly to the majors without making him rich, or clean-up hitter, in the bargain. These, said Mr. Agni, were his only conditions.

"Look," laughed the Mundys' man in Port Ruppert, "what about if we go you one better and don't pay him at all."

Mr. Agni leaped at the suggestion. "In other words, I would just continue to give him his allowance—?"

"Right. And of course his room, board, and supplies."

"In other words, he'd be playing for a professional team but still have his amateur status."

"Correct. Of course, we'd need a deposit from you right off, so's we can keep the eighth slot in the batting order open for him. And room and board we'd have to have in advance. You can understand that."

"Fine. Fine."

"All right, you're on. Now what's that name again? Angry?"

"*Ag*ni."

"First name?"

"Roland."

"Okey-dokey. Spring training begins March 1, Asbury Park, New Jersey—on account of the war. Be cheaper for you anyway than Florida. We'll hold the eighth spot for him until noon that day."

"Thank you. Thank you very much."

"Well, thank *you*, Mr. Angry, and thanks for calling the Mundys," said the fellow, with a chuckle, and hung up, believing that he had just indulged a practical joker, or perhaps a sportswriter having some fun at the expense of the Mundy front office. Maybe even a fella name a' Smitty.

To find himself in the P. League with the Ruppert Mundys, and batting eighth in their line-up—and not even getting paid for it—had something like the humbling effect upon their boy that the Agnis had hoped for. Still, crushed and bewildered as he was by this bizarre turn of events, Roland Agni led the league in batting that year with .362, in hits with 188, in home runs with 39, and in doubles with 44. Of course with the pitcher batting behind him, he hardly scored, unless he hit the ball out of the park, or stole second, third, and then home; after getting on with a hit he was generally cut down at second on a d.p. or left stranded as the pitcher went out on strikes. And given the eight who batted before him he had no chance of doing much of anything in the r.b.i. department.

In the middle of the season he was called for his Army physical and found unfit for service. First the Mundys, now 4F!

It took a team of physicians a whole morning to study his marvelous V-shaped physique, whispering all the while among themselves—in admiration, thought the innocent center-fielder —before arriving at their decision. "Okay, Roland," they asked, slumping wearily to the floor of the examination room after the three-hour ordeal, "what is it? Trick knee? Bad ticker? Night sweats? Nosebleeds? Sciatica?" "What do you mean?" "What's wrong with you, Roland, that you're too ashamed to say?" "Wrong with *me*? Nothin'! Just look," he cried, standing to show himself off in the nude, "I'm perfect." "Listen, Roland," said the doctors, "there's a war on, in case you haven't heard. A *world* war. What happens to be at stake isn't eighth place in the Patriot League but the future of civilization itself. We're doctors, Roland, and we have a responsibility. We don't want somebody going into a battle that may turn the tide of history, suddenly coming down with a sick headache and just lying down on the job in the trench. We don't want the lives of an entire platoon endangered just because somebody like you has to stop to scratch his pruritus ani." "But I don't get sick headaches, or the other thing either." "How do you know you don't get 'the other thing,'" they asked suspiciously, "if you don't even know what it is?" "Because I don't get *anything*— I have never even had a cavity, or a pimple. Smell my breath— it's like fresh-cut hay!" But when he blew his sweet odor into their nostrils, it only further infuriated the doctors. "Look here, Agni—we want to know what the hell is wrong with you, and we want to know now. Constipation? Sinusitis? Double vision? Get the shakes, do you? Hot flushes? Or is it the chills, Roland? How about epilepsy, does that ring a bell?" they asked, slamming him up against the white tile wall to have another go at him with their stethoscopes. "No! No! I tell you, I never been sick in my life! Sometimes I even think I am impregnable! And that ain't a boast—it's a fact!" "Oh it is, is it? Then how come according to our records here you are the only unpaid professional athlete in the business? How come your old man is paying them to keep you on the team, rather than the other way around? How come an impregnable boy like you isn't up with the Tycoons, Roland?" "That's what *I* want to know!" cried Agni, and collapsed onto the examination stool, where he sat weeping into his hands. They let him sob until it appeared he had no more resistance left in him. Then they stole upon him where he sat unclothed and gorgeous, and softly stroking his golden curls, whispered into his ear, "Wet the bed? Sleep with a night light? How come a big strong handsome boy like you, leading the league in base hits and doubles, is still batting eighth for Ruppert, Roland? Don't you like girls?"

"Daddy," Roland shouted into the phone when he was dressed again and back out in the world, "I am unfit for the service now too! I am 4F—ONLY THERE IS NOTHING WRONG WITH ME!"

"Well, there is that pride again, Rollie."

"BUT THE DOCTORS COULDN'T FIND ANYTHING, NOT EVEN THE THREE OF THEM TOGETHER!"

"Well, doctors aren't perfect, any more than the rest of us. That's the very point I am trying to make to you."

"But I should be 1A, not 4F! And not a Ruppert Mundy, either! Oh, Daddy, what am I doing on that team, where everybody is some kind of crackpot, thinking all the time about his name, or running into the walls, or having to have me sit on his chest to pull the darn baseball out of his *mouth!*"

"In other words, what you are telling me, Roland, is that you are too good for them."

"It ain't sayin' you are too good if you just happen to have all your arms and can stay awake for nine innings!"

"In other words then, you're just 'better' than everybody else."

"On this team, who wouldn't be!"

"And it doesn't occur to you that perhaps your teammates have had hardships in their lives about which you know nothing. Do you ever think that perhaps why you're 'better' is because you were fortunate enough to have all the opportunities in life that they were denied?"

"Sure I think about it! I thank my lucky stars about it! And that's why I don't belong with them, even if I was batting first and gettin' a million dollars!"

"Oh, son, what are we going to do with you, and this unquenchable thirst for fame and glory?"

"Trade me! Trade me away from these freaks and these oddballs! Daddy, they ain't even got a home park that's their own—what kind of major league ball club is that?"

"You mean for the great Roland Agni to be playing with?"

"For *anybody* to be playin' with—but me especially! Daddy, I am leading the league in batting in my rookie year! There's been nobody like me since Joe DiMaggio, and he was twenty-two!"

"And yet you're 4F. Doesn't that mean anything to you at all?"

"No! No! Nothin' means *nothin'* anymore!"


"Batting in ninth position and pitching for the Ruppert Mundys . . ."

The Mundy council of elders: starters Tuminikar, Buchis, Volos, and Demeter; relievers Pollux, Mertzeger, and the tiny Mexican right-hander, Chico Mecoatl—every last one of them flabby in the middle, arthritic in the shoulder, bald on the top. "The hairless wonders," said Jolly Cholly Tuminikar, who had discovered the fine art of self-effacement following the tragedy that destroyed his confidence and his career, "and a good thing too. Ain't a one of us could raise his arm to comb his hairs if he had any. Why, if I go three innings on a windy day, I got to use my other hand the next morning to wipe myself. Don't print that, Smitty, but it's the truth." Yes, has-beens, might-have-beens, should-have-beens, would-have-beens, never-weres and never-will-bes, Tuminikar and his venerable cohorts managed nonetheless to somehow get the ball the sixty feet and six inches to the plate, which was all the rule book required of them. The ball, to be sure, occasionally arrived on a bounce, or moved so slowly and with so little English on it that the patrons back of home plate would pretend to be reading General Oakhart's signature off the horsehide all the while the pitch was in transit. "What time you say she's due in?" they'd ask, holding up their pocket watches, and on and on, comically, in that vein. There was even one of them, Chico Mecoatl, who on occasion tossed the ball in *underhand*. "How about if he fungoes 'em, Chico, then you won't have to throw at all!" the sadistic hecklers called, heedless of the pain that caused Chico to resort sometimes to a style of pitching that had not been the custom now in baseball since the days of the buffalo and the Indian.

The fans who needled the wretched Mexican were not so plentiful actually as their vociferousness might make it appear. Most people seemed to find it eerie, rather than amusing or irritating, to watch him work in relief. Invariably it was dusk when Chico, the last bald man in the bullpen, would trudge across the darkening field to pitch for the Mundys, already brutally beaten with an inning or two of punishment still to come. By this hour, the hometown fans, filled to the gills on all the slugging they'd seen, would have begun to leave their seats, tugging their collars up against the cool breeze and smiling when they peered for a final time out at the scoreboard to what looked now like the score of a football game. Two, three touchdowns for the home team; a field goal for the visitors, if that . . . So, they would converge upon the exits, a swarm of big two-fisted creatures as drowsy with contentment as the babe whose face has dropped in bloated bliss from the sugary nipple. Ah, victory. Ah, triumph. How it does mellow the bearded sex! What are the consolations of philosophy or the affirmations of religion beside an afternoon's rich meal of doubles, triples, and home runs? . . . But then came Chico out to the mound, and made that little yelp of his as he tossed his single warm-up pitch in the general direction of Hothead's mitt, that little bleat of pain that passed from between his lips whenever he had to raise his arm above his waist to throw the ball. The fans, clustered now in the dark apertures that opened on to the ramps leading down to the city streets, would swing around upon hearing Chico's bleat, one head craning above the other, to try to catch a glimpse of the pitcher with the sorest arm in the game. For there was no one who had a motion quite like Chico's: in order to release the ball with a minimal amount of suffering, he did not so much throw it as push it, with a wiggling sort of straight-arm motion. It looked as though he might be trying to pass his hand through a hoop of flames without getting it burned—and it sounded as though he wasn't quite able to make it. "Eeeep!" he would cry, and there would be the ball, floating softly through the dusk at its own sweet pace, and then the solid retort of the bat, and all the base runners scampering for home.

Probably the fans themselves could not have explained what exactly it was that held them there sometimes five and ten minutes on end watching Chico suffer so. It was not pity—Chico could quit and go back to Mexico if he wanted, and do down there whatever it was Mexicans did. Nor was it affection; he was, after all, a spic, closer even to a nigger than the Frenchman, Astarte. Nor was it amusement, for after three hours of watching the Mundys on what even for them was an off day, you didn't have the strength to laugh anymore. It would seem rather that they were transfixed, perhaps for the first time in their lives, by the strangeness of things, the wondrous strangeness of things, by all that is beyond the pale and just does not seem to belong in this otherwise cozy and familiar world of ours. With the sun all but down and the far corners of the stadium vanishing, that noise he made might have originated in the swaying jungle foliage or in some dark pocket of the moon for the sense of fear and wonder that it awakened in men who only a moment earlier had been anticipating their slippers and their favorite chair, a bottle of beer and the lovely memories they would have forever after of all those runners they'd seen galloping around third that afternoon. "Hear it?" a father whispered to his young son. "Uh-huh," said the little boy, shifting on his little stick legs. "Hear that? It can give you the goose bumps. Chico Mecoatl—you can tell your grandchildren you heard him make that noise. *Hear* it?" "Oh, Poppy, let's go."

So home they went (home, to their homes!), leaving Chico, who hardly ever got anybody out anymore, to fill the bases two times over, and the relentless home team to clear them two times over, before, mercifully, the sun set, the field disappeared, and the disaster being played out now for the sake of no one, was called on account of darkness.

3

# IN THE WILDERNESS

## FINAL STANDINGS 1943

|  | W | L | PCT | GB |
|---|---|---|---|---|
| Tri-City Tycoons . . . . . . . . . . . . . . . . . | 90 | 64 | .584 | |
| Aceldama Butchers . . . . . . . . . . . . . . | 89 | 65 | .578 | 1 |
| Independence Blues . . . . . . . . . . . . . | 88 | 66 | .571 | 2 |
| Terra Incognita Rustlers . . . . . . . . . . . | 82 | 72 | .532 | 8 |
| Tri-City Greenbacks . . . . . . . . . . . . . | 79 | 75 | .513 | 11 |
| Asylum Keepers . . . . . . . . . . . . . . . . | 77 | 77 | .500 | 13 |
| Kakoola Reapers . . . . . . . . . . . . . . . . | 77 | 77 | .500 | 13 |
| Ruppert Mundys . . . . . . . . . . . . . . . | 34 | 120 | .221 | 56 |

# 3

*Containing a description of how it is to have your home away from home instead of having it at home like everybody else. Mister Fairsmith informs the team of the moral and spiritual benefits that can accrue from wretchedness. With predictable cynicism, Big John elucidates the advantages of homelessness. Frenchy forgets where he is. An insinuating incident in which a man dressed like a woman takes the field against the Mundys. A lively digression on the Negro Patriot League, the famous owner of the league, and a brief description of some fans, containing a scene which will surprise many who believe Branch Rickey the first major league owner courageous enough to invite colored players into organized baseball. The Mundys arouse the maternal instinct in three Kakoola spinsters and succumb to their wiles with no fight at all. Big John and Nickname visit the pink-'n-blue-light district, wherein Nickname gets what he is looking for, thus concluding the visit to Kakoola, in which city the Mundys will suffer more than the humiliation of their manliness before the downfall is complete. The Mundys are followed on a swing around the league and the particular manner in which they are intimidated in each of the league cities is described, including the train ride in and out of Port Ruppert, which, though short, may draw tears from some eyes. A victory for the Mundys in Asylum turns into another defeat, containing, for the curious, a somewhat detailed account of baseball as it is played by the mad. In this chapter the fortunate reader who has never felt himself a stranger in his own land, may pick up some idea of what it is like.*

$S$WINGING around the league for the first time in 1943, the Mundys were honored on the day of their arrival in each of the six P. League cities with a parade down the main commercial thoroughfare and a pregame ceremony welcoming them to the ball park. Because of war shortages, the vehicle which picked them up at the train station was, as often as not, borrowed for the hour from the municipal sanitation department. The twenty-five Mundys, having changed into their gray "away" uniforms on the train, and carrying their street clothes in suitcases or paper bags, would climb aboard to be driven from the station down the boulevard to their hotel, while over the loudspeaker fixed to the truck came the voice and guitar of Gene Autry doing his rendition of "Home on the Range." The record had been selected by General Oakhart's secretary, not only because the words to the song seemed to her appropriate to the occasion, but because it was reputed to be President Roosevelt's very own favorite, and would thus strengthen the idea that the fate of the Mundys and of the republic were inextricably bound together. Weary to death of the whole sordid affair, General Oakhart consented, for all that he would have been happier with something time-honored and to the point like "Take Me Out to the Ballgame."

Though it had been hoped that people in the streets would join in singing, most of the pedestrians did not even seem to realize what was going on when a city garbage truck drove past bearing the team that had finished last in the league the previous year. Of course, the tots out shopping with their mothers grew excited at the sound of approaching music, expecting, in their innocence, that they were about to see Santa or the Easter bunny; but excitement quickly faded and in some instances even turned to fear when the truck appeared, jammed full of men, most of them old and bald, waving their baseball caps around in the air, and singing, each in his own fashion—

> Oh, give me a home where the buffalo roam,
> Where the deer and the antelope play,
> Where seldom is heard a discouraging word,
> And the skies are not cloudy all day.

Judging from the racket they made, it couldn't be said that the Mundys were unwilling to give it the old college try, at least at the outset. Obviously a refuse van (as Mister Fairsmith preferred to call it) was not their idea of splendor anymore than it is yours or mine; still, scrubbed clean, more or less, and tricked up with red, white, and blue bunting, it was not really as bad as Hothead could make it sound when he started in, as per usual, being outraged. "Why, it looks to me like they are carting us off to the city dump! It looks to me as if they are about to flush us down the bowl!" cried Hot. "It looks to me like a violation of the worst sort there is of our inalienable human rights such as are guaranteed in the Declaration of Independence to all men *including Ruppert Mundys!*"

Yet, as the Mundys knew better than anyone in the game, there was a war on, and you had to make do with the makeshift for a while. It just did not help to complain. And hopefully, said Jolly Cholly T., hopefully the more they sacrificed, the sooner the war would be over and they would be home—and not home on the range either, but back in New Jersey, where they had been beloved and where they belonged.

Around the league the city officials were of course free to welcome the Mundys with a speech of their own composition; invariably, however, they chose to follow to the letter the text that had been composed for the pregame ceremony by General Oakhart's office, which also supplied the papier-mâché "key to the city" that was awarded at home plate to Mister Fairsmith, in behalf of the local fans. "Welcome Ruppert Mundys," the speech began, "welcome to ———, your home away from home!" Here the word "PAUSE" appeared in the prepared speech, capitalized and tucked between parentheses. Though the officials always correctly inserted the name of their fair city in the blank provided, they repeatedly read into the microphone at home plate the parenthetical direction intended to allow time for the fans to rise to their feet to applaud, if they should be so inclined. Fortunately nobody in the ball park ever seemed to notice this error; either they took the word for an electronic vibration coming over the p.a. system, or they weren't paying that much attention to the dronings of the nameless functionary in a double-breasted suit and pointed black shoes who had been dispatched by the mayor to take his place at the ceremonies. All the fans cared about was the ball game, and seeing the Mundys clobbered by the hometown boys. The Mundys, on the other hand, had become so accustomed to the ritual, that when, midway through the first road trip, a Kakoola city official neglected to make "PAUSE" the twelfth word in his welcoming speech, a contingent of disgruntled Mundys, led by Hot Ptah, accused the city of Kakoola of deliberately treating them as inferiors because they happened to be a homeless team. In point of fact, by actually pausing in his speech rather than just saying "PAUSE," Bridge and Tunnel Commissioner Vincent J. Efghi (brother to Boss Efghi, the mayor), had managed to evoke a ripple of applause from the crowd; nothing thunderous, mind you, but at least a response somewhat more sympathetic than the Mundys had received in those cities where the address was delivered by the local ward heeler, parenthetical instructions and all.

After the game that day, with Hot and his disciples still riled up, Mister Fairsmith decided to hold a meeting in the Mundy locker room, and give the team their first sermon of the season on the subject of suffering; for the first time since they had hit the road, he attempted to instruct them in the Larger Meaning of the experience that had befallen them, and to place their travail within the context of human history and divine intention. He began by reminding them that even as they were playing their baseball games on the road, American boys were bleeding to death in jungles halfway around the globe, and being blown to bits in the vast, uninhabited skies. He told them of the agony of those who had been crushed beneath the boot heel of the enemy, those millions upon millions who had lost not just a home in the world, but all freedom, all dignity, all hope. He told them of the volcanic eruptions that had drowned entire cities in rivers of fire in ancient times, and described to them earthquakes that had opened up beneath the world, delivering everything and everyone there was, like so much mail, into the churning bowels of the earth; then he reminded them of the sufferings of Our Lord. By comparison to such misery as mankind had known since the beginnings of time, what did it matter if the Bridge and Tunnel Commissioner of bridgeless and tunnelless Kakoola had neglected to read even *half* the welcoming speech to the Mundys? Solemn as he could be—and as he daily grew more venerable, that was very solemn indeed —Mister Fairsmith asked what was to become of them in the long hot months ahead, if they could not bear up beneath the tiny burden that they had had to shoulder thus far? What if they should have to partake of such sufferings as was the daily bread of the wretched of the wretched of the earth? "Gentlemen, if it is the Lord's will," he told them, "that you should wander homeless through this league, then I say leave off disputing with the Lord, and instead seize the opportunity He has thrust upon you to be strong, to be steadfast—to be saved."

"Horse *shit!*" snorted Hothead, after Mister Fairsmith had passed from the locker room in meaningful silence.

"Ah, forget it, Gimp," said Big John Baal. "It is only a word they left out of that speech there, you know. I mean it ain't exactly a sawbuck, or even two bits. If it was dough, that would *mean* somethin'. But a word, why it don't mean a thing that I could ever see. A whole speech is just a bunch of words from beginning to end, you know, that didn't fool nobody yet what's got half a brain in his head. Ain't that right, Damur?" he said, tossing his jock in the face of the fourteen-year-old whose guardian and protector he'd become. "A nose by any other name would smell as much sweat, ain't that so, *niño?* You fellers care too much about what folks say. Don't listen is my advice."

"You don't get it, Baal," snarled Hot. "You never do. Sure it starts with only a word. But how it ends is with them doin' whatever they damn well please, and kicking all your dreams down the drain."

"Hot," said John, leering suggestively, "maybe you is dreamin' about the wrong sort of things."

"Is justice the wrong thing? Is gettin' your rights like last licks the wrong thing?"

"Aww," said Big John, "it's only a game, for Christ's sake. I'm tellin' ya: it don't *mean* nothin'."

"To you nothin' means nothin'."

"Worryin' over shit like 'justice' don't, I'll tell you that much. I just do like I want anyway."

"Justice ain't shit!" Hot told him. "What they are doin' to us ain't *fair!*"

"Well, like Ulysses S. tole you boys, that's *good* for you that it ain't fair. That's gonna make champs out of you, if not in this here season, then in the next. Wait'll next year, boys! Haw! Haw!" Here he took a slug out of the liniment bottle that sat at the bottom of his locker. "You want me to tell you boys somethin'? This bein' homeless is just about the best thing that has ever happened to you, if you only had the sense to know it. What do you care that you don't have a home and the hometown fans that go with it? What the hell is hometown fans but a bunch of dodos who all live in the same place and

think that if we win that's good for 'em and if we lose it ain't?
And then we ain't none of us from that there town to begin
with—why, it could just as easy say PORT SHITHOLE across
your uniform as the name of the place you only happen to be
in by accident anyway. Ain't that so? Why, I even used to pretend like that's what it did say, years ago, instead of RUP-
PERT. I'd look down at my shirt and I'd say to myself, 'Hey,
Jawn, ain't you lucky to be playin' for PORT SHITHOLE and
the glory of the SHITHOLE fans. Boy, Jawn, you sure do
want to do your best and try real hard so you can bring honor
to the SHITHOLE name.' You damn fools," he said, "*you*
ain't from Rupe-it! You never was and you never would be,
not if you played there a million years. You are just a bunch of
baseball players whose asses got bought up by one place instead of the other. Come on, use your damn heads, boys—you
were visitors there just like you are visitors here. You are makin'
there be a difference where there ain't."

The Mundys went off to the shower in a silence that bespoke much confusion. First there had been Hothead to tell
them that the word dropped from the welcoming speech was
only the overture to the slights, insults, and humiliations that
were to be visited upon them in the months to come. Then
there was Mister Fairsmith to warn them that slights and insults weren't the half of it—they were shortly to begin to partake of the suffering that was the daily bread not just of the
wretched of the earth, but of the *wretched* of the wretched.
And now Big John informing them that the Rupe-it rootas, for
whom they had all begun to long with a feeling more intense
than any was even willing to admit, had been some sort of mi-
rage or delusion. Of course, that the son of Spit and the grandson of Base should speak with such contempt for their old
hometown hardly came as a surprise to any of his teammates;
having been raised in the sordid netherworld of Nicaraguan
baseball, he no more knew the meaning of "loyalty" than of
"justice" or "pride" or "fair play." Still, on the heels of Hothead's warning and Mister Fairsmith's apocalyptic prophecy, it
was not reassuring to be told that the place to which you
longed to return had never been "yours" to begin with.

"Well," cried Mike Rama, over the noise of the shower, "if
we ain't never been from Rupe-it, then the Reapers ain't from

Kakoola, either. Or the Rustlers from Terra Inc. Or the Blues from Independence. Or nobody from nowhere!"

"Right!" cried Nickname. "They's as worse off as we is!"

"Only then how come," said old Kid Heket, toweling himself down, "how come the Kakoolas is here in Kakoola and we ain't there in Rupe-it, or goin' back there all season long? How come instead of headin' back to Jersey, we are off to Independence and then all around the league to here again, and so on and so forth for a hundred and fifty-four games?"

"But what's the difference, Wayne," said Nickname, who was continually torn between parroting Big John, whose blasphemous nature had a strong hold upon a fourteen-year-old away from home for the first time in his life, and siding as any rookie would with the rest of the players *against* the Mundy renegade—"so what if we ain't goin' back there? It's more fun this way anyway. Stayin' in all them hotels, eatin' hamburgers whenever you want—winkin' at them girls in the lobby! And all them waitresses in them tight white un-ee-forms—wheee!"

"Nickname my lad, soon you will discover that it ain't 'fun' either way," said the old-timer, "it's only less confusin', that's all, wakin' up and knowin' where you are instead of where you ain't."

So, not much happier than when they went off to the shower, they returned to the locker room, there to be confronted by Frenchy, standing fully dressed before his locker, though not in his baggy brown suit and beret. No, the Frenchman was off in never-never land again. Half a dozen times already this season, one or another of the Mundys had come upon Frenchy making faces at himself in the washroom mirror, a grown man in need of a shave doing what little kids do when they want to look like something out of Charlie Chan—jutting his upper teeth out over his lower lip and holding back the flesh at the corner of either eye with an index finger. "Hey!" his teammate would shout, to wake him out of the trance he was in. "Hey, number one son!" and, caught in the traitorous act, Frenchy would run to hide in a toilet stall. What a character! Them foreigners!

But now it was not funny faces he was making in the mirror; no, nothing funny about this at all. There was Frenchy, dressed in the creamy white flannel uniform that none of them had worn all year, the Mundy home uniform, with the faint red chalk stripe and RUPPERT scrawled in scarlet across the chest, the final "t" ending in a flourish nearly as grand as John Hancock's. And what was so sad about it was how splendid he looked. The Mundys were stunned—so accustomed had they become to seeing one another in the drab gray "away" uniforms, they had nearly forgotten how stylish they used to be. No wonder they were beloved by the Rupe-it rootas, even in the worst of times. Just look how they'd looked only the season before!

"Hey, whatcha doin', Frenchman," asked Jolly Cholly, "kel sort of joke is this anyway, chair ol' pal? Ain't today been rough enough? Aw Christ, somebody, what's the French for knock it off?"

"Geem," replied Frenchy, whose English was incomprehensible to his teammates, except occasionally to Chico, who would pass on to Big John, the other Spanish-speaking Mundy, what he believed to be the general drift of Frenchy's zees and zoes—"geem zee wan, ooh zee was zow, zen ah geem zee, ah zee ull!" And he began to beat his skull against the door of his locker.

As best anyone could figure, coming back into the empty locker room from the shower, Frenchy had momentarily forgotten where he was, and begun to dress as though for the second game of a doubleheader back in Ruppert . . . "Crazy Canadian Frog," said Big John, "he still thinks it's on account of him not catchin' that pop-up that they give us the old heave-ho. Hey, Ass-start, don't lose your head over it," chuckled Big John while Cholly and Bud Parusha struggled to keep the shortstop from destroying himself, "look what they done to my daddy. And he didn't go around beatin' his brains out. Hell, he just figured it all out—and then passed it on to me. The wisdom of the ages, Ass-start: it's all shit. You jerk-offs take it too serious."

Here there was a noise at the clubhouse door, the timid peck of a tender knuckle, and then the quivering voice of a little lady inquiring as to whether the Mundys were "decent" . . .

But before narrating what next took place in Kakoola on May 5, 1943—a day that seems in retrospect to stand as the dividing line between the Mundy past and the Mundy future, between the Patriot League as it once had been and the Patriot League as it was to become in the two seasons before its dissolution—it is necessary to point out that Frank Mazuma, the innovative owner of the Reapers, had declared that afternoon "Ladies Day," hoping thus to beef up the skimpy crowd that would otherwise turn out to see the two lowliest P. League teams falling all over each other in their effort to lose. Play, in fact, had been interrupted in the top of the fifth when it was discovered that one of the ladies who had been admitted free of charge was in actuality a man. In a close-fitting dress of flamboyant design, all dolled up in a blond Hollywood wig, and swinging a gaudy handbag and hips, she had given herself away by making a brilliant one-handed stab on a near-miss home run lifted foul into the left-field seats by Big John, who, being perfectly sober, had swung late. At first the crowd got a bang out of the remarkable feat performed by the sexy gal, and stamped and hollered like a crowd at the burlesque show; then, in the next instant, realizing that no woman, no matter how proudly pronged her chest, could ever make a catch like that bare-handed, they began to converge upon the blond bombshell, piercing wolf whistles mixed with obscene threats. When police whistles joined in, the blond rushed down to the edge of the stands and with her dress parachuting up to her pink garters, leaped to the grass. Quickly she disposed of Rudra, the Kakoola left-fielder, with a stiff-arm block that sent him sprawling, and started for second. The Mundys, convinced by now that this was some sort of "half-time" entertainment cooked up by Frank Mazuma, had to join in laughing with the crowd when she sidestepped the charging Kakoola keystone combination (who wound up in one another's arms) and made for the pitcher's mound in those high-heeled, toeless shoes. Big John was still at the plate with his 0 and 2 count when the blond, swinging her purse at the Kakoola pitcher's head, drove him from the hill with his arms around his ears. Then, the purse still in her right hand, and the foul ball she had caught still in her left, she reared back—whew-whew! those garters again!—and threw the Mundy power hitter the biggest damn curve he'd seen in a decade. Christ, did John get a boot out of that! "A big-titted slit in a little-bitty dress, and she just struck me out! Haw! Haw! With stuff like that, just think what the rest of her looks like!" Next the blond broke for the Mundy dugout, throwing the boys big kisses as she headed their way. Oh brother. The visiting players were shrugging and grinning at one another and so hardly took seriously the cops charging after her, shouting, "Mundys, stop her! She ain't no lady! Stop her, boys—she's under arrest for pretending to be what she ain't!" Even when the police yanked their pistols from their holsters and drew a bead on the blond's behind, the Mundys just shook their heads, and, pretending to be stroking their whiskers, hid their titters behind their hands. Then *smack!* The blond had planted a kisseroo on Mister Fairsmith's mouth—and was down through the dugout and gone. They could hear her heels ringing on the concrete runway to the clubhouse. "Stop!" cried the cops, dashing right on after her. Then *bang!* Oh my God. They had opened fire on her fanny.

No one (except maybe Mazuma) knew what next to expect. Would the blond come back on out to take a bow, waving her wig at the crowd? Or would the cops come up out of the clubhouse dragging her "corpse" behind them? And what about her blood, would it be ketchup or real?

But all that happened next was that the game was resumed, an o and 2 count on Johnny Baal and the Mundys down by six . . . and the folks in the stands feverish with speculation. You should have heard the ideas they came up with. Some even began to wonder if maybe a real live homo hadn't got loose on the ball field. "Yep," said the old-timers out in the center-field bleachers, the boys with the green eyeshades who had been predicting the downfall of the game ever since the introduction of the lively ball, "I tole you—you start in foolin' with this here thing, and you start in foolin' with that one, and next thing you know, you got the cupcakes on your hands. You wait, you see—'Ladies Day' is only the beginnin'. They'll be havin' 'Fairy Day' around the league before this thing is over. *Yes*sir, every la-dee-da window-dresser in town will be out here in his girdle, and they'll be givin' away free nail polish to them fellers, so-called, at the door. Oh, it's acomin', don't worry about that. It's all acomin', every last damn thing you can think of that's rotten and dumb, on accounta they just could not leave the damn ball alone like it was!"

Among the sportswriters, speculation took a less pessimistic if no less bizarre turn; but then they were dealing with Frank Mazuma, who could out-bizarre you any day of the week. Those who had gotten a good look at the blond's sidearm delivery, and followed closely the course of that cruel curve, swore that the "lady" on the mound had been none other than Gil Gamesh done up in falsies and a dress—that's right, the big bad boy of yore, hired for the day as a female impersonator by Frank M. But Frank, who wore a black eyepatch (over the right eye one day, over the left the next) so as to look even more like the pirate he was, only clapped himself on the knee and said, "Hell, now why didn't I think of that!" "You mean, Frank, you are asking us to believe that you had nothing to do with those shameful shenanigans out there today?" "Smitty, I only wish I had. Whoever could stage a spectacle like that is just the kind of crowd-pleasing genius I would like to grow up to be. But in all honesty, I have to tell you that I think what happened there in the top of the fifth was something staged by the greatest crowd-pleaser of 'em all: fella name a' God."

Oh, there was little that Frank Mazuma would not say, or worse, do. Only the season before he had gotten the bright idea of turning the Reapers into the first colored team in Organized Baseball—yes, selling off all the white boys and bringing niggers in to replace them! As things stood in those days—days which must now seem as remote as the age of the Pharaohs to those who search in vain for a white face on the diamond when All-Star time comes around—the bigwigs of the national pastime understood that it was in the best interests of the game—and if of the game, the country; and if of the country, mankind itself—for the big leagues to be composed entirely of white men, with an occasional Indian, or Hawaiian, or Jew thrown in for the sake of color. Furthermore, the darkies had teams of their own, hundreds of them barnstorming around the country wherever colored folk were looking for a little Sunday entertainment; they even had their own "major" leagues, the Negro National, the Negro American, and the Negro Patriot League, composed of teams who made their homes in the real major league cities, and who were allowed to play in the big league parks when the white teams were out of town. Oftentimes these colored teams performed for Sunday crowds substantially larger than those that paid to see the white major league team play ball, and that, of course, was what most intrigued Frank Mazuma, and encouraged him to think along the lines of becoming the Abe Lincoln of big league ball.

What fans those colored boys had! Why, they would travel hundreds of miles, make overnight journeys in wagons drawn by mules and nags, to get to the ball park for a Sunday double-header between the Kakoola Boll Weevils and their first division rivals, the Ruppert Rastuses, or the champs playing out of Aceldama, known affectionately as the Shiftless Nine. In patched overalls and no shoes, they'd just come straight on out of the fields Saturday at quitting time, along the dusty country roads and on to the highways, walking all night long so as to reach the bubbling asphalt of the city by high noon of the next day. Batting practice was usually just getting under-way, when they emerged at last into those great coliseums raised by white men and white money and white might. Beneath their feet the cool concrete of the stadium runways was like soothing waters. (Yeah!) And that green pasture was greener than anything they knew, this side of the fields of heaven. (Yeah!) Oh, up, up went the sky-high stadium, up so high that those pennants seemed to be snappin' around God's very throne. (Yeah!) Oh them colorful flags, they might have been the fringes of His Robe! Yes suh, de Big Leagues! (Or, to be precise, a Negro facsimile of same.)

The owner of all eight teams in the Negro P. League was of course known to Americans primarily because of her picture on the flapjack box. With the fortune Aunt Jemima had amassed from the use of her name and her face on the pancake mix, she had managed to buy up one colored team after another in P. League towns, until she had organized the circuit and made it equal in status to the other two Negro "major" leagues. Of course, everywhere she went, she had that big smile full of white teeth shining out of her face, and she waxed her skin so it shone just as it did in her portrait on the box, and she was never without that checkered bandanna that made her look so cheery and sweet—but when it came to a business deal, she was a match for Mazuma himself; her name notwith-standing, she was nobody's aunt.

Aunt Jemima was always up in Kakoola on Sundays to watch her favorites, the Boll Weevils, take on whichever colored club was visiting with them that week; invariably she was accompanied by her brother, the famed valet of radio and motion picture fame, Washington Deesey, who year in and year out tap-danced the National Anthem from atop a bass drum set down on home plate the day the colored World Series opened. Other famous Negroes of the time who were frequent visitors to Aunt Jemima's box were the comedy duo "Teeth 'n Eyes," who were always seeing g-g-g-ghosts in horror movies, and would amuse the crowd at the ball park with their famous blood-curdling howl when a d-d-d-dangerous hitter came to the p-p-p-plate; and Li'l Ruby, the twittering maid of the airwaves, who had won America's heart with her ridiculous crying jags, and who arrived at the ball park riding sidesaddle on her great Dane, a strapping eighteen-year-old lad imported from Copenhagen, said to be something more than a means of transportation for the actress; "Now ain't that a surprise!" the fans would exclaim, when they saw the diamonds roped around her wrists and her ankles, "I thought she was a little bitty thing!" Yet another Boll Weevil fan was the man rumored to be Aunt Jemima's lover, the distinguished tragedian whose portrayal of the loyal old slave who saves his master's drowning child and subsequently dies of pneumonia in the Civil War epic *Look Away, Look Away* had earned him an Academy Award for the best supporting actor, Mr. Mel E. F. Lewis. And then over the years there were the numerous boxing champions who were like sons to Aunt Jemima: those who come immediately to mind are Kid Licorice, Kid Bituminous, Kid Smoke, Kid Crow, Kid Hershey, Kid Midnight, Kid Ink and his twin Kid Quink, Kid Tophat, Kid Coffee, Kid Mud, and of course, *the* champ, Kid Gloves, whose twenty-year reign as middleweight champion of the world ended in 1948 when he disowned fame, fortune, and country to become a worker in an aluminum factory in the Soviet Union. A moody and solitary man, he had always disdained the glitter of Aunt Jemima's box and instead preferred to sit on the bleacher benches in deep center, surrounded by barefoot children who clung to his powerful arms and to whom between innings he sang the songs of the Third International. In 1948, in a speech from the

center of the prizefight ring in Madison Square Garden, he infuriated Americans of all hues by denouncing the country that
had made him a hero, and the following day he left by steamer
for Murmansk.

Only weeks after his departure, news leaked from behind the
Iron Curtain (how, no one knew, given that the curtain was
iron) that the great Gloves had been exiled to Siberia for mur-
dering with one blow—ironically enough, said the gloating
tabloids, a left—a Commie foreman, who, in his impatience
with the new comrade unable to speak the mother tongue, had
called him by the one English word he had picked up from the
American G.I.s in the war. According to "highly authoritative"
reports released some years later by the U.S. State Department, in the Siberian labor camp poor Kid Gloves had been
cruelly teased and tormented by prisoners and guards alike,
until finally, in that far-off land of blizzards and collectives, the
broken-hearted boxer with the ravished utopian dream perished of homesickness, in his final days languishing for the
American prizefight ring as did his forebears in Georgia for
the jungle villages of the Ivory Coast.

Now, in order to scout the colored players he planned to
poach from Aunt Jemima's league, Frank Mazuma purchased
from a pawnshop a frayed clerical collar and a second-hand
black suit, painted himself with burnt cork, and, wearing beneath his derby a woolly gray wig, went out one Sunday in
1942 to see the Boll Weevils take on the Independence Field
Hands in a doubleheader in his own Reaper stadium. Needless
to say, Mazuma had no intention of "buying" these black boys
like so many slaves—he would just dangle the big leagues
before the best of them, and leave it to them to decide whether
they wished to continue to play for peanuts for the colored
version of the big leagues, or to run off to play for peanuts for
the real thing. So as to be privy to the inside dope on the star
colored players, Mazuma took a seat in a box directly behind
Aunt Jemima. Clever operator that she was, she instantly penetrated his disguise, but said nothing, choosing rather to pass
that scandalous information directly to General Oakhart the
next day. Let *him* handle the thief—it wasn't for Aunt Jemima
to admonish a white man with Mazuma's kind of money . . .
"Well," she said, welcoming the clergyman with her biggest,

shiningest smile, "howdydo, Reverend! Ain't we honored though!"

Mazuma bowed and presented her with a card from his tattered billfold. It read:

PARDON ME

I AM A NEGRO DEAF MUTE MINISTER

I SELL THIS CARD FOR A LIVING — MAY GOD

BLESS YOU

. . . But we stray from the story of the Mundys on the road. Suffice it to say that foolish and trivial as the events of that day may appear from the perspective of today, it nonetheless would appear that the death knell for the white man's game —and if for the white man's game, for a white man's country; and if for a white country, for a white world—that death knell's first faint tinkle was heard at the moment that Frank Mazuma, in that preposterous disguise, handed his outlandish business card to the famed "mammy" off the flapjack box at a doubleheader between the Boll Weevils and the Field Hands, with Teeth 'n Eyes, Li'l Ruby, and Washington Deesey looking on . . . Impossible, you may say. More than impossible— *outrageous*, to suggest that a greedy scoundrel like Mazuma in circumstances so ludicrous as these, initiated what was eventually to become the greatest advancement for the colored people to take place in America since the Emancipation Proclamation. But of course you must remember, fans, the turning points in our history are not always so grand as they are cracked up to be in the murals on your post office wall.

We return to that knock on the door of the visitors' clubhouse, where the dazed and troubled Mundys are still gathered, following the 14–3 "Ladies Day" loss to Kakoola, and all that had followed upon it. "Mundys? Ruppert Mundys?" A woman giggled. "Are—are you decent, boys?"

All but Frenchy were unclothed and dripping still from the shower, but Big John replied, "Oh sure, we're decent all right. And what about you, honey? Or is your name 'funny'?"

"That voice! It's Big John!"

"Big John!"

"Big John!"

"My, my," said Big John, his eyes darkening with desire, "there's three of 'em . . . Hey, who all are you girls, whatcha after, or can I take a guess?"

Now the three spoke in unison: "We're the Mundy Mommys!"

"The who?" asked John, laughing.

"The Mundy Mothers!"

"The Mundy Moms!"

"And," asked Big John, "just how old would such a Momma happen to be? Twenty-one or twenty-two?"

They giggled with delight.

"Fifty-four years young, John!"

"Sixty-eight years young, John!"

"Seventy-one years young, John!"

Baal pushed the door open a crack—"If she's fifty-four," he whispered to his mates, "Wayne here is a infant. Thanks, ladies," he called, "but we don't need none."

The other players had by now scrambled into their street clothes, and converging upon the door, peered out from behind the first-baseman at the three elderly ladies, wrinkled little walnuts in identical hats, shoes, and spectacles.

"Howdy," said Jolly Cholly, stepping into the hallway. "Now what can we do for you ladies?"

"It's Jolly Cholly!" the women cried. "Oh, look! It's Hothead! It's Chico! It's Deacon! It's Roland!" And then the three were talking all at once—"Oh you poor Mundys! You poor boys! How you must miss your sisters and your wives! Who sews your buttons? Who darns your socks? Who turns your collars and sees after your heels and your soles? Who takes *care* of you, always away from your home?"

"Oh," said Jolly Cholly, with a kindly smile, "we manage okay, more or less. It ain't so bad missin' a few buttons now and then. There's a war on, you know."

"But who feeds Frenchy his toast and his fries? Who looks after Bud to see he brushes his teeth after games? And Chico, with the sorest arm in the league—and nobody to cut his meat!"

"Oh," said Cholly, "don't you worry about Chico, he just sort of picks it up by the bone you know, with the other hand, and—and, look here, this is nice of you and all, but ain't you ladies from Kakoola anyway? How come you ain't sewin' buttons on for the Reapers over there, and bein' Moms to them?"

"They don't *need* Moms!" they cried, triumphantly.

"Well, we don't neither, ladies," said Jolly Cholly. "We're a big league club, you know, so of course thanks for the offer, very kind of you and all."

And yet within the hour the Mundys were marching through the darkening streets of Kakoola behind their self-appointed "Moms," each of the players obediently calling out the kind of home-baked pie he would like as the grand finale to his home-cooked meal. So what if it didn't accord with their "dignity"—so what if Roland Agni turned up his prima donna nose and refused to join in? Let Agni go back to brood in that lonely hotel! They might be a homeless ball team, but that didn't mean they had to do without their just desserts! Hell, if they were doomed the way Mister Fairsmith said they were, they would be doing without *everything* soon enough.

"Wayne?"

"Apple!"

"Bud?"

"Cherry!"

"Chico?"

"Bananna!"

"Mike?"

"Rhubarb, peach, chocolate cream—"

"Big John?"

"Hair!" and, laughing he ducked down a dark alleyway, dragging Nickname with him.

"Hey, Jawn—what about *my* pie?"

"You miss your momma, do you, Nickname?"

"Well, no."

"Is that why you was cryin' when she started in talkin' about sewin' on buttons?"

"I wasn't cryin', I got some shit in my eye, that's all."

"Come on, boy, you was bawlin' like a babe! She started in talkin' about darnin' socks, and you wuz about knee-deep in tears."

"Well," admitted the second-baseman, "I *am* homesick, a *little*."

"Haw! Haw! Sick for home are you? Miss your mom, do you?"

"Oh Jawn, don't kid with me—I—I—I—miss *everythin'* a little," he said, with a sob.

"Well, *niño*, then that's what we are going to get you— everythin'! Just like it used to be for you, boy, back in the good old days!"

And so they set out across Kakoola, Big John telling his pro-tégé, "In a town like this, Nickname, there ain't nothin' money can't buy. And if they ain't sellin' it here, they are sellin' it in Asylum—and if they ain't sellin' it in Asylum, there is always good old Terra Inc. down at the end of the line. Hell, a ball-player could spend a lifetime roamin' this league, and never lack for entertainment—if, *primo*, you know what I mean by entertainment, and *secondo*, what I mean by a ballplayer! Haw! Haw!" he roared, reaching for Nickname's little handful. "Come on, *muchacho*, I'll get you mothered all right—I'll get you a momma who really plies the trade!"

Oh, did Nickname's heart start in pounding then! A whore-house, he thought, his very first! What Ohio youngster's heart *wouldn't* be pounding!

But when they finally stopped running they were on a street that looked just like the streets where all the nice families lived in the movies he used to see on Saturdays back home. "Hey, John," he whispered, "this is the wrong place. Ain't it? Look at them houses. Look at them white fences and them green lawns."

"Yeah—and look up there at them street signs. This is it, Nickname. You heard of Broadway and 42nd Street. You heard of Hollywood and Vine. Well, this is the world-famous corner of Tigris and Euphrates. This is the world-renowned 'Cradle of Civilization.'"

"What's that?"

"Haw! Haw! Why, first time I ever heard of it, I guess I was only a lad your age too. Down Nicaragey way, from an ol' sailor off the Great Lakes. He was a shortstop for my paw, till he got the d.t.s and we traded him to a Guatemala farmer for a mule. He says, 'I been everywhere, I been to Shanghai, Rangoon, Bangkok, and the rest, I been to Bali and back—but what they got right up there in Kakoola, Wisconsin, U.S.A., ain't like nothin' in the whole wide wicked world for fixin' what ails you.'" Dragging Nickname with him, he started up the walk to 6 Euphrates Drive, which like numbers 2 through 20, was a white house with green shutters and a water sprinkler turning on the well-kept lawn.

John righted a tricycle overturned on the steps and rang the chimes.

"Hey," whispered Nickname, "some *kid* lives here."

"Kee-rect. And his name is you."

A little peephole opened in the door. "Whattayawant?"

"Say 'I'm home, Mom,'" whispered John.

"But I don't *live* here, Jawn!"

"That don't matter. *Say* it. It's like 'Joe sent me,' that's all."

"Awww—"But into the peephole, Nickname said, "Okay—I'm home."

"'*Mom*,'" said Johnny Baal.

"Okay! 'Mom,'" whispered Nickname, and the door swung open just as doors do when the magic words are spoken in fairy tales—and there was a woman looking nothing at all like what Nickname had had in mind. She wore no rouge, smoked no cigarettes, leered no leers. Oh, she was pretty enough, he supposed, and young too—but what the hell was she doing in a blue apron with yellow flowers on it? And holding an infant in her arms!

Instead of winking, or wiggling her hips, she smiled sweetly and said, "Why, my little . . ."

"Nickname," whispered Big John.

"Nicholas?"

"Nick*name*."

"My little Nickname's home!"

"Right on the nose, cutie," said Big John.

"Oh, Nickname," she said, leaning forward to kiss his cheek, "let me just put sister to bed. Oh, you must be so hungry and tired from playing all day with your friends! How you must need your little bath!"

Nickname made a face. "I just had a shower," he said to John. "Down the stadium."

"Well, now you're goin' to get a nice, warm soapy bath."

"Awww, Jawn!"

"Come, darling," said the woman and she turned and started up to the second floor, crooning to the tot in her arms as she mounted the stairs.

"Is she the one we do it to?" whispered Nickname.

"Nope," said Big John, leading the boy over the threshold. "She's the one what does it to you."

"Does *what*? And why's she got to have her baby here, in a place like this?"

"And what's wrong with this place, *niño*? This here is as cozy as you can get."

Sure enough, he could not complain about the accommodations. They were standing in a living room that had two big easy chairs pulled up to the fireplace, a sofa covered in chintz and plump with pillows, and hanging on every wall paintings of bowls of flowers. There was also a playpen in the center of the large round hooked rug. Stepping easily over the bars, Big John sat down among the stuffed animals. "Take your choice," he said, holding an animal in either hand, "the panda or the quack-quack? Well, what are you waitin' for, Nickname? Hop in, *muchacho*."

"Come on, Jawn. I ain't fourteen months—I'm fourteen *years*. I'm a big leaguer!"

"Hey—a rattle! Ketch!"

"But I'm second-baseman for the Ruppert Mundys!"

"And here's a little fire engine, all painted red! Ding-a-ling! Make way, here comes the fire department!"

"Aww, Jawn, you're makin' fun of me, I think."

"Hey, here she comes—now get in here, you!"

Reluctantly Nickname obeyed. He'd rather be in there with John than out on the rug with the woman with the apron and the apron strings.

"Ah, there's my darling little boy!" she chirped. "There's my . . ."

"Nickname," announced Nickname. "Nickname Damur, second-baseman, lady, for the Ruppert Mundys. In case you ain't heard."

"And all ready for his bath too, my little second-baseman!" Lovingly, she extended her two bare arms over the side of the playpen. "Come now, darling. Mommy's going to clean you and oil you, and then she's going to put you in your nice jammies and feed you and read to you and put you to beddy-bye—isn't that going to be fun?"

Nickname cocked his right arm. "Watch it, lady, I wouldn't come no closer with that kind a' talk!"

"*Bastante*, you little bastard," said John, "all she wants to do is take *care* of you. All she wants to do is give you all the comforts of *home*. Ain't this what all you big leaguers is pissin' and moanin' about? Ain't this what all that clubhouse croakin' is about? Now cut the shit, Nickname, this here is costin' me fifteen smackers! You know what I could get for that kind of dough in this town? Three different redhot nigger gals all at the same time!"

"Let's go get 'em then, John—let's get 'em, and split 'em!"

"You kiddin' me, *niño*? I'm talkin' about jungle pussy, boy, what's got fire in her belly! Now you just travel up them stairs, sonny—and do as your momma says. Go on, go on—here's your little quack-quack. Now git!"

So the second-baseman climbed out of the playpen and balefully followed his "mom" up to a bathroom whose wallpaper was a gay design of clowns and trumpets. There he was undressed and bathed, toweled down, powdered, diapered, and encased in a pair of pale-blue Doctor Dentons, with booties to cover his feet. Though he had long dreamed of being naked with a woman, all he felt while she kneeled on the floor beside the tub and cleaned the insides of his ears, was a desire to knock her down and run. And it didn't help any having Big John in the doorway making wisecracks, and reaching out with his toe to lift her dress and admire her behind.

"Now," said the "mom," "for your little hot dog."

"Hey, that there looks like fun!" roared John, as she soaped between Nickname's legs.

"Only it *ain't*," moaned the humiliated big leaguer.

After his bath came dinner of pea soup and applesauce, spoon-fed him by his "mom"—"Awwww, John!" "Eat it, Nickname—it's costin' fifteen smackers!"—and then he was released from his high chair and led up by the hand to his room, where she read to him the story of Little Red Riding Hood

("What a big pair you got too, Momma!" kibitzed Big John from the doorway) and finally she kissed him good night. "Go to sleep now, baby. It's way past your bedtime," she whispered, tucking the blanket in around his shoulders.

"Hey, Johnny!" cried Nickname from his enormous crib, "it's still light out! It ain't even eight! Enough joke is enough!"

Oh, that amused John greatly too. "Hey," he said to the "mom," "better sing him a lullaby, too."

She looked at her watch. "That'll be à la carte."

"Oh yeah? Since when?"

"It's either a lullaby or a story, Mac—not both."

"At fifteen smackers?"

"I don't make the rules around here, bud. I'm only a working girl. For fifteen dollars you get a Caucasian mother, patient and loving, but without the extras."

"Yeah? And since when is singin' a lullaby to a baby 'a extra'?"

"Look, there's a war on, in case you haven't heard. What with servicemen coming through on their way to the front, we're at it round the clock. Overtime, doubletime—you name it, we're workin' it. I can give you 'Rock-a-Bye-Baby' for ninety-eight cents, but that's the cheapest we got."

"Ninety-eight cents for 'Rock-a-Bye-Baby'? You know what I can get for ninety-eight cents down by the lake?"

"That's your business, Mac, I'm only tellin' you what we got here at the C."

"Where's Estelle?" said Big John.

"Down the office, I suppose."

"You wait here, Nickname! We're goin' to find out about this here war-profiteerin'!"

And Big John was down the stairs and gone. Despite the vehemence with which he had spoken to her, the woman seemed quite unperturbed; she extracted a pack of cigarettes from her apron, and offered one to Nickname.

"Smoke?" she said.

"Nope. I just chaw."

"Mind if I do?"

"Nope."

"Okay," she said, "take five, pal," and stepping to the window, lit a cigarette; she expelled the smoke with a long weary sigh.

"Look," said Nickname, "I don't need no lullaby, you know."

"Sure, I know," she said, laughing softly. "That's what they all tell me. The next morning they come down all spiffed up and shaved and Aqua Velvaed, and they say, 'You know, I didn't need the light on all night. I didn't need that glass of water, really. I didn't need to wet the bed, I didn't need to fill my diaper three times over'—but it's me who has to change 'em, see, irregardless of what they *really* needed. It's me who has to be up and down the stairs all night long, holding their hand when they wake up from a bad dream. It's me who has to be the nurse when they get a little tummy ache at 2 A.M. and cry like they're going to die. I don't know—maybe it's the war, but I've never seen such colic in my life. See, I used to work the day shift around here. Put 'em in the stroller, wheel 'em around to the park, give 'em a nap, a bottle, play patty-cake, and that was it, more or less. Oh, sure, they act up in the sand-box and comes four o'clock they start whining out of the blue, but believe me, it's nothing like this all-night-long business. Turn the light on. Turn the light off. Hold my hand. Sit over here. Don't go away. I got a pain in my nose. I got a pain in my finger. And on it goes, and I'm telling you, you begin to say to yourself, 'Honey, there's just got to be a better way to earn a living than this.' Sure, the tips are good and I don't have to bother with Internal Revenue, and I get to meet some pretty important people—but, let's face it, I can work the swing shift in a war plant and not do so bad either. I got kids of my own I'd like to see sometime too. You know something? I got a grandchild. You wouldn't know it to look at me, would you? Here, look here—" from the wallet she carried in her apron pocket, she extracted a small photograph. "Here, ain't he somethin'?"

The picture she handed Nickname was of a little tot dressed exactly as he was, and sitting up in a crib, though one not so large as his own.

"He's real cute," said Nickname, handing the photo back through the bars.

"Sure, he is," she said softly, looking at the photo, "but do I get a chance to enjoy him? It seems like half the naval training station was here just on Sunday alone."

"If you're a grandmother," asked Nickname, "how come— if you don't mind my askin'—how come you look so young?"

"I *used* to think it was because I was lucky. Now I'm starting to wonder. Look, look at these legs." She lifted her dress a ways. "Look at these thighs. I used to think they were some kind of blessing. Here, put your hand out here. Feel this." She placed her buttocks against the bars of the crib. "Feel how nice and firm that is. And look at my face—not a wrinkle anywhere. Not a gray hair on my head. And that isn't from the beauty parlor either. That's natural. I just do not age. Know what Estelle calls me? 'The Eternal Mom.' 'How can you quit, Mary?' she says to me. 'How can you go off and work in a factory, looking the way you do, and with your touch. With your patience. Why, I just won't have it.' Where's my loyalty, she asks me. Oh, I like that. Where's my loyalty to the wonderful people who come here to spit pea soup in my face? And what about the boys going off to war—how can I be so unpatriotic? So I stay, Nickname. Don't ask me why. Cleaning the mess out of the diaper of just about everybody and anybody who has fifteen bucks in his pocket and is out looking for a good time. Oh, there are nights when I've got applesauce running out of my ears, nights when they practically drown me in the tub—and I haven't even talked about the throwin' up. Oh, there's just nothing that's out-and-out disgusting, that they don't do it. Sometimes I say to myself, 'Face it, honey, you are just a mother at heart. Because if you weren't you would have been out of this life long ago.'"

When the trouble began down in the street, Nickname's "mother" motioned him over to the window to take a look. "Well," she said, in her unruffled way, "looks like your buddy is going to get it now."

Nickname crawled over the side of the crib and padded to her side. On the front walk, within the glow of the carriage lamp that had been turned up on the lawn, Big John was talking heatedly to two men in white uniforms who appeared to have stepped from a laundry truck parked at the curb; across the side of the truck it said,

C. OF C. DIAPER SERVICE
KAKOOLA

"Who are those guys?" Nickname asked.

"Oh," said Mary, with her soft laugh, "don't be fooled by the name. Those two don't happen to take any crap."

The three men entered the house. "Hey, Nickname!" Big John called up the stairs. "Come on! Put your jock on, *niño!* We're gettin' out of this clipjoint!"

"Whattaya say now, fella, this ain't a barroom," cautioned one of the diapermen. "It's a comfortable middle-class home in a nice neighborhood where people know how to behave themselves. If they know what's good for 'em, anyway."

"It's a racket, is what it is!" John said to the diaperman. "Fifteen bucks and he don't even got a piece of hamburger meat! You probably cut the pablum with water!"

"You're *supposed* to cut pablum with water, wiseguy. Now just quiet down, how about it? Maybe there are people tryin' to sleep around here, you know?"

Nickname by now had made his way to the head of the stairs. "Hi, Jawn . . . What's up?"

"Let's git, *niño.*"

"How come?" asked Nickname, nervously.

"How come? On accounta what they get around here for '*Alouette*,' that's how come!"

"What's an al-oo-etta?"

"It is a French song, that's all it is, keed—and it'll cost you two dollars and fifty cents! Know what they get for 'Happy Birthday'? Four dollars weekdays and five on Sundays! For 'Happy Birthday to You'!"

"Well," said Nickname, watching the two diapermen closing in on his protector, "it ain't my birthday anyhow—I already had it for this year."

"It ain't the birthday, damn it—it's the principle! You know what you can get for four bucks down by the lake? I hate to tell you. You know what you can get for two-fifty? You don't get no French song—you get Frenched itself! Come on, tweak your mom on the tittie, and let's get out of here!"

Nickname shrugged. "I guess we're goin' now," he said to Mary.

"Suits me. I been up since four. That'll be fifteen."

Nickname looked down the stairway to Big John. "Jawn? It'll be fifteen."

"Yeah, well, you tell her it'll be five, what with it bein' not even nine in the night."

"Sorry, Mac," said Mary. "Fifteen."

Big John said, "Five, slit," and reaching into his pocket for some change, added, "but here's two bits for yourself, for givin' us a glimpse of your can. Haw! Haw!"

One of the diapermen was beneath Big John, pinned to the floor of the playpen—an alphabet block stuffed in his mouth—and the other was preparing to bring the fire truck down on the first baseman's head, when the sirens came screaming into the street. "The cops!" cried the diaperman who could still speak, and he ran for the kitchen door—and there was a Kakoola policeman pointing a pistol.

"Pimp bastard," said the officer, and fired into the air.

Immediately, from the windows of the little white houses, men began to leap out onto the lawns, men in diapers and Doctor Dentons, some still holding bottles and clutching blankets in their hands. Nickname and Big John, charging out through the front door, found themselves on the front lawn beside a man in combat boots and a crew cut, clinging to a teddy bear; apparently he had been in another bedroom of the same house. "The Japs or the cops," he screamed, "which is it?"

"Haw! Haw!"

Now a squad car turned up off the street and came right at them there on the lawn, siren howling and searchlight a blinding white. The man with the teddy bear (a sergeant in the U.S. Marines according to the story in the morning paper about the raid on "the pink-'n-blue district") broke for the backyard. *Zing*, and he fell over into a forsythia bush, his teddy bear still in his arms.

They came out with their hands in the air after that; some were in tears and tried to hide their faces with their upraised arms. "Cry babies," mumbled a cop, and he beat them around the ankles with his nightstick as they stepped up into the police van one by one.

Meanwhile, they had begun to empty the houses of the "mothers." Storybooks in hand, they filed out, women more or less resembling Mary, wearing aprons and cotton dresses, and all, it would seem, very much in possession of themselves. They were lined up in the crossbeams of the squad cars and frisked by a policewoman; standing together in the street, they looked as though they might have been called together to give the neighborhood endorsement for 20 Mule Team Borax, rather than to be charged with a crime of vice.

When the policewoman reached into Mary's apron pocket and withdrew a handful of diaper pins, she exploded—"You and your diapers and your diaper pins and your diaper service! Filth! You live in filth! You're a disgrace to your sex!"

"Lay off," said the cop who was covering the "mothers" with a submachine gun.

"Shit and puke and piss! Just get a whiff of them!"

"Lay off, Sarge," said the armed policeman.

But she couldn't. "You perverts make a person sick, you stink so bad!" And she spat in Mary's face to show her contempt.

The "mothers" stood in the middle of Euphrates Drive listening with expressionless faces to the insults of the policewoman. A few like Mary had to laugh to themselves, however, for nothing the policewoman said could begin to approach the contempt that they felt for their own lives.

Nor did the "mothers" show any emotion when the diapermen, many of them badly beaten and covered with blood, were driven past them with nightsticks, and pushed on their faces into the police van. Only when the body of the dead customer with the teddy bear was carried to the ambulance—diapered down below, and above now too, where they had covered the fatal wound in his head—only then did one of them speak. It was the woman who had fed him that night. "He was just a boy," she said—to which a policeman replied, "Yeah, and so is Hitler."

"I wouldn't doubt it," the "mother" answered, and for her cheekiness was removed from the line and taken by two policemen into the back of a squad car. "What do you want to hear, officers," she asked as they led her away, "the Three Bears or—"

"Shut her up!" shouted the policewoman, and they did.

The van for the "mothers" was over an hour in arriving; it grew cold out in the street, and though the abuse from the policewoman grew more and more vile, the "mothers" never once complained.

*

Now because of the proximity of "the hog factory" to the ball park, playing against the Butchers in the Pork Capital of the World had never been considered a particularly savory experience by Patriot League players, and it was a long-standing joke among them that they would rather be back home cleaning out cesspools for a living than have to call Aceldama their home on a sultry August day. Of course, one full season at Butcher Field and a newcomer was generally as accustomed to the aromas wafting in from the abattoir as to the odors of the hot dogs cooking on the grill back of third. Only the visiting teams kept up their complaining year in and year out, and not so much because of the smell, as the sounds. Visiting rookies would invariably give a start at the noise that came from a pig having his throat slit just the other side of the left-field wall, and when a thousand of the terrified beasts started in screaming at the same time, it was not unheard of for a youngster in pursuit of a fly ball to fall cowering to his knees.

In '43, the Mundys had to come through Aceldama to play not just eleven, but twenty-two games, and from the record they made there that year, it would not appear that playing twice as many times in Butcher Field as each of the other six clubs did much to accustom them to the nearby slaughter-house and processing plant. "Lose to this mess of misfits," the Butcher manager, Round Ron Spam, had warned his team when the Mundys—fresh from their disasters in Kakoola— came to town to open their first four-game series of the year, "and it is worse than a loss. It is a disgrace. And it will cost you fifty bucks apiece. And I don't want just victory either—I want carnage." Subsequently the Bloodthirsty Butchers, as they came to be called that year, went on to defeat the Mundys twenty-two consecutive times, yet another of the records compiled against (or by) the roaming Ruppert team. The headlines of the Aceldama *Terminator* told the story succinctly enough:

MUNDYS MAULED
MUNDYS MALLETTED
MUNDYS MUZZLED
MUNDYS MURDERED
MUNDYS MOCKED
MUNDYS MINED

MUNDYS MOWED DOWN
MUNDYS MESMERIZED
MUNDYS MORGUED
MUNDYS MANGLED
MUNDYS MASHED
MUNDYS MUTILATED
MUNDYS MANHANDLED
MUNDYS MAUSOLEUMED
MUNDYS MACK-TRUCKED
MUNDYS MELTED
MUNDYS MAROONED
MUNDYS MUMMIFIED
MUNDYS MORTIFIED
MUNDYS MASSACRED
MUNDYS MANACLED

—and, after the final game of the season between the two clubs, in which "the meat end," so-called, of the Aceldama batting order hit five consecutive home runs in the bottom of the eighth—

MUNDYS MERCY-KILLED

From Aceldama, which was the third stop on the western swing after Asylum and Kakoola, the Mundys traveled overnight to the oldest Pony Express station in the Wild West and the furthest western outpost in any of the major leagues, Terra Incognita, Wyoming, there to play against the least hospitable crowd they had to put up with anywhere. No wonder Luke Gofannon had collapsed and called it quits in the middle of his first season as a Rustler. After twenty years as the hero of Rupe-it rootas—loving, tender, loyal, impassioned Rupe-it rootas!— how could he take those Terra Inc. fans in their bandannas and their undershirts, staring silently down at him in that open oven of a ball park? To be sure, in Luke's case, their silence had been punctuated with derisive insults and chilling coyote calls from the distant bleachers, but what nearly drove you nuts out there wasn't the noises, no matter how brutish, but that otherworldly quiet, that emptiness, and that *staring*: the miners, the farmers, the ranchers, the cowhands, the drifters, even the Indians packed into their little roped-off corner of the left-field stands, silent and staring. Or maybe the word is *glaring*. As though there was nothing more horrible to behold than these Mundys, a bunch of ballplayers who came from, of all places, *nowhere*.

Then there was this matter of the late, great Gofannon— fans out there hadn't forgotten yet the fast one that had been put over on them back in '32. Oh, you could see it plain as day in the set of the jaw of those Indians: a time would come when they would take their vengeance on these white men who had sold them a lemon for a hundred thousand dollars. As though Hothead, or Bud, or the Deacon had made a single nickel off that deal! As though these poor homeless bastards had any-thing to do with what had happened to the people of Terra Incognita ten long years ago! No, it was not pleasant being a Ruppert Mundy in the far western reaches of America. If the white ball emerging out of the acre of white undershirts in deep center wasn't enough to terrify a batsman who was a stranger to these parts, there were those cold, contemptuous, vengeful eyes looking him over from the seats down both foul lines. How they drew a bead on you with those eyes! Why, you had only to scoop up a handful of dust before stepping into the box, for those eyes to tell you, in no uncertain terms, "That there dirt ain't yours—it's ours. Put it back where you got it, pardner." And if you were a Ruppert Mundy and the year was 1943, you put it back all right, and pronto.

And then the long, long train ride back to the East, "the east-ern swing" as it was called by the four western clubs, and by the Mundys too, though always self-consciously, for they were hardly a western club in anybody's eyes, including their own. But then strictly speaking they weren't an eastern club any-more either, even if on those eastward journeys, when they turned their watches ahead, the rapid sweep of the minute hand around the dial encouraged them to imagine the present over and done with, and the future, the return to Ruppert, upon them.

Independence, Virginia, where tourists surge through cob-bled streets, and taxi drivers wear buckled shoes and powdered wigs, and in the restaurants the prices are listed in shillings and pence; where busloads of schoolkids line up next to the pillory in the town square to have their photo taken being punished, and a town crier appears in the streets at nine every night to shut the place down in accordance with the famous "Blue Laws" after which the baseball team is named. Talk about a place where they make a grown man feel welcome, and you are not talking about Independence, Virginia . . .

And then the worst of it, the coastal journey north from Independence to Tri-City, passing through Port Ruppert on the way . . .

Port Ruppert? Looked more like the Maginot Line. Soldiers everywhere. Two of them, fine-looking young fellows in gleaming boots and wearing pistols, hopped aboard the engine as it slowed in the railroad yard, awaiting clearance to enter the station. Guards in steel helmets and bearing arms stood some fifty feet apart all the way along the tracks, while still other soldiers, in shirt sleeves and blowing on whistles, directed empty flatcars into the roundhouse and back out onto the broad network of tracks. Where were the hobos who used to squat on their haunches cooking a potato at the track's edge, the bums who used to smile their toothless smiles up at the Mundys when they returned from the road? Where were the old signalmen who used to raise their lanterns in salute, and, win or loss, call out, "Welcome home, boys! You done okay!" Where, where were their hundred thousand loyal fans?

"Haven't you heard?" the Mundys chided themselves, "there's a war on."

With a gush from the train (and a sigh from the Mundys), they glided the last hundred yards into the station. "Rupe-it! Station Rupe-it!" the conductor called, and though many disembarked, nobody who played for the team of that name left his seat.

Rupe-it. Oh, how could something so silly as the way they pronounced those two syllables give you the gooseflesh? Two little syllables, Rupe and It, how could they give you the chills?

Hey, listen! They were announcing the arrival of their train in *four* different languages. Listen! English, French, Russian— and *Chinese*! In Rupe-it! And catch them faces? And all them uniforms! Why, you did not think there could *be* so many shades of khaki! Or kinds of hats! Or belts! Or salutes! Or shades of skin, for that matter! Why, there was a bunch of soldier boys wearing *earrings*, for Christ sake! Where the hell are they from—and how come they're on our side, anyway? Damn, who they gonna scare, dressin' up like that! Hey, am I seein' things or is that there big coon talkin' to that other coon in French? Hey, Ass-Start, is them niggers parlayvooin' French? Wee-wee? Hey, Frenchy's cousins is in town, haw haw! Hey— ain't those things Chinks? Yeah? And I thought they was supposed to walk in them little steps! I'll be darned—I never seen so many of 'em at the same time before. Kinda like a dream, ain't it? Hey—lookee there at them beards on *them* boys! Now where you figger those fellers hail from? Eskimos? In this heat? They would be leakin' at the seams, they would be dead. Zanzeebar? Never heard of 'em. And now what do you think them tiny little guys is? Some kind of wop looks like to me, only smaller. And now dang if that ain't some other kind of Chink altogether—over there! Unless it's their Navy! Christ, the Chinee Navy! I didn't even know they had one. And in Rupe-it!

Now the two soldiers who had leaped aboard in the yard came through each car checking the papers of all the service personnel. Because of the crowding the Mundys were huddled together now, three to a seat, in the last car of the train. "You fellas all flat-footed?" the soldier quipped, looking around at the bald pates of the pitching staff. He smiled. "Or are you enemy spies?"

"We are ballplayers, Corporal," said Jolly Cholly. "We are the Ruppert Mundys."

"I'll be darned," the young corporal retorted.

"We are on our way to play four games against the Tycoons up in Tri-City."

"I don't believe it," said the corporal. "The Mundys!"

"Right you are," said Jolly Cholly.

"And you know what I took you for?" said the corporal.

"What's that?"

"All squished up there, looking out the windows with them looks on your faces? I took you for a bunch of war-torn immigrants, just off the boat. I took you for somebody we just saved."

"Nope," said Jolly Cholly, "we ain't off no boat. We're from here. Matter of fact," he added, peering out the window, "probably the only folks in sight that is."

"I'll be darned," said the corporal. "Do you know, when I was just a little boy—"

But no sooner had he begun to reminisce, than the train was moving. "Uh-oh. See ya!" the corporal called, and in a flash he was gone. And so was Rupe-it.

*Ballplayers' ballplayers*—that was the phrase most commonly used to describe the Tycoon teams that in the first four decades of the twentieth century won eighteen pennants, eight World Series, and never once finished out of the first division. "Play," though, is hardly the word to describe what they were about down on the field. Leaving the heroics to others, without ferocity or even exertion, they concentrated on doing only what was required of them to win, neither more nor less: no whooping, no hollering, no guesswork, no gambling, no elation, no despair, nothing extreme or eccentric. Rather, efficiency, intelligence, proportion—four runs for the pitcher who needed the security, two for the pitcher who liked the pressure, one in the ninth for him who rose only to the challenge. You rarely heard of the Tycoons breaking out, as teams will on occasion, with fifteen or twenty hits, or winning by ten or eleven runs; just as rarely did you hear of them committing three errors in a game, or leaving a dozen men stranded on base, or falling, either individually or as a team, into a slump that a day's rest couldn't cure. Though they may not always have been the most gifted or spectacular players in the league considered one at a time, together they performed like nine men hatched from the same perfect egg.

Of course the fans who hated them—and they were legion, particularly out in the West—labeled them "robots," "zombies," and even "snobs" because of their emotionless, machine-like manner. Out-of-town fans would jeer at them, insult and abuse them, do everything they could think of to try to rattle them—and watched with awe and envy the quietly flawless, tactful, economical, virtually invisible way in which the Tycoons displayed their superiority year in and year out.

Afterwards it was not always clear how exactly they had done it. "Where was we when it happened?" was a line made famous by a Rustler who did not even know his team had been soundly beaten until he looked up at the end of the ninth and read the sad news off the scoreboard. "They ain't human," the other players complained, "they ain't all there," but out of their uniforms and in street clothes, the Tycoons turned out to be fellows more or less resembling themselves, if a little better dressed and smoother in conversation. "But they ain't that *good!*" the fans would cry, after the Tycoons had come through to sweep a four-game series—and yet there never did appear to be anybody that was better. "They *steal* them games! They take 'em while nobody's lookin'!" "It's that park of theirs, that's what kills us—that sunfield and all them shadows!" "The way they does it, they can win all they want, and I still ain't got no use for 'em! I wouldn't be a Tycoon fan if you paid me!" But the even-tempered Tycoons couldn't have cared less.

By '43, the Tycoons had lost just about every last member of the '41 and '42 pennant-winning teams to the Army, but to take their place for the duration, the Tri-City owner, Mrs. Angela Trust, had been able to coax out of retirement the world championship Tycoon team that in the '31 World Series against Connie Mack's A's had beaten Lefty Grove, Waite Hoyt, and Rube Walberg on three successive afternoons. To see those wonderful old-timers back in Tycoon uniforms, wearing the numerals each had made famous during the great baseball era that preceded the Depression, did much to assure baseball fans that the great days they dimly remembered really had been, and would be again, once the enemies of democracy were destroyed; the effect upon the visiting Mundys, however, was not so salutary. After having traveled on that train through a Port Ruppert station aswarm with foreigners of every color and stripe, after having been taken for strangers in the city whose name they bore, it was really more than the Mundys could bear, to hear the loudspeaker announce the names of the players against whom they were supposed to compete that afternoon. "Pinch me, I'm dreamin' again," said Kid Heket. "Why not raise up the dead," cried Hothead, "so we can play a series against the Hall of Fame!" "It must be a joke," the pitchers agreed. Only it wasn't. Funny perhaps to others—as so much was that year—but, alas, no joke for the Ruppert team. "For Tri-City, batting first, No. 12, Johnny Leshy, third base. Batting second, No. 11, Lou Polevik, left field. Batting third, No. 1, Tommy Heimdall, right field. Batting fourth, No. 14,

Iron Mike Mazda, first base. Batting fifth, No. 6, Vic Bragi, center field. Batting sixth, No. 2, Babe Rustem, shortstop. Batting seventh, No. 19, Tony Izanagi, second base. Batting eighth and catching for Tri-City, No. 4, Al Rongo . . ."

By the time the announcer had gotten to the Tycoons' starting pitcher, the Mundys would have passed from bewilderment through disbelief to giddiness—all on the long hard road to resignation. "Oh yeah, and who's the pitcher? Who is pitching the series against us—the Four Horsemen, I suppose."

They supposed right. They were to face the four Tycoon starters who had performed in rotation with such regularity and such success for over a decade, that eventually the sportswriter Smitty humorously suggested in "An Open Letter to the United States Congress" that they ought to call the days of the week after Sal Tuisto, Smoky Woden, Phil Thor, and Herman Frigg. By '42, Tuisto owned Tri-City's most popular seafood house, Woden was the baseball coach at the nearby Ivy League college, Thor was a bowling alley impresario, and Frigg a Ford dealer; nonetheless, despite all those years that had elapsed since the four had been big leaguers, against the Mundys in the first series played between the two clubs in Tycoon Park that year, each threw the second no-hitter of his career—four consecutive hitless games, a record of course for four pitchers on the same team . . . But then that was only the beginning of the records broken in that series, which itself broke the record for breaking records.*

One sunny Saturday morning early in August, the Ruppert Mundys boarded a bus belonging to the mental institution

---

*Some all-time records made by the '43 Mundys:
Most games lost in a season—120
Most times defeated in no-hitters in a season—6
Most times defeated in consecutive no-hitters in a season—4
Most triple plays hit into in one game—2
Most triple plays hit into in a season—5
Most errors committed by a team—302
Worst earned-run average for pitching staff—8.06
Most walks by a pitching staff—872
Most wild pitches by staff in an inning—8
Most wild pitches by staff in a game—14

and journeyed from their hotel in downtown Asylum out into
the green Ohio countryside to the world-famous hospital for
the insane, there to play yet another "away" game—a three-
inning exhibition match against a team composed entirely of
patients. The August visit to the hospital by a P. League team
in town for a series against the Keepers was an annual event of
great moment at the institution, and one that was believed to
be of considerable therapeutic value to the inmates, particularly the sports-minded among them. Not only was it their
chance to make contact, if only for an hour or so, with the real
world they had left behind, but it was believed that even so
brief a visit by famous big league ballplayers went a long way
to assuage the awful sense such people have that they are odious and contemptible to the rest of humankind. Of course the
P. League players (who like all ballplayers despised any exhibition games during the course of the regular season) happened
to find playing against the Lunatics, as they called them, a
most odious business indeed; but as the General simply would
not hear of abandoning a practice that brought public attention to the humane and compassionate side of a league that
many still associated with violence and scandal, the tradition
was maintained year after year, much to the delight of the insane, and the disgust of the ballplayers themselves.

The chief psychiatrist at the hospital was a Dr. Traum, a
heavyset gentleman with a dark chin beard, and a pronounced
European accent. Until his arrival in America in the thirties, he
had never even heard of baseball, but in that Asylum was the
site of a major league ball park, as well as a psychiatric hospital,
it was not long before the doctor became something of a student of the game. After all, one whose professional life involved ruminating upon the extremes of human behavior, had
certainly to sit up and take notice when a local fan decided to
make his home atop a flagpole until the Keepers snapped a
losing streak, or when an Asylum man beat his wife to death
with a hammer for calling the Keepers "bums" just like himself. If the doctor did not, strictly speaking, become an ardent
Keeper fan, he did make it his business to read thoroughly in
the literature of the national pastime, with the result that over
the years more than one P. League manager had to compliment the bearded Berliner on his use of the hit-and-run, and

the uncanny ability he displayed at stealing signals during their annual exhibition game.

Despite the managerial skill that Dr. Traum had developed over the years through his studies, his team proved no match for the Mundys that morning. By August of 1943, the Mundys weren't about to sit back and take it on the chin from a German-born baseball manager and a team of madmen; they had been defeated and disgraced and disgraced and defeated up and down the league since the season had begun back in April, and it was as though on the morning they got out to the insane asylum grounds, all the wrath that had been seething in them for months now burst forth, and nothing, but nothing, could have prevented them from grinding the Lunatics into dust once the possibility for victory presented itself. Suddenly, those '43 flops started looking and sounding like the scrappy, hustling, undefeatable Ruppert teams of Luke Gofannon's day—and this despite the fact that it took nearly an hour to complete a single inning, what with numerous delays and interruptions caused by the Lunatics' style of play. Hardly a moment passed that something did not occur to offend the professional dignity of a big leaguer, and yet, through it all, the Mundys on both offense and defense managed to seize hold of every Lunatic mistake and convert it to their advantage. Admittedly, the big right-hander who started for the institution team was fast and savvy enough to hold the Mundy power in check, but playing just the sort of heads-up, razzle-dazzle baseball that used to characterize the Mundy teams of yore, they were able in their first at bat to put together a scratch hit by Astarte, a bunt by Nickname, a base on balls to Big John, and two Lunatic errors, to score three runs—their biggest inning of the year, and the first Mundy runs to cross the plate in sixty consecutive innings, which was not a record only because they had gone sixty-seven innings without scoring earlier in the season.

When Roland Agni, of all people, took a called third strike to end their half of the inning, the Mundys rushed off the bench like a team that smelled World Series loot. "We was due!" yelped Nickname, taking the peg from Hothead and sweeping his glove over the bag—"Nobody gonna stop us now, babe! We was due! We was *over*due!" Then he winged the ball over to where Deacon Demeter stood on the mound, grinning. "Three big ones for you, Deke!" Old Deacon, the fifty-year-old iron-man starter of the Mundy staff, already a twenty-game loser with two months of the season still to go, shot a string of tobacco juice over his left shoulder to ward off evil spirits, stroked the rabbit's foot that hung on a chain around his neck, closed his eyes to mumble something ending with "Amen," and then stepped up on the rubber to face the first patient. Deacon was a preacher back home, as gentle and kindly a man as you would ever want to bring your problems to, but up on the hill he was all competitor, and had been for thirty years now. "When the game begins," he used to say back in his heyday, "charity ends." And so it was that when he saw the first Lunatic batter digging in as though he owned the batter's box, the Deke decided to take Hothead's advice and stick the first pitch in his ear, just to show the little nut who was boss. The Deacon had taken enough insults that year for a fifty-year-old man of the cloth!

Not only did the Deke's pitch cause the batter to go flying back from the plate to save his skin, but next thing everyone knew the lead-off man was running for the big brick building with the iron bars on its windows. Two of his teammates caught him down the right-field line and with the help of the Lunatic bullpen staff managed to drag him back to home plate. But once there they couldn't get him to take hold of the bat; every time they put it into his hands, he let it fall through to the ground. By the time the game was resumed, with a 1 and 0 count on a new lead-off hitter, one not quite so cocky as the fellow who'd stepped up to bat some ten minutes earlier, there was no doubt in anyone's mind that the Deke was in charge. As it turned out, twice in the inning Mike Rama had to go sailing up into the wall to haul in a long line drive, but as the wall was padded, Mike came away unscathed, and the Deacon was back on the bench with his three-run lead intact.

"We're on our way!" cried Nickname. "We are on our God damn way!"

Hothead too was dancing with excitement; cupping his hands to his mouth, he shouted across to the opposition, "Just watch you bastards go to pieces now!"

And so they did. The Deke's pitching and Mike's fielding

seemed to have shaken the confidence of the big Lunatic right-hander whose fastball had reined in the Mundys in the first. To the chagrin of his teammates, he simply would not begin to pitch in the second until the umpire stopped staring at him.

"Oh, come on," said the Lunatic catcher, "he's not staring at *you*. Throw the ball."

"I tell you, he's right behind you and he is too staring. Look you, I see you there behind that mask. What is it you want from me? What is it you think you're looking at, anyway?"

The male nurse, in white half-sleeve shirt and white trousers, who was acting as the plate umpire, called out to the mound, "Play ball now. Enough of that."

"Not until you come out from there."

"Oh, pitch, for Christ sake," said the catcher.

"Not until that person stops staring."

Here Dr. Traum came off the Lunatic bench and started for the field, while down in the Lunatic bullpen a left-hander got up and began to throw. Out on the mound, with his hands clasped behind his back and rocking gently to and fro on his spikes, the doctor conferred with the pitcher. Formal European that he was, he wore, along with his regulation baseball shoes, a dark three-piece business suit, a stiff collar, and a tie.

"What do you think the ol' doc's tellin' that boy?" Bud Parusha asked Jolly Cholly.

"Oh, the usual," the old-timer said. "He's just calmin' him down. He's just askin' if he got any good duck shootin' last season."

It was five full minutes before the conference between the doctor and the pitcher came to an end with the doctor asking the pitcher to hand over the ball. When the pitcher vehemently refused, it was necessary for the doctor to snatch the ball out of his hand; but when he motioned down to the bullpen for the left-hander, the pitcher suddenly reached out and snatched the ball back. Here the doctor turned back to the bullpen and this time motioned for the left-hander *and* a right-hander. Out of the bullpen came two men dressed like the plate umpire in white half-sleeve shirts and white trousers. While they took the long walk to the mound, the doctor made several unsuccessful attempts to talk the pitcher into relinquishing the ball. Finally the two men arrived on the mound and before the pitcher knew what had happened, they had unfurled a straitjacket and wrapped it around him.

"Guess he wanted to stay in," said Jolly Cholly, as the pitcher kicked out at the doctor with his feet.

The hundred Lunatic fans who had gathered to watch the game from the benches back of the foul screen behind home plate, and who looked in their street clothes as sane as any baseball crowd, rose to applaud the pitcher as he left the field, but when he opened his mouth to acknowledge the ovation, the two men assisting him in his departure slipped a gag over his mouth.

Next the shortstop began to act up. In the first inning it was he who had gotten the Lunatics out of trouble with a diving stab of a Bud Parusha liner and a quick underhand toss that had doubled Wayne Heket off third. But now in the top of the second, though he continued to gobble up everything hit to the left of the diamond, as soon as he got his hands on the ball he proceeded to stuff it into his back pocket. Then, assuming a posture of utter nonchalance, he would start whistling between his teeth and scratching himself, as though waiting for the action to *begin*. In that it was already very much underway, the rest of the Lunatic infield would begin screaming at him to take the ball out of his pocket and make the throw to first. "What?" he responded, with an innocent smile. "The ball!" they cried. "Yes, what about it?" "Throw it!" "But I don't have it." "You *do!*" they would scream, converging upon him from all points of the infield, "You do too!" "Hey, leave me alone," the shortstop cried, as they grabbed and pulled at his trousers. "Hey, cut that out—get your hands *out* of there!" And when at last the ball was extracted from where he himself had secreted it, no one could have been more surpised. "Hey, the *ball*. Now who put that there? Well, what's everybody looking at *me* for? Look, this must be some guy's idea of a joke . . . Well, Christ, *I* didn't do it."

Once the Mundys caught on, they were quick to capitalize on this unexpected weakness in the Lunatic defense, pushing two more runs across in the second on two consecutive ground balls to short—both beaten out for hits while the shortstop grappled with the other infielders—a sacrifice by Mike Rama, and a fly to short center that was caught by the fielder who then just stood there holding it in his glove, while Hothead, who was the runner on second, tagged up and hobbled to third, and then, wooden leg and all, broke for home, where he scored with a head-first slide, the only kind he could negotiate. As it turned out, the slide wasn't even necessary, for the center-fielder was standing in the precise spot where he had made the catch—and the ball was still in his glove.

With the bases cleared, Dr. Traum asked for time and walked out to center. He put a hand on the shoulder of the mute and motionless fielder and talked to him in a quiet voice. He talked to him steadily for fifteen minutes, their faces only inches apart. Then he stepped aside, and the center-fielder took the ball from the pocket of his glove and threw a perfect strike to the catcher, on his knees at the plate some two hundred feet away.

"Wow," said Bud Parusha, with ungrudging admiration, "now, that fella has a arm on him."

"Hothead," said Cholly, mildly chiding the catcher, "he woulda had you by a country mile, you know, if only he'd a throwed it."

But Hot, riding high, hollered out, "Woulda don't count, Charles—it's dudda what counts, and I dud it!"

Meanwhile Kid Heket, who before this morning had not been awake for two consecutive innings in over a month, continued to stand with one foot up on the bench, his elbow on his knee and his chin cupped contemplatively in his palm. He had been studying the opposition like this since the game had gotten underway, "You know somethin'," he said, gesturing toward the field, "those fellas ain't thinkin'. No sir, they just ain't usin' their heads."

"We got 'em on the run, Wayne!" cried Nickname. "They don't know *what* hit 'em! Damn, ain't nobody gonna stop us from here on out!"

Deacon was hit hard in the last of the second, but fortunately for the Mundys, in the first two instances the batsman refused to relinquish the bat and move off home plate, and so each was thrown out on what would have been a base hit, right-fielder Parusha to first-baseman Baal; and the last hitter, who drove a tremendous line drive up the alley in left center, ran directly from home to third and was tagged out sitting on the bag with what he took to be a triple, and what would have been one too, had he only run around the bases and gotten to third in the prescribed way.

The quarrel between the Lunatic catcher and the relief pitcher began over what to throw Big John Baal, the lead-off hitter in the top of the third.

"Uh-uh," said the Lunatic pitcher, shaking off the first signal given by his catcher, while in the box, Big John took special pleasure in swishing the bat around menacingly.

"Nope," said the pitcher to the second signal.

His response to the third was an emphatic, "N-O!"

And to the fourth, he said, stamping one foot, "Definitely *not!*"

When he shook off a fifth signal as well, with a caustic, "Are you kidding? Throw him that and it's bye-bye ballgame," the catcher yanked off his mask and cried:

"And I suppose that's what I want, according to you! To lose! To go down in defeat! Oh, sure," the catcher whined, "what I'm doing, you see, is deliberately telling you to throw him the wrong pitch so I can have the wonderful pleasure of being on the losing team again. Oh brother!" His sarcasm spent, he donned his mask, knelt down behind the plate, and tried yet once more.

This time the pitcher had to cross his arms over his chest and look to the heavens for solace. "God give me strength," he sighed.

"In other words," the catcher screamed, "I'm wrong *again*. But then in your eyes I'm *always* wrong. Well, isn't that true? Admit it! Whatever signal I give is *bound* to be wrong. Why? Because *I'm* giving it! I'm daring to give *you* a signal! I'm daring to tell *you* how to pitch! I could kneel here signaling for the rest of my days, and you'd just stand there shaking them off and asking God to give you strength, *because I'm so wrong and so stupid and so hopeless and would rather lose than win!*"

When the relief pitcher, a rather self-possessed fellow from the look of it, though perhaps a touch perverse in his own way, refused to argue, the Lunatic catcher once again assumed his squat behind the plate, and proceeded to offer a seventh signal, an eighth, a ninth, a tenth, each and every one of which the pitcher rejected with a mild, if unmistakably disdainful, remark.

On the sixteenth signal, the pitcher just had to laugh. "Well, that one really takes the cake, doesn't it? That really took brains. Come over here a minute," he said to his infielders. "All right," he called back down to the catcher, "go ahead, show them your new brainstorm." To the four players up on the mound with him, the pitcher whispered, "Catch this," and pointed to the signal that the catcher, in his mortification, was continuing to flash from between his legs.

"Hey," said the Lunatic third-baseman, "that ain't even a finger, is it?"

"No," said the pitcher, "as a matter of fact, it isn't."

"I mean, it ain't got no nail on it, does it?"

"Indeed it has not."

"Why, I'll be darned," said the shortstop, "it's, it's his thingamajig."

"Precisely," said the pitcher.

"But what the hell is that supposed to mean?" asked the first-baseman.

The pitcher had to smile again. "What do you think? Hey, Doc," he called to the Lunatic bench, "I'm afraid my battery-mate has misunderstood what's meant by an exhibition game. He's flashing me the signal to meet him later in the shower, if you know what I mean."

The catcher was in tears now. "He made me do it," he said, covering himself with his big glove, and in his shame, dropping all the way to his knees, "everything else I showed him wasn't *good* enough for him—no, he teases me, he taunts me—"

By now the two "coaches" (as they were euphemistically called), who had removed the starting pitcher from the game, descended upon the catcher. With the aid of a fielder's glove, one of them gingerly lifted the catcher's member and placed it back inside his uniform before the opposing players could see what the signal had been, while the other relieved him of his catching equipment. "He provoked me," the catcher said, "he always provokes me—"

The Lunatic fans were on their feet again, applauding, when their catcher was led away from the plate and up to the big brick building, along the path taken earlier by the starting pitcher. "—He won't let me alone, ever. I don't want to do it. I never wanted to do it. I *wouldn't* do it. But then he starts up teasing me and taunting me—"

The Mundys were able to come up with a final run in the top of the third, once they discovered that the second-string Lunatic catcher, for all that he sounded like the real thing— "Chuck to me, babe, no hitter in here, babe—" was a little leery of fielding a bunt dropped out in front of home plate, fearful apparently of what he would find beneath the ball upon picking it up.

When Deacon started out to the mound to pitch the last of the three innings, there wasn't a Mundy who took the field with him, sleepy old Kid Heket included, who didn't realize that the Deke had a shutout working. If he could set the Lunatics down without a run, he could become the first Mundy pitcher to hurl a scoreless game all year, in or out of league competition. Hoping neither to jinx him or unnerve him, the players went through the infield warm-up deliberately keeping the chatter to a minimum, as though in fact it was just another day they were going down to defeat. Nonetheless, the Deke was already streaming perspiration when the first Lunatic stepped into the box. He rubbed the rabbit's foot, said his prayer, took a swallow of air big enough to fill a gallon jug, and on four straight pitches, walked the center-fielder, who earlier in the game hadn't bothered to return the ball to the infield after catching a fly ball, and now, at the plate, hadn't moved the bat off his shoulder. When he was lifted for a pinch-runner (lifted by the "coaches") the appreciative fans gave him a nice round of applause. "That's lookin' 'em over!" they shouted, as he was carried from the field still in the batting posture, "that's waitin' 'em out! Good eye in there, fella!"

As soon as the pinch-runner took over at first, it became apparent that Dr. Traum had decided to do what he could to save face by spoiling the Deacon's shutout. Five runs down in the last inning and still playing to win, you don't start stealing bases—but that was precisely what this pinch-runner had in mind. And with what daring! First, with an astonishing burst of speed he rushed fifteen feet down the basepath—but then, practically on all fours, he was scrambling back. "No! No!" he cried, as he dove for the bag with his outstretched hand, "I won't! Never mind! Forget it!" But no sooner had he gotten back up on his feet and dusted himself off, than he was running again. "Why not!" he cried, "what the hell!" But having broken fifteen, *twenty*, feet down the basepath, he would come to an abrupt stop, smite himself on his forehead, and charge wildly back to first, crying, "Am I crazy? Am I out of my *mind*?"

In this way did he travel back and forth along the basepath some half-dozen times, before Deacon finally threw the first pitch to the plate. Given all there was to distract him, the pitch was of course a ball, low and in the dirt, but Hothead, having a great day, blocked it beautifully with his wooden leg.

Cholly, managing the club that morning while Mister Fair-smith rested back in Asylum—of the aged Mundy manager's spiritual crisis, more anon—Cholly motioned for Chico to get up and throw a warm-up pitch in the bullpen (one was enough —one was too many, in fact, as far as Chico was concerned) and meanwhile took a stroll out to the hill.

"Startin' to get to you, are they?" asked Cholly.

"It's that goofball on first that's doin' it."

Cholly looked over to where the runner, with time out, was standing up on first engaged in a heated controversy with himself.

"Hell," said Cholly, in his soft and reassuring way, "these boys have been tryin' to rattle us with that there bush league crap all mornin', Deke. I told you fellers comin' out in the bus, you just got to pay no attention to their monkeyshines, because that is their strategy from A to Z. To make you lose your concentration. Otherwise we would be rollin' over them worse than we is. But Deke, you tell me now, if you have had it, if you want for me to bring the Mexican in—"

"With six runs in my hip pocket? And a shutout goin'?"

"Well, I wasn't myself goin' to mention that last that you said."

"Cholly, you and me been in this here game since back in the days they was rubbin' us down with Vaseline and Tabasco sauce. Ain't that right?"

"I know, I know."

"Well," said the Deke, shooting a stream of tobacco juice over his shoulder, "ain't a bunch of screwballs gonna get my goat. Tell Chico to sit down."

Sure enough, the Deacon, old war-horse that he was, got the next two hitters out on long drives to left. "Oh my God!" cried the base runner, each time the Ghost went climbing up the padded wall to snare the ball. "Imagine if I'd broken for second! Imagine what would have happened then! Oh, that'll teach me to take those crazy leads! But then if you don't get a jump on the pitcher, where are you as a pinch-runner? That's the whole idea of a pinch-runner—to break with the pitch, to break *before* the pitch, to score that shutout-breaking run! That's what I'm in here for, that's my entire purpose. The whole thing is on *my* shoulders—so then what am I doing *not* taking a good long lead? But just then, if I'd broken for second, I'd have been doubled off first! For the last out! But then suppose he hadn't made the catch? Suppose he'd dropped it. Then where would I be? Forced out at second! *Out*—and all because I was too cowardly. But then what's the sense of taking an unnecessary risk? What virtue is there in being fool-hardy? None! But then what about playing it too safe?"

On the bench, Jolly Cholly winced when he saw that the batter stepping into the box was the opposing team's shortstop. "Uh-oh," he said, "that's the feller what's cost 'em most of the runs to begin with. I'm afraid he is goin' to be lookin' to right his wrongs—and at the expense of Deacon's shutout. Dang!"

From bearing down so hard, the Deacon's uniform showed vast dark continents of perspiration both front and back. There was no doubt that his strength was all but gone, for he was re-lying now solely on his "junk," that floating stuff that in times gone by used to cause the hitters nearly to break their backs swinging at the air. Twice now those flutter balls of his had damn near been driven out of the institution and Jolly Cholly had all he could do not to cover his eyes with his hand when he saw the Deke release yet another fat pitch in the direction of home plate.

Apparently it was just to the Lunatic shortstop's liking too. He swung from the heels, and with a whoop of joy, was away from the plate and streaking down the basepath. "Run!" he shouted to the fellow on first.

But the pinch-runner was standing up on the bag, scanning the horizon for the ball.

"Two outs!" cried the Lunatic shortstop. "Run, you idiot!"

"But—where is it?" asked the pinch-runner.

The Mundy infielders were looking skywards themselves, wondering where in hell that ball had been hit to.

"Where *is* it!" screamed the pinch-runner, as the shortstop came charging right up to his face. "I'm not running till I know where the *ball* is!"

"I'm coming into first, you," warned the shortstop.

"But you can't overtake another runner! That's against the law! That's *out*!"

"Then *move*!" screamed the shortstop into the fellow's ear.

"Oh, this *is* crazy. This is exactly what I *didn't* want to do!" But what choice did he have? If he stood his ground, and the shortstop kept coming, that would be the ballgame. It would be all over because he who had been put into the game to run, had simply refused to. Oh, what torment that fellow knew as he rounded the bases with the shortstop right on his tail. "I'm running full speed—and I don't even know where the ball is! I'm running like a chicken with his head cut off! I'm running like a madman, which is just what I don't want to do! Or be! I don't know where I'm going, I don't know what I'm doing, I haven't the foggiest idea of what's happening—and I'm running!"

When, finally, he crossed the plate, he was in such a state, that he fell to his hands and knees, and sobbing with relief, began to kiss the ground. "I'm home! Thank God! I'm safe! I made it! I scored! Oh thank God, thank God!"

And now the shortstop was rounding third—he took a quick glance back over his shoulder to see if he could go all the way, and just kept on coming. "Now where's *he* lookin'?" asked Cholly. "What in hell does he see that I can't? Or that Mike don't either?" For out in left, Mike Rama was walking round and round, searching in the grass as though for a dime that might have dropped out of his pocket.

The shortstop was only a few feet from scoring the second run of the inning when Dr. Traum, who all this while had been walking from the Lunatic bench, interposed himself along the foul line between the runner and home plate.

"Doc," screamed the runner, "you're in the way!"

"That's enough now," said Dr. Traum, and he motioned for him to stop in his tracks.

"But I'm only inches from pay dirt! Step aside, Doc—let me score!"

"You just stay vere you are, please."

"*Why?*"

"You know vy. Stay right vere you are now. And giff me the ball."

"What ball?" asked the shortstop.

"You know vat ball."

"Well, I surely don't have any ball. I'm the *hitter*. I'm about *to score*."

"You are not about to score. You are about to giff me the ball. Come now. Enough foolishness. Giff over the ball."

"But, Doc, I haven't got it. I'm on the offense. It's the *de-fense* that has the ball—that's the whole idea of the game. No criticism intended, but if you weren't a foreigner, you'd probably understand that better."

"Haf it your vay," said Dr. Traum, and he waved to the bull-pen for his two coaches.

"But, Doc," said the shortstop, backpedaling now up the third-base line, "*they're* the ones in the field. *They're* the ones with the gloves—why don't you ask them for the ball? Why me? I'm an innocent base runner, who happens to be rounding third on his way home." But here he saw the coaches coming after him and he turned and broke across the diamond for the big brick building on the hill.

It was only a matter of minutes before one of the coaches returned with the ball and carried it out to where the Mundy infield was now gathered on the mound.

The Deacon turned it over in his hand and said, "Yep, that's it, all right. Ain't it, Hot?"

The Mundy catcher nodded. "How in hell did *he* get it?"

"A hopeless kleptomaniac, that's how," answered the coach. "He'd steal the bases if they weren't tied down. Here," he said, handing the Deacon a white hand towel bearing the Mundy laundrymark, and the pencil that Jolly Cholly wore behind his ear when he was acting as their manager. "Found this on him too. Looks like he got it when he stumbled into your bench for that pop-up in the first."

The victory celebration began the moment they boarded the asylum bus and lasted nearly all the way back to the city, with Nickname hollering out his window to every passerby, "We beat 'em! We shut 'em out!" and Big John swigging bourbon from his liniment bottle, and then passing it to his happy teammates.

"I'll tell you what did it," cried Nickname, by far the most exuberant of the victors, "it was Deacon throwin' at that first guy's head! Yessir! Now that's my kind of baseball!" said the fourteen-year-old, smacking his thigh. "First man up, give it to 'em right in the noggin'."

"Right!" said Hothead. "Show 'em you ain't takin' no more of their shit no more! Never again!"

"Well," said Deacon, "that is a matter of psychology, Hot, that was somethin' I had to think over real good beforehand. I mean, you try that on the wrong feller and next thing they is all of them layin' it down and then spikin' the dickens out of you when you cover the bag."

"That's so," said Jolly Cholly. "When me and the Deke come up, that was practically a rule in the rule book—feller throws the beanball, the word goes out, 'Drag the ball and spike the pitcher.' Tell you the truth, I was worried we was goin' to see some of that sort of stuff today. They was a desperate bunch. Could tell that right off by their tactics."

"Well," said the Deke, "that was a chance I had to take. But I'll tell you, I couldn't a done it without you fellers behind me. How about Bud out there, throwin' them two runners out at first base? The right-fielder to the first-baseman, *two times in a row.* Buddy," said the Deacon, "that was an exhibition such as I have not seen in all my years in organized ball."

Big Bud flushed, as was his way, and tried to make it sound easy. "Well, a' course, once I seen those guys wasn't runnin', I figured I didn't have no choice. I *had* to play it to first."

Here Mike Rama said, "Only that wasn't what *they* was fig-urin', Buddy-boy. You got a one-arm outfielder out there, you figure, what the hell, guess I can get on down the base line any old time I feel like it. Guess I can stop off and get me a beer and a sangwich on the way! But old Bud here, guess he showed 'em!"

"You know," said Cholly, philosophically, "I never seen it to fail, the hitters get cocky like them fellers were, and the next thing you know, they're makin' one dumb mistake after another."

"Yep," said Kid Heket, who was still turning the events of the morning over in his head, "no doubt about it, them fellers just was not usin' their heads."

"Well, maybe they wasn't—but *we* was! What about Hot?" said Nickname. "What about a guy with a wooden leg taggin' up from second and scorin' on a fly to center! How's that for heads-up ball?"

"Well," said Wayne, "I am still puzzlin' that one out myself. What got into that boy in center, that he just sort of stood there after the catch, alookin' the way he did? What in hell did he want to wait fifteen minutes for anyway, before throwin' it? That's a awful long time, don't you think?"

They all looked to Cholly to answer this one. "Well, Wayne," he said, "I believe it is that dang cockiness again. Base runner on second's got a wooden leg, kee-rect? So what does Hot here do—he *goes*. And that swellhead out in center, well, he is so darned stunned by it all, that finally by the time he figures out what hit him, we has got ourselves a gift of a run. Now, if I was managin' that club, I'd bench that there prima donna and slap a fine on him to boot."

"But then how do you figure that shortstop, Cholly?" asked the Kid. "Now if that ain't the strangest ballplayin' you ever seen, what is? Stickin' the ball in his back pocket like that. And then when he is at bat, with a man on and his team down by six, and it is their last licks 'n all, catchin' a junk pitch like that inside his shirt. Now I cannot figure that out nohow."

"Dang cockiness again!" cried Nickname, looking to Cholly. "He figures, hell, it's only them Mundys out there, I can do any dang thing I please—well, I guess we taught him a thing or two! Right, Cholly?"

"Well, nope, I don't think so, Nickname. I think what we have got there in that shortstop is one of the most tragic cases I have seen in my whole life long of all-field-no-hit."

"Kleptomaniac's what the coach there called him," said the Deacon.

"Same thing," said Cholly. "Why, we had a fella down in Class D when I was just startin' out, fella name a' Mayet. Nothin' got by that boy. Why, Mayet at short wasn't much different than a big pot of glue out there. Fact that's what they called him for short: Glue. Only trouble is, he threw like a girl, and when it come to hittin', well, my pussycat probably do better, if I had one. Well, the same exact thing here, only worse."

"Okay," said Kid Heket, "I see that, sorta. Only how come he run over to field a pop-up and stoled the pencil right off your ear, Cholly? How come he took our towel away, right in the middle of the gosh darn game?"

"Heck, that ain't so hard to figure out. We been havin' such rotten luck this year, you probably forgot just who we all are, anyway. What boy *wouldn't* want a towel from a big league ball club to hang up and frame on the wall? Why, he wanted that thing so bad that when the game was over, I went up to the doc there and I said, 'Doc, no hard feelin's. You did the best you could and six to zip ain't nothin' to be ashamed of against big leaguers.' And then I *give* him the towel to pass on to that there kleptomaniac boy when he seen him again. So as he didn't feel too bad, bein' the last out. And know what else I told him? I give him some advice. I said, 'Doc, if I had a shortstop like that, I'd bat him ninth and play him at first where he don't *have* to make the throw."

"What'd he say?"

"Oh, he laughed at me. He said, 'Ha ha, Jolly Cholly, you haf a good sense of humor. Who efer heard of a first-baseman batting ninth?' So I said, 'Doc, who ever heard of a fifty-year-old preacher hurlin' a shutout with only three days' rest—but he done it, maybe with the help of interference on the last play, but still he done it.'"

"Them's the breaks of the game anyway!" cried Nickname. "About time the breaks started goin' our way. Did you tell him that, Cholly?"

"I told him that, Nickname. I told him more. I said, 'Doc, there is two kinds of baseball played in this country, and maybe somebody ought to tell you, bein' a foreigner and all—there is by the book, the way you do it, the way the Tycoons do it—and I grant, those fellers win their share of pennants doin' it that way. But then there is by hook and crook, by raw guts and all the heart you got, and that is just the way the Mundys done here today.'"

Here the team began whooping and shouting and singing with joy, though Jolly Cholly had momentarily to turn away, to struggle against the tears that were forming in his eyes. In a husky voice he went on—"And then I told him the name for that. I told him the name for wanderin' your ass off all season long, and takin' all the jokes and all the misery they can heap on your head day after day, and then comin' on out for a exhibition game like this one, where another team would just go through the motions and not give two hoots in hell how they played—and instead, instead givin' it everything you got. I told the doc the name for that, fellers. It's called courage."

Only Roland Agni, who had gone down twice, looking, against Lunatic pitching, appeared to be unmoved by Cholly's tribute to the team. Nickname, in fact, touched Jolly Cholly's arm at the conclusion of his speech, and whispered, "Somebody better say somethin' to Rollie. He ain't takin' strikin' out too good, it don't look."

So Cholly the peacemaker made his way past the boisterous players and down the aisle to where Roland still sat huddled in a rear corner of the bus by himself.

"What's eatin' ya, boy?"

"Nothin'," mumbled Roland.

"Why don'tcha come up front an'—"

"Leave me alone, Tuminikar!"

"Aw, Rollie, come on now," said the sympathetic coach, "even the best of them get caught lookin' once in a while."

"Caught *lookin*?" cried Agni.

"Hey, Rollie," Hothead shouted, "it's okay, slugger—we won anyway!" And grinning, he waved Big John's liniment bottle in the air to prove it.

"Sure, Rollie," Nickname yelled. "With the Deke on the mound, we didn't need but one run anyway! So what's the difference? Everybody's gotta whiff sometimes! It's the law a' averages!"

But Agni was now standing in the aisle, screaming, "You think I got caught *lookin'*?"

Wayne Heket, whose day had been a puzzle from beginning to end, who just could not really take any more confusion on top of going sleepless all these hours, asked, "Well, wasn't ya?"

"You bunch of morons! You bunch of idiots! Why, you are bigger lunatics even than they are! Those fellers are at least locked up!"

Jolly Cholly, signaling his meaning to the other players with a wink, said, "Seems Roland got somethin' in his eye, boys—seems he couldn't see too good today."

"You're the ones that can't see!" Agni screamed. "*They were madmen! They were low as low can be!*"

"Oh, I don't know, Rollie," said Mike Rama, who'd had his share of scurrying around to do that morning, "they wasn't *that* bad."

"They was *worse*! And you all acted like you was takin' on the Cardinals in the seventh game of the Series!"

"How else you supposed to play, youngster?" asked the Deacon, who was beginning to get a little hot under the collar.

"And you! You're the worst of all! Hangin' in there, like a regular hero! Havin' conferences on the mound about how to pitch to a bunch of hopeless maniacs!"

"Look, son," said Jolly Cholly, "just on account you got caught lookin'—"

"*But who got caught lookin'*? How could you get caught lookin' against pitchers *that had absolutely nothin' on the ball!*"

"You mean," said Jolly Cholly, incredulous "you took a *dive*? You mean you throwed it, Roland? *Why?*"

"*Why?* Oh, please, let me off! Let me off this bus!" he screamed, charging down the aisle toward the door. "I can't take bein' one of you no more!"

As they were all, with the exception of the Deacon, somewhat pie-eyed, it required virtually the entire Mundy team to subdue the boy wonder. Fortunately the driver of the bus, who was an employee of the asylum, carried a straitjacket and a gag under the seat with him at all times, and knew how to use it. "It's from bein' around them nuts all mornin'," he told the Mundys. "Sometimes I ain't always myself either, when I get home at night."

"Oh," said the Mundys, shaking their heads at one another, and though at first it was a relief having a professional explanation for Roland's bizarre behavior, they found that with Roland riding along in the rear seat all bound and gagged, they really could not seem to revive the jubilant mood that had followed upon their first shutout win of the year. In fact, by the time they reached Keeper Park for their regularly scheduled afternoon game, one or two of them were even starting to feel more disheartened about that victory than they had about any of those beatings they had been taking all season long.

# 4

## EVERY INCH A MAN

# 4

*A chapter containing as much as has ever been written anywhere on the subject of midgets in baseball. In which all who take pride in the nation's charity will be heartened by an account of the affection bestowed by the American public upon such unusual creatures. Being the full story of the midget pinch-hitter Bob Yamm, his tiny wife, and their nemesis O.K. Ockatur. How the Yamms captured the country's heart. What the news-papers did in behalf of midgets. The radio interview between Judy Yamm and Martita McGaff. A description of O.K. Ockatur, who be-lieved the world owed him something because he was small and mis-shapen. What happened when the midgets collided in the Kakoola dugout. The complete text of Bob Yamm's "Farewell Address." Exception taken to the Yamms by Angela Trust. In which the Mundys arrive in Kakoola to defeat the demoralized Reapers. A Chinese home run by Bud Parusha travels all the way to the White House; a telegram (purport-edly) from Eleanor Roosevelt; wherein a trade is arranged, the one-armed outfielder for the despised dwarf. A conversation between Jolly Cholly Tuminikar and the aging members of the Mundy bench, surprising in its own way. An account of "Welcome Bud Parusha Day," with the difficulties and discourage-ments that may attend those who would exchange one uniform for another. The disastrous conclusion to the foregoing adventures.*

IN SEPTEMBER of that wartime season, with the Keepers and the Reapers battling for sixth, Kakoola owner Frank Mazuma signed on a midget to help his club as a pinch-hitter in the stretch. The midget, named Yamm, was the real thing; he stood forty inches high, weighed sixty-five pounds, and when he came to the plate and assumed the crouch that Mazuma had taught him, he presented the pitcher with a strike zone not much larger than a matchbox. At the press conference called to introduce the midget to the world, the twenty-two year-old Yamm, fresh from the University of Wis-consin, where he'd been the first midget ever in Sigma Chi, praised Mazuma for his courage in defying "the gentleman's agreement" that had previously excluded people of his stature from big league ball. He said he realized that as baseball's first midget he was going to be subjected to a good deal of ridicule; however, he had every hope that in time even those who had started out as his enemies would come to judge him by the only thing that really mattered in this game, his value to the Kakoola Reapers. In the final analysis, Yamm asked rhetorically, what difference was there between a midget such as himself and an ordinary player, provided he contributed to the success of his team?

"The difference? About two and a half feet," said Frank Mazuma, taking the mike from the midget. "And let me tell you something else about little Mr. Yamm here, gentlemen. Every time he comes to bat, I am going to be perched up on top of the grandstand with a high-powered rifle aimed at home plate. And if this little son of a buck so much as raises the bat off his shoulder, I'll plug him! Hear that, Pee Wee?"

Chuckling, the reporters rushed off to the phones (supplied by Mazuma) to get the story to their papers in time for the evening edition.

Sure enough, the first time the midget was announced over the public address system—"Your attention, ladies and gentlemen, pinch-hitting for the Reapers, No. ¼, Bob Yamm"—a man wearing a black eyepatch, an Army camouflage uniform, a steel helmet, and carrying a rifle, was seen to climb out through a trapdoor atop the stadium at Reaper Field and take up a firing position on the roof. Needless to say, he did not find it necessary to pull the trigger; in Yamm's first ten pinch-hitting assignments, not only did he draw ten walks, but he was not even thrown a strike. Even the sinking stuff sailed by the bill of his cap, and of course when the opposing pitchers began to press, invariably they threw the ball into the dirt, bouncing it past the midget, as though he were the batsman in cricket.

In the interest of league harmony, the other P. League owners had been willing to indulge the maverick Mazuma for a game or two, expecting that either the fans would quickly tire of the ridiculous gimmick, or that General Oakhart would make Mazuma see the light; but as it turned out, Kakoolians couldn't have been more delighted to see Yamm drawing balls in the batter's box (and Mazuma taking aim at him from the stadium roof), and General Oakhart was as powerless as ever against Mazuma's contempt for the time-honored ways. When the General telephoned to remind Mazuma of the dignity of the game and the integrity of the league (and vice versa), Mazuma responded by calling a second press conference for the articulate Bob Yamm.

"I have it on very good authority," said Yamm, impeccably dressed in a neat pin-striped business suit and a boy's clip-on necktie, "that the powers-that-be have threatened to pass a law at the next annual winter meeting of the owners of the Patriot Baseball League of America that will bar forever from any team in the league anyone under forty-eight inches in height. This, may I add, even as our country is engaged in a brutal and costly war in behalf of freedom and justice for all. To be sure, such a law, if passed, would only be the outright codification of that very same 'gentleman's agreement' that has operated since the inception of the eight-team Patriot League in 1898 to prevent people of my stature and proportions from competing as professional baseball players.

"It is my understanding that these people now intend to launch a systematic campaign of slander against me, suggesting that I, Bob Yamm, am not entitled to the rights and privileges such as our Constitution guarantees to every American, but rather that I am—and I quote—'a gimmick,' 'a joke,' 'a farce' —and what is more, that my presence on a major league diamond constitutes a 'disgrace' to the game that calls itself our national pastime. Gentlemen of the press, I am sure I speak not only for myself, but for all midgets everywhere, when I say that I will not for a single moment permit these self-styled protectors of the game to deny me my rights as an American and a human being, and that I will oppose this conspiracy against myself and my fellow midgets with every fiber of my being."

Frank Mazuma, whose motto was "Always leave 'em laughin'," immediately quipped, "Every fiber of his being— that's sixty-five pounds worth, fellas!"—and so the reporters departed once again in high spirits; but that Yamm had made a strong claim upon their feelings was more than obvious in the evening's papers. "A midget to be proud of," one writer called him. "A credit to his size," wrote another. "A little guy with a lot on his mind." "Only forty inches high, but every inch a man." One columnist, in as solemn (and complex) a sentence as he had ever written, asked, "Why are our brave boys fighting and dying in far-off lands, if not so that the Bob Yamms of this world can hold high their heads, midgets though they may be?" And the following week a famous illustrator of the era penned a tribute to Yamm on the cover of *Liberty* magazine that was subsequently reprinted by the thousands and came to take its place on the walls of just about every barber shop in America in those war years—the meticulously realistic drawing entitled "The Midgets' Midget," showing Bob in his baseball togs, his famous fraction on his back, waving his little bat toward an immense cornucopia decorated with forty-eight stars; marching out of the cornucopia are an endless stream of what appear to be leprechauns and elves from all walks of life: tiny little doctors with stethoscopes, little nurses, little factory workers in overalls, little tiny professors wearing glasses and carrying little books under their arms, little policemen and firemen, and so on, each a perfect miniature of his or her fully grown counterpart.

All at once—to the astonishment even of Frank Mazuma—the entire nation took not only brave Bob Yamm to its heart, but all American midgets with him, a group previously unknown to the vast majority of their countrymen. Until Bob Yamm's entrance into baseball, how many Americans had even taken a good long look at a midget, let alone heard one speak? How many Americans had ever been in a midget's house? How many Americans had ever taken a meal with a midget, or exchanged ideas with one? What did midgets eat anyway? And how much? Where did they live? Did midgets marry, and if so, whom? Other midgets? Where did they go to *find* other midgets? What did midgets do for entertainment? Religion? Clothes? To all of these questions the ordinary, full-grown man in the street had to confess his ignorance; either he knew nothing whatsoever about the American midget, or what was worse, shared the general misconception that they were people of dubious morality and low intelligence, belonging to no religious order, befriended only by the sleaziest types, and constitutionally unable to rise in life above the station of bellhop, if that.

Following the publication of that cover drawing of Bob Yamm, photo stories began to appear with almost weekly regularity in Sunday papers around the country, reporting on the valuable work that local midgets were doing, particularly in behalf of the war effort: photos of midgets with blowtorches crawling down into sections of airplane fuselage far too small for an ordinary aircraft worker to enter; photos of midgets in munitions plants, their feet sticking up out of heavy artillery pieces—according to the caption, spot-checking the weapons against sabotage prior to shipment to the front. There was even a contingent of midgets, recruited from all around the country, shown in training for a highly secret intelligence mission; for security reasons their faces were blacked out in the photo, but there they sat, in what appeared to be a kindergarten classroom, taking instruction from a full-grown Army colonel.

On the lighter side, there were photos of midgets having fun, the men dressed in tuxedos, the women in floor-length gowns, celebrating New Year's Eve at a party complete with champagne, streamers, noisemakers, false noses, and paper hats. There was a photo story one week in the nation's largest Sunday supplement showing a pair of married midgets at home eating a spaghetti dinner ("Doris does the cooking usually, but spaghetti 'n meatballs is Bill's own specialty. From the looks of that big smile—and even bigger portion!—it sure seems like *somebody* enjoys his own cooking in the Peterson household") and another of a midget standing in the Victory Garden out back of his house, pointing up at the corn. ("'Just growin' like Topsy!' says Tom Tucker, of his prize-winning vegetable patch. Tom, known throughout his neighborhood for his green thumb, modestly chalks his outstanding harvest up to 'dumb luck.'")

What one photo story after another revealed, and what was at first so difficult for their fellow Americans to believe, was that midgets were exactly like ordinary people, only smaller. Indeed, after Mrs. Bob Yamm had appeared on Martita McGaff's daytime radio show, the network received letters from over fifteen thousand women, congratulating them for their courage in having as a guest the utterly charming wife of the controversial little baseball player. Only a very small handful found the program distasteful, and wrote to complain that hearing a midget on the radio had frightened their young children and given them nightmares.

"I only wish all of you out there in radioland," Martita began, "could be here in the studio to *see* my guest today. She is Mrs. Bob Yamm, her husband is the pinch-hitter who has major league pitchers going round in circles, and she herself is cute as a button. Welcome to the show, Mrs. Yamm—and just what is that darling little outfit you're wearing? I've been admiring it since I laid eyes on you. And the little matching shoes and handbag! I've never *seen* anything so darling!"

"Thank you, Martita. Actually the sunsuit is something I designed and made myself."

"You didn't! Well, watch out, Paris—there's a little lady in Kakoola, Wisconsin, who just may run you out of business! *Have* you ever thought of designing clothes specifically for women midgets, Mrs. Yamn? Am I correct—it *is* 'women midgets'; or *does* one say 'midgetesses'? Our announcer and myself were talking that over just before the show, and Don says he believes he *has* heard the term 'midgetesses' used on occasion . . . No?"

"No," said Mrs. Yamm.

"Tell me then, what *do* women midgets do about clothes? I'm sure all our listeners have wondered. Do most of them design and make their own, or are you out of the ordinary in that respect?"

"Yes, I guess you could say I was out of the ordinary in that respect," replied Mrs. Yamm. "But since I'm rather thin for my height, and most children's clothes just swim on me, I took to making my own—I guess as a matter of necessity."

"It *is* the mother of invention, isn't it?"

"Yes," agreed Mrs. Yamm.

"And may I say," said Martita, "for the benefit of our radio audience, you are *marvelously* thin. I'm sure the ladies listening in, some of whom have *my* problem, would like to know your secret. Do you watch your diet?"

"No, I more or less eat whatever I want."

"And continue to remain so wonderfully petite?"

"Yes," said Mrs. Yamm.

"Oh, that we were all so lucky! I just *look* at a dish of ice cream—well, let's not go into *that* sad story! Now—what is it like suddenly being the wife of a famous man? Do you find people staring at you now whenever you two step out?"

"Well, of course, they always stared, you know, even before."

"Well, I wouldn't doubt that. You *are* a darling couple. How did you meet Bob? Is there a funny story that goes with that? Did Bob get down on his knees to ask for your hand—or just how did he pop the question?"

"He just asked me if I'd marry him."

"Not on bended knee, eh? Not the old-fashioned type."

"No."

"And just what do you think it was that made you attractive to a man like Bob Yamm?"

"Well, my size, primarily. My being another midget."

"And a very *lovely* midget, if I may say for the benefit of the radio audience what Mrs. Yamm is too modest to say herself. Just to give our radio audience an idea of *how* lovely I'm going to run the risk of embarrassing our guest—I hope she won't mind—but coming into the studio today, for the first moment I did not even realize that she was real. I had seen photographs of her, of course, and knew she would be my guest today—and yet in that first moment, seeing her in that darling outfit, with matching purse and shoes, sitting straight up in the corner of my office sofa with her legs out in front of her, one demurely crossed over the other, I actually thought she was a doll! I thought, 'My granddaughter Cindy has been here and she's left her new doll. She'll be sick, wondering where it is, such a lovely and expensive one too, with real hair and so on'—and then the doll's mouth opened and said, 'How do you do, I'm Judy Yamm.' Well, you're blushing, but it's true. I was literally and truly in wonderland for a moment. And I wouldn't doubt that Bob Yamm was, when he first laid eyes upon you."

"Thank you."

"Was it love at first sight for you, too? Did you ever expect when you first met him that Bob would be a major league baseball player?"

"No, I didn't."

"What a thrill then for two young people who only a few months ago thought of themselves as just an ordinary American couple. By the way, are there any little Yamms at home?"

"Pardon? Oh, no—just Bob and myself."

"Uh-oh, I'm being told to cut it short, time for only one more question—so at the risk of being as ultracontroversial as your ultracontroversial husband, Bob Yamm, brilliant pinch-hitter for the Kakoola Reapers, I'm going to ask it. Do you think a midget can ever get to be President of the United States? Now you don't have to answer that one."

"I think I won't."

"Well, I'm no political pundit either, but let me say that I've been talking to a midget who could certainly get to be First Lady in my book—and that is the utterly delightful and charming, *and* beautiful Judy Yamm, wife of the famous baseball star, and clothes designer in her own right—and I only hope our granddaughter Cindy isn't waiting outside here, because one look at you, Judy Yamm, and she's going to want to take you home for her own! This is Martita McGaff—have a happy, everyone!"

The enthusiasm that Bob Yamm had generated around the nation took even the audacious Frank Mazuma by surprise, and though the owner continued to delight the fans by making unscheduled appearances on the stadium roof when Yamm came to bat, he let it be known to the press that of course his high-powered rifle was loaded only with blanks; in public, he even stopped referring to Bob as "Squirt" and "Runt," allowing the fans to enjoy the midget however they liked. If they wanted to make a hero out of somebody who was only forty inches high, that was their business—especially as it was good for business. In fact, when a midget a full three inches shorter than Yamm turned up at Mazuma's office one day, claiming to be a right-handed pitcher, Mazuma promptly pulled a catcher's mitt out of his desk drawer and took him down beneath the stands for a tryout. The following day, a new name was added to the Reaper roster: No. ½, O.K. Ockatur.

For a week, Ockatur sat alone in a corner of the Reaper dugout, pounding his little glove and muttering to himself what were taken at the time to be analyses of the weaknesses of the opposing batsmen. Then the Mundys arrived in town direct from a series in Asylum, and the right-hander climbed down off the Reaper bench, and with his curious rolling gait—for he was not so perfectly formed as Yamm, nor so handsome either—made his way out to the mound, where he pitched a four-hit shutout. Using a sidearm delivery, he started low as he could, actually dragging his knuckles in the dust, and then released the ball on a rising trajectory, so that it was still climbing through the strike zone when it passed the batter. "Why, I never seen nothin' like it," said Wayne Heket. "That little boy out there, or whatever he is, was throwin' *up* at us." "The mountain climber," some called the Ockatur pitch; "the skyrocket," "the upsydaisy"—and as for Ockatur's right arm, inevitably it was dubbed "the ack-ack gun," and with characteristic wartime enthusiasm little No. ½ was labeled "Kakoola's Secret Weapon"—until the players around the league got the knack of laying into that odd, ascending pitch, and began to send it out of the ball park, "where," said the writers, who weren't fooled for too long either, "it belonged to begin with."

What caused the disenchantment, when it came, to be so profound was the discovery of Ockatur's fierce hatred of all men taller than himself, including Bob Yamm. At the outset, his refusal to be photographed shaking Yamm's hand on the steps of the Reaper dugout had startled those who had drawn around, in a spirit of good cheer, to observe the historic event. Visibly shaken by the rebuff, Yamm had nonetheless told the reporters present that *he* understood perfectly why Mr. Ockatur had turned away in a huff; in fact, he *admired* him for it! "What O.K. Ockatur has made clear, gentlemen, and in no uncertain terms, is that he has no intention of walking in Bob Yamm's shadow." And, in the face of increasingly blatant provocations, Bob continued to conduct himself as he had earlier with Frank Mazuma, when the Reaper owner would do whatever he could to get a laugh out of Bob's size: he ignored him, and went about his job, which was to draw bases on balls as a pinch-hitter. Only with an adversary like Ockatur, it required a far more heroic effort of restraint, for where Mazuma was a clown who invariably could be counted on to compromise himself by his own exceedingly bad taste, Ockatur was a crazed and indefatigable enemy, who despised him and attacked him with all the ingrained bitterness of a man who is not only a midget by normal standards, but an exceedingly short person even by the standards of the average midget. Though it was not a word Bob himself would ever have used either publicly or privately to describe Ockatur, in the end he had silently to agree with Judy, when she broke down crying one night at dinner, and called Ockatur, who was trying her husband to the breaking point, "nothing but a dirty little dwarf."

If Ockatur came to seem to the Yamms and to the press an insult to the good name of midgets everywhere, to Ockatur, Bob Yamm seemed the last man in the world to bear the title of "the midgets' midget." The sight of Yamm wearing a smaller number than his own made him wild with anger (or envy, as most interpreted it) : why, if Yamm was Number ¼, then *he* should be ⅛, if not ¹⁄₁₆! *He* was the shorter of the two, and with his oversized head and bandy legs, was far more representative of the average little person than this perfectly proportioned, well-spoken, college-educated, smartly dressed, "courageous," "dignified," forty-inch fraternity-boy Adonis, with his spic-and-span Kewpie-doll of a wife! Oh how he hated the kind of midget who went around pretending that he was nothing but a smaller edition of everybody else! who wanted no more than "an even break like everybody else"! As if it were possible for a midget's life to be anything but a trial and a nightmare! As if it were possible sitting in a high chair in a restaurant eating your dinner to feel like "everybody else," while as a matter of fact "everybody else" was either looking the other way in disgust, or openly staring in wonder. And that, only if the management would seat you to begin with. Sorry sir, no room—*no room*, to somebody who weighs only fifty-five pounds and could take his dinner in the phone booth! And what *about* phone booths? What about having to ask the policeman on his beat if he will be kind enough to pick you up so you can dial—is that like "everybody else," Bob Yamm? Is it like "everybody else" to go into a public urinal and stand on tiptoes at the trough, while "everybody else" is pissing over your shoulder? And what about the movie show, where either you sit in the front row, and look straight up at figures that loom over you even worse than in life, or you go all the way to the back, to the last row, and stand there on your seat—if the usher will permit. Ushers—*those* compassionate souls! And what about doorknobs, Bob? What about stairways! Turnstiles! Water coolers! Is there a single object that a midget confronts in this entire world that does not say to him loud and clear, "Get out of here, you, you're the wrong size." An even break like everybody else! Oh, *that's* whose midget Bob Yamm was, all right—*everybody else's!* And that's whose midget he wanted to be, too!

Is it any wonder then that on the afternoon they were to be photographed shaking hands outside the Reaper dugout, Ockatur muttered at Yamm that insult of midget argot ordinarily applied to the so-called normal-sized people? Chin to chin, looking into Yamm's clear, kind blue eyes, Ockatur snarled, "I didn't know they piled shit that high!" then turned and angrily walked—waddled, alas, would be a more accurate description —down into the Reaper clubhouse, leaving Bob to interpret Ockatur's appalling behavior in what he hoped would be the best interest of their mutual cause.

OCKATUR, YAMM IN DUGOUT SLUGFEST;
BRAWLING MIDGETS DRAW SUSPENSION, FINE
FROM MAZUMA; PINCH-HIT STAR ADMITS
GUILT, ADDS: "THIS CLUB NOT BIG ENOUGH
FOR BOTH OF US"; TO QUIT GAME, MAY RUN
FOR CONGRESS AFTER HOLLYWOOD FILMS LIFE

Sept. 14—The much-feared volcano the Reapers have been worrying over privately for two weeks erupted yesterday in the team dugout, when the first two midgets in baseball, pinch-hitter Bob Yamm and pitcher O.K. Ockatur, came to blows. Yamm was just about to leave the Reaper dugout to pinch-hit against Asylum in the eighth [Asylum won the game 5–4, tumbling the Reapers into seventh place. See story p. 43.] when a remark from Ockatur sparked the feud that has been developing between the two since the midget pitcher joined the Reapers in the stretch drive for sixth.

Following the bloody battle, both players were taken by ambulance to Kakoola Memorial for treatment of cuts and bruises.

WOULD SUSPEND POPE

Owner Frank Mazuma promptly slapped a one hundred dollar fine and a ten-day suspension on each player for "conduct unbecoming a

Reaper." Mazurna said: "Of course it's going to hurt the club. If Bob had walked yesterday he would have forced in the tying run and we might well be in sixth right now, where we belong. But there is more to this game than winning."

Mazuma replied with some salty language when asked if he would have meted out such punishment to the players if either had been "someone your own size." "It strikes me," said an angry Mazuma, "as somewhat odd that the guy who has single-handedly lifted the barrier against midgets should now be accused of picking on them because they happen to be small. I don't care if they were giants. Throw a punch in my dugout, and I don't care if you are the Pope himself, out you go on your ——."

[In the Vatican, sources close to the Pontiff said the Holy Father had not yet been informed of Mazuma's remark. Photo story on local Catholic reaction, pro and con, p. 7.]

### BRILLIANT MIDGETS

No one knows yet what exactly passed between the two players as Yamm was moving out of the dugout to pinch-hit against the Keepers with the bases loaded and one out. According to other players, ever since Ockatur came up and began his brilliant winning streak—3–0 to date—he has been needling Yamm, asking him why he doesn't go ahead and swing away. In the fifteen times he came to bat prior to his suspension, Yamm had not swung at a pitched ball. To date there have been only three strikes called against the forty-inch-high pinch-hitter, each coming in a different game.

His fifteen consecutive bases on balls already exceed the old major league record by seven.

### SECOND VOLCANO

The second volcano erupted in Kakoola—and the nation—at exactly 9:07 P.M. Central Daylight Saving Time, when Bob Yamm went on station KALE to read to Reaper fans the letter which he had just sent by special messenger to owner Frank Mazuma. [See back page for photo story on midget messenger and his reactions.]

Yamm appeared at the studio with a bandaged head and hand, accompanied by his wife, Judith. Both were dressed in the style they have made a nationwide fad in only a matter of weeks. Bob wore his famous gray double-breasted pin-striped suit, and Mrs. Yamm a monogrammed yellow sunsuit, with matching yellow purse, shoes, and hair barrette. Mrs. Yamm maintained her composure throughout, but was seen to dab at her face with a yellow handkerchief when her husband read the final paragraph of his prepared statement. [See story "Grown Men Weep" for reaction of studio technicians to Yamm Farewell Speech, p. 9.]

## THE FAREWELL ADDRESS

The following is the complete text of the Yamm speech, as broadcast over KALE:

Good evening. I am Bob Yamm. I have in the past hour sent a letter to Mr. Frank Mazuma, owner of the Kakoola Reapers, which I shall now read to you in its entirety.

Dear Mr. Mazurna: I want to tell you that I am wholly to blame for the violent incident that occurred this afternoon at 3:56 P.M., as I was leaving the dugout to pinch-hit against the Asylum Keepers. In the five hours that have elapsed since, I have remained silent as to my responsibility, and have thus caused a great injustice to be visited upon my teammate O.K. Ockatur.

### NO EXCUSE

I have no more excuse to make for this unconscionable delay than for the incident itself. If I told you that I was too "dazed" at the time to collect my thoughts, I would be reporting only a fraction of the truth. I fear that it was unjustifiable anger, and a cowardly fear of the consequences, that served to seal both my lips and O.K. Ockatur's fate.

### IN ANGUISH SINCE FIVE-THIRTY

I was discharged from the hospital at 5:14 P.M., clinging still to my self-righteous attitude and fully intending to maintain my silence. I will tell you now that my conscience has not given me a moment's peace since 5:30 when I returned home, and, in anguish, heard the news bulletin announcing your decision to punish O.K. Ockatur and myself equally. That I allowed three hours and two minutes more to intervene between your press conference and my decision to come on the air (reached at 8:32 C.D.S.T.), is, I fear, yet another black mark against my integrity.

### KEEPS PITCHERS HONEST

Mr. Mazuma, it will not do any longer to intimate—if only by my silence—that even if I am responsible for this ugly affair, I should be excused from blame because of the burdens I have borne since entering the big leagues. I do not wish to minimize the difficulties and hardships that must befall any man who is a pioneer in his field. I mean rather to suggest that the pressures—and the prejudices—that I have had to withstand as the first midget in baseball, have been as nothing beside those under which my teammate and fellow midget, O.K. Ockatur, has had to labor.

That there might one day be a midget pinch-hitting in the big leagues had long ago occurred to baseball men, if only as a "funny" idea, a curiosity to draw fans to the ball park. Moreover, on the basis of the thousands of letters I have received from midgets around the country since joining the Reapers, I think I can safely say that this dream of a midget pinch-hitter, who one day would stand at home plate testing the control of the best pitchers in the game, has been a secret ambition of American midgets from time immemorial. I have even received letters from nonmidgets, from full-grown baseball fans, who write to wish me well, and to say that the presence of a midget in the batter's box may well be what is necessary to prevent big league pitching from deteriorating any further—to keep the pitchers, as they like to put it, "honest." And many of these correspondents are fans who admit to having scoffed at the idea just a short month ago.

Unfortunately, they continue to scoff at the idea of a midget on the mound. Victorious though he has been in three consecutive outings, in many ways the spark plug of the Reaper drive on sixth, O.K. Ockatur continues to remain to many something less than a major league pitcher. Sad to say, in their estimations he is still "a freak."

### OUTSTANDING FREAKS

Yes, "freak" is the word that some Americans will use to describe a man whose style of pitching is his own and no one else's, a man who is unusual, unorthodox—in a word, an individualist. Well, if to be one's own man, if to pursue excellence and accomplishment with all that is unique to your being is what is meant by "a freak," then I guess O.K. Ockatur is a freak, all right. And so too, I submit, were the Founding Fathers of this country, so too were the great Greek philosophers, so too were the lonely geniuses who invented the wheel, the steam engine, the cotton gin, and the airplane. And so too is every hero in history who has lived and died by his own lights.

But perhaps what makes O.K. Ockatur "a freak" isn't his unyielding individualism, but the determination he has displayed in the face of every conceivable obstruction, his courage in the face of the most heartbreaking adversity. Yes, perhaps it is his bravery that makes him "a freak"—perhaps it is that to which the fans are paying tribute, when they lean over the dugout roof and cry, "Hey it *is* a midget—I thought it was a monkey!" or when they write letters to him, un-signed of course, in which they tell him to go back to the sideshow. Well, that must be some sideshow, including as it does such freaks as George Washington, Abraham Lincoln, Socrates, the Wright Brothers, and Thomas Alva Edison—in short, every man who has ever dared to pit himself against the ingrained habits and customs of his time, who has dared to brave the jeers of the rabble, the envy of the cowardly, the smugness of the complacent, the sarcasm of the know-it-alls, and the unremitting opposition of the vested interests.

### FAILS ALL BUT DOG

Mr. Mazuma, knowing as I did the extent of the abuse and ridicule that have been O.K. Ockatur's daily fare since arriving in the big leagues, knowing too how even the most proud and independent of men may come to be poisoned by such venom, it was surely incumbent upon me to be understanding, if not forgiving, of his stronger moods. Surely it was not too much to ask that I overlook conduct that might vex an ordinary person, and grant remission where another might condemn. But I failed him, at the very moment that he most needed a friendly smile, a kind remark, a brotherly gesture of solidarity. I failed him, and failed as well: my wife; my teammates; you, Mr. Mazuma; the Patriot League; General Oakhart; Judge Landis; organized baseball; midgets throughout the country, many of them in important war work; those everywhere who have supported the midget in his drive for equal opportunities; and, last but not least, our soldiers across the Atlantic and the Pacific, hundreds of whom have written asking for autographed photos of me at the plate. I don't think it is an exaggeration to say that I failed everyone everywhere, regardless of faith, creed, color, or size, who has clung to the vision of a better world, even as this bloody war rages on. And, of course, most unforgivable of all, I have failed myself.

Though it may seem insensitive of me to be momentarily lighthearted, may I add that just about the only one I seem *not* to have failed is my chihuahua pup, Pinch-hit, who has sat in my lap all the while I have been composing this letter, blissfully ignorant of the fact that his master is not the same man today that he was yesterday, and that he will never be again.

### BOWS OUT

Mr. Mazuma, I fear that my usefulness to the Reapers has come to an end. Much as I continue to respect O.K. Ockatur as an athlete and a man, I cannot expect that, following today's atrocious episode, we two will ever be able to resolve our difficulties amicably. And surely the last thing our team needs, in the midst of a battle for sixth, is a smoldering battle simultaneously taking place on the bench, between an occasional pinch-hitter and a starting pitcher who has not yet lost a game in the majors.

Nor do I think it would be in the interests of O.K. Ockatur himself, if I were to remain with the Reapers as his teammate. Mr. Mazuma, if any of what I have said here will cause you to rescind, or even miti-gate, the punishment you have leveled upon O.K., perhaps that may repair to some degree the damage that I have done his reputation. But I do not really believe there is any way to meet his justifiable sense of grievance, or fully to restore his manly dignity, short of my departure from the club.

### GREAT WIFE

Because of "the gentleman's agreement" that as we all know con-tinues to exist among the other clubs, leaving the Reapers is of course tantamount for me to retirement from big league baseball. I only re-gret that I, who entered the drama of this great game so auspiciously, find myself exiting in disgrace. To be absolutely frank, for almost a week now, I have felt an increasing strain, and had begun to worry for my self-control. So too did my wife Judy, who I want to say now, has been a tower of strength right from the day I signed my Kakoola con-tract. Even though she dreaded the changes my new career would bring to our settled and comfortable domestic life, she knew that I would never be able to count myself a man if I refused to accept the challenge to break down the big league barrier against midgets. However, as each day she saw more and more evidence of my mental and moral faltering, she could not help but become alarmed, and only yesterday, fearful of just such an incident as erupted this afternoon, begged me to remain at home and take a rest.

Unfortunately, I did not heed her wifely wisdom, and told her that I owed it to the club to continue to play, regardless of my own inner turmoil. Had I the humility to have heeded Judy's advice, a good deal of suffering would have been spared us all. But I would be less than honest if I suggested that it was ever within my power to relinquish a single second of the experience of being a big leaguer. Mr. Mazuma, the time has come for Bob Yamm to bow out of the great game of baseball, but I want you to know, sir, that for these three weeks that I have worn the Kakoola uniform, I have been, not merely the happiest midget, but the happiest man on the face of the earth.

Sincerely,
Robert Yamm

### ALL MEN MIDGETS

Yamm concluded his radio address with an appeal for "human soli-darity and brotherhood under God, Our Maker." "I say 'Our' Maker," he continued, "though as we all know there are those in this country who would still have us believe that He who made the full-grown did not make the midget also. Well, let me assure these skeptics, that ever since my own Hour of Crisis began in the Reaper dugout at 3:56 P.M.

Central Daylight Saving Time, I have heard His Voice, and it is not runty or pint-sized; let me assure the skeptics that He Who exhorts, chastens, and comforts me is not less a God, nor is He any other God, than He Who made and judges the fully grown. On high, there is but one God Who made us all, and to Him, *all* men are midgets."

## OVERWHELMING REACTION

Reactions to Yamm's forty-two-minute address began coming in from around the nation almost immediately—sports authorities cannot remember another athlete who off the playing field has so captivated the country. Reaper owner Mazuma called Yamm's speech "certainly one of the top ten farewell addresses I've ever heard and just possibly the greatest in history." Mazuma declined to comment further at this time, except to say, "Whether it will be Bob's swan song remains to be seen. The fans are yet to be heard from." [See story on fan mail, "Christmas in September at Kakoola P.O.," p. 26.]

Meanwhile a movement has gotten underway overnight to send Bob Yamm to Congress in the next elections. Republican and Democratic spokesmen declined to comment until Yamm makes known his party affiliation, but interest was more than apparent in the headquarters of both parties here. The sentiment seems to be that perhaps the time is ripe to send a midget to Washington.

"The tragedy of it," said one highly placed political observer, who preferred to remain unidentified, "is that the midgets themselves have always lived scattered about, singly and in pairs around the country, and frankly haven't shown much political savvy. I'm sure they've had other things to worry about, but banded together there's no doubt they would have had one of their own kind in the House long ago. Whether full-grown citizens will elect a midget to represent them in Congress remains to be seen. Up until tonight I would have had to say no. With Yamm's speech, it's a new ballgame. He just could go all the way."

From Hollywood comes word that three major film companies are already bidding for the movie rights to the Bob Yamm story. Talk in the film capital has it that Bob and Judy Yamm will agree to play themselves for one million dollars, with Bob writing the screenplay, to be called "All Men Are Midgets." Part of the proceeds from the projected film are already earmarked to charitable organizations that aid needy and aged midgets.

## ANGELA TRUST OUTSPOKEN

Strong criticism of Bob Yamm's speech came from Mrs. Angela Whittling Trust, owner of the Tri-City Tycoons, currently in first place

in the Patriot League. Mrs. Trust is the outspoken widow of Spenser
Trust, who forged Tri-City dynasties in baseball and banking. Of
those owners opposed to midgets in the majors, Mrs. Trust has been
the most unyielding and vociferous. Newsmen were called to her
underground apartment in Tycoon Park at 11:00 P.M., where Mrs.
Trust, 72, read the following statement from her wheelchair. Her hip
was broken July 4, when she failed in her attempt to field a foul ball
lined at her box.

### NIX ON SIAMESE

"I never heard such rubbish in my life," Mrs. Trust's statement began. "Just who does he think he is? This Mr. Bob Yamm has delusions
of grandeur that would be offensive in a Tri-City Tycoon, but are utterly bizarre in a player who has pinch-hit a dozen times for a team
battling to stay out of seventh, and is a midget besides, with no more
business in the major leagues than a sword-swallower or Siamese
twins. Yes, you can tell Frank Mazuma that Angela Trust is against
Siamese twins too, in case he was planning to bring a pair of them up
as a switch-hitter. I know, I am a terrible old New England biddy with
a closed mind and the rest of that poppycock, but if Mr. Mazuma's
Reapers come to Tri-City, Mass., with a shortstop and a second-
baseman who are joined back to back, he will find the door to the visitors' clubhouse locked. I will forfeit the game, I would forfeit the
pennant, rather than subject my team to any more of his shenanigans.

### CALLS YAMM SWISS

"Unfortunately," the Angela Trust statement continued, "what we
are witnessing in this country is what I would describe as an outburst
of war hysteria. Suddenly anything goes. People are desperate for diversion. Reading the battlefront news I cannot say that I blame them.
American women are in tears and cannot sleep. Families are separated, husbands and fathers and sons are gone. The strongest ten million men in America are not with us. We are trying to accustom
ourselves to their absence. What could be harder? No wonder the nation appears to be losing its sense of proportion. Who would have believed just one month ago that two ill-tempered midgets dressed up
in children's uniforms, with absurd fractions on their backs, would
fall to brawling in a major league baseball dugout—and then, *and
then*, that one of them would go on the radio for a special broadcast,
to bow out of baseball as though he were the King of England abdi-
cating the throne. Yes, a country at war hungers for distractions of a
strange sort, but I ask you, my fellow Americans: *how much of this
strangeness are we built for?* We must maintain standards! We must return to our senses! We must not account a man 'great' who is nothing

more than a presumptuous self-seeking midget with an elephantine sense of his own importance, cashing in during a time of national catastrophe. Truly, I have never in my life heard such cornstarch as he uttered tonight. Why, from the sound of it, you would think Mr. Yamm's conscience was as delicately made as a five hundred dollar Swiss watch. You would think that nobody had a conscience in the world before he appeared at the microphone, with his perfect little wheels whirring away underneath that pretentious little pin-striped suit!

### SORRY FOR MIDGETS

"Of course I'm delighted he's out of baseball," Mrs. Trust continued. "Good riddance. And his wife with him. Frankly, no baseball wife has ever given me a bigger pain in the neck than this one with her matching shoes and handbags. 'Tower of strength'? Little fashion plate is all she is. Little clotheshorse. A Shetland pony in a child's sunsuit. In this business, the towers of strength are the men on the field. That's why they are there. That's what people pay good money to see. It just will not do to start calling things what they are not. We do not need any more applesauce than there already is in the world. A midget is a midget. I am sorry for them that that has to be the case. I would not wish to be one myself. It must be ghastly. If it were up to me, there wouldn't be any midgets in the world at all. But for some reason that is beyond my understanding, there are, and there is no sense pretending otherwise. As I said, luckily I happen not to be one, but if I were, I assure you I would know my place and have pride enough to make the best of it. And without whining, or what is even worse, going to the opposite extreme and pretending I was some special kind of saint because of it. *That* is what a tower of strength would do, in my judgment.

### WON'T SEE HUBBY BELITTLED

"Finally, I will not sit silently by while this sanctimonious, self-inflated, self-admiring, holier-than-thou, stuck-on-himself windbag of a midget announces to the entire country that in his opinion *and* God's, all men are midgets. I have never heard anything so idiotic and insulting in my life. All men are *not* midgets. My husband, Mr. Spenser Trust, who built Trust Savings and Loan, Trust Guaranty Trust, Trust Mutual of Tri-City, as well as the Tri-City Tycoons and Tycoon Park, all before he died at the age of sixty-three, was not a midget in any sense of the word. Nor was my father a midget. He began life as a lumberjack at the age of twelve and by the time he was thirty-five was the greatest timber baron in North America. If the rest of the women in America want to sit idly by while someone calls their

men a bunch of midgets, that is their affair. Maybe they know something I don't. But nobody belittles my father or my husband and gets
away with it."

The day after Bob Yamm's dramatic broadcast stunned Kakoola
and the nation, the Mundys arrived in town. So rattled were
the Reapers by the unlikely events of the preceding afternoon
and evening, that the Mundys piled up more runs in nine
innings than they ordinarily scored in a week, edging Kakoola
6–5 in the ninth. Roland Agni hit two home runs, bringing his
season total to thirty-three (most by a Mundy in a single season since Gofannon), and with one on and two out in the last
inning, Bud Parusha set a record of his own, lofting the first
and only home run he or any other one-armed man would
ever hit in the majors. Of course there was a stiff late afternoon
breeze blowing in off the lake and out the left-field line, and
the Kakoola left-fielder also helped to turn into a four-bagger
what should have been an easy out by tipping the high pop-up
off his mitt and into the stands—and then too the pitch
Parusha swung at was described later by the disgusted Kakoola
catcher, Ducky Rig, as "a Lady Godiva ball," meaning it had
absolutely nothing on it at all; yet none of this did anything to
diminish the joy in Bud's heart. Obviously under the sway of
Bob Yamm's radio address of the previous night, Bud told reporters that *he* was the happiest man on the face of the earth,
and then beaming with pride, showed them the telegram that
had arrived in the visitors' clubhouse from Washington, D.C.,
signed "Eleanor Roosevelt," and inviting him to be co-
chairman along with her husband of the upcoming drive for
the March of Dimes.

The Kakoola fans, no less distracted than their players,
seemed for the moment not even to care about the loss that
pushed their team yet another full game behind the Keepers. It
was not to watch the seventh place Reapers take on the eighth
place Mundys that a record-breaking forty-two thousand had
assembled in Reaper Field on a weekday afternoon—rather,
they had come, some from as far as two hundred miles upstate,
to see justice done.

For nine full innings of play, whenever the Reapers came to
bat, the fans began their voodoo-like chant. No wonder Jolly

Cholly, throwing his usual wastebasket full of trash, was able to set the Reapers down looking inning after inning. The Mundys themselves were accustomed by now to all sorts of noise assaulting their eardrums when they stepped up to the plate, but the Reapers, for all that they were the property of showman Frank Mazuma, and might have been expected to be somewhat more inured to the outlandish, seemed actually to fall into a state of hypnosis when the fans started in calling for the return of their hero. Ptah passed balls (two), Tuminikar wild pitches (two), Mundy fielding errors (five) were as nothing to the transfixed Reaper offense when forty thousand voices set the ball park to rumbling like the heart of a volcano: "YAMM! YAMM! YAMM! YAMM! YAMM! YAMM! YAMM!" Starving savages invoking their potato god for an abundant crop could not have offered up a more impassioned and sustained cry of yearning.

And by nightfall, the deity had delivered. "The fans have spoken," announced Mazuma, his one piratical eye agleam. "As of six o'clock this evening, Bob Yamm, the Midgets' Midget and now the People's Choice, has been reinstated as a Kakoola Reaper. And, in a straight player deal, O.K. Ockatur has been traded to the Ruppert Mundys for slugging outfielder Bud Parusha."

Those sportswriters who hated him of course derided Mazuma for compounding one cruel, corrupt publicity stunt with another. Clearly Mazuma had acquired Parusha—and in the process unloaded the washed-up dwarf—because of the telegram that had converted the Mundy right-fielder from a baseball curiosity into a symbol of courage on a par with the paralyzed President. And even *more* clearly, the telegram purportedly from Mrs. Roosevelt had been composed in his own front office by Mazuma and dispatched by some low-down pal of his in the nation's capital . . . or so whispered his enemies, who claimed that it was only to spare the feelings of poor Bud Parusha that the First Lady, justifiably outraged, had nonetheless decided to allow the telegram to stand as her own—exactly as Mazuma had predicted to his cronies the tender-hearted Eleanor would behave! Admittedly, the name Parusha had once been to the Patriot League what Waner was to the National and DiMaggio to the American, but that was before Angelo and Tony, the Joe and Dom, the Big and Little Poison of the Tycoon outfield, went off to the wars; surely a woman as well informed as Mrs. Roosevelt understood that if Bud Parusha's presence in the big time symbolized anything, it was only the awful depths to which the depleted leagues had fallen. Still, she held her tongue. Oh, that God damn Mazuma! He would even go so far as to shit on Eleanor Roosevelt and the March of Dimes in order to make himself a buck!

To fill the right-field slot left vacant by the departure of Bud Parusha, Mister Fairsmith had now to look to his bench, and like schoolchildren who had not done their homework, Mokos, Omara, Skirnir, Terminus, Hunaman, Khovaki, Kronos, and Garuda looked the other way. Said Mister Fairsmith's emissary, Jolly Cholly T., "All right, who wants to play right field?" and the eight, whom he had called together in the visitors' clubhouse, continued studying the scarred floorboards.

"Look," said Cholly, "you boys are forty and fifty years old. When will you ever get a chance like this again? Don't you want to have somethin' to tell your grandchildren about?" he asked, figuring this last might have some appeal, in that all of the Mundy utility players were proud, doting grandfathers, who passed much of their time on the bench exchanging snapshots of their offsprings' offspring, while their less fortunate teammates were out on the field being beaten to a pulp. "Come on, Mule," said Cholly to Mokos, a great glove man with the Greenbacks prior to their scandalous demise, "think how proud little Mickey would be to see your name in the box score every day. Think how he could say to his school-chums, 'That's my Grampa out there!' Now how many kids can do that?"

"Cholly," said Mokos, sighing, "God knows I'd like to help you. But frankly it's too much standin' on your feet out there to suit me."

"Suppose I say you can sit down, Mule. Suppose I say you can sit down on the grass and rest up whenever there's an intentional pass or a new pitcher comes in to warm up. Now you know with us that can be as much as two, three times an innin' late in the game, and that's exactly when you'd be needin' it most."

The old, tired Mule shook his head. "Sorry, Cholly, I'll sit here on the bench for you, and watch these games every afternoon, even though the truth be known, I got me a thousand and one things back home I could do better with my time—but to be perfectly frank with you, I'll be darned if I'm going to *stand* to watch a ballgame, especially when one of the teams is a last-place club fifty games out of first. I gotta be honest with you, Cholly. You and me know each other too many years to start pullin' our punches at a time like this."

Cholly turned next to Clever Carl Khovaki.

"Can't hear you, Cholly."

"I said," shouted the Mundy coach, "how would you like to play right field on a regular basis?"

"Write to who about the bases? I can't but sign my name with a X, you know that."

"No, *play right field on a regular basis.*"

"Me?" bellowed Carl, and broke into a big smile. "You must be kiddin'. Can't hear."

"You don't have to hear!" shouted Cholly. "Just field and hit!"

"Can't hear, though. Can't hear the crowd. Can't hear the ball bein' struck. Can't hear Agni if he calls for me to catch it." Then, with that wonderful ability to laugh at himself that had made him the beloved dunderhead of the fans in years gone by, Clever Carl said, "Can't even hear myself think. That's how come I give it up."

It was true: even in his heyday with Aceldama, though he could regularly drive a high hard one into the seats, Carl would be as apt to run back to first as on to third, if someone hit a single while he was on second. In the thick of things he seemed to have no more idea as to how the game was played than a Saudi Arabian. Then he went deaf and lost what little contact he had with those who could holler and scream at him what to do next—and then he became a Mundy. "Get a feller can hear, Cholly, that's my advice. That is," said Carl, "if we got one on the club. Otherwise my advice is buy one, and the hell with the price. Should be one of us ain't hard of hearin' anyway, just in case of some kind of emergency."

"Now, look," said Cholly, "somebody has got to play right

field on this club, and it ain't me. I am already pitcher, coach, mother, and father around here, and that's enough."

"Well," snapped Wally Omara, "it ain't me, either! Let's get that clear. Not with my blood pressure—no, sir! If we had even a shot at seventh, well, that would be a arguin' point, Cholly. But we ain't got a shot at shit as far as I can see, and in the light of that, I really am flabbergasted that you have had the raw nerve, Charles, to even suggest to a feller with my blood pressure—"

"And you?" asked Cholly, turning to Applejack Terminus, who was sitting off by himself, as though nursing some private misery.

"Cholly," said Applejack, looking sadly down at the belly bulging over his belt, "Cholly, if I could still go back for 'em the way I did when I come up, I'd be out there for you every afternoon for the rest of the month. But," said the Apple, closing his eyes against the tears, "them days is gone, Cholly."

"Suppose I say you don't have to go back, Apple. Suppose I say you can play up against the wall, so you only have to come in."

"Cholly," said Terminus, "ain't *nobody* can't catch 'em comin' *in*. Why, that's a insult!"

"But I ain't even sayin' *catch* 'em, Apple. Let 'em drop in for singles and take 'em on the hop. And we'll call that playin' right field. What do you say, fella?"

"Cholly," he moaned, again struggling not to weep, "in my prime, Cholly, when I was playin' center for the Blues, there was times I covered *second* on account of how close in I would play. And you know, 'cause you seen it. You seen where the smart fans used to sit back in them days when I was with the Blues—right out there in the bleachers! And not just paupers either, but millionaires with their chauffeurs. And why? 'Cause they knew. You want to watch a ace outfielder like Apple ply his trade, why, that's the only place *to* sit—right back of him! Yessir! And then watch him go when that ball is hit! Just *watch* him! But then a' course," said Apple, suddenly bitter, "then a' course they put that rabbit in the ball, didn't they? That's what moved us back a' course—*and ruined the whole gosh darn game!* Hell, I remember the first time this feller struck a triple

over my head with that new ball a' theirs. Can't even recall his
name no more—I don't think he lasted in the big time but fifteen minutes. Anyhow, he struck this darn triple. It was
openin' day of 1920. Know what I did? I was so dang mad, I
didn't even bother to throw that ball in from center, nosir; I
ran all the way to the infield, holdin' that new ball a' theirs in
my hand, see, and I run all the way up to that hoofenpoofer,
who was a smilin' away to beat the band on third there, as
though he had done somethin' special, you understand, and I
said, 'Listen, you sorry excuse of a whangdoodle, last year you
couldn't a hit the ball above your waist if we give it to you to
hold in your hand!' 'Oh no?' says that grinnin' gaboon, 'then
how come I done it just now, Apple?' 'How *come*?' says I. '*Here's*
how come!' And I ripped off his cap and stuck that ball right
up to his ear: 'Juss listen, you wampus cat, juss hold that right
up to yer ear you tree squeak of a gazook, and you can *hear*
that rabbit's heart a-beatin' away in there!'" And on and on
went the fat man, fifteen minutes more on the subject that invariably threw him into a tirade—the introduction twenty-odd
years earlier of the lively ball. "Nope," he concluded, spitting
on the clubhouse floor to register his vote, "the day I have to
rest my fanny on the fence, that is the day I bow out of this
game for good. Either you play the outfield shallow, Cholly,
like it was meant to be played back before the era of the
stitched golf ball, *or you don't play it at all!*"

In the end it was the undernourished six-footer, skinny
Specs Skirnir, the Mundy with a year of college education and
the least confident of them all, who took the job.

"I just don't want to break my glasses, Cholly."

"You won't, Specs."

"I'm not used to them yet, and I'm afraid I'm going to
break them."

"Specs, you've had 'em since '34."

"I know, Cholly, but I just can't get used to them."

"Well, it may just be a matter of playin' with 'em regular.
That may do it for you, boy."

"But what happens when they get steamed up?"

"Just take 'em off and clean 'em with your hankie."

"What if it's in the middle of a play, Cholly?"

"Do it before the play."

"But they don't get steamed up *before*. They get steamed up *during*."

"Well, then," said Cholly, patiently, "do the best you can, and clean 'em after."

"But *after's* too late! What if because they're steamed up I can't see—and get hit with the ball! Suppose I'm at bat and get hit in the mouth! Suppose a grounder jumps up and breaks my nose! And all because my glasses got steamed up!"

"Ah, come on, Specs, none of that's goin' to happen. It hasn't yet."

"That's because since I got them in 1934 I've been *benched*! And even with *that* they get steamed! Look, look how I chipped my tooth on the water fountain in Independence. My glasses got steamed up on account of the heat, and I went in too close for a drink, and I chipped my tooth on the spout. Look, Cholly, look at my shins, they're all black and blue— tripped over Big Jawn's foot just going down to the clubhouse in Terra Inc. to take a leak. Imagine—just taking a leak is dangerous in these damn things! Cholly, I shouldn't even really be in the *dugout* during the game, let alone on the *field*! Nine innings just on the bench and at the end of the game I'm a wreck! If I don't go in and get a rubdown and a hot shower, I ache in every muscle for a week! Cholly, this is crazy—this is insane! I don't get what's going on around here at all. I've been to school, Cholly, and I can tell you this much—you don't trade away a perfectly decent one-armed outfielder to put in his place a guy who wears *glasses*. What kind of baseball strategy is that? And look what we got in return, Charles—a dwarf! It wasn't bad enough to have Chico with that awful squeak of his, now we got to have a twisted little dwarf coming in out of the bullpen for the grand finale every afternoon! Cholly, I don't like it! Nine years now, Cholly, one way or another, I've managed to stay alive wearing these God damn things—and now suddenly this crazy little dwarf shows up to help us finish last, and I'm supposed to take my life in my hands playing in glasses for a big league team. *Cholly, I'm only forty-three years old!*"

"Specs," said Cholly, laying a fatherly hand upon the sopping uniform of the terrified utility player on the brink of becoming a regular again, "I have just spent a mornin' here goin' over this club's reserve strength, and if it'll be any comfort to you, I don't believe this here *is* a big league team any more, in the original way that they meant that word."

"Well, maybe *we* ain't a big league team, but we're playing *against* big league teams—and, Cholly, that's what's scariest of all!"

After a moment's reflection, Cholly said, "I suppose that is what's scariest, come to think of it. Still and all, we gotta do it," and he entered Specs Skirnir on the line-up card for that day's game. "You're battin' seventh, son. And don't forget your hankie."

*Query:* Who back in Port Ruppert had arranged the trade anyway? As far as the players knew, the paneled, carpeted stadium offices of the Mundy management had been turned over to the Army, along with the beautifully manicured field, and the patriotic Mundy brothers had rented for the duration a nondescript cubbyhole in a rundown office building at the very edge of Port Ruppert's colored section. According to one of the rumors with which the players around the league liked to tease and taunt the Mundys, the office was tended only by an old woolly-haired janitor who came in to raise and lower the blackout shade each day, and to forward whatever mail had accumulated on to the exotic cities of Latin America, where the Mundy brothers were said to be recuperating from the hard winter of negotiation that had landed their ball club on the road.

"Hey," said Big John, laughing as usual, "maybe the nigger done it. Maybe Mazuma called when he was sweepin' up, and the nigger said, 'Okay wiff me, boss,' and hung up. What do you say to that, Venus de Milo? Some nigger janitor back in Rupe-it swapped you even up for a fella the size of a mosquito!"

"Hey, would that be legal?" asked Nickname. "If a nigger done it? I mean, ain't they got their own leagues?"

"That depends whether the Mundy brothers give 'im the authority," said old Wayne Heket. "Why, down home I know a feller signed everythin' over to his dog, then just lay down and died."

"Could be Nickname's right, though," said Hot. "I'm gonna look that up. It just could be that if a nigger has done it, that

Bud here ain't got no choice but to go over to their leagues—
and for life!"

"Now wouldn't that be somethin'! If on top of havin' just
one arm for hittin' and throwin' and wipin' his bee-hind, poor
Buddy wound up by mistake playin' outfield for a bunch of
niggers!"

"Hell, I'druther go on home and shovel hoss manure than
have to play ball with jigaboos every day!"

"At least you'd have your self-respect!"

"Poor Buddy! Eatin' all that shit they eat too, instead a' real
food!"

"And how's he ever goin' to know what they're sayin' when
they're talkin' to him? I hear tell over in them leagues, that instead of havin' signals they just holler out 'Bunt!', figurin' the
other team don't know enough English to guess what's comin'
next. Them spades is always scratchin' themselves so much,
half the time what you figure for a hit-'n-run sign ain't nothin'
but the manager goin' after his cooties."

"Poor Buddy!"

"Poor Bud!"

While this exchange took place in the Mundy locker room,
Bud continued to separate out of his locker what belonged to
the Mundys and what belonged to him. Earlier in the day he
had wondered just how unhappy he would be when the time
to leave his old teammates rolled around. He was a sentimental sucker from way back, and he knew it. But as it turned out,
he found he was just too damn happy about going to be sad.
Why, if anything it was the other players who looked to be on
the brink of tears, as they watched him pack his cardboard suitcase with his few things, and render unto Ruppert what was
the team's.

"Poor Buddy," they said, "I don't envy him if he winds up
with a bunch of blooches to have to sit down next to in the
dugout on a hundred degree day. Pee-*you*!"

Oh, but did they envy him! With exception perhaps of John
Baal, who considered a home a joke, there was hardly a Mundy
who wouldn't have given his right arm to have been Big Bud
Parusha, the new Kakoola Reaper.

"Well, fellas," said Bud, "that's it, I guess." He waited a moment to see if he might stop being so damn happy and start in

being just a little sad, if only for auld lang syne. But it was not for him to be miserable that day—not quite yet. "Well, I won't forget you fellers, don't worry," said Bud, and suitcase in hand, he left the Mundy clubhouse, never to wear that uniform again.

O.K. Ockatur arrived shortly thereafter to take his place; no observations about niggers from the Mundys, either, not a word in fact about anything in this whole wide world, while the misshapen midget stripped out of his little street clothes and climbed into the scarlet and gray.

Frank Mazuma, having already designated the opener of the Mundy-Reaper series "Welcome Bud Parusha Day," held one of his press conferences before the game, this one to introduce Buddy to the Kakoola newspapermen, and even more important, "to squelch at the outset a most detestable rumor that," said Mazuma, "reflects not simply upon that doormat known as Frank Mazuma's integrity, or upon the integrity of this fine young man bearing the honored baseball name of Parusha, but what is of far greater moment, upon the integrity of the wife of the President of the United States, and, by extension, of the Commander-in-Chief himself, the leader of the world's greatest democracy in its do-or-die battle against the forces of evil."

Bud, standing sheepishly beside the Reaper owner, wore a Reaper home uniform of creamy white flannel, bearing on its back the orange numeral 1½. The fraction, of course, had come off O.K. Ockatur's uniform; as Mazuma explained to the reporters, it was not intended to suggest that Bud was missing anything ("the empty right sleeve of his uniform, gentlemen, tells that story eloquently enough") but rather that he was endowed with about fifty per cent more courage than the ordinary mortal.

"Why not go all the way then, Frank," asked one reporter, "and give him 1–5–0 for a number?"

"Well, the fact is, Len, I talked that over with Bud here, but he said he thought it might seem to the other ballplayers that he was trying to lord it over them, if he had three numbers to their two. So we settled on the half. In fact, I said to him, 'Bud, do you think you can restore this fraction to a place of dignity in the baseball world?' and Buddy here said in reply, 'I sure can try, Mr. Mazuma.'"

Then a reporter asked, "How the hell does he tie his shoelaces, Frank?"

"Good question, Red, but if you don't mind, we're going to save those exhibitions for the pregame ceremonies. Right now I want, for everyone's sake, to turn to that rumor that has swept the league ever since I purchased Buddy from the Mundys late yesterday afternoon. I needn't tell you gentlemen that over the years I have grown somewhat accustomed to having my motives maligned by the self-styled protectors of this game—the people I call (and I'm not mincing initials here either) the s.o.b.s of O.B. But I really must confess that I was not prepared for their latest smear campaign. I simply did not believe that they could sink to such depths as to claim that this fine young ballplayer whom you see before you, who only yesterday struck the first four-bagger ever hit in the majors by a one-armed player, is not in fact one-armed at all, but that beneath his uniform he has a perfectly good second arm tied down to his left side."

"They *didn't!*" someone cried (someone perhaps in Mazuma's employ?).

"Gentlemen of the press, I have asked you here to help me scotch this despicable lie of theirs before this boy goes out on the field today to have bestowed upon him the honors he earned yesterday with one mighty swing of his bat, and I remind you, against my own ball club. I am going to ask my little daughter, Doubloon, to come out here to assist Bud in removing his new Reaper shirt. She's been clamoring all summer for a job out at the ball park, and I thought maybe this would be as good a time as any. Honey? Doubloon?"

Here a voluptuous young woman in brief white shorts and a clinging orange blouse (and the word "Over" stitched across her back, just above the number "21") rushed in a clatter of high heels up to the microphone, kissed her daddy on the mouth, and then, to the applause and catcalls of the assembled reporters, began to fumble with the buttons of Bud's uniform shirt.

"By the way," ad-libbed Mazuma, "'Doubloon' doesn't

mean what some of you fellas think it does. Strange to say, it has nothing to do with things that come in pairs."

The newspapermen had to chuckle at the famous Mazuma humor which he could direct even at the members of his own family.

"I'm all thumbs," giggled Doubloon, as she loosened Bud's belt so as to extract his shirttails from his trousers. "Oh what a stupid thing to say to *you!*" she cried, fluttering her eyelids at the new Kakoola Reaper.

"Nor," said Mazuma, lighting up a cigar, "is 'Doubloon' a mispronunciation of the capital of Ireland, for all that this kid could get anybody's Irish up, if you know what I mean by 'Irish.' "

By now Bud's shirt had been removed and Doubloon was drawing his orange sweatshirt out of his shorts.

"Actually," said Mazuma, continuing with the witty patter, " 'Doubloon' is just another way of saying 'Do-re-mi.' Tell the boys the names of your brothers and sisters, sweetheart."

Turning momentarily from her task, she wiped the perspiration from her upper lip with a raised shoulder ("Oh baby!" cried one of the reporters, oddly moved by the gesture) and in her whispery voice, said, "Jack, Buck, Gelt, and Dinero."

Then, with a little jump into the air, Doubloon yanked the sweatshirt over Bud's head and the athlete was nude to the waist.

"Ucch," cried Doubloon, unable to suppress a shiver of revulsion.

"Well," said Mazuma, gravely now, "there it is, gentlemen. The truth for all to behold. Not a trace of a left arm. Not a *suggestion* of a left arm."

Here, at a nod from Mazuma, the photographers surged forward and the room was incandescent with flashbulbs.

"How about from the back, Bud!"

"Smile, Bud, cheer up! This is your day, boy!"

"Make a muscle, Bud, with the one you got!"

"Cheese, Bud, cheese! *Thatta* boy!"

When the photographers receded—with a promise from Mazuma that there was more to come—one of the reporters said, "Frank, you may not like this, but how do we know that this isn't some kind of trick make-up job such as they do in the movies? How do we know that Bud's missing arm isn't in fact hidden away under a phony layer of skin made out of wax or some such substance?"

"Doubloon," said Mazuma, "would you do Daddy a favor? To assure the reporters that there's no arm hidden away inside a false covering of skin, would you just pass your hand up and down Bud's side?"

"Do *what*?"

"Just press lightly up and down his left side, so they see that it is really and truly him. Well, come on now, honey."

"Oh, *Daddy*."

"Now, Dubby, you're the one who wanted a summer job, you know that. You're the one who wanted to wear the number 'Over 21,' remember? You're a big girl now and sometimes big people have to do things they don't necessarily like to do. Touch his side, sweetheart."

"Oh, Daddy, I *can't*. It's so *uccchy*."

"Look, young lady either you touch him as I tell you to, or I am going to put you over my knee! You may be over twenty-one, you know, but you're still not too old for your daddy to give you a good old-fashioned spanking, press conference or no press conference!"

Here the photographers came surging forward again, cameras in the air.

"What a clown," mumbled a reporter known to be no great admirer of Mazuma's.

"Clown my ass, Smitty!" snapped the Reaper owner. "Do you think I want you boys leaving here half-believing that you've been had? *Do* you? Do you think I want the people of this country to suspect that the wife of the President of the United States, the First Lady of the Land, has asked somebody to be honorary co-chairman of the March of Dimes who has been disguised by me, Frank Mazuma, for reasons of publicity or profit, to look like some kind of freak, when in fact he isn't? Do you think I want our brave allies to harbor the slightest suspicion that this is a country run by con-men and crooks? Do you boys know what Tokyo Rose could do with a little tidbit like this? Do *you*, Doubloon, my innocent daughter? Do you realize the kind of venom that Jap bitch could pour into the ears of—?"

"Oh, *please*," cried Doubloon, "I can't *bear* you, Daddy, when you sound like a minister!"

"And what's wrong with sounding like a minister, may I ask? Since when is religion a dirty word in this country, may I ask?"

"Oh, all right, I'll *touch* him—just stop *lecturing* me!"

"Okay then, okay," said Mazuma, subsiding, and nodded to the photographers to get ready.

Doubloon meanwhile readied herself. First, she squeezed her eyes shut very tightly like a little girl preparing to swallow a spoonful of cod-liver oil. Then she rose up on tiptoes so that her narrow white heels came popping up out of her orange shoes ("Oh baby!" cried that same reporter, now moved apparently by the sight of her heels); and then, with great reluctance and much wiggling of the can, she extended the finger of one hand very, very slowly in the direction of Bud Parusha's body, which all the while he had been standing shirtless before the crowd, had been turning a deep shade of crimson.

Because of the lightning storm of flashbulbs that accompanied the contact of Doubloon's fingertip with Buddy's flesh, the effect of her gesture upon the former Mundy was not immediately apparent. But when at last everyone's vision was restored, there for all to see was a bulge of substantial proportions in Buddy's new flannel trousers.

"My, my," laughed the reporters.

Mazuma, never at a loss for words, quipped, "Well, gentlemen, I'll tell you one thing my new right-fielder ain't missin'," and with that, brought the house down.

What a clown indeed. Is it any wonder that when Mazuma beckoned, the reporters came in droves? And is it any wonder that those like General Oakhart, who had struggled all their lives to prevent the great American game from becoming just another cheap form of popular entertainment, wished that Frank Mazuma, and all his kind, might be lined up against the outfield wall and shot?

The jubilant mood in which the press conference ended continued on through the pregame ceremonies of "Welcome Bud

Parusha Day"—baseball stunts and feats of skill performed by the visiting Mundys. "Their tribute," announced Frank Mazuma, to the forty-odd thousand who had of course turned out not to welcome Bud Parusha but to witness the return of Bob Yamm, "their tribute to their former teammate, a great ballplayer and an even greater human being, brother of the great Tycoon Parushas, now serving so gallantly with the United States Marines, Angelo and Tony—" here the fans rose and accorded Angelo and Tony a standing ovation that lasted two full minutes—"Bud Parusha!"

Scattered applause as Bud ran from the Reaper dugout waving his mitt at the stands. From the steps of the visitors' dugout, the Mundys looked on in awe at Buddy all in home team white. How like a bride he seemed to them in their own tattered road uniforms of gray! Jolly Cholly, the kindest coach who ever lived, flashed the V for Victory sign—"Good luck, kid!" he called, and Parusha was all at once washed over with an emotion so strong, so engulfing, that he even felt it in his missing limb. *Take me back*, cried the heart of the bride-to-be, *take me back before it's too late. Maybe you're where I belong!* But what American in his right mind ever wanted to be back with an eighth place team when he could be up with one in seventh? So, instead of bolting for the Mundy dugout, Bud continued on to home plate, to his deliverers, Mazuma and Doubloon.

And now the first of the Mundys who had agreed to perform that afternoon was introduced to the fans. On the sly, Mazuma had approached each of the disgruntled Ruppert players, but in the end only two of the regulars and one of the relief pitchers was so desperate, or so gullible, as to be taken in when the owner promised to make Reapers out of them too if they proved to be "crowd pleasers" in the manner of Buddy P.

"Ladies and gentlemen," Mazuma announced into the mike that had been set up at home plate, "it is a pleasure and an honor to introduce to you the youngest player in the history of the major leagues, Mundy second-sacker, fourteen-year-old Nickname Damur!"

Nickname came charging full-speed from the visiting team's dugout and made a perfect (and he hoped, crowd-pleasing) hook slide around Doubloon's leg and into the plate.

"Cut it *out*," snapped Doubloon.

"Reputed to be the fastest base runner in the game today—
by those, that is, who've had the rare opportunity of *seeing* him
on base—only kidding, Nickname!" quipped Mazuma, clapping the boy on the back, while the mob howled—"Nickname
Damur is today going to match his speed around the bases
with none other than the second cousin by marriage to the
great Seabiscuit, my own Doubloon's polo pony—Graham
Cracker!"

Here a snorting little chestnut filly danced up out of the
Reaper dugout. "Grahams!" called Doubloon, and she ran to
where the batboy, who had led the horse up past the water
cooler and on to the playing field, was holding the pony by the
reins. "Oh Grammies!" cried Doubloon and buried her lips in
the pony's mane. Then, in high-heeled shoes, shorts, and
blouse, she was hoisted up onto her mount by the batboy; her
riding crop was tossed up to her and she was off—galloping all
the way to the center-field wall and back.

"Graham Cracker will be carrying one hundred and seven
pounds. Or," said Mazuma, "to put it so that you folks who
don't follow the ponies understand, 38–22–36."

Now Nickname and Graham Cracker lined up with their
noses even at home plate and pointed in the direction of first
base. "As you fans know," said Mazuma, "thanks to General
Douglas D. Oakhart there are still no pari-mutuel windows
allowed in Patriot League parks. But speaking for myself and
fun-loving men everywhere, I don't see what's to stop you
from placing a friendly little wager with your neighbor . . ."

While the hubbub of betting excitement swept through the
stadium, Doubloon took the opportunity to lean down across
Graham Cracker's neck, and as though talking into the horse's
ear, whispered to the Mundy second-baseman, "Wouldn't
crowd us on the turn, Nickname—not if you want to come
out of this thing in one piece."

And they were off!

"It's Graham Cracker in the lead as they break from the
plate," announced Mazuma, dropping into a deep gravelly
voice and firing his words like bullets— "It's Graham by half a
length down the first-base line! At the bag, Graham turns wide
—and it's Nickname making his dash on the inside as they

head for second! And now they're neck and neck, Nickname's right there! So is Graham! They're around second heading for third, and it's Nickname now by a length, a length and a half with a third of the way to come—and now Graham Cracker is making her move as they pass the shortstop position! Graham Cracker is not beaten yet! She's coming with a rush! If she don't get blocked, she'll give that Mundy an awful drive! Now they're around third, they're heading for home, *and here comes Graham Cracker*—" and now forty thousand screaming, hollering fans were on their feet, and even as Doubloon's whip curled across his mouth, even as the blood sprang from his nose, Nickname could imagine victory—himself a Kakoola Reaper, second-baseman for an authentic big league team, a club with a park of its own, fans of its own, and an owner of whose presence you could never for a moment be in doubt—ah, but there was the blur of Graham Cracker pulling past him, and once again that whip as it flailed backwards to crack open the skin of his brow, and no, he would *not* be defeated, no, he would *not* be a Mundy for the rest of his born days—"Don't!" hollered Jolly Cholly, as Nickname began to go into his slide—but he did, he did: at the risk of being crushed to powder beneath Graham Cracker's four plunging legs, the ambitious fourteen-year-old, who wanted only to improve his lot in life (as who doesn't?), who wanted only to better himself (as who wouldn't?), went in under the horse's hoofs.

"Crazy little prick!" cried Doubloon, and swerving to avoid a collision at the plate, allowed Nickname to score. She herself went hurtling headlong out of the saddle and flew some thirty feet through the air, then bounced into the Mundy dugout, where Big John, taking her on the short hop, was able to squeeze just about whatever he wanted before the stretcher arrived to hurry the broken body of the unconscious young woman to the emergency operating room of Kakoola Memorial. Then, with forty thousand flabbergasted fans looking on—yes, even the Kakoola fans were staggered, even their expectations of a lively afternoon of thrills were exceeded by this calamitous turn of events—Mazuma borrowed a pistol from a stadium guard and put a bullet through Graham Cracker's skull.

"Gee," gulped Nickname, as the pony, who had lain

twitching in agony only inches from home plate, died with a whish of fumes from her exhaust, "I was *only* tryin' to win."

In his grief, Mazuma had to smile. "Well, if Doubloon kicks the bucket, Damur, you'll see what you won. When the fans get through with you, Nickname, you'll envy the unenviable Gamesh. My educated guess, kid, is that even if Doubloon survives, you yourself are washed up. To coin an appropriately paradoxical phrase, 'You're out of the running, flash-in-the-pan.'"

"At fourteen?" cried the bloodied Mundy.

"Kee-rect," said Mazuma. "I believe you have just Mundied yourself for life."

"But how *could* I? I *won!*"

"Tell it to them, Nickname," said Mazuma, lifting his gaze to the mob howling now for Nickname's unsportsmanlike hide. "Like the feller says," quipped Mazuma, covering his ears, "where you're concerned, it's all over but the shouting."

Minutes passed before Mazuma could even hope to make himself heard; then he stepped to the microphone, raised one hand, and into the red roaring mouth of the crowd, tossed this tender filet: "Official time, fourteen and four-fifths seconds. The winner—Damur!"

"Murderer! Killer! Monster! Fiend!"—yes, those were the nicknames they were now suggesting for the youth perennially in search of the right monicker for himself.

After the groundskeepers had dragged Graham Cracker's carcass across the field and out through the Mundy bullpen, and had raked away the last of her poignant hoof prints, Mazuma announced to the crowd that he intended to continue with "Welcome Bud Parusha Day" ceremonies as planned. And when, in a breaking voice, he said, "I can't help but think that Doubloon would want it that way," the fans once again came to their feet to deliver a standing ovation.

To the surprise and delight of everyone, the next person to be introduced was a stout, gray-haired woman in a longish print dress and sturdy shoes who was helped up out of the Reaper dugout and escorted to the microphone by a small army of Boy Scouts. "Ladies and gentlemen," said Mazuma, pecking her once on the cheek, "this little lady happens to be—my mom! And with her, Troop 40 of Mazuma Avenue School!"

The Boy Scouts came instantly to attention and saluted—
some saluted Mother Mazuma, others Frank Mazuma, still
others the American flag in center field, and a few simply saluted
each other. Mrs. Mazuma waved shyly at the crowd with her
handbag. "Today," she said into the mike, but so softly the
fans had to lean forward in their seats to hear . . . *Today*,
came the even gentler echo . . . "I consider myself—" *I consider myself* . . . "the happiest mother—" *the happiest mother*
. . . "on the face of the earth—" *of the earth* . . .

Yet another standing ovation

"Now, fans," said Mazuma, "as you all know, there is a custom in baseball, old as the great game itself, for the team at bat
to attempt to rile up the team on the field by that benign form
of badinage known as bench-jockeying. And as you also know
if you've been out to the park this year to see our erstwhile
visitors at play, there is probably no player in the entire league
who the bench-jockeys can rile up quicker and easier than the
man I am about to introduce. All you have to shout from the
bench is, 'Hothead, bet you a bottle of suds you couldn't throw
out my own mother!' and then watch that Mundy fume. Folks,
let's give a big welcome to Bud Parusha's former teammate
and fellow defective, Ruppert Mundy catcher, Hothead Ptah!"

Wearing but one shin guard—"Only got but one shin!" Hot
would snarl at the wiseguys—and his chest protector, and
carrying his mask and his glove, Hot came racing out of the
Mundy dugout at what for him was top speed. Oh, was he
eager!

"Well," said Mazuma when the laughter died down, "here
she is, Hot—my mom!"

"Howdy!"

"Good day, Mr. Ptah."

"Well, Hot," said Mazuma, "think you can throw her out at
second, two out of three? Personally, I have to say I got my
doubts, knowin' Mom here and her speed."

The crowd went wild as Hothead proceeded instantly to
lose his temper. "You'll eat those words, Mazuma!"

"And—and," said Mazuma, having to wait now for his own
laughter to subside ("His daughter's in the hospital, surgery is
being performed on her spinal column at this very moment,
and he can still laugh! What a guy!" said the Reaper sports-

caster to the hundreds of thousands tuned to KALE), "to assist Hothead in his attempt to cut down my mother stealing two times out of three, here is the proud owner of the sorest arm in baseball, Mundy relief ace—"

Yes, to the delight of the multitude, Chico Mecoatl began the long sad walk in from the Mundy bullpen. "Eeeep!" they cried, "eeeep!" imitating that little yelp he made when he pitched. Oh, how the crowd loved it—while the Mundys themselves were dumbstruck. Chico, even *Chico*, with an E.R.A. of 14.06, could no longer bear the indignity of wearing the Ruppert R!

"And," continued Mazuma, "covering second, to take the throw from Hothead—" "No!" the fans roared. "—Mundy second-sacker—" "No! No!" "—Nickname—"

"MURDERER! KILLER! THUG!" they shrieked, as Nickname, tipping his cap, ran gamely out to his position.

When Big John rose from the Mundy bench to go out to cover first, he quickly assured his startled teammates that *he* was only doing it for the kicks involved. "Don't worry, boys. I ain't no turncoat. Only trade I'd consider is to the Gypsys—wouldn't mind dancin' with a bear before I die! Haw! Haw!"

Mrs. Mazuma, meanwhile, had retired to the Reaper dugout, to leave her purse for safekeeping with the Boy Scouts of Troop 40, and to change into her spikes.

To spare himself some suffering, Chico rolled his warm-up pitch on the ground to Hot, who then pegged the ball down to Nickname at second. Ducky Rig, the Reaper catcher, came out to pretend to be the batter, and to yet another standing ovation—seven in all during the pregame ceremony, "let me check—yes sir, that's it all right, a major league record," said the sportscaster, "for standing ovations in a pregame ceremony in regular season competition"—Mazuma's mom walked to first in her baseball shoes, being careful to avoid stepping down on the freshly laid foul line.

"How do you do, Mr. Baal," she said, and Big John gave the fans their money's worth by sweeping off his cap and bowing in the manner of Sir Walter Raleigh.

Then the Mexican right-hander went into his stretch; he looked cursorily back over his left shoulder to first—and sure enough, the old lady in the print dress came climbing down off the bag, and taking one inch, and then another, and then another, wound up taking herself a very healthy lead indeed. Engaging Chico's eyes, she began to move her arms in a slow swinging motion, looking for all the world as though she would be breaking for second as soon as he went into his delivery.

Well, let her. Chico hadn't thrown to first to hold a *regular* base runner to the bag so far this year, and he wasn't starting up at this late date with an old lady. Not with *his* arm, he wasn't. So, into his snake-like wind-up he went, and with that yelp of his—"Eeeeep!"—looped the ball into the dirt. Hot blocked it neatly with his wooden leg, and Mrs. Mazuma held at first.

On the second pitch she went! The pitch, when it finally arrived, was high, but Hot, playing inspired ball, leaped to grab it and still in the air, fired down to Nickname.

Dress and all, Mrs. Mazurna slid, and her son, who was serving now as umpire at second, called, "Y'r out!"

The look she gave him when she rose to brush the dirt off herself could hardly be described as maternal. "He missed the tag, Frank."

"I call 'em the way I see 'em, Mom," said Mazuma into the hand mike he was carrying.

"He never touched me, Frank," said Mrs. Mazuma, kicking angrily at the bag.

"Look, no favors around here just because you happened once upon a time to have nursed the umpire! If I said 'Y'r out!', y'r out!"

Shaking her head in dismay, she trotted back to first, but not before turning to toss a few words Nickname's way.

Nickname now walked the ball to the mound, waving for Hot and Big John to join him and Chico for a conference. "Look," he said, "you ain't gonna believe this—but know what Mrs. Mazuma just told me? She flashes me this look, see, and she says, 'Don't block that bag, sonny, or next time I'll cut your ears off!'"

"Well, whattayaknow! Just as I suspicioned! That card Mazuma done it to us again—the she is really a he! Haw!"

"Look," snarled Hot, "I don't care if it's a *it*! You block that bag good, Nickname! And Chico, don't you give her no jump like that, you hear? Fire to first when she takes that lead!"

"Oh, Caldo, no, please Caldo, I don't be happy fire to first
—too much hurt, Caldo—"

"And what about bein' a friggin' Mundy, don't that hurt?
Hold that slit to first, you yelpin' little spic, or the whole lot of
us is doomed to Rupe-it forever!"

"Haw! Doomded we is anywhichway," said Big John, and
strode back to first base as though doom was so much lemon-
ade to him. "How they hangin', honey?" he asked Mrs. Mazuma, placing a wad of tobacco juice between her spikes.

"Here, here," retorted Mrs. Mazuma, "we don't need any
of that, young man," and stepped down off the bag with her
lead.

Chico's sorry throw to first, preceded as it was by a squeak,
enabled Mrs. Mazuma to get back to the bag in plenty of time.

"Ain't you afraid you'll tear your nice dress, sweetie, if you
have to hit the dirt again?" asked Big John.

"I can look after myself perfectly well, thank you," and she
broke for second! Again Hot's peg was perfect, but with a
slide reminiscent of the Georgia Peach himself, Mrs. Mazuma
swept in on her back to the right of the bag—and the tag—
while reaching behind to tick the base with the fingers of her
left hand.

"Safe!" called Mazuma, extending his arms, palms down.
"She is *safe!*"

With the crowd on its feet again, Mrs. Mazuma rose to clap
the dust out of her dress and to adjust her rubberized hose.
And all the while, in a voice that was no less menacing for
being muted, she issued a warning to the Mundy second-
baseman, who though he could not believe his ears, listened
as politely as he would to any lady her age dressed in that kind
of dress: "Now back in the kitchen, sonny," she told him,
brushing herself clean, "I have got me a special grinding stone
for honing my carving knives—and you know what I do with
it? I sit around with the other nice ladies in the afternoon over
a cup of coffee and some petit fours, and I sharpen up my spikes.
Now this is the last time I'm telling you: that basepath, in case
you ain't heard, belongs to the runner. You get in the runner's
way one more time, and she is going to take you, buster, clothes
and all. I'm stealing this next one for a kid in the hospital,

Nickname, little girl name a' Doubloon—so just you give me room, boy, if you want to have a face left."

"But," replied Nickname, "she *whipped* me—with her *whip*! Look, this blood is *mine*!" But Mrs. Mazuma was trotting back to first, accompanied by a joyous roar from the crowd.

As the two stood together on the bag, Big John came up to within an inch of her jaw, and inquired, "Just couldn't be, under that wig and make-up and all, that you are the outlawed and unfamous Gil Gamesh pickin' up a few pesos—could it, Mrs. M.? That couldn't be you under there, playin' the slit again, could it, Gilly boy?"

"Now you just watch your tongue, Mr. Baal. One more crack—"

"You call it how you want—haw! haw!"

"—and I will report you to General Oakhart for even mentioning that name on a big league diamond, and what's more, to an American Mom." And like a big, calm, cunning cat, she started inching away from that bag.

Behind the plate, Hothead was already screaming, "Hold her to the—!" But it was too late now; the old lady had gotten the jump and was already midway to second while Hot was still waiting for Chico's slow ball to arrive at the plate. According to some of the ironists in the league, you really had to feel sorry for that pitch—slow is slow, but that poor thing was retarded. Hot, too frantic to think, did the unthinkable: while the ball was still on its way to the plate, he rushed forward to meet it, thus putting himself directly in the path of the bat, should the man at the plate decide to take a cut at either the ball or the catcher.

"Swing!" the fans cried to Duck Rig. "Knock the cover off his skull!"

Ducky was really of a kindly nature (and the fans of course were only kidding), but still and all, it was his job up there to keep the whole thing honest, and so he swung—a kind of golf stroke, was all, at Hothead's wooden leg, driving it cleanly off the stump and down the third-base line—"Foul!" according to the sportscaster up in the radio box. One of the Boy Scouts ran instantly out to retrieve it, even as Hot, balancing on just one leg, burned one down to second and then went toppling after it on to his face. God, did ever a man want to be traded as much as Hothead Ptah?

"A perfect peg!" the sportscaster cried—only Mrs. Mazuma was sliding in with her right leg so high in the air, you could for a moment see the sunlight glinting off her spikes. Then shoe, leg, and the flying folds of her long dress disappeared into the crumbling figure of Nickname, who went down as if in slow motion, closing over Mrs. Mazuma's lower extremities like the jaws of a crocodile.

Silence in the ball park, the silence of the spheres, while the dust cleared and Mazuma looked to ascertain whether the runner had managed to separate the second-baseman from his head, which had pretty much seemed her intention. But no, though she had sliced his uniform open diagonally from the shoulder to the waist, Nickname himself was intact; the second-baseman had, however, been separated from the ball, which lay fifteen feet beyond him at the edge of the grass.

"Safe!" exclaimed Mazuma, and as they said next day in the papers, you could have renamed Reaper Field Pandemonium Park.

Halfway to the mound, the Mundy catcher lay pounding the dirt with his fists, and howling, as though those tears he wept were scalding his face.

Suddenly a Boy Scout appeared at the side of the fallen catcher, holding the wooden limb in his two outstretched hands. "Here, sir, your leg."

"Aww, stick it up your ass," wept Hothead. "*You* go through life a jelly-apple!"

"You mean," cried the Boy Scout, a look of pure delight breaking across his freckled face, "I can keep it? And the baseball shoe, too? Wow! Hothead Ptah's leg!" he called, running back with his prize to the troop in the Reaper dugout. "He said I can *have* it!"

And now Nickname was kneeling beside him, and Big John too. "How could you do it?" Hot cried, grabbing the second-baseman by the shirt, "How could you be afraid of a sixty-year-old lady's spikes?"

"Aw, lay off, Hot," said Big John. "It warn't no old lady. If you ask me, it was a ringer named Gamesh."

But Nickname, wiping the warpaint of his own blood and tears across his cheek with the back of his mitt, blubbered, "But it *was* a old lady, Jawn, that's the worst of it. *That's* how come I dropped the ball! It weren't them spikes that scared me, Hot. Look, I took 'em full in the letters."

"Then *what?*" screamed Hot. "Was you bein' *polite* to her that you lost the ball?"

"No! No! It's, it's when she raised up her leg—that's how come I lost it! I damn near went unconscious."

"Why?" demanded Hothead.

"Aw jeez, Hot, I ain't never smelled nothin' like that at second base before. Or in a cathouse even. It stunk like somethin' that's been left out somewhere and turned green. I ain't lyin' to you, Hot—I thought maybe it was a shrimp boat dockin' at the bag. Only worse! Then my whole life flashed before my eyes, and I thought, by Jesus, I'm gonna *die* from whatever it is!"

"That keen, huh?" said Big John.

"Keen? I'druther be drownin' in a swamp!"

"Well," said Big John, consoling the catcher as he and Nickname each took the dumbstruck Hothead by an arm and helped him back to the Mundy dugout, "old or young, they all of them knows how to get the use out of that thing, don't they? Cheer up now, ol' Hothead, you ain't the first feller to get done in by the black hole of Calcutta—or the last either."

And Chico? No sooner had Hot's leg been driven foul than he ran from the field to the visitors' clubhouse, climbed inside his locker and pulled the door shut behind him. A devout and simple man (albeit an ingrate), he had taken what happened as a judgment upon himself. Through the airholes of the locker he whispered a plea, "I like Mundy! I be Mundy! I stay Mundy!" and though Jolly Cholly shortly appeared to open the locker and remove the trembling reliever from his makeshift confessional, thereafter Chico's sleep was plagued with visions of limbs being batted back at him out of the box, of eyeballs dropping like bunts, and whole heads, severed at the neck, that he took with a shriek on one hop . . . oh, in torment he would roll from his hotel bed to the floor, and there on his face, in yet another strange town, beg to be forgiven for his disloyalty to the team that owned him, and his hatred of the uniform he wore. He prayed to the Holy Mother to keep him a Mundy forever—hoping against hope of course, that because he was so unworthy, his prayers would go unanswered.

In the name of mercy (and narrative brevity, fans), let us pass over Bud Parusha's protracted demonstration of how he tied his shoelaces, and over the eight and two-thirds innings of baseball that ensued, to arrive at the final bloodletting of "Welcome Bud Parusha Day," wherein the refugees from Ruppert, bereft of the player whose name at least had endowed their line-up with some small claim to big league legitimacy, went from being simply the most inept and ludicrous team in the history of Organized Baseball, to the most universally despised. In that nobody on the Kakoola club had any idea of how to remove the ball from between their new right-fielder's jaws when in his anxiety it would become lodged there (as it did in one out of every two chances he had during his first day as a Reaper), what should have been an easy 8–0 victory for the home team, went to the last of the ninth with the score tied 8–8, thanks to Bud Parusha's big mouth.

The bottom of the ninth then, score tied, two men down, and the bases full of Reapers—could it have happened any more dramatically in a storybook? With a weary, wild fifty-year-old on the hill for the Mundys, and the winning run on third, the longed-for words were uttered:

"Your attention, please. Pinch-hitting for Kakoola, Number ¼—"

His name was lost in the roar.

But for a small (a very small) Band-Aid across the bridge of his nose, Bob Yamm bore no marks of the fierce combat of the previous afternoon. Nor was there any indication in his bearing that the decision made by an entire nation "in the long dark night of its soul" (to hear Frank M. describe it) "to bring Bob back to baseball and baseball back to Bob" had affected by so much as one iota, by so much as one micron, by so much as one *millimicron*, his exquisite sense of propriety. He emerged from the Reaper dugout swinging his two little bats and proceeded on to home plate with the grave, determined manner of a man with a job to do, no more, no less. The tumultuous ovation being accorded him he acknowledged only by pulling on the bill of his cap. And when he looked for the briefest second to the stands, it was not to the roaring multitude, but to a seat in Frank Mazuma's box back of first, where Judy Yamm, perched on two Kakoola telephone directories, chewed upon her manicured and polished nails. To her alone Bob smiled.

On the mound, Deacon Demeter, who had already walked fourteen full-grown men in the course of the long, harrowing afternoon, leaned way down off the rubber and searched for that narrow slot in space through which the ball must now pass to be considered a strike. He looked and he looked and he looked—the Deacon was a patient man—and then instead of rearing back to pitch, he walked off the field and out of the game, all on his own. "Believe me, Cholly," he told the Mundy coach in the dugout, "if it was possible, I'd a tried. But, hell, you couldn't even a got a nickel in there to make a phone call."

"Ladies and gentlemen, your attention please: coming in to pitch for the Mundys, Number ¹⁄₁₆—"

The rest is Patriot League history, or was, when P. League history was still extant around here. Pitching to someone approximately his own size, Number ¹⁄₁₆—who was of course O.K. Ockatur, wearing on his Mundy shirt the number of his dreams and of his own devising—cut loose with two overhand curveballs, quite normal little pitches such as a pretty good fifth-grader might throw; each broke in across the waist of the immobile Yamm and over the outside corner for strikes one and two. Now, Yamm was as unfamiliar with an o and 2 situation as a man from Mars, or Budapest; likewise he was utterly without ability as a hitter, which was why Mazuma had warned him at the outset that he wasn't to lift the bat off his shoulder if he wanted to live to tell the tale. But Bob did not intend to go down looking at called strike three. It wasn't a matter of sparing *his* pride, either; what concerned him was the pride of respectable, honest, hardworking midgets everywhere, the average American midget whose dignity he embodied and trust he bore. He stood for too much to too many little people, to stand there helpless and impotent before Ockatur's third strike.

It came down to this: he was loved and Ockatur was loathed. One had only to listen to that crowd to know that.

Of course with two quick strikes on the hitter, Ockatur decided to waste his next pitch—as who wouldn't, freak or Hall of Famer? Yamm, however, imagining that the high hard one sailing toward his hands was going to break down and away like the two preceding curveballs, went lunging after it with his hat. He swung with all his might, and he missed, even as the ball kept right on coming at his face.

The first bulletins from the hospital were hopeful. Millions of Americans went to bed at midnight September 15, 1943, believing that the crisis had passed. Then, at 4:17 A.M. Central Daylight Saving Time, Frank Mazuma emerged from Kakoola Memorial and wearily mounted the hood of a police car. He was unshaven and his face was streaked with tears. To the gathering of newsmen, to the hundreds of fans and well-wishers who had continued to stand vigil outside the hospital even as a fine morning drizzle had begun to fall, Mazuma announced that the ball that had struck Bob Yamm between the eyes had blinded him for life. When he came to deliver the rest of his report, he broke down completely and had to be helped from the police car by his sons Jack and Gelt, and hurried away. It was only a matter of minutes, however, before a hospital orderly who wanted his picture in the paper collared the sportswriter Smitty and revealed that the curvaceous Doubloon would never wiggle her sweet ass again, as she was paralyzed from her twenty-two-inch waist clear to the ground.

And after those two stories went crackling out over the wire services, not even Bud Parusha, miserable and solitary misfit that he was to be with a team of commonplace duffers like the Reapers, ever longed to return to the Mundys again.

5

# THE TEMPTATION OF
# ROLAND AGNI

# 5

*A word on the Mundy winning streak and an observation on the law of averages. The secret meeting between Roland Agni and Angela Whittling Trust, in which Roland delivers a monologue on his batting prowess that approaches the condition of poetry. The history goes backward to recount the adventures of Mrs. Trust: a description of her love affairs with Ty Cobb, Babe Ruth, Jolly Cholly Tuminikar, Luke Gofannon, and Gil Gamesh. Her great address to Agni on her transformation from a selfish woman into a responsible human being. A dire warning to Agni, in which the reader will be no less astonished than the rookie to learn of the international conspiracy against the Patriot League. Concluding with an account of the history of the Greenbacks under Jewish management, including scenes of Jewish family life which will appear quite ordinary to most of our readers, albeit they are enacted in a ball park.*

NEAR the end of September, just as the '43 season was coming to a close, a phenomenon so unlikely occurred in the Patriot League that for a couple of weeks the nation ceased speculating upon when and where the Allied invasion of the European fortress would be launched and turned its attention to the so-called "miracle" of the sports world. The pennant races themselves had people yawning: in a hapless American League, the Yanks were running away with the flag on an un-Yankeeish team batting average of .256, and in the National, the Cardinals, who still had Musial to hit and Mort Cooper to pitch, were eighteen games ahead of the second place Reds and twenty-three in front of Durocher's Dodgers. The only race that might have been worth watching was over in the P. League, where for months the Tycoons had remained only percentage points ahead of the Butchers; by September, however, both clubs were playing such uninspired ball that it seemed each had secretly come around to thinking that winning the flag in that league in that year might not be such an honor after all. No, the "miracle" in the Patriot League wasn't taking place at the top of the standings, but at the bottom. The Ruppert Mundys were winning.

The streak began on September 18, with a fourteen-run explosion against Independence, and it did not end until the final day of the season, and it took Tri-City to do it: Tycoons 31, Mundys 0, the worst defeat suffered by the Mundys all season, and unquestionably the worst game ever to be played by any team in the history of the major leagues.

Nonetheless, that the Mundys should give up thirty-one runs on twenty-seven hits and twelve errors—nineteen runs in a single inning—on the final day of that grim year was not beyond human comprehension; what was, were those eleven consecutive victories by scores of 14–6, 8–0, 7–4, 5–0, 3–1, 6–4, 11–2, 4–1, 5–3, 8–1, and 9–3. How in the world had a team like that managed to score eighty runs in little more than a week, when they had barely scored two hundred in the five months before?

"They wuz due maybe," said the fans.

"Law of averages," wrote the sportswriters.

But neither explanation made any sense; nobody who is down and out the way the Mundys were is *ever* due—that is not the *meaning* of "down and out"—and as for the "law of averages," it doesn't exist, certainly not in the sense that he who has lost over a considerable length of time must, on the strength of all that accumulated defeat, inevitably begin to win. There is no mechanism in life, any more than at the gaming tables, that triggers any such equalizing or compensatory "law" into operation. A gambler at the wheel who bets the color black because the red has turned up on ten successive turns may tell himself that he is wisely heeding the law of averages, but that is only a comforting pseudoscientific name that he has attached to a wholly unscientific superstition. The roulette wheel has no memory, unless, that is, it has been fixed.

### HOW THE MIRACLE CAME TO PASS

It all began when Roland Agni, an Ace bandage wound round his face and over his blond curls, broke into Tycoon Park one night, bound and gagged the night watchman, and then, having relieved the old man of his key-ring, made his way to the underground bunker of Angela Whittling Trust, owner of

Tri-City's team of aging immortals. The only weapon Agni carried was his bat.

Silently he pushed open the heavy steel door and slipped into the vestibule of her apartment. From floor to ceiling the walls were lined with glass showcases containing cups and trophies two and three feet high, topped like wedding cakes with figurines in baseball togs, and lit from above by spotlights: the Patriot League Cup, the Honey Boy Evans Trophy, the World Series Cup, the Douglas D. Oakhart Triple Crown Award . . . Roland could identify each by its size and shape even before stealing down the corridor to gaze upon the hallowed objects. Further on gleamed a row of goldfish bowls, each containing a single baseball bearing the Patriot League insignia and hung with a small silver medallion identifying the relic within:

Phil Thor's
61⅓ Scoreless Innings
in a Row
1933

Vic Bragi's
535th Lifetime Home Run
1935

Smoky Woden's
Perfect Sixteen-Inning Game
1934

Double Play Number
216 of the 1935 Season
"Rustem-to-Izanagi-to-Mazda"

Like any American who had been a kid growing up in the era of the faultless Tycoon clubs of the early thirties, Agni was overcome when he discovered himself only inches from these record-breaking baseballs out of the Patriot League past. To be sure, the Tycoon stars of the Depression years whose names Agni read with such reverence were the same old-timers against whom he and the Mundys had been playing baseball all season long. Yet, to see *the* very ball with which Smoky Woden had registered the last out against the Butchers in that perfect sixteen-inning game back in '34 was a thrill bearing no resemblance to playing against old Smoky himself. *That* was no thrill at all, but downright humiliating. Yes, the more legendary the star, the more anguished was Roland to take the field with his eight clownish teammates, and thus come to be associated with them in the mind of someone he had idolized ever since he was a nine-year-old boy, dreaming of the Patriot League as of Paradise.

Now to the naked eye the ball with which Smoky had finished up his sixteen perfect innings back in '34 looked to be an exact replica of the one Vic Bragi had driven into the stands for his five hundred and thirty-fifth P. League home run in '35—be that as it may, there was no confusing the depth and quality of the awe that each inspired in someone with Agni's exquisitely refined feel for the game, one who could sense within his own motionless body that synchronization of strength, timing, and concentration that each achievement must have called forth. For all that he was an outfielder—and what an outfielder!— Roland had only to read "Double Play Number 216" for his muscular frame to vibrate with the rhythms that carry a ball from short to second to first, from second to short to first, from first to second and back to first for two! "Ah oh ee," he moaned, "ee oh ah . . . ah ah ah . . . whoo-up whoo-up pow . . ." Two hundred and sixteen times and never the same way twice! Every double play as different from the next as one snowflake from another—and each just as perfect! Oh this game, thought Roland, shuddering with ecstasy, how I love and adore this game!

Tommy Heimdall's
65th Double
1932

Tuck Selket's
23rd Pinch-Hit
1933

"All right, Agni," said Angela Trust, who had rolled her wheelchair to within point-blank range of her ecstatic and spellbound intruder, "drop the bat."

At the sight of the black revolver, Agni instinctively fell back from the display of famous balls, as though from a wild pitch.

"Drop it, Roland," repeated Mrs. Trust. "Pretend you've just drawn ball four, and drop it at your feet—or I'll send you to the showers for life."

The Louisville Slugger slipped from his hands to the carpet. "How," he muttered through the Ace bandage, while raising his hands over his head, "how do you even know for sure it's me?"

The elderly woman, a beauty still beneath the wrinkles, and imposing even in a wheelchair, kept the revolver trained on his groin. "Who else has been sending me candy and flowers for a week?" she said coldly.

"You didn't answer my letters!" cried Agni. "I didn't know what to do. *I had to see you.*"

"So you decided on this," she said, contemptuously. "Take that absurd thing off your face."

He did as he was told, returning the bandage to his right knee, which he had twisted the previous week stealing home against the Blues. "Boy," he said, adjusting his trousers, "that was really startin' to ache, too. I just didn't want the night watchman to recognize me, that was all."

"And is he dead? Did you crack his head for a home run, you fool?"

"No! Of course not! I just tied him up and gagged him . . . with . . . well . . . with a couple of my jocks. But I didn't do him no harm, I swear! Look, I wouldn't have done nothin' like this—but I had to! If I call, you don't even come to the phone. When I write you, you ignore me even worse. My telegrams—do you even *get* them?"

"Daily."

"Then why don't you answer! I am the league's leading batter and the outstanding candidate for rookie of the year—or I would be, if I was a Tycoon! Oh, Mrs. Trust, how can you be like this to someone who is hittin' .370!"

"The answer is no."

"But that don't make *sense*! *Nothin'* makes sense no more! *I don't understand!*"

"You're a center-fielder, Agni; nobody expects you to understand. There is more at stake than you can ever comprehend."

"But the pennant's what's at stake right now! Bragi can hardly swing from his rheumatism killin' him so—and Tommy

Heimdall's so darn tired he don't even come out for battin' practice! And Lou Polevik is pooped even worse! Them guys are goin' on sheer nerve! On what they was, not what they are!"

Sharply, she replied, "They are fine, courageous men. There will never be another outfield like them. In their prime, they made Meusel, Combs, and Ruth look nothing more than competent."

"But you'll lose the pennant—and to them two-bit Butchers! I could put you over the top, I swear!"

"And is that what you came here to tell me? Is that why you tied a night watchman in athletic supporters and stole in here with your mighty bat? Did you actually think I would negotiate a trade just because you threatened to fungo my brains against the wall? Or did you plan to rape me, Roland, to assault a seventy-two-year-old woman with a Louisville Slugger if she did not give in to your wishes? My God! Not even Cobb was that crazy!"

"But, holy gee, neither am I! I wouldn't *dream* of anything like that! Gosh, Mrs. Trust, what a thing to say to—to me! About you! And my bat!"

"Why then *bring* the bat, Roland?" she snapped.

"Why else?" he said, shrugging—and smiling. "To show you my form."

"And you expect me to believe that? Don't you think I've had the wonderful privilege of seeing your perfect form already?"

Of course he could tell from her tone that Angela Trust was being sarcastic, but that didn't make what she had said any less true: his form *was* perfect, and he knew it. Blushing, he said, "Not close up, though."

God, it's so, she thought. He wasn't going to bludgeon her into buying him—he was only going to try to seduce her with his form. Oh, he was a .370 hitter, all right—a peacock, a princeling, a prima donna, just like all the other .370 hitters she had known. They think they have only to step to the plate for the whole of humankind to fall to its knees in adoration. As though there is nothing in this world so beautiful to behold as the stride and the swing and the follow-through of a man who can hit .370 in the big leagues. *And is there?*

"Pick it up," she said, without, however, lowering the pistol, "and come into my parlor. But one false move, Roland, and you're out."

"I swear, Mrs. Trust, I only want to show you my swing. In slow motion."

At each end of Mrs. Trust's parlor was a life-sized oil painting, one of her husband, wearing a dark suit and a no-nonsense expression, and seated before a vault at Trust Guaranty Trust; the other was of her father, also in a business suit, but posed with an ax over his shoulder; behind him stretched a sea of stumps. Projecting from the two side walls, some fifteen feet above the floor and at an angle of forty-five degrees, were several dozen baseball bats; at first glance, they looked like two rows of closely packed flagpoles. Slowly walking the length of this old lady's parlor, from the portrait of the great banker who had been her husband, to the portrait of the great lumber baron who had been her father, one could gaze up on either hand at the bat of each and every Tri-City Tycoon who had ever hit .300 or more in a single season. They formed an unbroken shelter beneath which Angela Whittling Trust conducted her affairs.

Agni pointed with his own bat to the one directly over his head.

"Wow. Who's *that* belong to?"

"A forty-two ouncer," she replied. "Who else? Mike Mazda."

"Look at the length of that thing!"

"Thirty-eight inches."

Agni whistled. "That's a lot a' bat, ain't it?"

"He was a lot of man."

"Mine here is thirty-four inches, thirty-two ounces, ya' know. That's how come the writers say I 'snap the whip.' That's how come I got that drivin' force, see. It ain't because my wrists is weak that I like the narrow handle, it's because they're so damn strong. And that's the truth. My forearms and my wrists are like steel, Mrs. Trust. Want to feel them and see for yourself? Want to see me take my cut now? In slow motion? I can swing real slow for ya', and ya' can follow it to see just how damn level it is. Hey, want to try an experiment with a coin? When I'm standin' in there, waitin' for the pitch, ya' know, I hold the big end of the bat so straight and so still, ya' can balance a dime on the end of it. And that's the truth. Most fellas, when they start that sweep forward, they got some kind of damn hitch or dip in there, so tiny sometimes you can't even see it without a microscope—but just try to balance a coin on that big end there when they start their swing, and you see what happens. They see that ball acomin' at them, and they will drop their hands, maybe only that much, but that is all it takes to throw your timin' to hell. And your power too. Nope, there is only one way to be a great hitter like me, and it ain't movin' the bat in two directions, I'll tell ya'. Same with the stride. Me, I just raise up my front foot and set it back down just about where I raised it up from. You don't *need* no more stride than that. I see fellas take a big stride, I got to turn away—that's true, Mrs. Trust, it actually makes me nauseous to look at, and I don't care if it's Ott himself. They might just as easy put a knife to themselves and slice off two inches of good shoulder muscle, because that's what they are givin' away in leverage. I just don't understand why they want to look like tightrope walkers up there, when all you got to do with that foot is just *raise* it up and *set* it down. A' course, you got to have eyes too, but then I don't have to tell you about my eyes. They say my eyes are so sharp that I can read the General's signature off a fastball comin' up to the plate. Well, if that's what the pitchers wanna tell each other, that's okay with me. But between you and me, Mrs. Trust, I ain't some eagle that can read handwritin' comin' at me at sixty miles a hour—all I *can* tell is if the thing is goin' to break or not, because of the way them stitches are spinnin'. If you want, I could stand behind home plate with you durin' battin' practice, and you tell the pitcher to mix 'em up however he likes and ninety per cent of the time I promise I will holler out the curveballs even before they break. Maybe I *could* read General Oakhart's signature on a change-up, but frankly I ain't never bothered to try. It ain't goin' to help me get a base hit, is it—so why bother? Want to see me swing again?"

By now the pistol lay in her lap like a kitten.

"Want to see me take my cut now?" Agni repeated, when the old woman remained frozen, seemingly uncomprehending in her chair. "Mrs. Trust?"

*He's Luke Gofannon*, she was thinking, *it's Luke Gofannon all over again.*

*

There had been five men in her life who mattered, and none
had been her husband; her affair with him had begun only
after he was in the ground. Of the five—two Mundys, a Greenback, a Yankee, and a Tiger—she had loved only one with all
her heart, the Loner, Luke Gofannon. Not that he was a fiercely
passionate man in the way of a Cobb or a Gamesh; no, it was
the great haters who made the great lovers, or such had been
Angela's experience with America's stars. To yield to the man
who had stolen more bases than anyone in history—by terrifying as many with his menacing gaze as with his surgical
spikes—was like nothing she had ever known before as a
woman; it was more like being a catcher, blocking home plate
against a bloodthirsty base runner, than being a perfumed
beauty with breasts as smooth as silk and a finishing school education; she felt like a base being stolen—no, like a bank being
robbed. Throughout he glared down at her like a gunman,
snarling in his moment of ecstasy, "Take that, you society slit!"
But then, where another would collapse with a shudder,
shrivel up, and sleep, the great Ty would (as it were) just continue on around the bag and try for two; and then for three!
And then he would break for the plate, and to Angela's weary
astonishment, make it, standing! a four-bagger, where another
player would have been content with a solid base hit! The clandestine affair that had begun in his hotel room in 1911—on the
day he won the batting crown with an average of .420—came
to a violent end at the conclusion of the 1915 season, when he
decided to perform upon her an unnatural act he described as
"poling one out of the ball park foul." Actually she did not so
much resist as take longer to think it over than he had patience
for, or pride. Having stolen his record-breaking ninety-six
bases that year, he was not accustomed to waiting around for
what he wanted.

According to the next day's newspapers, Mrs. Trust suffered
her broken nose in the bath of a Detroit hotel room; true
enough, only she had not got it by "slipping in the tub," as the
papers reported.

The Yankee was Ruth. How could she resist?

"George? This is Angela Whittling Trust. We happen to be
in the same hotel."

"Come on up."

"With Spenser or without?"

"Surprise me." He laughed. It was October of 1927; he had already hit sixty home runs in the course of the regular season, and that afternoon, in the third World Series game against the Pirates, he'd hit another in the eighth with two on.

*Surprise me*, the Bambino had said, but the surprise was on her when he answered her knock, for the notorious bad boy was unclothed and smoking a cigar. Still slender, still silken, Angela was nonetheless a white-haired woman of fifty-five in the fall of '27, and in her silver-fox cape the last woman in the world one would think to greet in anything but the manner prescribed by society. Which was of course why the Babe had chosen to appear nude at the door—and why Mrs. Trust had entered without any sign that she was discomfited in the slightest. Of course he was a clown, a glutton, an egomaniac, a spoiled brat, and a baby through and through . . . but what was any of that beside those tremendous home runs?

"I been expectin' ya', Whittlin' Trust."

"Have you now." She removed her cape and draped it over a trophy that the Babe had placed to ice in a champagne bucket. What wit. What breeding. She took a good look at him—what legs. But who cared, with all those home runs?

"Since when?" Angela asked, removing her gloves in a most provocative way.

"Since 1921, Whittlin' Trust."

"Really? You thought I'd ring you up for fifty-nine home runs, did you?"

He smiled and sucked his cigar. "And one hundred seventy r.b.i.s. And a hundred seventy-seven runs. And a hundred nineteen extra-base hits. Yeah, Whittlin' Trust," said the Yankee immortal, chortling, "as a matter of fact, I thought you might."

"No," she said, as she set down her watch and her rings and began to unbutton her blouse, "I thought it would be best to wait. I have my reputation to consider. How was I to know you weren't just another flash-in-the-pan, George?"

"Come 'ere, W.T., and I'll show you how."

A season with Ruth—and then in '29, the first of her pitchers, the first of her Mundys, the speedballer, Prince Charles

Tuminikar. Yes, they called him a prince when he came up, and they called swinging and missing at that fastball of his "chasin' Charlies." That was all he bothered to throw back then, but it was enough: 23–4 his rookie year, and by July 4 of the following season, 9–0. Then one afternoon, locked in a 0–0 tie going into the fourteenth, he killed a man. Everyone agreed it was a chest-high pitch, but it must have been coming a hundred miles an hour at least, and a dumb rookie named O'del, the last pinch-hitter off the Terra Inc. bench, stepped into the damn thing—exactly as Bob Yamm was to do against Ockatur thirteen years later—and he was pronounced dead by the umpire even before the trainer could make it out to the plate with an ice pack. Everyone agreed O'del was to blame, except Tuminikar. He left the mound and went immediately to the police station to turn himself in.

Of course no one was about to bring charges against a man for throwing a chest-high pitch in a baseball game, though maybe if they had, he could have served four or five years for manslaughter, and come on out of jail to be his old self on the mound. As it was, he never threw a fastball of any consequence again, or won more games in a season than he lost. Or was worth much of anything to Angela Whittling Trust.

And so it was, in her sixtieth year, that she came to Luke Gofannon, the silent Mundy center-fielder who had broken Ruth's record in 1928, as great a switch-hitter as the game had ever known, a man who made both hitting and fielding look like acts of meditation, so effortless and tranquil did he appear even in the midst of running with the speed of a locomotive, or striking at the ball with the force of a pile driver.

"You're poetry in motion," said Angela, and Luke, having reflected upon this observation of hers for an hour (they were in bed), remarked at last:

"Could be. I ain't much for readin'."

"I've never seen anything like you, Luke. The equanimity, the composure, the serenity . . ."

To this he answered, in due time, "Well, I ain't never been much for excitement. I just take things as they come."

His exquisitely proportioned, powerful physique in repose —the repose itself, that pensive, solitary air that had earned him his nickname—filled Angela with a wild tenderness that she had not known as mistress to the ferocious Tiger, the buffoonish Yankee, and the ill-fated fireballer they now called Jolly Cholly T.; he awakened an emotion in her at once so wistful and so full of yearning, that she wondered if perhaps she should not have been a mother after all, as Spenser had wanted her to be, a good mother and a good wife. But before another season began, she would be sixty. Her face, her breasts, her hips, her thighs, for all that she had given them everything money could buy (yes, these had been her children), soon would be the face, breasts, and thighs of a thirty-five-year-old woman. And then what would she do with her time?

"I love you, Luke," she told the Loner.

Another hour passed.

"Luke? Did you hear me, darling?"

"I heard."

"Don't you want to know *why* I love you?"

"I know why, I guess."

"Why?"

"My bein' a pome."

"But you *are* a poem, my sweet!"

"That's what I said."

"Luke—tell me. What do you love most in the world? Because I'm going to make you love me just as much. More! What do you love most in the entire world?"

"In the entire world?"

"Yes!"

It was dawn before he came up with the answer.

"Triples."

"Triples?"

"Yep."

"I don't understand, darling. What about home runs?"

"Nope. Triples. Hittin' triples. Don't get me wrong, Angela, I ain't bad-mouthin' the home run and them what hits 'em, me included. But smack a home run and that's it, it's all over."

"And a triple?" she asked. "Luke, you must tell me. I have to know. What is it about the triple that makes you love it so much? Tell me, Luke, tell me!" There were tears in her eyes, the tears of jealous rage.

"You sure you up to it?" asked Luke, as astonished as it was in his nature to be. "Looks like you might be gettin' a little cold."

"You love the triple more than Horace Whittling's daughter, more than Spenser Trust's wife—*tell me why!*"

"Well," he said in his slow way, "smackin' it, first off. Off the wall, up the alley, down the line, however it goes, it goes with that there crack. Then runnin' like blazes. 'Round first and into second, and the coach down there cryin' out to ya', 'Keep comin'.' So ya' make the turn at second, and ya' head for third—and now ya' know that throw is comin', ya' know it is right on your tail. So ya' slide. Two hunerd and seventy feet of runnin' behind ya', and with all that there momentum, ya' hit it—whack, into the bag. Over he goes. Legs. Arms. Dust. Hell, ya' might be in a tornado, Angela. Then ya' hear the ump—'Safe!' And y're in there . . . Only that ain't all."

"What then? Tell me everything, Luke! What then?"

"Well, the best part, in a way. Standin' up. Dustin' off y'r breeches and standin' up there on that bag. See, Angela, a home run, it's great and all, they're screamin' and all, but then you come around those bases and you disappear down into the dugout and that's it. But not with a triple . . . Ya' get it, at all?"

"Yes, yes, I get it."

"Yep," he said, running the whole wonderful adventure through in his mind, his eyes closed, and his arms crossed behind him on the pillow beneath his head, "big crowd . . . sock a triple . . . nothin' like it."

"We'll see about that, Mr. Loner," whispered Angela Trust.

Poor little rich girl! How she tried! Did an inning go by during the two seasons of their affair, that she did not know his batting average to the fourth digit? You're batting this much, you're fielding that much, nobody goes back for them like you, my darling. Nobody swings like you, nobody runs like you, nobody is so beautiful just fielding an easy fly ball!

Was ever a man so admired and adored? Was ever a man so worshipped? Did ever an aging woman struggle so to capture and keep her lover's heart?

But each time she asked, no matter how circuitously (and prayerfully) she went about it, the disappointment was the same.

"Lukey," she whispered in his ear, as he lay with his fingers interlaced beneath his head, "which do you love more now, my darling, a stolen base, or me?"

"You."

"Oh, darling," and she kissed him feverishly. "Which do you love more, a shoestring catch, or me?"

"Oh, you."

"Oh, my all-star Adonis! Which do you love more, dearest Luke, a fastball letter-high and a little tight, or me?"

"Well . . ."

"Well what?"

"Well, if I'm battin' left-handed, and we're at home—"

"Luke!"

"But then a' course, if I'm battin' rightie, you, Angel."

"Oh, my precious, Luke, what about—what about a home run?"

"You or a home run, you mean?"

"Yes!"

"Well, now I really got to think . . . Why . . . why . . . why, I'll be damned. I got to be honest. Geez. I guess—you. Well, isn't that somethin'."

He who had topped Ruth's record, loved her more than all his home runs put together! "My darling," and in her joy, the fading beauty offered to Gofannon what she had withheld even from Cobb.

"And Luke," she asked, when the act had left the two of them weak and dazed with pleasure, "Luke," she asked, when she had him just where she wanted him, "what about . . . your triples? Whom do you love more now, your triples, or your Angela Whittling Trust?"

While he thought that one through, she prayed. *It has to be me. I am flesh. I am blood. I need. I want. I age. Someday I will even die. Oh Luke, a triple isn't even a person—it's a thing!*

But the thing it was. "I can't tell a lie, Angela," said the Loner. "There just ain't nothin' like it."

Never had a man, in word or deed, caused her such anguish and such grief. This illiterate ballplayer had only to say "Nothin' like it" about those God damn triples for a lifetime's desire to come back at her as frantic despair. Oh, Luke, if you had only known me in my prime, back when Ty was hitting

.420! God, I was irresistible! Back before the lively ball, oh you should have seen and held me then! But look at me now, she thought bitterly, examining herself later that night in her mirrored dressing room—just *look* at me! Ghastly! The body of a thirty-five-year-old woman! She turned slowly about, till she could see herself reflected from behind. "Face it, Angela," she told her reflection, "thirty-six." And she began to sob.

"Luke! Luke! Luke! Luke! Luke!"

It was only the name of a Patriot League center-fielder that she howled, but it came so piercingly from her throat, and with such pitiable yearning, that it might have stood for all that a woman, no matter how rich, beautiful, powerful, and proud she may he, can never hope to possess.

And then he was traded, and then he was dead.

And so that spring she took up with a Greenback rookie, a beautiful Babylonian boy named Gil Gamesh.

"Till I was eight or nine, I knew we was the only Babylonian family in Tri-City, but I figured there was more of us out in California or Florida, or some place like that, where it was warm all the time. Don't ask me how a kid gets that kind of idea, he just gets it. Bein' lonely, I suppose. Then one day I got the shock of my life when my old man sat me down and he told me we wasn't just the only ones in Tri-City, or even in Massachusetts, but in the whole damn U.S.A. Oh, my old man, he was a proud old son of a bitch, Angela—you would a' liked that old fire-eater. He wouldn't change his ways for nobody or nothin'. 'What do you mean you're a Babylonian?' they'd ask him when he filled out some kind of form or somethin'—'what the hell is God damn Babylonian supposed to be? If you're some kind of wop or Polack or somethin', say it, so we know where we stand!' Oh, that got him goin' all right, callin' him those things. 'I Babylonian! Free country! Any damn thing—that *my* damn thing!' That's just what he'd tell 'em, whether it meant gettin' the job or losin' it. And so that's what I wrote down in school too, under what I was: Babylonian. And that's how come they started throwin' them rocks at me. Livin' down by the docks in those days, there wasn't any kind of person you didn't see. We even had some Indians livin' there, Red Indians, workin' as longshoremen, smokin' God damn peace pipes on their lunch hour. Christ, we had Arabs, we had *everythin'*. And they'd all take turns chasin' me home from school. First for a few blocks the Irish kids threw rocks at me. Then the German kids threw rocks at me. Then the Eye-talian, then the colored, then them Mohawk kids, whoopin' at me like it was some honest to Christ war dance; then down by the chop suey joint, the Chink's kid; then the Swedes—hell, even the Jew kids threw rocks at me, while they was runnin' away from the kids throwin' rocks at them. I'm tellin' you, it was somethin', Angela. Belgian kids, Dutch kids, Spanish kids, even some God damn kid from Switzerland—I never seen one before, and I never ever heard of one since, but there he is, on my tail, shoutin' at the top of his lungs, 'Get outta here, ya' lousy little Babylonian bastard! Go back to where you belong, ya' dirty bab!' Me, I didn't even know what a bab was. Maybe those kids didn't either. Maybe it was somethin' they picked up at home or somethin'. I know my old man never heard it before. But, Christ, did it get him mad. 'They you call bab? Or *bad*? Sure not *bad*?' 'I'm sure, Poppa,' I told him. 'Bab,' he'd say, 'bab . . .' and then he'd just start goin' wild, tremblin' and screamin' so loud my old lady went into hidin'. 'Nobody my boy bab call if here I am! Nobody! Country *free*! God damn *thing*! Bab they want—we them bab show all right *good*!' Only I didn't show them nothin', 'ceptin' my tail. When those rocks started comin' my way, I just up and run for my life. And that just made my old man even madder. 'Free! Free! Underneath me?' That's how he used to say 'understand.' Or maybe that's how all Babylonians say it, when they speak En-glish. I wouldn't know, since we was the only ones I ever met. Don't worry, it got him into a lot of fights in bars and stuff, sayin' 'underneath' for 'understand' like that. 'Don't again to let you them call bab on my boy—underneath? *Ever*!' 'But they're throwin' rocks big as my head—at my head!' I told him. 'Then back throw rock on them!' he told me. 'Throw them big rock, throw you more big!' 'But there are a hundred of them throwin', Poppa, and only one a' me.' 'So,' he says, grabbin' me by the throat to make his point, 'throw you more *hard*. And *strong*! *Underneath?*'

"So that's how I come to pitchin', Angela. I got myself a big pile a' rocks, and I lined up these beer and whiskey bottles that I'd fish outta the bay, and I'd stand about fifty feet away, and then I'd start throwin'. You mick bastard! You wop bastard! You kike bastard! You nigger bastard! You Hun son of a bitch! That's how I developed my pick-off play. I'd shout real angry, 'Run, nigger!' but then I'd spin around and throw at the bottle that was the wop. In the beginnin', a' course, out on the street, bein' so small and inexperienced and all, and with the pressure on and so forth, I was so damn confused, and didn't know what half the words meant anyway, I'd be callin' the wops kikes and the niggers micks, and damned if I ever figured out what in hell to call that kid from Switzerland to insult him—'Hey,' I'd say, 'you God damn kid from God damn Switzerland,' but by the time I got all that out, he was gone. Well, anyway, by and by I got most of the names straightened around, and even where I didn't, they stopped laughin', on account of how good I got with them rocks. And about then I picked up this here fierce way I got too, just by imitatin' my dad, mostly. Oh, those little boys didn't much care to chase me home from school anymore after that. And you should a' heard my old man crowin' then. 'Now you them show what bab do! Now they underneath! And good!' And I was so damn proud and happy, and relieved a' course, and a' course I was only ten, so I just didn't think to ask him right off what else a bab could do. And then he up and died around then—they beat the shit out of him in a bar, a bunch of guys from Tierra del Fuego, who had it in for Babylonians, my mother said— and, well, that was it. I didn't have no father no more to teach me, so I never did know how to be the kind of Babylonian he wanted me to be, except by throwin' things and sneerin' a lot. And that's more or less what I been doin' ever since."

A callow, untutored boy, a wharf rat, enraged son of a crazed father—no poem he, but still the greatest left-handed rookie in history, and nothing to sneer at at sixty-one . . . But then he threw that pitch at Mike Masterson's larynx, and Gil was an ex-lover too. To be sure, in the months after his disappearance, she had waited for some message from the exile, a plea for her to intervene in his behalf. But none came, perhaps because he knew that she was not the kind of woman whose intervention anyone would ever take seriously. "Speak a word to the Commissioner about that maniac," her husband had cautioned her, "and I will expose you to the world, Angela, for the tramp that you are. Every loudmouth Ty and Babe and Gil who comes along!"

Even in her grief she found the strength to taunt him. "Would you prefer I slept with bullpen catchers?"

"Look at you, the carriage of Caesar's wife, and the morals of a high school harlot who pulls down her pants for the football team."

"I have my diversions, Spenser, and you have yours."

"Diversions? I happen to be the patron and the patriarch of a great American metropolis. I have made Tri-City into the Florence of America. I am a financier, a sportsman, and a patron of the arts. I endow museums. I build libraries. My baseball team is an inspiration to the youth and the men of the U.S.A. I could have been the Governor of this state, Angela. Some say I could have been the President of the country, if only I did not have as my wife a woman whose name is scribbled on locker room walls."

"You diminish my accomplishments, Spenser, though, I must say, you certainly do justice to your own."

"Babe Ruth," he said contemptuously.

"Yes, Babe Ruth."

"What do you do after you make love to Babe Ruth? Discuss international affairs? Or Benvenuto Cellini?"

"We eat hot dogs and drink pop."

"I wouldn't doubt it."

"Don't," said Angela Whittling Trust.

"A woman," he said bitterly, "with your aristocratic profile."

"A woman does not live by her profile alone, my dear."

"Oh? And in what ways is a baseball player able to gratify you that a billionaire is not?" He was a fit and handsome man, with no more doubt of his prowess in sex than in banking. "I'd be interested to learn wherein Babe Ruth is more of a man than Spenser Trust."

"But he isn't more of a man, darling. He's more of a boy. That's the whole point."

"And that is irresistible to you, is it?"

"To me," said his wife, "and about a hundred million other American citizens as well."

"You gum-chewing, star-struck adolescent! Hear me now,

Angela: if at the age of sixty-one you should now take it into your selfish, spoiled head to sirenize a Tri-City Tycoon—"

"I assured you long ago that I would not cuckold you with any of your players. I realize by what a slender thread your authority, as it were, hangs."

"Because I am not running a stud farm for aged nymphomaniacs!"

"I understand what you are running. It is something more on the order of a money-making machine."

"Call it what you will. They are the most accomplished team in Organized Baseball, and they are not to be tampered with by a bored and reckless bitch who is utterly without regard for the rules of civilized life. A fastball pitcher's floozie! Whore to whomever hits the longest home run! That's all you are, Angela—a stadium slut!"

"Or slit, as the players so neatly put it. No, it wouldn't do for the Governor of the state to be married to a slit instead of a lady, would it, Spenser? And whoever heard of the President being married to a wayward woman? It isn't done that way in America, is it, my patron and patriarch?"

"To think, you have kept me from the White House just for the sake of debauching yourself with baseball stars."

"To think," replied his wife, "you would keep me from debauching myself with baseball stars, just for the sake of getting into the White House."

That winter, while Angela waited in dread for the news that Gil Gamesh was dead (if not beaten to a pulp like his father before him, stomped to death by Tierra del Fuegans whom he had insulted in some poolroom somewhere, then dead by his own wrathful hand), her own husband was fatally injured in a train wreck. His broken body was removed from the private car that had been speeding him to Chicago for a meeting with Judge Landis, and Angela was summoned to the hospital to bid him farewell. When she arrived she found his bed surrounded by his lawyers, whom he had called together to be sure that the dynasty was in order before he took his leave of it; all fifteen attorneys were in tears when they left the room. Then the Tri-City Tycoons were called in. The regulars, like eight sons, stood on one side of the bed, the pitching staff

lined up on the other, and the remaining players gathered together at his feet, which he himself could no longer feel; they
had come in uniform to say goodbye. Hospital regulations had
made it necessary for them to remove their spikes in the corridor, but once inside his room, they had donned them again
and crossed the floor to the dying owner's bedside with that
clackety-clack-clack that had always been music to his ears.

Angela stood alone by the window, hers the only dry eyes in
the room. Dry, and burning with hatred, for Spenser had just
announced that he had passed the ownership of the club on to
his wife.

The players moved up to say farewell, in the order in which
they batted. He grasped their powerful hands with the little
strength that remained in his own, and when he spoke his last
words to each of them, they had virtually to put their ears to
his lips to understand what he was saying. He was fading
quickly now.

"Lay off the low ones, Tom, you're golfin' 'em."

"I will, Mr. Trust, I will—s'long, Mr. Trust . . ."

"Mike, your ass is in the dugout on those curveballs. Stand
strong in there, big fella."

"Yes, sir. Always, sir . . . See ya', sir . . ."

"If I had a son, Tuck, I'd have wanted him to be able to
pinch-hit like you."

"Oh, jeez, Mr. Trust, I won't forget that, ever . . ."

"Victor—Victor, what can I say, lad? If it's 3 and 0, and he
lays it in there, suit yourself."

"I will, Boss, I will. Oh thank you, Mr. Trust."

"Just make sure it's in there. No bad pitches."

"No, never, sir, never . . ."

Finally there was just his wife and himself.

She had never despised him more. "And me, Spenser?" she
asked, shaking with rage at the thought of all he had burdened
her with. "Just what am I supposed to do with your wonderful
team?"

He beckoned for her to come around to the side of his pillow. In one of his bandaged hands, it turned out, he was
clutching a baseball. With a final effort of his patriarchal will,
he tossed it to her. "Learn to be a responsible human being,

Angela," and with that, the Lorenzo de' Medici of Massachusetts closed his eyes and passed into oblivion.

. . . Now, to the Roland Agni who would woo her with his swing and his follow-through, Angela Trust said, "For your information, Agni, I had you scouted when you were eleven years old. What do you think of that?" Nothing wistful in her voice, nothing flirtatious or lascivious, much as he reminded her of the Loner who had been the love of her life; no, remembering what she had been, she remembered who she was—*a responsible human being.*

Yes, a decade earlier Spenser had died, leaving her holding the ball, and the ball had been her salvation.

"You *did*?" Agni said.

"I have a dossier on you going back to the fifth grade. I have photographs of you at bat against your uncle Art on a family picnic in the year 1936, him in his shirtsleeves and mustache, and you in overalls and sneakers."

"You *do*?"

"Young man, the day you graduated from high school, who was the first on line to offer you a contract? That was no 'hunch' on my part, I wasn't just hopping on the bandwagon like the rest of my colleagues. I had arrived at my decision about you when you were still playing in that vacant lot at the corner of Chestnut and Summit."

"You *had*?"

"But you and your dad went with the Mundys instead. Well, so be it. Life must go on. I have reports on my desk right now of six-year-old boys, little tykes who still won't even go to sleep with the light off, who nonetheless have the makings of big leaguers. They're my concern now, not you."

"*But*—"

"But what? Win the pennant? I'd give my eyeteeth for that flag. If any Tycoon team ever deserved it, it's these stars of a decade ago, who have come out of retirement so as to keep us all above water during these terrible years. Sure they need help right now. But there are the Mundys to think of, too."

"But the Mundys are fifty games out of first! They're finishing the lowest last in history!"

"And without you, they would not finish at all."

"So what! They don't *deserve* to finish! *And they don't deserve me!* Mrs. Trust, I am a Tycoon dressed up in a Mundy baseball suit, and that's the truth! Ya' have to trade for me, Mrs. Trust —ya' gotta!"

"And win the flag in a seven-team league? You are all that makes the Mundys major league. I tremble to think of them without you."

"I tremble thinkin' of them *with* me! Now we even got Ockatur! The dwarf who blinded Yamm! And Nickname Damur, who crippled that beautiful girl! It's like livin' with criminals—and all I want to do is just play *ball*!" And here, seated beneath Mike Mazda's forty-two-ounce bat, the .370 hitter fell to weeping.

"Roland," she said, unable to bear the sight of him in tears, "I'm going to tell you something now that's going to astound you. Stop crying, Roland, and listen carefully to what I have to say."

"You're tradin' for me!" he shouted triumphantly.

"*Listen* to me, I said. You may not understand this, it may well be beyond you—God knows, it's beyond older and more worldly men than yourself—but the fact is this: there is nothing that the enemies of this country would like *better* than for Angela Whittling Trust to buy Roland Agni from the Ruppert Mundys."

"The who?"

"The enemies of America. Those who want to see this nation destroyed."

"And if you buy me, they'll like it?"

"If I buy you, they will adore it."

"But—"

"But why? But how? Believe me, I do not talk tommyrot. I do not have the largest army of baseball scouts in America in my employ for nothing. It isn't just about exceptional young athletes that my scouts keep me informed. They live close to the people. In many cases they are not even suspected of being Tycoon scouts at all, but appear to their friends and neighbors to be ordinary townsfolk like themselves. As a result, I know what goes on in this country. Not even the Federal Bureau of Investigation knows what I do, until I tell them."

"But—but why me? I don't get it, Mrs. Trust. Why does Hitler—"

"Hitler? Who mentioned that madman? Oh no, Roland, we are dealing with an enemy far more cunning and insidious than that deluded psychopath out to conquer the world with bombs and bullets. No, even while this war rages on against the Germans and the Japs, the other war against us has already begun, the invisible war, the silent assault upon the very fabric that holds us together as a nation. You look puzzled. What *does* hold this nation together, Roland? The stars and the stripes? Is that what men talk about over a beer, how much they love Old Glory? On the streetcars, on the trains, on the jitneys, what does one American say to another, to strike up a conversation, 'O say can you see by the dawn's early light?' No! He says, 'Hey, how'd the Tycoons do today?' He says, 'Hey, did Mazda get himself another homer?' Now, Roland, now do you remember what it is that links in brotherhood millions upon millions of American men, makes kin of competitors, makes neighbors of strangers, makes friends of enemies, if only while the game is going on? *Baseball!* And that is how they propose to destroy America, young man, that is their evil and ingenious plan—*to destroy our national game!*"

"But—but *how?* How can they do a thing like that?"

"By making it a joke! By making it a laughingstock! They are planning to laugh us into the grave!"

"But—*who* is?"

"The Reds," said Mrs. Trust, studying his reaction.

"Aww, but they're finishin' in the money, Mrs. Trust, back a' the Cards. I don't get it. What's their kick?"

"No, no, not Cincinnati, my boy. If only it were . . . No, it's not Bill McKechnie's boys we're up against this year, but General Joe Stalin's. The *Russian* Reds, Roland. From Stalin-to-Lenin-to-Marx."

"Well, I'm sure glad to hear it don't involve Johnny Vander Meer. That'd be like Shoeless Joe again."

He could not understand—but then could General Oakhart? Could Kenesaw Mountain Landis? "Roland, it may sound outlandish and far-fetched to you, and yet, I assure you, *it is true.* In order to destroy America, the Communists in Russia and their agents around the world are going to attempt to destroy the major leagues. They have selected as their target the weakest link in the majors—our league. And the weakest link within our league—the Mundys. Roland, why do you think the Mundys are homeless? Whose idea do you think that was?"

"Well . . . the Mundy brothers . . . no?"

"The Mundy brothers are only *pawns*. Not even fellow travelers—just stupid pawns, who can be manipulated for a few hundred thousand dollars without their even knowing it. Much as I despise those playboys, the fact remains that the plan to send the Mundys on the road while the U.S. government takes over the stadium in Port Ruppert was not hatched in the Mundy front office. *It began in our own War Department.* Do you understand the implications of what I have just said?"

"Well, I don't know . . . for sure."

"The plan was conceived in our own War Department. In other words, *there are Communists in the War Department of the United States government. There are Communists in the State Department.*"

"Gee, there are?"

"Roland, there are even Communists in the Patriot League itself . . . *right* . . . *this* . . . *minute!*"

"There *are*?"

"The owner of the Kakoola Reapers, to name but one."

"Mr. *Mazuma*?"

"Yes, Mr. 'Mazuma,' as you call him, is a Communist Spy."

"But—"

"Roland, who else is making such a mockery of baseball? Who else so mocks and shames the free enterprise system? Yes, through the person of our friend, Mr. Frank Mazuma, they are going to turn the people, not only against the national game, but simultaneously against the profit system itself. Midgets! Horse races! And he'll have colored on that team soon enough, just wait and see. I've had him under surveillance now since the day he came into the league, I know every move he makes before he makes it. Colored, Roland, colored major league players! And that is only the beginning. Only wait until Hitler is defeated. Only wait until the international Communist conspiracy can invade every nook and cranny of our national life. They will do to every sacred American institution, to everything we hold dear, just what Mazuma has done to the integrity and honor of our league. They will make a travesty of it! Our own people will grow ashamed and bewildered as everything they once lived by is reduced to the level of a joke. And in our ridiculousness, our friends and our neighbors, those who have looked to us as a model and an inspiration, will come to despise us. And all this the Communists will have accomplished without even dropping a bomb or firing a bullet. They will have Frank Mazumas everywhere, they will do to General Motors and to U.S. Steel just what they have done to us—turn those great corporations into cartoons out of a Russian newspaper! They've given up on the idea of taking over the working class, Roland—that didn't work, so now they are going to take over the *free enterprise system itself*. How? By installing spies as presidents of great companies, and saboteurs as chairmen of the board! Mark my word, the day will come when in the guise of an American capitalist, a friend of Big Business and a member of the Republican Party, a Communist will run for President of the United States. And if he is elected, he will ring down the curtain on the American tragedy—a tragedy because it will have been made into a farce! And when that terrible day comes, Roland, when a President Mazuma is installed in the White House, they won't need a Red Army marching down Trust Street to blow up the Industrial and Maritime Exchange; the poor bewildered American people will do it themselves . . . But then they won't be Americans by then, no, no, not as you and I know them. No, when baseball goes, Roland, you can kiss America goodbye. Try to imagine it, Roland, an American summer Sunday without doubleheaders, an American October without the World Series, March in America without spring training. No, they can call it America, but it'll be something very different by then. Roland, once the Communists have made a joke of the majors, the rest will fall like so many dominoes.

"You don't believe me, do you? Well, neither do the men at the top of the leagues—'Angela, you're blaming the Communists for what you people have brought upon yourselves. You've let the league go to pot, and now you are paying the price with playboys like the Mundys, and clowns like Mazuma, and undesirables like the little Jew.' But, Roland, who *is* the little Jew? Now, I have no final proof as yet, this is still only conjecture, but it all fits together too neatly to he dismissed out of hand. The Jew who bought the Greenbacks in 1933, this seemingly comical little fellow in his dark suit and hat, this foreigner with an accent who plunged what we believed to be his life's earnings into those scandal-ridden Greenbacks, *is a Communist agent too.* Yes, taking his orders from Moscow—*and* his money! But tell this to Frick, or Harridge, or Oakhart, or even Judge Landis. Behind my back, they call me a fanatic, a bitter old woman who has lost her looks and her lovers and now has nothing better to do than cause them trouble. But I have not 'lost' anything—I have only fulfilled the request my husband made of me on his deathbed. 'Become a responsible human being,' he told me. I hated him for saying that, Roland. In my selfish womanish ignorance, I did not even know the meaning of the words. I wanted poetry, passion, romance, adventure. Well, let me tell you, there is more poetry and passion and romance and adventure in being a responsible human being than in all the boudoirs in France! And I do not intend to be irresponsible ever again!"

"In other words," said Agni, tears once more welling up in his eyes now that he saw that she was finished, "in other words, on account of your husband and what he said and so on, and all that other stuff you just said, I am stuck with the Mundys for the rest of my life!"

"Would you prefer to be 'stuck' with Communism, you stupid boy? Would you rather that you and your children and your children's children be 'stuck' with atheistical totalitarian Communism till the end of time?"

"But I ain't *got* no children—or children's children. *I swear!*"

"Roland Agni, if you make a deal to be traded you will have to make it with the enemies of the United States, *as* an enemy of the United States. However, if you care more for your country than for yourself, you will play ball not with the Communists, but with the Ruppert Mundys!"

"But you could win the *pennant*, Mrs. Trust—"

"And enslave mankind in the bargain? You must be mad!"

As usual in Tri-City, while the Tycoons battled to win the flag, across town the team once considered their rivals, if not in league standings then in the hearts of the local fans, made their annual attempt to climb out of the second division and finish in the money. It was a feat that the Greenbacks had not managed yet in the years since Gil Gamesh and the Whore House Gang had been driven from the league, not even when they won more games than they lost. Eager and accomplished as the players might be, invariably they began to falter in August, and by the season's end the team was firmly ensconced in fifth or sixth. At first glance it seemed (to the moralists, that is) that the scandals that had destroyed the fiery Greenback teams of '33 and '34 had left behind "a legacy of shame" which inevitably eroded the confidence of newcomers to the club, just as it had poisoned the spirit of the veterans of those unfortunate years. Comparison had only to be made to what had befallen the Chicago White Sox of the American League, after it was discovered at the tail-end of the 1920 season that the pennant-winning 1919 team, the team of Shoeless Joe Jackson and Eddie Cicotte, had thrown the World Series to Cincinnati: as all the world knows, it was sixteen years before the demoralized White Sox finished in the first division again.

Popular as such explanations proved to be with the punitive masses, those inside the game suggested that what stood between these perfectly competent Greenback teams and a first division finish was really the odd family who were now the Greenback owners. In actuality, none of the rookies who joined the club after the '34 season ever appeared at the outset to be intimidated by the team's scandalous past; the youngsters were mostly country kids, and when a Greenback scout appeared in the midst of the Depression with a fistful of bills and a big league contract, they grinned for the camera, and right out there in the pasture, beside their overalled dads, signed on the dotted line. How were they to know, those eager innocent kids and their impoverished dirt farmer dads, that when the rookie got up north to Tri-City to meet the owner, he would turn out to be a *Jew*, an oily, overweight, excitable little Jew, whose words came thick and fast from his mouth, in sentences the likes of which none of them had ever heard before. Down on the farm a pig was a pig and a cow was a cow—whoever heard of a Jew with the same name as an island in New York harbor? A real Goldberg—only called Ellis!

"De immigration took one look at de real name," explained the Greenback owner to the farmboy who sat before him, his cardboard suitcase in his lap and tears of disappointment in his eyes, "and dat vas dat. Vee vuz Ellis."

"But . . ." the rookie stammered.

"But vat? Speak up. Dun' be shy."

"Well, sir . . . well, I don't think . . . well, that you is what my daddy and me had in mind."

"I ain't vat my daddy and me had in mind needer, Slugger. But dis is de land of opportunities."

"But—what kind of opportunity," the boy blurted out, "is playin' big league ball for a *Jew*!"

Ellis shrugged; sarcastically he said, "A vunz in a lifetime. Okay? Now, vipe de tears and go put on de uniform. Let's take a look on you, all dressed up."

Reluctantly, the boy changed out of his threadbare church suit and his frayed white shirt into a fresh Greenback home uniform. "Nice," Ellis said, smiling, "*very* nice."

"Ain't the seat kind a' baggy?"

"The seat I can take in."

"And the waist—"

"De vaist I can fix, please. I'm talkin' general appearance. Sarah," he called, "come look at de new second-baseman."

A roundish woman, her hair up in a bun and wearing an apron, came into the office, bucket and mop in hand.

"Vat do you t'ink?" he asked his wife.

She nodded her head, approvingly. "It's him."

"Toin aroun'," said Ellis, "show her from de beck."

The rookie turned.

"It's him," said Mrs. Ellis. "Even the number is him."

"But—but how about down here, M'am," asked the rookie, "in the seat here—?"

"Dun' *vurry* vit de seat," said Ellis. "De important t'ing is de shoulder. If it fits in de shoulder, it fits."

The rookie squirmed inside the suit, miserable as he could be.

"Go ahead, swing. Take a cut—be sure you got room. I don't vant it should pinch in de shoulder."

The rookie pretended to swing. "It don't," he admitted.

"Good! Vundaful! She'll pin de seat and de vaist, and you'll pick up Vensday."

"*Wednesday?* What about tomorrow?"

"Please, she already got t'ree rookies came in yesterday. Vensday! Now, how about a nice pair of spikes?"

Dear Paw [the letters went, more or less] we bin trikt. The owner here is a ju. He lives over the skorbord in rite so he can keep his i on the busnez. To look at him cud make you cry like it did me just from lookin. A reel Nu York ju like you heer about down home. It just aint rite Paw. It aint big leeg like I expeck atal. But worse of all is the sun. Another ju. A 7 yr old boy who is a Gene Yuss. Izik. He duz not even go to skule he is that much of a Gene Yuss. His i cue is 424 same ex-ack as Wee Willie Keeler hit in '97. Only it aint base hits but brains. Paw he trys to manig the team. A seven yr old. It just aint what we had in mind is it Paw. What shud I do now. Yor sun Slugger.

Isaac. *There* (according to those in the know) was *precisely* what had stood between the Greenbacks and the first division all these years. In the end most of the players could swallow being fathered and mothered by the Ellises—but that crazy little genius kid of theirs, this Isaac, with his charts, his tables, his graphs, his calculations, his formulae—with his *ideas!* According to him, every way they had of playing baseball in the majors before he came along was absolutely *wrong*. The sacrifice bunt is *wrong*. The intentional pass is *wrong*. With less than two outs the hit-and-run is preferable to hitting away, *regardless of who is at the plate*. "Oh yeah?" the players would say, "and just how'd you figure that one out, Izzy?" Whereupon the seven-year-old would extract his clip-on fountain pen from his shirt pocket, and set out to show them how on his pad of yellow paper.

"First off, you must understand that the hit-and-run is the antithesis of the sacrifice bunt, a maneuver utterly without value, which by my calculations results in a *loss* of seventy-two runs over the season. I calculate this loss by the following formula," and here he wrote on the paper which he held up for them to see—

$$1 \; \Upsilon_s = 5.4376 \; CRy + .2742 = .4735$$

"On the other hand," said Isaac, "compare the total runs scored by hitting away versus the hit-and-run, which of course is your remaining alternative with a man on base. As you can see from the graph—" Shuffling through his briefcase, he came up with a chart, prepared on the cardboard from a laundered shirt, a maze of intersecting lines, each carefully labeled in block letters, "$CRy$ performance," "$Ys$ probability," "probable total DG attempts," etc.—"as you can see, wherein the broken line represents hitting away—"

"Uh-huh," said the ballplayers, winking at one another, "oh, sure, clear as day—you're a real smart little tyke, Izzy—" they said, signaling with an index finger to the temple that actually in their estimation the child was a little touched in the head.

"If then," concluded Isaac, "the hit-and-run were employed at four times the ordinary frequency of the sacrifice bunt, we could anticipate another sixty-five to seventy-five runs per year for the Greenbacks. Now you ask, what are the consequences in the standings of these sixty-five to seventy-five runs per year for the Greenbacks? Let us look at Table 11, which I have here, keeping in mind as we do that of course the fundamental equation for winning a baseball game is $1 \Upsilon = (Rw)(Pb/Pd)$."

But by now most of his audience would have drifted away, some to the batting cage, others off to sprint and shag flies in the outfield, and so Isaac would pack his briefcase, and with his pad under his arm, wander down to the bullpen to give the day's lesson to the utility catchers and relief pitchers. He removed a cardboard from his briefcase and attempted to pass it among them. It read—

$$d = \frac{{}^{c}L \, P \, V^2 \, t^2 \, g \, C^2}{7230 \; W} \text{ feet}$$

"Aww, what the hell is that, Izzy?" they said, handing it right back.

"A formula I've prepared to tell how much a ball will curve. Don't you think that is something you ought to be familiar with ?"

"Well, we is already, kid—so go on out of here."

"All right, if that is the case, what does $d$ stand for?"

"Doggie. Now get out. Scat."

"$d$ equals displacement from a straight line."

"Oh sure it does, everybody knows that."

"Or should," said Isaac, "if they pretend to any knowledge whatsoever of the game. How about ${}^{c}L$?"

Silence. Weary silence.

"$^c L$ equals the circulation of the air generated by friction when the ball is spinning," said Isaac. "And $P$ equals the density of the air, of course—normal at .002–.378. $V$ equals the speed of the ball, $t$ equals the time for delivery. And $g$ equals the acceleration of gravity—32.2 feet per second. $C$ equals—well, you tell me. What *does* $C$ equal?"

"Cat," they said, as though the joke were on him.

"Wrong. $C$ equals the circumference of the ball—9 inches. And $W$? What about $W$?"

"$W$ is for Watch Your Little Ass, sonny," whispered a rookie, in disgust.

"No, $W$ equals the ball's weight, which is .3125 pound. 7230 relates other values of pounds, inches, feet, seconds, and so forth, to arrive at an answer in feet."

"Yeah? And so what! What of it!"

"Only that I know whereof I speak, gentlemen. You must believe me. If only you would cease being slaves to the tired, conventional, and wholly speculative strategies of the game as it has been mistakenly played these fifty years, and would apply the conclusions I have reached by the mathematical analysis of the official statistics, you could add three hundred runs to the team's total production, thus lifting the Tri-City Greenbacks from fifth to *first*. *Your* conclusions are based on nothing but traditional misconceptions; *mine* are developed from the two fundamental theorems of the laws of chance, proposed by Pascal in the seventeenth century. Now, if you will agree to be patient, I am willing to try once again—"

"Well, we ain't! Get lost, Quiz Kid! This is a game for men, not boys!"

"If I may, it is 'a game' for neither. It is an applied science and should be approached as such."

"F off, Isaac! F-U-C-K off, if you know what *that* equals!"

As the seasons passed, and Isaac developed into even more of a genius than he had been when he first came to the Greenbacks at the age of seven, relations with his father's team became increasingly bitter; having confirmed his theories over the years by subjecting the entire canon of baseball records to statistical analysis, he found he no longer had the patience to explain ad infinitum to these nincompoops why they were playing the game all wrong. The antagonism he had had to face in his first years in the majors had hardened him considerably, and by the age of ten the charming pedantry and professional thoroughness of the seven-year-old (who had deemed it necessary to convince as much by his eloquence as by the facts and the figures) had given way to a strident and demanding manner that did not serve to endear him to players two and three times his own age. For this tone he now regularly took toward the Greenback regulars, he more than once had been rewarded with a wad of tobacco juice. "I'll worry about *why*, you idiot—*just do as I say!* You wouldn't understand *why* if I told you—which I have anyway, *a thousand times. Just no more sacrifice bunts!* Because what you are sacrificing is sixty-two runs a year! When he says bunt, *I want the hit-and-run!* Do you understand that! *Do not bunt under any circumstances.* Hit-and—" And just about then came the tobacco juice, a neat stream, or a dripping wad, expertly placed right down through his open mouth, putting that voice box of his out of commission, at least for a time.

"Isaac," said his father, "I'm payink a high-class baseball manager fifteen t'ousand dollars a year, dat he should tell dem to bunt, dat behind his back, you should tell dem hit-and-run?"

"But I am a mathematical genius!"

"And *he* is a baseball genius!"

"He is a baseball *ignoramus.* They *all* are!"

"And so who should be de manager, Isaac—you? At de ripe age of ten?"

"Age has nothing to do with it! We are talking about conclusions I have reached through the scientific method!"

"*Enough* vit dat method! You ain' gung to manage a major leek team at age ten—*and dat's dat!*"

"But if I did, we would be in first place within a month!"

"And day vud t'row me from de leek so fast you vud'n know vat *hit* you! Isaac, day ain' lookin' already for somet'ink day could tell me goodbye and good riddintz? Huh? Day ain' sorry enough day let a Jew in to begin vit, now I got to give dem new ammunition to t'row me out on my ear? *Listen* to me, Isaac: I didn't buy no baseball team juss for my own healt'—I bought it for *yours*! So you could grow up in peace an American boy! So ven came time to give it to de Jews again, day couldn't come around to my door! Isaac, dis is a business vere you could grow up safe and sound! Jewish geniuses, go look how long is de average life span in a pogrom! But own a big leek team, my son, and you ain' got for to vurry never again!"

"But what good is a big league team if the big league team plays the game *all wrong*!"

"In *your* eyes all wrong. But not to de big leekers! Isaac, please, if de goyim say bunt, let dem bunt!"

"But the hit-and-run—"

"*Svallow* de hit-and-run! *Forget* de hit-and-run! It ain' de vay day do here!"

"But the way they do it here is *wrong*!"

"But here is vere it *comes* from!"

"But I can prove they're wrong SCIENTIFICALLY!"

"You're such a genius, do me a favor, prove day're *right*!"

"But that's not what geniuses do!"

"I dun *care* about de oder geniuses! I only care about *you*! Dis is big leek baseball, Isaac—vat vuz here for a t'ousand years already! *Leaf vell enough alone!*" And here he related to Isaac yet again the long, miserable story of anti-Semitism; he told him of murder and pillage and rape, of peasants and Cossacks and crusaders and kings, all of whom had oppressed the Jewish people down through the ages. Only in America, he said, could a Jew rise to such heights! Only in America could a Jew ever hope to become the owner of a major league baseball team!

"That's because they only *have* baseball in America," said Isaac, scowling with disgust.

"Oh yeah? Vat about Japan, viseguy?" snapped Ellis. "Day dun' got baseball dere? You t'ink a Jew could own a baseball team in Japan so easy? Isaac—listen to me, for a Jewish pois'n dis is de greatest country vat ever vas, in de history of de *vold*!"

"Sure it is, 'Dad'," said the contemptuous son, "as long as he plays the game their way."

Thus the seasons passed, the Greenbacks regularly finishing fifth and sixth in the Patriot League, and the genius son no less contemptuous of his father's old-country fearfulness than of the Greenbacks, who were bound by ignorance and superstition and habit to self-defeating taboos. Before Isaac's tirades and tongue-lashings, even the staunchest players eventually came to lose faith in the instructions they received from the bench, and by midseason most of them would wind up playing entirely on their own, heeding neither the conventional tactics of that season's manager, nor the unorthodox strategies of "the little kike" as the little tyke was now called; or, what was even worse, rather than following their own natural instincts, independent of seasoned manager or child prodigy, they would try to *reason* their way out of the dilemma, with the result that time and again, in the midst of straining to think the problem through, they would go down looking at a fat one. Finally, it was not the increase in Greenback strike-outs, but a sense of all the bewilderment that lay back of them, that caused the Greenback fans to become increasingly uneasy in the stands, and to emerge from the stadium at the end of nine innings as exhausted as if they had spent the preceding two hours watching a tightrope walker working without benefit of a net. So exhausting did it become to watch their team's strained performance, that even those Greenback fans whose interest had survived the expulsion of Gamesh and who had made their peace with the idea of a true-blue Yid as owner, eventually preferred to stay at home and wash the car on their day off, rather than going out to Greenback Stadium to see a perfectly competent ball club struggling in vain against eighteen men—the nine on the opposing team and the nine on their own.

# 6

# THE TEMPTATION OF ROLAND AGNI
*(continued)*

# 6

*The arrival of Agni at Greenback Stadium; what befalls him amongst the Jews he there meets with, containing several dialogues between a Jew and a Negro that cause Roland to consider taking his life. Newspaper coverage of his suicide imagined by the rookie sensation. Isaac Ellis makes another appearance; a conversation on "the Breakfast of Champions," wherein the desperate hero of this great history learns the difference between the Wheaties that are made in Minneapolis by General Mills and those that are manufactured in an underground laboratory by a Jewish genius, and something too about Appearance and Reality. Roland succumbs. Concerning winning and losing. A short account of the Mundy miracle, with assorted statistics. The bewilderment of Roland; his fears and hallucinations. In which the character of Mister Fairsmith appears, with an explanation as to why he disappeared from the scene so early in the book. A long digression on baseball and barbarism, with a very full description of Mister Fairsmith's adventures in Africa; his success there with our national pastime, his disappointment, his bravery, and his narrow escape from the savages who blaspheme all he holds sacred and dear. His faith in a Supreme Being is tested by the Mundys. A disputation between a devout and the manager on whether Our Lord loves baseball. The Mundy winning streak settles the issue. A heartwarming scene on a train to Tri-City. The disastrous conclusion of the foregoing adventure, in which Nickname's attempt to stretch a double into a triple with the Mundys thirty-one runs behind the Tycoons in the ninth constitutes the coup de grâce. Isaac and Agni have it out. Mister Fairsmith is laid to rest.*

L ATE one night, not very long after his visit to Mrs. Trust, Roland Agni once again stole out of his hotel room after Jolly Cholly's bed check and made his way through the unfamiliar streets of Tri-City, this time toward the harbor instead of the business district. The Tycoons were at home fattening themselves on the visiting Mundys, the Greenbacks were on the road; nonetheless, a light was shining in a window above the scoreboard in right field, exactly as it had on each of the two previous excursions that Agni had secretly made to Greenback Stadium. As yet, however, he had not found the courage to ring the bell in the recessed doorway on the street side of the right-field wall. But was "courage" the word? Wasn't it more like "treachery"?

*If you make a deal, Roland,* Mrs. Trust had told him, *you'll have to make it with the enemies of America, as an enemy of America . . .*

"Vat *is* dis? Who *is* dis?" came a voice from a window some twenty-five feet above his head. For he (or the traitor in him) had rung the bell at last!

"Vat kind of joke is dis! Vat's gung on down dere!"

"I—I thought there was a night game . . . sorry . . ."

"At 2 A.M.?" cried Ellis. "Get outta here, viseguy, de Greenbacks is on de road!"

"I—I have to see the owner."

"Write de complaint department, dummy!"

But as the Jew's head withdrew, the miserable Mundy star cried out, "It's—it's Roland Agni, Mr. Ellis!"

"It's *who*?"

"Me! Roland! The leading hitter in the league!"

Agni was led up a steep circular stairway through the interior of the scoreboard, as terrified as if he were climbing the spinal column of a prehistoric monster. A single bulb burned at the very top, no larger than you would imagine a monster's brain to be, and with about as much intensity. Black squares of wood were fitted into the thirty or forty apertures that faced out onto the field, as though the mouths, ears, and nostrils, as well as all the eyes, had lids to pull shut when the great beast wasn't out breathing fire. . . . In all, mounting the dim hollow interior of the scoreboard produced the most eerie sensation in Roland—or maybe it was just walking behind a Jew. He did not believe he had ever even seen one up close before, though of course he'd heard the stories.

Mrs. Ellis immediately put up some hot water for tea. "A .370 hitter," she said, pulling a housecoat over her nightgown, "and he goes out in the middle of the night without a jacket!"

"I wasn't thinkin', ma'm. I wanted a little air, ya' see, and got lost . . ."

She put her hand to his forehead. "This I don't like," she told her husband, and left the room, returning in a moment with a thermometer. "Please," she said to Agni, who at first refused to rise from his chair, "you wouldn't be the first big leaguer what I seen with his pants down."

So, scaling new heights of humiliation in his desperate attempt to shed the scarlet-and-gray, Roland did as he was told.

While Mrs. Ellis sat beside him, waiting for his fever to register, the Jew owner returned to the ledgers which lay open beneath the lamp on his desk. "You know vat I clear in a veek?" he asked the Mundy star. "Last veek, know vat I cleared in cash, after salaries, after rent and repairs, after new balls and new resin bags? Take a guess."

"A thousand?" said Agni.

"Who you talkin' to, Mrs. Trust from de Tycoons, or me? Guess again."

"Shucks, I can't, Mr. Ellis, with this here thing stickin' in me . . ."

"Sha," whispered Mrs. Ellis, checking the second hand on her watch.

"Guess again, Roland!" said Ellis.

"A hundred a week?"

"Come again!"

"Ninety? Eighty? Look, how do I know—I got my own troubles, Mr. Ellis!"

*With the enemies, as an enemy* . . .

"Twenty-t'ree dollars a veek!" cried Mr. Ellis. "Less den de ushers! Less den de groundkipper! Less den de hooligan vat sells de beer! *And I'm de owner!*"

Mrs. Ellis extracted the thermometer. "Well," she said, "I'll tell you the name of one .370 hitter who ain't running around Tri-City no more tonight! The league's leading hitter and he's out looking for pneumonia!"

"It's . . . it's bein' a Mundy, Mrs. Ellis . . ." whispered Agni.

"It's *what?*"

"Nothin'," he said, but instead of getting up and getting the hell out, he allowed himself (or the traitor in him) to be bundled into a pair of Mr. Ellis's pajamas and buried beneath three blankets on the sofa.

It wasn't making a deal with the enemy, was it, to stay overnight?

In the morning his temperature was normal, but Mrs. Ellis would not hear of his returning to his hotel without breakfast. "Please, you're not playing against the Tycoons on an empty stomach." And he had to agree that that made no sense.

"Tell me somet'ink," grumbled Ellis from across the breakfast table, "vy do vee haf all dese pitchers? Can somebody give me vun good reason?"

"Abe," said his wife, from the stove, "enough with the pitchers."

"God forbid dey should lift a finger around here between assignments! To get dem to pinch-*run* even, you got to get down on your knees and beg! Years ago, a pitcher who vas a pitcher would t'row bot' ends of a doubleheader! Ven I fois' came to dis country, belief me, you didn't *haf* eight pitchers sittin' dere on dere behinds for every vun vat was on de mound! You had two, t'ree iron men, and dat vas it! Today, *nine pitchers*! No vunder I'm goink to de poor house! And *you*—" he cried, as into the room came his worst enemy of all, "Mr. Argument! Mr. Ideas! Mr. Sabotage-his-own-fad'er!"

"You sabotage yourself," mumbled Isaac, and stuffed a sugar bun into his mouth.

"Isaac," said Mrs. Ellis, "see who's here? Roland Agni! The league's leading hitter!"

"Bat him first," said Isaac, "instead of eighth, and he'd be leading the league in runs scored, too."

"I *would*?" said Agni. "I thought fourth."

"First!" shouted Isaac. "Players should bat in the descending order of run-productiveness! $Dy = rp \times 1275$. But try to explain that to the morons who manage this game!"

"Mr. Know-it-all!"

"They don't see eye-to-eye," explained the kindly Mrs. Ellis.

"Neither does me and my dad," Agni said.

"Vell, listen to him den!" snapped Ellis. "Maybe you'll loin somet'ink!"

"I did," whined Agni, "that's how come everthin' that's wrong with me is wrong. On account of my father! Oh, Mr. Ellis," cried Agni, "I—I—I—"

*As an enemy, with the enemies, Roland.*

"I—I want—I want—"

"What is it?" cried Mrs. Ellis, clutching her heart at the sight of the young hero suddenly in tears.

"I—I want to be a Greenback! To play for you! Oh, buy me, Mr. Ellis—and I'll play for nothin'! But I just can't be a Mundy no more!"

Stunned, Ellis said, "For nuttink?"

"Yes! Yes! I play for my allowance of two-fifty a week as it is! Oh, buy me, please! I'll bring in fans by the tens of thousands! I'll be the greatest Greenback since Gil Gamesh!"

"A star like you—you vud play for a Jewish pois'n?"

"Mr. Ellis, I don't care if you was the worst Jew in the world—*I'll do anything! I'll eat scraps! I'll sleep on the clubhouse floor!*"

"Not in my stadium," said Mrs. Ellis.

"Sarah," said Ellis, "get me de Mundy front office. Ve're makink a deal!"

Isaac Ellis stood by, sneering, while his mother called long distance to Port Ruppert. "Hello?" she said. "This is the Ruppert Mundys? . . . You *sure*?" Shrugging she handed the phone to her husband.

"Vat?" he asked her.

"To me," she said, "sounds like the *shvartze*."

"Abe Ellis talkink here."

"What you want, Abe Ellis dere?"

"To speak vit one of de Mundy boys, if you dun' mind."

"Day ain' here. Day in South America. What you want?"

"Who is dis talking to me like dis?" demanded Ellis.

"Dis here George. Now what you want befo' I hang up?"

"I vant to talk to de Mundy brut'ers about a trade, if dat's all right vit' you!"

"Who all you wanna trade?"

"Listen, who is dis, may I ask, de colored janitor or somebody?"

"Das right. Dis here is George Washington, de colored janitor. Who all you wanna trade? Don' tell me no dwarf now, 'cause I jus' bought me a li'l dwarf."

"*You* bought?"

"Das right."

"And since ven you got de right to buy and sell in de Patriot Leek?"

"Since when do *you*, Jew?" and the Ruppert front office hung up.

"A *shvartze* janitor," said Ellis, "runnink a big leek team!"

"A what?" asked Agni.

"A colored pois'n!" cried Ellis. "George Vashington no less! He sveeps de floor—and he makes de trades!"

"Then that's him," said Agni, "who traded Buddy to Kakoola —just like the fellers said!"

"I dun' belief it! Sarah," said Ellis, "call again—and call *right*!"

"This the Mundys?" she asked, after dialing long distance and waiting to be connected. "Yes?" She handed the phone to her husband. "It's him."

"Hello?" said Ellis, "Ruppert Mundys?"

"Das right."

"Look—I vant to buy from you a center-fielder."

"Well, ain' dat somethin'. De Jew, he wanna buy de bess playuh we done got! And how much you wanna pay, Jew?"

"Vatch de vay you talk to me, sonny boy!"

"How much you wanna pay, Jew? Dis here de league leadin' batter we's talkin' about. Dis here a nineteen-year-ol' boy, strong as de ox, quick as de rabbit, smart as de owl, and hungry as de wolf!"

"How much *you* vant?"

"Oh, jus about as much as you ready to part wid, Jew—and den some!"

"Vell, frankly I vas t'inkink more alonk de line of a svop— svoppink players."

"Oh, I betch you wuz," chuckled George. "Only we don' *need* no mo' players."

"De Mundys dun' need *players*?"

"We juss fine in de player department. We wan' yo' *money*."

"Listen, vat is dis! Vat's goink on! Who gave you de right— I demand to know!"

"Same one gave *you*," and the phone went dead.

"Can't be!" cried the Greenback owner. "Dis is somebody

tryink to drive me crazy! It couldn't be a real *shvartze*—no, it can't be true!"

Sneering, Isaac said, "Why not, Dad? It's the land of opportunity, *Dad*."

"For everybody," thought Agni, bursting into tears again, "but me! And *I'm* the All-American star! It ain't fair! It don't make sense no more! I'm the greatest rookie of all time! I'm another Cobb! I'm another Ruth! I'm everybody great rolled up into one—and a Jew and a nigger is bargainin' for my hide!"

This time Ellis himself did the phoning. "You sure," he asked the operator, "dis is de big leek team? You sure dis ain't a practical joke?"

"This is not A Practical Joke, sir," the operator informed him. "If you want A Practical Joke you will have to get that number from information. I have the Ruppert Mundy Baseball Organization of the Patriot League on the wire. Go ahead, please."

"Hello—Mundys? *Ruppert* Mundys?"

"De same."

"Dis is de *shvartze* again?"

"De same."

"How much for Roland Agni?"

"A cool qwata of a million."

"*Dollars?*"

"De *same*, Jew."

Agni descended through the dim interior of the right-field scoreboard; halfway down he walked out along a gangway to lift one of the boards and peer through the aperture at the playing field that might have been his home, if only he wasn't so great and didn't cost so much to buy . . . Far below, the pasture beckoned. He saw the headlines.

AGNI LEAPS FROM SCOREBOARD
Rookie Slugger Suicide; Jews, Niggers, Commies, Cripples, Dwarfs, and Other Freaks Held Responsible; Landis Orders Disreputable Elements Barred from Game Forever; "Clean-up long overdue," says Mrs. Trust; "Could have been greatest of all time," Managers agree; Mundy Brothers Jailed; Mazuma Gets Death Penalty; Agni's Father Weeps at Funeral: "I was only trying to teach him humility"—Stoned by Grief-Stricken Fans; "This day shall live in infamy," says F.D.R.;

Nation-wide Mourning Ordered; Pathetically Broken Beautiful Body To Be Cremated in Ceremony at Hall of Fame; Ashes To Be Scattered from Air Force Bomber on Fans at Opening Game of World Series; Number To Be Retired; Shoes To Be Bronzed; Bat and Glove To Be Taken on Round-the-World Tour of G.I.s by Bob Hope; Name To Live Forever; "Lesson to Mankind," says Pope; Fred Waring's "Ballad of Roland Agni" Number One on Hit Parade; Big Four to Meet

It almost seemed worth it . . .

Except, thought Agni, that's not what would happen at all—not with my luck! No, even if he leaped to his death in a perfect swan dive, he would get no more than a few grudging lines on page seventy-two, he was sure . . .

MUNDY DEAD IN FALL, AS IF ANYONE CARES

Tri-City, Sept. 16—One of Ruppert Mundys, the joke team of organized baseball, in a typical stupid Mundy stunt, fell out of the scoreboard at Greenback Stadium and died. God only knows what he was doing there. His name was Nagi or something like that and he was said to be their best player. The Mundys' best player. Terrific.

"No luck, Agni?"

"What!"

"It's me."

"Who? It's so dark!"

"Down here. Isaac Ellis. The ungrateful son."

"Oh . . ."

"Down here. Keep coming, Roland, keep coming."

"What—what is all this?"

"My laboratory."

"Where am I?"

"Under the stadium. You missed the door to the street."

"What—what are you doing?"

"Oh, this? Splitting the atom."

"What—what's that mean?"

"Just something to pass the time, Roland, until I get to manage the Greenbacks the way they ought to be managed."

"But you're only seventeen."

"And a Jew and a genius, I know."

"Boy, you must be lonely to sit down here like this, doin' that. Well, I better be going, you know. How do I get out a' here?"

"Not so fast. Sit down. I wanted to talk to you, Roland."

"But I got to be at Tycoon Park—I gotta game to play."

"Don't be frightened, Roland. I only want to talk, that's all. You're a great baseball player, Roland. They don't make them like you anymore."

"I know they don't. They never did, like me. I've got practically everything you could want."

"Roland, I'd like to manage you some day. Your body, my brains—there'd be nothing like it in the history of the game."

"But I'm a Mundy, in case you ain't heard."

"I could buy you from the Mundys, don't worry about that."

"Oh yeah! And where *you* goin' get two hundred and fifty thousand dollars from?"

"A seventeen-year-old Jewish genius can always lay his hands on a few bucks, Rollie."

"Oh sure."

"My friend, I could make the quarter of a million just between now and the end of the season by betting on the Mundys to win all their remaining games."

"You could, huh? And how they gonna do that? A miracle from God?"

"See this that I am holding in my hand? You can read by the light of my Bunsen burner."

"It's just a box of Wheaties."

"Wheaties, the Breakfast of Champions."

"Well, that's pure baloney, that champion stuff. We get 'em free, by the case. And look at all the good they done us."

"You get your Wheaties from the General Mills Company in Minneapolis, Minnesota. That is why they don't do what they're advertised to do. These Wheaties are manufactured by a seventeen-year-old Jewish genius."

"But—it's the same box, ain't it?"

"The same box. The same flavor. The same in every visible way. Only one invisible difference."

"What?"

"They do the job. If the Ruppert Mundys were to eat these Wheaties made by me in Tri-City, if only a few little flakes were to be sprinkled on top of those Wheaties they already eat made by the Wheaties company in Minneapolis, your team would be unbeatable."

"Oh yeah? And what makes them so special again?"

"Let's call it extra energy."

"That's what they all say. Vitamin X, Y, and Z. It's all words."

"Roland, if only you will slip these Wheaties into their breakfast in the morning, there will be no holding down the Mundys on the field."

"I suppose they're going to wake up old Wayne Heket while they're at it, too."

"They'll do more than just wake him up, I can assure you of that."

"Oh sure, sure."

"Stupid *goy*, I am splitting the atom! I am fifty years ahead of my time in nuclear physics alone! The Wheaties I could do with a frontal lobotomy! I am telling you the scientific facts— the Mundys will eat my Wheaties, and they will win all of their remaining games! And by betting on them I will win a quarter of a million dollars—and buy you for my father's team—and become the Greenback manager, at long last! And either my old man says yes, or he winds up on the street, begging with a cup!"

"But—but, if I feed the boys these Wheaties—is that what you want me to do?"

"Exactly! Every morning, just a little sprinkle!"

"And we win—?"

"Yes! You win!"

"But—that'd be like throwin' a game."

"Like *what*?"

"Like throwin' it. I mean, we'd be winnin' when we're sup- posed to be losin'—and that's wrong. That's illegal!"

"Throwing a game, Roland, is *losing* when you're supposed to be *winning*. Winning instead of losing is what you're *sup- posed* to do!"

"But not by eatin' Wheaties!"

"*Precisely* by eating Wheaties! That's the whole *idea* of Wheaties!"

"But that's *real* Wheaties! And they don't make you do it anyway!"

"Then how can they be 'real' Wheaties, if they don't do what they're supposed to do?"

"That's what *makes* them 'real'!"

"No, that's what makes them *unreal*. *Their* Wheaties say they're supposed to make you win—and they don't! *My* Wheaties say they're supposed to make you win—and they do! How can that be wrong, Roland, or illegal? That is keeping your promises! That is being true to your word! I am going to make the most hopeless baseball team in history into a team of red-blooded American boys! And you call that 'throwing a game'? I am talking about *winning*, Roland, *winning*—what made this country what it is today! Who in his right mind can be against *that*?"

Who, indeed. Winning! Oh, you really can't say enough good things about it. There is nothing quite like it. Win hands down, win going away, win by a landslide, win by accident, win by a nose, win without deserving to win—you just can't beat it, however you slice it. Winning is the tops. Winning is the name of the game. Winning is what it's all about. Winning is the be-all and the end-all, and don't let anybody tell you otherwise. All the world loves a winner. Show me a good loser, said Leo Durocher, and I'll show you a loser. Name one thing that losing has to recommend it. You can't. Losing is tedious. Losing is exhausting. Losing is uninteresting. Losing is depressing. Losing is boring. Losing is debilitating. Losing is compromising. Losing is shameful. Losing is humiliating. Losing is infuriating. Losing is disappointing. Losing is incomprehensible. Losing makes for headaches, muscle tension, skin eruptions, ulcers, indigestion, and for mental disorders of every kind. Losing is bad for confidence, pride, business, peace of mind, family harmony, love, sexual potency, concentration, and much much more. Losing is bad for people of all ages, races, and religions; it is as bad for infants as for the elderly, for women as for men. Losing makes people cry, howl, scream, hide, lie, smolder, envy, hate, and quit. Losing is probably the single biggest cause of suicide in the world, and of murder. Losing makes the benign malicious, the generous stingy, the brave fearful, the healthy ill, and the kindly bitter. Losing is universally despised, as well it should be. The sooner we get rid of losing, the happier everyone will be.

But winning. To win! It was everything Roland remembered.

*

14–6 against Independence, nine runs scored in the first inning. Seven Mundy home runs! Eight Mundy stolen bases! WAYNE HEKET STEALS HOME!

8–0, knocking the Blues out of the pennant race. THE MUNDYS KNOCK THE BLUES OUT OF THE PENNANT RACE! Deacon Demeter goes all the way, scattering three hits. Four Mundy double plays. WAYNE HEKET STEALS TWO BASES! FIFTY YEARS OLD AND HE STEALS TWO BASES! Home runs: Rama (2), Skirnir, Agni, and Damur. NICKNAME DAMUR, FOURTEEN YEARS OLD AND NINETY-TWO POUNDS, HITS A HOME RUN INTO THE UPPER DECK!

Asylum. Four home games against the Mundys for the Keepers. This should land them in fifth for sure. This is their chance to overtake the Greenbacks for sure. MUNDYS SWEEP FOUR IN A ROW. Demeter, Tuminikar, Volos, Buchis hurl COMPLETE GAMES! TUMINIKAR UNLEASHES FAST-BALL OF YORE! HEKET STEALS FIVE BASES! PTAH HITS SAFELY IN SIXTH CONSECUTIVE GAME! Home runs in Asylum: Rama (4), Skirnir (3), Baal (6), Agni (2).

Kakoola. Mundys take three in a row. Ho-hum. Ockatur two-hits old mates. Rama-Baal home run barrage continues. Heket scores from first on long Damur single! Steals everything except the catcher's underwear. Skirnir's great catch breaks back of Reaper rally! Reliever Chico Mecoatl fans last seven Reaper batters! Tuminikar whiffs sixteen with blazing fastball. Mazuma delighted as incredulous capacity crowds witness massacre of locals. "Know that R that used to stand for 'Ridiculous'?" says Mazuma. "Stands for 'Renegades' now. One more season without a home, and they'll be the greatest team in the history of the game. And the most dreaded!"

Then Terra Inc. 8–1, 9–3. Simple as that. The Mundys, boom, boom, boom; the Rustlers, swish, swish, swish. Eleven in a row.

Assorted statistics for the miracle: Heket, 14 stolen bases; Rama, 12 home runs; Baal, 10 home runs, 4 triples, 2 doubles; Ptah, hit safely 11 consecutive games; Damur, batting average for 11 games, .585 (in contrast to .087 for previous 142); complete games pitched, Tuminikar 3, Ockatur 2, Demeter 2, Volos 1, Buchis 1. Wild pitches, none. Passed balls, none. Errors, 3, all on Skirnir, trying to make acrobatic never-say-die shoestring catches.

Oh it was wonderful, it was glorious, it was heavenly—except at night, when he could not sleep because of those nightmares in which he stood before the conscience of the game, the Commissioner himself, and received his just deserts. "But I didn't eat any myself, Your Honor—I swear I didn't! Not a one!" "You fed the others, Roland." "They fed *themselves*. They lifted the spoons to their own mouths and chewed and swallowed all on their own, I swear!" "But who brought those boxes of illegal Wheaties to the table, Roland? Who sprinkled them in with the others?" "But it was that smart little Jew that put me up to it, Commissioner! He forced me to, by playin' on my hopes!" "Roland, I have no more love for a smart little Jew than the next fellow. Baseball has always been a Christian game, and so it shall remain, if I have anything to do with it. But if Jews don't belong here, neither do ballplayers who fall for their schemes to make an easy buck." "But *I* don't want to make a buck. The little *Jew* did. I only wanted to play baseball with a real big league team!" "Well, that's unfortunate, because as it now stands, you are never going to play baseball with any team again. You are banished for life, Roland Agni. You are a traitor and a crook." "No! No!"

And leaping from his bed he would run down into the hotel lobby to telephone Tri-City.

"Look, Isaac, what if somebody dies!"

"Nobody's going to die, Roland."

"But maybe this stuff can kill somebody who isn't supposed to have any."

"Roland, you just keep feeding them the Breakfast of Champions, and don't worry about a thing."

"But—but you should see Old Wayne. He starts packin' it away—well, I get worried! Suppose he ups and croaks. That'd be murder!"

"You want to be a Mundy forever, do you?"

"Well, no. But I don't want to get the chair, either! Or get banished! I mean, you watch those guys out there, the way they're playin', and you think, if they keep this up, they're going to *die*!"

"Die? Why?"

"Well, they're too good, that's why! I just think sometimes in the middle of an innin', when we're battin' around and scorin' and goin' crazy on the bases, that all of a sudden, I'm goin' to look in the dugout *and they'll all be dead!*"

"Nobody's died yet from winning, Roland, not that I've ever heard of."

"But maybe if they lost *one*, sort of to give their systems a rest . . ."

"Just what the bookies are waiting for. Why I'm still getting six and seven to one, Agni, is because Las Vegas expects the collapse to come every day, and it doesn't. And it won't, so long as you do your job. Understand me?"

"Well, just so long as nobody gets harmed . . . or paralyzed . . . or somethin' like that. I keep thinkin', one mornin' they're all goin' to be eatin' breakfast, and then they're all just goin' to get paralyzed from head to toe. That could happen too, you know."

"No, it couldn't."

"Why not!"

"Because I'm a scientific genius, Roland, that's why not."

But, thought Roland, if you're such a scientific genius, you smart little Jew, why don't you use them Jewish Wheaties on the Greenbacks to make them win? Why don't you use them on your own father's team? Because they give people something awful, that's why! Because one day, right out on the field, the whole damn team is going to turn purple in the face and fall down dead! I know it!

But of course all that happened to the Ruppert Mundys from eating "the Jewish Wheaties" was that they kept on winning games—and started in giving Roland friendly tips on how to hit the ball, for as it happened, during the course of the winning streak his was the lowest batting average on the club. "You're pressin', kid," said Nickname, at the pregame batting practice, "just meet the ball." "Believe you're droppin' your head there, Rollie," advised Skirnir, "keep the old bean up." "You're uppercuttin' the low ones, Agni—give in the knees more." And who said that? The dwarf, Ockatur, who barely *came* to Agni's knees!

\*

And what of Ulysses S. Fairsmith? Do you fans even remember the name? If not, then you are in about the same fix by this time as the players themselves.

Where has the Mundy manager been all season long? Why isn't he in his famous wooden rocker in the corner of the Mundy dugout, moving the defense around with the gold tip of his bamboo cane? What happened to *him*?

Sadly, this: managing the Mundys on the road was worse than anything the grand old man of baseball could ever have imagined. Of course, ever since the death of Glorious Mundy in 1931, he had known his share of disappointment and frustration, beginning with the Mundy brothers selling out from under him the pennant-winning clubs of the twenties and replacing all those greats with the lowest-priced players they could find; certainly when they sold Luke the Loner to the Rustlers, no one would have thought any the less of the venerable manager had he bid Ruppert goodbye. But out of loyalty to the city of Port Ruppert and all the friends he had made there, out of loyalty to the memory of the incomparable Glorious M., Mister Fairsmith accepted without complaint what any other manager of his record would have interpreted as a cynical disregard for his professional dignity. Even his enemies, who ridiculed him behind his back for his ministerial ways, had to admire so impressive a display of character. "There is more to human life than what you read in the won-and-lost column, my good friends," said Mister Fairsmith, and he was a manager, mind you, who had known the taste of victory and who had cherished it.

But what happened to the Mundys in '43 was more even than a man of his forbearance and compassion could bear to witness —or be a party to. Calamity, catastrophe, cataclysm—of course he had expected no less; he had *prayed* for no less, praying too that the Lord would give him the strength, the will, and the wisdom to inspire his homeless flock to prevail over every conceivable form of suffering that he expected would be visited upon them. But what shook Mister Fairsmith's faith, what brought him at the age of eighty to the very edge of an abyss even more terrifying than the one he had glimpsed twenty years earlier in Africa, was that rather than being the most profoundly

religious experience of a Christian life, shepherding the Ruppert Mundys from one P. League town to the next had turned
into a farce and a travesty. Where there was to have been
meaningful torment and uplifting anguish and ennobling despair, there was ridiculousness—and worse. These were the
most unprofessional, undignified, *immoral* athletes he had ever
seen gathered together on a playing field in his life—if you
could even call them "athletes"! This wasn't suffering deserving
of his compassion—this was just downright disgusting behavior! Why, not even those African savages, with their filed teeth
and carved flesh, not even those black devils with their hateful
abominations, had sickened and revolted him as did the '43
Ruppert Mundys!

. . . And those savages had sickened him, all right. The barbaric ceremony that they had forced him to witness some
twenty years earlier had been the most hideous culmination
imaginable to a round-the-world trip that, till then, the American newspapers had hailed as a brilliant success, particularly
those wonderful weeks proselytizing for the national pastime
in Japan. With the assistance of an erudite young theology student, a nephew of his who was as adept with a fungo bat as
with the language of this remote jungle tribe, Mister Fairsmith
had penetrated a thousand miles into the primitive interior of
Africa, the last thirty miles by foot through the jungle, with native carriers bearing upon their backs the bags of bats, gloves,
and bases he had borne from America. The villagers, numbering
no more than a hundred and fifty men, women, and children,
lived in a circle of grass huts not so much larger than a regulation infield. Beyond the village in all directions was half a mile
of high grass—beyond that, the jungle.

Using a machete-like tool with a hooked blade that they
swung two-handed—using a nice level stroke and practically
no stride at all—the men of the village cleared a hundred square
yards of grass for their white visitors, solemn and silent as grave-
diggers while they worked. Here Mister Fairsmith conducted
his classes and organized the first game of baseball ever played
on the continent of Africa between all-native teams. With
equipment donated at their playgrounds by the schoolkids of
Ruppert, and which was to be left behind with the villagers
once they had mastered the skills of the game, Mister Fairsmith

demonstrated the fundamentals of hitting, bunting, catching, pitching, fielding, baserunning, sliding, and umpiring. The moment he saw the men clearing the field, he realized that he had stumbled upon a tribe of great long-ball hitters. Stumbled? Or had the Lord a hand in this? They were something to watch in the batter's box; not even their fastest pitcher could intimidate a hitter once he had dug in with his bare feet at the plate, and when they swung it was as though the bat was a blade with which they intended to cut the ball in two. No, Mister Fairsmith did not have to remind these savages, as he did his own rookies throughout spring training, to follow through on the swing. The follow-through was in their blood. They were naturals.

The trouble erupted over sliding. Though the men were clothed only in genital pouches tied around the waist with rawhide, they did not for a moment flinch from "hitting the dirt." To the contrary, they slid with abandon whether a slide was in order or not, with the result that by the time a runner had come round to score he was covered with dust from head to foot. No matter how sternly Mister Fairsmith would address them on this matter, they would not even remain on their feet going into *first*.

It was not a decision that it pleased him to make, but at the end of the first week, he called the native men together and through the person of his young nephew announced that henceforth any runner sliding into first base would automatically be called out. He regretted having to resort to a measure of this kind, but he simply did not know how else to curb this stupid passion of theirs.

The spears appeared from out of nowhere. One moment the tribesmen were standing around, listening in their silent, solemn way to what they must have imagined was to be an impromptu class on the finer points of the game—a review, perhaps, of the previous day's lesson in the squeeze play—and the next they were pressing in upon him with their long weapons of warfare. And to protect himself, Mister Fairsmith, in khaki short pants, half-sleeved shirt, and pith helmet, had nothing but a thirty-four-ounce Hillerich and Bradsby.

Then came the wailing of the women, as horrifying a sound as Mister Fairsmith had ever heard—and he had spent his life in baseball parks, he had known crowds to cry for blood before. But not even in Aceldama, Ohio, or Brooklyn, New York, had he ever heard anything to match this. All at once the shaven-headed women were rushing from the circle of huts, some with painted babies still at their scarred breasts, and making a noise as though they were gargling with fire. Oh they were ecstatic, these savage women—tonight they would be dining out on the flesh of Christian gentlemen!

Incredible! Horrendous! Or—or was it not a miracle? Yes! They were going to eat him *because he had decided to add to baseball a rule of his own devising, a rule that did not really exist.* In their own savage African way, they were responding as would the fans at any major league park in America, if the umpire had arbitrarily suspended or altered the code that governs their national pastime. What they had come to understand in one short week was that this was no game for children he had come six thousand miles to teach them, this was no summertime diversion for adults—it was a sacred institution. And who was he, who was *anyone*, to forbid sliding into first when not even the Official Playing Rules Committee of the three leagues forbade it?

The natives were right and he was wrong, and being the man he was, Sam Fairsmith told them so.

At once the women ceased their yowling and the men fell back with their spears. And his young nephew, who had already had voice enough to translate his uncle's words, removed the catcher's mask and began to undo the chest protector behind which he'd taken refuge when the tribesmen had charged Mister Fairsmith; however, like a catcher who may or may not get a turn at bat in the inning, he continued to wear the shin guards.

Now the leader of the village, a giant of a man for whom Mister Fairsmith had high hopes as a fastballing right-handed pitcher on the style of Walter Johnson, separated himself from his fellows and stepped forward to address Mister Fairsmith in the language of his tribe. He spoke—as they all did on the rare occasions they were moved to speak—with much glowering and eye-rolling.

Mister Fairsmith's nephew translated. "Walter Johnson says that it pleases his people that Mister Baseball has chosen not to burden them with a regulation against sliding that would be punishable by an out."

"Tell Walter Johnson," replied "Mister Baseball," "that I shall try never again to be so mindless and foolish as to place such a burden upon them."

The gigantic native glowered upon hearing the good news, and spoke again.

"Walter Johnson says that he is grateful. He says, however, that now that the issue of sliding has been raised, he wishes to make it known that he and his braves believe they have been deprived of still another opportunity to enjoy the pleasure and thrill of the slide. He says that players wish to know if there is any rule that forbids them from sliding into first following a base on balls."

Mister Fairsmith said, "You mean, after receiving a *walk*, they want to slide into first?"

"It would appear from his tone," said Fairsmith's nephew, reaching for the catcher's mask again, "to be on the order of a smoldering grievance, Uncle Sam."

"Now, that *is* ridiculous. The primary object of the slide is to reach the base without being tagged out by the fielder. As they surely must understand by now, if a batter in his turn at bat receives four pitches outside of the strike zone he is *awarded* first base. Consequently there is no need to avoid being tagged or thrown out; all that is required of the batsman is that he proceed to first base, where, merely by touching the bag it becomes 'his'."

"You want me to tell him all that?"

"Why, of course I do. And over and over, until he gets it into his head. Now, why are you putting that chest protector on again? Good Lord, son, don't show *fear*, of all things."

"But—I'm frightened."

"Of a tribe of heathen black men?"

"Of their *spears*, Uncle. Look!"

Sure enough, the men of the village who had fallen back when Mister Fairsmith had rescinded the prohibition of sliding into first, were advancing again with spears upraised, ready to lunge, it would appear, if he should fail to grant this new request. Nonetheless, the Mundy manager said, "You will repeat my words to Walter Johnson. You will tell him that sliding into first after a walk is just plain foolishness and I won't have it. I wouldn't allow American players to do it, and I surely am not going to extend to a village of black Africans a prerogative that I would deny my own countrymen and kin."

When Walter Johnson had heard Mister Fairsmith's message, he responded in a voice so thunderous that it caused the scrawny village dogs to go yelping off into the high grass. And then the women started instantly to yowl and screech in *their* bone-chilling fashion.

"What now?" asked the exasperated American.

"He says, 'On what authority will Mister Baseball not allow us to slide into first following a walk?' He demands to know the number of *that* rule in the Official Baseball Rules as recorded, amended, and adopted by the Professional Baseball Playing Rules Committee."

Chagrined as he was by this renewed outburst of wailing from the women, and distracted as he was by the spears pressing toward his throat, Mister Fairsmith was once again deeply gratified by all that Walter Johnson had remembered from his very first lecture on the Rules. Not only did he have a hopping fastball and fine control, not only was he an excellent hitting pitcher, but he appeared to have, in that head decorated with triangular scars on either cheekbone, a brain. "Well, of course," said Mister Fairsmith, "my authority in this instance does not derive from a written regulation, and consequently I cannot give him the number of the rule. You must explain to him that what we are dealing with here is a matter of *unwritten* law, or custom, but one so universally respected as to have the force and effect of every last rule in the rulebook."

No sooner were these words translated, than the women, like a flock of squawking crows, rushed off to the far end of the village circle, and then swept back again, pushing through the dust a black kettle, five times the size of a beer keg. Meanwhile the children, who had disbanded in search of wood, were already carrying it to a spot at the outskirts of the village, where the older girls of the tribe had begun to assemble the branches for a fire.

When his nephew pulled the catcher's mask over his face, Mister Fairsmith instantly snatched it away and threw it to the ground. "Now, you must stop this nonsense immediately. I want to know what exactly is going on with these people. Why in God's name are they behaving like this *now*? What did he just say to me?"

"He—he said they were a proud race."

"Pride he calls it? The men with spears? The women screaming like banshees? And from the looks of it, preparations underway for an outright act of cannibalism? That isn't pride in my book, and you may tell him as much!"

"But, Uncle, he says that though they will follow to the letter the *rules* of the white man's game, they refuse to be enslaved by arbitrary strictures designed to rob them of their inalienable cultural rights. By denying the men the right to slide into first after having been awarded a base on balls, you have grievously insulted their masculinity."

"To the contrary," said Mister Fairsmith, while only fifty feet away the women set to scrubbing the interior of the immense kettle with sand and river water, "sliding into first after a walk is as sure a way as I know of for a ballplayer to compromise himself *and* his professional stature in the eyes of the spectator."

"Apparently," said the younger, after translating Mister Fairsmith's remarks to Walter Johnson, "that isn't the way they see it."

"Oh, isn't it? In other words, a tribe of black men who had not even seen a ball or a bat prior to last week, is going to tell Ulysses S. Fairsmith, manager of the Ruppert Mundys, what constitutes professionalism in baseball?"

"I think that is the meaning of the spears, Uncle, yes."

"Well, suppose you just make it perfectly clear to Mr. Walter Johnson here that if there is anything in the world I hate worse than a cheat, it's a bully. I am afraid these people are really starting to rub me the wrong way, and I am a man who is known and respected throughout the world of sport for his patience."

"But, Uncle—what if they eat us! What if because you won't let them slide into first after a walk, they put us into that pot and boil us alive!"

"My dear young fellow, if despite all we have tried to teach them in this last week they want to continue to be loathed and despised by civilized men the world over, in the final analysis, that is their business. They're the ones who are going to have to live with themselves, once the 'fun' is over. I, however, have a responsibility to my countrymen and to the game which is their national pastime. Surely, it must be clear to you now that where sliding is concerned, if you give these people a finger, they will take a hand. Allow them to slide into second, third, and home and they want to slide into first for no good reason. Allow them to do so on a batted ball and they want to do it after a *walk*. And where will it stop, I ask you? No, either I draw the line right here, at the cost of my life if need be, or else, simply to save my skin, I yield to force, I yield to just the kind of violence I detest with all my heart and soul, and give baseball over, lock, stock, and barrel, to these savages to pervert and destroy."

"Listen!" cried the young seminarian. "A drum!"

Yes, somewhere in this village, the hands of a warrior had begun to thump out a rhythm whose ominous meaning was all too clear . . .

"No," said Mister Fairsmith, "I will not be the man who allowed baseball to become a primitive rite for savages. I would rather die a martyr to the national pastime, if such is the will of the Lord."

"But—" cried his young champion, "what about *me*?"

"You?" said Mister Fairsmith. "I believed when I took you with me, that your ambition in life was to be a Christian missionary."

"It was! It is! But why should I die for *baseball*?"

Mister Fairsmith raised his face to the African sun: "Father, forgive him, he knows not what he says."

By midnight two fires burned. The one back of home plate had been ignited by an ancient bony creature of indeterminate sex, who seemed weighted to the ground only by virtue of the mask and the chest protector that he (or she) wore. The fire midway between the pitcher's mound and second base appeared to be the special property of the women of the tribe, who throughout the evening had chanted a monotonous incantation in rhythm with the village drum, meanwhile feeding the flames with oil so that they reared high into the air, casting a red gleam over the entire infield. The outfield was lit by the moon and the stars. From beyond the black wall of foliage, there came a shrill, insistent piping, as though all the beasts of the jungle were being directed to seats in the treetops by the African night birds.

The two white men were bound by their wrists and ankles to stakes driven into the coaching boxes, Mister Fairsmith at third, young Billy Fairsmith at first. They had been hanging there since noon.

When the kettle was rolled by six naked warriors across the infield and hoisted up over the fire back of the pitcher's mound, the villagers who had gathered two and three deep along the infield foul lines began to wail with excitement. They too were unclothed now, and all their protuberances seemed swollen to the bursting point in the flickering shadows; many bore white phosphorescent markings on their heels and shoulder blades, and when they leaped in place, their movements dazzled and confused the eye. As what didn't?

Two tiny boys—matchsticks with bellies—now appeared upon the diamond, dragging Mister Fairsmith's ball bag. Hobbling behind, making signs in the air, came the creature in the mask and the chest protector. When the little boys had finally pulled the heavy bag up on the rubber, this creature—wise man? wise woman?—directed them to empty the bag of its contents. Meanwhile, the water crested and slid over the edge of the kettle and into the fire, the sizzle greatly exciting the villagers, causing them to wail as though in torment—though in fact they appeared from their sporadic leaping about to be in some savage version of seventh heaven.

And now Walter Johnson strode out to the mound. He dismissed the tiny boys with a wave of the hand, and immediately took to examining the several dozen baseballs they had emptied on to the ground. It was a while before he found the one that most suited him. After rubbing it three times in his immense hands—"*Omoo! Omoo! Omoo!*" the women chanted—he passed it, with a deep bow and a friendly bark, to the Wise One in the mask and chest protector. The Wise One, ball in hand, hobbled toward the fire. Raising the ball once toward the villagers lined up along the first-base foul line—"*Omoo!*"—then to the villagers lined up along third—"*Omoo*"—the Wise One

went into a windup more elaborate than any Mister Fairsmith
had seen in his entire career, and let fly the ball in the direction
of the kettle.

When the wailing had subsided, the boy children of the tribe
ran out to the mound, where they squatted on their haunches
around Walter Johnson. He addressed them in so fearsome a
manner that several instantly wet the ground beneath them.
Then each was handed a baseball, and just as the Wise One
had earlier, threw it into the kettle. "*Omoo! Omoo! Omoo!*" With
the mound empty of baseballs, the women moved in again,
chanting in rhythm to the drum, and swaying now, as they
watched the balls jump and spin like fabulous curves and knuck-
lers in the roiling waters. From time to time a woman approached the fire, and dipping a net on a long pole into the
kettle, extracted a ball. Walter Johnson tested the stitches with
a thumb, and then directed her to return the steaming ball to
the pot. In the end he took the pole himself and dipped deep
into the kettle, collecting all the balls in the net. Then, swinging
the pole three times over his head—"*Omoo! Omoo! Omoo!*"—
he sent the boiled baseballs sailing into the air.

As though unchained, the tiny boys broke across the diamond, two or three of them invariably leaping upon the same
ball, biting simultaneously into the cover, teeth to teeth, nose
to nose—and kicking all the while at one another's shins in wild
windmill fashion. When, finally, one or another of the boys
had the ball to himself and firmly in his own grasp, he dropped
to his knees to devour the covering with the ferocity of one
who had been denied food for twenty-four hours; perhaps that
was the case. Having eaten clear down to the yarn, the child
then raced to the sidelines to deposit the carcass with one of the
village elders—presumably his own grandfather—and sped off
in search of another ball. Along the sidelines, the parents and
relatives of the children shrieked directions at them, pointing
and shouting to draw their attention to balls that remained un-
claimed at the far edges of the diamond. For all their ardor,
however, they were obviously amused by the ceremony, and
the most ancient members of the community had to be held
up on their feet, so wracked were they with laughter. To be sure,
here and there spectators were covering their eyes with their

fingertips—a gesture apparently signifying shame. These, it would seem, were relatives of the few youngsters who kneeled retching in the basepaths or rolled around the mound, in the full glow of the fire, clutching their stomachs and whimpering with pain.

Finally there was not a ball that had been donated by the generous little boys of Port Ruppert whose cover had not been wholly devoured. On their haunches again, the panting, sweating little children waited while Walter Johnson and the Wise One moved along the foul lines, counting the skinned baseballs that had been dropped at the feet of the village elders.

The winner of the competition was a burly little fellow, no more than seven, who had eaten the covers off five regulation baseballs. Hoisted up on to Walter Johnson's marvelous shoulders, he was carried ceremoniously around the basepaths, while the villagers chanted, "*Typee! Typee! Typee!*"

The next competition turned out to be not so amusing, or so successful, and left the villagers oddly dispirited, as though they might be wondering, "What's the matter with the kids these days?"

It was a hitting contest. The object fired down off the hill by Walter Johnson was not a baseball, however—there was no longer a single baseball intact on the entire continent of Africa —but a black, shriveled head, slightly larger in circumference than the nine and a quarter inch ball considered "official" in the big leagues. Invariably Johnson got two quick strikes past a youngster before he had even gotten the bat off his bare little shoulder; then he would throw him a head wide or low of the plate, and strike him out swinging. Now, from the way the spectators hissed and spat at the children from the sidelines, it would seem that to bring the meat-end of a bat into contact with what had once been the face of a tribal enemy, or traitor, appeared to them to be as easy as pie; the fact that the youngsters could not even rouse themselves to swing until they were already down by two strikes, bespoke a timidity that particularly enraged the menfolk. Yet, for all that the fathers barked angry instructions at the tiny little hitters, leaping high into the air and showing their filed teeth to communicate their disappointment, their offspring remained frozen in fear at the plate, even though Walter

Johnson was clearly throwing nothing but half-speed pitches, and curves that turned so slowly you could virtually see the glum expression on the face as it broke down the middle.

Only the burly little seven-year-old who had skinned and eaten the most hides managed to get so much as a *piece* of a head, ticking an ear or an eyelid so lightly however, that after examination by the Wise One, the head was deemed undamaged enough to be thrown back into play. Nonetheless, he managed to stay alive in the batter's box longer than any of his little friends, and was thus declared the winner once again.

Now the tribesman whom Mister Fairsmith had come to call Babe Ruth—as much for his barrel-chested, bandy-legged physique as his power at the plate—was called out of the crowd of spectators to satisfy the expectations that the fledglings of the village had so miserably disappointed. And did he! *There* was the old sound of wood against bone! The moment the bat met the skull, you just knew that that old head was *gone*. What a night for the Babe! Fourteen heads thrown, fourteen heads smashed to smithereens.

No sooner was the exhibition over, than the village children, and even some of the men, surged forward to capture a sliver of cranial bone as a souvenir of the occasion.

And now came the ceremony of the virgins and the baseball bats. The tribe, stirred to a frenzy by Babe Ruth's performance at the plate, went silent as worshippers when the first demure native girl, with brass hoops dangling from her ears, and her shaved head covered by a Mundy baseball cap, was led slowly in from the bullpen and across the dark outfield by the Wise One. The women tending the fire reached out to touch the lithe naked body when she moved past the flames, and on the sidelines the spectators whispered excitedly to see the tears of joy in her large brown eyes. Under the direction of Walter Johnson —as gentle now with the maiden as he had been severe with the young boys—the girl arranged herself upon home plate, as she did so darting a shy glance toward the "hitter" in the on-deck circle. Then Walter Johnson gently pulled the oversized Mundy cap down over her eyes and the women of the tribe began to sing.

A jug of boiling water dipped from the kettle was used to wash down the plate after the initiate had taken her turn in the box. With a broom of twigs the Wise One brushed away every last grain of dust, and then examined the bat to be used next, giving particular attention to the handle, to be sure that it had been cleansed of the resin that Mister Fairsmith had encouraged the players to use in order to improve their grip in this tropical climate. From the meticulous hygienic ritual that preceded each deflowering—and too from the tender way in which Walter Johnson covered their eyes to prevent them from growing skittish, in the manner of fillies—it would appear that the girls of this tribe were a pampered lot indeed. Each bat was used but once and then discarded, yet another indication of the singular care and concern lavished upon the pubescent female in this remote corner of the world.

Then came the feast.

Gloves had been boiling in the kettle all the while the girls had been up at the plate. By now they were cooked to a turn, and when they were removed from the water and scattered about the field the villagers fell upon them with ferocity—in the end they did not even leave uneaten the tough lacing that edged the first-basemen's mitts. The eyelets through which the lacing was drawn they spit on the ground like so many pits, but everything else they devoured, thirty-six gloves in all: four right-handed catchers' mitts, four first-basemen's mitts (two left-handed, two right-handed), and eighteen right-handed fielders' gloves eaten by the men; ten left-handed fielders' mitts divided among the women and the children. The chest protectors were boiled for dessert, and while the adults sucked and chewed on the canvas, the children gobbled down the filling. Some of the tots were carried off to sleep still clutching tufts of hairy wadding in their little pink palms.

Long after the village was asleep, when only embers burned where the huge fires had illuminated the infield, Mister Fairsmith, hanging still from his post in the third-base coaching box, was stirred to consciousness by the noise of creatures scurrying back and forth across the diamond. In the dim light he gradually was able to bring his eyes to focus upon the crones of the village, bone-thin women, bent and twisted in the spine, who were scrambling and darting about like a school of crabs over the ocean floor. Combing the playing field, they had collected all the bats that had been discarded earlier on, and now with no regard for the sanctity of the ritual, for hygiene or for decorum, they proceeded to ape the ceremony of the virgins and the bats. Two or three together would roll in the dust around home plate, cackling and moaning, whether in mockery of the young virgins or in imitation, it was impossible for Mister Fairsmith to tell.

Then, with a blast of heat right up from Hades, the African dawn—and fast as they could, the old women departed, using the serviceable Louisville Sluggers for crutches and canes.

Across the field Billy still hung from his pole in the first-base coaching box. He too had escaped the kettle. But that was all he had escaped.

"Old . . . old-timers' day . . ." he called to his uncle, looking with a lopsided smile after the departing hags.

To which Mister Fairsmith cried out twice, a cry that was no more than a breath: "The horror! The horror!"

In the morning, with the sun really cooking, one of the village boys came skipping out to the field, apparently without any idea at all that the season in the Congo had come to an end. Or maybe he was hoping that even if his friends and their fathers had returned to the round of life such as had existed in the village before Mister Fairsmith and his bearers had emerged from the jungle, the Mundy manager might at least play a game of "pepper" with him. It was the boy Mister Fairsmith had christened Wee Willie, after Wee Willie Keeler, whose famous dictum, "Hit 'em where they ain't," had taken a strong hold upon the youngster's imagination. He was exceedingly bright for a dusky little fellow, and in the week's time had even come to learn a few words of English, along with learning how to switch his feet and punch the ball through to the opposite field.

For several minutes he stood before the stake to which Mister Fairsmith was fastened, waiting to receive his instructions. Then he spoke. "Mistah Baseball?" He reached up and tugged at the Patriot League buckle on the manager's belt. "Mistah Baseball?"

Nothing. So he ran clockwise around the diamond, sliding into second on his bare behind, then into first, before approaching the white man hanging from the stake in the first-base coaching box. Looking up into the lopsided smile, he gave him the bad news. "Mistah Baseball—he dead."

The canoe in which the two Americans were discovered was decorated on either side with what must have been the tribe's symbol for Death, a stick figure holding in one of his outstretched arms an oval shield looking something like an oversized catcher's mitt. The bodies had been wrapped from head to foot in the yarn off the two dozen balls whose hides had been eaten by the boys of the tribe. They were discovered (just barely this side of the afterlife) in a stream twenty miles from Stanleyville, from whence they were borne by friendly natives through the jungle to a hospital in the city. And there they lay for weeks and weeks, first Mister Fairsmith, then young Billy, about to land, like a called third strike, in the Great Mitt of Death.

When they could walk again, it was the older man who led the younger through the gardens. Every time they came upon a doctor or a nun, Billy would launch into a description of the marvelous night game that he and his uncle had witnessed in the interior. He told them of the nine girls who had come up to the plate to "pinch-hit," he told them of "the Old-Timers' Game," that had taken place just before dawn, but in that by and large the staff was composed of Belgians, they listened politely, without any understanding that the young American had lost his mind.

Thereafter, for so long as the Mundys made their home in Port Ruppert, Mister Fairsmith arranged for Billy and a nurse from the institution to be chauffeured out to the ball park on Opening Day, and for the two to be seated in a box directly beside his honor the mayor. That was the least he could do, for, loosely speaking, he was responsible for the boy's mind having become forever unhinged. Not, mind you, that Mister Fairsmith would have conducted himself any differently if he'd had to live through that nightmare again. True, a bright young man whose ambition had been to become a missionary in the service of Christ had lost his bearings in the world. But suppose, on the other hand, Ulysses S. Fairsmith had consented to allow African baseball players to slide into first after a walk . . . suppose he had been the one responsible for an entire continent of black men turning the great American game of baseball into so much wallowing in the mud . . . No, he could never have borne that upon his conscience.

*

To return to the trial facing the venerable manager in his eighti-
eth year, the hopeless '43 Ruppert Mundys—how could they
disgust and horrify him even more than those African savages?
Precisely because they were *not* African savages, but Americans! (by and large), big leaguers! (supposedly). For heathen
barbarians to defile the national pastime was one thing, but
American men wearing the uniform of the major league team
to which Ulysses S. Fairsmith had devoted his entire life? That
was beyond compassion and beneath contempt.

So far-reaching was his disgust that when they arrived (on
separate trains) in a P. League town, Mister Fairsmith would
not even stay at the hotel where he might have the misfortune
of running into one of his players in the lobby or the dining
room. Instead he went off as a guest to the home of the local
evangelist, as much for the sake of religious succor as for the
relief it afforded him to be out of sight of those degenerates
impersonating his beloved Mundys.

"First African savages. Then the Emperor of Japan. And now,
now my own Mundys. Billy," he asked the evangelist, "how
can God exist and sanction such as this?"

"The Lord has his reasons, Samuel."

"But have you ever been to watch this team on the field of
play?"

"No. But I read the box scores. I know what they are
suffering."

"Billy, the box scores are as nothing beside the games
themselves."

"We can only pray, Samuel. Let us pray."

And so instead of traveling out to the ball park, where
nothing he could say or do would change these imposters into
Mundys, Mister Fairsmith would remain on his knees throughout the afternoon, praying that the Lord might accomplish the
transformation that was beyond his own managerial powers.

Each evening, after dinner, Jolly Cholly traveled out from
the hotel to tell Mister Fairsmith the results of that day's game.
The minister's wife always prepared a plate of cookies to bring
to the Mundy coach while he sat in a chair beside Mister Fairsmith's bed and, scorecard in hand, described the horrors of
the afternoon, play by play.

Down in the living room, the minister asked his wife, "How is he taking it?"

"He just lies there, looking into space."

"I'll go to him, when Jolly Cholly leaves."

"I think you had better."

At the door, the minister would say to the Mundy coach, "And who will be the starting pitcher tomorrow, Mr. Tuminikar?"

And as often as not, Jolly Cholly shrugged and answered, "Whoever feels like it, I guess. We sort of have given up on any kind of rotation, Reverend. Whoever wants the exercise, he just grabs his mitt and goes on out there."

Carrying his Bible and wearing his collar, the minister would enter Mister Fairsmith's room.

"In victory," cried the Mundy manager, "I was magnanimous. In defeat I was a gentleman. In Africa, I would have martyred myself rather than permit those savages to sully the national game. Why, why is this happening!"

"Tell *me* why, Samuel. Say what is in your heart. Why has the Lord chosen you for such suffering and pain?"

"Because," said Mister Fairsmith, bitterly, "because the Lord hates baseball."

"But our Lord is just and merciful."

"No, He hates baseball, Billy. Either that, or He does not exist."

"Our Lord exists, Samuel. Moreover, He loves baseball with a love that is infinite and all-encompassing."

"Then why is there such a team as the '43 Mundys? Why a Hothead Ptah! Why a Nickname Damur! And now a dwarf who blinded a midget! A dwarf in a Ruppert uniform! *Why?*"

"Samuel, you must not lose faith. He will answer our prayers, albeit in His own time."

"But they are already in last place *by fifty games!*"

"Many that are first by fifty games shall be last, Samuel, and the last by fifty, first. Let us pray."

So he prayed: in Tri-City with the Reverend Billy Tollhouse, in Aceldama with the Reverend Billy Biscuit, in Independence with the Reverend Billy Popover, in Terra Incognita with the Reverend Billy Scone, in Asylum with the Reverend Billy Zwieback, in Kakoola with the Reverend Billy Bun. Yes, the most famous radio preachers of the era sought to save the great manager from apostasy; but, alas, by the middle of September, with the Mundys having won but twenty-three of one hundred and forty-two games, those who patiently tried to explain to him that perhaps he would have to wait until next year for his prayers to be answered, feared that if the Lord did not intervene in behalf of the Mundys before the season's end, Ulysses S. Fairsmith's faith would be extinguished forever.

And then it happened. Mundys 14, Blues 6. Mundys 8, Blues 0. Mundys 7, Keepers 4. Mundys 5, Keepers 0.

Hallelujah! Hallelujah! Hallelujah!

"So there is a God on high, and He does love baseball."

"It would appear so, Billy."

"And He has tested His servant, Ulysses S. Fairsmith, and He has not found him wanting."

"Then *that* was His reason."

Hallelujah! Hallelujah!

Perhaps they were a last place team with the worst record ever compiled in the history of the three leagues, but on the train ride back across the country following the 9–3 home-run extravaganza against Terra Incognita—their eleventh in a row—they were as joyous and confident as any Ruppert team Mister Fairsmith could recall, including the great pennant winners of the twenties.

The train was bound for Tri-City, where they were to play their final game of the year, a contest rained out earlier in the season against the Tycoons. And what a victory that was going to be! Oh sure, the bookmakers had them down as four-to-one underdogs (how on earth could they do it again? how could the Mundys knock the Tycoons out of first on the last day of the season?) but there wasn't a Ruppert Mundy who heard those odds, who didn't have to laugh. "Well, you want to be a rich man, George," they told the grinning porter, "you lay down two bits and see if you ain't got yourself a dollar in your pocket by tomorrow night."

Soldiers on board the eastbound train continually drifted back to the dining car during the evening meal to get a peek at the miracle team of the Patriot League. "Our pleasure, our pleasure," the Mundys said, when the G.I.s asked for autographs. The soldiers said, "You don't know what it means to a feller headed to he-don't-know-where, just to be ridin' the same train with a team what's done what you guys have. Wait'll I write home!"

"Good luck, soldier! Good luck, G.I. Joe!" the Mundys called after them. "You make it hot for old Hitler now!"

"We will! We will!"

"Good luck, lads! You're brave boys!"

"And good luck to you—in Tri-City!"

"Oh, tell that to them Tycoons! Them's the ones need luck!"

They were up till midnight in the diner, playing spit-in-the-ocean and smoking Havana cigars. The waiters, who ordinarily would have shooed them off to their berths hours ago—after having flung their food at them, cold and greasy—were more than happy to stay and do their bidding, just for the privilege of hearing the rampaging Ruppert recount inspirational anecdotes from their amazing eleven-game streak. After all, if the Mundys could rise from ignominy to glory virtually overnight, who in this world could consider himself doomed?

"Yes, *suh*, Mistah Hothead! Yes, *suh*, Mistah Nickname! Mistah O.K.—you want sump'n, suh?"

"A new pack of Bicycles, George!"

"Yes, *suh*!"

At midnight, leaning on Jolly Cholly's arm, Mister Fairsmith entered the dining car. Nickname doused his cigar in his beer, and Ockatur, who had the lion's share of the winnings piled on the tray of the high chair in which he was seated, slipped the money surreptitiously into his pocket.

Following the two victories in Independence and the four in Asylum, Mister Fairsmith had rejoined the team in the dugout, remaining with them throughout their last five triumphs in Kakoola and Terra Inc. His cane across his lap, a beatific gleam in his blue eyes, he slowly rocked to and fro on his chair, as one Mundy runner after another crossed home plate. He was a far more decrepit figure than they remembered from Opening Day—the wear and tear of all that prayer. Indeed, if anything had the power to subdue these spirited Mundys, who now virtually quivered with energy from breakfast to bedtime, it was that look in Mister Fairsmith's eye of exceeding wisdom and benevolence.

With Jolly Cholly's assistance, Mister Fairsmith was helped into a chair drawn into the aisle at the head of the car. "I have a telegram to read to you before I retire for the night," he said, studying the face of each of the redeemed. "It has just this minute arrived, and was brought back to me by the engineer. 'Dear Sam. No matter what the outcome of tomorrow's game, I want you to know how proud I am of you and the Ruppert Mundys. As a result of what you have accomplished against the most insuperable odds, the R that once stood for Ruppert must henceforth be considered to stand for nothing less than this great Republic. The Mundys are a homeless team no more— they belong to an entire nation. Sam, I will consider it a great privilege if I may board the train in Port Ruppert tomorrow morning and accompany you and your team to their final game in Tri-City.' Signed, 'General Douglas D. Oakhart, President of the Patriot League.' "

With this, Mister Fairsmith signaled for Jolly Cholly to help him to his feet. "Good night, Mundys. Good night, my Ruppert Mundys," and his creased and craggy face beamed with love.

Rupe-it!

There was a band to greet them—at 6 A.M.! And all along the tracks into the station, Rupe-it rootas, waving hand-lettered signs wildly in the air.

MUNDYS WE MISS YOU!
GONE BUT NOT FORGOTTEN!
MUNDYS COME HOME ALL IS FORGIVEN!

The players pressed their noses to the windows and waved at the crowd that had turned out at dawn just to watch their train pass through on the way to Massachusetts.

When the train stopped to receive passengers, mobs of schoolchildren surged to the side of the sleeping car to gape at the heroes whose names had all at once become legendary throughout the land. The players winked and laughed and blew kisses, and then, when they were moving again, lay back

in their berths, not a few with tears on their faces. Winning!
Winning! Oh, you just can't say enough good things about
winning!

Festooned with ribbons, General Oakhart stood at the entrance
to the dining car to receive them; Mister Fairsmith, supported
by Jolly Cholly, introduced the victorious players one by one.
When the last Mundy was seated before his orange juice, the
President of the league addressed them:

"Before I drink a toast to this brave and courageous ball
club"—he amused the players, who were easy to amuse these
days, by tapping a fingernail on his juice glass—"I have a telegram to read to you date-marked yesterday noon. 'Dear General. No one could be more delighted than I am by the
remarkable Mundy winning streak. As you know, at the outset
of the season, I shared your fears that the burden they had
chosen to bear might ultimately do serious damage to their
morale. And indeed, there were moments during the season
when being a permanent road club seemed to be weighing too
heavily upon the shoulders of the Ruppert team. But just when
it appeared that our worst fears were about to be realized, they
have astounded and heartened the entire country with the
most incredible display of Big League ball many a fan has seen
this season, or *any* season. It is a great moment, not only for the
Mundys and Mister Fairsmith, not only for you and the Patriot
League, not only for baseball, but for the nation. I am deeply
honored by your invitation to join you in your box at Tycoon
Park to watch this final contest of the Patriot League season,
and wish to inform you that despite pressing business here in
the Commissioner's office, I will leave Chicago in time to be in
Tri-City to address the Mundys in their clubhouse before the
game begins.' And, gentlemen, the telegram is signed by the
Commissioner of Baseball, Judge Kenesaw Mountain Landis."

And there he was, craggier even than Mister Fairsmith, the
czar of baseball, waiting to greet them as they entered the visitors' clubhouse at noon. If till then the Mundys had any doubt
that they had passed from being the most despised to the most
beloved baseball team in America, it surely disappeared when
the Commissioner, of his own accord, kneeled to exchange a
few pleasantries with O.K. Ockatur. Then, while the flashbulbs

popped, the fearless judge—so aptly named for an American mountain—read the following telegram to the team:

"'My dear Judge Landis. It has been a bracing experience for me, as for my fellow Americans, to watch the Ruppert Mundys turn a season of seeming catastrophe into a gallant triumph. I firmly believe that the farmers and the factory workers, the children in our schools and the women who keep the home fires burning, and above all, our brave fighting men around the globe, cannot but draw inspiration from the "Never Say Die" spirit of these illustrious men. Though I cannot join you today at Tri-City to watch this undiscourageable nine in their final battle of the season, I assure you I will, from the War Room, be in continual telephone contact with the stadium in order to remain abreast of the inning-by-inning developments. Accepting your most kind and thoughtful invitation in my behalf will be my wife, a baseball fan in her own right, and one who has seen in the resurgence of the team everyone had counted out, a stirring example for all underdogs everywhere. With every best wish, very sincerely yours, Franklin D. Roosevelt.'"

So, along with Mrs. Trust and General Oakhart and Judge Kenesaw Mountain Landis, the wife of the President of the United States sat that afternoon in a box behind the Tri-City dugout, there to pay tribute to the Ruppert team in behalf of America's Chief Executive. The game, in fact, was delayed thirty minutes while Mrs. Roosevelt went down into the visitors' dugout to shake the hands of the players and ask them what states they were from. Then she rejoined the other dignitaries in the box, and the Tycoons, weary from their season-long battle against the surging Butchers, and visibly unnerved by all the attention being heaped upon their adversaries, took the field. Though the day was breezy, and he had taken no more than a dozen warm-up pitches, Smoky Woden's uniform was already gray with perspiration when Frenchy Astarte stepped up to the plate and the umpire cried, "Play ball!"

No need to chronicle here the records compiled in a game about which tens of thousands of words were written during that fall and winter: the record number of times Hothead Ptah tripped on his mask going back for foul pop-ups, the record number of times that Mike Rama knocked himself unconscious against the left-field wall, the record number of times Specs Skirnir "lost" ground balls in the sun—every stupid and humiliating mishap of that afternoon was recounted by the sports columnists of the nation no less frequently than the third strike that Mickey Owen dropped in the '41 World Series, or the error that earned Bonehead Merkle his nickname in 1908, and lost the Giants the pennant.

With two out in the ninth and his team down by thirty-one runs, Nickname Damur got the fifth Mundy hit of the day— Agni had the other four—a clean shot up the alley in left center, and then was out when he tried to stretch the double into a three-bagger. The Tycoon fans, by reputation as sober and scholarly a crowd as you could find anywhere, were so busy laughing at the sheer idiocy of Nickname's base-running, that it was a while before they even realized that their team had just won the '43 flag. In the dugout, streaming tears, Nickname stood before Mister Fairsmith and tried to think of some sort of explanation for what he had just done.

"I don't know, sir," he said, shrugging. "I guess you could say I gambled."

"Thirty-one runs behind in the ninth . . . and you say . . . you say you *gambled*? My God," moaned Mister Fairsmith, "my God, why hast thou forsaken me?" and rolling off his rocker, died on the floor of the visitors' dugout.

"What happened, you son of a bitch?"

"I couldn't—I couldn't do it."

"Why, Roland, *why* couldn't you?"

"Don't you know who all was eatin' breakfast with us? General Oakhart! You know who all was in the box? Judge Landis, the Commissioner! And Mrs. Eleanor Roosevelt! And you know who sent us a telegram? *The President of the United States!*"

"And what do they have to do with anything?"

"They just happen to be the most important people in the world, that's all!"

"Idiot! They are the most important people in the world just like the Wheaties they make in Minneapolis are the Breakfast of Champions!"

"But they kept sending these *telegrams*. Everybody kept

sayin', 'I just got this telegram,' and it would get all hushed and everythin', and then when they start in readin' it, it would sound just like the Gettysburg Address or somethin'! It would give me the gooseflesh!"

"And that's why you couldn't do it—because of the goose-flesh?"

"But we had enough money anyway, Isaac! You said we had the quarter million to buy me already!"

"Oh, we had it all right."

"What—what do you mean, Isaac! You said on the phone we had *more*—two hundred and seventy-five thousand dollars—you told me that just last night!"

"And just last night we did."

"But if you lost twenty-five today, you still have enough—well, *don't you?* They didn't go raise the price on me, on account of my goin' four for four—*did they?*"

"You know what the odds were today, Roland? 4–1. Two hundred and seventy-five thousand dollars would get you a million and change, if the Mundys did it again."

"Yeah—*so?*"

"So I thought, since the Mundys *are* going to win, why buy just Roland Agni? Why not a whole franchise while I'm at it?"

"*So?*"

"So I bet the wad, Rollie."

"You *did?*"

"See, I didn't figure on the league's leading hitter getting gooseflesh from all those telegrams. I didn't figure on being betrayed by a weakling and a coward!"

"You bet it *all?*"

"All."

"Then—*there's nothin' left!*"

"Correct. I go back to splitting atoms, you go back to being a Ruppert Mundy for the rest of your life."

"But *I can't!*"

"Oh yes you can, you All-American asshole. Gooseflesh from telegrams!"

"But it was just my *respect* comin' out!"

"*Respect?* For *who*, for *what?*"

"For the President of the United States! For—for the whole country!"

"But *I'm* the one you should respect, Roland. The one you should have gooseflesh over is *me*! Ah, go on back to the Mundys, Agni. That's where you belong anyway."

"I *don't*!"

"You do, my cowardly, simple-minded, patriotic pal. Because that's all you really are when it comes down to it—a Ruppert Mundy."

"And you—you're a lousy loudmouth little kike! You're a dirty greedy money-mad mocky! You're a Shylock! You're a sheeny! *You killed Christ!* I'd rather be a *nigger* than be one of you!"

"Well, good, Roland. Because before this is over, you may get your chance."

And so the '43 season came to an end.

Mister Fairsmith's body was borne by train directly from Tri-City to Cooperstown, New York. The journey of less than three hundred miles lasted through a day and a night, for in every village and hamlet along the way the train would draw to a halt to allow those who had gathered together at the station to say goodbye to the great Mundy manager. The local high school team, with heads bowed and eyes closed, was invariably to be found at the siding with their coach, as were numerous children in baseball togs, some so small they had to be held in their mother's arms.

In the village of Cooperstown, the flag-draped coffin was removed from the train by members of the Mundy team and placed upon a horse-drawn caisson. To the slow, mournful pace set by the corps of drummers from the service academies, and escorted by an honor guard drawn from every team in the three leagues, each wearing his gray "away" uniform, the Mundys walked behind the coffin down the main street of Cooperstown. At the National Baseball Hall of Fame, the coffin was unlashed and the pallbearers—Astarte, Damur, Baal, Ptah, Rama, Heket, Skirnir, and Agni—carried it through the gate and up the steps of the Museum and into the gallery of the Hall of Fame, a room nearly as long as the distance from home to first, and flanked by black marble columns hewn from the earth of Mister Fairsmith's native Vermont.

There, beneath the bronze plaques upon which are sculpted

the faces of baseball's immortals, brief eulogies were delivered by General Oakhart and Judge Landis. Each noted that Ulysses S. Fairsmith and the pillars came from the same state, and drew the appropriate conclusions. Judge Landis described him as "baseball's ambassador to mankind," and said that throughout the world, people of all races and nations would mourn the passing of the man known to many of them simply as "Mister Baseball." Slowly, he read the "roll call" of the seven continents to which Mister Fairsmith had traveled as the ambassador of the national pastime. "Yes," he said, in conclusion, "even Antarctica. That was the kind of human being that this man was." Then the doors to the street were opened and throughout the afternoon the fans filed past the open coffin, made of hickory wood by Hillerich and Bradsby.

They buried him on a hillside that looks down upon the spot where (legend has it) Abner Doubleday invented the game in 1839. And if it *is* only legend? Does this make the shrine any less holy?

"Oh God," said the Reverend Billy Bun, "Thy servant, having played his nine innings upon this earth  . . ."

When the last prayer had been uttered by the last of the Billies, each of the Mundy regulars stepped up to the grave, and with a bat handed him by the minister, fungoed a high fly ball in the direction of the setting sun. Then a solitary bugle played "Take Me Out to the Ballgame," and the mourners turned and made their way back down into the town that is to baseball fans the Lourdes, the Canterbury, the Kyoto of America.

# 7

## THE RETURN OF
## GIL GAMESH; OR,
## MISSION FROM MOSCOW

# 7

*An extraordinary letter of reference. A project of Mrs. Trust's, and her
trip with General Oakhart to visit a penitent sinner. Gil Gamesh relates
his history; his wonderings; student days at SHIT, and other adventures
in Soviet Russia. The Soviet spy system revealed to the General. The author puts in a brief recorded appearance. In which the history leaps
ahead seven months with an excerpt from General Oakhart's testimony
before a Congressional Committee. The press conference wherein Gamesh
is reinstated; he relates a history appropriate to the occasion. America
opens its heart—with a notable exception. A series of lectures on Hatred
and Loathing. Roland returns to a vengeful team; his chagrin; the surprising discovery he makes in the locker room; his death. In which General Oakhart names names and Gil Gamesh pays tribute to a great
American. The Patriot League cleans house and the Mundy
Thirteen appear before the House Un-American Activities Committee. In which the author puts in an
appearance before the Congressional Committee and expresses his opinion in no uncertain terms. Wherein the history draws
to a conclusion, with a few last-
minute disasters.*

## McWILEY'S GROCERY STORE
### 141 KAKOOLA BLVD., KAKOOLA, WISCONSIN
Wm. McWiley, Prop.

March 1, 1944

To Whom It May Concern:

This is to affirm that Gil Gamesh was formerly employed under a
variety of aliases by the Kakoola Citizens Action Committee for
Americanism and the Kakoola Council to Keep America Free in doing
investigative and research work.

During the period of his employment, Mr. Gamesh's services were
entirely satisfactory and I have no hesitation in recommending him
for any type of work in which a thorough knowledge of Communism
and Communist methods is necessary. He made an excellent witness
in executive session of the statewide Citizens Action Committee for
Americanism held here in Kakoola at McWiley's Grocery Store for
November 23–24, 1943, and his services were much in demand by

the investigative units of both the Committee and the Council throughout the Middle West.

His knowledge of Communism and Communist methods can be utilized in the fields of dissemination of information concerning Communism, as well as the field of investigation.

Yours very truly,
Wm. McWiley
President, Kakoola CACA
Legal Director, Kakoola KAF

"Mrs. Trust," said the General, returning the letter to the old lady of the league, "the Ruppert Mundys have just this afternoon lost their first exhibition game of the '44 season by a score of 12–4 to Asbury Park High. I have just this moment learned by phone that they would not even have scored their four runs if the high school coach hadn't put in his junior varsity for a couple of innings' experience against a big league club, once he had the game sewed up. I have Roland Agni, the league's leading hitter, out there in Michigan sulking in his bedroom, refusing to join the Mundys in New Jersey for spring training, or ever again, from what he tells his poor father—I have a league, in other words, that is just about coming apart at the seams, Mrs. Trust, and you arrive here with a letter for me to read from some greengrocer in Kakoola."

"This greengrocer happens also to be the President of the Kakoola Citizens Action Committee for Americanism and the Legal Director of the Kakoola Council to Keep America Free."

"Organizations unknown to me, I'm afraid."

"And I suppose the name Gil Gamesh is unknown to you as well?"

Wearily he said, "It rings a bell, Madam."

"You banished him from baseball."

"And would again, for all that it appears to have cost us."

"*And* him."

"That a criminal should be stigmatized for his crime seems to me one of the few reassuring facts of this life; that the victim should be stigmatized, therein lies the tragedy. My dear lady, I long ago lost interest in the fate of Gil Gamesh. I assumed, as I think you did, that the man was dead. Nor did I grieve at the thought that he might have come to a violent end. At the risk of being indecorous, let me say that I understood how your feelings might have been otherwise. I would not have expected them to be my own. Nonetheless, ever since you assumed the ownership of the Tycoons, I have had every reason to believe that you joined in the opinion of baseball's leaders that I had acted in the best interests of the game and the league, and the cause of decency and justice, when I expelled Gamesh in '33. I can't believe that with all that threatens the integrity and existence of our league at this moment, you would want now to divert my attention in any way from the serious work at hand."

"To the contrary," said Angela Trust, hammering the floor with her cane, "I want you to see how much more serious it is than you may wish to know!"

"Madam, we have had our conversations on the subject of Communism. Surely you know I am no friend of the Reds."

"Nor is Will Harridge! Nor is Ford Frick! Nor is that eminent jurist Kenesaw Mountain Landis! And yet all the while you four stalwarts are not befriending the Reds, the Reds continue making inroads into the Patriot League! General, you talk to me of *stigmas*, but there is no stigma—there is only subversion! There is only conspiracy and sabotage!"

"Mrs. Trust, that is just so much foolishness."

"And is *this*?" she cried, rattling the letter in the air. "Would it still seem foolish if what I have been telling you for years were told to you now by a man who has consorted with the Communists for a decade? Would it be foolishness if you heard my own warnings from the mouth of a man who studied for four years in Moscow at the International Lenin School of Subversion, Hatred, Infiltration, and Terror? Who now takes his orders directly from *the highest placed Communist agent in America*?"

"You mean this *grocer*, this McWiley?"

"*I mean Gil Gamesh.*"

"Gamesh? A Communist *spy*?"

"As far as the Communists are concerned, yes. But I know otherwise. And now, General, so too do you: Gil Gamesh, who loathed America, loves it once again. He has defected back to us."

"How can you say these things *seriously*? Who *told* you all this?"

Beneath the thousand wrinkles, she was suddenly as radiant as she had ever been. "Gil," she answered.

Mrs. Trust's limousine carried them to the no-man's land between Greenback Stadium and the waterfront, amidst the looming warehouses and grimy factories of what had been Tri-City's "Docktown," a workers' quarter once as lively with petty intrigue, as squalid, as "colorful" as anything bordering the docks of Marseilles or Singapore. Here and there a dirt path still opened up through the weeds back of a trucking platform, and beside a heap of charred rubbish or the rusted-out bones of a dismantled car, stood one of those lean-to shacks that used to house Docktown families of five, six, and seven—a brawling immigrant couple, their ragged children, the toothless Old World parents. By 1944, of course, a few two-by-fours nailed together in Tri-City at the tail-end of the previous century hardly resembled any sort of human habitation, and, in fact, seemed to be home only to the barnswallows that swooped toward the General's glittering Army insignia as he followed angrily along the rutted path behind the grande dame, who set a feverish pace, cane and all.

The General looked at him in disbelief. No yellow linen suit; no perforated two-tone shoes; no brilliantine making patent leather of the hair; no *hair*; no swagger either; no scowl; no crooked smile; no *smile*—no expression at all, other than a terrifying blankness fixed upon bones as prominent as the handles of a valise. The man appeared to have been stripped of hide, meat, and muscle, boiled down to bone, then wired together again like the extinct displayed in the biology lab—and finally covered over in a shroud of wax a size too small for his carcass. The clothes too looked like retreads, just such outfits as are issued to those corpses selected to rise from the dead to go and walk among the living in Automats and public library reading rooms: fraying gray cotton jacket, thread-worn tweed trousers thickly cuffed, narrow black knit tie, and dark shoes with a wedge of heel thin as a wafer and the leather worn membranous over the corns. The uniform, not of the dandy, but the "loner."

"General Oakhart," said the ghost, gravely.

"I am he. But who may I ask are you?"

"Just who Angela says I am."

"I don't believe it. You don't look like the Gil Gamesh I knew. You don't *sound* like that Gil Gamesh, either."

"Nor do I feel like that Gil Gamesh any longer. Nonetheless, that is the Gil Gamesh I am doomed to remain forever. I can never hope to unburden myself of his foolishness, his treachery, or his despair. My hair is gone. My arm is gone. My looks are gone. So what. I am what I have been. Can I now become what I would be? It seems once again, General, that my future is in your hands."

"What future? Who are you, man? Do you live in this dump?"

"This dump and worse dumps. This dump and palaces. I've driven dynamite over the Rockies in a broken-down Ford. I've fought gun duels in the Everglades with the F.B.I. Prison in Poland. Sturgeon with Stalin. Cocktails with Molotov."

"Mrs. Trust, only listen to this impostor—just *look* at him! This is not Gil Gamesh!"

"If you like, General," said the ghost, "I will recount to you in detail the substance of my meetings with you and Mike the Mouth in the summer of '33. 'Gil,' he said, 'somebody in this world has got to run the game. Otherwise, you see, it wouldn't be baseball, it would be chaos. We would be right back where we were in the Ice Ages . . .'"

"If you are Gamesh, where did you learn to speak like a radio announcer, instead of a roughneck off the streets?"

"Where else?" said Gamesh. "Night school."

"And how do you come to *look* like this?"

"Rage, hatred, suffering—you name it."

"And you live here, is that the idea? Is this your hideout, or some such nonsense?"

"It is my *yafka*, yes."

"Meaning what! Speak English!"

"I hide here, General, from time to time. It also happens to be the house where I was born. A fitting place to be reborn. General, there is no need for you to doubt my identity. I am Gil Gamesh, an agent of the Communist Party, just returned from six years in Moscow, four of them at the International Lenin School from which I received the equivalent of a Ph.D. in espionage and sabotage. My mission is to complete the destruction of the Patriot League of Professional Baseball Clubs."

"Madness!" cried General Oakhart to Mrs. Trust. "Sheer madness, all of it!"

"I agree, General," replied Gamesh. "I have indeed been a mad, enraged creature. All my life I found my strength in rancorous resentment, but only after my banishment from baseball did I plunge headlong into a barbarous world of violence and vengeance, and dedicate myself wholly to destroying what had destroyed me. Only listen to my story, General, and perhaps it will explain even to your satisfaction how I come to look as I do . . ."

After he had been banished, he said, he had made his way west, robbing and raping as he went, teaming up along the way with other vengeful men. In those years they were not hard to come by. There was no Germany or Japan to hate then—only one's own, one's native land. Whom did he meet in those Depression years who had not been abused, humiliated, cheated, thwarted, and wrecked (to hear the victim tell it) by America? Was there a man in a bar between Port Ruppert and Seattle without a score to settle, without reparations due him, without hatred boiling in his heart? While busting miners' heads for a copper company in Nevada, he met a man named "Bill Smith" —a Commie in scab's clothing. It was the Communists who sent him to night school to learn the three Rs; Russian they taught him on their own. They gave him books to read. They gave him fraudulent birth certificates. They gave him dynamite. They gave him guns. They told him America was on its last legs—brave revolutionary leaders like Gil Gamesh would deal the deathblow to their homeland. They told him a new day was dawning for mankind, and he pretended to be happy to hear the news. But what did he care about mankind? That was just another highfalutin' name for the sons of bitches who screwed you out of what was yours. Mankind? That was for "Bill Smith" and "Bob White" and "Jim Adams," and the hundreds of others with names out of grade school primers, Yids most of them, who kept him awake at night with fervent speeches about "the new day that was dawning." Only it wasn't dawn that interested Gil Gamesh, it was night.

"In 1938 I was called to Moscow, the highest honor that can be accorded a struggling young Communist agent. I was enrolled in the International Lenin School for Subversion, Hatred, Infiltration and Terror, known popularly as SHIT."

"You expect me to believe that that is the name of a school in Moscow, Mr. Gamesh?" asked the skeptical General.

"General, they are nothing if not contemptuous of human decency and dignity. Irreverence and blasphemy are their business, and they know how to practice it, too. Let me go on, please. As a student at SHIT I attended classes fourteen hours a day, seven days a week. To school in the dark, home in the dark, and once a week in winter, out of bed again to perfect the 4 A.M. arrest on somebody down the hall. Summers off in the country, in slave labor camps, administering beatings and conducting interrogations while the regular torturers are on vacation—occasionally driving a prisoner insane or tormenting an intractable suspect into a confession, but by and large the usual student stuff, cleaning up after suicides, seeing that the bread is stale and there's nothing nourishing in the soup, and so on. And the talk, General. The unending lectures. The study groups. And then the murders, of course. Three roommates murdered in their beds during my senior year. My freshman year at SHIT there were eighty-seven of us, handpicked from around the globe. We graduated a class of twenty-four. Sixteen strangled, nineteen poisoned, five run over, eleven shot, three knifed, one electrocuted by a high-voltage toilet seat, and thirteen 'suicides'—out of windows, off roof-tops, and down the stairwell. I pushed two of them myself to pass 'Defenestration.' General Stalin spoke at our graduation. I was class valedictorian. When Stalin shook my hand, he said, 'The final conflict will be between the Communists and the ex-Communists.' The idea startled me. I had thought the final conflict would be between the Communists and the Wall Street Dogs. Only in the next year did I understand Uncle Joe's curious remark, or warning, to the SHIT valedictorian of '42. The higher I rose in espionage circles the more disillusioned I became. Oh, I could stomach the brutality easily enough—it didn't take more than two minutes, if that, to get over missing a murdered friend, and of course a murdered enemy was so much gravy. Then to be graduated directly from SHIT to one of the highest planning positions in Sabotage in the Kremlin restored me to just the sort of power and prestige that I had known so briefly and that I had imagined I had lost forever. No, for that monster of vengeance, Gil Gamesh, Communism was like a dream come true, it was an evil man's paradise, except for one small thing. No baseball.

"Yes, after all those years away, I began missing the hell out of baseball. It wasn't so bad during the winter, but when spring finally came I found myself turning to the back pages of *Pravda* looking for the scores. I'd walk by a vacant lot, hear some kids screaming, and expect to see a gang of boys shagging flies— instead they would be playing 'Purge,' running around arresting each other and dragging the girls into the bushes for mock trials. World Series time was the worst. I understood then what it meant to have betrayed my country. You see, it was the first time in my life that I realized that it *was* my country, that a country, that *anything*, could really be mine. God knows, I wasn't a Russian. Nor was I ever a Babylonian, really, in anything other than name. Least of all was I a member of mankind. No, it wasn't for humanity, or the working class, that my heart ever bled, but only for *me*, Number 19. Or so I thought, until I looked out of my window on Red Square one night last October and saw that while I had been eighteen hours at my desk, planning the destruction of the Patriot League, three feet of snow had fallen on Moscow. And I thought: what the hell am I doing in snow-covered Russia, when in Mother America it is crisp, bright fall? The Cardinals, the Tycoons, and the Yanks are playing in the World Series, even as I sit here! *Who's pitching? What's the score?* And then I did a stupid, reckless thing—I fear still that one day it will cost me my life. At 3 A.M. I walked down the corridor into the shortwave radio room of Soviet Military Intelligence, where I knew there was a man on duty monitoring the opening game, and I sat there until dawn, listening to Spud Chandler pitch a three-hitter against the Tycoons. When Keller grand-slammed Woden I let out a cheer. That's right, Angela, still the Greenback in my heart—still the crosstown rival, even in Moscow! Fortunately the radioman was asleep. Though was he? Who knows? I left before Etten hit his in the eighth, but Keller's was enough. I knew then that I wasn't any longer just Gil Gamesh looking out for himself, I wasn't just Number 19 in this world and no more—I knew then that down beneath the dreams of glory and vengeance, beneath the contempt, the isolation, the loneliness and the hatred, I happened to be an American.

"Of course it was pretty late in the day to be making such a discovery. I was due to return to America in only one week, my mission to personally initiate and oversee our next, and, hopefully, our final assault upon your league, General. As I have said, planning the infiltration and the destruction of the Patriot League has been my primary task ever since my graduation from SHIT. It was with a program such as this in mind that the Party had latched on to me back in '34, though of course it was not until I had proved myself as an underground agent in twenty-two states that I was called to my training in Moscow. In that time the Politburo handed down a different directive on baseball each season. Not only was the program uncoordinated and haphazard, but it became a dangerous battleground for party factions. That is what invariably happens when there is no firm theoretical grasp of the issues. Nine comrades who opposed the destruction of baseball were tried and sentenced to death in 1940 for Incurable Right-Wing Deviationism, and the following year, directly after the All-Star game, nine who *favored* the destruction of baseball were tried and sentenced for the same crime. The fact of the matter is that nobody in all of Russia had the slightest understanding of the political and cultural significance of baseball and its relationship to the capitalist mystique, until I arrived on the scene. It is no secret that my senior honors paper entitled 'The Exploitation of Regional Pride by the Profit-Mongers of Professional Sport' provided the theoretical foundation for the revised plan of attack that eventually resulted in the expulsion of the Mundys from Port Ruppert. Stalin himself, you should know, tended to side at the outset with the faction, now jailed, who were for the expulsion of the Tycoons from Tri-City. Or so he led us to believe. I realize now that he was only testing my strength and my staying power. I am sure he understood from the beginning that any attempt to dislodge the Tycoons would inevitably result in failure, and even worse, exposure of the entire conspiracy against the league. Furthermore, ironic as General Stalin can be at the expense of Mrs. Trust, he is a shrewd judge of character, and a careful student of the reports filed by Colonel Chichikov. He knows just how tough and wily a foe International Communism is up against in the person of Angela Whittling Trust."

"Colonel Chichikov?" said General Oakhart. "And just who is this Colonel Chichikov, if I may ask?"

"Colonel Chichikov of the General Staff. You know him under the alias Frank Mazuma."

"Oh, this *is* preposterous! You're telling me now that Frank Mazuma, the owner of the Kakoola Reapers, is a member of the General Staff of the Red Army?"

"Was at one time, yes. Since 1928, Colonel Chichikov has been one of Russia's most valuable agents in America."

"But in 1928 the man was a well-known bootlegger!"

"Among other things, General, among other things. It is Colonel Chichikov who through his American experiences has provided Stalin with the witticisms he has been dining out on for years. Chichikov's definition of capitalism, for example, is one of Stalin's favorites: 'From each according to his stupidity, to each according to his greed.'"

"Please, Mrs. Trust, how much more of this hallucinatory, psychopathetic rot must I stand here and listen to!"

"As much as it takes," said Mrs. Trust, "to make you face the facts! To make you see that the greatest conspiracy in the nation's history is taking place right under your nose! Of *course* Colonel Chichikov is operating within our midst. Who with eyes in his skull and a brain in his head could have watched the antics of our Mr. Mazuma just this last season and concluded otherwise? *I* have been calling that man a Communist for years, General—now here is Gil Gamesh, fresh from six years in Moscow, four of them a student at SHIT, to tell you that in actuality Mazuma is none other than Colonel Chichikov of the General Staff, and you *still* refuse to believe! What will it take, General, to rouse you from this mindless sloth to do your duty as an American, as a soldier, and as President of the Patriot League? General Oakhart, fail to heed this warning, sir, and you will go down in history with Benedict Arnold, your name like his will be a synonym for treason and betrayal for as long as decent patriots draw breath! For the sake of God, for the sake of America, attend to what this man is telling you. He has been there—he knows!"

"True," said Gamesh, nodding sadly. "I have seen the future, General, and it stinks."

"Gil, tell him who else is an officer in the Russian armed forces. Tell him the name of the man you met in Moscow in 1941."

"O.K. Ockatur," said Gamesh.

"You mean—the dwarf who pitches for the Mundys?" cried Oakhart.

"The dwarf who pitches for the Mundys," said Gamesh. "Formerly Captain Smerdyakov, a tank officer in the Leningrad Military Unit of the Red Army."

"You met him, you're telling me, in *Moscow*?"

"He came to address the school."

The words "Benedict Arnold" had undermined the General's confidence more even than he knew. It simply could not *be* that he who had devoted his entire life to defending the Rules and Regulations could go down in history as neglectful of his responsibilities to be vigilant, honorable, and upright! "Gamesh," cried the aging warrior, "are you sure of this? Are you telling me the truth? Are you absolutely sure it wasn't some *other* dwarf?"

"After four years in the Communist underground, and four more at SHIT, you learn to be able to distinguish between dwarfs, General, easily enough. It was Ockatur. The fact of it is, I am here to spy on him as well as to become the manager of the Mundys."

"Become *what*?"

"That is my mission. I was assigned here the very night news was flashed to the Kremlin of the death of Ulysses S. Fairsmith. 'You will return to America, Comrade Gamesh. You will become the manager of the Mundys. The last there will ever be.' Those were Stalin's words. I said to him, 'Comrade Stalin, that is more easily said than done.' To which he replied, 'Where there is an iron will, Comrade, there is a way.' On my departure, there were those in my own faction who said that Stalin is grooming me to be his heir—on the other hand, there are those among my adversaries who maintain that whether I fail or succeed, my usefulness to the Party will have been exhausted and I will be earmarked for liquidation, precisely as Ockatur is now."

"Liquidation? Ockatur? *Why?*"

"No complicated political motive there, General. Simple, in fact. Stalin is a heartless man who despises dwarfs. Of course, he is curiously drawn to them as well—undoubtedly for pathological reasons. As soon as a new dwarf appears in the Party, he is inevitable elevated with great rapidity to a position of trust in the Kremlin. And then even more quickly annihilated, so that not a trace of him remains. General, if the life of the ordinary citizen in the Soviet Union is fraught with danger and uncertainty, the life of a dwarf there is even worse. That is why you see so very few dwarfs these days in Russia. In the time of the czars, nearly every village and hamlet had at least one misshapen little gnome-like person, if not a dwarf, then a hunchback, if not hunchback, at least a hydrocephalic or something along that line. Today there's hardly a trace of them. You can ride from one end of Russia to the other on the Trans-Siberian Railroad and look in vain for somebody, other than a child, under four feet tall. Either they have risen to the top in the Kremlin, only to be swallowed up in the void, or else, if they have any wits at all, they are in the forests, in hiding, living off nuts and berries, and there they will remain so long as this madman is the ruler over Russia. This madman, General, who would rule the world. And will—unless we stop him, here and now."

"But—but—" There were a thousand questions, a million, a hundred million. And for a Douglas D. Oakhart who would not be a Benedict Arnold, the gravest of all: *what if this is so?*

"But this letter?" said Gamesh.

"Well, yes! Among other things, this letter—from the grocer named McWiley. In Kakoola!"

"Colonel Raskolnikov of the Russian Secret Police."

"You mean—*he* is a spy too?"

"He is *the* spy, General. Raskolnikov is the number one underground espionage agent in the United States. As President of CACA and Legal Director of 'Keep America Free,' he's able to keep abreast of just who in the Middle West has information about the Communist conspiracy to destroy the American way of life. At the same time, his own humble position as a grocer, and his deliberately crackpot behavior, tend to give the whole anti-Communist crusade a bad name. But that's the least of his cunning. Every deadly plan begins with him. In the Soviet Union they say there has never been a hatchet man to match him. At SHIT, of course, his name is legend."

"Mrs. Trust," said the confused and demoralized General, "you—you know this? When you showed me this letter, you knew that William McWiley was in actuality—"

"Of course."

"In other words, you deliberately deceived me!"

"As the Communists learned to their satisfaction a long time ago, to deceive the President of the Patriot League is not such a difficult task."

"True enough," said Gamesh. "Comrade Stalin himself said to me triumphantly at dinner one night, 'Roosevelt in Washington, Oakhart in Massachusetts—as the great Russian proverb has it, When the farmer and his wife hold the jug too long to their lips, the wolf steals through the snow to sink his teeth in the throat of the cackling chicken.'"

*The following phone conversation was monitored and recorded on the evening of March 16, 1944, by agents of the F.B.I. and subsequently introduced into the hearings of a subcommittee of the House Un-American Activities Committee, presided over by Congressman Martin Dies of Texas, and held in Room 1105, United States Court House, Port Ruppert, New Jersey, October 8, 1944.*

SMITTY: Why doesn't he go to the F.B.I.?

OAKHART: He claims the F.B.I. is infiltrated from top to bottom with Communists and Communist sympathizers. He says he wouldn't get out of there alive.

SMITTY: Why not Landis then?

OAKHART: He doesn't trust him. Smitty, neither do I. Landis would use the scandal to make us look bad and himself like a hero. He'd use this thing to shut the league down once and for all. Exactly, Gamesh says, what the Communists would want him to do in the first place.

SMITTY: Then why doesn't he go to the top?

OAKHART: According to him, the Soviet agents in the War Department who arranged the leasing of Mundy Park are Roosevelt appointees. They'd bury it, he says—and him too.

SMITTY: And the papers? What about talking to me? I know the son of a bitch.

OAKHART: Because that would be premature. Right now he could finger only Mazuma and Ockatur—but there are others, just as highly placed, whose identities are a mystery even to him. Then there are the party members and fellow travelers among the players—

SMITTY: And where does he find evidence for that, General?

OAKHART: That's what he's *out* to find. As manager of the Mundys he'll appear to Stalin to be carrying out his mission, but in actuality he'll be in the best possible position to work in our behalf to uncover and expose the entire conspiracy. Up close, inside, managing the team that's been their number one target, he'll be right at the center, able to employ all the skills he's learned from them, against them. At SHIT he was first in his class, Smitty—so he tells us, anyway.

SMITTY: Also at bullshit, my old friend.

OAKHART: You don't buy it?

SMITTY: Do *you*? The guy is crazy. Some lunatic off the street hired by that dried-up old slit. Whatever it is, it ain't on the level.

OAKHART: You think it's not even Gamesh?

SMITTY: Suppose that it is. Why would you believe *him*, of all people? If ever there was a grievance-monger with a score to settle, it's that maniacal bastard. "Sturgeon with Stalin. Cocktails with Molotov." It's all too ridiculous.

OAKHART: Ridiculous, yes—*but what if it's also true?* What if baseball *is* destroyed from within?

SMITTY: When that happens, my dear General, it'll be a sad day indeed, but it won't be the atheistical materialistic Communists who will have done it.

OAKHART: Who then?

SMITTY: Who? The atheistical materialistic capitalists, that's who! A' course that's just one man's opinion, General—fella name a' Smith.

*The following is excerpted from General Oakhart's testimony before the subcommittee of the House Un-American Activities Committee on October 8, 1944, in Port Ruppert.*

THE CHAIRMAN: General, would you tell the Committee why, having solicited the advice and opinion of your friend Mr. Word Smith, the well-known sportswriter, you decided the following morning to disregard it and to recommend the appointment of Gamesh as manager of the Mundys?

GENERAL OAKHART: Well, Mr. Dies, it was because of that startling phrase that Mr. Smith used, "atheistical materialistic capitalists."

MR. THOMAS: In other words, General, until he used that phrase, it just had not entered your head at any time during the previous years that this man might have Communist leanings or might even be an outright agent of a foreign power dedicated to overthrowing our government by violent means.

GENERAL OAKHART: Frankly, sir, I have to say no, it did not. I am afraid I had been completely taken in by him until that evening. Perhaps I might not even have been alert to the implications of the phrase "atheistical materialistic capitalists" if I had not spent those hours earlier in the day with Mrs. Trust and Mr. Gamesh. You must realize—indeed, I know you do—that I have not been alone in believing the Russians and General Stalin to be, in President Roosevelt's words, "our brave allies in the fight against Fascism."

MR. THOMAS: Along that line, General—would it be your opinion, as a former military man, that the war against the Germans and the Japanese has been used by the Communists to mask their subversive activities here in the United States?

GENERAL OAKHART: Absolutely. There is no better example of that particular kind of Communist treachery than the cynical way in which patriotic feelings were manipulated by the Communist agents in the War Department in order to secure the lease to Mundy Park and drive the Ruppert Mundys from their home. I'd like to take this opportunity, if I may, Mr. Thomas, to inform the Committee that I was one of those who from the very outset opposed leasing Mundy Park to the War Department. At that time, of course, I had no idea that Communists had so thoroughly infiltrated the executive branch of the United States government, and that it was they who were plotting the destruction of my league. On the other hand, that destruction was imminent if the Mundys should be dispossessed from Mundy Park—well, that seemed to me a foregone conclusion.

THE CHAIRMAN: General, following your March 16 phone

conversation with Mr. Smith, in which he used the phrase "atheistical materialistic capitalists," did you have any specific recollections of other catchphrases or slogans he had used in the past, either in conversation or in his writings, that had a subversive or propagandistic flavor?

GENERAL OAKHART: Well, of course, his speech and his writings were peppered with phrases that caught you up short by their sardonic or barbed quality, but generally speaking, I shared the view of most everyone, that this show of irreverence was more or less in the nature of a joke, much like all that alliteration he's so famous for.

MR. MUNDT: A joke at the expense of his country.

GENERAL OAKHART: It seemed benign enough, Mr. Mundt, at the time. As everybody knew, he had been a pinochle-playing crony to several American presidents.

MR. THOMAS: Did you know, General, that he has also been a ghostwriter for the present incumbent of the White House?

GENERAL OAKHART: No, sir. I have only learned that through these hearings. But let me tell you, Mr. Thomas, that when he used that phrase, "atheistical materialistic capitalists," I could not have been any more shocked had I known that the man who spoke such a phrase happened also to be a speechwriter for the President of the United States.

MR. THOMAS: Well, I'm glad to hear that. Because it would have shocked *me* profoundly to learn that the hero of the Argonne Forest and the President of a major American baseball league could permit such a traitorous, slanderous, propagandistic remark to leave no impression on him whatsoever.

GENERAL OAKHART: Well, you needn't be shocked, sir, because it didn't. It is not for me, Mr. Thomas, to describe the action I took within the next twenty-four hours as "daring" or "courageous" or "far-sighted," but given the tone of your last remark, I feel I must remind the Committee that Angela Trust and myself, alone in the entire world of baseball, have been fighting tooth and nail against the hammer and sickle —and to this day, *to this day*, have earned little more than the scorn of our colleagues and the disbelief of the nation. Admittedly, it was not until that fateful night in March that I came to recognize the enemy for who and what he was, but since that time, as I am sure you know, I have been in the forefront of the battle against the Red menace, and no less than the members of this Committee, have done everything within my power to fight to preserve the Constitution of the United States and the great game of baseball against Communist subversion and treachery.

(*Loud applause. The Chairman raps his gavel.*)

THE CHAIRMAN: I appreciate that the spectators may from time to time wish to express their admiration for a witness, but I must ask you to restrain your enthusiasm in the hearing room. I'm sure that General Oakhart, who just prior to this morning's hearings announced his intention to run for the presidency of the United States in the coming election, would just as soon you express yourselves through the ballot box anyway.

(*Laughter.*)

GENERAL OAKHART: And, Mr. Dies, I am equally sure that if in August either of our great political parties had nominated for the presidency a candidate who had seen at first hand how the Communists work, a man who knew from hard and tragic experience what an unscrupulous, ruthless, and murderous gang they are, if the American people had been given the opportunity by either the Democrat or the Republican parties to vote for a man who was equipped to fight and to defeat the Communist enemy in our midst, then they might not be roused to display such enthusiasm for my words. But the fact of the matter is, sir, that the people will be silent no longer. Their eyes have been opened—they know the struggle that America will face in the postwar years with those who now pose as her friends. And so do I. And if Mr. Franklin D. Roosevelt and the Democrat Party do not know—and Mr. Roosevelt does not!—and if Mr. Thomas E. Dewey and the Republican Party do not know—and Mr. Dewey does not!—then the American people will look elsewhere for leadership. They will look at one who is not afraid to speak the unspeakable and to do the undoable, to one who is not afraid to call an enemy an enemy, at whatever cost and peril to himself! To one whose party is his country and whose platform is the law of the land!

(*Loud applause.*)

*

It was a warm and hospitable welcome that Gil Gamesh received when General Oakhart announced to the members of the press assembled in his Tri-City office on St. Patrick's Day 1944 that the former Greenback pitching ace standing beside him, whom he himself had banished a decade earlier, was now to be reinstated in the league, as manager of the Ruppert Mundys. With one notable exception, the writers broke into spontaneous applause as the ghostly Gamesh (bewigged, as he would be henceforth, in a raven-black hairpiece, and wearing his old Number 19) stepped to the microphone, removed his spectacles (the General's idea—adds seriousness) to wipe at an eye with the back of his big left paw, and then proceeded to express his gratitude, first to General Oakhart, for granting him amnesty and a chance to begin life anew; then to Mrs. Trust, for going to bat for him with the General; and then to the American people, who by giving him a second chance, attested to nothing less than their faith in mankind itself . . . Then he told them what he had seen and what he had learned in his ten years of exile. It was not the story he had told to the General and Mrs. Trust, but one devised for public consumption by the three of them. It had mostly to do with "our greatest natural resource, the kids of America, this country's future and its hope." In his guilt and his shame, said Gamesh, he had wandered the length and breadth of the land under a number of aliases—Bill Smith, Bob White, Jim Adams—working for weeks and months at a time as dishwasher, handyman, grocery clerk, and farmhand; he had lived beneath forty-watt bulbs in rooming houses in each of the forty-eight states, lonely as a man could be, without a friend in the world, except, except for "the kids." At the end of the work day, having downed his bowl of chili at the counter of the local greasy spoon, he would step out into the street and listen. For what? For the sound of the ball striking the bat, or landing with a whack in the pocket of a catcher's mitt. On many a night he had walked a mile just to watch a bunch of kids batting a taped-up ball around. Was he even alive in those years, other than during those twilight hours on the sandlots of America? Did his heart stir otherwise? No, no—the remaining twenty-three hours of the day and night he was a corpse embalmed in shame. "Hey, mister," they'd call over to him as he stood on the sidelines smoking his two-cent after-dinner cigar, "wanna ump?" "Hey, mister, fungo some out to us, hey?" "Hey, mister, ain't that right? Ain't Gil Gamesh the greatest that ever lived?" "Walter Johnson!" "Gil Gamesh!" "Rube Waddell!" "Gil Gamesh!" "Grover Alexander!" "No, Gamesh! Gamesh! Gamesh!" Dangerous as it was for this man who wished to be forgotten by America to come anywhere near a pitcher's mound, it was simply beyond him sometimes not to give a youngster in need a little advice. "Here, boy, do it this way," and taking the ball from the little pitcher's hand, he'd show him how to set the curveball spinning. Oh, there were idyllic summer nights in small Middle Western towns when he just couldn't resist, when he would rear back with that taped-up lopsided ball and hurl a perfect strike into the mitt of the twelve-year-old catcher—in the process (Gil added, with a tender laugh) knocking him onto his twelve-year-old fanny. Oh, the mouths of those youngsters sure hung open then! "Hey, who are you anyway, mister?" "Nobody," Gil answers, "Bob White, Bill Smith, Jim Adams . . ." "Hey, know who he looks a little like, guys? Hey, guys, know who he *is*?" But by then Gil would be shambling off to the sidelines, headed for his rooming house, there to pack up and move on out to some place new, a strange town where he could live another day, another week, another month, as an anonymous drifter . . . Then, said Gil, the war came. He went around after Pearl Harbor trying to enlist, but always they would ask to see his birth certificate and always he would refuse to show it; oh, he had one all right, only it did not say Bob or Bill or Jim—it said, for all the world to see, this here is Gil Gamesh, the man who hated his fellow man. Then one day down in Winesburg, Ohio, unable to bear any longer his life as a lonely grotesque, he turned that self-incriminating document over to the recruiting sergeant. "Yep, he's me," he finally admitted— and the fellow turned red, white, and blue and immediately ran back to show the thing to his commanding officer. For over an hour Gil sat in that office, praying that his exile had ended— instead, the sergeant came back with a captain and a major at his side and handed Gil a little card stamped U, meaning that as far as the U.S. government was concerned he was and forever would be an "Undesirable." The major warned him that if he did not present the card to his draft board whenever they might call him up for induction, he would be liable for arrest and imprisonment. Then the officers withdrew, and while the Undesirable stood there wondering where he might steal a belt to hang himself with, the sergeant, in a whisper, asked if he might have his autograph.

Months of wandering followed, months too desperate to describe—Black Hawk, Nebraska; Zenith, Minnesota; up in Michigan; Jefferson, Mississippi; Lycurgus, New York; Walden, Massachusetts . . . One night he found himself in Tri-City— it had taken a decade to wend his way back to the scene of the crime. There he waited outside Tycoon Park for a glimpse of the great lady of baseball, Angela Whittling Trust. It was she whom he begged to intercede in his behalf. "For I knew then," said Gil, "that if I could not regain my esteem and my honor in the world whose rules I had broken and whose traditions I had spat upon, I would be condemned to wander forever, a stranger and an outcast, in this, my own, my native land. Of course I knew my pitching days were over, but what with the war raging and so many major leaguers gone, I thought perhaps I might be taken on as a bullpen catcher, as someone to throw batting practice, as a batboy perhaps . . . Gentlemen, I did not dream, I did not dare to dream" et cetera and so forth, until he came around again to the kids of America, who were his inspiration, strength, salvation, and hope. To them he owed his redemption—to them he now committed heart and soul.

ONE MAN'S OPINION
By Smitty
*Talking to Myself*

"And not a word about Mike the Mouth. Has anyone happened to notice?"

Look, that was a decade ago. Isn't it a sign of human goodness and mercy to be able to forget about what happened to the other guy ten years back? Besides, Mike the Mouth is dead by now anyway. Or else out there still in the boondocks, demanding some nutcake's version of Justice. Be reasonable, Smitty. So Gamesh robbed him of his voice —the old geezer happened to rob Gil of something too, remember? A *perfect* perfect game. Look, Smitty, don't you believe in people changing for the better? Don't you believe in human progress? Why don't you see the good in people sometimes, instead of always seeing the bad?

"I'm not talking about good men or bad men," said Smitty, signaling for another round for the two of them. "I'm talking about madmen."

Oh sure, everybody in this world is cracked, except you know who.

"Not everybody," said Smitty. "Just the crackpots who run it. Crackpots, crooks, cretins, creeps, and criminals."

You left out cranks—how come? Cranks who write columns and cry crocodile tears. Maybe you scribblers worry too much.

"If we don't, who will?"

What the h. do you think you are, anyway? The unacknowledged legislator of mankind?

"Well, that was one man's opinion."

Whose, Smith? Yours?

"No. Fella name a' Percy Shelley."

Never heard of him.

"Well, he said it."

Well, don't believe everything you hear.

"I don't. But what about what I don't hear?"

What's that?

"A word, a single word," said Smitty, "about Mike the Mouth," and called sharply this time to the waiter for drinks for himself and his friend.


Said Frank Mazuma: "Gamesh? Great gimmick. Why don't I think of things like that? Who'd they get to coach at first, Babyface Nelson?"


### FIRST DAY BACK IN THE BIG TIME

Gentlemen, the name is Gil Gamesh. I am the manager who is replacing the gentle Jolly Cholly Tuminikar, who himself replaced the saintly Ulysses S. Fairsmith. My lecture for today is the first in our spring training series on the subject of Hatred and Loathing. Today's talk is entitled "Ha Ha."

Let me begin by telling you that I think you gentlemen are vermin, cowards, weaklings, milksops, toadies, fools, and jellyfish. You are the scum of baseball and the slaves of your league. And why? Because you finished last by fifty games? Hardly. *You are scum because you do not hate your oppressors. You are slaves and fools and jellyfish because you do not loathe your enemies.*

And *why* don't you? They certainly loathe *you*. They mock you, they ridicule you, they taunt you; your suffering moves them not to tears, but to laughter. You are a joke, gentlemen, in case you haven't heard. They laugh at you. To your face, behind your back, they laugh and they laugh and they laugh.

And what do you do about it? You take it. You try not to hear. You pretend it isn't happening. You shrug your shoulders and tell yourself, "It's fate." You say, "What difference does it make, no skin off my nose," and other such philosophical remarks. No wonder they laugh. A team not of baseball players, but philosophers! Stoics and fatalists instead of hitters and fielders! Of *course* they laugh. Gentlemen, *I* laugh! Ha ha ha ha ha ha ha ha ha ha! Hear me, Mundys? I am laughing, *at you.* Along with the rest of America! At your resignation! At your fatalism! At your jellyfish philosophy of life! Ha ha ha ha ha ha ha ha ha ha! Ha ha ha ha ha ha ha ha ha! Ha ha ha ha ha ha ha ha!

### SECOND DAY BACK

Welcome, Mundys, to another in our spring lecture series on Hatred and Loathing. Before I begin I have to tell you that you surely did outdo yourselves yesterday on the playing field in being laughable. What a wonderful comedy show that was! A regular *Hellzapoppin'*! I near wet my pants watching you standing out there on the field with your heads hanging like the old tried and true victims you are, while those high school lads (or were they lasses?) scored those eight runs in the first inning. What got you down so, "men"? I figured you were going to go out there and really start hating and loathing your enemies and oppressors, and instead you were the jellyfish and cowards and vermin of old, if not more so. Maybe you are ready for our second lecture then, entitled "How To Hate, and Whom."

Boys, it's easy. Just think of all the things you haven't got that other people have. Shall I name a few just to get you going? The obvious first. Other people have all their limbs. Other people have all their hair. Other people have all their teeth and twenty-twenty vision in both eyes. Other people have admiration, luck, fun, something to look forward to. Other people—and this may come as a surprise—have something to be *proud* of: self-respect, love, riches, peace of mind, friends—why, other people have sirloin for breakfast, champagne for lunch, and dancing girls for dinner. And more!

Now you may ask, "Okay, I ain't got one of that and they

got all of that—where's the hatred come in?" Mundys, that you can ask such a question is the measure of just how ruthlessly oppressed you have been. Don't you *understand*, boys? It isn't *fair*! It isn't *just*! It isn't *right*! Why should those who have have and those who have not have not? For what reason do they have everything and you nothing? In the name of what and whom? It makes my blood boil just talking about it! I feel the hatred for those haves coursing through my veins just thinking about all that you boys live without that other people have more of than they know what to do with! Brains! Strength! Self-confidence! Courage! Fortitude! Wit! Charm! Good looks! Perfect health! Wisdom! Why, *even Common Sense*! Oh, I could go on forever naming the things that other people have in excess, but that you Mundys haven't a trace of, singly, or taken all together. Talk about being deprived! My cowards, my jellyfish, my fools, you have absolutely *nothing* to recommend you—and on top of that, *you haven't even got a home!* A *home*, such as every little birdie has in a tree, such as every little mole has in the ground, such as every major league team in creation has, *excepting you!* Talentless, witless, luckless, and as if all that wasn't unfair and unjust enough, *homeless too!*

And you ask me, "But what's there to hate about, Gil?" *They robbed you of your home! They drove you out like dogs!* and you say, "Hey, where's the hatred come in?"

### THIRD DAY BACK

Fellas, we had to cut it short yesterday so you could go out there and get your asses whipped by the naval station team, with the result that I did not get around to telling you whom to hate for having deprived you of just about everything a baseball team could want. Let me make it easy for you. Just so you don't go wrong—being new as you are to this great adventure of loathing—why don't you begin by hating your fellow man *across the board*? That way you won't grow confused. If you see a guy in a Mundy uniform, he's all right, *but everybody who is not in the Ruppert scarlet and gray, you are to hate, loathe, despise, vilify, threaten, curse, slander, betray, mock, deceive, revile, and have nothing further to do with*. Is that clear? All mankind except those in the scarlet and gray. Any questions?

Nickname, did I happen to hear you say " *Why?*" Because they live off your misery, Damur! Because the nightmare that is your life at second base *gives them pleasure*! Your errors are their solace, your strike-outs their consolation. Mundys, don't you get it yet? You bear their blame! You suffer in their stead! The worse your luck, the better for them—the greater your misery, the happier they will be! Look, haven't you heard? Do I have to tell you *everything*? THE RUPPERT MUNDYS ARE THE OFFICIAL SCAPEGOATS OF THE U.S.A.!

And who *made* you scapegoats, boys? Was it writ in the stars, Specs? God's will, Tuminikar? Well, that's what they tell the peasants, all right, when those poor bastards don't happen to like their lot anymore. That's what they tell the slaves, when they happen to look up from their shackles and ask, "Hey, what the hell is goin' on around here?" Sorry, sorry, nothing to be done for you downtrodden today. God's will. He wants it this way, with you on the bottom and us on the top. Back to work now—we'll tell you if and when there's to be any change with those chains . . .

Mundys, it isn't *God* that put you on the road! It isn't *fate*, and it isn't *nothing*, either. *It is your fellow man!* Who made you scapegoats, Mundys? The United States government and the brothers M.! The country whose flag you salute, the owners whose names you bear! That's who joined forces to rob you of honor and dignity and home! The state and the owners! Your country and your bosses!

It did not come easy at first, but that's what spring training is for, Gil told them, getting that old unused venom running again, getting out there first thing in the morning to start in working on those old weaknesses of character, like ingrained habits of courtesy and that old bugaboo, the milk of human kindness. Get that gee-whiz out of your voice, Damur—this is no high school dance! Cut out that grinning, Rama, nothing is funny about hate! *Snarl*, Heket, *snarl* at your oppressor—he lives off your old age! I want to hear some *hatred* in there when you shout "Hate!"

Ah, but it was hard. How could you go around insulting some player on the other team when you knew he was better than you by far? How could you expect to frighten somebody with your bark or your bite who had you pegged for a busher long ago—somebody who in fact frightened *you*. No, it just wouldn't work. Besides, it wasn't that the other players *always* teased and kidded them—sometimes they were downright amiable, even sympathetic with the Mundys for having to be Mundys. Why, if they went around hating everybody, they were going to wind up losing what few friends they still had left in the league.

"You have no friends! You have only enemies! Their smiles oppress you as much as their sneers! You don't want their sympathy—you want their *blood*!"

Oh, but it was so hard. How do you go about hating and loathing those crowds you've been working so hard to placate and appease? How can you possibly hate all those people who you don't even know? Christ, when you come down to it, they're just people, like you and me.

"No, they are not! They are your tormentors! They imprison you by their ridicule! You are in bondage to their contempt! You are shackled by their smirks and their smart-ass remarks! There is no such *thing* as 'people just like you and me' if you are Ruppert Mundys! There are the oppressed and the oppressors! The Mundys and the rest of mankind—or mancruel, to be precise!"

Oh, but it was hard spreading that hatred around the way Gil wanted. Hate the Mundy brothers *too*? Hell, they didn't even know what they looked like. How can you hate somebody you wouldn't even recognize if he sat down next to you on the trolley car? And they don't even travel on trolleys—those guys travel in limousines! These are important people, these are powerful men!

"And they sold you down the river, boys, kicked you and your pitiful asses out of the inn, just like Jesus and his Mom! That's what important people do. That's how they get to *be* important."

But, but we're their team, they pay the wages—their father was *the* Glorious Mundy who is back in Port Ruppert buried in deep center field. Their name is our name. How can we hate our own name, if you know what we mean?

"Because their name *isn't* Mundy anymore. It's Muny, good old-fashioned dough! They have maligned the name—mangled it beyond repair! *You* are the true Mundys, boys, and not because it was the name of your robber-baron father, either! No, because it is short for Mundane! Meaning *common*, meaning *ordinary*—meaning the man in the street who's fed up to here with the Muny brothers and their ilk dancing the rhumba down in Rio while the ordinary Joe toils without honor and without reward! The Mundane, who do the dirty work of this world, their noses to the ground or the grounder, their tails to the whip, while the Muny boys stash it away in Fort Knox! Their name your name? Their team your team? *Says who!*"

Oh, but it was hard, hardest of all hating the U.S. of A. Why, if it wasn't for our country 'tis of thee, there wouldn't even be baseball to begin with!

"Or homeless baseball teams! Look," cried Gamesh, "what the hell good is a country to you anyway, if there is no place in it you can call your own?"

Oh, it was hard, but as it turned out in the end, not *that* hard. By the time the '44 season had begun, they had trampled out the vintage where the grapes of wrath are stored. Their hatred knew no bounds.

### SECRET SPRING TRAINING REPORT ON COMMUNIST INFILTRATION OF PATRIOT LEAGUE

Excerpts from Memorandum prepared by Gil Gamesh, Manager of the Ruppert Mundys and Chief Investigator, Patriot League Internal Security Affairs Division, for General Douglas D. Oakhart, President of Patriot League, and Mrs. Angela Whittling Trust, Presidential Adviser for Internal Security Affairs, submitted 4/17/44:

1. *Summary.* It is now clear that (a) Communist infiltration of the Patriot League is far more extensive than our most pessimistic preseason estimates; and (b) that the Ruppert Mundys, as had been hypothesized, occupy a pivotal position in the Communist plans for the subversion of the Patriot League. The clarification of (a) has been achieved by (c) continuous surveillance of Ruppert Mundy activities throughout spring training and (d) an analysis of same. Clarification of (b) has been achieved by way of (a) (c) and (d), with equal emphasis given to each. Current trends, unless reversed before conclusion of '44 season, will lead to a Communist-controlled league, with complete dissolution to follow, from all indications, during '45 season, so as to coincide with Communist takeovers in Europe and Asia at conclusion of international hostilities. The situation is very disturbing, as will be reflected in the following percentages, based on the evidence supplied by (c) and (d):

|  | Mundys | | P. League as Whole | |
|  | April 1933 | April 1944 | April 1933 | April 1944 |
|---|---|---|---|---|
| Communist agents | 0% | 8% | 0% | 6% |
| Communist Party members | 4% | 16% | 3% | 14% |
| Fellow travelers | 8% | 24% | 6% | 16% |

2. *Analysis of percentages* (charts attached) . . .

3. *Communists detected*

    a. Communist espionage agents

        (1) O.K. Ockatur (P). As reported earlier, Ockatur is in actuality Captain Smerdyakov, formerly a tank officer in the Leningrad Military Unit of the Red Army, now affiliated with the Main Intelligence Directorate of GRU of the Armed Forces General Staff. Because of the blinding of Bob Yamm his reputation is currently at a low ebb in Moscow, where the latest official explanation of that act is that it was committed solely out of personal animosity, in direct defiance of orders. Ockatur argues that he acted in direct *compliance* with orders and accuses his enemies of attempting to ruin him with a charge of "incurable dwarfism." It would appear from all this that Stalin, in the Russian phrase, has already begun "turning the little fellow on his head in the earth," and that sooner or later he will be liquidated, perhaps by being beaned by a Communist pitcher during his turn at bat. We must be prepared for this eventuality.

        (2) Hothead Ptah (C). Ptah is none other than Major Stavrogin, the infamous "One-Legged Man," probably the most admired *agent provocateur* ever to be graduated from SHIT.

    b. Communist Party members

        (1) Frenchy Astarte (SS). Astarte was an active member of the Communist Party in Canada, Latin America, and the Far East before entering the United States under the guise of an infielder. He is fluent in six languages, though pretends to understand nothing but French. On instruction from Moscow Astarte dropped the pop fly in the last of the ninth of the last game of the '42 season, the error that cost the Mundys a tie for seventh, and set the stage for the expulsion from Port Ruppert.

        (2) Big John Baal (1B). Trained in the jungles of Central America by local Communist insurrectionists; highly motivated. Cell leader of Mundys, certainly one of the top two or three party members in the league.

        (3) Chico Mecoatl (P). Roots in Mexican insurgency movement.

Two brothers, three sisters, six cousins, and two stepfathers jailed in Mexico for political activities. Noises he makes while pitching may be code signals.

(4) Deacon Demeter (P). "The Red Deacon," liaison between party members in organized baseball and party members infiltrating organized religion. Top Southern "white trash" Communist in U.S.

c. Fellow travelers

(1) Jolly Cholly Tuminikar (P)

(2) Nickname Damur (2B)

(3) Specs Skirnir (RF)

(4) Carl Khovaki (UT)

(5) Applejack Terminus (UT)

(6) Mule Mokos (UT)

4. *The Isaac Ellis Development*

a. Background and summary; or, "From Surmise to Certainty." It has long been suspected by the Presidential Adviser and the Chief Investigator of the Internal Security Affairs Division of the Patriot League that the owner of the Tri-City Greenbacks, Abraham Ellis, and his wife, Sarah Ellis, were, like so many of their co-religionists, either "tools" of the Communists, party members, or fellow travelers. It has now been established with maximal certainty *that the entire Ellis family comprises the key intelligence and secret police unit in all of organized baseball.*

b. J.E.W.; or, "The Ellis Mission." The Ellis mission appears to be threefold: (J) to contribute by their very presence to undermining faith in the Patriot League; (E) to mastermind ad hoc espionage activities within the league; and (W) to spy on their fellow Communists within the league and transmit all data as to the loyalty, dedication, and competence of agents and party functionaries to the appropriate Kremlin offices. With a foot in both the GRU (Main Intelligence Directorate of the Armed Forces General Staff) and the KGB (Intelligence Service of the Soviet State Security Service, or Secret Police), the Ellises hold the position of *highest-ranking Communist agents in the Patriot League*, outranking Frank Mazuma (Colonel Chichikov) and the Chief Investigator of the Internal Security Affairs Division of the Patriot League. Their identity is probably known only to Colonel Raskolnikov himself.

c. Isaac Ellis; or, "Moscow Makes Her Move." On April 12, 1944, three days before the opening of the Patriot League season, Isaac Ellis, the seventeen-year-old son of Abraham Ellis, requested an interview with Gil Gamesh in a cafeteria in Tri-City, where the

Mundys were playing a final exhibition game against the Green-backs. There Ellis made the following proposal:

(1) That he become a Ruppert Mundy "coach" under manager Gil Gamesh

(2) That he be given complete managerial control over team strategy until the All-Star break

(3) That during this "trial" period he be permitted to institute the following changes—

    (a) Do away with the sacrifice bunt as an offensive maneuver and the intentional pass as a defensive maneuver

    (b) With a runner or runners on base and less than two outs, rely almost exclusively on the hit-and-run

    (c) Bat the hitters in descending order of run productiveness

    (d) Instead of removing pitchers "randomly and haphazardly" in a game for defensive reasons, rotate for offensive reasons; start with "a relief pitcher" who works approximately two innings, follow with "a starting pitcher" who goes approximately five, and finish up with "a second relief pitcher" who pitches the final two

    (To justify this bizarre and outlandish system, Ellis offered a wealth of spurious statistics and pseudoscientific explanations [see charts attached]; he argued that if instituted on opening day, the system would land the Mundys in the first division by the All-Star break and the team would be in contention for the pennant by the season's end.)

d. Analysis. It was of course immediately apparent to the Chief Investigator that (J) Isaac Ellis was a Communist agent assigned to spy on Gil Gamesh; (E) that if hired by Gil Gamesh to be a Ruppert Mundy coach he might well be able to act to inhibit the counterespionage activities of Gamesh; but (W) that if he were *not* hired, it would be immediately apparent to Moscow that Gamesh, by refusing to capitalize on Ellis's brilliantly destructive scheme, had acted to preserve rather than to undermine the Patriot League—in short, that he had (as indeed he has) resumed his loyalty to his native land.

When, at the end of June, the Mundys moved up into undisputed possession of fourth place, Roland Agni found himself unable to justify any longer, either to his father or to Manager Gamesh, his refusal to honor his Ruppert contract. Never mind that a day didn't pass now without a Mundy player being thrown out of a ballgame for cursing the ump or taking a poke at an opposing player; never mind that there were fist fights with fans and rumors of knives in the Mundy dugout; never mind the invective spewed forth from the Mundy bench, the likes of which had never before been heard in big league ball. The point was this: how could he continue to call them the worst team in history when there now appeared to be four teams even worse in the Patriot League alone—and only three that were better! Just what kind of prima donna was he to refuse to play ball on a major league team with a better than .500 average? "What about Walter Johnson, Roland—twenty years with the Senators and only two pennants—and did he complain? Did he run home and refuse to leave his room?" "But it's a fluke, Daddy!" cried Roland from the bed where he now lay for weeks on end. "I know these fellas—they can't even *field* .500!" "Yet," said his father, peering into the darkened room, "here are today's official standings, for all to see. Tycoons first. Butchers second. Keepers third. And Mundys fourth, with thirty wins and twenty-nine losses. In ten weeks, they have won almost as many without you as they won *with* you during the entire season of play." "But that wasn't my fault—*I won the batting championship of the entire league!*" "Yet oddly it didn't help that team one bit. From the looks of things, it may even be what hindered them. You and your superior ways may well have been what crushed the confidence of that entire team. Oh, son, when will you understand that no man is an island unto himself?"

So the fatal, final step was taken: the incomparable Roland Agni, who had never wanted any more from life than that it should reward him with the dignity and honor commensurate with his talent, returned to don the uniform whose scarlet R— heretofore the initial letter of "Ridiculous" and "Refugee"— was now said to stand for "Ruthless" and "Revenge."

And it was ghastlier than ever. Winning every other game through a systematic program of hatred and loathing was worse even than losing them all through ineptness and stupidity. Enraged, his teammates were even more repulsive to Roland than they had been cowed and confused; at least then, in a weak moment, he could feel a little *pity*. But now they could not even step bareheaded to the top step of the dugout to listen to the National Anthem without hissing among themselves like a pack of venomous snakes—despicable bastards!

"Fuckin' Betsy Ross!"

"Fuckin' Francis Scott Key!"

"Fuckin' stripes!"

"Fuckin' stars!"

And that was just the pregame vitriol. By the time nine innings had elapsed there was nothing around that had not been traduced and vilified by the Ruppert team, beginning of course with the opposing ballplayers, their parents, wives, sweethearts, and children, and proceeding right on down to the local transportation system and the drinking water. It did not let up for a moment, neither from the field nor the bench, and certainly not from the third-base coaching box, where No. ⅟₁₆, the most vengeful of the vengeful, could turn an opposing pitcher into a raving madman by saying what was more disgusting even than what Hothead used to whisper to the Southern boys about their moms—referring as it did, in O.K.'s case, to their little tiny daughters in kindergarten, girls just about the right size and shape, insinuated O.K., for a fella of his dimensions. Oh, could that vile little dwarf make those pitchers balk! Why, he could score a man all the way around from first on three well-timed remarks about some little bit of a girl just out of diapers.

And could old Jolly Cholly make them bastards jump! Oh, did they go down when he threw that fast one back of their shoulder blades! "Know who that is out there?" Hothead would whisper to the batter with his face in the dust. "Tuminikar, that once killed a guy. Fella just about your size too."

"Tag 'em, Kid, right in the gazoo!" Nickname would shout across to third, and Heket—grinning sheepishly—would feint one way, and then, the old man's revenge, slam the ball and the glove right up between the base runner's thighs.

"Yeeeeowwwwwww!" cries the base runner.

"Out!" cries the ump, even as the fans swarm on to the field screaming for Heket's scalp, and the most aged of the Mundys swarm up out of the dugout, armed with two bats apiece to protect their decrepit brother.

Inning after inning, day in and day out, Gil Gamesh sends

his pitcher back out to the mound with only three words of instruction: "Knock somebody down."

"Who?"

"Anybody. They live off your suffering, *each and every one.*"

"Those dirty bastards!"

"What right have they to be batting last all the time?"

"The filthy pricks!"

"Who are they to mock and ridicule you?"

"They're nobody! They're nothin'!"

"They're *worse* than nothing, boys! They're *not Ruppert Mundys*! They're baseball players *who don't wear scarlet and gray*! They're Keepers, they're Greenbacks, they're fucking *Tycoons*!"

"The filthy slimy shits!"

"Ah, that's the spirit! *That's* my Mundanes! Cut his face, Nickname! Crush his balls, Kid! Defame his wife! Threaten his life! Calumniate his kids! I want blood! I want brawls! I want hate! I want a baseball team that nobody is ever going to laugh at again!"

### CHANSON DE ROLAND

"The end justifies the means. All we're trying to do out there is win a ballgame."

"But it ain't a ballgame anymore—not by anybody's standards!"

"What then?"

"It's hatin', threatenin', and cursin'—it's wantin' to kill the other guy, wantin' him dead—*and that ain't a game!*"

"Never heard of Ty Cobb, did you? Mugsy McGraw? Leo the Lip?"

"But they ain't nothin' compared to this! And that's only three. This is a whole team that's gone crazy! And you goadin' and goadin' em, till one day they is goin' to take the ump and rip him into little pieces! It's got to stop, Mr. Gamesh! Why do they have to hate the whole country? Even Cobb didn't do that! And Leo Durocher don't go around cursin' Abraham Lincoln and Valley Forge! *What does that have to do with baseball?*"

"Hatred makes them brave and strong—it's as simple as that."

"But it ain't brave *or* strong—it's just stupid! They are just a bunch of stupid fellers to begin with, and all you are doin' is makin' them stupider!"

"And what was so smart about being in last?"

"I ain't sayin' it was smart—it was just *right*. That's where they belong!"

"And you, where do you belong? Let me tell you, Roland. Away where they put the rest of you guys who go around trading in *phony breakfast foods*."

"But they weren't *mine*. Who told you *that*?"

"Who do you think?"

"But *he's* the one who made 'em, the little Jew! Did he tell you that, too? *He* made 'em, not me!"

"But you're the one who dropped them in their breakfast bowls, All-American Boy."

"But I *had* to."

"Tell it to the Commissioner, Roland, tell it to General O. Or would you prefer me to?"

"No! No!"

"Then keep your clean-cut ideas to yourself, Roland—underneath me? That's Babylonian, Star, for understand. The Mundys are fourth in the league—and without the benefit of your clean-cut advice."

"But they don't *deserve* to be fourth!"

"What about all that winning, Roland?"

"But they don't deserve to be *winning*!"

"And who does in this world, Roland? Only the gifted and the beautiful and the brave? What about the rest of us, Champ? What about the wretched, for example? What about the weak and the lowly and the desperate and the fearful and the deprived, to name but a few who come to mind? What about losers? What about failures? What about the ordinary fucking outcasts of this world—who happen to comprise *ninety per cent of the human race*! Don't they have dreams, Agni? Don't they have hopes? Just who told you clean-cut bastards you own the world anyway? Who put you clean-cut bastards in charge, that's what I'd like to know! Oh, let me tell you something, All-American Adonis: you fair-haired sons of bitches have had your day. It's all over, Agni. We're not playing according to your clean-cut rules anymore—we're playing according to our own! The Revolution has begun! Henceforth, the Mundys are the master race!"

*

"Ellis."

"What do *you* want?"

"Ellis, why did you tell the skipper about them Wheaties? *Nobody's supposed to know.*"

"Nobody's supposed to know what, Agni? That Mr. Perfect isn't Mr. Perfect after all?"

"He's goin' to blackmail me!"

"Not if you keep your clean-cut mouth shut, Roland."

"But this ain't baseball anymore at all! This is worse than last year even! Him and his hatin' and you and your charts— you two are destroyin' the game!"

"Let's say we're changing things."

"But it's all wrong! A Jew at first, a dwarf at third—whoever heard of coaches like that! You can't even catch a ball, Isaac! All you know is numbers! To you we're just pieces of arithmetic! Somethin' you can multiply and divide—and to him, to him we're wild savages! We're somethin' that you open the cage and let 'em out to run wild! It's gotta stop, Isaac!"

"Why is that?"

"Because—this ain't the time-honored way!"

"Neither was feeding them 'Jewish Wheaties' the time-honored way. But you did it."

"But I *had* to!"

"In order to be the hero you are, right, Golden Boy?"

"Oh, why is everybody against me bein' great—when I am! Why does everybody hate me for somethin' I can't help! It ain't my fault I was born superior!"

"Well, maybe the same holds true for the inferior, Roland."

"But I ain't tellin' them *not* to be inferior. That is their right! Only give me mine! Instead there is this plot to beat me down!"

"Poor little .370 hitter."

"But if I wasn't always goin' crazy with this here team, I could hit more! I could be a .400 hitter—instead they're drivin' me mad!"

### THE SHOT HEARD ROUND THE LEAGUE

Then, fans, it was over: Roland Agni was dead and the Mundys were no more.

Fifty-five thousand Kakoolians were already in their seats when the Ruppert team came out for batting practice on the Fourth of July 1944. All around the P. League now the sight of the Mundys emerging from their dugout set the spectators' mouths to foaming, but nowhere did the resentment reach such a pitch even before the first pitch as in Kakoola, in part, of course, because the ingenious Kakoola entrepreneur was always on hand to get the day's frenzy under way—"Renegades! Roughnecks! Rogues! Rapscallions! Rowdies"—but also because Gamesh's snarling, scowling nine was still the bunch that had crippled Doubloon and blinded Bob Yamm, and sold the Reapers that one-armed lemon named Parusha.

(Afterwards, when that day's tragedy was history, the editorialists around the nation were to lament this "climate of hatred" that had gripped the city of Kakoola on "the fateful Fourth" and prepared the way for the bloodshed—though Mayor Efghi was quick to remind the papers that it was not a Kakoolian who had pulled the trigger, but "a deranged, embittered loner . . . whose barbarous and wanton act is as repugnant to Kakoolians as it is to civilized men the world over.")

When the visitors departed the clubhouse that day for the pregame workout, one Mundy stayed behind. Seated before his locker wearing only his support, he was as striking and monumental a sufferer as any sculptor had ever hewn from stone. "What am I to do? Go home again? No, no," he realized, "you *can't* go home again. Who ever heard of anybody great going home—who ever heard of a great man who lived with his mom and his dad!" Oh, he could just see himself, lying there in his bedroom till his hair turned white and his teeth fell out, his high school trophies and that year in the majors all he had to prove that he would have been and *should* have been the greatest center-fielder of all time. He could just imagine those meals at the family dinner table, himself ninety and his father a hundred and twenty-five. "No man is an island unto himself, Roland." "But they were not men!" "All ballplayers are men, Roland. The Ruppert Mundys were ballplayers. Therefore the Ruppert Mundys are men." "But all ballplayers are not men. Some are freaks and bums!" "But freaks and bums are men. The freak and the bum are your brothers, my son." And would it be any better down in the town? "See that one there, with the cane and the beard. That's old Roland Agni. Let him be a warning to you, children." "Why, what'd he do wrong, Mommy?" "He never thought about others, that's what, only about himself and how wonderful he was . . ."

Roland was drawn from the horrible vision of a lifetime of paternal reprimand and unjust obscurity by the strange conversation coming from the clubhouse entryway. What the hell language was that anyway? It wasn't German, it wasn't Japanese— he knew what they sounded like from the war movies. What was that language then—and who was talking it anyway?

When he peered around the row of lockers he saw a stolid little man wearing a big padded blue suit conversing with the manager of the Ruppert Mundys. Gamesh had his eyes riveted to the foreigner's face, a face broader than it was long and heavily padded, like the suit. The stranger was holding a baseball bat at his side. He handed it to Gamesh, *Gamesh saluted*, and the man in the suit was gone.

That was all he heard and saw, but it left the center-fielder reeling.

Then Gamesh saw *him*.

"You again? What are you sulking about now, Goldilocks? Who excused you from batting practice, Big Star?"

"That—that was Russian!" Agni cried.

"Get out on the field, Glamor Puss, and fast."

"But you were talkin' *Russian* to that man!"

"That man, Agni, happened to be my uncle from Babylonia, and what we were talking was pure, unadulterated Babylonian. Now get your immortal ass out on the ball field."

"If it was your uncle, why did you salute him?"

"Respect, Roland—ever hear of it? All Babylonians salute their uncles. Don't you know ancient history, don't you know anything except what a star you are?"

"But—but why did he give you a bat?"

"Jesus, what a question! Why shouldn't he? Don't Babylonians have kids? Don't Babylonian kids like autographs, too?"

"Well, sure, I guess so . . ."

"You guess so . . ." snorted Gamesh, that master of intimidation. "Here," he said, handing Agni a pen to finish him off, "ink your famous monicker—be the first on your team. And then get out of here. You've got hitting to do. You've got *hating* to do. And loathing, God damn it! Oh, we'll make a Mundy out of you yet, Mr. All-American Boy!"

Thirty-two was the number chiseled into the wood at the butt end of the bat, but Roland Agni had only to lift it in his right hand to know that it did not weigh a gram over thirty-one ounces. An ounce of bat was missing. *Somewhere it was hollow.*

He reeled again, but not so the Soviet terrorist and saboteur could see.

Even from deepest center, Agni followed the skipper's every movement down in the dugout: he watched him use it as a pointer to move his infield around, watched him hammer with it on the dugout floor to rattle the Kakoola hitters, watched between pitches when he rested his chin on the flat end, as though it were a bat and he were a manager like any other. For six full innings the center-fielder kept one eye on the game and the other on Gamesh—with that great pair of eyes, he could do it—and then at the top of the seventh, a Damur foul zinged back into the Mundy dugout, and when the players went scrambling, Agni landed like a blockbuster in the manager's lap.

"Hey! Give that here!" snarled Gamesh. "Hey—!"

But on the very next pitch, Nickname drew a walk; Terminus, pinch-hitting for the pitcher, moved up to the plate; and Roland, who according to the Isaac Ellis Rotation Plan (and with the reluctant permission of his father) batted first, leaped from the dugout to the on-deck circle, swinging round and round over his head the bat he had wrested from the Mundy manager with all the strength in his body, the bat that was missing an ounce.

Now rarely during that season did the Mundy manager step onto the field if he could help it; he had his reasons—and they were to prove to be good ones. To remove a pitcher from the game, he sent the Jewish genius out to the mound, and to talk to the batters he had the notorious Ockatur waddle on down from the third-base coaching box. Those two misfits gave a crowd plenty to holler about, without Gamesh (who was of course *the* Mundy they had turned out to see and to censure—though his popularity had plummeted, the charisma held) running the risk of liquidation.

But now the threatening notes he had been receiving daily since opening day must have seemed to him as nothing beside the danger of discovery by the incomparable center-fielder, whose demoralization and incipient derangement (any inning now, Gamesh reported daily to his superiors) had fit precisely into his sinister timetable. So he called for time and came up out of the Mundy dugout as though to talk strategy with Terminus at home plate. What a Fourth of July treat for that crowd! At the sight of the cadaverous Mundy manager, wearing on his back the number he had made infamous a decade earlier, the Reaper fans roared as only they could. *There he was* at last, the hero who spoke to them of rage, ruination, and rebirth, a white Jack Johnson, a P. League Jesse James—the martyred intransigent, the enviable transgressor, and something too of the resurrected who had died for their sins and returned.

At home plate, Gamesh took Applejack Terminus aside to tell the fifty-two-year-old to remember to keep his eye on the ball, then headed back to the Mundy dugout by way of the on-deck circle, the crowd raving on all the while. With Gamesh looming over him, Roland remained down on one knee, the fingers of his right hand curled like a python around the handle of the Babylonian's bat.

"Okay, Champ," said the manager, clapping him lightly on the back, "give it here and go back down and get your own."

"Communist! Dirty Communist!"

"Tsk, tsk. What sort of language is that for a clean-cut lad from a big middlewestern state?"

"*True* language!" said the center-fielder, and opening his clenched left fist, showed Gamesh that he had the goods on him at last. "It's all clear now—you traitor!"

"What's clear, Roland? To me you sound confused, boy."

"That you're a spy, a secret Soviet spy! Just like Mrs. Trust warned me about!"

"Now what on earth are you holding in your hand, Roland?"

"Film! A tiny little roll of secret film!"

"Where'd you buy it, from some dirty old pervert downtown? Tsk, tsk, Roland Agni."

"I got it out of this here bat! You know that! By unscrewin' the bottom of the bat! And out it dropped, right in my hand!"

"Play ball!" the umpire called. "You gave 'em their thrill, Gil—they've seen your frightenin' mug—now let's play the game!"

"Film?" said Gamesh. "Oh, sure. My uncle. He's the super-duper photographer in the family. Babylonians love pictures, you know—worth a thousand words, we say."

"Your uncle's a Communist spy! You're one too! *That's* why you're teachin' them hate!"

"*Play ball!*"

Before the umpire could descend upon them, Gamesh started back to the dugout—but his parting words were chilling, their meaning as well as their tone: "Use your head, Hero. I can ruin your life, destroy your reputation forevermore."

After working the count to 2 and 2, Terminus popped up foul on an Ellis hit-and-run and not all the abuse in the new Mundy lexicon could cause the Kakoola third-baseman to drop the fly ball, nor was he intimidated by Applejack's bat as it came careening toward his ankles. The put-out made, how-ever, the third-baseman started after Ockatur (later, from his hospital bed, he claimed that the dwarf had spit in his eye as he crossed the coaching box in pursuit of the pop-up), where-upon the Mundys sprang from the bench and were kneeing (some said knifing) the fielder before he could lay hold of the misshapen coach. Scores of police charged on to the field from beneath the stands—on hand, as of old, when Gamesh came to town—and when finally spikes were plucked from flesh and fingers from eyeballs, Ockatur, Astarte, and Rama were ejected from the game, and the Kakoola third-baseman, as well as the shortstop—the sole Reaper who had dared to come to his defense—were carried unconscious from the diamond. How times do change! Who would have believed this of the Mundys only the season before?

The field clear at last of law-enforcement officers (and their horses), Gamesh came off the Mundy bench once again and started out to home plate, where Agni waited for the Reaper utility infielders to take a practice throw before stepping in for his turn at bat.

Making no effort to hide his disgust, the umpire said, "Now

what, Gamesh? You gotta start in too? Ain't they crazy enough
from Mazuma?" he asked, motioning out to the bleachers,
where the irrepressible Kakoola owner, in an Uncle Sam beard
and suit to celebrate the day, and with the assistance of daughter Dinero, was loading an iron ball into a mock cannon aimed
in the direction of the Mundy bullpen.

"So what do you say, Rollie," Gamesh whispered, "you
don't want to go down in recorded history like Shoeless Joe,
do you? You wouldn't want the world to know about those
W-h-e-a-t-i-e-s, would you? Why not give over the fil-um
then, okay? And then go get yourself a nice new bat, and we
will forget we ever crossed swords today—what do you say,
Roland? *Otherwise your name will be anathema for centuries to
come. Like Caligula. Like Judas. Like Leopold and Loeb.*"

"What—what's anathema?" asked the young center-fielder,
weakening under Gamesh's maniacal, threatening gaze.

"*Mud*, my boy, *mud*. You will be an outcast from decent
society worse even than me. You who could be greater than
Gofannon, greater than Cobb, greater than the great Joe D."

"But—but you're out to destroy America!"

"America?" said Gamesh, smiling. "Roland, what's America
to you? Or me, or those tens of thousands up in the stands?
It's just a word they use to keep your nose to the grindstone
and your toes to the line. America is the opiate of the people,
Goldilocks—I wouldn't worry my pretty little reflexes about it,
if I was a star like you."

When the bang sounded, all faces turned—grinning—
toward the open center-field bleachers, where the bearded, top-
hatted Mazuma, and daughter Dinero, clad for a summer day
in a strip of red, a cup of white, and a cup of blue, were still
wrestling with the cannonball (and one another). The fans
whooped and barked with delight. Then came the second report, and with it the realization that it wasn't Mazuma setting
off fireworks, and it wasn't a joke.

Spectators turned up afterwards (publicity hounds, one and
all) who claimed to have heard as many as six and seven shots
ring out, thus giving rise to the "keystone combo" conspiracy
theory of assassination bandied about for months and months
in the letters column of the Kakoola papers; however, the inves-

tigation conducted by General Oakhart's office in cooperation with the Kakoola Police Department concluded "beyond a shadow of a doubt" that only two bullets had been fired, the one that shattered Gil Gamesh's left shoulder before ricocheting into Roland's throat, and the bullet that penetrated Agni's head directly between his baby-blue eyes, at the very instant, it would seem, that he was either to betray his country so as to save his name, or sacrifice his name so as to save his country.

From the stands it was at first assumed that the bodies lying atop one another across home plate were both dead; but though Gamesh's famed left arm lay stretched in the dust, lifeless as a length of cable, the right edged slowly down Roland's bloody shirtfront, and while pandemonium reigned in the stadium, Gamesh reached into Roland's pants and fished the microfilm out from where the innocent youngster had (predictably) secreted it.

The assassin was dead within minutes. Kakoola mounted police, low in their saddles, charged the scoreboard, placing as many as twenty bullets into each of the apertures from which the shots appeared to have come. As a result, they got not just the assassin, but also the scorekeeper—a father of four, two of whom, being boys, were assured within the week of admission to West Point when they should come of age. At a memorial service at Kakoola City Hall, a service academy spokesman standing in full-dress uniform beside the two small boys, Mayor Efghi, Frank Mazuma, and a veiled, voluptuous Dinero, would call the appointments "a tribute to the brave father of those two proud young Americans, who had perished," as he put it, "in the line of duty" (perished along with Mike the Mouth Masterson, who was, as the reader will already have surmised, the murderer).

The coroner's inquest revealed that of the two hundred and fifty-six slugs fired by the Kakoola police, one had grazed Mike's ear; however, the long night he had spent with his high-powered rifle in a remote corner of the scoreboard, sucking chicken bones and drinking soda pop and dreaming his dreams of vengeance, followed by the excitement of the assassination itself, apparently had been enough to cause him to keel over, at eighty-one, a victim of heart failure.

## THE ENEMY WITHIN

Two days after Agni's death, from the studios of TAWT, Angela Whittling Trust's Tri-City radio station, General Oakhart revealed to the American people the magnitude of the plot to destroy the Patriot League, Organized Baseball, the free enterprise system, democracy, and the republic. Seated to either side of the microphone from which the General read his statement were Gil Gamesh, Angela Trust, and Mr. and Mrs. Roland Agni, Senior, parents of the slain center-fielder, who, it was now revealed, had not been the accidental victim of a vengeful madman, "a loner" acting on his own, but had been murdered deliberately for refusing to play ball with America's enemies.

"My fellow Americans, and ladies and gentlemen of the press," General Oakhart began. "I have here in my hand the names of thirteen members of the Ruppert Mundy baseball team who have been named as dues-paying, card-carrying members of the Communist Party, secret agents of a Communist espionage and sabotage ring, and Communist sympathizers."

He proceeded then to outline the scheme hatched over a decade ago in the inner sanctum of the Kremlin, and that had erupted in violence two days earlier with the tragic murder of the 1943 Patriot League batting champ, and the attempt upon the life of Gil Gamesh. "I am shortly going to ask the Mundy manager to tell you his own remarkable story in his own words. It is a story of defeat and dejection, of error and of betrayal; it is a story of the horror of treason and the circle of loneliness and misery in which the traitor moves. I know that some of you will ask, How can you have any respect for the integrity of a man who now admits to such a heinous past, who admits to us now that he did not tell anything like the whole truth about himself the first time he appeared before the nation only a few brief months ago? My answer is not one of justification but of extenuation. My fellow Americans, is it not better to tell the whole truth in the end than to refuse to tell the truth at all? Is it not better to be one who has been a Communist than one who may still be one? I think one need only contrast the searing frankness and the soul-searching courage of Gil Gamesh with the deviousness and treachery of the Mundy Thirteen—

twelve of whom still staunchly refuse to admit to the crime of treason—to conclude that Gil Gamesh is indeed an American who deserves not only our respect, but our undying gratitude for this warning he has given us of the conspiracy we face and the battle that lies ahead."

General Oakhart now read into the microphone the names of the Mundys whom he was suspending that day from the Patriot League for their Communist activities. Full files, he said, were available on each and every one of these cases, and had been turned over that morning to the F.B.I., along with the files on another thirty-six Communists and pro-Communists presently active in the league. In that the Thirty-Six hadn't yet been afforded an opportunity, in closed session with the General, either to refute the charges or to make a full confession, General Oakhart said that he did not consider it "fair play" to make their names known to the public at this time. To date, he reported, not a single one of the Mundy Thirteen that he had interrogated in his office had been able to disprove the allegations to the satisfaction of himself or Mrs. Trust, who had served throughout as his associate in this investigation; and so far only one Mundy—after having laughingly denied his Communist affiliations in the morning—had returned to the General's office in the afternoon and made a clean breast of his lifelong service as an agent of the Soviet Union. He was John Baal, the Mundy first-baseman. Having confessed to his own conspiratorial role, he had then proceeded to confirm the identities of his twelve Communist teammates, who were, in alphabetical order, Jean-Paul Astarte, Oliver Damur, Virgil Demeter, coach Isaac Ellis, Carl Khovaki, Chico Mecoatl, Eugene Mokos, Donald Ockatur, Peter Ptah, George Skirnir, Cletis Terminus, and Charles Tuminikar.

General Oakhart concluded his remarks with the assurance that the Patriot League would be cleansed of its remaining thirty-six Communists and the plot against American baseball destroyed before the week was out.

Now Gamesh, his left arm in a sling beneath his Ruppert warm-up jacket, stepped to the microphone. After being accorded a standing ovation by the assembled reporters (with one notable exception), he delivered himself of the story he had previously told the General in the old family hovel in Docktown. At the request of the reporters, he twice recounted his experience in the radio room of Soviet Military Intelligence, where he had listened one night to the first Yankee-Tycoon World Series game while snow fell upon the Communist capital he never could call home. "I feared that some day I would pay with my life for the longing that had drawn me to that room. And so," said Gamesh, as the reporters (with one notable exception) scribbled furiously, "I nearly did, two days ago. My fellow Americans, that the Communists should have chosen from their ranks former Patriot League umpire Mike Masterson to be my assassin is an indication of just how shrewd and cynical is the enemy secretly conspiring against us. For had I been killed two days back by the bullet that has instead only shattered my arm, it would have appeared to the world that I was the victim of an act of vengeance taken against me and me alone by a crazed and senile old man who could never find it in his heart to forgive and forget. And it would have been assumed, as indeed it has been until this moment, that Roland Agni was merely an unintended victim of the homicidal umpire's bullets. But the truth is far more tragic and far more terrifying. Mike Masterson, the umpire who never called one wrong in his heart, was no less a dupe of the Communists than I was—and in his obedience to his Communist masters, deliberately and in cold blood destroyed the life of a very great American—a great hitter, a great fielder, and a great anti-Communist crusader. I am speaking of the youngster I came to know so well, and admire so deeply, in the few brief weeks I was privileged to be his manager. I am speaking of the one Mundy who did not jump to the bait that I dangled before his teammates to determine just which were the Red fish swimming in the Ruppert Mundy sea. I am speaking of the young American who the Communists so feared that in the end they ordered his execution, the youngster who fought the Reds at every turn, at times blindly and in bewilderment, but always armed with the conviction that there was only one way to play the game, and that was the way Americans played it. I am speaking of the player, who, had he lived in happier times, would have broken all the records in the book and surely one day would have been enshrined in Cooperstown with the greats of yesteryear, but whose name will live on nonetheless in the Anti-Communist Hall of Fame soon to be constructed here in Tri-City by Angela Whittling Trust: I am speaking of Ruppert center-fielder Roland Agni."

Here Gamesh turned to the parents of the slain young man. The elder Mr. Agni, no less impressive a physical specimen than his son, rose to his feet and extended a hand to Roland's mother; together the bereaved father and his petite and pretty wife stepped to the microphone. Mr. Agni's voice was husky with emotion when he began, and his wife, who had been so brave all along, now gave in to tears and wept quietly at his side while he spoke. Mrs. Trust, in a gesture recorded in the Pulitzer Prize photograph of that year, reached up and with her own withered hand took hold of Mrs. Agni's arm to comfort the younger woman.

Said Mr. Agni: "My wife and I have lost our nineteen-year-old son. Of course we cannot but grieve, of course our hearts are heavy. But I should like to tell you that we have never in our lives been prouder of him than we are today. To others Roland was always a hero because he was a consummate athlete—to us, his parents, he is now a hero because he was a patriot who made the ultimate sacrifice for his country and for mankind. Where is there an American mother and father who could ask for anything more?"

The last word that afternoon was Mrs. Trust's. It was her answer to the Communists, and it was "Applesauce!"

As General Oakhart had promised, within the week thirty-six more Communists and Communist sympathizers were suspended from the Patriot League and their names released to the press: nine Reapers, eight Greenbacks, seven Keepers, six Butchers, four Blues, and two Rustlers. Even more shocking than this list of thirty-six was the exposure of the Communist owners, Frank Mazuma and Abraham Ellis, as well as the Soviet "courier," Ellis's wife Sarah. When both owners immediately issued statements in which they categorically denied the charges—calling them outrageous, nonsensical, and wickedly irresponsible—General Oakhart traveled to Chicago to confer with Judge Landis. The incensed Commissioner had already informed reporters that he for one did not intend to do the job of "rodent extermination" for General Oakhart that the P. League President should have been doing for himself while the Communists were infiltrating his league over the last decade; nonetheless, following their three-hour meeting, Landis made a brief statement to reporters in which he announced that Organized Baseball lent its "moral support" to the General's decision to suspend from league play the Kakoola Reapers and the Tri-City Greenbacks until such time as the accused owners either proved their innocence or divested themselves of their franchises. But in the matter of any legal suits resulting from the suspension of the two teams, Judge Landis made it altogether clear that they would be the sole responsibility of those who had gotten themselves into this mess to begin with.

Thereafter chaos reigned in General Oakhart's league. The teams decimated by suspensions had to call on local high school boys to fill out their rosters, if, that is, they could find high school boys of any ability whose fathers were foolish enough to compromise their sons' prospects by associating them with a P. League club. The suspended players meanwhile loudly proclaimed their innocence in bars and poolrooms all over the country—causing brawls aplenty—or else, following the example of Big John Baal, willingly admitted to whatever it was they were being charged with in the hope that an admission of guilt and a humble apology ("I'm just a country boy, I didn't know no better") would lead to reinstatement. Frank Mazuma did go ahead and bring a damage suit for four and a half million dollars against the Patriot League President, but the Ellises seemed virtually to acknowledge their guilt by locking the gates to Greenback Stadium and disappearing from Tri-City without leaving a trace. Even dedicated P. League fans indifferent to the dangers of Marxist-Leninism (and there were many) grew increasingly exasperated by the shifting schedule, by fourteen- and fifteen-year-old relief pitchers, and by the vociferous American Legion pickets forbidding them entrance to the bleachers. Consequently, by the end of the '44 season there wasn't a team in the league, not even the untainted Tycoons, who could draw more than three hundred people into the park to watch them play baseball.

The day after Max Lanier picked up the final Cardinal victory in the '44 World Series, the House Un-American Activities Committee began hearings on Communist infiltration of the Patriot League in Room 1105 of the federal court house in Port Ruppert, New Jersey. The Vice President of the United States, Mr. Henry Wallace, in a speech that very morning before the convention of the East-West Educational and Rehabilitation Alliance of the Congress for the Promotion of Humanitarianism in the United Post-War World, described the investigation as "a despicable affront to our brave Russian allies," and Mrs. Roosevelt, in her daily newspaper column, agreed, calling it "an insult to the people and the leaders of the Soviet Union." F.D.R. was reported to have laughed the whole thing off as so much "electioneering." "By whom, Mr. President?" "Doug Oakhart," the Chief Executive was supposed to have said. "The old war-horse still wants my job."

Each day hundreds of Port Ruppert citizens congregated near the statue of Lincoln at the foot of the Port Ruppert court house steps to watch the subpoenaed witnesses arrive; so did they once line the sidewalk ten and fifteen deep outside the Mundy clubhouse door to catch a glimpse of the great Gofannon as the shy star exited Mundy Park in an open-neck shirt and overalls at the end of a good day's work. Only the crowd back in those days was head over heels in love.

One by one the Mundys whom General Oakhart had suspended arrived with their lawyers to testify before the Committee.

"Traituh!"

"Toincoat!"

"Spy!"

In that entire week only one Port Rupe-it roota was seen weeping, a midget in a messenger's uniform who broke from between a policeman's legs at the sight of Ockatur stepping out of his taxi, and called in a high, breaking voice, "Say it ain't so, O.K.!"

"It ain't, you little asshole!" replied Ockatur, and waddled arrogantly up the steep court house steps one at a time.

Of the thirteen, ten maintained their innocence right down to the end, despite repeated warnings from the chairman that they were testifying under oath and if found guilty of perjury would receive stiff fines and heavy jail sentences; at least half of these ten would undoubtedly have made a confession too, had it not been for Ockatur, who emerged as the strong man of the group, tongue-lashing the fainthearted like Skirnir and appealing to the conscience of the preacher, Demeter, in night-long arguments at their hotel. Of the three who admitted to being Communists, Big John Baal had of course done so prior to being called before the Committee—indeed, he had just gone around the corner from General Oakhart's office and after an hour in a bar "seen the light": "Sure I was a Communist for the Communists," he told the press. "Sure I was trained by the Reds down there in Nicaragey—hell, they wuz all over the place. Sure the Mundys is mostly Commies. I think some of 'em is queers, too. Ha ha ha ha!" The two who changed their story at the hearings and admitted to affiliations they had previously denied, and of which they were now deeply ashamed, were Nickname Damur (reportedly whipped by his daddy till he told the truth) and Chico Mecoatl, who testified with the aid of an interpreter. At the conclusion of their testimony, in which they fingered not only themselves but the other Communist members of the team, they were lauded by the Committee chairman. "Mr. Damur, Mr. Mecoatl, we appreciate your cooperation with our Committee," said Congressman Dies. "It is only through the assistance of people such as you that we have been able to make the progress that has been made in bringing the attention of the American people to the machinations of this Communist conspiracy for world domination."

"*Muchas gracias, Señor Dies,*" said Chico, but Nickname wept.

The most troublesome of the Mundy Thirteen were the coaches, Isaac Ellis and O.K. Ockatur, both of whom created such commotion at the hearings that they had to be forcibly removed by federal marshals and subsequently were found in contempt of a Congressional committee and each sentenced to a year in jail, Ockatur to the federal penitentiary at Lewisburg, Pennsylvania, and Isaac to a farm for delinquent boys in Rahway, New Jersey, where, within a month of his arrival, he was beaten to death in the shower by his entire dormitory, apparently for suggesting that the great Mundy martyr, Roland

Agni, had been involved with him in feeding doped-up break-fast food to his teammates toward the end of the '43 season.

Frenchy Astarte was the only other Mundy to die after giving testimony to the Committee, he by his own hand on the family farm at Gaspé.

The "surprise" witness called by the committee in Port Ruppert was the sports columnist of the Finest Family Newspapers, Word Smith, who refused to answer questions having to do with purported friends of his, "highly placed officials in the executive branch of the government" allegedly involved in the leasing of Mundy Park by the War Department, in accordance, it now turned out, with the Soviet plot to destroy the Patriot League.

"Mr. Chairman," said Smitty, after supplying his name, his address, and his occupation, "this Committee and its investigation is a farce. I refuse to be a party to it. I refuse to answer any more of your questions, particularly questions about my associations, past, present, or in the life to come. I refuse to answer any questions having to do with my political beliefs, my health habits, my sex habits, my eating habits, and my good habits, such as they are. I refuse to apologize or explain or verify any remarks I have ever made to anyone over the telephone, face to face, in my sleep, in my cups, or in my solitude. I refuse to participate in this lunatic comedy in which American baseball players who could not locate Russia on a map of the world—who could not locate *the world* on a map of the world—denounce themselves and their teammates as Communist spies out of fear and intimidation and howling ignorance, or, as is the case with that case named Baal, out of incorrigible human perversity and curdled genes. Truly, sir, I have never seen anything in sixty years of astonishment to compare with these shameful shenanigans. Over the past two seasons it has been my misfortune to follow the Patriot League through one incredible and ludicrous crisis after another. Things have happened on the field of play that I would not have believed if I had not been there to see them with my own eyes. Frankly, I still don't believe them. But for sheer unabashed, unabetted, unabridged, unaccountable, unadorned, unallayed, unamusing, unanticipated, unassailable—"

(*Laughter. Scattered applause.*)

CHAIRMAN: Now, just a minute—

SMITTY: —uncalled for, unchecked, uncoherent, unconditional—

CHAIRMAN: Counsel, I think you had better advise your client—

SMITTY: —unconnected, unconscionable, unconstrained—

CHAIRMAN: It is you, sir, who is unconstrained. I think you are describing yourself. Now—

SMITTY: —uncontrollable, uncurbed, undecipherable, undefinable—

CHAIRMAN (*pounding gavel*): Now, you will have to stop or you will leave the witness stand. And you will leave the witness stand because you are in contempt. And if you are just trying to force me to put you in contempt, you won't have to try much harder. You won't have to get to the end of the alphabet to go to jail, you know.

SMITTY: —undesirable, undiluted, undisguised, undreamt-of, unearthly, unequaled, unfaltering, unfathomable, unforgettable—

CHAIRMAN: Officers, take this man away from the stand.

　　(*Applause and boos as witness is approached by federal marshals.*)

SMITTY: —unreality, Mr. Chairman, for sheer *unununununreality*, I cannot think of anything to compare with what has transpired at these hearings.

CHAIRMAN: Is that all you wanted to tell us?

SMITTY (*being led from the stand by two marshals*): That ain't exactly nothin'.

CHAIRMAN: But surely as a writer, Mr. Smith, you know the old saying that truth is stranger than fiction.

SMITTY: So are falsehoods, Mr. Chairman. Truth is stranger than fiction, but stranger still are lies.

　　(*Applause and boos as he is led out of the room.*)

For his defiance Smitty was held in contempt of the Committee and was sentenced to a year in the federal penitentiary at Lewisburg; he was paroled after six months, but never again did his by-line appear in an American newspaper.

\*

*November 1944.* General Douglas D. Oakhart runs as a write-in candidate for President of the United States. Receives one-tenth of one per cent of the popular vote.

*February 1945.* HUAC concludes investigation of all Patriot League teams; calls for federal grand jury to investigate baseball.

*March 1945.* Twenty-three more Communists expelled from Patriot League, bringing total (exclusive of owners) to seventy-two. General Oakhart regretfully suspends league operations until end of war when returning veterans will restore P. League play to "peacetime caliber."

*August 1945.* Destruction of Fairsmith Stadium in Hiroshima.

*October 1945.* Publication of *Communism Strikes Out*, by Douglas D. Oakhart (Stand Up and Fight Press, Tri-City, Mass.).

*January 1946.* First contingent of P. League ex-G.I.s proclaim themselves "free agents." Refuse to honor reserve clause of contracts drawn with "Communist-dominated" teams. Backed by American Legion and Veterans of Foreign Wars. Frank Mazuma promises to carry case to Supreme Court.

*March 1946.* Gil Gamesh disappears from Tri-City editorial office of Angela Trust weekly national newsletter, *Stand Up and Fight!* Revenge by Communists feared. Mrs. Trust offers hundred thousand dollars for information pertaining to Gamesh's whereabouts.

*April 1946.* Angela Whittling Trust, in surprise preseason move, releases "loyal" Tycoon players from contracts, signaling demise of Patriot League. Says of third major league, "Better dead than Red." Mazuma labels act "mad," promises to fight to restore league "integrity." Publication of *Switch-Hitter, or I Led Two Lives*, by John Baal (Stand Up and Fight Press, Tri-City).

*September 1946.* War Department dismisses four who engineered lease of Mundy Park from Ruppert franchise. Department of Justice reconvenes grand jury investigating baseball.

*March 1947.* Wreckers begin demolition of Mundy Park for exclusive harborside luxury apartments. Port Ruppert City Council votes unanimously to change city name by January

1948; contest announced for name appropriate to "new era of expansion and prosperity."

*April 1947.* Aceldama, Asylum, Independence (Va.), Kakoola, and Terra Incognita follow Port Ruppert example, to be rechristened by '48. Frank Mazuma courtroom heart attack victim; survivors drop legal actions instituted by embittered entrepreneur named by P. League as Soviet spy. "Our family," says Doubloon Mazuma from wheelchair, "has suffered enough from this savage national pastime."

*November 1948.* General Oakhart runs for President of the United States on Patriot Party ticket; running mate Bob Yamm. Receives surprising two per cent of popular vote; strongest in California. "Crusade under way," says General.

*May 1949. Pravda* photograph of Moscow May Day celebration reprinted in American papers; hatted figure between Premier Stalin and Minister of State Security Beria identified as Marshal Gilgamesh. Angela Whittling Trust May 2 suicide in underground stadium bunker. May 3, Tri-City councilmen vote to join former P. League towns in search for new name.

*June 1952.* Tycoon Park, last remaining P. League stadium in U.S., to make way for multi-billion dollar "Maine to Montevideo" highway.

*October 1952.* Oakhart-Yamm seek McCarthy endorsement; share TV platform when Wisconsin Senator raps Stevenson: "If somebody would only smuggle me aboard the Democratic campaign special with a baseball bat in my hand, I'd teach patriotism to little Ad-lie." Political analysts interpret remark as boost to Patriot Party presidential ticket. Splinter Republicans wave signs, "General E, no! General O, yes!"

*November 1952.* Oakhart-Yamm receive 2.3 per cent of popular vote, despite charge by Dems. and Reps. that Oakhart dupe of Soviet agent.

*March 1953. Pravda* photograph of Stalin funeral mourners reprinted in American press; hatted figure between Minister of State Beria and First Secretary Malenkov identified as Marshal Gilgamesh.

*December 1953.* Lavrenti P. Beria executed in Soviet Union by Stalin's heirs; hatted figure between First Secretary Khrushchev and Minister of Defense Bulganin identified as Marshal Gilgamesh in *Pravda* photo.

*March 1954.* Marshal Gilgamesh sentenced to death as "double agent" and executed. *Pravda* carries full confession wherein "enemy of people" admits secret connection to American and National Baseball leagues. Leagues in joint statement label Gamesh confession "a preposterous fraud . . . typical act of Communist treachery to which no American in his right mind could possibly give credence." Oakhart calls for full-scale investigation of league presidents Frick and Harridge; McCarthy reported "ready and willing."

*August 1956.* Private plane en route to Patriot Party Convention in Palm Springs disappears without trace; General Douglas D. Oakhart, Bob and Judy Yamm, and aircraft millionaire pilot assumed dead. Communist sabotage suspected.

# Epilogue

THE DRAMA's done. Why then here does one step forth?—
Because one did survive the wreck of the Patriot League.
One did survive the madness, the ignorance, the betrayals, the
hatred, and the lies! One did survive the Fairsmiths and Oak-
harts and Trusts and Baals and Mazumas and Gil Gameshes!
Survived (somehow!) the writing of this book! O fans, forgive
the hubris, but I'm a little in awe of my own fortitude. Rage,
we know, can carry a writer a long long way, but O the anguish
en route, the loneliness, the exhaustion, the self-doubt. But I
will not describe again the scorn and the derision to which I've
been subjected (see Prologue); believe me when I say, *they
don't let up, they're out there being smug and self-satisfied and
stupid every single day!* Charges of lunacy from senile old goats!
Literary criticism from philistine physicians! Vile aspersions
cast upon my probity, my memory, my dignity, my honor—
and by whom? By the fogeys in the TV room watching *The
Price Is Right*! O try it, fans, try plying your trade day in and
day out with all around you sneering and calling you cracked.
Do an old man a favor and see how far you get laying your
bricks and selling your salamis, with every passerby crying,
"Liar! Madman! Fool!" See how *you* hold up. O fans, it's been
no picnic scratching out the truth here at Valhalla.

Or surviving those publishers down in New York. Let me
share with you a representative sampling of their prose—and
prudence, you might call it, if you were of a generous turn of
mind.

Dear Mr. Smith:
   I find what I have read of your novel thoroughly objectionable. It
is a vicious and sadistic book of the most detestable sort, and your
treatment of blacks, Jews, and women, not to mention the physically
and mentally handicapped, is offensive in the extreme; in a word, sick.

Dear Mr. Smith:
   We find your novel far-fetched and lacking authenticity and are returning it herewith.

Dear Mr. Smith:

Book blew my mind. Great put-down of Estab. Wild and zany black humor à la Bruce & Burroughs. The Yamms are a gas. I'd publish tomorrow if I was in charge here. But the Money Men tell me there's no filthy lucre in far-out novel by unknown ab't mythical baseball team. What can ya' do? Fallen world. I make what inroads I can but they are a CONGLOMERATE and I am just a "Smitty" to them. Anyhoo: let me buy you a lunch if you're ever down from Valhalla. And please let me see your next. Y'r 'umble.

Dear Mr. Smith:

I am returning your manuscript. Several people here found portions of it entertaining, but by and large the book seemed to most of us to strain for its effects and to simplify for the sake of facile satiric comment the complex realities of American political and cultural life.

Dear Mr. Smith:

Too long and a little old-hat. Sorry.

No need to quote from the other twenty-two filed here in my pocket, nor from my replies.

And now? Yet another year has passed—and I and the truth remain buried alive. Around me the other aged endear themselves to the doctor by playing checkers by day and dying by night. Weekly the incoming arrive on canes, the outgoing depart in polyethylene sacks. "Well," says the nurse to each decrepit newcomer, "I think you're going to like it here, Gramps. We look after you and you look after yourself, and the world outside can just worry about its own problems for a change." "Oh," comes the codger's reply, "sounds good to me. No more teachers, no more books." "That's the spirit," chirps the slit, and sets him out in the sun to start in drying up for the grave. "Some folks," she growls, as I hand her a letter to post, "know how to enjoy the old age the good Lord has been kind enough to grant them." To which *I* reply, "Tampering with the mails is a federal offense. Be sure that goes out tonight."

Yes, I fire off letter after letter—to Walter Cronkite, to William Buckley, to David Susskind, to Senator Kennedy, to Ralph Nader, to the Human Rights Commission of the UN, to renowned American authors, to Ivy League professors, to columnists, to political cartoonists, to candidates for public office looking for an "issue"; alert to the danger of appearing just another crank to the savvy secretaries of the great, I employ in my correspondence a style as dignified as any an invest-ment banker or a funeral director might use on a prospective client: I am respectful, I am thoughtful, I am restrained. I wres-tle insistence into submission; I smother upper case howls in the crib; exclamation points, those bloody daggers, I drive back into my own innards; and I don't alliterate (if I can help it). Yes, I forgo everything and anything smacking of seething, seething all the more so as I do so. And still I never get a seri-ous reply.

The latest and, admittedly, most desperate of my letters fol-lows. Beyond this there seems to me nowhere to go, except to that undiscovered country from which no traveler returns. Needless to say, when my fellows here learned of my letter's destination, my reputation as resident laughingstock soared. "There's the feller I tole you that writes them letters to China," they inform the local do-gooders who bring us their cakes and cookies once a week. "A real screwball, that one. Imagination up and run away with him, and the two just never come back. Cracked right down the middle, he is." "Well," say the good ladies of Valhalla, New York, "I myself feel more pity than con-tempt for such a person," whereupon they are informed that that is compassion misspent.

The plight of the artist, fans. Meanwhile, no answer from China as yet. But I will wait. I will wait, and I will wait, and I will wait. And need I tell you what that's like, for a man with-out the time for waiting, or the temperament?

Valhalla Home for the Aged
Valhalla, New York
January 15, 1973

Chairman Mao Tse-tung
Great Hall of the People
Peking, China

My dear Chairman Mao:

I am sure you are aware of the recent publication in the United States of a great historical novel by the Soviet writer and Nobel Prize winner for Literature, Alexander I. Solzhenitsyn. As you must know, Mr. Solzhenitsyn was not able to find a publisher for this work in the Soviet Union and subsequently has been vilified and traduced by his fellow Soviet writers for allowing his manuscript to be smuggled out to the West for publication. The reason Mr. Solzhenitsyn is despised

in Russia is that his version of Russian history happens not to corre-
spond with the version that is promulgated by the powers-that-be
over there. In short, he refuses to accept lies for the truth and myth
for reality. For this he has been expelled from the Soviet writers'
union and designated an enemy of the people by the Russian government. I understand that he lives now in isolation from society, virtually under arrest, in his apartment in Moscow.

If I have followed Mr. Solzhenitsyn's tragic circumstances with
more than ordinary interest and concern during the months he has
been in the news here, it is because I am an author who has for years
lived in something like the same situation in America as he does in Soviet Russia. Presently I am as good as imprisoned in a county home
for the destitute aged in upstate New York, where, by staff and inmates alike, I am considered deranged. Why? Because I have written a
historical novel that does not accord with the American history with
which they brainwash our little children in the schools. I say "historical," doubtless they would say "hysterical." Not a single American
publisher dares to present the American people with the true story I
have told, nor is there anyone here at Valhalla who considers me and
my book anything but a joke. I have every reason to believe that upon
my death, which like yours, Mr. Chairman, could occur any minute—
I am nearing ninety, sir—the manuscript that is continually at my side
for safekeeping will be destroyed, and with it all record of this heinous
chapter in my country's history.

Now you may wonder why I am not addressing this letter to Party
Chairman Brezhnev in Moscow. At first glance it might appear that
he would pounce upon the opportunity for retaliation against the
United States and the "traitor" Solzhenitsyn, by printing in Russia,
and in Russian, a book that for all intents and purposes has been suppressed in America because it is at variance with the U.S. Government
Officially Authorized Version of Reality. Once you have read the last
chapter of my book, however, you will understand quickly enough
why the Russians would find this work no less compromising than the
Americans do. On the other hand, I would think that precisely what
makes it so odious to these two fearful giants, is what would make it
attractive to you.

I am writing to you, Chairman Mao, to propose the publication of
my book in the People's Republic of China. I assure you that nobody
knows better than I the difficulties of translation that are posed by a
work like mine, particularly into Chinese. Still, I cannot believe that
such obstacles would prove insurmountable to the people whose labor raised the Great Wall, or the leader whose determination has carried them on their Long March to Communism. I do not mean, by

the way, to give the impression that I turn to you because I sympathize with your state and its methods, or feel a special kinship with your people or your system or yourself. I turn to Mao Tse-tung because I have no one else to turn to. Likewise, you should know that I am under no illusion about the devotion of politicians either to truth or to art, not even those like yourself who write poetry on the side. If you ran China on the side and wrote poetry in front, that would be another matter. But nations and leaders being what they are, I realize full well that if you publish my book, it will be because you consider it in the interest of your revolution to do so.

Mr. Chairman, we are two very old men who have survived great adversity and travail. In our own ways, on our own continents, with our own people, each has led an embattled life, and each continues to survive on the strength of an impassioned belief: yours is China, mine is art—an art, sir, not for its own sake, or the sake of national pride or personal renown, but art for the sake of the record, an art that reclaims what is and was from those whose every word is a falsification and a betrayal of the truth. "In battle with the lie," said Alexander I. Solzhenitsyn, "art has always been victorious, always wins out, visibly, incontrovertibly for all! The lie can stand against much in the world— but not against art." Thus my defiant Russian colleague in a Nobel Prize lecture that he was prevented from delivering in Stockholm by the falsifiers who govern in his land. O would that I might draw upon his courage, his strength, and his wisdom in the days and months to come, if they come. For I will need all that and more to survive in upstate New York when (and if) *The Great American Novel* is published in Peking.

Respectfully yours,
Word Smith
(Author of "One
Man's Opinion")

MY LIFE AS A MAN

*To Aaron Asher and Jason Epstein*

I could be his Muse, if only he'd let me.

—*Maureen Johnson Tarnopol,*
*from her diary*

# I

# USEFUL FICTIONS

# Salad Days

Fɪʀsᴛ, foremost, the puppyish, protected upbringing above his father's shoe store in Camden. Seventeen years the adored competitor of that striving, hot-headed shoedog (that's all, he liked to say, a lowly shoedog, but just you wait and see), a man who gave him Dale Carnegie to read so as to temper the boy's arrogance, and his own example to inspire and strengthen it. "Keep up that cockiness with people, Natie, and you'll wind up a hermit, a hated person, the enemy of the world—" Meanwhile, downstairs in his store, Polonius displayed nothing but contempt for any employee whose ambition was less fierce than his own. Mr. Z.—as he was called in the store, and at home by his little son when the youngster was feeling his oats—Mr. Z. expected, *demanded*, that by the end of the workday his salesman and his stock boy should each have as stupendous a headache as he did. That the salesmen, upon quitting, invariably announced that they hated his guts, always came to him as a surprise: he expected a young fellow to be grateful to a boss who relentlessly goaded him to increase his commissions. He couldn't understand why anyone would want less when he could have more, simply, as Mr. Z. put it, "by pushing a little." And if they wouldn't push, he would do it for them: "Don't worry," he admitted proudly, "I'm not proud," meaning by that apparently that he had easy access to his wrath when confronted with another's imperfection.

And that went for his own flesh and blood as well as the hired help. For example, there was the time (and the son would never forget it—in part it may even account for what goaded him to be "a writer"), there was the time the father caught a glimpse of his little Nathan's signature across the face of a booklet the child had prepared for school, and nearly blew their house down. The nine-year-old had been feeling self-important and the signature showed it. And the father knew it. "This is the way they teach you to sign your name, Natie? This is supposed to be the signature that somebody on the other end is supposed to read and have respect for? Who the hell can read something that looks like a train wreck! Goddam it, boy, *this is your name*. Sign it *right*!" The self-important child of the self-important shoedog bawled in his room for hours afterward, all the while strangling his pillow with his bare hands until it was dead. Nonetheless, when he emerged in his pajamas at bedtime, he was holding by its topmost corners a sheet of white paper with the letters of his name, round and legible, engraved in black ink at the center. He handed it over to the tyrant: "Is *this* okay?" and in the next instant was lifted aloft into the heaven of his father's bristly evening stubble. "Ah, now *that's* a signature! *That's* something you can hold your head up about! *This* I'm going to tack up over the counter in the store!" And he did just that, and then led the customers (most of whom were Negroes) all the way around behind the register, where they could get a really close look at the little boy's signature. "What do you think of *that*!" he would ask, as though the name were in fact appended to the Emancipation Proclamation.

And so it went with this bewildering dynamo of a protector. Once when they were out fishing at the seashore, and Nathan's Uncle Philly had seen fit to give his nephew a good shake for being careless with his hook, the shoedog had threatened to throw Philly over the side of the boat and into the bay for laying a hand on the child. "The only one who touches him is me, Philly!" "Yeah, that'll be the day . . ." Philly mumbled. "Touch him again, Philly," his father said savagely, "and you'll be talking to the bluefish, I promise you! You'll be talking to *eels*!" But then back at the rooming house where the Zuckermans were spending their two-week vacation, Nathan, for the first and only time in his life, was thrashed with a belt for nearly taking his uncle's eye out while clowning around with that goddam hook. He was astonished that his father's face, like his own, should be wet with tears when the three-stroke beating was over, and then—more astonishing—he found himself crushed in the man's embrace. "An *eye*, Nathan, a person's *eye*—do you know what it would be like for a grown man to have to go through life without *eyes*?"

No, he didn't; any more than he knew what it would be like to be a small boy without a father, or wanted to know, for all that his ass felt on fire.

Twice his father had gone bankrupt in the years between the wars: Mr. Z.'s men's wear in the late twenties, Mr. Z's kiddies' wear in the early thirties; and yet never had a child of Z.'s gone without three nourishing meals a day, or without prompt medical attention, or decent clothes, or a clean bed, or a few pennies "allowance" in his pocket. Businesses crumbled, but never the household, because never the head of the house. During those bleak years of scarcity and hardship, little Nathan hadn't the faintest idea that his family was trembling on the brink of anything but perfect contentment, so convincing was the confidence of that volcanic father.

And the faith of the mother. *She* certainly didn't act as though she was married to a businessman who'd been bankrupt and broke two times over. Why, the husband had only to sing a few bars of "The Donkey Serenade" while shaving in the bathroom, for the wife to announce to the children at the breakfast table, "And I thought it was the radio. For a moment I actually thought it was Allan Jones." If he whistled while washing the car, she praised him over the gifted canaries who whistled popular songs (popular maybe, said Mr. Z., among other canaries) on WEAF Sunday mornings; dancing her across the kitchen linoleum (the waltz spirit oftentimes seized him after dinner) he was "another Fred Astaire"; joking for the children at the dinner table he was, at least to her way of thinking, funnier than anyone on "Can You Top This"—certainly funnier than that Senator Ford. And when he parked the Studebaker—it never failed—she would look out at the distance between the wheels and the curbstone, and announce—it never failed—"Perfect!" as though he had set a sputtering airliner down into a cornfield. Needless to say, never to criticize where you could praise was a principle of hers; as it happened, with Mr. Z. for a husband, she couldn't have gotten away with anything else had she tried.

Then the just deserts. About the time Sherman, their older son, was coming out of the navy and young Nathan was entering high school, business suddenly began to boom in the Camden store, and by 1949, the year Zuckerman entered college, a brand new "Mr. Z." shoe store had opened out at the two-million-dollar Country Club Hills Shopping Mall. And then at last the one-family house: ranch style, with a flagstone fireplace, on a one-acre lot—the family dream come true just as the family was falling apart.

Zuckerman's mother, happy as a birthday child, telephoned Nathan at college the day the deed was signed to ask what "color scheme" he wanted for his room.

"Pink," Zuckerman answered, "and white. And a canopy over my bed and a skirt for my vanity table. Mother, what is this 'your room' crap?"

"But—but why did Daddy even buy the house, if not for you to have a real boy's room, a room of your own for you and all your things? This is something you've wanted all your life."

"Gee whiz, could I have pine paneling, Mother?"

"Darling, that's what I'm telling you—you can have *anything*."

"And a college pennant over my bed? And a picture on my dresser of my mom and my girl?"

"Nathan, why are you making fun of me like this? I was so looking forward to this day, and all you have for me when I call with such wonderful news is—sarcasm. College sarcasm!"

"Mother, I'm only trying very gently to break it to you— you just cannot delude yourself into thinking there is something called 'Nathan's room' in your new house. What I wanted at the age of ten for all 'my things,' I don't necessarily want any longer."

"Then," she said weakly, "maybe Daddy shouldn't pay your tuition and send you a check for twenty-five dollars a week, if you're that independent now. Maybe it works both ways, if that's the attitude . . ."

He was not much impressed, either by the threat or the tone in which it was delivered. "If you want," said he in the grave, no-nonsense voice one might adopt to address a child who is not acting his age, "to discontinue paying for my education, that is up to you; that is something you and Dad will have to decide between you."

"Oh darling, what's turned you into this cruel person—you, who were always so so sweet and considerate—?"

"Mother," replied the nineteen-year-old, now a major in English language and literature, "try to be precise. I'm not cruel. Only direct."

Ah, the distance he had traveled from her since the day in 1942 when Nathan Zuckerman had fallen in love with Betty Zuckerman the way men seemed to fall in love with women in the movies—yes, smitten by her, as though she weren't his mother but a famous actress who for some incredible reason happened also to cook his meals and keep his room in order. In her capacity as chairwoman of the war bond drive at his school, she had been invited to the assembly hall that morning to address the entire student body on the importance of saving war stamps. She arrived dressed in the clothes she ordinarily wore only when she and her "girl friends" went in to Philadelphia to see the matinee performance of a stage show: her tailored gray suit and a white silk blouse. To top it off, she delivered her talk (without notes) from back of the lectern luxuriantly draped with red, white, and blue bunting. For the rest of Nathan's life, he was to find himself unduly susceptible to a woman in a gray suit and a white blouse, because of the glamour his slender, respectable, well-mannered mother radiated from the stage that day. Indeed, Mr. Loomis, the principal (who may have been somewhat smitten himself), compared her demeanor as chairwoman of the bond drive and president of the PTA to that of Madame Chiang Kai-shek. And in shyly acknowledging his compliment, Mrs. Zuckerman had conceded from the platform that Madame Chiang was in fact one of her idols. So too, she told the assembled students, were Pearl Buck and Emily Post. True enough. Zuckerman's mother had a deep belief in what she called "graciousness," and a reverence, such as is reserved in India for the cow, toward greeting cards and thank you notes. And while they were in love, so did he.

One of the first big surprises of Zuckerman's life was seeing the way his mother carried on when his brother Sherman entered the navy to serve his two-year hitch in 1945. She might have been some young girl whose fiancé was marching off to die in the front lines, while the fact of the matter was that America had won World War Two in August and Sherman was only a hundred miles away, in boot camp in Maryland. Nathan did everything he could possibly think of to cheer her up: helped with the dishes, offered on Saturdays to carry the groceries home, and talked nonstop, even about a subject that ordinarily embarrassed him, his little girl friends. To his father's consternation he invited his mother to come and look over his shoulder at his hand when "the two men" played gin rummy on Sunday nights at the bridge table set up in the living room. "Play the game," his father would warn him, "concentrate on my discards, Natie, and not on your mother. Your mother can take care of herself, but you're the one who's going to get schneidered again." How could the man be so *heartless*? His mother could *not* take care of herself—*something had to be done*. But what?

It was particularly unsettling to Nathan when "Mamselle" was played over the radio, for against this song his mother simply had no defense whatsoever. Along with "The Old Lamplighter," it had been her favorite number in Sherman's entire repertoire of semi-classical and popular songs, and there was nothing she liked better than to sit in the living room after dinner and listen to him play and sing (at her request) his "interpretation." Somehow she could manage with "The Old Lamplighter," which she had always seemed to love equally well, but now when they began to play "Mamselle" on the radio, she would have to get up and leave the room. Nathan, who was not exactly immune to "Mamselle" himself, would follow after her and listen through the door of her bedroom to the muffled sounds of weeping. It nearly killed him.

Knocking softly, he asked, "Mom . . . you all right? You want anything?"

"No, darling, no."

"Do you want me to read you my book report?"

"No, sweetheart."

"Do you want me to turn off the radio? I'm finished listening, really."

"Let it play, Nathan dear, it'll be over in a minute."

How awful her suffering was—also, how odd. After all, for *him* to miss Sherman was one thing—Sherman happened to be *his only older brother*. As a small boy Nathan's attachment to Sherman had been so pronounced and so obvious that the other kids used to make jokes about it—they used to say that if Sherman Zuckerman ever stopped short, his kid brother's nose would go straight up Sherm's ass. Little Nathan could indeed be seen following behind his older brother to school in the morning, to Hebrew school in the afternoon, and to his

Boy Scout meetings at night; and when Sherman's five-piece high-school band used to go off to make music for bar mitzvahs and wedding parties, Nathan would travel with them as "a mascot" and sit up in a chair at the corner of the stage and knock two sticks together during the rumbas. That he should feel bereft of his brother and in their room at night grow teary at the sight of the empty twin bed to his right, that was to be *expected*. But what was his mother carrying on like this about? How could she miss Sherman so, when *he* was still around— and being nicer, really, than ever. Nathan was thirteen by this time and already an honor student at the high school, but for all his intelligence and maturity he could not figure that one out.

When Sherman came home on his first liberty after boot camp, he had with him a ditty bag full of dirty photographs to show to Nathan as they walked together around the old neighborhood; he also had a pea jacket and a sailor cap for his younger brother, and stories to tell about whores who sat on his lap in the bars around Bainbridge and let him stick his hand right up their dresses. *And for nothing.* Whores *fifty* and *sixty* years old. Sherman was eighteen then and wanted to be a jazz musician à la Lennie Tristano; he had already been assigned to Special Services because of his musical talent, and was going to be MCing shows at the base, as well as helping the chief petty officer organize the entertainment program. He was also that rarity in show business, a marvelous *comic* tap dancer, and could give an impression of Bojangles Robinson that would cause his younger brother to double over with laughter. Zuckerman, at thirteen, expected great things from a brother who could do all this. Sherman told him about pro kits and VD films and let him read the mimeographed stories that the sailors circulated among themselves during the nights they stood guard duty. Staggering. It seemed to the adolescent boy that his older brother had found access to a daring and manly life.

And when, upon being discharged, Sherman made directly for New York and found a job playing piano in a bar in Greenwich Village, young Zuckerman was ecstatic; not so, the rest of the family. Sherman told them that his ambition was to play with the Stan Kenton band, and his father, if he had had a gun, would probably have pulled it out and shot him. Nathan, in the meantime, confided to his high-school friends stories about his brother's life "in the Village." They asked (those bumpkins), "What village?" He explained, scornfully; he told them about the San Remo bar on MacDougal Street, which he himself had never seen, but could imagine. Then one night Sherman went to a party after work (*which was four in the morning*) and met June Christie, Kenton's blonde vocalist. June Christie. *That* opened up a fantasy or two in the younger brother's head. Yes, it began to sound as though the possibilities for someone as game and adventurous as Sherman Zuckerman (or Sonny Zachary, as he called himself in the cocktail lounge) were going to be just about endless.

And then Sherman was going to Temple University, taking pre-dent. And then he was married, not to June Christie but to *some girl*, some skinny Jewish girl from Bala-Cynwyd who talked in baby talk and worked as a dental technician somewhere. Nathan couldn't believe it. Say it ain't so, Sherm! He remembered those cantaloupes hanging from the leering women in the dirty pictures Sherman had brought home from the navy, and then he thought of flat-chested Sheila, the dental technician with whom Sherman would now be going to bed every night for the rest of his life, and he couldn't figure the thing out. What had happened to his glamorous brother? "He saw the light, that's what," Mr. Z. explained to relatives and friends, but *particularly* to young Nathan, "he saw the handwriting on the wall and came to his goddam senses."

Seventeen years then of family life and love such as he imagined everyone enjoyed, more or less—and then his four years at Bass College, according to Zuckerman an educational institution distinguished largely for its lovely pastoral setting in a valley in western Vermont. The sense of superiority that his father had hoped to temper in his son with Dale Carnegie's book on winning friends and influencing people flourished in the Vermont countryside like a jungle fungus. The apple-cheeked students in their white buck shoes, the *Bastion* pleading weekly in its editorial column for "more school spirit," the compulsory Wednesday morning chapel sermons with visiting clergy from around the state, and the Monday evening dormitory "bull sessions" with notables like the dean of men—the ivy on the library walls, the dean told the new freshmen boys, could be heard on certain moonlit nights to whisper the word "tradition"—none of this did much to convince Zuckerman that he ought to become more of a pal to his fellow man. On the other hand, it was the pictures in the Bass catalogue of the apple-cheeked boys in white bucks crossing the sunlit New England quadrangle in the company of the apple-cheeked girls in white bucks that had in part drawn Zuckerman to Bass in the first place. To him, and to his parents, beautiful Bass seemed to partake of everything with which the word "collegiate" is so richly resonant for those who have not been beyond the twelfth grade. Moreover, when the family rode up in the spring, his mother found the dean of men—who three years later was to tell Zuckerman that he ought to be driven from the campus with a pitchfork for the so-called parody he had written in his literary magazine about the homecoming queen, a girl who happened to be an orphan from Rutland—this same dean of men, with briar pipe and football shoulders swathed in tweed, had seemed to Mrs. Zuckerman "a perfectly gracious man," and that about sewed things up—that and the fact that there was, according to the dean, "a top-drawer Jewish fraternity" on the campus, as well as a sorority for the college's thirty "outstanding" Jewish girls, or "gals," as the dean called them.

Who knew, who in the Zuckerman family knew, that the very month he was to leave for his freshman year of college, Nathan would read a book called *Of Time and the River* that was to change not only his attitude toward Bass, but toward Life Itself?

After Bass he was drafted. Had he continued into advanced ROTC he would have entered the service as a second lieutenant in the Transportation Corps, but almost alone among the Bass undergraduates, he disapproved of the skills of warfare being taught and practiced at a private educational institution, and so after two compulsory years of marching around the quadrangle once a week with a rifle on his shoulder, he had declined an invitation from the colonel in charge to proceed further with his military training. This decision had infuriated his father, particularly as there was another war on. Once again, in the cause of democracy, American young men were leaving this world for oblivion, this time at a rate of one every sixty minutes, and twice as many each hour were losing parts of themselves in the snowdrifts and mudfields of Korea. "Are you crazy, are you *nuts* to turn your back on a deal in the Transportation Corps that could mean life or death? You want to get your ass shot off in the infantry, instead? Oh, you are looking for trouble, my son, and you are going to find it, too! The shit is going to hit the fan, buddy, and you ain't going to like it one bit! Especially if you are dead!" But nothing the elder Zuckerman could think to shout at him could change his stubborn son's mind on this matter of principle. With somewhat less intensity (but no less befuddlement) Mr. Zuckerman had responded to his son's announcement in his freshman year that he intended to drop out of the Jewish fraternity to which he had begun to pledge only the month before. "Tell me, Nathan, how do you quit something you don't even belong to yet? How can you be so goddam superior to something when you don't even know what it's like to *belong* to the thing yet? Is this what I've got for a son all of a sudden—a *quitter*?"

"Of some things, yes," was the undergraduate's reply, spoken in that tone of cool condescension that entered into his father's nervous system like an iron spike. Sometimes when his father began to seethe, Zuckerman would hold the telephone out at arm's distance and just look at it with a poker face, a tactic he had seen people resort to, of course, only in the movies and for comic effect. Having counted to fifty, he would then try again to address the entrepreneur: "It's beneath my dignity, yes, that's correct." Or: "No, I am not against things to be against them, I am against them on matters of principle." "In other words," said—seethed—Mr. Zuckerman, "you are right, if I'm getting the idea, and the rest of the world is wrong. Is that it, Nathan, you are the new god around here, and the rest of the world can just go to hell!" Coolly, coolly, so coolly that the most sensitive seismograph hooked into their long-distance connection would not have recorded the tiniest quaver in his voice: "Dad, you so broaden the terms of our discussion with a statement like that—" and so on, temperate, logical, eminently "reasonable," just what it took to bring on the volcano in New Jersey.

"Darling," his mother would plead softly into the phone,

"did you talk to Sherman? At least did you think to talk this over with him first?"

"Why should I want to talk it over with 'him'?"

"*Because he's your brother!*" his father reminded him.

"And he loves you," his mother said. "He watched over you like a piece of precious china, darling, you remember that—he brought you that pea jacket that you wore till it was rags you loved it so, oh Nathan, *please*, your father is right, if you won't listen to us, listen to him, because, when he came out of the navy, Sherman went through an independent stage exactly like the one you're going through now. To the T."

"Well, it didn't do him very much good, Mother, did it."

"WHAT?" Mr. Zuckerman, flabbergasted yet again. "What kind of way is that to talk about your brother, damn it? Who *aren't* you better than—please just tell me one name, for the record book at least. Mahatma Gandhi maybe? Yehudi? Oh, do you need some humility knocked into you! Do you need a good stiff course in Dale Carnegie! Your brother happens to be a practicing orthodontist with a wonderful practice and also *he is your brother.*"

"Dad, brothers can have mixed feelings about one another. I believe you have mixed feelings about your own."

"But the issue is *not* my brothers, the issue is *yours*, don't confuse the issue, which is your KNOW-IT-ALL ARRO-GANCE ABOUT LIFE THAT DOESN'T KNOW A GOD-DAM THING!"

Then Fort Dix: midnights on the firing range, sit-ups in the rain, mounds of mashed potatoes and Del Monte fruit cup for "dinner"—and again, with powdered eggs, at dawn—and before even four of the eight weeks of basic infantry training were over, a graduate of Seton Hall College in his regiment dead of meningitis. Could his father have been *right*? *Had* his position on ROTC been nothing short of insane, given the realities of army life and the fact of the Korean War? Could he, a summa cum laude, have made such a ghastly and irrevers-ible mistake? Oh God, suppose he were to come down now with spinal meningitis from having to defecate each morning with a mob of fifty! What a price to pay for having principles about ROTC! Suppose he were to contract the disease while

scrubbing out the company's hundred stinking garbage cans—
the job that seemed always to fall to him on his marathon stints
of KP. ROTC (as his father had prophesied) would get on very
nice without him, ROTC would *flourish*, but what about the
man of principle, would he keel over in a garbage pail, dead
before he'd even reached the front lines?

But like Dilsey (of whom Zuckerman alone knew, in his platoon of Puerto Ricans), he endured. Basic training was no small
trial, however, particularly coming as quickly as it did upon
that last triumphant year at Bass, when his only course but one,
taken for nine hours' credit, was the English honors seminar
conducted by Caroline Benson. Along with Bass's two other
most displaced Jews, Zuckerman was the intellectual powerhouse of "The Seminar," which assembled every Wednesday
from three in the afternoon until after six—dusk in the autumn
and spring, nightfall in the winter—on Queen Anne dining
chairs pulled around the worn Oriental rug in the living room
of Miss Benson's cozy house of books and fireplaces. The seven
Christian critics in The Seminar would hardly dare to speak
when the three dark Jews (all refugees from the top-drawer
Jewish fraternity and founders together of Bass's first literary
magazine since—ah, how he loved to say it—the end of the
nineteenth century), when these three Jews got to shouting
and gesticulating at one another over *Sir Gawain and the
Green Knight*. A spinster (who, unlike his mother, happened
not to look half her age), Caroline Benson had been born, like
all her American forebears, over in Manchester, then educated
at Wellesley and "in England." As he would learn midway
through his college career, "Caroline Benson and her New
York Jew" was very much a local tradition, as much a part of
Bass as the "hello spirit" the dean of men was so high on, or
the football rivalry with the University of Vermont that annually brought the ordinarily respectable campus to a pitch of religious intensity only rarely to be seen in this century beyond
the Australian bush. The wittier New Englanders on the faculty spoke of "Caroline's day-vah Jew experience, it always
feels like something that's happened to her in a previous semester . . ." Yes, he was, as it turned out, one of a line—and
didn't care. Who was Nathan Zuckerman of Camden, New
Jersey, to turn his untutored back on the wisdom of a Caroline

Benson, educated in England? Why, she had taught him, within the very first hour she had found him in her freshman literature class, to pronounce the *g* in "length"; by Christmas vacation he had learned to aspirate the *h* in "whale"; and before the year was out he had put the word "guy" out of his vocabulary for good. Rather *she* had. Simple to do, too.

"There are no 'guys,' Mr. Zuckerman, in *Pride and Prejudice*."

Well, he was glad to learn that, delighted to, in fact. She could singe him to scarlet with a line like that, delivered in that clipped Vermont way of hers, but vain as he was he took it without so much as a whimper—every criticism and correction, no matter how minute, he took unto himself with the exaltation of a martyred saint.

"I think I should learn to get along better with people," he explained to Miss Benson one day, when she came upon him in the corridor of the literature building and asked what he was doing wearing a fraternity pledge pin (wearing it on the chest of the new V-neck pullover in which his mother said he looked so collegiate). Miss Benson's response to his proposed scheme for self-improvement was at once so profound and so simply put that Zuckerman went around for days repeating the simple interrogative sentence to himself; like *Of Time and the River*, it verified something he had known in his bones all along, but in which he could not place his faith until it had been articulated by someone of indisputable moral prestige and purity: "Why," Caroline Benson asked the seventeen-year-old boy, "should you want to learn a thing like that?"

The afternoon in May of his senior year when he was invited —not Osterwald who had been invited, not Fischbach, but Zuckerman, the chosen of the Chosen—to take tea with Caroline Benson in the "English" garden back of her house, had been, without question, the most civilized four hours of his life. He had been directed by Miss Benson to bring along with him the senior honors paper he had just completed, and there in a jacket and tie, amid the hundreds of varieties of flowers, none of whose names he knew (except for the rose), sipping as little tea as he could politely get away with (he was unable as yet to dissociate hot tea with lemon from the childhood sickbed) and munching on watercress sandwiches (which he had never even heard of before that afternoon—and wouldn't miss, if he didn't hear of them again), he read aloud to Miss Benson his thirty-page paper entitled, "Subdued Hysteria: A Study of the Undercurrent of Agony in Some Novels of Virginia Woolf." The paper was replete with all those words that now held such fascination for him, but which he had hardly, if ever, uttered back in the living room in Camden: "irony" and "values" and "fate," "will" and "vision" and "authenticity," and, of course, "human," for which he had a particular addiction. He had to be cautioned repeatedly in marginal notes about his relentless use of that word. "Unnecessary," Miss Benson would write. "Redundant." "Mannered." Well, maybe unnecessary to her, but not to the novice himself: human character, human possibility, human error, human anguish, human tragedy. Suffering and failure, the theme of so many of the novels that "moved" him, were "human conditions" about which he could speak with an astonishing lucidity and even gravity by the time he was a senior honors student—astonishing in that he was, after all, someone whose own sufferings had by and large been confined up till then to the dentist's chair.

They discussed first the paper, then the future. Miss Benson expected him after the army to continue his literary studies at either Oxford or Cambridge. She thought it would be a good idea for Nathan to spend a summer bicycling around England to see the great cathedrals. That sounded all right to him. They did not embrace at the end of that perfect afternoon, but only because of Miss Benson's age, position, and character. Zuckerman had been ready and willing, the urge in him to embrace and be embraced all but overpowering.

His eight unhappy weeks of basic infantry training were followed by eight equally unhappy weeks of military police training with a herd of city roughnecks and southern hillbillies under the equatorial sun at Fort Benning, Georgia. In Georgia he learned to direct traffic so that it flowed "through the hips" (as the handbook had it) and to break a man's larynx, if he should wish to, with a swat of the billy club. Zuckerman was as alert and attentive at these army schools as he had been earning his summa cum laude degree from Bass. He did not like the environment, his comrades, or "the system," but he did not wish to die in Asia either, and so applied himself to every detail of his training as if his life depended upon it—as it would. He did not pretend, as did some of the other college graduates in his training company, to be offended or amused by the bayonet drill. One thing to be contemptuous of soldierly skills while an undergraduate at Bass, another when you were a member of an army at war. "KILL!" he screamed, "KILL!" just as "aggressively" as he was instructed to, and drove the bayonet deep into the bowels of the sandbag; he would have spat upon the dying dummy too if he had been told that that was standing operating procedure. He knew when to be superior and when not to be—or was beginning at least to find out. "What are you?" Sergeant Vinnie Bono snarled at them from the instructor's platform (a jockey before Korea, Sergeant Bono was reputed to have slain a whole North Korean platoon with nothing but an entrenching tool)—"What are you with your stiff steel pricks, you troopers—pussycats or lions?" "LIONS!" roared Zuckerman, because he did not wish to die in Asia, or anywhere for that matter, ever.

But he would, and, he feared, sooner rather than later. At those Georgia reveille formations, the captain, a difficult man to please, would be giving the troopers their first dressing down of the long day—"I guaranfuckintee you gentlemen, not one swingin' dick will be leavin' this fiddlefuckin' area to so much as chew on a nanny goat's tittie—" and Zuckerman, ordinarily a cheery, a dynamic morning riser, would suddenly have a vision of himself falling beneath the weight of some drunken redneck in an alley back of a whorehouse in Seoul. He would expertly crack the offending soldier in the larynx, in the groin, on the patella, in all the places where he had crippled the dummy in the drill, but the man facedown in the mud would be Zuckerman, crushed beneath the drunken lawbreaker's brute strength—and then from nowhere, his end would come, by way of the knife or the razor blade. Schools and dummies were one thing—the world and the flesh something else: How would Zuckerman find the wherewithal to crack his club against a real human patella, when he had never been able to do so much as punch somebody's face with his fist in a schoolyard fight? And yet he had his father's short fuse, didn't he? And the seething self-righteousness to go with it. Nor was he wholly without physical courage. After all, as a boy he had never been much more than skin and bones beneath his shoulder pads and helmet, and yet in the sandlot football games he played in weekly every fall, he had not flinched or cried aloud when the stampede had come sweeping around his end of the line; he was fast, he was shifty—"wiry" was the word with which he preferred to describe himself at that time, "Wiry Nate Zuckerman"—and he was "smart," and could fake and twist and fight his way through a pack of thirteen-year-old boys built like hippos, for all that he was a boy built like a giraffe. He had in fact been pretty fearless on the football field, *so long as everybody played according to the rules and within the spirit of the game.* But when (to his surprise) that era of good fellowship came to an end, Wiry Nate Zuckerman retired. To be smashed to the ground because he was left end streaking for the goal line with the ball had always been all right with him; indeed he rather liked the precarious drama of plucking a spiral from the air one moment, and then in the next, tasting dirt, as the pounds piled up above him. However, on a Saturday morning in the fall of 1947, when one of the Irish kids on the Mount Holly Hurricanes came flying onto the pileup (at the bottom of which lay Zuckerman, with the ball) screaming, "Cream that Yid!" he knew that his football career was over. Henceforth football was no longer to be a game played by the rules, but a battle in which each of the combatants would try to get away with as much as he could, for whatever "reasons" he had. And Zuckerman could get away with nothing—he could not even hit back when attacked. He could use what strength he had to try to restrain somebody else from going at him, he would struggle like hell to prevent damage or disfigurement to himself, but when it came to bringing his own knuckles or knees into violent contact with another, he just could not make it happen. Had never been up to it on the neighborhood playground, would be paralyzed for sure on the mainland of Asia. An attentive and highly motivated student, he had earned the esteem of a trained killer for the manner in which he disemboweled the sandbag in basic training—"That's it, Slim," Sergeant Bono would megaphone down to his favorite college graduate, "that's grabbin' that gook by his gizzard, that's cuttin' off the Commie bastard's cock!"—but face to face with a real live enemy, he might just as well be carrying a parasol and wearing a bustle for all the good his training as a warrior was going to do himself or the Free World.

So, it looked as though he would not be taking that pilgrimage to Canterbury Cathedral after all, nor would he get to see the Poets' Corner in Westminster Abbey, or the churches where John Donne had preached, or the Lake District, or Bath, the setting of *Persuasion* (Miss Benson's favorite novel), or the Abbey Theatre, or the River Liffey, nor would he live to be a professor of literature some day, with a D. Litt. from Oxford or Cambridge and a house of his own cozy with fireplaces and walled with books; he would never see Miss Benson again, or her garden, or those fortunate 4Fs, Fischbach and Osterwald —and worse, no one, ever again, would see him.

It was enough to make him cry; so he did, invariably after being heroically lighthearted on the telephone with his worried mother and father in New Jersey. Yes, outside the phone booth, within hearing distance of the PX jukebox—"Oh, the red we want is the red we got in th' old red, white, and blue" —he would find himself at the age of twenty-one as tearful and panic-stricken as he had been at four when he had finally had to learn to sleep with all the lights off in his room. And no less desperate for his mommy's arms and the feel of his daddy's unshaven cheek.

Telephoning Sharon, being brave with her, would also reduce him to tears afterward. He could hold up all right during the conversations, while *she* cried, but when it came time to give up the phone to the soldier standing next in the line, when he left the phone booth where he had been so good at cheering her up and started back through the dark across that alien post— "Yes, the red we want is the red we got in th' old red, white, and blue"—he had all he could do not to scream out against the horrible injustice of his impending doom. No more Sharon. *No more Sharon!* NO MORE SHARON! What proportions the loss of Sharon Shatzky assumed in young Zuckerman's mind. And who was she? Who was Sharon Shatzky that the thought of leaving her forever would cause him to clap a hand over his mouth to prevent himself from howling at the moon?

Sharon was the seventeen-year-old daughter of Al "the Zipper King" Shatzky. With her family she had recently moved into Country Club Hills, the development of expensive ranch-type houses where his own parents now lived, on the outskirts of Camden, in a landscape as flat and treeless as the Dakota badlands. Zuckerman had met her in the four weeks between his graduation from Bass and his induction into the army in July. Before their meeting his mother had described Sharon as "a perfect little lady," and his father had said she was "a lovely lovely child," with the result that Zuckerman was not at all prepared for the rangy Amazon, red-headed and green-eyed, who arrived in short shorts that night, trailing sullenly behind Al and Minna. All four parents present fell over themselves treating her like a baby, as though that might convince the college graduate to keep his eyes from the powerful curve of haunch beneath the girl's skimpy summer outfit. Mrs. Shatzky had just that day taken Sharon shopping in Philadelphia for her "college wardrobe." "Mother, *please*," Sharon said, when Minna began to describe how "adorable" Sharon looked in each of her new outfits. Al said (proudly) that Sharon Shatzky here now owned more pairs of shoes than he owned undershorts. "*Daddy*," moaned Sharon, closing her jungle eyes in exasperation. Zuckerman's father said that if Sharon had any questions about college life she should ask his son, who had been editor up at Bass of "the school paper." It had been the literary magazine that Zuckerman had edited, but he was by now accustomed to the inaccuracies that accompanied his parents' public celebration of his achievements. Indeed, of late, his tolerance for their failings was growing by leaps and bounds. Where only the year before he might have been incensed by some line of his mother's that he knew came straight out of *McCall's* (or by the fact that she did not know what an "objective correlative" was or in what century Dryden had lived), now he was hardly perturbed. He had also given up trying to educate his father about the ins and outs of the syllogism; to be sure, the man simply could not get it through his head that an argument in which the middle term was not distributed at least once was invalid—but what difference did that make to Zuckerman any more? He could afford to be generous to parents who loved him the way they did (illogical and uneducated though they were). Besides, if the truth be known, in the past four years he had become more Miss Benson's student than their offspring . . . So he was kind and charitable to all that night, albeit "amused" by much of what he saw and heard; he answered the Shatzkys' questions about "college life" without a trace of sarcasm or snobbishness (none, at any rate, that he could hear), and all the while (without success) tried to keep his eyes from their daughter's perky breasts beneath her shrunken polo shirt, and the tempting cage of her torso rising from that slender, mobile waist, and the panthery way she moved across the wall-to-wall carpet on the balls of her bare feet . . . After all: what business did a student of English letters who had taken tea and watercress sandwiches only a few weeks earlier in the garden of Caroline Benson have with the pampered middle-class daughter of Al "the Zipper King" Shatzky?

By the time Zuckerman was about to graduate (third in his class, same rank as at Bass) from MP school, Sharon was a freshman at Juliana Junior College, near Providence. Every night she wrote him scandalous letters on the monogrammed pink stationery with the scalloped edges that Zuckerman's mother had given the perfect young lady for a going-away present: "dearest dearest all i could think about while playing tennis in gym class was getting down on my hands and knees and crawling across the room toward your prick and then pressing your prick against my face i love it with your prick in my face just pressing your prick against my cheeks my lips my tongue my nose my eyes my ears wrapping your gorgeous prick in my hair—" and so on. The word, which (among others) he had taught her and encouraged her to use during the sex act and also, for titillation's sake, on the phone and through the mails —had a strong hold over the young girl locked up in the dormitory room in Rhode Island: "every time the ball came over the net," wrote Sharon, "i saw your wonderful prick on top of it." This last, of course, he didn't believe. If Sharon had a fault as a student of carnality, it was a tendency to try a little too hard, with the result that her prose (to which Zuckerman, trained by Miss Benson in her brand of the New Criticism, was particularly attuned) often offended him by a too facile hyperbole. Instead of acting upon him as an aphrodisiac, her style frequently jarred him by its banal insistence, reminding him less of Lawrence than of those mimeographed stories his brother used to smuggle home to him from the navy. In particular her use of "cunt" (modified by "hot") and "prick" (modified by "big" or "gorgeous" or both) could be as mannered and incantatory, in a word, as sentimental, as his own use, or misuse, in college of the adjective "human." Nor was he pleased by her refusal to abide by the simple rules of grammar; the absence of punctuation and capitalization in her obscene letters was not exactly an original gesture of defiance (or an interesting one either, to Zuckerman's mind, whether the iconoclast was Shatzky or cummings), and as a device to communicate the unbridled flow of passion, it seemed to him, a votary not only of *Mrs. Dalloway* and *To the Lighthouse*, but also of *Madame Bovary* and *The Ambassadors* (he really could not read Thomas Wolfe any more), to have been conceived at a rather primitive level of imagination.

However, as for the passion itself, he had no criticism to make.

Practically overnight (correction: overnight), the virgin whose blood had stained his thighs and matted his pubic hair when he had laid her on a blanket in the back seat of his father's new Cadillac, had developed into the most licentious creature he'd ever known. Nobody like Sharon had been in attendance at Bass, at least nobody he had ever undressed, and he had traveled with the college's half dozen bohemians. Even Barbara Cudney, leading lady of the Bass Drama Society and Zuckerman's companion during his final year of success and celebrity at college, a girl who had thrown herself all over the stage in *Medea* and was now studying at the Yale Drama School, had nothing like Sharon's sensual adventurousness or theatricality, nor had it ever occurred to Zuckerman to ask of Barbara, free and uninhibited spirit that she was, such favors as Sharon virtually begged to bestow upon him. Actually the teacher was not so far out in front of his pupil as he led her to think he was, though of course his surprise at her willingness to satisfy his every whim and farfetched desire was something he kept to himself. In the beginning it exceeded all understanding, this bestiality he had awakened in her simply by penetration, and recalled to mind those other startling and baffling metamorphoses he had witnessed—his mother's transformation into the Maiden Bereft when Sherman left home for the navy, and the descent of Sherman himself from glamor boy to orthodontist. With Sharon, he had only to *allude* to some sexual antic or other, give the slightest *hint* of an interest —for *he* was not without inhibitions—for her to fall into the appropriate posture or turn up with the necessary equipment. "Tell me what you want me to say, Nathan, tell me what you want me to do—" As Zuckerman was a highly imaginative boy, and Sharon so anxious to please, there was, that June, very nearly something new and exciting to do every night.

The sense of adventure that surrounded their lovemaking (if such is the term that applies here) was heightened further by the presence often of the four parents in some other part of the house, or out on the back terrace, drinking iced tea and gabbing. While buggering Sharon on the floor beneath the ping-pong table in the basement of her parents' house, Zuckerman would call out from time to time, "Nice shot," or "Nice return, Sharon"—even as the feverish young girl whispered up from the canine position, "Oh it's so strange. It hurts, but it doesn't hurt. Oh Nathan, it's *so strange.*"

Very spicy stuff; more reckless than made him comfortable (Al Shatzky hadn't risen to the top of the zipper industry by being a gentle or forgiving fellow), but irresistible. At the suggestion of the adults, they would go off to the kitchen late at night and there like good little children eat oversized syrup-covered portions of ice cream out of soup bowls. Out on the terrace the adults would laugh about the appetite on those two kids—yes, those were his father's very words—while beneath the table where they sat, Zuckerman would be bringing Sharon to orgasm with his big toe.

Best of all were "the shows." For Zuckerman's pleasure and at his instigation, Sharon would stand in the bathroom with the door open and the overhead light on, performing for him as though she were on a stage, while he would be seated in the dark living room at the other end of the corridor, seemingly looking in the direction of the television set. A "show" consisted of Sharon unfastening her clothes (very slowly, deftly, very much the teasing pro) and then, with the little under-things at her feet, introducing various objects into herself. Transfixed (by the Phillies game, it would appear), Zuckerman would stare down the hallway at the nude girl writhing, just as he had directed her to, upon the plastic handle of her hairbrush, or her vaginal jelly applicator, or once, upon a zucchini purchased for that purpose earlier in the day. The sight of that long green gourd (uncooked, of course) entering into and emerging from her body, the sight of the Zipper King's daughter sitting on the edge of the bathtub with her legs flung apart, wantonly surrendering all five feet nine inches of herself to a vegetable, was as mysterious and compelling a vision as any Zuckerman had ever seen in his (admittedly) secular life. Almost as stirring as when she crawled to him across the length of her parents' living room that night, her eyes leveled on his exposed member and her tongue out and moving. "I want to be your whore," she whispered to him (without prompting too), while on the back terrace her mother told his mother how adorable Sharon looked in the winter coat they'd bought for her that afternoon.

It was not, it turned out, a complicated sort of rebellion Sharon was engaged in, but then she wasn't a complicated girl. If her behavior continued to exceed understanding it was now because it seemed so pathetically *transparent*. Sharon hated her father. One reason she hated him—so she said—was because of that ugly name of theirs *which he refused to do anything about*. Years and years ago, when she was still an infant in the crib, all five brothers on the Shatzky side had gotten together to decide to change the family name, "for business reasons." They had decided on Shadley. Only her father, of the five, refused to make the improvement. "I ain't ashamed," he told the other four—and went on from there, he informed his daughter, to become the biggest success of them all. As if, Sharon protested to Zuckerman, that proved anything! What about the sheer *ugliness* of that *name*? What about the way it *sounded* to people? Especially for a girl! Her cousin Cindy was Cindy Shadley, her cousin Ruthie was Ruthie Shadley—she alone of the girls in the family was still Shatzky! "Come on, will you please—I'm a trademark," her father told her, "I'm known nationwide. What am I supposed to become all of a sudden, Al 'the Zipper King' *Shadley*? Who's *he*, honey?" Well, the truth was that by the time she was fifteen she couldn't bear that he called himself "the Zipper King" either. "The Zipper King" was as awful as Shatzky—in ways it was worse. She wanted a father with a name that wasn't either a joke or an outright lie;

she wanted *a real name*; and she warned him, some day when she was old enough, she would hire a lawyer and go down to the county courthouse and get one. "You'll get one, all right—and you know how? The way all the other nice girls do. You'll get married, and why I'll cry at the wedding is out of happiness that I won't have to hear any more of this *name* business—" and so on, in this vein, for the five tedious years of Sharon's adolescence. Which wasn't quite over yet. "What is Shatzky," she cried sorrowfully to Zuckerman, "but the past tense of Shitzky? Oh why won't he change it! How stubborn can a person *be*?"

In her denunciations of the family name, Sharon was as witty as she would ever be—not that the wit was intentional. The truth was that when she was not putting on a three-ring circus for him, Sharon was pretty much of a bore to Zuckerman. She didn't know anything about anything. She did not pronounce the *g* in "length," nor did she aspirate the *h* in "when" or "why," nor would she have in "whale" had the conversation ever turned to Melville. And she had *the* most Cockney Philadelphia *o* he had ever heard on anyone other than a cabdriver. If and when she did get a joke of his, she would sigh and roll her eyes toward heaven, as though his subtleties were on par with her father's—Zuckerman, who had been the H. L. Mencken of Bass College! whose editorials (on the shortcomings of the administration and the student body) Miss Benson had likened in their savage wit to Jonathan Swift! How could he ever take Sharon up to Bass with him to visit Miss Benson? What if she started telling Miss Benson those pointless and interminable anecdotes about herself and her high-school friends? Oh, when she started talking, she could bury you in boredom! Rarely in conversation did Sharon finish a sentence, but rather, to Zuckerman's disgust, glued her words together by a gummy mixture of "you knows" and "I means," and with such expressions of enthusiasm as "really great," "really terrific," and "really neat" . . . the last usually to describe the gang of kids she had traveled with at Atlantic City when she was fifteen, which, to be sure, had only been the summer before last.

Coarse, childish, ignorant, utterly lacking in the exquisiteness of feeling and refinement of spirit that he had come to admire so in the novels—in the person—of Virginia Woolf, whose photograph had been tacked above his desk during his last semester at Bass. He entered the army after their feverish, daredevil month together secretly relieved at having left behind him (seemingly as he had found her) Al and Minna's five-foot nine-inch baby girl; she was a tantalizing slave and an extraordinary lay, but hardly a soul mate for someone who felt as he did about great writers and great books. Or so it seemed, until that day they issued him his M1 rifle, and he found he needed everyone he had.

"I love your prick," the girl wept into the phone. "I miss your prick *so much*. Oh, Nathan, I'm touching my cunt, I'm touching my cunt and making believe it's you. Oh, Nathan, should I make myself come on the phone? Nathan—?"

In tears, in terror, he went reeling from the phone booth: think of it, both he and his genitals would shortly be extinct! Oh what if just the genitals went, and *he* lived on—suppose a land mine were to explode beneath his boots, and he was returned to a girl like Sharon Shatzky, a blank between the legs. "No!" he told himself. "Stop having such thoughts! Lay off! Use your brains! That is only irrational guilt over Sharon and the zucchini—it is only fear of punishment for buggering the daughter right under the father's nose! Casebook fantasies of retribution! *No such thing can happen!*" To *him*, was what he meant, because of course in warfare such things do happen, they happen every day.

And then, after the eight weeks of infantry training followed by eight more at MP school, he was assigned as a clerk-typist to a quartermaster unit at Fort Campbell, in the southwestern corner of Kentucky, sixty miles east of Paducah, eight thousand east of the land mines. Lucky Zuckerman! Beneficiary of one of those administrative errors by which doomed men are suddenly pardoned, and the happy-go-lucky are, overnight, earmarked for death. These things also happen every day.

Zuckerman could type only with his index fingers, and he knew nothing about filing or making out forms, but fortunately for him, the captain in charge of the supply room to which he was assigned was so pleased to have a Jew around to bait—and that too has been known to happen—that he was willing to make do with an inept assistant. He did not—as the inept assistant continuously feared he would—report the error in classification that had sent Zuckerman to Fort Campbell instead of to his bloody demise in the mud behind a brothel in Seoul, nor did he request a replacement for him from personnel. Instead, each afternoon before departing for the links over by the air base, Captain Clark would tune up for his game by driving cotton golf balls out of his office in the direction of the cubicle occupied by the clerk-typist manqué. Zuckerman did his best to look unperturbed when the golf balls glanced off his shirt. "On target, sir," said he with a smile. "Not kwat," replied his superior, all concentration, "not kwat . . ." and would continue to swat them out through the open door of his office until at last he'd found the mark. "Ah, they we go, Zuckuhmun, rat on the nose."

Sadistic bully! Southern bigot! Zuckerman left the supply room at the end of each day bound for the office of the adjutant general, where he intended to bring charges against Captain Clark (who, for all he knew, held secret membership in the KKK). But since actually Zuckerman was not even supposed to *be* in Kentucky, but had been allocated for destruction in Korea (and might wind up there yet, if he gave Clark any trouble), he invariably saw fit to suppress his indignation and proceed on over to the mess hall for dinner, and then on to the post library, to continue to read his way through the Bloomsbury group, with time out every hour or so for another look at the day's bawdy letter from the teenage debauchee he hadn't been able to bring himself to relinquish quite yet. But, oh Christ, was he mad! His human dignity! His human rights! His *religion*! Oh, each time a golf ball caromed softly off his flesh, how he seethed with indignation . . . which isn't, however (as Private Zuckerman well knew), the same as running with blood. Nor is it what is meant in literature, or even in life for that matter, by suffering or pain.

Though pain would come to Zuckerman in time—in the form of estrangement, mortification, fierce and unremitting opposition, antagonists who were not respectable deans or loving fathers or dim-witted officers in the Army Quartermaster Corps; oh yes, pain would enter his life soon enough, and not entirely without invitation. As the loving father had warned him, looking for trouble, he would find it—and what a surprise that would be. For in severity and duration, in sheer *painfulness*, it would be like nothing he had known at home, in school, or in the service, nor would it be like anything he had imagined while contemplating the harrowed, soulful face of Virginia Woolf, or while writing his A+ honors paper on the undercurrent of agony in her novels. Only a short time after having been shipped by providential error—his last big dose, as it turned out, of beginner's luck—to the rural American southland instead of the Korean slaughter, adversity was to catch up with the young conquistador. He would begin to pay . . . for the vanity and the ignorance, to be sure, but above all for the contradictions: the stinging tongue and the tender hide, the spiritual aspirations and the lewd desires, the softy boyish needs and the manly, the *magisterial* ambitions. Yes, over the next decade of his life he was to learn all that his father might have wished Dale Carnegie to teach him about humility, and then some. And then some more.

But that is another story, and one whose luridness makes the small-time southern Jew-baiter lofting cotton golf balls toward his nose, makes even seventeen-year-old Sharon Shatzky, performing for him on a gourd like a Pigalle whore at an exhibition, seem as much a part of his idyllic and innocent youth as that afternoon he once spent sipping tea and eating watercress in Caroline Benson's garden. The story of Zuckerman's suffering calls for an approach far more *serious* than that which seems appropriate to the tale of his easeful salad days. To narrate with fidelity the misfortunes of Zuckerman's twenties would require deeper dredging, a darker sense of irony, a grave and pensive voice to replace the amused, Olympian point of view . . . or maybe what that story requires is neither gravity nor complexity, but just another author, someone who would see it too for the simple five-thousand-word comedy that it very well may have been. Unfortunately, the author of this story, having himself experienced a similar misfortune at about the same age, does not have it in him, even yet, midway through his thirties, to tell it briefly or to find it funny. "Unfortunate" because he wonders if that isn't more the measure of the man than of the misfortune.

# Courting Disaster

## or, Serious in the Fifties

No, I did not marry for conventional reasons; no one can accuse me of that. It was not for fear of loneliness that I chose my wife, or to have "a helpmate," or a cook, or a companion in my old age, and it certainly was not out of lust. No matter what they may say about me now, sexual desire had nothing to do with it. To the contrary: though she was a pretty enough woman—square, strong Nordic head; resolute blue eyes that I thought of admiringly as "wintry"; straight wheat-colored hair worn in bangs; a handsome smile; an appealing, openhearted laugh—her short, heavy-legged body struck me as very nearly dwarfish in its proportions and was, from first to last, unremittingly distasteful. Her gait in particular displeased me: mannish, awkward, it took on a kind of rolling quality when she tried to move quickly, and in my mind associated with images of cowhands and merchant seamen. Watching her run to meet me on some Chicago street—after we had become lovers—I would positively recoil, even at a distance, at the prospect of holding that body against me, at the idea that voluntarily I had made her *mine*.

Lydia Ketterer was a divorced woman, five years my senior, and mother of a ten-year-old girl who lived with Lydia's former husband and his second wife in a new suburban housing development south of Chicago. During their marriage, whenever Lydia dared to criticize or question her husband's judgment he would lift her from the floor—a massive man twice her weight and a foot taller—and heave her against the nearest wall; in the months following the divorce he abused her through her child, who was then six and in Lydia's custody; and when Lydia broke down, Ketterer took the child to live with him, and subsequently, after Lydia had been released from the hospital and was back in her apartment, refused to return the little girl.

He was the second man nearly to destroy her; the first, Lydia's father, had seduced her when she was twelve. The mother had been bedridden since Lydia's birth, a victim it would seem of nothing more than lumbago, but perpetually weak unto dying. After the father fled, Lydia had been taken to be raised in the home of two spinster aunts in Skokie; until she ran off with Ketterer at the age of eighteen, she and her mother shared a room at the rear of this haven whose heroes were the aviator Lindbergh, the senator Bilbo, the cleric Coughlin, and the patriot Gerald L. K. Smith. It had been a life of little but punishment, humiliation, betrayal, and defeat, and it was to this that I was drawn, against all my misgivings.

Of course, the contrast to my own background of familial devotion and solidarity was overwhelming: whereas Lydia remembered a thousand and one nights of rubbing Sloan's liniment into her mother's back, I could not remember a single hour of my childhood when my mother was incapable of performing the rites of her office. If indeed she ever had been indisposed, it seemed not even to interfere with her famous whistling, that continuous medley of "show tunes" she chirped melodiously away at through her day of housework and family chores. The sickly one in our home was me: suffocating diphtheria, subsequent annual respiratory infections, debilitating glandular fevers, mysterious visitations of "allergies." Until puberty, I spent as much time at home in my bed or under a blanket on the sofa in the living room as I did in my seat in the classroom, all of which makes the disposition of my mother, the whistler—"Mrs. Zuckerbird" the postman called her—even more impressive. My father, though not so sunny in his indestructibility, and constitutionally a much more solemn person than my peppy peasant of a mother, was no less equal to the hardships our family endured: specifically, the Depression, my ailments, and my older sister Sonia's inexplicable marriages, *twice* to the sons of Sicilians: the first an embezzler and in the end a suicide; the second, honest in his business but otherwise "common as dirt"—in the Yiddish word, which alone seemed to carry the weight of our heartbreak and contempt, *prust.*

We ourselves were not elegant, but surely we were not coarse. Dignity, I was to understand, had nothing to do with one's social station: character, conduct, was everything. My mother used to laugh and make cracks about the ladies around who had secret dreams of mink coats and Miami Beach vacations.

"To her," she would say disparagingly of some silly neighbor, "the be-all and end-all is to put on a silver fox and go gallivanting with the hoi polloi." Not until I got to college and misused the word myself did I learn that what my mother took to mean the elite—perhaps because "hoi polloi" sounded like another of her disdainful expressions for people who put on airs, "the hoity-toity"—actually referred to the masses.

So much for the class struggle as a burning issue in my house, or social resentment or ambitiousness as a motive for action. A strong character, not a big bankroll, was to them the evidence of one's worth. Good, sensible people. Why their two offspring should have wasted themselves as they did, why both children should have wed themselves to disaster, is difficult to understand. That my sister's first husband and my only wife should both have taken their own lives would seem to suggest something about our common upbringing. But what? I have no theories. If ever a mother and father were not responsible for the foolishness of their children, it was mine.

My father was a bookkeeper. Because of his excellent memory and his quickness with figures, he was considered the local savant in our neighborhood of hardworking first-generation Jews and was the man most frequently consulted by people in trouble. A thin, austere, and humorless person, always meticulous in a white shirt and a tie, he communicated his love for me in a precise, colorless fashion that makes me ache with tenderness for him, especially now that he is the bedridden one, and I live in self-exile thousands of miles from his bed.

When *I* was the sickly, feverish patient, I felt something more like mystification, as though he were a kind of talking electrical toy come to play with me promptly each evening at six. His idea of amusing me was to teach me to solve the sort of arithmetical puzzles at which he himself was a whiz. " 'Marking Down,' " he would say, not unlike a recitation student announcing the title of a poem. "A clothing dealer, trying to dispose of an overcoat cut in last year's style, marked it down from its original price of thirty dollars to twenty-four. Failing to make a sale, he reduced the price still further to nineteen dollars and twenty cents. Again he found no takers, so he tried another price reduction and this time sold it." Here he would pause; if I wished I might ask him to repeat any or all of the details. If not, he proceeded. "All right, Nathan; what was the selling price, if the last markdown was consistent with the others?" Or: "'Making a Chain.' A lumberjack has six sections of chain, each consisting of four links. If the cost of cutting open a link—" and so on. The next day, while my mother whistled Gershwin and laundered my father's shirts, I would daydream in my bed about the clothing dealer and the lumberjack. To whom had the haberdasher finally sold the overcoat? Did the man who bought it realize it was cut in last year's style? If he wore it to a restaurant, would people laugh? And what did "last year's style" look like anyway? "'Again he found no takers,'" I would say aloud, finding much to feel melancholy about in that idea. I still remember how charged for me was that word "takers." Could it have been the lumberjack with the six sections of chain who, in his rustic innocence, had bought the overcoat cut in last year's style? And why suddenly did he need an overcoat? Invited to a fancy ball? By whom? My mother thought the questions I raised about these puzzles were "cute" and was glad they gave me something to think about when she was occupied with housework and could not take the time to play go fish or checkers; my father, on the other hand, was disheartened to find me intrigued by fantastic and irrelevant details of geography and personality and intention instead of the simple beauty of the arithmetical solution. He did not think that was intelligent of me, and he was right.

I have no nostalgia for that childhood of illness, none at all. In early adolescence, I underwent daily schoolyard humiliation (at the time, it seemed to me there could be none worse) because of my physical timidity and hopelessness at all sports. Also, I was continually enraged by the attention my parents insisted upon paying to my health, even after I had emerged, at the age of sixteen, into a beefy, broad-shouldered boy who, to compensate for his uncoordinated, ludicrous performances in right field or on the foul line, took to shooting craps in the fetid washroom of the corner candy store and rode out on Saturday nights in a car full of "smoking wise guys"—my father's phrase—to search in vain for that whorehouse that was rumored to be located somewhere in the state of New Jersey. The dread I felt was of course even greater than my parents':

surely I would awaken one morning with a murmuring heart, or gasping for air, or with one of my fevers of a hundred and four . . . These fears caused my assault upon them to be particularly heartless, even for a teenager, and left them dazed and frightened of me for years thereafter. Had my worst enemy said, "I hope you die, Zuckerman," I could not have been any more provoked than I was when my well-meaning father asked if I had remembered to take my vitamin capsule, or when my mother, to see if a cold had made me feverish, did so under the guise of giving my forehead a lingering kiss at the dinner table. How all that tenderness enraged me! I remember that it was actually a relief to me when my sister's first husband got caught with his fist in the till of his uncle's heating-oil firm, and Sonia became the focus of their concern. And of my concern. She would sometimes come back to the house to cry on my seventeen-year-old shoulder, after having been to visit Billy in jail where he was serving a year and a day; and how good it felt, how uplifting it was, not to be on the receiving end of the solicitude, as was the case when Sonia and I were children and she would entertain the little shut-in by the hour, and without complaint.

A few years later, when I was away at Rutgers, Billy did my parents the favor of hanging himself by a cord from the drapery rod in their bedroom. I doubt that he expected it would hold him; knowing Billy, I guess he wanted the rod to give under his weight so that he might be found, still breathing, in a heap on the floor when my parents came back from their shopping. The sight of a son-in-law with a sprained ankle and a rope around his neck was supposed to move my father to volunteer to pay Billy's five-thousand-dollar debt to his bookie. But the rod turned out to be stronger than Billy had thought, and he was strangled to death. Good riddance, one would think. But no; the next year Sunny married (in my father's phrase) "another one." Same wavy black hair, same "manly" cleft in his chin, same repellent background. Johnny's weakness was not horses but hookers. The marriage has flourished, nonetheless. Each time my brother-in-law gets caught, he falls to his knees and begs Sunny's forgiveness; this gesture seems to go a long way with my sister—not so with our father: "Kisses her shoes," he would say, closing his eyes in disgust; "actually kisses *shoes*, as though that were a sign of love, of respect—of anything!" There are four handsome wavy-haired children, or were when last I saw them all in 1962: Donna, Louis, John Jr., and Marie (that name the unkindest cut of all). John Sr. builds swimming pools and brings in enough each week to be able to spend a hundred dollars on a New York call girl without feeling a thing, financially speaking. When last I saw it, their summer house in the Italian Catskills had even more pink "harem" pillows in the living room than the one in Scotch Plains, and an even grander pepper mill; in both "homes," the silver, the linens, and the towels are monogrammed SZR, my sister's initials.

*How come?* I used to be plagued by that question. How could it be that the sister of mine who had rehearsed for hours on end in our living room, over and over again singing to me the songs from *Song of Norway* and *The Student Prince* until I wished I were Norwegian or nobility; the sister who took "voice" from Dr. Bresslenstein in his studio in North Philadelphia and at fifteen was already singing "Because" for money at weddings; a sister who had the voluptuous, haughty airs of a prima donna when the other little girls were still fretting over boys and acne—how could *she* wind up in a house with a harem "motif," mothering children taught by nuns, and playing "Jerry Vale Sings Italian Hits" on the stereo to entertain our silent parents when they come for a Sunday visit? *How? Why?*

I used to wonder, when Sonia married for the second time, if perhaps she were involved in a secret and mysterious religious rite: if she had not deliberately set out to mortify herself, so as to sound to the depths her spiritual being. I would imagine her in bed at night (yes, in bed), her pretty-boy slob of a husband asleep beside her, and Sonia exultant in the dark with the knowledge that unbeknownst to everyone—everyone being the bewildered parents and incredulous college-boy brother—she continued to be the very same person who used to enchant us from the stage of the Y with what Bresslenstein (a poor refugee from Palestine, but according to himself formerly the famous impresario of Munich) described to my mother as "a beautiful beautiful coloratura quality—the beginnings of another Lily Pons." I could imagine her one evening at dinnertime knocking on the back door to our apartment, her black hair to her shoulders again, and wearing the same long embroidered dress in which she had appeared in *The Student Prince*—my graceful and vivacious sister, whose appearance on a stage would cause tears of pride to spring to my eyes, our Lily Pons, our Galli-Curci, returning to us, as bewitching as ever *and uncorrupted*: "I had to do it," she explains, when we three rush as one to embrace her, "otherwise it meant nothing."

In brief: I could not easily make peace with the fact that I had a sister in the suburbs, whose pastimes and adornments—vulgar to a snobbish college sophomore, an elitist already reading Allen Tate on the sublime and Dr. Leavis on Matthew Arnold with his breakfast cereal—more or less resembled those of millions upon millions of American families. Instead I imagined Sonia Zuckerman Ruggieri in Purgatorio.

Lydia Jorgenson Ketterer I imagined in Hell. But who wouldn't have, to hear those stories out of her lurid past? Beside hers, my own childhood, frailty, fevers, and all, seemed a version of paradise; for where I had been the child served, she had been the child servant, the child slave, round-the-clock nurse to a hypochondriacal mother and fair game to a benighted father.

The story of incest, as Lydia told it, was simple enough, so simple that it staggered me. It was simply inconceivable to me at the time that an act I associated wholly with a great work of classical drama could actually have taken place, without messengers and choruses and oracles, between a Chicago milkman in his Bloomfield Farms coveralls and his sleepy little blue-eyed daughter before she went off to school. Yet it had. "Once upon a time," as Lydia liked to begin the story, early on a winter morning, as he was about to set off to fetch his delivery truck, her father came into her room and lay down beside her in the bed, dressed for work. He was trembling and in tears. "You're all I have, Lydia, you're all Daddy has. I'm married to a corpse." Then he lowered his coveralls to his ankles, all because he was married to a corpse. "Simple as that," said Lydia. Lydia the child, like Lydia the adult, did not scream out, nor did she reach up and sink her teeth into his neck once he was over her. The thought of biting into his Adam's apple occurred to her, but she was afraid that his screams would awaken her mother, who needed her sleep. *She was afraid that his screams would awaken her mother.* And, moreover, she did not want to hurt him: he was her father. Mr. Jorgenson showed up for work that morning, but his truck was found abandoned later in the day in the Forest Preserve. "And where he went," said Lydia, in mild storybook fashion, "nobody knew," neither the invalid wife whom he had left penniless nor their horrified little child. Something at first made Lydia believe that he had run away "to the North Pole," though simultaneously she was convinced that he was lurking in the neighborhood, ready to crush her skull with a rock if she should tell any of her little friends the thing he had done to her before disappearing. For years afterward—even as a grown woman, even after her breakdown—whenever she went to the Loop at Christmastime, she would wonder if he might not be one of the Santa Clauses standing outside the department stores ringing a little bell at the shoppers. In fact, having decided in the December of her eighteenth year to run away from Skokie with Ketterer, she had approached the Santa Claus outside Goldblatt's and said to him, "I'm getting married. I don't care about you any more. I'm marrying a man who stands six feet two inches tall and weighs two hundred and twenty-five pounds and if you ever so much as follow me again he'll break every bone in your body."

"I still don't know which was more deranged," said Lydia, "pretending that that poor bewildered Santa Claus was my father, or imagining that the oaf I was about to marry was a man."

Incest, the violent marriage, then what she called her "flirtation" with madness. A month after Lydia had divorced Ketterer on grounds of physical cruelty, her mother finally managed to have the stroke she had been readying herself for all her life. During the week the woman lay under the oxygen tent in the hospital, Lydia refused to visit her. "I told my aunts that I had put in all the hours I owed to the cause. If she were dying, what help could I be in preventing it? And if she were faking again, I refused to participate." And when the mother did expire at long last, Lydia's grief, or relief, or delight, or guilt, took the form of torpor. Nothing seemed worth bothering to do. She fed and clothed Monica, her six-year-old daughter, but that was as far as she went. She did not change her own clothes, make the bed, or wash the dishes; when she opened a can to eat something she invariably discovered that she was eating the cat's tinned food. Then she began to write on the walls with her lipstick. The Sunday after the funeral, when Ketterer came to take Monica away for the day, he found the child in a chair, all dressed and ready to go, and the walls of the apartment covered with questions, printed in big block letters with a lipstick: WHY NOT? YOU TOO? WHY SHOULD THEY? SAYS WHO? WE WILL? Lydia was still at her breakfast, which consisted that morning of a bowl full of kitty litter, covered with urine and a sliced candle.

"Oh, how he loved that," Lydia told me. "You could just see his mind, or whatever you'd call what he's got in there, turning over. He couldn't bear, you see, that I had divorced him, he couldn't bear that a judge in a courtroom had heard what a brute he was. He couldn't bear losing his little punching bag. 'You think you're so smart, you go to art museums and you think that gives you a right to boss your husband around—' and then he'd pick me up and throw me at the wall. He was always telling me how I ought to be down on my knees for saving me from the houseful of old biddies, how I ought to *worship* him for taking somebody who was practically an orphan and giving her a nice home and a baby and money to spend going to art museums. Once, you see, during the seven years, I had gone off to the Art Institute with my cousin Bob, the bachelor high-school teacher. He took me to the art museum and when we were all alone in one of the empty rooms, he exposed himself to me. He said he just wanted me to look at him, that was all. He said he didn't want me to touch it. So I didn't; I didn't do anything. Just like with my father—I felt sorry for *him*. There I was, married to an ape, and here was Cousin Bob, the one my father used to call 'the little grind.' Quite a distinguished family I come from. *Anyway:* Ketterer broke down the door, saw the handwriting on the wall was mine, and couldn't have been happier. Especially when he noticed what I was pretending to be eating for my breakfast. Because it was all pretense, you see. I knew exactly what I was doing. I had no intention of drinking my own urine, or eating a candle and kitty litter. I knew he was coming to call, that was the reason I did it. You should have heard how solicitous he was: 'You need a doctor, Lydia, you need a doctor real bad.' But what he called was a city ambulance. I had to smile when two men came into my apartment actually wearing white coats. I didn't have to smile, that is, but I did. I said: 'Won't you gentlemen have some kitty litter?' I knew that was the kind of thing you were supposed to say if you were mad. Or at least that's what everybody else thought. What I really say when I'm insane are things like 'Today is Tuesday,' or 'I'll have a pound of chopped meat, please.' Oh, that's just cleverness. Strike that. I don't know *what* I say if I'm mad, or if I've even *been* mad. Truly, it was just a mild flirtation."

But that was the end of motherhood, nonetheless. Upon her release from the hospital five weeks later, Ketterer announced that he was remarrying. He hadn't planned on "popping the question" so soon, but now that Lydia had proved herself in public to be the nut he had had to endure in private for seven miserable years, he felt duty bound to provide the child with a proper home and a proper mother. And if she wanted to contest his decision in court, well, just let her try. It seemed he had taken photographs of the walls she had defaced and had lined up neighbors who would testify to what she had looked like and *smelled* like in the week before "you flipped your Lydia, kid," as it pleased Ketterer to describe what had happened to her. He did not care how much it would cost him in legal fees; he would spend every dime he had to save Monica from a crazy woman who ate her own filth. "And also," said Lydia, "to get out of paying support money in the bargain."

"I ran around frantically for days, begging the neighbors not to testify against me. They knew how much Monica loved me, they know that I loved her—they knew it was only because my mother had died, because I was exhausted, and so on and so forth. I'm sure I terrified them, telling them all they 'knew' that they didn't begin to know about my life. I'm sure I *wanted* to terrify them. I even hired a lawyer. I sat in his office and wept, and he assured me that I was within my rights to demand the child back, and that it was going to be a little harder for Mr. Ketterer than he thought, and so on and so forth, very encouraging, very sympathetic, very optimistic. So

I left his office and walked to the bus station and took a bus to Canada. I went to Winnipeg to look for an employment agency—I wanted to be a cook in a logging camp. The farther north the better. I wanted to be a cook for a hundred strong, hungry men. All the way to Winnipeg in the bus I had visions of myself in the kitchen of a big mess hall up in the freezing wilds, cooking bacon and eggs and biscuits and pots and pots of coffee for the morning meal, cooking their breakfast while it was still dark—the only one awake in the logging camp, me. And then the long sunny mornings, cleaning up and beginning preparations for the evening meal, when they'd all come in tired from the heavy work in the forest. It was the simplest and most girlish little daydream you can imagine. *I* could imagine. I would be a servant to a hundred strong men, and they in return would protect me from harm. I would be the only woman in the entire camp, and because there was only one of me, no one would ever dare to take advantage of my situation. I stayed in Winnipeg three days. Going to movies. I was afraid to go to a logging camp and say I wanted work there—I was sure they would think I was a prostitute. Oh, how banal to be crazy. Or maybe just banal being me. What could be more banal than having been seduced by your own father and then going around being 'scarred' by it forever? You see, I kept thinking all the while, 'There's no need for me to be behaving in this way. There is no need to be acting crazy—and there never was. There is no need to be running away to the North Pole. I'm just pretending. All I have to do to stop is *to stop*.' I would remember my aunts telling me, if I so much as uttered a whimper in objection to anything: 'Pull yourself together, Lydia, mind over matter.' Well, it couldn't be that I was going to waste my life defying *those* two, could it? Because making myself their victim was sillier even than continuing to allow myself to be my father's. There I sat in the movies in Canada, with all these expressions I used to hate so, going through my head, *but making perfect sense*. Pull yourself together, Lydia. Mind over matter, Lydia. You can't cry over spilled milk, Lydia. If you don't succeed, Lydia—and you don't—try, try again. Nothing could have been clearer to me than that sitting in the movies in Winnipeg was as senseless as anything I could do if I ever hoped to save Monica from her father. I could only conclude that I didn't want to save her from him. Dr. Rutherford now tells me that that was exactly the case. Not that it requires a trained therapist to see through somebody like me. How did I get back to Chicago? According to Dr. Rutherford, by accomplishing what I set out to do. I was staying in a two-dollar-a-night hotel on what turned out to be Winnipeg's skid row. As if Lydia didn't know, says Dr. Rutherford. The third morning that I came down to pay for the room, the desk clerk asked me if I wanted to pick up some easy cash. I could make a lot of money posing for pictures, especially if I was blonde all over. I began to howl. He called a policeman, and the policeman called a doctor, and eventually somehow they got me home. And that's how I managed to rid myself of my daughter. You would have thought it would have been simpler to drown her in the bathtub."

To say that I was drawn to her story because it was so lurid is only the half of it: there was the way the tale was told. Lydia's easy, familiar, even cozy manner with misery, her droll acceptance of her own madness, greatly increased the story's appeal —or, to put it another way, did much to calm whatever fears one might expect an inexperienced young man of a conventional background to have about a woman bearing such a ravaged past. Who would call "crazy" a woman who spoke with such detachment of her history of craziness? Who could find evidence of impulses toward suicide and homicide in a rhetorical style so untainted by rage or vengeful wrath? No, no, this was someone who had *experienced* her experience, who had been *deepened* by all that misery. A decidedly ordinary looking person, a pretty little American blonde with a face like a million others, she had, without benefit of books or teachers, mobilized every ounce of her intelligence to produce a kind of *wisdom* about herself. For surely it required wisdom to recite, calmly and with a mild, even forgiving irony, such a ghastly narrative of ill luck and injustice. You had to be as cruelly simpleminded as Ketterer himself, I thought, not to appreciate the moral triumph this represented—or else you just had to be someone other than me.

I met the woman with whom I was to ruin my life only a few months after arriving back in Chicago in the fall of 1956, following a premature discharge from the army. I was just short of twenty-four, held a master's degree in literature, and prior to my induction into the service had been invited to return to the College after my discharge as an instructor in the English composition program. Under any circumstances my parents would have been thrilled by what they took to be the eminence of that position; as it was, they looked upon this "honor" as something like divine compensation for the fate that had befallen their daughter. Their letters were addressed, without irony, to "Professor Nathan Zuckerman"; I'm sure many of them, containing no more than a line or two about the weather in New Jersey, were mailed solely for the sake of addressing them.

I was pleased myself, though not so awestruck. In fact, the example of my own tireless and resolute parents had so instilled in me the habits that make for success that I had hardly any understanding at all of failure. Why *did* people fail? In college, *I* had looked with awe upon those fellows who came to class *un*-prepared for examinations and who did *not* submit their assignments on time. Now why should they want to do it that way, I wondered. Why would anyone prefer the ignobility of defeat to the genuine pleasures of achievement? Especially as the latter was so easy to effectuate: all you had to be was attentive, methodical, thorough, punctual, and persevering; all you had to be was orderly, patient, self-disciplined, undiscourageable, and industrious—and, of course, intelligent. And that was it. What could be simpler?

What confidence I had in those days! What willpower and energy! And what a devourer of schedules and routines! I rose every weekday at six forty-five to don an old knit swimsuit and do thirty minutes of pushups, sit-ups, deep knee bends, and half a dozen other exercises illustrated in a physical-fitness guide that I had owned since adolescence and which still served its purpose; of World War Two vintage, it was titled *How To Be Tough as a Marine*. By eight I would have bicycled the mile to my office overlooking the Midway. There I would make a quick review of the day's lesson in the composition syllabus, which was divided into sections, each illustrating one of a variety of rhetorical techniques; the selections were brief—the better to scrutinize meticulously—and drawn mostly from the work of

Olympians: Aristotle, Hobbes, Mill, Gibbon, Pater, Shaw, Swift, Sir Thomas Browne, etc. My three classes of freshman composition each met for one hour, five days a week. I began at eight thirty and finished at eleven thirty, three consecutive hours of hearing more or less the same student discussion and offering more or less the same observations myself—and yet never with any real flagging of enthusiasm. Much of my pleasure, in fact, derived from trying to make each hour appear to be the first of the day. Also there was a young man's satisfaction in authority, especially as that authority did not require that I wear any badge other than my intelligence, my industriousness, a tie, and a jacket. Then of course I enjoyed, as I previously had as a student, the courtesy and good-humored seriousness of the pedagogical exchange, nearly as much as I enjoyed the sound of the word "pedagogical." It was not uncommon at the university for faculty and students eventually to call one another by their given names, at least outside the classroom. I myself never considered this a possibility, however, any more than my father could have imagined being familiar in their offices with the businessmen who had hired him to keep their books; like him, I preferred to be thought somewhat stiff, rather than introduce considerations extraneous to the job to be done, and which might tempt either party to the transaction to hold himself less accountable than was "proper." Especially for one so close to his students in age, there was a danger in trying to appear to be "a good guy" or "one of the boys"—as of course there was equally the danger of assuming an attitude of superiority that was not only in excess of my credentials, but distasteful in itself.

That I should have to be alert to every fine point of conduct may seem to suggest that I was unnatural in my role, when actually it was an expression of the enthusiasm with which I took to my new vocation and of the passion I had in those days to judge myself by the strictest standard in every detail.

By noon I would have returned to my small quiet apartment, eaten a sandwich I had prepared for myself, and already have begun work on my own fiction. Three short stories I had written during the evenings when I was in the army had all been accepted for publication in a venerable literary quarterly; they were, however, no more than skillful impersonations of the sort of stories I had been taught to admire most in college—stories of "The Garden Party" variety—and their publication aroused in me more curiosity than pride. I owed it to myself, I thought, to find out if I might have a talent that was my own. "To owe it to oneself," by the way, was a notion entirely characteristic of a man like my father, whose influence upon my thinking was more pervasive than might have been apparent to anyone—myself included—who had listened to me, in the classroom, discussing the development of a theory in Aristotle or a metaphor in Sir Thomas Browne.

At six P.M., following five hours of working at my fiction and an hour brushing up on my French—I planned to travel to Europe during the summer vacation—I bicycled back to the university to eat dinner in the Commons, where I had formerly taken my meals as a graduate student. The dark wood tones of the paneled hall, and the portraits of the university's distinguished dead hanging above the refectory tables, satisfied a strong taste in me for institutional dignity. In such an environment I felt perfectly content to eat alone; indeed, I would not have considered myself unblessed to have been told that I would be dining off a tray in this hall, eating these stews and salisbury steaks, for the rest of my days. Before returning to my apartment to mark one seventh of my weekly stack of sixty-odd freshmen essays (as many as I could take in a sitting) and to prepare for next day's lesson, I would browse for half an hour or so in the secondhand bookstores in the neighborhood. Owning my own "library" was my only materialistic ambition; in fact, trying to decide which two of these thousands of books to buy that week, I would frequently get so excited that by the time the purchase was accomplished I had to make use of the bookseller's toilet facilities. I don't believe that either microbe or laxative has ever affected me so strongly as the discovery that I was all at once the owner of a slightly soiled copy of Empson's *Seven Types of Ambiguity* in the original English edition.

At ten o'clock, having completed my classroom preparation, I would go off to a local graduate-student hangout, where generally I ran into somebody I knew and had a glass of beer—one beer, one game of pinball soccer, and then home, for before I went to sleep, there were still fifty pages to be underlined and annotated in some major work of European literature that either I hadn't yet read or had misread the first time around. I called this "filling in the gaps." Reading—and noting—fifty pages a night, I could average three books a month, or thirty-six a year. I also knew approximately how many short stories I might expect to complete in a year, if I put in thirty hours at it a week; and approximately how many students' essays I could mark in an hour; and how large my "library" would be in a decade, if I were to continue to be able to make purchases in accordance with my present budget. And I liked knowing all these things, and to this day like myself for having known them.

I seemed to myself as rich as a young man could be in spiritual goods; as for worldly goods, what could I possibly need that I didn't have? I owned a bicycle to get around the neighborhood and provide me with exercise, a Remington portable (my parents' gift for my graduation from high school), a briefcase (their gift for my grade-school graduation), a Bulova watch (their gift for my bar mitzvah); I had still from my undergraduate days a favorite well-worn tweed jacket to teach my classes in, complete with leather elbow patches, my army khakis to wear while writing and drinking my beer, a new brown glen plaid suit for dressing up, a pair of tennis sneakers, a pair of cordovan shoes, a ten-year-old pair of slippers, a V-neck sweater, some shirts and socks, two striped ties, and the kind of jockey shorts and ribbed undershirts that I had been wearing since I had graduated from diapers, Fruit of the Loom. Why change brands? They made me happy enough. All I wanted to be happier still were more books to inscribe my name in. And to travel to Europe for two months to see the famous cultural monuments and literary landmarks. Two times each month I would be surprised to find in my mailbox a check from the university for one hundred and twenty-five dollars. Why on earth were they sending me money? It was I, surely, who should be paying them for the privilege of leading such a full, independent, and honorable life.

In the midst of my contentment there was one difficulty: my headaches. While a soldier I had developed such severe migraines that I had finally to be separated with a medical discharge after serving only eleven months of my two-year term.

Of course, I didn't miss the tedium and boredom of peacetime army life; from the day I was drafted I had been marking off the time until I could return to a life no less regimented and disciplined than a soldier's, but overseen by me and for the sake of serious literary studies. However, to have been released back into a studious vocation because of physical incapacity was disconcerting to one who had spent nearly ten years building himself, by way of exercise and diet, into a brawny young man who looked as though he could take care of himself out in the harsh world. How doggedly I had worked to bury the frail child who used to lie in his bed musing over his father's puzzles, while the other little children were out on the streets learning to be agile and fearless! I had even been pleased, in a way, when I had found myself assigned by the army to military police school in Georgia: they did not make sissy invalids into MPs, that was for sure. I was to become a man with a pistol on his hip and starch in the knifelike creases of his khakis: a humanist with a swagger, an English teacher with a billy club. The collected stories of Isaac Babel had not appeared yet in the famous paperback edition, but when I read them five years later, I recognized in Babel's experience as a bespectacled Jew with the Red cavalry something like a highly charged version of what I had experienced during my brief tour of duty as an MP in the state of Georgia. An MP, until those headaches knocked me off my spit-shined boots . . . and I lay mummified on my bed for twenty-four hours at a stretch, the most ordinary little sound outside the barracks window—a soldier scratching at the grass with a rake, some passerby whistling a tune between his teeth—as unbearable as a spike being driven in my brain; even a beam of sunlight, filtering through the worn spot in the drawn green shade back of my bunk, a sunbeam no larger than the head of a pin, would be, in those circumstances, intolerable.

My "buddies," most of them without a twelfth-grade education, assumed that the college genius (and Jewboy) was malingering, especially when I discovered that I could tell *the day before* that one of my disabling headaches was on its way. It was my contention that if only I were allowed to retire to my bed prior to the onset of the headache, and to remain there in the dark and quiet for five hours or so, I could ward off an otherwise inevitable attack. "Look, I think you could too," said the wise sergeant, while denying me permission to do so, "I have often thought the same thing about myself. You can't beat a day in the sack for making you feel good all over." Nor was the doctor on sick call much more sympathetic; I convinced no one, not even myself. The "floating" or "ghostly" sensation, the aura of malaise that served as my warning system was, in truth, so unsubstantial, so faint, that I too had to wonder if I wasn't imagining it; and then subsequently "imagining" the headache to justify the premonition.

Eventually, when headaches began to flatten me regularly every ten or twelve days, I was admitted to the post hospital for "observation," which meant that, except if I was actually in pain, I was to walk around in a pair of blue army pajamas pushing a dry mop. To be sure, when the aura of a headache came upon me, I could now retire immediately to my bed; but that, as it turned out, worked only to forestall the headache for another twelve hours or so; on the other hand, if I were to remain *continually* in bed . . . But I couldn't; in the words of Bartleby the Scrivener (words that were with me frequently in the hospital, though I had not read the story for several years), I preferred not to. I preferred instead to push my mop from one ward to another and wait for the blow to fall.

Rather quickly I came to understand that my daily work routine had been devised as a combination punishment and cure by the hospital authorities. I had been assigned my mop so as to be brought into contact with those who were truly ill, irreversibly and horribly so. Each day, for instance, I went off to mop between the beds of patients in "the burn ward," young men so badly disfigured by fire that in the beginning either I had to turn away at the sight of them or else could not withdraw my gaze at all. Then there were amputees who had lost limbs in training accidents, in automobile collisions, in operations undertaken to arrest the spread of malignancies. The idea seemed to be that I would somehow be shamed out of my alleged illness by the daily contact that I made on my rounds with these doomed mortals, most of them no older than myself. Only after I was called before a medical board and awarded a discharge did I learn that no such subtle or sadistic therapy had been ordered in my case. My internment in the hospital had been a bureaucratic necessity and not some sly form of purifying and healing imprisonment. The "cure" had been wholly of my own devising, my housecleaning duties having been somewhat less extensive than I had imagined. The nurse in charge of my section, an easygoing and genial woman, was amused to learn from me, on the day of my discharge, that I had been wandering through the hospital from nine to five every day, cleaning the floors of all the open wards, when the instructions she had given me had been only to clean up each morning around my own bed. After that I was to have considered myself free to come and go as I wished, so long as I did not leave the hospital. "Didn't anyone ever stop you?" she asked. "Yes," I said, "in the beginning. But I told them I'd been ordered to do it." I pretended to be as amused as she was by the "misunderstanding," but wondered if bad conscience was not lending her to lie now about the instructions she had given me on the day I had become her patient.

In Chicago, a civilian again, I was examined by a neurologist at Billings Hospital who could offer no explanation for the headaches, except to say that my pattern was typical enough. He prescribed the same drugs that the army had, none of which did me any good, and told me that migraines ordinarily diminish in intensity and frequency with time, generally dying out around the age of fifty. I had vaguely expected that mine would die out as soon as I was my own man again and back at the university; along with my sergeant and my envious colleagues, I continued to believe that I had induced this condition in myself in order to provide me with grounds for discharge from an army that was wasting my valuable time. That the pain not only continued to plague me, but in the months following my discharge began to spread until it had encompassed both halves of my skull, served to bolster, in a grim way, a faltering sense of my own probity.

Unless, of course, I was covering my tracks, "allowing" the headaches a somewhat longer lease on my life than might be physically desirable, for the sake of my moral well-being. For who could accuse me of falling ill as a means of cutting short my tour of army duty when it was clear that the rewarding academic life I had been so anxious to return to continued to be as marred by this affliction as my purposeless military existence had been? Each time I had emerged from another twenty-four-hour session of pain, I would think to myself, "How many more, before I've met my obligation?" I wondered if it was not perhaps the "plan" of these headaches to visit themselves upon me until such time as I would have been discharged from the service under ordinary conditions. Did I, as it were, *owe* the army a migraine for each month of service I had escaped, or was it for each week, or each day, or each hour? Even to believe that they might die out by the time I was fifty was hardly consolation to an ambitious twenty-four-year-old with as strong a distaste for the sickbed as I had developed in my childhood; also to one made buoyant by fulfilling the exacting demands of schedules and routines, the prospect of being dead to the world and to my work for twenty-four hours every ten days for the next thirty-six years, the thought of all *that* waste, was as distressing as the anticipation of the pain itself. Three times a month, for God only knew how long, I was to be sealed into a coffin (so I described it to myself, admittedly in the clutch of self-pity) and buried alive. Why?

I had already considered (and dismissed) the idea of taking myself to a psychoanalyst, even before the neurologist at Billings informed me that a study in psychosomatic medicine was about to be initiated at a North Shore clinic, under the direction of an eminent Freudian analyst. He thought it was more than likely that I might be taken on as a patient at a modest fee, especially as they were said to be interested particularly in the ailments that manifested themselves in "intellectuals" and "creative types." The neurologist was not suggesting that migraines were necessarily symptomatic of a neurotic personality disturbance; rather he was responding, he said, to what he took to be "a Freudian orientation" in the questions I asked him and in the manner in which I had gone about presenting the history of the disorder.

I did not know that it was a Freudian orientation so much as a literary habit of mind which the neurologist was not accustomed to: that is to say, I could not resist reflecting upon my migraines in the same supramedical way that I might consider the illnesses of Milly Theale or Hans Castorp or the Reverend Arthur Dimmesdale, or ruminate upon the transformation of Gregor Samsa into a cockroach, or search out the "meaning" in

Gogol's short story of Collegiate Assessor Kovalev's temporary loss of his nose. Whereas an ordinary man might complain,
"I get these damn headaches" (and have been content to leave
it at that), I tended, like a student of high literature or a savage
who paints his body blue, to see the migraines as *standing for
something*, as a disclosure or "epiphany," isolated or accidental
or inexplicable only to one who was blind to the design of a
life or a book. What did my migraines *signify*?

The possibilities I came up with did not satisfy a student as
"sophisticated" as myself; compared with *The Magic Mountain* or even "The Nose," the texture of my own story was
thin to the point of transparency. It was disappointing, for instance, to find myself associating the disability that had come
over me when I had begun to wear a pistol on my hip with
either my adolescent terror of the physical life or some traditional Jewish abhorrence of violence—such an explanation
seemed too conventional and simplistic, too "easy." A more
attractive, if in the end no less obvious, idea had to do with a
kind of psychological civil war that had broken out between
the dreamy, needy, and helpless child I had been, and the independent, robust, manly adult I wanted to be. At the time I recalled it, Bartleby's passive but defiant formula, "I would
prefer not to," had struck me as the voice of the man in me defying the child and his temptation to helplessness; but couldn't
it just as well be the voice of the frail and sickly little boy answering the call to perform the duties of a man? Or of a *policeman*? No, no, much too pat—my life surely must be more
complex and subtle than that; *The Wings of the Dove* was. No, I
could not imagine myself *writing* a story so tidy and facile in
its psychology, let alone living one.

The stories I *was* writing—the fact of the writing itself—did
not escape my scrutiny. It was to keep open the lines to my
sanity and intelligence, to engage in a solitary, thoughtful
activity at the end of those mindless days of directing traffic
and checking passes at the gate into town, that I had taken up
writing for three hours each evening at a table in the corner of
the post library. After only a few nights, however, I had put
aside my notes for the critical article I had planned on some
novels of Virginia Woolf (for an issue of *Modern Fiction Studies* to be devoted entirely to her work) to begin what was to

turn out to be my first published short story. Shortly thereafter, when the migraines began, and the search for a cause, a reason, a meaning, I thought I saw in the unexpected alteration the course of my writing had taken something analogous to that shift in my attention that used to disconcert my father when he presented the little boy in the sickbed with those neat arithmetical puzzles of his—the movement from intellectual or logical analysis to seemingly irrelevant speculation of an imaginary nature. And in the hospital, where in six weeks' time I had written my second and third stories, I could not help wondering if for me illness was not a necessary catalyst to activate the imagination. I understood that this was not an original hypothesis, but if that made it more or less applicable to my situation I couldn't tell; nor did I know what to do with the fact that the illness itself was the one that had regularly afflicted Virginia Woolf and to some degree contributed to the debilitation that led to suicide. I knew about Virginia Woolf's migraines from having read her posthumous book, *A Writer's Diary*, edited by her husband and published in my senior year of college. I even had the book with me in my footlocker, for the essay I had been going to write on her work. What was I to think then? No more than a coincidence? Or was I imitating the agony of this admirable writer, as in my stories I was imitating the techniques and simulating the sensibilities of still other writers I admired?

Following my examination by the neurologist, I decided to stop worrying about the "significance" of my condition and to try to consider myself, as the neurologist obviously did, to be one hundred and eighty pounds of living tissue subject to the pathology of the species, rather than a character in a novel whose disease the reader may be encouraged to diagnose by way of moral, psychological, or metaphysical hypotheses. As I was unable to endow my predicament with sufficient density or originality to satisfy my own literary tastes—unable to do "for" migraines what Mann had done in *The Magic Mountain* for TB or in *Death in Venice* for cholera—I had decided that the only sensible thing was to have my migraine and then forget about it till the next time. To look for meaning was fruitless as well as pretentious. Though I wondered: Couldn't the migraines themselves be diagnosed as "pretentious" in origin?

I also withstood the temptation to take myself for an interview to the North Shore clinic where the study of psychosomatic ailments was getting under way. Not that I was out of sympathy with the theories or techniques of psychotherapy as I had grasped them through my reading. It was, rather, that aside from these headaches, I was as vigorous in the execution of my duties, and as thrilled with the circumstances of my life, as I could ever have dreamed of being. To be sure, to try to teach sixty-five freshmen to write an English sentence that was clear, logical, and precise was not always an enchanting experience; yet, even when teaching was most tedious, I maintained my missionary spirit and with it the conviction that with every clichéd expression or mindless argument I exposed in the margins of my students' essays, I was waging a kind of guerrilla war against the army of slobs, philistines, and barbarians who seemed to me to control the national mind, either through the media or the government. The presidential press conference provided me with material for any number of classroom sessions; I would have samples of the Eisenhower porridge mimeographed for distribution and then leave him to the students to correct and grade. I would submit for their analysis a sermon by Norman Vincent Peale, the president's religious adviser; or an ad for General Motors; or a "cover story" from *Time*. What with television quiz shows, advertising agencies, and the Cold War all flourishing, it was a period in which a composition teacher did not necessarily have to possess the credentials or doctrines of a clergyman to consider himself engaged in the business of saving souls.

If the classroom caused me to imagine myself to be something of a priest, the university neighborhood seemed to me something like my parish—and of course something of a Bloomsbury—a community of the faithful, observing the sacraments of literacy, benevolence, good taste, and social concern. My own street of low, soot-stained brick apartment buildings was on the grim side, and the next one over, run-down only the year before, was already in rubble—leveled as though by blockbusters for an urban renewal project; also, in the year I had been away, there had been a marked increase of random nighttime violence in the neighborhood. Nonetheless, within an hour of my return, I felt as comfortable and at home as someone whose family had dwelled in the same small town for generations. Simultaneously I could never forget that it was not in such a paradise of true believers that I had been born and raised; and even if I should live in the Hyde Park neighborhood for the next fifty years—and why should I ever want to live elsewhere?—the city itself, with streets named for the prairie and the Wabash, with railroad trains marked "Illinois Central" and a lake bearing the name "Michigan," would always have the flavor of the faraway for one whose fantasies of adventure had been nurtured in a sickbed in Camden, New Jersey, over an aeon of lonely afternoons. How could *I* be in "Chicago"? The question, coming at me while shopping in the Loop, or watching a movie at the Hyde Park Theatre, or simply opening a can of sardines for lunch at my apartment on Drexel, seemed to me unanswerable. I suppose my wonderment and my joy were akin to my parents', when they would address those envelopes to me in care of Faculty Exchange. How could *he* be a professor, who could barely breathe with that bronchitis?

All this by way of explaining why I did not betake myself to that clinic for the study of psychosomatic ailments and offer up my carcass and unconscious for investigation. I was too happy. Everything that was a part of getting older seemed to me to be a pleasure: the independence and authority, of course, but no less so the refinement and strengthening of one's moral nature —to be magnanimous where one had been selfish and carping, to be forgiving where one had been resentful, to be patient where one had been impetuous, to be generous and helpful where one had previously been needful . . . It seemed to me at twenty-four as natural to be solicitous of my sixty-year-old parents as to be decisive and in command with my eighteen- and nineteen-year-old students. Toward the young girls in my classes, some as lovely and tempting as the junior at Pembroke College with whom I had just concluded a love affair, I behaved as I was expected to; it went without saying that as their teacher I must not allow myself to take a sexual interest in them or to exploit my authority for personal gratification. No difficulty I encountered seemed beyond my powers, whether it was concluding a love affair, or teaching the principles of logic to my dullest composition students, or rising with a dry mouth to address the Senate of the Faculty, or writing a short story four times over to get it "right" . . . How could I turn my-self over to a psychoanalyst as "a case"? All the evidence of my life (exclusive of the migraines) argued too strongly against that, certainly to one to whom it meant so much never to be classified as a patient again. Furthermore, in the immediate aftermath of a headache, I would experience such elation just from the *absence* of pain that I would almost believe that what-ever had laid that dose of suffering upon me had been driven from my body for good—that the powerful enemy (yes, more feeble interpretation, or superstition) who had unleashed upon me all his violence, who had dragged me to the very end of my endurance, had been proved unable in the end to do me in. The worse the headache the more certain I was when it was over that I had defeated the affliction once and for all. *And was a better man for it.* (And no, my body was not painted blue in these years, nor did I otherwise believe in angels, demons, or deities.) Often I vomited during the attacks, and afterward, not quite daring to move (for fear of breaking), I lay on the bathroom floor with my chin on the toilet bowl and a hand mirror to my face, in a parody perhaps of Narcissus. I wanted to see what I looked like having suffered so and survived; in that feeble and euphoric state, it would not have frightened me—might even have thrilled me—to have observed black vapors, something like cannon smoke, rolling out of my ears and nostrils. I would talk to my eyes, reassuring them as though they were somebody else's: "That's it, the end, no more pain." But in point of fact there would be plenty more; the experiment which has not ended was only beginning.

In the second semester of that—no other word will do; if it smacks of soap opera, that is not unintentional—of that fateful year, I was asked if I should like to teach, in addition to my regular program, the night course in "Creative Writing" in the downtown division of the university, a single session each Monday night running for three consecutive hours, at a salary of two hundred and fifty dollars for the semester. Another windfall it seemed to me—my round-trip tourist-class fare on the *Rotterdam*. As for the students, they were barely versed in the rules of syntax and spelling, and so, I discovered, hardly able to make head or tail of the heady introductory lecture that, with characteristic thoroughness, I had prepared over a period of a week for delivery at our first meeting. Entitled "The Strategies and Intentions of Fiction," it was replete with lengthy (and I had thought) "salient" quotations from Aristotle's *Poetics*, Flaubert's correspondence, Dostoevsky's diaries, and James's critical prefaces—I quoted only from masters, pointed only to monuments: *Moby Dick, Anna Karenina, Crime and Punishment, The Ambassadors, Madame Bovary, Portrait of the Artist as a Young Man, The Sound and the Fury.* " 'What seems to me the highest and most difficult achievement of Art is not to make us laugh or cry, or to rouse our lust or our anger, but to do as nature does—that is, fill us with wonderment. The most beautiful works have indeed this quality. They are serene in aspect, incomprehensible . . . *pitiless.*' " Flaubert, in a letter to Louise Colet ("1853," I told them, in responsible scholarly fashion, "a year into the writing of *Madame Bovary*"). " 'The house of fiction has in short not one window but a million . . . every one of which is pierced, or is still pierceable, in its vast front, by the need of the individual vision and by the pressure of the individual will. . . .' " James, the preface to *The Portrait of a Lady*. I concluded with a lengthy reading from Conrad's inspirational introduction to *The Nigger of the "Narcissus"* (1897): " '. . . the artist descends within himself, and in that lonely region of stress and strife, if he be deserving and fortunate, he finds the terms of his appeal. His appeal is made to our less obvious capacities: to that part of our nature which, because of the warlike conditions of existence, is necessarily kept out of sight within the more resisting and hard qualities—like the vulnerable body within a steel armor. His appeal is less loud, more profound, less distinct, more stirring—and sooner forgotten. Yet its effect endures forever. The changing wisdom of successive generations discards ideas, questions facts, demolishes theories. But the artist appeals to that part of our being which is not dependent on wisdom: to that in us which is a gift and not an acquisition—and, therefore, more permanently enduring. He speaks to our capacity for delight and wonder, to the sense of mystery surrounding our lives; to our sense of pity, and beauty, and pain; to the latent feeling of fellowship with all creation—to the subtle but invincible conviction of solidarity that knits together the loneliness of innumerable hearts, to the solidarity in dreams, in joy, in sorrow, in aspirations, in illusions, in hope, in fear, which binds men to each other, which binds together all humanity—the dead to the living and the living to the unborn. . . .'"

When I finished reading my twenty-five pages and asked for questions, there was to my surprise and disappointment, just one; as it was the only Negro in the class who had her hand raised, I wondered if it could be that after all I had said she was going to tell me she was offended by the title of Conrad's novel. I was already preparing an explanation that might turn her touchiness into a discussion of frankness in fiction—fiction as the secret and the taboo disclosed—when she rose to stand at respectful attention, a thin middle-aged woman in a neat dark suit and a pillbox hat: "Professor, I know that if you're writing a friendly letter to a little boy, you write on the envelope 'Master.' But what if you're writing a friendly letter to a little girl? Do you still say 'Miss'—or just what *do* you say?"

The class, having endured nearly two hours of a kind of talk none of them had probably ever heard before outside of a church, took the occasion of her seemingly ludicrous question to laugh uproariously—she was the kid who had farted following the principal's lecture on discipline and decorum. Their laughter was *pointedly* directed at student, not teacher; nonetheless, I flushed with shame and remained red all the while Mrs. Corbett, dogged and unperturbed in the face of the class's amusement, pursued the knowledge she was there for.

Lydia Ketterer turned out to be by far the most gifted writer in the class and, though older than I, still the youngest of my students—not so young, however, as she looked in the bleak heart of a Chicago winter, dressed in galoshes, knee stockings, tartan skirt, "reindeer" sweater, and the tassled red wool hat, from which a straight curtain of wheat-colored hair dropped down at either side of her face. Outfitted for the ice and cold, she seemed, amid all those tired night-school faces, a junior-high-school girl—in fact, she was twenty-nine and mother of a lanky ten-year-old already budding breasts more enticing than her own. She lived not far from me in Hyde Park, having moved to the university neighborhood four years earlier, following her breakdown—and in the hope of changing her luck. And indeed when we met in my classroom, she probably was living through what were to be the luckiest months of her life: she had a job she liked as an interviewer with a university-sponsored social science research project at two dollars an hour, she had a few older graduate students (connected to the project) as friends, she had a small bank account and a pleasant little apartment with a fireplace from which she could see across the Midway to the Gothic façades of the university. Also at that time she was the willing and grateful patient of a lay psychoanalyst, a woman named Rutherford, for whom she dressed up (in the most girlish dress-up clothes I'd seen since grade school, puffed sleeves, crinolines, etc.) and whom she visited every Saturday morning in her office on Hyde Park Boulevard. The stories she wrote were inspired mostly by the childhood recollections she delivered forth to Dr. Rutherford on these Saturdays and dealt almost exclusively with the period after her father had raped her and run, when she and her mother had been taken on as guests—her mother as guest, Lydia as Cinderella—by the two aunts in their maidenly little prison house in Skokie.

It was the accumulation of small details that gave Lydia's stories such distinction as they had. With painstaking diligence she chronicled the habits and attitudes of her aunts, as though with each precise detail she was hurling a small stone back through her past at those pinch-faced little persecutors. From the fiction it appeared that the favorite subject in that household was, oddly enough, "the body." "The body surely does not require that much milk on a bowl of puffed oats, my dear." "The body will take only so much abuse, and then it will *balk*." And so on. Unfortunately, small details, accurately observed and flatly rendered, did not much interest the rest of the class unless the detail was "symbolic" or sensational. Those who most hated Lydia's stories were Agniashvily, an elderly Russian émigré who wrote original "Ribald Classics" (in Georgian, and translated into English for the class by his stepson, a restaurateur by trade) aimed at the *Playboy* "market"; Todd, a cop who could not go two hundred words into a narrative without a little something running in the gutter (blood, urine, "Sergeant Darling's dinner") and was a devotee (I was not—we clashed) of the O. Henry ending; the Negro woman, Mrs. Corbett, who was a file clerk with the Prudential during the day and at night wrote the most transparent and pathetic pipe dreams about a collie dog romping around a dairy farm in snow-covered Minnesota; Shaw, an "ex-newspaperman" with an adjectival addiction, who was always quoting to us something that "Max" Perkins had said to "Tom" Wolfe, seemingly in Shaw's presence; and a fastidious male nurse named Wertz, who from his corner seat in the last row had with his teacher what is called "a love-hate" relationship. Lydia's most ardent admirers, aside from myself, were two "ladies," one who ran a religious bookshop in Highland Park and rather magnified the moral lessons to be drawn from Lydia's fiction, and the other, Mrs. Slater, an angular, striking housewife from Flossmoor, who wore heather-colored suits to class and wrote "bittersweet" stories which concluded usually with two characters "inadvertently touching." Mrs. Slater's remarkable legs were generally directly under my nose, crossing and uncrossing, and making that whishing sound of nylon moving against nylon that I could hear even over the earnestness of my own voice. Her eyes were gray and eloquent: "I am forty years old, all I do is shop and pick up the children. I live for this class. I live for our conferences. Touch me, advertently or inadvertently. I won't say no or tell my husband."

In all there were eighteen of them and, with the exception of my religionist, not one who seemed to smoke less than a pack a night. They wrote on the backs of order forms and office stationery; they wrote in pencil and in multicolored inks; they forgot to number pages or to put them in order (less frequently, however, than I thought). Oftentimes the first sheet of a story would be stained with food spots, or several of the pages would be stuck together, in Mrs. Slater's case with glue spilled by a child, in the case of Mr. Wertz, the male nurse, with what I took to be semen spilled by himself.

When the class got into a debate as to whether a story was "universal" in its implications or a character was "sympathetic," there was often no way, short of gassing them, of getting them off the subject for the rest of the night. They judged the people in one another's fiction not as though each was a collection of attributes (a mustache, a limp, a southern drawl) to which the author had arbitrarily assigned a Christian name, but as though they were discussing human souls about to be consigned to Hades or elevated to sainthood—depending upon which the class decided. It was the most vociferous among them who had the least taste or interest in the low-keyed or the familiar, and my admiration for Lydia's stories would practically drive them crazy; invariably I raised *somebody's* hackles, when I read aloud, as an example they might follow, something like Lydia's simple description of the way in which her two aunts each had laid out on a doily in the bedroom her hairbrush, comb, hairpins, toothbrush, dish of Lifebuoy, and tin of dental powder. I would read a passage like this: "Aunt Helda, while listening to Father Coughlin reasoning with the twenty thousand Christians gathered in Briggs Stadium, would continually be clearing her throat, as though it were she who was to be called upon to speak next." Such sentences were undoubtedly not so rich and supple as to deserve the sort of extensive, praiseful exegesis I would wind up giving them, but by comparison with most of the prose I read that semester, Mrs. Ketterer's line describing Aunt Helda listening to the radio in the 1940s might have been lifted from *Mansfield Park*.

I wanted to hang a sign over my desk saying ANYONE IN THIS CLASS CAUGHT USING HIS IMAGINATION WILL BE SHOT. I would put it more gently when, in the parental sense, I lectured them. "You just cannot deliver up fantasies and call that 'fiction.' Ground your stories in what you know. Stick to that. Otherwise you tend, some of you, toward the pipe dream and the nightmare, toward the grandiose and the romantic—and that's no good. Try to be precise, accurate, measured . . ." "Yeah? What about Tom Wolfe," asked the lyrical ex-newspaperman Shaw, "would you call that measured, Zuckerman?" (No Mister or Professor from him to a kid half his age.) "What about prose-poetry, you against that too?" Or Agniashvily, in his barrel-deep Russian brogue, would berate me with Spillane—"And so how come he's got ten million in prrrint, Prrrofessor?" Or Mrs. Slater would ask, in conference, inadvertently touching my sleeve, "But *you* wear a tweed jacket, Mr. Zuckerman. Why is it 'dreamy'—I don't understand—if Craig in my *story* wears—" I couldn't listen. "And the pipe, Mrs. Slater: now why do you think you have him continually puffing on that pipe?" "But men *smoke* pipes." "Dreamy, Mrs. Slater, too damn dreamy." "But—" "Look, write a story about shopping at Carson's, Mrs. Slater! Write about your afternoon at Saks!" "Yes?" "Yes! Yes! Yes!"

Oh, yes, when it came to grandiosity and dreaminess, to all manifestations of self-inflating romance, I had no reservations about giving them a taste of the Zuckerman lash. Those were the only times I lost my temper, and of course losing it was always calculated and deliberate: scrupulous.

*Pent-up rage,* by the way—that was the meaning the army psychiatrist had assigned to my migraines. He had asked whether I liked my father better than my mother, how I felt about heights and crowds, and what I planned to do when I was returned to civilian life, and concluded from my answers that I was a vessel of *pent-up rage.* Another poet, this one in uniform, bearing the rank of captain.

My friends (my only real enemy is dead now, though my censurers are plentiful)—my friends, I earned those two hundred and fifty dollars teaching "Creative Writing" in a night school, every penny of it. For whatever it may or may not "mean," I didn't once that semester get a migraine on a Monday, not that I wasn't tempted to take a crack at it when a tough-guy story by Patrolman Todd or a bittersweet one by Mrs. Slater was on the block for the evening . . . No, to be frank, I counted it a blessing of sorts when the headaches happened to fall on the weekend, on my time off. My superiors in the college and downtown were sympathetic and assured me that I wasn't about to lose my job because I had to be out ill "from time to time," and up to a point I believed them; still, to be disabled on a Saturday or a Sunday was to me far less spiritually debilitating than to have to ask the indulgence of either my colleagues or students.

Whatever erotic curiosity had been aroused in me by Lydia's pretty, girlish, Scandinavian block of a head—and odd as it will sound to some, by the exoticism of the blighted middle western Protestant background she wrote about and had managed to survive in one piece—was decidedly outweighed by my conviction that I would be betraying my vocation, and doing damage to my self-esteem, if I were to take one of my students to bed. As I have said, suppressing feelings and desires extraneous to the purpose that had brought us together seemed to me crucial to the success of the transaction—as I must have called it then, the pedagogical transaction—allowing each of us to be as teacherly or as studently as was within his power, without wasting time and spirit being provocative, charming, duplicitous, touchy, jealous, scheming, etc. You could do all that out in the street; only in the classroom, as far as I knew, was it possible to approach one another with the intensity ordinarily associated with love, yet cleansed of emotional extremism and free of base motives having to do with profit and power. To be sure, on more than a few occasions, my night class was as perplexing as a Kafka courtroom, and my composition classes as wearisome as any assembly line, but that our effort was characterized at bottom by modesty and mutual trust, and conducted as ingenuously as dignity would permit, was indisputable. Whether it was Mrs. Corbett's innocent and ardent question about how to address a friendly letter to a little girl or my own no less innocent and ardent introductory lecture to which she was responding, what we said to one another was not uttered in the name of anything vile or even mundane. At twenty-four, dressed up like a man in a clean white shirt and a tie, and bearing chalk powder on the tails of my worn tweed jacket, that seemed to me a truth to be held self-evident. Oh, how I wanted a soul that was pure and spotless!

In Lydia's case, professorial discretion was helped along some, or I should have thought it would be, by that rolling, mannish gait of hers. The first time she entered my class I actually wondered if she could be some kind of gymnast or acrobat, perhaps a member of a women's track and field association; I was reminded of those photographs in the popular magazines of the strong blue-eyed women athletes who win medals at the Olympic games for the Soviet Union. Yet her shoulders were as touchingly narrow as a child's, and her skin pale and almost luminously soft. Only from the waist to the floor did she seem to be moving on the body of my sex rather than her own.

Within the month I had seduced her, as much against her inclination and principles as my own. It was standard enough procedure, pretty much what Mrs. Slater must have had in mind: a conference alone together in my office, a train ride side by side on the IC back to Hyde Park, an invitation to a beer at my local tavern, the flirtatious walk to her apartment, the request by me for coffee, if she would make me some. She begged me to think twice about what I was doing, even after she had returned from the bathroom where she had inserted her diaphragm and I had removed her underpants for the second time and was hunched, unclothed, over the small, ill-proportioned body, preparatory to entering her. She was distressed, she was amused, she was frightened, she was mystified.

"There are so many beautiful young girls around, why pick on me? Why choose me, when you could have the cream of the crop?"

I didn't bother to answer. As though she were the one being coy or foolish, I smiled.

She said: "Look, look at me."

"I'm doing that."

"Are you? I'm five years older than you. My breasts sag, not that they ever amounted to much to begin with. Look, I have stretch marks. My behind's too big, I'm hamstrung— 'Professor,' listen to me, I don't have orgasms. I want you to know that beforehand. I never have."

When we later sat down for the coffee, Lydia, wrapped in a robe, said this: "I'll never know why you wanted to do that. Why not Mrs. Slater, who's *begging* you for it? Why should anyone like you want me?"

Of course I didn't "want" her, not then or ever. We lived together for almost six years, the first eighteen months as lovers, and the four years following, until her suicide, as husband and wife, and in all that time her flesh was never any less distasteful to me than she had insistently advertised it to be. Utterly without lust, I seduced her on that first night, the next morning, and hundreds of times thereafter. As for Mrs. Slater, I seduced her probably no more than ten times in all, and never anywhere but in my imagination.

It was another month before I met Monica, Lydia's ten-year-old daughter, so it will not do to say that, like Nabokov's designing rogue, I endured the uninviting mother in order to have access to the seductive and seducible young daughter. That came later. In the beginning Monica was without any attraction whatsoever, repellent to me in character as well as appearance: lanky, stringy-haired, undernourished, doltish, without a trace of curiosity or charm, and so illiterate that at ten she was still unable to tell the time. In her dungarees and faded polo shirts she had the look of some mountain child, the offspring of poverty and deprivation. Worse, when she was dressed to kill in her white dress and round white hat, wearing her little Mary Jane shoes and carrying a white handbag and a Bible (white too), she seemed to me a replica of those overdressed little Gentile children who used to pass our house every Sunday on their way to church, and toward whom I used to feel an emotion almost as strong as my own grandparents' aversion. Secretly, and despite myself, I came close to despising the stupid and stubborn child when she would appear in that little white church-going outfit—and so too did Lydia, who was reminded by Monica's costume of the clothes in which she had had to array herself each Sunday in Skokie, before being led off to Lutheran services with her aunts Helda and Jessie. (As the story had it: "It did a growing body good to sit once a week in a nice starched dress, and without squirming.")

I was drawn to Lydia, not out of a passion for Monica—not yet—but because she had suffered so and because she was so brave. Not only that she had survived, but *what* she had survived, gave her enormous moral stature, or glamor, in my eyes: on the one hand, the puritan austerity, the prudery, the blandness, the xenophobia of the women of her clan; on the other, the criminality of the men. Of course, I did not equate being raped by one's father with being raised on the wisdom of the *Chicago Tribune*; what made her seem to me so valiant was that she had been subjected to every brand of barbarity, from the banal to the wicked, had been exploited, beaten, and betrayed by every last one of her keepers, had finally been driven crazy—and in the end had proved indestructible: she lived now in a neat little apartment within earshot of the bell in the clock tower of the university whose atheists, Communists, and Jews her people had loathed, and at the kitchen table of that apartment wrote ten pages for me every week in which she managed, heroically I thought, to recall the details of that brutal life in the style of one very long way from rage and madness. When I told the class that what I admired most in Mrs. Ketterer's fiction was her "control," I meant something more than those strangers could know.

Given all there was to move me about her character, it seemed to me curious that I should be *so* repelled by her flesh as I was that first night. I was able myself to achieve an orgasm, but afterward felt terrible for the "achievement" it had had to be. Earlier, caressing her body, I had been made uneasy by the unexpected texture of her genitals. To the touch, the fold of skin between her legs felt abnormally thick, and when I looked, as though to take pleasure in the sight of her nakedness, the vaginal lips appeared withered and discolored in a way that was alarming to me. I could even imagine myself to be staring down at the sexual parts of one of Lydia's maiden aunts, rather than at a physically healthy young woman not yet into her thirties. I was tempted to imagine some connection here to the childhood victimization by her father, but of course that was too literary, too poetic an idea to swallow—this was no stigma, however apprehensive it might make me.

The reader may by now be able to imagine for himself how the twenty-four-year-old I was responded to his alarm: in the morning, without very much ado, I performed cunnilingus upon her.

"Don't," said Lydia. "Don't do that."

"Why not?" I expected the answer: *Because I'm so ugly there.*

"I told you. I won't reach a climax. It doesn't matter what you do."

Like a sage who'd seen everything and been everywhere, I said, "You make too much of that."

Her thighs were not as long as my forearm (about the length, I thought, of one of Mrs. Slater's Pappagallos) and her legs were open only so far as I had been able to spread them with my two hands. But where she was dry, brownish, weather-worn, I pressed my open mouth. I took no pleasure in the act, she gave no sign that she did; but at least I had done what I had been frightened of doing, put my tongue to where she had been brutalized, as though—it was tempting to put it this way—that would redeem us both.

*As though that would redeem us both.* A notion as inflated as it was shallow, growing, I am certain, out of "serious literary studies." Where Emma Bovary had read too many romances of her period, it would seem that I had read too much of the criticism of mine. That I was, by "eating" her, taking some sort of sacrament was a most attractive idea—though one that I rejected after the initial momentary infatuation. Yes, I continued to resist as best I could all these high-flown, prestigious interpretations, whether of my migraines or my sexual relations with Lydia; and yet it surely did seem to me that my life was coming to resemble one of those texts upon which certain literary critics of that era used to enjoy venting their ingenuity. I could have done a clever job on it myself for my senior honors thesis in college: "Christian Temptations in a Jewish Life: A Study in the Ironies of 'Courting Disaster.'"

So: as often during a week as I could manage it, I "took the sacrament," conquering neither my fearful repugnance nor the shame I felt at being repelled, and neither believing nor disbelieving the somber reverberations.

During the first month of my love affair with Lydia, I continued to receive letters and, on occasion, telephone calls from Sharon Shatzky, the junior at Pembroke with whom I had concluded a passionate romance prior to my return to Chicago. Sharon was a tall, handsome, auburn-haired girl, studious, enthusiastic, and lively, an honor student in literature, and the daughter of a successful zipper manufacturer with country-club affiliations and a hundred-thousand-dollar suburban home who had been impressed with my credentials and entirely hospitable to me, until I began to suffer from migraines. Then Mr. Shatzky grew fearful that if he did not intervene, his daughter might one day find herself married to a man she would have to nurse and support for the rest of her life. Sharon was enraged by her father's "lack of compassion." "He thinks of my life," she said, angrily, "as a business investment." It enraged her even more when I came to her father's defense. I said that it was as much his paternal duty to make clear to a young daughter what might be the long-range consequences of my ailment as it had been years before to see that she was inoculated against smallpox; he did not want her to suffer for no reason. "But I love you," Sharon said, "that's my 'reason.'" I want to be with you if you're ill. I don't want to run out on you then, I want to take care for you." "But he's saying that you don't know all that 'taking care of' could entail." "But I'm telling you—I *love* you."

Had I wanted to marry Sharon (or her family's money) as much as her father assumed I did, I might not have been so tolerant of his opposition. But as I was just into my twenties then, the prospect of marriage, even to a lovely young woman toward whom I had so strong an erotic attachment, did not speak to the range of my ambitions. I should say, *particularly* because of this strong erotic attachment was I suspicious of an enduring union. For without that admittedly powerful bond, what was there of consequence, of *importance*, between Sharon and myself? Only three years my junior, Sharon seemed to me vastly younger, and to stand too much in my shadow, with few attitudes or interests that were her own; she read the books I recommended to her, devouring them by the dozen the summer we met, and repeated to her friends and teachers, as hers, judgments she had borrowed from me; she had even switched from a government to a literature major under my influence, a satisfaction to me at first, in the fatherly stage of my infatuation, but afterward a sign, among others, of what seemed to me an excess of submissiveness and malleability.

It did not, at that time, occur to me to find evidence of character, intelligence, and imagination in the bounteousness of her sexuality or in the balance she managed to maintain between a bold and vivacious animality and a tender, compliant nature. Nor did I begin to understand that it was in that tension, rather than in the sexuality alone, that her appeal resided. Rather, I would think, with something like despair, "That's all we really have," as though unself-consciously fervent love-making, sustained over a period of several years, was a commonplace phenomenon.

One night, when Lydia and I were already asleep in my apartment, Sharon telephoned to speak with me. She was in tears and didn't try to hide it. She could not bear any longer the *stupidity* of my decision. Surely I could not hold her accountable for her father's cold-blooded behavior, if that was the explanation for what I was doing. What *was* I doing anyway? And *how* was I doing? Was I well? Was I ill? How was my writing, my teaching—I *had* to let her fly to Chicago . . . But I told her she must stay where she was. I remained throughout calm and firm. No, I did not hold her accountable for anybody's behavior but her own, which was exemplary. I reminded her that it was not I who had judged her father "cold-blooded." When she continued to appeal to me to come to "my senses," I said that it was she who had better face facts, especially as they were not so unpleasant as she was making them out to be: she was a beautiful, intelligent, passionate young woman, and if she would stop this theatrical grieving and make herself available to life once again—

"But if I'm all those things, then why are you throwing me away like this? Please, I don't understand—make it clear to me! If I'm so exemplary, why don't *you* want me? Oh, Nathan," she said, now openly weeping again, "you know what I think? That underneath all that scrupulousness and fairness and reasonableness, you're a madman! Sometimes I think that underneath all that 'maturity' you're just a crazy little boy!"

When I returned from the kitchen phone to the living room, Lydia was sitting up in my sofa bed. "It was that girl, wasn't it?" But without a trace of jealousy, though I knew she hated her, if only abstractly. "You want to go back to her, don't you?"

"*No.*"

"But you know you're sorry you ever started up with me. *I* know it. Only now you can't figure how to get out of it. You're afraid you'll disappoint me, or hurt me, and so you let the weeks go by—and I can't stand the suspense, Nathan, or the confusion. If you're going to leave me, please do it now, tonight, this minute. Send me packing, please, I beg you—because I don't want to be endured, or pitied, or rescued, or whatever it is that's going on here! What *are* you doing with me—what am *I* doing with someone like *you*! You've got success written all over—it's in every breath you take! So what is this all about? You know you'd rather sleep with that girl than with me—so stop pretending otherwise, and go back to her, and do it!"

Now *she* cried, as hopeless and bewildered as Sharon. I kissed her, I tried to comfort her. I told her that nothing she was saying was so, when of course it was true in every detail: I loathed making love to her, I wished to be rid of her, I couldn't bear the thought of hurting her, and following the phone call, I did indeed want more than ever to go back to the one Lydia referred to always as "that girl." Yet I refused to confess to such feelings or act upon them.

"She's sexy, young, Jewish, *rich*—"

"Lydia, you're only torturing yourself—"

"But I'm so *hideous*. I have *nothing*."

No, if anyone was "hideous," it was I, yearning for Sharon's sweet lewdness, her playful and brazen sensuality, for what I used to think of as her *perfect pitch*, that unfailingly precise responsiveness to whatever our erotic mood—wanting, remembering, envisioning all this, even as I labored over Lydia's flesh, with its contrasting memories of physical misery. What was "hideous" was to be so queasy and finicky about the imperfections of a woman's body, to find oneself an adherent of the most Hollywoodish, *cold-blooded* notions of what is desirable and what is not; what was "hideous"—alarming, shameful, astonishing—was the significance that a young man of my pretensions should attach to his lust.

And there was more which, if it did not cause me to feel so peculiarly desolated as I did by what I took to be my callow sexual reflexes, gave me still other good reasons to distrust myself. There were, for instance, Monica's Sunday visits—how brutal they were! And how I recoiled from what I saw! Especially when I remembered—with the luxurious sense of having been blessed—the Sundays of my own childhood, the daylong round of visits, first to my two widowed grandmothers in the slum where my parents had been born, and then around Camden to the households of half a dozen aunts and uncles. During the war, when gasoline was rationed, we would have to walk to visit the grandmothers, traversing on foot five miles of city streets in all—a fair measure of our devotion to those two queenly and prideful workhorses, who lived very similarly in small apartments redolent of freshly ironed linen and stale coal gas, amid an accumulation of antimacassars, bar mitzvah photos, and potted plants, most of them taller and sturdier than I ever was. Peeling wallpaper, cracked linoleum, ancient faded curtains, this nonetheless was my Araby, and I their little sultan . . . what is more, a sickly sultan whose need was all the greater for his Sunday sweets and sauces. Oh how I was fed and comforted, washerwoman breasts for my pillows, deep grandmotherly laps, my throne!

Of course, when I was ill or the weather was bad, I would have to stay home, looked after by my sister, while my father and mother made the devotional safari alone, in galoshes and under umbrellas. But that was not so unpleasant either, for Sonia would read aloud to me, in a very actressy way, from a book she owned entitled *Two Hundred Opera Plots*; intermittently she would break into song. " 'The action takes place in India,' " she read, " 'and opens in the sacred grounds of the Hindoo priest, Nilakantha, who has an inveterate hatred for the English. During his absence, however, a party of English officers and ladies enter, out of curiosity, and are charmed with the lovely garden. They soon depart, with the exception of the officer, Gerald, who remains to make a sketch, in spite of the warning of his friend, Frederick. Presently the priest's lovely daughter, Lakmé, enters, having come by the river. . . .' " The phrase "having come by the river," the spelling of Hindu in Sunny's book with those final twin *o*'s (like a pair of astonished eyes; like the middle vowels in "hoot" and "moon" and "poor"; like a distillation of everything and anything I found mysterious), appealed strongly to this invalid child, as did her performing so wholeheartedly for an audience of one . . . Lakmé is taken by her father, both of them disguised as beggars, to the city market: " 'He forces Lakmé to sing, hoping thus to attract the attention of her lover, should he be amongst the party of English who are buying in the bazaars.' " I am still barely recovered from the word "bazaars" and its pair of *a*'s (the sound of "odd," the sound of a sigh), when Sunny introduces "The Bell Song," the aria "*De la fille du paria*," says my sister in Bresslenstein's French accent: the ballad of the pariah's daughter who saves a stranger in the forest from the wild beasts by the enchantment of her magic bell. After struggling with the soaring aria, my sister, flushed and winded from the effort, returns to her highly dramatic reading of the plot: "And this cunning plan succeeds, for Gerald instantly recognizes the thrilling voice of the fair Hindoo maiden—' " And is stabbed in the back by Lakmé's father; and is nursed back to health by her " 'in a beautiful jungle' "; only there the fellow " 'remembers with remorse the fair English girl to whom he is betrothed' "; and so decides to leave my sister, who kills herself with poisonous herbs, " 'the deadly juices of which she drinks.' " I could not decide whom to hate more, Gerald, with his remorse for "the fair English girl," or Lakmé's crazy father, who would not let his daughter love a white man. Had I been "in India" instead of at home on a rainy Sunday, and had I weighed something more than sixty pounds, I would have saved her from them both, I thought.

Later, at the back landing, my mother and father shake the water off themselves like dogs—our loyal Dalmatians, our life-saving Saint Bernards. They leave their umbrellas open in the bathtub to dry. They have carried home to me—two and a half miles through a storm, and with a war on—a jar of my grandmother Zuckerman's stuffed cabbage, a shoe box containing my grandmother Ackerman's strudel: food for a starving Nathan, to enrich his blood and bring him health and happiness. Later still, my exhibitionistic sister will stand exactly in the center of the living-room rug, on the "oriental" medallion, practicing her scales, while my father reads the battlefront news in the *Sunday Inquirer* and my mother gauges the temperature of my forehead with her lips, each hourly reading ending in a kiss. And I, all the while, an Ingres odalisque languid on the sofa. Was there ever anything like it, since the day of rest began?

How those rituals of love out of my own antiquity (no nostalgia for me!) return in every poignant nostalgic detail when I watch the unfolding of another horrific Ketterer Sunday. As orthodox as we had been in performing the ceremonies of familial devotion, so the Ketterers were in the perpetuation of their barren and wretched lovelessness. To watch the cycle of disaster repeating itself was as chilling as watching an electrocution—yes, a slow electrocution, the burning up of Monica Ketterer's life, seemed to me to be taking place before my eyes Sunday after Sunday. Stupid, broken, illiterate child, she did not know her right hand from her left, could not read the clock, could not even read a slogan off a billboard or a cereal box without someone helping her over each syllable as though it were an alp. Monica. Lydia. Ketterer. I thought: "What am I doing with these people?" And thinking that, could see no choice for myself but to stay.

Sundays Monica was delivered to the door by Eugene Ketterer, just as unattractive a man as the reader, who has gotten the drift of my story, would expect to find entering the drama at this point. Another nail in Nathan's coffin. If only Lydia had been exaggerating, if only I could have said to her, as it isn't always impossible to say to the divorced of their former spouses, "Come on now, he isn't nearly so bad as all that." If only, even in a joking way, I could have teased her by saying, "Why, I rather like him." But I hated him.

The only surprise was to discover him to be physically uglier than Lydia had even suggested. As if that character of his wasn't enough. Bad teeth, a large smashed nose, hair brilliantined back for church, and, in his dress, entirely the urban yokel . . . Now how could a girl with a pretty face and so much native refinement and intelligence have married a type like this to begin with? Simple: he was the first to ask her. Here was the knight who had rescued Lydia from that prison house in Skokie.

To the reader who has not just "gotten the drift," but begun to balk at the uniformly dismal situation that I have presented here, to the reader who finds himself unable to suspend his disbelief in a protagonist who voluntarily sustains an affair with a woman sexless to him and so disaster-ridden, I should say that in retrospect I find him nearly impossible to believe myself. Why should a young man otherwise reasonable, farsighted, watchful, judicious, and self-concerned, a man meticulously precise in the bread-and-butter concerns of life, and the model of husbandry with his endowment, why should he pursue, in this obviously weighty encounter, a course so *defiantly* not in his interest? For the sake of defiance? Does that convince *you*? Surely some protective, life-sustaining instinct—call it common sense, horse sense, a kind of basic biological alarm system—should have awakened him to the inevitable consequences, even as a glass of cold water thrown in his face will bring the most far-gone sleepwalker back from the world of stairwells without depth and boulevards without traffic. I look in vain for anything resembling a genuine sense of religious mission—that which sends missionaries off to convert the savages or to minister to lepers—or for the psychological abnormality pronounced enough to account for this preposterous behavior. To make *some* sort of accounting, the writer emphasizes Lydia's "moral glamor" and develops, probably with more thoroughness than is engrossing, the idea of Zuckerman's "seriousness," even going so far, in the subtitle, as to describe that seriousness as something of a social phenomenon; but to be frank, it does not seem, even to the author, that he has, suggestive subtitle and all, answered the objection of implausibility, any more than the young man Zuckerman's own prestigious interpretations of his migraines seemed to him consonant with the pain itself. And to bring words like "enigmatic" and "mysterious" into the discussion not only goes against my grain, but hardly seems to make things any less inconceivable.

To be sure, it would probably help some if I were at least to mention in passing the pleasant Saturday strolls that Lydia and Nathan used to take together down by the lake, their picnics, their bicycle rides, their visits to the zoo, the aquarium, the Art Institute, to the theater when the Bristol Old Vic and Marcel Marceau came to town; I could write about the friendships they made with other university couples, the graduate-student parties they occasionally went to on weekends, the lectures by famous poets and critics they attended at Mandel Hall, the evenings they spent together reading by the fire in Lydia's apartment. But to call up such memories in order to make the affair more credible would actually be to mislead the reader about the young man Nathan Zuckerman was; pleasures and comforts of the ordinary social variety were to him inconsequential, for they seemed *without moral content*. It wasn't because they both enjoyed eating Chinese food on Sixty-third Street or even because both admired Chekhov's short stories that he married Lydia; he could have married Sharon Shatzky for that, and for more. Incredible as it may seem to some—and I am one of them—it was *precisely* "the uniformly dismal situation" that did more for Lydia's cause than all the companionable meals and walks and museum visits and the cozy fireside conversations in which he corrected her taste in books.

To the reader who "believes" in Zuckerman's predicament as I describe it, but is unwilling to take such a person as seriously as I do, let me say that I am tempted to make fun of him myself. To treat this story as a species of comedy would not require more than a slight alteration in tone and attitude. In graduate school, for a course titled "Advanced Shakespeare," I once wrote a paper on *Othello* proposing just such a shift in emphasis. I imagined, in detail, several unlikely productions,

including one in which Othello and Iago addressed each other
as "Mr. Interlocutor" and "Mr. Bones," and another, somewhat more extreme, in which the racial situation was entirely
reversed, with Othello acted by a white man and the rest of the
cast portrayed by blacks, thus shedding another kind of light (I
concluded) on the "motiveless malignity."

In the story at hand, it would seem to me that from the
perspective of this decade particularly, there is much that
could be ridiculed having to do with the worship of ordeal and
forbearance and the suppression of the sexual man. It would
not require too much ingenuity on my part to convert the
protagonist here into an insufferable prig to be laughed at, a
character out of a farce. Or if not the protagonist, then the
narrator. To some, the funniest thing of all, or perhaps the
strangest, may not be how I conducted myself back then, but
the literary mode in which I have chosen to narrate my story
today: the decorousness, the orderliness, the underlying sobriety, that "responsible" manner that I continue to affect. For
not only have literary manners changed drastically since all this
happened ten years ago, back in the middle fifties, but I myself
am hardly who I was or wanted to be: no longer am I a member in good standing of that eminently decent and humane
university community, no longer am I the son my parents
proudly used to address by mail as "professor." By my own
standards, my private life is a failure and a disgrace, neither
decorous, nor sober, and surely not "responsible." Or so it
seems to me: I am full of shame and believe myself to be a scandalous figure. I can't imagine that I shall ever have the courage
to return to live in Chicago, or anywhere in America.

Presently we reside in one of the larger Italian cities; "we"
are myself and Monica, or Moonie, as I eventually came to call
her in our intimacy. The two of us have been alone together
now since Lydia gouged open her wrists with the metal tip of
a can opener and bled to death in the bathtub of our ground-
floor apartment on Woodlawn, where the three of us were
living as a family. Lydia was thirty-five when she died, I was
just thirty, and Moonie sixteen. After Ketterer's second divorce, I had gone to court, in Lydia's behalf, and sued him to
regain custody of her daughter—and I won. How could I lose?
I was a respectable academic and promising author whose

stories appeared in serious literary quarterlies; Ketterer was a wife beater, two times over. That was how Moonie came to be living with us in Hyde Park—and how Lydia came to suffer her final torment. For she could not have been any more excluded from their lives by the aunts in Skokie, or more relegated to the position of an unloved Cinderella, than she was by what grew up between Moonie and myself and constituted during those years my only sexual yearning. Lydia used to awaken me in the middle of the night by pounding on my chest with her fists. And nothing Dr. Rutherford might do or say could stop her. "If you ever lay a finger on my daughter," she would cry, "I'll drive a knife into your heart!" But I never did sleep with Moonie, not so long as her mother was alive. Under the guise of father and daughter, we touched and fondled one another's flesh; as the months went by we more and more frequently barged in upon one another—unknowing, inadvertently—in the midst of dressing or unclothed in the bathtub; raking leaves in the yard or out swimming off the Point we were playful and high-spirited, as a man and his young mistress might be expected to be . . . but in the end, as though she were my own offspring or my own sister, I honored the incest taboo. It was not easy.

Then we found Lydia in the tub. Probably none of our friends or my colleagues assumed that Lydia had killed herself because I had been sleeping with her daughter—until I fled with Moonie to Italy. I did not know what else to do, after the night we finally did make love. She was sixteen years old—her mother a suicide, her father a sadistic ignoramus, and she herself, because of her reading difficulties, still a freshman in high school: given all that, how could I desert her? But how ever could we be lovers together in Hyde Park?

So I at last got to make the trip to Europe that I had been planning when Lydia and I first met, only it wasn't to see the cultural monuments and literary landmarks that I came here.

I do not think that Moonie is as unhappy in Italy as Anna Karenina was with Vronsky, nor, since our first year here, have I been anything like so bewildered and disabled as was Aschenbach because of his passion for Tadzio. I had expected more agony; with my self-dramatizing literary turn of mind, I had even thought that Moonie might go mad. But the fact is that to our Italian friends we are simply another American writer and his pretty young girl friend, a tall, quiet, somber kid, whose only distinction, outside of her good looks, appears to them to be her total devotion to me; they tell me they are unused to seeing such deference for her man in a long-legged American blonde. They rather like her for this. The only friend I have who is anything like an intimate says that whenever I go out of a room, leaving her behind, Moonie seems almost to cease to exist. He wonders why. It isn't any longer because she doesn't know the language; happily, she became fluent in Italian as quickly as I did and, with this language, suffers none of those reading difficulties that used to make her nightly homework assignments such hell for the three of us back in Chicago. She is no longer stupid; or stubborn; though she is too often morose.

When she was twenty-one, and legally speaking no longer my "ward," I decided to marry Moonie. The very worst of it was over by then, and I mean by that, voracious, frenzied lust as well as paralyzing fear. I thought marriage might carry us beyond this tedious second stage, wherein she tended to be silent and gloomy, and I, in a muted sort of way, to be continually anxious, as though waiting in a hospital bed to be wheeled down to the operating room for surgery. Either I must marry her or leave her, take her upon me forever or end it entirely. So, on her twenty-first birthday, having firmly decided which was the choice for me, I proposed. But Moonie said no, she didn't ever want to be a wife. I lost my temper, I began to speak angrily in English—in the restaurant people looked our way. "You mean, *my* wife!" "*E di chi altro potrei essere?*" she replied. *Whose could I ever be anyway?*

That was that, the last time I attempted to make things "right." Consequently, we live on together in this unmarried state, and I continue to be stunned at the thought of whom my dutiful companion is and how she came to be with me. You would think I would have gotten over that by now, but I seem unable, or unwilling, to do so. So long as no one here knows our story, I am able to control the remorse and the shame.

However, to stifle the sense I have that I am living *someone else's life* is beyond me. I was supposed to be elsewhere and otherwise. This is not the life I worked and planned for! Was made for! Outwardly, to be sure, I am as respectable in my dress and manner as I was when I began adult life as an earnest young academic in Chicago in the fifties. I certainly *appear* to have no traffic with the unlikely or the unusual. Under a pseudonym, I write and publish short stories, somewhat more my own by now than Katherine Mansfield's, but still strongly marked by irony and indirection. To my surprise, reading through the magazines at the USIS library one afternoon recently, I came upon an article in an American literary journal, in which "I" am mentioned in the same breath with some rather famous writers as one whose literary and social concerns are currently out of date. I had not realized I had ever become so well known as now to be irrelevant. How can I be certain of anything from here, either the state of my pseudonymous reputation or my real one? I also teach English and American literature at a university in the city, to students more docile and respectful than any I have ever had to face. The U. of C. was never like this. I pick up a little extra cash, very little, by reading American novels for an Italian publishing house and telling them what I think; in this way I have been able to keep abreast of the latest developments in fiction. And I don't have migraines any more. I outgrew them some twenty years before the neurologist said I might—make of that what you wish . . . On the other hand, I need only contemplate a visit to my aging and ailing father in New Jersey, I have only to pass the American airline offices on the Via ——, for my heart to go galloping off on its own and the strength to flow out of my limbs. A minute's serious thought to being reunited with those who used to love me, or simply knew me, and I am panic-stricken . . . The panic of the escaped convict who imagines the authorities have picked up his scent—only I am the authority as well as the escapee. *For I do want to go home.* If only I had the wherewithal to extradite myself! The longer I remain in hiding like this, the more I allow the legend of my villainy to harden. And how do I even know from here that such a legend exists any longer outside my imagination? Or that it ever did? The America I glimpse on the TV and read about once a month in the periodicals at the USIS library does not strike me as a place where people worry very much any more about who is sleeping with whom. Who cares any longer that this twenty-four-year-old woman was once my own stepdaughter? Who cares that I took her virginity at sixteen and "inadvertently" fondled her at twelve? Who back there even remembers the late Lydia Zuckerman or the circumstances surrounding her suicide and my departure in 1962? From what I read it would appear that in post-Oswald America a man with my sort of record can go about his business without attracting very much attention. Even Ketterer could cause us no harm, I would think, now that his daughter is no longer a minor; not that after we ran off he felt much of anything anyway, except perhaps relief at no longer having to fork over the twenty-five bucks a week that the court had ordered him to pay us for Moonie's support.

I know then what I must do. I know what must be done. I do know! Either I must bring myself to leave Moonie (and by this action, rid myself of all the confusion that her nearness keeps alive in me); either I must leave her, making it clear to her beforehand that there is another man somewhere in this world with whom she not only could survive, but with whom she might be a gayer, more lighthearted person—I must convince her that when I go she will not be left to dwindle away, but will have (as she will) half a hundred suitors within the year, as many serious men to court a sweet and statuesque young woman like herself as there are frivolous ones who follow after her here in the streets, hissing and kissing at the air, Italians imagining she is Scandinavian and wild—either I must leave Moonie, and *now* (even if for the time being it is only to move across the river, and from there to look after her like a father who dwells in the same city, instead of the lover who lies beside her in bed and to whose body she clings in her sleep), either that, or return with her to America, where we will live, we two lovers, like anybody else—like *everybody* else, if I am to believe what they write about "the sexual revolution" in the newsmagazines of my native land.

But I am too humiliated to do either. The country may have changed, I have not. I did not know such depths of humiliation were possible, even for me. A reader of Conrad's *Lord Jim* and Mauriac's *Thérèse* and Kafka's "Letter to His Father," of Hawthorne and Strindberg and Sophocles—of Freud!—and still I did not know that humiliation could do such a job on a man. It seems either that literature too strongly influences my ideas about life, or that I am able to make no connection at all between its wisdom and my existence. For I cannot fully believe in the hopelessness of my predicament, and yet the line that concludes *The Trial* is as familiar to me as my own face: "it was as if the shame of it must outlive him"! Only I am not a character in a book, certainly not *that* book. I am real. And my humiliation is equally *real*. God, how I thought I was suffering in adolescence when fly balls used to fall through my hands in the schoolyard, and the born athletes on my team would smack their foreheads in despair. What I would give now to be living again back in that state of disgrace. What I would give to be living back in Chicago, teaching the principles of composition to my lively freshmen all morning long, taking my simple dinner off a tray at the Commons at night, reading from the European masters in my bachelor bed before sleep, fifty monumental pages annotated and underlined, Mann, Tolstoy, Gogol, Proust, in bed with all that genius—oh to have that scene of worthiness again, and migraines too if need be! How I wanted a dignified life! And how confident I was!

To conclude, in a traditional narrative mode, the story of that Zuckerman in that Chicago. I leave it to those writers who live in the flamboyant American present, and whose extravagant fictions I sample from afar, to treat the implausible, the preposterous, and the bizarre in something other than a straightforward and recognizable manner.

In my presence Eugene Ketterer did his best to appear easygoing, unruffled, and nonviolent, just a regular guy. I called him Mr. Ketterer, he called me Nathan, Nate, or Natie. The later he was in delivering Monica to her mother, the more offhand and, to me, galling was his behavior; to Lydia it was infuriating, and in the face of it she revealed a weakness for vitriolic rage which I'd seen no evidence of before, not at home or in class or in her fiction. It did not help any to caution her against allowing him to provoke her; in fact, several times she accused me—afterward, tearfully asking forgiveness—of taking Ketterer's side, when my only concern had been to prevent her from losing her head in front of Monica. She responded to Ketterer's taunting like some animal in a cage

being poked with a stick, and I knew, the second Sunday that
I was on hand to witness his cruelty and her response, that I
would shortly have to make it clear to "Gene" that I was not
just some disinterested bystander, that enough of his sadism
was enough.

In the beginning, before Ketterer and I finally had it out, if
Lydia demanded an explanation from him for showing up at
two P.M. (when he had been due to arrive with Monica at ten
thirty in the morning) he would look at *me* and say, fraternally,
"Women." If Lydia were to reply, "That's idiotic! That's
meaningless! What would a thug like you know about 'women,'
or men, or children! Why are you late with her, Eugene?" he
would just shrug and mumble, "Got held up." "That will not
do—!" "Have to, Lyd. 'Fraid that's the way the cookie crum-
bles." Or without even bothering to give her an answer, he
would say, again to me, "Live 'n' learn, Natie." A similarly unpleasant scene would occur in the evening, when he arrived to
pick Monica up either much too early or too late. "Look, I
ain't a clock. Never claimed to be." "You never claimed to be
anything—because you're *not* anything!" "Yeah, I know, I'm a
brute and a slob and a real bad thug, and you, you're Lady
Godiva. Yeah, I know all that." "You're a tormentor, that's
what you are! That you torture me is not even the point any
more—but how can you be so cruel and heartless as to torture
your own little child! How can you play with us like this, Sunday after Sunday, year after year—you caveman! you hollow
ignoramus!" "Let's go, Harmonica"—*his* nickname for the
child—"time to go home with the Big Bad Wolf."

Usually Monica spent the day at Lydia's watching TV and
wearing her hat. Ready to go at a moment's notice.

"Monica," Lydia would say, "you really can't sit all day
watching TV."

Uncomprehending: "Uh-huh."

"Monica, do you hear me? It's three o'clock. Maybe that's
enough TV for one day—do you think? Didn't you bring your
homework?"

Completely in the dark: "My *what*?"

"Did you bring your homework this week, so we can go
over it?"

A mutter: "Forgot."

"But I told you I'd help you. You *need* help, you know that."

Outrage: "Today's *Sunday.*"

"And?"

Law of Nature: "Sundays I don't *do* no homework."

"Don't talk like that, please. You never even spoke like that when you were a little six-year-old girl. You know better than that."

Cantankerous: "What?"

"Using double negatives. Saying I don't do *no*—the way your father does. And please don't sit like that."

Incredulous: "*What?*"

"You're sitting like a boy. Change into your dungarees if you want to sit like that. Otherwise sit like a girl your age."

Defiant: "I am."

"Monica, listen to me: I think we should practice your subtraction. We'll have to do it without the book, since you didn't bring it."

Pleading: "But today's *Sunday.*"

"But you need help in subtraction. That's what you need, not church, but help with your math. Monica, take that hat off! Take that silly hat off this minute! It's three o'clock in the afternoon and you just can't wear it all day long!"

Determined. Wrathful: "It's my hat—I can too!"

"But you're in my house! And I'm your mother! And I'm telling you to take it off! Why do you insist on behaving in this silly way! I *am* your mother, you know that! Monica, I love you and you love me—don't you remember when you were a little girl, don't you remember how we used to play? Take that hat off *before I tear it off your head!*"

Ultimate Weapon: "Touch my head and I'll tell my dad on you!"

"And don't call him 'Dad'! I cannot stand when you call that man who tortures the two of us 'Dad'! And sit like a girl! Do as I tell you! Close your legs!"

Sinister: "They're close."

"They're *open* and you're showing your underpants and stop it! You're too big for that—you go on buses, you go to school, if you're wearing a dress then behave as though you're wearing one! You cannot sit like this watching television

Sunday after Sunday— not when you cannot even add two and two."

Philosophical: "Who cares."

"I care! *Can* you add two and two? I want to know! Look at me—I'm perfectly serious. I have to know what you know and what you don't know, and where to begin. How much is two and two? *Answer me.*"

Dumpish: "Dunno."

"You *do* know. And pronounce your syllables. And answer me!"

Savage: "I don't know! Leave me alone, you!"

"Monica, how much is eleven minus one? Eleven take away one. If you had eleven cents and someone took away one of them, how many would you have left? Dear, please, what number comes before eleven? You must know *this.*"

Hysterical: "*I don't know it!*"

"You do!"

Exploding: "Twelve!"

"How can it be *twelve*? Twelve is *more* than eleven. I'm asking you what's *less* than eleven. Eleven take away one—is how much?"

Pause. Reflection. Decision: "One."

"No! You *have* eleven and you take *away* one."

Illumination: "Oh, take *away.*"

"Yes. Yes."

Straight-faced: "We never had take-aways."

"You *did*. You *had* to."

Steely: "I'm telling you the truth, *we don't have take-aways in James Madison School.*"

"Monica, this is *subtraction*—they have it everywhere in every school, and you have to know it. Oh darling, I don't care about that hat—I don't even care about him, that's *over*. I care about *you* and what's going to happen to *you*. Because you cannot be a little girl who knows nothing. If you are you'll get into trouble and your life will be awful. You're a girl and you're growing up, and you have to know how to make change of a dollar and what comes before eleven, which is how old you'll be *next year*, and you have to know how to sit—please, please don't sit like that, Monica, please don't go on buses and sit like that in public even if you insist on doing it here in order to frustrate me. Please. Promise me you won't."

Sulky, bewildered: "I don't understand you."

"Monica, you're a developing girl, even if they do dress you up like a kewpie doll on Sundays."

Righteous indignation: "This is for *church*."

"But church is beside the *point* for you. It's reading and writing—oh, I swear to you, Monica, every word I say is only because I love you and I don't want anything awful to happen to you, ever. I do love you—*you must know that!* What they have told you about me *is not so*. I am not a crazy woman, I am not a lunatic. You mustn't be afraid of me, or hate me—I was sick, and now I'm well, and I want to strangle myself every time I think that I gave you up to him, that I thought he could begin to provide you with a mother and a home and everything I wanted you to have. And now you don't have a mother—you have this person, this woman, this ninny who dresses you up in this ridiculous costume and gives you a Bible to carry around that you can't even *read!* And for a father you have that man. Of all the fathers in the world, *him!*"

Here Monica screamed, so piercingly that I came running from the kitchen where I had been sitting alone over a cup of cold coffee, not even knowing what to think.

In the living room all Lydia had done was to take Monica's hand in her own; yet the child was screaming as though she were about to be murdered.

"But," wept Lydia, "I only want to hold you—"

As though my appearance signaled that the *real* violence was about to begin, Monica began to froth at the mouth, screaming all the while, "*Don't! Don't! Two and two is four! Don't beat up on me! It's four!*"

Scenes as awful as this could be played out two and three times over in the course of a single Sunday afternoon—amalgams, they seemed to me, of soap opera (that genre again), Dostoevsky, and the legends of Gentile family life that I used to hear as a child, usually from my immigrant grandmothers, who had never forgotten what life had been like amid the Polish peasantry. As in the struggles of soap opera, the emotional ferocity of the argument exceeded by light-years the substantive issue, which was itself, more often than not, amenable to a little logic, or humor, or a dose of common sense. Yet, as in the scenes of family warfare in Dostoevsky, there was murder in the air on those Sundays, and it could not be laughed or reasoned away: an animosity so deep ran between those two females of the same blood that though they were only having that standard American feud over a child's schoolwork (the subject not of *The Possessed* or *The Brothers Karamazov* but of Henry Aldrich and Andy Hardy) it was not impossible (from another room) to imagine them going about it with firebrand, pistol, hanging rope, and hatchet. Actually, the child's cunning and her destructive stubbornness were nothing like so distressing to me as Lydia's persistence. I could easily envision, and understand, Monica's pulling a gun— bang, bang, you're dead, no more take-aways—but it was imagining Lydia trying to *bludgeon* the screaming child into a better life that shocked and terrified me.

Ketterer was the one who brought to mind those cautionary tales about Gentile barbarity that, by my late adolescence, I had rejected as irrelevant to the kind of life that I intended to lead. Exciting and gripping as they were to a helpless child— hair-raising tales of "their" alcoholism, "their" violence, "their" imperishable hatred of us, stories of criminal oppressors and innocent victims that could not but hold a powerful negative attraction for any Jewish child, and particularly to one whose very body was that of the underdog—when I came of age and began the work of throwing off the psychology and physique of my invalid childhood, I reacted against these tales with all the intensity my mission required. I did not doubt that they were accurate descriptions of what Jews had suffered; against the background of the concentration camps I hardly would dare to say, even in my teenage righteousness, that these stories were exaggerated. Nonetheless (I informed my family), as I happened to have been born a Jew not in twentieth-century Nuremberg, or nineteenth-century Lemberg, or fifteenth-century Madrid, but in the state of New Jersey in the same year that Franklin Roosevelt took office, et cetera, et cetera. By now that diatribe of second-generation American children is familiar enough. The vehemence with which I advanced my position forced me into some ludicrous positions: when my sister, for instance, married her first husband, a man who was worthless by most anyone's standards (and certainly repulsive to me at fifteen, with his white shirt cuffs rolled back twice, his white calfskin loafers, his gold pinkie ring, and the way he had with his well-tanned hands of touching everything, his cigarette case, his hair, my sister's cheek, as though it were silk— the whole effeminate side of hooliganism), I nonetheless berated my parents for opposing Sunny's choice of a mate on the grounds that if she wished to marry a Catholic that was her right. In the anguish of the moment they missed my point, as I, with my high-minded permissiveness, missed theirs; in the end it was they of course who turned out to be prophetic, and with a vengeance. Only a few years later, at last a free agent myself, I was able to admit that what was so dismal and ridiculous about my sister's marriages wasn't her penchant for Italian boys from South Philly, but that both times out she chose precisely the two who confirmed, in nearly every detail, my family's prejudice against them.

Dim-witted as it may seem in retrospect—as much does, in my case—it was not until Ketterer and Monica came into my life that I began to wonder if I was being any less perverse than my sister; *more so*, because unlike Sunny, I was at least alert to what I might be up to. Not that I had ever been unaware of all there was in Lydia's background to lend support to my grandmothers' observations about Gentile disorder and corruption. As a child, no one of course had mentioned incest to me, but it went without saying that if either of these unworldly immigrants had been alive to hear the whole of Lydia's horror story, they would not have been so shocked as was I, their college-professor grandson, by the grisliest detail of all. But even without a case of incest in the family, there was more than enough there for a Jewish boy to break himself upon: the unmotherly mother, the unfatherly father, the loveless bigoted aunts—my grandmothers could not themselves have invented a shiksa with a more ominous and, to their way of thinking, representative dossier than the one their fragile Nathan had chosen. To be sure, Dr. Goebbels or Air Marshal Goering might have a daughter wandering around somewhere in the world, but as a fine example of the species, Lydia would do nicely. I knew this; but then the Lydia I had chosen, unlike Sunny's

elect, *detested this inheritance herself.* In part what was so stirring about her (to me, to me) was the price she had paid to
disown it—it had driven her crazy, this background; and yet
she had lived to tell the tale, to *write* the tale, and to write it
for *me.*

But Ketterer and his daughter Monica, who as it were came
*with* Lydia, in the same deal, were neither of them detached
chroniclers or interpreters or enemies of their world. Rather,
they were the embodiment of what my grandparents, and
great-grandparents, and great-great-grandparents, had loathed
and feared: shagitz thuggery, shiksa wiliness. They were to me
like figures out of the folk legend of the Jewish past—only they
were real, just like my sister's Sicilians.

Of course I could not stand around too long being mesmerized by this fact. Something had to be done. In the beginning
this consisted mostly of comforting Lydia in the aftermath of
one of her tutorial disasters; then I tried to get her to leave
Monica alone, to forget about saving her on Sundays and just
try to make her as happy as she could for the few hours they
had together. This was the same sort of commonsense advice
that she received from Dr. Rutherford, but not even the two of
us together, with the considerable influence we had over her,
could prevent her from collapsing into frantic instruction
before the day was out and bombarding Monica with a crash
course in math, grammar, and the feminine graces before Ketterer arrived to spirit her back to his cave in the Chicago suburb of Homewood.

What followed, followed. I became the child's Sunday
schoolteacher, unless I was down with a migraine. And she
began to learn, or to try to. I taught her simple take-aways, I
taught her simple sums, I taught her the names of the states
bordering Illinois, I taught her to distinguish between the Atlantic and the Pacific, Washington and Lincoln, a period and a
comma, a sentence and a paragraph, the little hand and the big
hand. This last I accomplished by standing her on her feet and
having her pretend hers were the arms of the clock. I taught
her the poem I had composed when I was five and in bed with
one of my fevers, my earliest literary achievement, according
to my family: "Tick tock, Nathan is a clock." "Tick tock," she
said, "Monica is a clock," and thrust her arms into the nine

fifteen position, so that her white church dress, getting tighter on her by the month, pulled across the little bubbles of her breasts. Ketterer came to hate me, Monica to fall in love with me, and Lydia to accept me at last as her means of salvation. She saw the way out of her life's misery, and I, in the service of Perversity or Chivalry or Morality or Misogyny or Saintliness or Folly or Pent-up Rage or Psychic Illness or Sheer Lunacy or Innocence or Ignorance or Experience or Heroism or Judaism or Masochism or Self-Hatred or Defiance or Soap Opera or Romantic Opera or the Art of Fiction perhaps, or none of the above, or maybe all of the above and more—I found the way into mine. I would not have had it in me at that time to wander out after dinner at the Commons to spend a hundred dollars on the secondhand books that I wanted to fulfill my dream of a "library" as easily and simply as I squandered my manhood.

## II

## MY TRUE STORY

*Peter Tarnopol was born in Yonkers, New York, thirty-four years ago. He was educated in public schools there, and was graduated summa cum laude from Brown University in 1954. He briefly attended graduate school, and then served for two years as an MP with the U.S. Army in Frankfurt, Germany, the setting for A Jewish Father, the first novel for which in 1960 he received the Prix de Rome of the American Academy of Arts and Letters as well as a Guggenheim Fellowship.*

*Since then he has published only a handful of stories, devoting himself almost exclusively in the intervening years to his nightmarish marriage to the former Maureen Johnson of Elmira, New York. In her lifetime, Mrs. Tarnopol was a barmaid, an abstract painter, a sculptress, a waitress, an actress (and what an actress!), a short-story writer, a liar, and a psychopath. Married in 1959, the Tarnopols were legally separated in 1962, at which time Mrs. Tarnopol accused the author, before Judge Milton Rosenzweig of the Supreme Court of the County of New York, of being "a well-known seducer of college girls." (Mr. Tarnopol has taught literature and creative writing at the University of Wisconsin and lately at Hofstra College on Long Island.) The marriage was dissolved in 1966 by Mrs. Tarnopol's violent death. At the time of her demise she was unemployed and a patient in group therapy in Manhattan; she was receiving one hundred dollars a week in alimony.*

*From 1963 to 1966, Mr. Tarnopol conducted a love affair with Susan Seabury McCall, herself a young widow residing in Manhattan; upon the conclusion of the affair, Mrs. McCall attempted unsuccessfully to kill herself and is currently living unhappily in Princeton, New Jersey, with a mother she cannot abide. Like Mr. Tarnopol, Mrs. McCall has no children, but would very much like to before time runs out, sired preferably by Mr. Tarnopol. Mr. Tarnopol is frightened of remarrying, among other things.*

*From 1962 until 1967, Mr. Tarnopol was the patient of the psychoanalyst Dr. Otto Spielvogel of New York City, whose articles*

*on creativity and neurosis have appeared in numerous journals,
most notably the* American Forum for Psychoanalytic Studies,
*of which he is a contributing editor. Mr. Tarnopol is considered by
Dr. Spielvogel to be among the nation's top young narcissists in
the arts. Six months ago Mr. Tarnopol terminated his analysis
with Dr. Spielvogel and went on leave from the university in order to take up temporary residence at the Quahsay Colony, a
foundation-supported retreat for writers, painters, sculptors, and
composers in rural Vermont. There Mr. Tarnopol keeps mostly to
himself, devoting nights as well as days to considering what has
become of his life. He is confused and incredulous much of the
time, and on the subject of the late Mrs. Tarnopol, he continues to
be a man possessed.*

*Presently Mr. Tarnopol is preparing to forsake the art of fiction
for a while and embark upon the autobiographical narrative, an
endeavor which he approaches warily, uncertain as to both its ad-
visability and usefulness. Not only would the publication of such
a personal document raise serious legal and ethical problems, but
there is no reason to believe that by keeping his imagination at
bay and rigorously adhering to the facts, Mr. Tarnopol will have
exorcised his obsession once and for all. It remains to be seen
whether his candor, such as it is, can serve any better than his art
(or Dr. Spielvogel's therapeutic devices) to demystify the past and
mitigate his admittedly uncommendable sense of defeat.*

> *P. T.*
> *Quahsay, Vt.*
> *September 1967*

## 1. PEPPY

Has anything changed?

I ask, recognizing that on the surface (which is not to be
disparaged—I live there too) there is no comparing the thirty-
four-year-old man able today to manage his misfortunes without collapse, to the twenty-nine-year-old boy who back in the
summer of 1962 actually contemplated, however fleetingly,
killing himself. On the June afternoon that I first stepped into
Dr. Spielvogel's office, I don't think a minute elapsed before I

had given up all pretense of being an "integrated" personality and begun to weep into my hands, grieving for the loss of my strength, my confidence, and my future. I was then (miraculously, I am no longer) married to a woman I loathed, but from whom I was unable to separate myself, subjugated not simply by her extremely professional brand of moral blackmail—by that mix of luridness and corn that made our life together resemble something serialized on afternoon TV or in the *National Enquirer*—but by my own childish availability to it. Just two months back I had learned of the ingenious strategy by which she had deceived me into marrying her three years earlier; instead of serving me as the weapon with which finally to beat my way out of our bedlam, what she had confessed (in the midst of her semi-annual suicide attempt) seemed to have stripped me of my remaining defenses and illusions. My mortification was complete. Neither leaving nor staying meant anything to me any more.

When I came East that June from Wisconsin, ostensibly to participate as a staff member in a two-week writing workshop at Brooklyn College, I was as bereft of will as a zombie—except, as I discovered, the will to be done with my life. Waiting in the subway station for an approaching train, I suddenly found it advisable to wrap one hand around the links of a chain that anchored a battered penny weighing machine to the iron pillar beside me. Until the train had passed in and out of view, I squeezed that chain with all my strength. "I am dangling over a ravine," I told myself. "I am being hoisted from the waves by a helicopter. *Hang on!*" Afterward I scanned the tracks, to be certain that I had in fact succeeded in stifling this wholly original urge for Peter Tarnopol to be transformed into a mangled corpse; amazed, terrified, I had also, as they say, to laugh: "Commit suicide? Are you kidding? You can't even walk out the door." I still don't know how near I may actually have come that day to springing across the platform and, in lieu of taking my wife head-on, taking on that incoming IRT train. It could be that I didn't have to *cling* to anything, that too could have been so much infantile posturing; then again I may owe my survival to the fact that when I heard blessed oblivion hurtling my way, my right hand fortunately found something impressively durable to hang on to.

At Brooklyn College over a hundred students were present in the auditorium for the opening session; each member of the workshop staff of four was to give a fifteen-minute address on "the art of fiction." My turn came, I rose—and couldn't speak. I stood at the lectern, notes before me—*audience* before me—without air in my lungs or saliva in my mouth. The audience, as I remember it, seemed to me to begin to *hum*. And all I wanted was to go to sleep. Somehow I didn't close my eyes and give it a try. Neither was I entirely there. I was nothing but heartbeat, just that drum. Eventually I turned and left the stage . . . and the job . . . Once, in Wisconsin, after a weekend of quarreling with my wife (she maintained, over my objections, that I had talked too long to a pretty graduate student at a party on Friday night; much discussion on the relativity of time), she had presented herself at the door of the classroom where I taught my undergraduate fiction seminar from seven to nine on Monday evenings. Our quarrel had ended at breakfast that morning with Maureen tearing at my hands with her fingernails; I had not been back to our apartment since. "It's an emergency!" Maureen informed me—and the seminar. The ten middle western undergraduates looked first at her, standing so determinedly there in the doorway, and then with comprehension at my hands, marked with mercurochrome—"The cat," I had explained to them earlier, with a forgiving smile for that imaginary beast. I rushed out into the corridor before Maureen had a chance to say more. There my sovereign delivered herself of that day's manifesto: "You better come home tonight, Peter! You better not go back to some room somewhere with one of those little blondes!" (This was the semester before I went ahead and did just that.) "Get out of here!" I whispered. "Go, Maureen, or I'll throw you down those fucking stairs! Go, *before I murder you!*" My tone must have impressed her—she took hold of the banister and retreated a step. I turned back to the seminar room to find that in my haste to confront Maureen and send her packing, I had neglected to shut the door behind me. A big shy farm girl from Appleton, who had spoken maybe one sentence all semester, was staring fixedly at the woman in the corridor behind me; the rest of the class stared into the pages of *Death in Venice*—no book had ever been so riveting. "All right," said the quavering voice that entered the room—an arm had violently flung the door shut in Maureen's face, I'm not wholly sure it was mine—"why does Mann send Aschenbach to Venice, rather than Paris, or Rome, or Chicago?" Here the girl from Appleton dissolved into tears, and the others, usually not that lively, began answering the question all at once . . . I did not recall every last detail of this scene as I stood yearning for sleep before my expectant audience at Brooklyn College, but it accounts, I think, for the vision that I had as I stepped to the lectern to deliver my prepared address: I saw Maureen, projected like a bullet through the rear door of the auditorium, and shouting at the top of her lungs whatever revelation about me had just rolled off the presses. Yes, to that workshop audience that took me to be an emerging literary figure, a first novelist whose ideas about writing were worth paying tuition to hear, Maureen would reveal (without charge) that I was not at all as I would present myself. To whatever words, banal or otherwise, that I spoke from the platform, she would cry, "Lies! Filthy, self-serving lies!" I could (as I intended to) quote Conrad, Flaubert, Henry James, she would scream all the louder, "Fraud!" But I spoke not a syllable, and in my flight from the stage, seemed to be only what I was—terrified, nothing any longer but my fears.

My writing by this time was wholly at the mercy of our marital confusion. Five and six hours a day, seven days a week, I went off to my office at the university and ran paper through the roller of my typewriter; the fiction that emerged was either amateurishly transparent—I might have been drawing up an IOU or writing the instructions for the back of a detergent box for all the imagination I displayed—or, alternately, so disjointed and opaque that on rereading, I was myself in the dark, and manuscript in hand, would drag myself around the little room, like some burdened figure broken loose from Rodin's "Bourgeois of Calais," crying aloud, "Where was *I* when this was written?" And I asked because I didn't know.

These pounds and pounds of pages that I accumulated during the marriage had the marriage itself as the subject and constituted the major part of the daily effort to understand how I had fallen into this trap and why I couldn't get out. Over the three years I had tried easily a hundred different ways to penetrate that mystery; every other week the whole course of the novel would change in midsentence, and within any one month the surface of my desk would disappear beneath dozens of equally dissatisfying variants of the single unfinished chapter that was driving me mad. Periodically I would take all these pages—"take" is putting it mildly—and consign them to the liquor carton filling up with false starts at the bottom of my closet, and then I would begin again, often with the very first sentence of the book. How I struggled for a description. (And, alas, struggle still.) But from one version to the next nothing of consequence ever happened: locales shifted, peripheral characters (parents, old flames, comforters, enemies, and allies) came and went, and with about as much hope for success as a man attacking the polar ice cap with his own warm breath, I would attempt to release a flow of invention in me by changing the color of her eyes or my hair. Of course, to give up the obsession would surely have made the most sense; only, obsessed, I was as incapable of not writing about what was killing me as I was of altering or understanding it.

So: hopeless at my work and miserable in my marriage, with all the solid achievements of my early twenties gone up in smoke, I walked off the stage, too stupefied even for shame, and headed like a sleepwalker for the subway station. Fortunately there was a train already there receiving passengers; it received me—rather than riding over me—and within the hour I was deposited at the Columbia campus stop only a few blocks from my brother Morris's apartment.

My nephew Abner, surprised and pleased to see me in New York, offered me a bottle of soda and half of his salami sandwich. "I've got a cold," he explained, when I asked in a breaking voice what he was doing home from school. He showed me that he was reading *Invisible Man* with his lunch. "Do you really know Ralph Ellison, Uncle Peppy?" "I met him once," I said, and then I was bawling, or barking; tears streamed from my eyes, but the noises that I made were novel even to me. "Hey, Uncle Pep, what's the matter?" "Get your father." "He's teaching." "*Get him, Abbie.*" So the boy called the university—"This is an emergency; his brother is very sick!"—and Morris was out of class and home in minutes. I was in the bathroom by this time; Moe pushed right on in, and then, big two-hundred pounder though he is, kneeled down in that tiny tiled room beside the toilet, where I was sitting on the seat, watery feces running from me, sweating and simultaneously trembling as though I were packed in ice; every few minutes my head rolled to the side and I retched in the direction of the sink. Still, Morris pressed his bulk against my legs and held my two limp hands in his; with a rough, rubbery cheek he wiped the perspiration from my brow. "Peppy, ah, Peppy," he groaned, calling me by my childhood nickname and kissing my face. "Hang on, Pep, I'm here now."

A word about my brother and sister, very different creatures from myself.

I am the youngest of three, always "the baby" in everyone's eyes, right down to today. Joan, the middle child, is five years my senior and has lived most of her adult life in California with her husband Alvin, a land developer, and their four handsome children. Says Morris of our sister: "You would think she'd been born in a Boeing jet instead of over the store in the Bronx." Alvin Rosen, my brother-in-law, is six foot two and intimidatingly handsome, particularly now that his thick curls have turned silvery ("My father thinks he *dyes* it that color," Abner once told me in disgust) and his face has begun to crease like a cowboy's; from all the evidence he seems pretty much at one with his life as Californian, yachtsman, skier, and real estate tycoon, and utterly content with his wife and his children. He and my trim stylish sister travel each year to places slightly off the main tourist route (or just on the brink of being "discovered"); only recently my parents received postcards from their granddaughter, Melissa Rosen, Joannie's ten-year-old, postmarked Africa (a photo safari with the family) and Brazil (a small boat had carried friends and family on a week-long journey up the Amazon, a famous Stanford naturalist serving as their guide). They throw open their house for an annual benefit costume party each year in behalf of *Bridges*, the West Coast literary magazine whose masthead lists Joan as one of a dozen advisory editors—frequently they are called upon to bail the magazine out of financial trouble with a timely donation from the Joan and Alvin Rosen Foundation; they are also generous contributors to hospitals and libraries in the Bay Area and among the leading sponsors of an annual fund drive

for California's migrant workers ("Capitalists," says Morris,
"in search of a conscience. Aristocrats in overalls. Fragonard
should paint 'em."); and they are good parents, if the buoy-
ancy and beauty of their children are any indication. To dismiss
them (as Morris tends to) as vapid and frivolous would be
easier if their pursuit of comfort, luxury, beauty, and glamor
(they number a politically active movie star among their inti-
mates) weren't conducted with such openness and zest, with a
sense that they had discovered *the* reason for being. My sister,
after all, was not always so fun loving and attractive or adept at
enjoying life. In 1945, as valedictorian of Yonkers High, she
was a hairy, hawk-nosed, undernourished-looking little "grind"
whose braininess and sallow homeliness had made her just
about the least popular girl in her class; the consensus then was
that she would be lucky to find a husband, let alone the rich,
lanky, Lincolnesque Wharton School graduate, Alvin Rosen,
whom she carried away from the University of Pennsylvania
along with her A.B. in English. But she did it—not without
concentrated effort, to be sure. Electrolysis on the upper lip
and along the jawbone, plastic surgery on the nose and chin,
and the various powders and paints available at the drugstore
have transformed her into a sleek, sensual type, still Semitic,
but rather more the daughter of a shah than a shopkeeper.
Driving around San Francisco in her Morgan, disguised as a
rider off the pampas one day and a Bulgarian peasant the next,
has gained her in her middle years something more than mere
popularity—according to the society page of the San Francisco
paper (also sent on to my mother by little Melissa) Joan is "the
most daring and creative tastemaker" alive out there. The photograph of her, with Alvin in velvet on one bare arm and the
conductor of the San Francisco Symphony on the other (captioned, by Melissa, "Mom at a party"), is simply staggering to
one who remembers still that eight-by-ten glossy of the '45
senior prom crowd at Billy Rose's Diamond Horseshoe in
New York—there sits Joan, all nose and shoulder blades, adrift
in a taffeta "strapless" into which it appears she will momentarily sink out of sight, her head of coarse dark hair (since
straightened and shined so that she glows like Black Beauty)
mockingly framed by the Amazonian gams of the chorus girl
up on the stage behind her; as I remember it, sitting beside

her, at their "ringside" table, was her date, the butcher's large shy son, bemusedly looking down into a glass with a Tom Collins in it . . . And this woman today is the gregarious glamor girl of America's most glamorous city. To me it is awesome: that she should be on such good terms with pleasure, such a success at satisfaction, should derive so much strength and confidence from how she looks, and where she travels, and what she eats and with whom . . . well, that is no small thing, or so it seems to her brother from the confines of his hermit's cell.

Joan has recently written inviting me to leave Quahsay and come out to California to stay with her and her family for as long as I like. "We won't even bother you with our goatish ways, if you should just want to sit around the pool polishing your halo. If it pleases you, we will do everything we can to prevent you from having even a *fairly* good time. But reliable sources in the East tell me that you are still very gifted at that yourself. My dearest Alyosha, between 1939, when I taught you to spell 'antidisestablishmentarianism,' and now, you've changed. Or perhaps not—maybe what sent you into ecstasy over that word was how difficult it was. Truly, Pep, if your appetite for the disagreeable should ever slacken, I am here and so is the house. You're fallen sister, J."

For the record, my reply:

Dear Joan: What's disagreeable isn't being where I am or living as I do right now. This is the best place for me, probably for some time to come. I can't stay on indefinitely of course, but there are approximations to this sort of life. When Maureen and I lived in New Milford, and I had that twelve-by-twelve shack in the woods behind the house—and a bolt to throw on the door—I could be content for hours on end. I haven't changed much since 1939: I still like more than anything to sit alone in a room spelling things out as best I can with a pencil and paper. When I first got to New York in '62, and my personal life was a shambles, I used to dream out loud in my analyst's office about becoming again that confident and triumphant college kid I was at twenty; now I find the idea of going back beyond that even more appealing. Up here I sometimes imagine that I am ten— and treat myself accordingly. To start the day I eat a bowl of hot cereal in the dining room as I did each morning in our kitchen at home; then I head out here to my cabin, at just about the time I used to go off to school. I'm at work by eight forty-five, when "the first bell" used to ring. Instead of arithmetic, social studies, etc., I write on the typewriter till noon. (Just like my boyhood idol, Ernie Pyle; actually I may have grown up to become the war correspondent I dreamed of being in 1943—except that the front-line battles I report on aren't the kind I'd had in mind.) Lunch out of a lunch pail provided by the dining hall here: a sandwich, some carrot sticks, an oatmeal cookie, an apple, a thermos of milk. More than enough for this growing boy. After lunch I resume writing until three thirty, when "the last bell" used to ring at school. I straighten up my desk and carry my empty lunch pail back to the dining hall, where the evening's soup is cooking. The smell of dill, mother's perfume. Manchester is three miles from the Colony by way of a country road that curves down through the hills. There is a women's junior college at the edge of town, and the girls are down there by the time I arrive. I see them inside the laundromat and at the post office and buying shampoo in the pharmacy—reminding me of the playground "after school," aswarm with long-haired little girls a ten-year-old boy could only admire from afar and with wonder. I admire them from afar and with wonder in the local luncheonette, where I go for a cup of coffee. I have been asked by one of the English professors at the college to speak to his writing class. I declined. I don't want them any more accessible than they would be if I were back in the fifth grade. After my coffee I walk down the street to the town library and sit for a while leafing through the magazines and watching the schoolkids at the long tables copying their book reports off the jacket flaps. Then I go out and hitch a ride back up to the Colony; I couldn't feel any more trusting and innocent than when I hop out of the car and say to the driver, "Thanks for the ride—s'long!"

I sleep in a room on the second floor of the big three-story farmhouse that houses the guests; on the main floor are the kitchen, dining hall, and the living room (magazines, record player, and piano); there's a ping-pong table on a side porch, and that's just about it. On the floor of my room, in my undershorts, I do half an hour of calisthenics at the end of each afternoon. In the last six months, through dint of exercise and very little appetite, I have become just about as skinny as I was when you used to pretend to play the xylophone on my ribs. After "gym" I shave and shower. My windows are brushed by the needles of an enormous spruce; that's the only sound I hear while shaving, outside of the water running into the sink. Not a noise I can't account for. I try each evening to give myself a "perfect" shave, as a shaving ten-year-old might. I *concentrate*: hot water, soap, hot water, coat of Rise, with the grain, coat of Rise, against the grain, hot water, cold water, thorough investigation of all surfaces . . . perfect.

The vodka martini that I mix for myself at six, I sip alone while listening to the news on my portable radio. (I am on my bed in my bathrobe: face ivory smooth, underarms deodorized, feet powdered, hair combed—clean as a bridegroom in a marriage manual.) The martini was of course not my habit at ten, but something like Dad's when he came home with his headache (and the day's receipts) from the store: looking as though he were drinking turpentine, he would toss down his shot of Schenley's, and then listen in "his" chair to "Lyle Van and the News." Dinner is eaten at six thirty here, in the company of the fifteen or so guests in residence at the moment, mostly novelists and poets, a few painters, one composer. Conversation is pleasant, or annoying, or dull; in all, no more or less taxing than eating night after night with one's family, though the family that comes to mind isn't ours so much as the one Chekhov assembled in *Uncle Vanya*. A young poetess recently arrived here mired in astrology; whenever she gets going on somebody's horoscope I want to jump up from the table and get a pistol and blow her brains out. But as we are none of us bound by blood, law, or desire (as far as I can tell), forbearance generally holds sway. We drift after dinner into the living room, to chat and scratch the resident dog; the composer plays Chopin nocturnes; the *New York Times* passes from hand to hand . . . generally within the hour we have all drifted off without a word. My understanding is that with only five exceptions, all those in residence right now happen to be in flight, or in hiding, or in recovery—from bad marriages, divorces, and affairs. I have overheard tag ends of conversation issuing from the phone booth down in the kitchen to support this rumor. Two teacher-poets in their thirties who have just been through the process of divesting themselves of wives and children and worldly goods (in exchange for student admirers) have struck up a friendship and compare poems they're writing about the ordeal of giving up little sons and daughters. On the weekends when their dazzling student girl friends come to visit, they disappear into the bedsheets at the local motel for forty-eight hours at a clip. I recently began to play ping-pong again for the first time in twenty years, two or three fierce games after dinner with an Idaho woman, a stocky painter in her fifties who has been married five times; one night last week (only ten days after her arrival) she drank everything she could find on the premises, including the vanilla extract in the cook's pantry, and had to be taken away the next morning in a station wagon by the mortician who runs the local AA. We all left our typewriters to stand glumly out on the steps and wave goodbye. "Ah, don't worry," she called to us out the car window, "if it wasn't for my mistakes I'd still be back on the front porch in Boise." She was our only "character" and far and away the most robust and spirited of the survivors hereabouts. One night six of us went down into Manchester for a beer and she told us about her first two marriages. After she finished, the astrologist wanted to know her sign: the rest of us were trying to figure out how come she wasn't dead. "Why the hell do you keep getting married, Mary?" I asked her. She chucked me on the chin and said, "Because I don't want to die shriveled up." But she'd gone now (probably to marry the mortician), and except for the muffled cries rising from the phone booth at night, it's as quiet here as a hospital zone. Perfect for homework. After dinner and the *Times*, I walk back out to my studio, one of twenty cabins scattered along a dirt road that winds through the two hundred acres of open fields and evergreen woods. In the cabin there's a writing desk, a cot, a Franklin stove, a couple of straight-backed chairs painted yellow, a bookcase painted white, and the wobbly wicker table where I eat lunch at noon. I read over what I've written that day. Trying to read anything else is useless; my mind wanders back to my own pages. I think about that or nothing.

Walking back to the main house at midnight I have only a flashlight to help me make my way along the path that runs between the trees. Under a black sky by myself, I am no more courageous at thirty-four than I was as a boy: there is the urge to run. But as a matter of fact invariably I will turn the flashlight off and stand out there in the midnight woods, until either fear subsides or I have achieved something like a Mexican standoff between me and it. What frightens me? At ten it was only oblivion. I used to pass the "haunted" Victorian houses on Hawthorne Avenue on my way home from Cub Scout meetings, reminding myself, *There are no ghosts, the dead are dead*, which was, of course, the most terrifying thought of all. Today it's the thought that the dead *aren't* that turns my knees to water. I think: the funeral was another trick—she's alive! Somehow or other, she will reappear! Down in town in the late afternoon, I half expect to look into the laundromat and see her stuffing a machine with a bag of wash. At the luncheonette where I go for my cup of coffee, I sometimes sit at the counter waiting for Maureen to come charging through the door, with finger pointed—"What are you doing in here! You said you'd meet me by the bank at four!" "By the bank? Four? You?" And we're at it. "You're dead," I tell her, "you cannot meet anyone by any bank if you are, *as you are*, dead!" But still, you will have observed, I keep my distance from the pretty young students buying shampoo to wash their long hair. Who ever accused a shy ten-year-old of being "a well-known seducer of college girls"? Or, for that matter, heard of a plaintiff who was ashes? "She's dead," I remind myself, "and it is over." But how can that be? Defies credulity. If in a work of realistic fiction the hero was saved by something as fortuitous as the sudden death of his worst enemy, what intelligent reader would suspend his disbelief? Facile, he would grumble, and fantastic. Fictional wish fulfillment, fiction in the service of one's dreams. Not True to Life. And I would agree. Maureen's death is not True to Life. Such things simply do not happen, except when they do. (And as time passes and I get older, I find that they do with increasing frequency.)

I'm sending along Xerox copies of two stories I've written up here, both more or less on the Subject. They'll give you an idea as to why I'm here and what I'm doing. So far no one has read the stories but my editor. He had encouraging things to say about both of them, but of course what he would like to see is that novel for which my publisher advanced twenty thousand dollars back when I was a boy wonder. I know how much he would like to see it because he so scrupulously and kindly avoided mentioning it. He gave the game away, however, by inquiring whether "Courting Disaster" (one of the two stories enclosed) was going "to develop into a longer work about a guilt-ridden Zuckerman and his beautiful stepdaughter in Italy—a kind of post-Freudian meditation on themes out of *Anna Karenina* and *Death in Venice*. Is that what you're up to, or are you planning to continue to write Zuckerman variations until you have constructed a kind of full-length fictional fugue?" Good ideas all right, but what I am doing, I had to tell the man standing there holding my IOU, is more like trying to punch my way out of a paper bag. "Courting Disaster" is a post-cataclysmic fictional meditation on nothing more than my marriage: what if Maureen's personal mythology had been biographical truth? Suppose that, and suppose a good deal more—and you get "C.D." From a Spielvogelian perspective, it may even be read as a legend composed at the behest and under the influence of the superego, my adventures as seen through its eyes—as "Salad Days" is something like a comic idyll honoring a Pannish (and as yet unpunished) id. It remains for the ego to come forward then and present *its* defense, for all parties to the conspiracy-to-abscond-with-my-life to have had their day in court. I realize now, as I entertain this idea, that the nonfiction narrative that I'm currently working on might be considered just that: the "I" owning up to its role as ringleader of the plot. If so, then after all testimony has been heard and a guilty verdict swiftly rendered, the conspirators will be consigned to the appropriate correctional institution. You suggest your pool. Warden Spielvogel, my former analyst (whose job, you see, I am now doing on the side), would suggest that the band of desperados be handed back over to him for treatment in the cell block at Eighty-ninth and Park. The injured plaintiff in this action does not really care where it happens, or how, so long as the convicted learn their lesson and NEVER DO IT AGAIN. Which isn't likely: we are dealing with a treacherous bunch here, and that this trio has been entrusted with my well-being is a source of continuous and grave concern. Having been around the track with them once already, I would as soon consign my fate to the Marx Brothers or the Three Stooges; buffoons, but they at least *like* one another. P.S. Don't take personally the brother of "Salad Days" or the sister of "Courting Disaster." Imaginary siblings serving the design of the fiction. If I ever felt superior to you and your way of life, I don't any longer. Besides, it's to you that I may owe my literary career. Trying on a recent afternoon walk to figure out how I got into this line of work, I remembered myself at age six and you at age eleven, waiting in the back seat of the car for Mother and Dad to finish their Saturday night shopping. You kept using a word that struck me as the funniest thing I'd ever heard, and once you saw how much it tickled me, you wouldn't stop, though I begged you to from the floor of the car where I was curled up in a knot from pure hilarity. I believe the word was "noodle," used as a synonym for "head." You were merciless, somehow you managed to stick it somewhere into every sentence you uttered, and eventually I wet my pants. When Mother and Dad returned to the car I was outraged with you and in tears. "Joannie did it," I cried, whereupon Dad informed me that it was a human impossibility for one person to pee in another person's pants. Little he knew about the power of art.

Joan's prompt reply:

Thanks for the long letter and the two new stories, three artful documents springing from the same hole in your head. When that one drilled she really struck pay dirt. Is there no bottom to your guilty conscience? Is there no other source available for your art? A few observations on literature and life—1. You have no reason to hide in the woods like a fugitive from justice. 2. You did not kill her, in any way, shape, or form. Unless there is something I don't know. 3. To have asked a pretty girl to have intercourse with a zucchini in your presence is morally inconsequential. Everybody has his whims. You probably made her day (if that was you). You announce it in your "Salad Days" story with all the bravado of a naughty boy who knows he has done wrong and now awaits with bated breath his punishment. *Wrong*, Peppy, is an ice pick, not a garden vegetable; *wrong* is by force or with children. 4. You do disapprove of me, as compared with Morris certainly; but that, as they say, is your problem, baby. (And brother Moe's. And whoever else's. Illustrative anecdote: About six weeks ago, immediately after the Sunday supplement here ran a photo story on our new ski house at Squaw Valley, I got a midnight phone call from a mysterious admirer. A lady. "Joan Rosen?" "Yes." "I'm going to expose you to the world for what you are." "Yes? What is that?" "A

Jewish girl from the Bronx! Why do you try to hide it, Joan? It's written all over you, you phony bitch!") So then, I don't take either of those make-believe siblings for myself. I know you can't write about me—you can't make pleasure credible. And a working marriage that works is about as congenial to your talent and interests as the subject of outer space. You know I admire your work (and I do like these two stories, when I can ignore what they imply about your state of mind), but the fact is that you couldn't create a Kitty and a Levin if your life depended on it. Your imagination (hand in hand with your life) moves in the other direction. 5. Reservation ("Courting Disaster"): I never heard of anyone killing herself with a can opener. Awfully gruesome and oddly arbitrary, unless I am missing something. 6. Idle curiosity: was *Maureen* seduced by her father? She never struck me as broken in that way. 7. After the "nonfiction narrative" on the Subject, what next? A saga in heroic couplets? Suggestion: Why don't you plug up the well and drill for inspiration elsewhere? Do yourself a favor (if those words mean anything to you) and FORGET IT. Move on! Come West, young man! P.S. Two enclosures are for your edification (and taken together, right up your fictional alley—if you want to see unhappiness, you ought to see this marriage in action). Enclosed note #1 is to me from Lane Coutell, *Bridges'* new, twenty-four-year-old associate editor (good-looking and arrogant and, in a way, brilliant; more so right now than is necessary), who was here with his wife for supper and read the stories. He and the magazine would (his "reservations" notwithstanding) give anything (except money, of which there's none) to publish them, though I made it clear that he'd have to contact you about that. I just wanted to know what someone intelligent who didn't know your true story would make of what you've made out of it here. Enclosed note #2 is from Frances Coutell, his wife, who runs *Bridges'* office now. A delicate, washed-out beauty of twenty-three, bristling with spiritual needs; also a romantic masochist who, as you will surmise, has developed a crush on you, not least because she doesn't like you that much. Fiction does different things to different people, much like matrimony.

#1

Dear Joan: As you know I wasn't one of those who was taken by your brother's celebrated first novel. I found it much too proper a book, properly decorous and constrained on the formal side, and properly momentous (and much too pointed) in presenting its Serious Jewish Moral Issue. Obviously it was mature for a first novel—too obviously: the work of a gifted literature student straitjacketed by the idea that fiction is the means for proving righteousness and displaying intelligence; the book seems to me very much a relic of the fifties. The

Abraham and Isaac motif, rich with Kierkegaardian overtones, reeks (if I may say so) of those English departments located in the upper reaches of the Himalayas. What I like about the new stories, and why to my mind they represent a tremendous advance over the novel, is that they seem to me a deliberate and largely conscious two-pronged attack upon the prematurely grave and high-minded author of *A Jewish Father*. As I read it, in "Salad Days" the attack is frontal, head-on, and accomplished by means of social satire, and, more notably, what I'd call tender pornography, a very different thing, say, from the pornography of a Sade or a Terry Southern. For the author of that solemn first novel, a story like "Salad Days" is nothing less than blasphemous. He is to be congratulated heartily for triumphing (at least here) over all that repressive piety and fashionable Jewish angst. "Courting Disaster" is a more complicated case (and as a result not so successful, in a purely literary sense). As I would *like* to read it, the story is actually a disguised critical essay by Tarnopol on his own overrated first book, a commentary and a judgment on all that *principledness* that is *A Jewish Father*'s subject and its downfall. Whether Tarnopol intended it or not, I see in Zuckerman's devotion to Lydia (its joylessness, its sexlessness, it scrupulosity, its madly ethical motive) a kind of allegory of Tarnopol and his Muse. To the degree that this is so, to the degree that the character of Zuckerman embodies and represents the misguided and morbid "moral" imagination that produced *A Jewish Father*, it is fascinating; to the degree that Tarnopol is back on the angst kick, with all that implies about "moving" the reader, I think the story is retrograde, dull, and boring, and suggests that the conventional (rabbinical) side of this writer still has a stranglehold on what is reckless and intriguing in his talent. But whatever my reservations, "Courting Disaster" is well worth publishing, certainly in tandem with "Salad Days," a story that seems to me the work of a brand new Tarnopol, who, having objectified the high-minded moralist in him (and, hopefully, banished him to Europe forevermore, there to dwell in noble sadness with all the other "cultural monuments and literary landmarks"), has begun at last to flirt with the playful, the perverse, and the disreputable in himself. If Sharon Shatzky is your brother's new Muse, and a zucchini her magic wand, we may be in for something more valuable than still more fiction that is "moving." Lane.

#2

Joan: My two cents worth, only because the story L. admires most seems to me smug and vicious and infuriating, all the more so for being so *clever* and *winning*. It is pure sadistic trash and I pray (actually) that *Bridges* doesn't print it. Art is long, but the life of a little magazine is short, and much too short for *this*. I hate what he does with that suburban college girl—and I don't even mean what Zuckerman (the predictable prodigal son who *majors* in English) does but what the author does, which is just to twist her arm around behind her back and say, "You are not my equal, you can never be my equal—*understand?*" Who does he think he is, anyway? And why would he want to be such a thing? How could the man who wrote "Courting Disaster" want to write a heartless little story like that? And vice versa? Because the long story is absolutely heart*rending* and I think (contrary to L.'s cold-blooded analysis) that *this* is why it works utterly. I was moved to tears by it (but then I didn't perform brain surgery on it) and moved to the most aching admiration for the man who could just *conceive* such a story. The wife, the daughter, the husband are painfully true (I'm sure because he made me sure), and I shall never forget them. And Zuckerman *here* is completely true too, sympathetic, interesting, a believable observer and center of feeling, all the things he has to be. In a strange way they were all sympathetic to me, even the awful ones. Life is awful. Yours, Franny. P.S. I apologize for saying that something your brother wrote is hateful. I don't know him. And I don't think I want to. There are enough Jekyll and Hydes around here as it is. You're an older women, tell me something. What's the matter with men? What do they *want?*

My brother Morris, to whom copies of my latest stories were also sent in response to a letter inquiring about my welfare, had his own trenchant comments to make on "Courting Disaster"—comments not so unlike Joan's.

What is it with you Jewish writers? Madeleine Herzog, Deborah Rojack, the cutie-pie castrator in *After the Fall*, and isn't the desirable shiksa of *A New Life* a kvetch and titless in the bargain? And now, for the further delight of the rabbis and the reading public, Lydia Zuckerman, that Gentile tomato. Chicken soup in every pot, and a Grushenka in every garage. With all the Dark Ladies to choose from, you luftmenschen can really pick 'em. Peppy, why are you still wasting your talent on that Dead End Kid? Leave her to Heaven, okay? I'm speaking at Boston University at the end of the month, not that far from you. If you're still up on the mountain, come down and stay at the Commander with me. My subject is "Rationality, Planning, and Gratification Deferral." You could stand hearing about *a* and *b*; as for *c*, would you, a leading contender for the title in the highly competitive

Jewish Novelist Division, agree to give a black belt demonstration in same to the assembled students of social behavior? Peppy, *enough with her already!*

Back in 1960, following a public lecture *I* had delivered (my first) at Berkeley, Joan and Alvin gave a party for me at the house they had then up on a ridge in Palo Alto. Maureen and I had just returned to the U.S. from our year at the American Academy in Rome, and I had accepted a two-year appointment as "writer-in-residence" at the University of Wisconsin. In the previous twelve months I had become (according to an article in the Sunday *Times* book section) "the golden boy of American literature"; for *A Jewish Father*, my first novel, I had received the Prix de Rome of the American Academy of Arts and Letters, a Guggenheim grant of thirty-eight hundred dollars, and then my invitation to teach at Wisconsin. I myself had expected no less, back then; it was not my good fortune that surprised me at the age of twenty-seven.

Some sixty or seventy of their friends had been invited by Joan and Alvin to meet me; Maureen and I lost sight of one another only a few minutes after our arrival, and when she turned up at my side some time later I was talking rather self-consciously to an extremely seductive looking young beauty of about my own age, self-conscious precisely for fear of the scene of jealous rage that proximity to such a sexpot would inevitably provoke.

Maureen pretended at first that I was talking to no one; she wanted to go, she announced, all these "phonies" were more than she could take. I decided to ignore the remark—I did not know what else to do. Draw a sword and cut her head off? I didn't carry a sword at the time. I carried a stone face. The beautiful girl—from her décolletage it would have appeared that she was something of a daring tastemaker herself; I was too ill at ease, however, to make inquiries of a personal nature— the girl was asking me who my editor was. I told her his name; I said he happened also to be a good poet. "Oh, how could you!" whispered Maureen, and her eyes all at once flooded with tears; instantly she turned and disappeared into a bathroom. I found Joan within a few minutes and told her that Maureen and I had to go—it had been a long day and Maureen wasn't feeling well. "Pep," said Joan, taking my hand in hers, "why are you doing this to yourself?" "Doing what?" "Her," she said. I pretended not to know what she was talking about. Just presented her with my stone face. In the taxi to the hotel, Maureen wept like a child, repeatedly hammering at her knees (and mine) with her little fists. "How could you embarrass me like that—how could you say that, with me right there at your side!" "Say *what*?" "You know damn well, Peter! Say that *Walter* is your editor!" "But he *is*." "What about *me*?" she cried. "You?" "I'm your editor—you know very well I am! Only you refuse to admit it! I read every word you write, Peter. I make suggestions. I correct your spelling." "Those are typos, Maureen." "*But I correct them!* And then some rich bitch sticks her tits in your face and asks who your editor is and you say *Walter*! Why must you demean me like this—oh, why did you do that in front of that empty-headed girl? Just because she was all over you with those tits of hers? Mine are as big as hers—touch them some day and you'll see!" "Maureen, not this, not again—!" "Yes, again! And again and again! Because *you will not change!*" "But she meant my editor *at my publishing house!*" "But I'm your editor!" "You're not!" "I suppose I'm not your wife either! Why are you so ashamed of me! In front of those phonies, no less! People who wouldn't look twice at you if you weren't this month's cover boy! Oh, you baby! You infant! You hopeless egomaniac! Must you always be at the center of *everything*?" The next morning, before we left for the airport, Joan telephoned to the hotel to say goodbye. "We're always here," she told me. "I know." "If you want to come out and stay." "Well, thank you," I said, as formally as if I were acknowledging an offer from a perfect stranger, "maybe we'll take you up on it sometime." "I'm talking about you. Just you. You don't have to suffer like this, Peppy. You're proving nothing by being miserable, nothing at all." As soon as I hung up, Maureen said, "Oh, you could really have all the beautiful girls, couldn't you, Peter—with your sister out procuring for you. Oh, she would really enjoy that, I'm sure." "What the hell are you talking about *now*?" "That deprived little look on your face—'Oh, if I wasn't saddled with this witch, couldn't I have a time of it, screwing away to my heart's content at all the vapid twittering ingenues!'" "Again, Maureen? *Again?* Can't you at least let twenty-four hours go by?" "Well, what about that girl last night who wanted to know who your *editor* was? Oh, she really cared about that, I'm sure. Well, be honest, Peter, didn't you want to fuck her? You couldn't take your *eyes* off those tits of hers." "I suppose I noticed them." "Oh, I suppose you did." "Though apparently not so much as you, Maureen." "Oh, don't use your sardonic wit on me! Admit it! You *did* want to fuck her. You were *dying* to fuck her." "The fact of it is, I was close to catatonic in her presence." "Yes, *suppressing all that goddam lust!* How hard you have to work to suppress it—with everybody but me! Oh, admit it, tell the truth for *once*—if you had been alone, you know damn well you would have had her back here in this hotel! On this very bed! And *she* at least would have gotten laid last night! Which is more than I can say for me! Oh, why do you punish me like this— why do you lust after every woman in this whole wide world, *except your own wife.*"

My family . . . In marked contrast to Joan and Alvin and their children, Mab, Melissa, Kim, and Anthony, are my elder brother Morris, his wife Lenore, and the twins, Abner and Davey. In their home the dominant social concern is not with the accumulation of goods, but the means by which society can facilitate their equitable distribution. Morris is an authority on underdeveloped nations; *his* trips to Africa and the Caribbean are conducted under the auspices of the UN Commission for Economic Rehabilitation, one of several international bodies to which Moe serves as a consultant. He is a man who worries over everything, but nothing (excluding his family), nothing so much as social and economic inequality; what is now famous as "the culture of poverty" has been a heartbreaking obsession with him since the days he used to come home cursing with frustration from his job with the Jewish Welfare Board in the Bronx—during the late thirties, he worked there days while going to school nights at N.Y.U. After the war he married an adoring student, today a kindly, devoted, nervous, quiet woman, who some years ago, when the twins went off to kindergarten, enrolled at the School of Library Service at Columbia to take a master's degree. She is now a librarian for the city of New York. The twins are fifteen; last year both refused to leave the local upper West Side public school to become students at Horace Mann. On two consecutive days they were roughed up and robbed of their pennies by a Puerto Rican gang that has come to terrorize the corridors, lavatories, and basketball courts back of their school—nonetheless, they have refused to become "private school hypocrites," which is how they describe their neighborhood friends, the sons and daughters of Columbia faculty who have been removed from the local schools by their parents. To Morris, who worries continuously for their safety, the children shout indignantly, "How can you, of all people, suggest Horace Mann! How can you betray your own ideals! You're just as bad as Uncle Alvin! Worse!"

Moe has, he says, only himself to congratulate for their moral heroics; ever since they could understand an English sentence, he has been sharing with them his disappointment with the way this rich country is run. The history of the postwar years, with particular emphasis upon continuing social injustice and growing political repression, has been the stuff of their bed-time stories: instead of Snow White and the Seven Dwarfs, the strange adventures of Martin Dies and the House Un-American Activities Committee; instead of Pinocchio, Joe McCarthy; instead of Uncle Remus, tales of Paul Robeson and Martin Luther King. I can't remember once eating dinner at Moe's, that he was not conducting a seminar in left-wing politics for the two little boys wolfing down their pot roast and kasha— the Rosenbergs, Henry Wallace, Leon Trotsky, Eugene Debs, Norman Thomas, Dwight Macdonald, George Orwell, Harry Bridges, Samuel Gompers, just a few whose names are apt to be mentioned between appetizer and dessert—and, simultaneously, looking to see that everybody is eating what is best for him, pushing green vegetables, cautioning against soda pop gulped too quickly, and always checking the serving bowls to be sure there is Enough. "Sit!" he cries to his wife, who has been on her feet all day herself, and like an enormous lineman going after a loose fumble, rushes into the kitchen to get another quarter pound of butter from the refrigerator. "A glass of ice water, Pop!" calls Abner. "Who else for ice water? Peppy? You want another beer? I'll bring it anyway." His big paws full, he returns to the table, distributes the goods, waving for the boys to go on with what they were saying—intently he listens to them both, the one little boy arguing that Alger Hiss *must* have been a Communist spy, while the other (in a voice even louder than his brother's) tries to come to grips with the fact that Roy Cohn is a Jew.

It was to this household that I went to collapse. Moe, at my request, telephoned Maureen the first night after the Brooklyn College episode to say that I had been taken ill and was resting in bed at his apartment. She asked to speak to me; when Moe said; "He just can't talk now," she replied that she was getting on the next plane and coming East. Moe said, "Look, Maureen, he can't see anybody right now. He's in no condition to." "I'm his wife!" she reminded him. "But he cannot see *anybody*." "What is going on there, Morris, behind my back? He is not a baby, no matter how *you* people think of him. Are you listening to me? I demand to speak to my husband! I will not be put off by somebody who wants to play big brother to a man who has won the Prix de Rome!" But he was not intimidated, my big brother, and hung up.

At the end of two days of hiding behind his bulk, I told Moe I was "myself" again; I was going back to the Midwest. We had rented a cabin for the summer in the upper peninsula of Michigan, and I was anxious to get out of the apartment in Madison and up to the woods. I said I had to get back to my novel. "And to your beloved," he reminded me.

Moe made no secret ever of how much he disliked her; Maureen maintained that it was because, unlike his own wife, she, one, was a Gentile, and, two, had a mind of her own. I tried to give him the same stone face that I had given my sister when she had criticized my marriage and my mate. I hadn't yet told Moe, or anyone, what I had learned from Maureen two months earlier about the circumstances under which we had married—or about my affair with an undergraduate that Maureen had discovered. I just said, "She's my wife." "So you spoke to her today." "She's my *wife*, what do you expect me to do!" "She telephoned and so you picked it up and talked to her." "We talked, right." "Ah, you jerk-off! And do me a favor, will you, Peppy? Stop telling me she's your 'wife.' The word does not impress me to the extent it does you two. She's ruining you, Peppy! You're a wreck! You had a nervous breakdown here only *two* mornings ago! I don't want my kid brother cracking up—*do you understand that?*" "But I'm fine now." "Is that what your 'wife' told you you were on the phone?" "Moe, lay off. I'm not a frail flower." "But you are a frail flower, putz. You are a frail flower if I ever saw one! Look, Peppy— you were a very gifted boy. That should be obvious. You stepped out into the world like a big, complicated, hypersensitive million-dollar radar system, and along came Maureen, flying her four-ninety-eight model airplane right smack into the middle of it, and the whole thing went on the fritz. And it's still on the fritz from all I can see!" "I'm twenty-nine now, Moey." "But you're still worse than my fifteen-year-old kids! *They're* at least going to get killed in behalf of a noble ideal! But you I don't understand—trying to be a hero with a bitch who means *nothing*. *Why*, Peppy? Why are you destroying your young life with *her*? The world is full of kind and thoughtful and pretty young girls who would be *delighted* to keep a boy with your bella figura company. Peppy, you used to take them out by the dozens!"

I thought (not for the first time that week) of the kind and thoughtful and pretty young girl, my twenty-year-old student Karen Oakes, whose mistake it had been to involve herself with a Bluebeard like me. Maureen had just that afternoon— during the course of our *fifth* phone conversation of the hour; if I hung up, she just called back, and I felt duty bound to answer—Maureen had threatened once again to create a scandal at school for Karen—"that sweet young thing, with her bicycle and her braids, blowing her creative writing teacher!" —if I did not get on a plane and come home "instantly." But it wasn't to prevent the worst from happening that I was returning; no, whatever reckless act of revenge I thought I might forestall by doing as I was told and coming home, I was not so deluded as to believe that life with Maureen would ever get better. I was returning to find out what it would be like when it got even worse. How would it all end? Could I imagine the grand finale? Oh, I could, indeed. In the woods of Michigan she would raise her voice about Karen, and I would split her crazy head open with an ax—if, that is, she did not stab me in my sleep or poison my food, first. But one way or another, *I would be vindicated.* Yes, that was how I envisioned it. I had by then no more sense of reasonable alternatives than a character in a melodrama or a dream. As if I ever had, with her.

I never made it to Wisconsin. Over my protests, Moe went down in the elevator with me, got in the taxi with me, and rode with me all the way out to LaGuardia Airport; he stood directly behind me in the Northwest ticket line, and when his turn came, bought a seat on the same plane I was to take back to Madison. "You going to sleep in bed with us too?" I asked, in anger. "I don't know if I'll sleep," he said, "but I'll get in there if I have to."

Whereupon I collapsed for the second time. In the taxi back to Manhattan I told him, through my tearful blubbering, about the deception that Maureen had employed to get me to marry her. "Good Christ," he moaned, "you were really up against a pro, kiddo." "Was I? Was I?" I had my face pressed into his chest, and he was holding me in his two arms. "And you were still going back to her," he said, now with a groan. "I was going to kill her, Moey!" "You? *You* were?" "Yes! With an ax! With my bare hands!" "Oh, I'll bet. Oh, you poor, pussy-whipped bastard, I'll just bet you would have." "I would have," I croaked through my tears. "Look, you're just the same as when you were a kid. You can give it, but you can't take it. Only now, on top of that, you can't give it either." "Oh, why is that? *What happened?*" "The world didn't turn out to be the sixth-grade classroom at P.S. 3, that's what happened. With gribben on a fat slice of rye bread waiting for you when you got home from a day of wowing the teachers. You weren't ex-actly trained to take punishment, Peppy." Still weeping, but bitterly now, I asked him, "Is anybody?" "Well, from the look of things, your 'wife' got very good instruction in it—and I think she was planning to pass the torch on to you. She sounds to me just from our phone conversation like one of the great professors in the subject." "Yes?" You see, driving back from the airport that day I felt like somebody being filled in on what had transpired on earth during the sabbatical year he had just spent on Mars; I could have just stepped off a space ship, or out of steerage—I felt so green and strange and lost and dumb.

By late afternoon I was in Dr. Spielvogel's office; out in the waiting room Moe sat like a bouncer with his arms folded and his feet planted solidly on the floor, watching to be sure I did not slip off by myself to the airport. By nightfall Maureen was on her way East. Within two days I had notified the chairman of my department that I would be unable to return to my job in the fall. By the end of the week Maureen—having failed in several attempts to get past the door to Moe's apartment—had returned to Madison, cleared our stuff out of our apartment, and come East a second time; she moved into a hotel for transients on lower Broadway, and there she intended to remain, she said, until I had let go of my brother's apron strings and returned to our life together. Failing that, she said, she would do what I was "forcing" her to do through the courts. She told me on the phone (when it rang, I picked it up, Moe's instructions to the contrary notwithstanding) that my brother was a "woman hater" and my new analyst a "fraud." "He's not even licensed, Peter," she said of Spielvogel. "I looked him up. He's a European quack—practicing here without any credentials at all. He's not attached to a single psychoanalytic institute —no *wonder* he tells you to leave your wife!" "You're lying again, Maureen—you just made that up! You'll say anything!" "But *you're* the liar! You're the betrayer! You're the one who deceived me with that little student of yours! Carried on with her for months behind my back! While I cooked your dinner and washed your socks!" "And what did you do to get me to marry you in the first place! Just *what*!" "Oh, I *knew* I should never have told you that—I knew you would use that against me some day, to excuse yourself and your rotten philandering! Oh, how can you allow two such people to turn you against your own wife—when you were the guilty one, you were the one who was screwing those students left and right!" "I was *not* screwing students left and right—" "Peter, I caught you red-handed with that girl with the braids!" "*That is not left and right, Maureen!* And you are the one who turned me against you, with your crazy fucking paranoia!" "When? When did I do that, I'd like to know?" "From the *beginning*! Before we were even married!" "Then why on earth did you marry me, if I was so hateful to you even then? Just to punish me like this?" "I married you because you *tricked* me into marrying you! Why else!" "But that didn't mean you *had* to—you still could decide on your own! And you did, you liar! Don't you even remember what *happened?* You *asked* me to be your wife. You *proposed.*" "Because among other things you *threatened to kill yourself if I didn't!*" "And you mean to say you *believed* me?" "*What?*" "You actually believed that I would kill myself over *you?* Oh, you terrible narcissist! You selfish egomaniacal maniac! You actually do think that you are the be-all and end-all of human existence!" "No, no, it's *you* who think I am! Why else won't you leave me *alone!*" "Oh, Jesus," she moaned, "oh Jesus—haven't you ever heard of *love?*"

## 2. SUSAN: 1963–1966

It is now nearly a year since I decided that I would not marry Susan McCall and ended our long love affair. Until last year marrying Susan had been legally impossible because Maureen continued to refuse to grant me a divorce under the existing New York State matrimonial laws or to consent to a Mexican or out-of-state divorce. But then one sunny morning (only one short year ago), Maureen was dead, and I was a *widower*, free at last of the wife I had taken, entirely against my inclinations but in accordance with my principles, back in 1959. Free to take a new one, if I so desired.

Susan's own absurd marriage to the right Princeton boy had also ended with the death of her mate. It had been briefer even than my own, and also childless, and she wanted now to have a family before it was "too late." She was into her thirties and frightened of giving birth to a mongoloid child; I hadn't known how frightened until I happened by accident to come upon a secret stockpile of biology books that apparently had been picked up in a secondhand bookstore on Fourth Avenue. They were stuffed in a splitting carton on the floor of the pantry where I had gone in search of a fresh can of coffee one morning while Susan was off to her analyst's. I assumed at first that they were books she had accumulated years ago at school; then I noticed that two of them, *The Basic Facts of Human Heredity* by Amram Scheinfeld and *Human Heredity* by Ashley Montagu, hadn't been published until she was already living alone and widowed in her New York apartment.

Chapter Six of the Montagu book, "The Effects of Environment Upon the Developing Human Being in the Womb," was heavily marked with a black crayon, whether by Susan, or by whoever had owned the book before her, I had no sure way of knowing. "Studies of the reproductive development of the female show that from every point of view the best period during which the female may undertake the process of reproduction extends on the average from the age of twenty-one to about twenty-six years of age. . . . From the age of thirty-five years onward there is a sudden jump in the number of defective children that are born, especially of the type known as *mongoloids*. . . . In mongolism we have the tragic example of what may be an adequately sound genetic system being provided with an inadequate environment with resulting disordered development in the embryo." If it was not Susan who had done the heavy underlining, it was she who had copied out into the margin, in her round, neat schoolgirlish hand, the words "an inadequate environment."

A single paragraph describing mongoloid children was the only one on the page that had not been framed and scored with the black crayon; in its own simple and arresting way, however, it gave evidence of having been read no less desperately. The seven words that I italicize here had, in the book, been underlined by a yellow felt-tipped pen, the kind that Susan liked to use to encourage correspondents to believe that she was in the highest of spirits. "Mongoloid children may or may not have the fold of skin over the inner angle of the eye (epicanthic fold) or the flat root of the nose that goes with this, but they do have smallish heads, fissured tongues, a transverse palmar crease, with extreme intellectual retardation. Their I.Q. ranges between 15 and 29 points, from idiocy to the upper limit of about seven years. *Mongoloids are cheerful and very friendly personalities*, with often remarkable capacities for imitation and memories for music and complex situations which far outrank their other abilities. The expectation of life at birth is about nine years."

After almost an hour with these books on the pantry floor, I returned them to the carton, and when I saw Susan again that evening said nothing about them. Nothing to her, but thereafter I was as haunted by the image of Susan buying and reading her biology books as she was of giving birth to a monstrosity.

But I did not marry her. I had no doubt that she would be a loving and devoted mother and wife, but having been unable ever to extricate myself by legal means from a marriage into which I'd been coerced in the first place, I had deep misgivings about winding up imprisoned once again. During the four years that Maureen and I had been separated, her lawyer had three times subpoenaed me to appear in court in an attempt to get Maureen's alimony payments raised and my "hidden" bank accounts with their hidden millions revealed to the world. On each occasion I appeared, as summoned, with my packet of canceled checks, my bank statements, and my income tax returns to be grilled about my earnings and my expenses, and each time I came away from those proceedings swearing that I would never again put authority over my personal life into the hands of some pious disapproving householder known as a New York municipal judge. Never again would I be so stupid and reckless as to allow some burgher in black robes to tell me that I ought to "switch" to writing movies so as to make sufficient money to support the wife I had "abandoned." Henceforth *I* would decide with whom I would live, whom I would support, and for how long, and not the state of New York, whose matrimonial laws, as I had experienced them, seemed designed to keep a childless woman who refused to hold a job off the public dole, while teaching a lesson to the husband (me!) assumed to have "abandoned" his innocent and helpless wife for no other reason than to writhe in the fleshpots of Sodom. At those prices, would that it were so!

As my tone suggests, I had found myself as humiliated and compromised, and nearly as disfigured, by my unsuccessful effort to get unmarried as I had ever been by the marriage itself: over the four years of separation I had been followed to dinner by detectives, served with subpoenas in the dentist's chair, maligned in affidavits subsequently quoted in the press, labeled for what seemed like all eternity "a defendant," and judged by a man with whom I would not eat my dinner—and I did not know if I could undergo these indignities again, and the accompanying homicidal rage, without a stroke finishing me off on the witness stand. Once I even took a swing at Maureen's dapper (and, let it be known, elderly) lawyer in the corridor of the courthouse, when I learned that it was he who had invited the reporter from the *Daily News* to attend the hearing at which Maureen (for the occasion, in Peter Pan collar and tears) testified that I was "a well-known seducer of college girls." But that story of my swashbuckling in its turn. My point is that I had not responded with much equanimity to the role in which I was cast by the authorities and did not want to be tested by their system of sexual justice ever again.

But there were other, graver reasons not to marry, aside from my fear of divorce. Though I had never taken lightly Susan's history of emotional breakdown, the fact is that as her lover it had not weighed upon me as I expected it would if I were to become her husband and her offspring's father. In the years before we met, Susan had gone completely to pieces on three occasions: first, in her freshman (and only) year at Wellesley; then after her husband had been killed in a plane crash eleven months into their marriage; and most recently, when her father, whom she doted upon, had died in great pain of bone cancer. Each time she fell into a kind of waking coma and retired to a corner (or a closet) to sit mutely with her hands folded in her lap until someone saw fit to lift her onto a stretcher and carry her away. Under ordinary circumstances she managed to put down what she called her "everyday run-of-the-mill terror" with pills: she had through the years discovered a pill for just about every phobia that overcame her in the course of a day, and had been living on them, or not-living on them, since she had left home for college. There was a pill for the classroom, a pill for "dates," a pill for buying clothes, a pill for *returning* clothes, and needless to say, pills for getting started in the morning and dropping into oblivion at night. And a whole mixed bag of pills which she took like M&Ms when she had to converse, even on the phone, with her formidable mother.

After her father's death she had spent a month in Payne Whitney, where she'd become the patient of a Dr. Golding, reputedly a specialist with broken china. He had been her analyst for two years by the time I came along and had by then gotten her off everything except Ovaltine, her favorite childhood narcotic; in fact, he had encouraged the drinking of Ovaltine at bedtime and during the day when she was feeling distressed. Actually during the course of our affair Susan did not take so much as an aspirin for a headache, a perfect record, and one that might have served to assure me that *that* past was past. But then so had her record been "perfect" when she had enrolled at Wellesley at the age of eighteen, an A student from Princeton's Miss Fine's School for Young Ladies, and immediately developed such a fear of her German professor, a caustic young European refugee with a taste for leggy American girls, that instead of going off to his class she took a seat in the closet of her room every Monday, Wednesday, and Friday at ten A.M., and until the hour was over, hid out there, coasting along on the belladonna that she regularly obtained from Student Health for her menstrual cramps. By chance one day (and a merciful day it was) a dormitory chambermaid opened the closet door during Susan's German hour, and her mother was summoned from Princeton to take her out from behind her winter coats and away from Wellesley for good.

The possibility of such episodes recurring in the future alarmed me. I believe my sister and brother would argue that Susan's history of breakdowns was largely what had *intrigued* me and *attracted* me, and that my apprehension over what might happen to her, given the inevitable tensions and pressures of marriage, was the first sign I had displayed, since coming of age, that I had a modicum of common sense in matters pertaining to women. My own attitude toward my apprehensiveness is not so unambiguously approving; I still do not know from day to day whether it is cause for relief or remorse.

Then there is the painful matter of the elusive orgasm: no matter how she struggled to reach a climax, "it" never happened. And of course the harder she worked at it, the more like labor and the less like pleasure erotic life became. On the other hand, the intensity of her effort was as moving as anything about her—for in the beginning, she had been altogether content just to open her legs a little way and lie there, a well to pump if anyone should want to, and she herself couldn't imagine why anyone would, lovely and well formed as she was. It took much encouragement and, at the outset, much berating, to get her to be something more than a piece of meat on a spit that you turned this way and that until you were finished; *she* was never finished, but then she had never really begun.

What a thing it was to watch the appetite awaken in this shy and timid creature! And the daring—for if only she dared to, she might actually have what she wanted! I can see her still, teetering on the very edge of success. The pulse beats erratically in her throat, the jaw strains upward, the gray eyes *yearn*—just a yard, a foot, an inch to the tape, and victory over the self-denying past! Oh yes, I remember us well at our honest toil—pelvises grinding as though to grind down bone, fingers clutching at one another's buttocks, skin slick with sweat from forehead to feet, and our flushed cheeks (as we near total collapse) pressing so forcefully into one another that afterward her face is blotchy and bruised and my own is tender to the touch when I shave the following morning. Truly, I thought more than once that I might die of heart failure. "Though in a good cause," I whisper, when Susan had signaled at last a desire to throw in the towel for the night; drawing a finger over the cheekbone and across the bridge of the nose, I would check for tears—rather, *the* tear; she would rarely allow more than one to be shed, this touching hybrid of courage and fragility. "Oh," she whispers, "I was almost almost almost . . ." "Yes?" Then that tear. "Always," she says, "almost." "It'll happen." "It won't. You know it won't. What I consider almost is probably where everybody else begins." "I doubt it." "You don't . . . Peter, next time—what you were doing . . . do it—harder." So I did it, whatever it was, harder, or softer, or faster, or slower, or deeper, or shallower, or higher, or lower, as directed. Oh, how Mrs. Susan Seabury McCall of Princeton and Park Avenue tried to be bold, to be greedy, to be *low* ("Put it . . ." "Yes, say it, Suzie—" "Oh, in me from behind, but don't hurt—!")—not of course that living on bennies in a Wellesley dormitory in 1951 hadn't constituted an act of boldness for a society-bred, mother-disciplined, father-pampered young heiress from a distinguished New Jersey family, replete on the father's side with a U.S. senator and an ambassador to England, and on the mother's, with nineteenth-century industrial barons. But that diversion had been devised to annihilate temptation; now she *wanted* to want . . . Exhilarating to behold, but over the long haul utterly exhausting, and the truth was

that by the third year of our affair both of us were the worse
for wear and came to bed like workers doing overtime night
after night in a defense plant: in a good cause, for good wages,
but Christ how we wished the war was over and won and we
could rest and be happy.

I have of course to wonder now if Susan wouldn't have been
better off if I had deferred to her and simply left her alone
about coming. "I don't care about that," she had told me,
when I first broached the distressing subject. I suggested that
perhaps she *should* care. "Why don't you just worry about your
own fun . . ." said she. I told her that I was not worrying
about "fun." "Oh, don't be pretentious," she dared to mumble
—then, *begging*: "Please, what difference does it make to you
anyway?" The difference, I said, would be to her. "Oh, stop
trying to sound like the Good Sex Samaritan, will you? I'm
just not a nymphomaniac and I never was. I am what I am, and
if it's been good enough for everyone else—" "Has it?" "No!"
and out came the tear. So the resistance began to crumble, and
the struggle, which I initiated and to which I was accomplice
and accessory, began.

I should point out here that the distressing subject had been
a source of trouble between Maureen and myself as well: she
too was unable to reach a climax, but maintained that what
stood in her way was my "selfishness." Characteristically she
had confused the issue somewhat by leading me to believe for
the longest while that she and orgasms were on the very *best* of
terms—that I, in fact, had as much chance of holding her back
as a picket fence has of obstructing an avalanche. Well into the
first year of our marriage, I continued to look on in wonder at
the crescendo of passion that would culminate in her sustained
outcry of ecstasy when *I* began to ejaculate; you might even
say that my ejaculations sort of faded off into nothing beside
her clamorous writhings. It came as a surprise then (to coin a
phrase appropriate to these adventures) to learn that she had
actually been pretending, faking those operatic orgasms, she
explained, so as to protect me from the knowledge of just how
inadequate a lover I was. But how long could she keep up that
pretense in order to bolster my sense of manliness? What about
*her*, she wanted to know. Thereafter I was to hear repeatedly
how even Mezik, the brute who was her first husband, even

*Walker*, the homosexual who was her second, knew more about how to satisfy a woman than the selfish, inept, questionable heterosexual who was I.

Oh, you crazy bitch (if the widower may take a moment out to address the ghost of his wife), death is too good for you, really. Why isn't there a hell, with fire and brimstone? Why isn't there a devil and damnation? Why isn't there *sin* any more? Oh, if I were Dante, Maureen, I'd go about writing this another way!

At any rate: in that Maureen's accusations, no matter how patently bizarre, had a way of eating into my conscience, it very well might be that what Susan derided as my sexual good samaritanism was in part an attempt by me to disprove the allegations brought against me by a monumentally dissatisfied wife. I don't really know. I believe I meant well, though at the time I came to Susan there is no denying how dismayed I was by my record as a pleasure-giving man.

Obviously what drew me to Susan to begin with—only a year into my separation and still reeling—was that in temperament and social bearing she was as unlike Maureen as a woman could be. There was no confusing Maureen's recklessness, her instinct for scenes of wild accusation, her whole style of moral overkill, with Susan's sedate and mannerly masochism. To Susan McCall, speaking aloud and at length of disappointment, even to one's lover, was like putting an elbow on the dinner table, something One Just Didn't Do. She told herself that by making her heartache her business and nobody else's, she was being decorous and tactful, sparing another the inconsequential bellyaching of "a poor little rich girl," though of course the person she was sparing (and deluding) by being so absurdly taciturn and stoically blind about her life was herself. She was the one who didn't want to hear about it, or think about it, or do anything about it, even as she continued to suffer it in her own resigned and baffled way. The two women were wholly antithetical in their response to deprivation, one like a dumb, frightened kid in a street fight who knows no way to save his hide but to charge into the melee, head down and skinny arms windmilling before him, the other docile and done in, resigned to being banged around or trampled over. Even when Susan came to realize that she needn't settle any longer for a diet of bread and water, that it wasn't simply "okay" with me (and the rest of mankind) that she exhibit a more robust appetite, but that it made her decidedly more attractive and appealing, there was the lifelong style of forbearance, abstemiousness in all things but pharmaceuticals, there was the fadeaway voice, the shy averted glance, the auburn hair drawn austerely back in a knot at the back of the slender neck, there was the bottomless patience, the ethereal silence, that single tear, to mark her clearly as a member of another tribe, if not another sex, from Maureen.

It need hardly be pointed out that to me hers was a far more poignant struggle to witness (and be a party to) than that one in which Maureen had been so ferociously engaged—for where Maureen generally seemed to want to have something largely because someone else was able to have it (if I had been impotent, there is no doubt she would have been content to be frigid), Susan now wanted what she wanted in order to rid herself of the woman she had been. Her rival, the enemy whom she hoped to dispossess and drive into exile, if not extinction, was her own constrained and terrified self.

Poignant, moving, admirable, endearing—in the end, too much for me. I couldn't marry her. I couldn't do it. If and when I was ever to marry again, it would have to be someone in whose wholeness I had abounding faith and trust. And if no one drawing breath was *that* whole—admittedly I wasn't, my own capacity for faith and trust, among other things, in a state of serious disrepair—maybe that meant I would never remarry. So be it. Worse things had happened, one of them, I believed, to me.

So: freed from Maureen by her death, it seemed to me that I had either to go ahead and make Susan a wife and mother at thirty-four, or leave her so that she might find a man who would do just that before she became, in Dr. Montagu's words, a totally "inadequate environment" for procreation. Having been to battle for nearly all of my adult life, first with Maureen and then with the divorce laws of the state of New York—laws so rigid and punitive they came to seem to me the very codification of Maureen's "morality," the work of her hand—I no longer had the daring, or the heart, or the confidence to marry again. Susan would have to find some man who was braver, or stronger, or wiser, or maybe just more foolish and deluded—

Enough. I still don't know how to describe my decision to leave her, nor have I stopped trying to. As I asked at the outset: Has anything changed?

Susan tried to kill herself six months after I had pronounced the affair over. I was here in Vermont. After I left her, my days in New York, till then so bound up with hers, had become pointless and empty. I had my work, I had Dr. Spielvogel, but I had become used to something more, this woman. As it turned out, I was no less lonely for her here in my cabin, but at least I knew that the chances were greatly reduced that she would show up in the Vermont woods at midnight, as she did at my apartment on West Twelfth Street, where she could call into the intercom, "It's me, I miss you." And what do you do at that hour, *not* let her in? "You could," Dr. Spielvogel advised me, "take her home in a taxi, yes." "I did—at two." "Try it at midnight." So I did, came downstairs in my coat, to escort her out of the building and back to Park and Seventy-ninth. Sunday the buzzer went off in the morning. "Who is it?" "I brought you the *Times*. It's Sunday." "I know it's Sunday." "Well, I miss you like mad. How can we be apart on Sunday?" I released the lock on the downstairs door ("Take her home in a taxi; there are taxis on Sunday"—"But I miss *her*!") and she came on up the stairs, beaming, and invariably, Sunday after Sunday, we wound up making love in our earnest and strenuous way. "See," says Susan. "What?" "You do want me. Why are you acting as though you don't?" "You want to be married. You want to have children. And if that's what you want you should have it. But I myself don't, can't, and won't!" "But I'm not *her*. I'm *me*. I'm not out to torture you or coerce you into anything. Have I ever? Could I possibly? I only want to make you happy." "I can't do it. *I don't want to.*" "Then don't. You're the one who brought up marriage. I didn't say a word about it. You just said I can't do it and I have to go—and you went! But this is intolerable. Not living with you doesn't make sense. Not even seeing each other—it's just too bizarre." "I don't want to stand between you and a family, Susan." "Oh, Peter, you sound like some dope on a soap opera when you say that. If I have to choose between you and a family, I choose *you*." "But you want to be married, and if you want to be married, and if you want to have children, then you should have them. *But I don't, can't, and won't.*" "It's because I don't come, isn't it? And never will. Not even if you put it in my ear. Well, isn't it?" "No." "It's because I'm a junkie." "You are hardly a junkie." "But it is that, it's those pills I pop. You're afraid of having somebody like me on your hands forever—you want somebody better, somebody who comes like the post-man, through rain and snow and gloom of night, and doesn't sit in closets and can live without her Ovaltine at the age of thirty-four—and why shouldn't you? I would too, if I were you. I mean that. I understand completely. You're *right* about me." And out rolled the tear, and so I held her and told her no-no-it-isn't-so (what else, Dr. Spielvogel, is there to say at that moment—yes, you're absolutely correct?). "Oh, I don't blame you," said Susan, "I'm not even a person, really." "Oh, what are you then?" "I haven't been a person since I was sweet sixteen. I'm just symptoms. A collection of symptoms, instead of a human being."

These surprise visits continued sporadically over a period of four months and would have gone on indefinitely, I thought, if I just stayed on there in New York. Certainly, I could refuse to respond to the doorbell, pretend when she came by that I wasn't at home, but as I reminded Dr. Spielvogel when he suggested somewhat facetiously that I "marshal" my strength and forget about the bell—"it'll stop soon enough"—this was Susan I was dealing with, not Maureen. Eventually I packed a bag and, marshaling my strength, came up here.

Just before I left my apartment, however, I spent several hours writing Susan notes telling her where I was going—and then tearing them up. But what if she "needed" me? How could I just pick up and *disappear*? I ended up finally telling a couple who were our friends where I would be hiding out, assuming that the wife would pass this confidence on to Susan before my bus had even passed over the New York State line.

I did not hear a word from Susan for six weeks. Because she had been told where I was or because she hadn't?

Then one morning I was summoned from breakfast to the phone here at the Colony—it was our friends informing me that Susan had been found unconscious in her apartment and rushed by ambulance to the hospital. It seemed that the previous night she had finally accepted an invitation to dinner with a man; he had left her at her door around eleven, and she had come back into the apartment and swallowed all the Seconal and Tuinal and Placidyl that she had been secreting under her lingerie over the years. The cleaning lady had found her in the morning, befouled and in a heap on the bathroom floor, surrounded by empty vials and envelopes.

I got an afternoon flight from Rutland and was at the hospital by the evening visiting hours. When I arrived at the psychiatric ward, I was told she had just been transferred and was directed to a regular private room. The door was slightly ajar and I peered in—she was sitting up in bed, gaunt and scraggly looking and still very obviously dazed and disoriented, like a prisoner, I thought, who has just been returned from an all-night session with her interrogators. When she saw that it was me rapping on the door, out came the tear, and despite the presence of the formidable mother, who coolly took my measure from the bedside, she said, "I love you, that's why I did it."

After ten days in the hospital getting her strength back—and assuring Dr. Golding when he came around to visit each morning, that she would never again lay in a secret cache of sleeping pills—she was released in the care of her mother and went back home to New Jersey, where her father had been a professor of classics at Princeton until his death. Mrs. Seabury, according to Susan, was a veritable Calpurnia; in grace, in beauty, in carriage, in icy grandeur (and, said Susan, "in her own estimation") very much a Caesar's wife—and to top it off, Susan added hopelessly, she happened also to be *smart*. Yes, top marks, it turned out, from the very college where Susan hadn't been able to make it through her freshman year. I had always suspected that Susan might be exaggerating somewhat her mother's majesty—it was, after all, *her* mother—but at the hospital, when by chance our daily visits overlapped, I found myself not a little awed by the patrician confidence radiated by this woman from whom Susan had obviously inherited her own striking good looks, though not a Calpurnian presence. Mrs. Seabury and I had next to nothing to say to one another. She looked at me in fact (or so I imagined it, in those circumstances) as though she did not see there much opposition to be brooked. Only further evidence of her daughter's prodigality.

"Of course," her silence seemed to me to say, "of course it would be over the loss of a hysterical Jewish 'poet.'" In the corridors outside the hospital room of my suicidal mistress, it was difficult to rise to my own defense.

When I came down to Princeton to visit Susan, we two sat in the garden back of the brick house on Mercer Street, next door to where Einstein had lived (legend had it that as a little redheaded charmer, back in the years before she was just "symptoms," Susan used to give him candy to do her arithmetic homework); Madame Seabury, wearing pearls, sat with a book just inside the terrace door, no more than ten yards away—it was not *A Jewish Father* she was reading, I was sure. I had taken the train to Princeton to tell Susan that now that she was being looked after by her mother, I would be going back to Vermont. So long as she had been in the hospital, I had, at Dr. Golding's suggestion, been deliberately vague about my plans. "You don't have to tell her anything, one way or another." "What if she asks?" "I don't think she will," Golding said; "for the time being she's content that she got you down here. She won't push her luck." "Not yet. But what about when she gets out? What if she tries it again?" "I'll take care of that," said Golding, with a businesslike smile meant to close off conversation. I wanted to say: "You didn't take such marvelous care of 'that' last time!" But who was the runaway lover to blame the devoted doctor for the castoff mistress's suicide attempt?

It was a warmish March day, and Susan was wearing a clinging yellow jersey dress, looking very slinky for a young woman who generally preferred to keep her alluring body inconspicuous. Her hair, unknotted for the occasion, was a thick mane down her back; a narrow band of girlish freckles faintly showed across the bridge of her nose and her cheekbones. She had been out in the sun every afternoon—in her bikini, she let me know—and looked gorgeous. She could not keep her hands from her hair, and continuously, throughout our conversation, took it from behind her neck and pulled it like a thick, auburn rope over either shoulder; then, raising her chin just a touch, she would push the mass of hair back behind her neck with two open palms. The wide mouth and slightly protrusive jaw that gave a decisive and womanly quality to her delicate beauty, struck me suddenly as *prehistoric*, the sign of what was still raw and forceful in this bridled daughter of propriety and wealth. I had always found her beauty stirring, but never before had it seemed so thoroughly dominated by the sensuous. That was new. Where was Susan the interrogated prisoner? Susan the mousy widow? Susan the awesome mother's downtrodden Cinderella? All gone! Was it having toyed with suicide and gotten away with it that gave her the courage to be so blatantly tempting? Was it the proximity of the disapproving mother that was goading her on? Or was this her calculated last-ditch effort to arouse and lure back the fugitive from matrimony?

Whatever, I was aroused.

With her legs thrown over the filigreed arm of the white wrought-iron chaise, Susan's yellow dress rode high on her tanned thigh—I thought it must be the way she used to sit at age eight with Einstein, before she had begun to be educated by her fears. When she shifted in the chaise, or simply raised her arms to fool with her hair, the edge of her pale underpants came into view.

"Coming on very shameless," I said. "For my benefit or your mother's?"

"Both. Neither."

"I don't think she thinks the world of me to begin with."

"Nor of me."

"Then that won't help any, will it?"

"Please, *you're* 'coming on' like somebody's nanny."

Silence, while I watch that hair fan out in her two hands. One of her tanned legs is swinging to the slowest of beats over the arm of the garden chaise. This is not at all the scenario that I had constructed on the train coming down. I had not counted on a temptress, or an erection.

"She always thought I had the makings of a whore anyway," says Susan, frowning like any victimized adolescent.

"I doubt that."

"Oh, are you siding with my mother these days? It's a regular phalanx. Only you're the one who turned me against her."

"That tack won't work," I said flatly.

"What will then? Living here in my old room like the crazy daughter? Having college boys ask me for dates over the card catalogue in the library? Watching the eleven o'clock news, with my Ovaltine and my mom? What ever *has* worked?"

I didn't answer.

"I ruin everything," she announced.

"You want to tell me that I do?"

"I want to tell you that Maureen does—still! Now why did she have to go and get killed? What are all these people trying to do anyway, dying off on me this way? Everything was really just fine, until *she* upped and departed this life. But out of her clutches, Peter, you're even more haywire than you were *in*. Leaving me like that was *crazy*."

"I'm not haywire, I'm not crazy, and everything was not 'just fine.' You were biding your time. You want to be married and a mother. You dream about it."

"You're the one who dreams about it. You're the one who's obsessed with marriage. I told you I was willing to go ahead without—"

"But I don't want you going ahead 'without'! I don't want to be responsible for denying you *what you want*."

"But that's my worry, not yours. And I don't want it any more, I told you that. If I can't, I won't."

"Yes?—then what am I to make of all those books, Susan?"

"Which *books*?"

"Your volumes on human heredity."

She winced. "Oh." But the mildness of what she said next, the faint air of self-mockery, surprised me. And relieved me too, for in my impatience with what I took to be rather self-deluded assertions about living "without," I had gone further than I'd meant to. "Are *they* still around?" she asked, as though it was a teddy bear that I'd uncovered from a secret hiding place.

"Well, *I* didn't move them."

"I was going through a stage . . . as they say."

"What stage?"

"Pathetic. Morbid. Blue. That stage . . . When did you find them?"

"One morning. Only about a year ago."

"I see . . . Well—" All at once she seemed crushed by my discovery; I thought that she might scream. "Well," she said, inhaling deeply, "what next? What else have you found out about me?"

I shook my head.

"You should know—" she stopped.

I said nothing. But what should I know? *What should I know?*

"A Princeton hippie," said Susan, slyly smiling, "is taking me to a movie tonight. You should know that."

"Very nice," I said. "A new life."

"He picked me up at the library. Want to know what I'm reading these days?"

"Sure. What?"

"Everything about matricide I can get my hands on," she told me, through her teeth.

"Well, reading about matricide in a college library never killed anybody."

"Oh, I just went there because I was bored."

"In that dress?"

"Yes, in this dress. Why not? It's just a little dress to wear around the stacks, you know."

"I can see that."

"I'm thinking of marrying him, by the way."

"Who?"

"My hippie. He'd probably 'dig' a two-headed baby. And a decrepit 'old lady.'"

"That thigh staring me and your mother in the face doesn't look too decrepit."

"Oh," said Susan, "it won't kill you to look at it."

"Oh, it's not killing me," I said, and suppressed an urge to reach out and up and stroke what I saw.

"Okay," she said abruptly—"you can tell me what you came to tell me, Peter. I'm 'ready.' To use a serviceable phrase of my mother's, I've come to grips with reality. Shoot. You're never going to see me again."

"I don't see what's changed," I answered.

"You don't—I know you don't. You still think I'm Maureen. You still think I'm that terrible person."

"Hardly, Susan."

"But how can you go around never trusting anyone ever again just because of a screwball like that! *I* don't lie, Peter. *I* don't deceive. I'm *me. And don't give me that look.*"

"What look?"

"Oh, let's go up to my bedroom. The hell with Mother, I want to make love to you, terribly."

"*What look?*"

She closed her eyes. "Stop," she whispered. "Don't be furious with me. I swear to you, I didn't mean it that way. It was not blackmail, truly. I just could not bear any longer Being Brave."

"Then why didn't you call your doctor—instead of taking Maureen's favorite home remedy!"

"Because I didn't want him—I wanted *you*. But I didn't pursue you, did I? For six weeks you were up there in Vermont, and I didn't write, and I didn't phone, and I didn't get on an airplane—did I? Instead I went around day after day Being Brave, and not in Vermont either, but in the apartment where I used to eat and sleep with *you*. Finally I even came to grips with reality and accepted an invitation for dinner—and that was my biggest mistake. I tried to Start My Life Again, just like Dr. Golding told me to, and this very upright man that I went out with went ahead and gave me a lecture on how I oughtn't to depend upon people who were 'lacking in integrity.' He told me that he heard from a reliable source in publishing that you were lacking in integrity. Oh, he made me furious, Peter, and I told him I was going home, and so he got up and left with me, and when I got home I wanted to call you so, I wanted to speak to you so badly, and the only way I couldn't do it was to take the pills. I know it makes no sense, it was so utterly stupid, and I would never ever do it again. You don't know how sorry I am. And you may tell yourself that I did it out of anger with you, or to try to blackmail you, or to punish you, or because I actually took what that man said about you to heart—but it was none of that. It was just that I was so worn down from going around for six weeks Being Brave! Oh, let's go somewhere, to a motel room or *somewhere*. I want terribly to be fucked. That's all I've been thinking about down here for days. I feel like—a *fiend*. Oh, please, I'm going to scream, living with this mother of mine!"

Here that mother of hers was out through the terrace doors, across the patio, and into the garden before Susan could even brush away the tear or I could respond to her appeal. And what response would I have made? Her explanation did seem to me at that moment truthful and sufficient. Of course she did not lie or deceive, of course she was not Maureen. If I didn't want

Susan, I realized then, it was not because I didn't want her to sacrifice for me her dream of a marriage and a family; it was because I didn't want Susan any more, under any conditions. Nor did I want anyone else. I wanted only to be placed in sexual quarantine, to be weaned from the other sex forever.

Yet everything she said was so convincing.

Mrs. Seabury asked if I could come inside with her a moment.

"I take it," she said, when we were standing together just inside the terrace doors, "that you told her you don't plan to see her again."

"That's right."

"Then perhaps the best thing now would be to go."

"I think she's expecting me to take her to lunch."

"She has no such expectation that I know of. I can see to her lunch. And her welfare generally."

Outside Susan was now standing up beside the chaise. Both Mrs. Seabury and I were looking her way when she pulled the yellow jersey dress up over her head and let it fall to the lawn. It wasn't pale underpants I'd seen earlier beneath the skimpy dress, but a white bikini. She adjusted the back rest of the chaise until it was level with the seat and the foot rest, and then stretched herself out on it, face down. An arm hung limply over either side.

Mrs. Seabury said, "Staying any longer will only make it more difficult for her. It was very good of you," she said in her cool and unruffled way, "to visit her at the hospital every day. Dr. Golding agreed. That was the best thing to do in the situation, and we appreciate it. But now she must really make an effort to come to grips with reality. She must not be allowed to continue to act in ways that are not in her own interest. You must not let her work on your sympathies with her helplessness. She has been wooing people that way all her life. I tell you this for your own good—you must not imagine yourself in any way responsible for Susan's predicament. She has always been all too willing to collapse in other people's arms. We have tried to be kind and intelligent about this behavior always— she is what she is—but one must also be firm. And I don't think it would be kind, intelligent, or firm for you to forestall the inevitable any longer. She must begin to forget you, and the sooner the better. I am going to ask you to go now, Mr. Tarnopol, before my daughter once again does something that she will regret. She cannot afford much more remorse or humiliation. She hasn't the stamina for it."

Out in the garden, Susan had turned over and was lying now on her back, her legs as well as her arms dangling over the sides of the chaise—four limbs seemingly without strength.

I said to Mrs. Seabury, "I'll go out and say goodbye. I'll tell her I'm going."

"I could as easily tell her you've gone. She knows how to be weak but she also knows something about how to be strong. It's a matter of continually making it clear to her that people are not going to be manipulated by the childish ploys of a thirty-four-year-old woman."

"I'll just say goodbye."

"All right. I won't make an issue over a few more minutes," she said, though it was altogether clear now how little she liked being crossed by a hysterical Jewish poet. "She has been carrying on in that swimsuit for a week now. She greets the mailman in it every morning. Now she is exhibiting herself in it for you. Given that less than two weeks ago she tried to take her life, I would hope that you could summon up as much self-control as our mailman does and ignore the rather transparent display of teenage vampirism."

"That is not what I am responding to. I lived with Susan for over three years."

"I don't wish to hear about that. I was never delighted by that arrangement. I deplored it, in fact."

"I was only explaining to you why I'd prefer not to leave without at least telling her that I'm going."

She said, "It is not possible for you to leave because she is lying on her back with her legs spread apart and—"

"And," I replied, my face ablaze, "suppose that were the reason?"

"Is that all you people can think about?"

"Which 'people' are you referring to?"

"People like yourself and my daughter, experimenting with one another's genitals, up there in New York. When do you stop being adolescent transgressors and grow up? You know you never had the slightest intention of making Susan your wife. You are too much of a 'swinger' for that. Such people used to be called 'bohemians.' They don't believe in marriage, with its risks and its trials and its difficulties—only in sex, till it bores them. Well, that is your business—and your prerogative, I am sure, as an artist. But you should not be so reckless as to foist your elitist values upon someone like Susan, who happens to come from a different background and was raised according to more traditional standards of conduct. Look at her out there, trying so hard to be a sexpot for your benefit. How could you have wanted to put such a ridiculous idea in that girl's head? Of all the things to encourage a person like Susan to become! Why on earth couldn't you have left such an unlikely candidate alone? Must she be driven crazy with sex too? Must every last woman in the world be 'turned on' by you modern Don Juans? To what end, Mr. Tarnopol, other than to quench your unquenchable sexual vanity? Wasn't she confused and broken enough—without *this*?"

"I don't know where to begin to tell you that you're wrong."

I walked out into the garden and looked down at a body as familiar to me as my own.

"I'm going now," I said.

She opened her eyes against the sun, and she laughed, a small, rather surprisingly cynical laugh; then after a moment's contemplation, she raised the hand nearest to me from where it dangled to the ground and placed it between the legs of my trousers, directly on my penis. And she held me like that, her face now stolid and expressionless in the strong light. I did nothing but stand there, being held. From where she had stepped out onto the patio, Mrs. Seabury looked on.

This all couldn't have lasted as long as a minute.

She lowered her hand to her own bare stomach. "Go ahead," Susan whispered. "*Go.*" But just before I moved away she raised her body and pressed her cheek to my trousers.

"And I was 'wrong,'" said Mrs. Seabury, her voice harsh at last, as I passed through the living room to the street.

At the time we met, Susan was just thirty and had been living for eleven years in the co-op apartment at Park and Seventy-ninth that had become hers (along with the eighteenth-century

English marquetry furniture, the heavy velvet draperies, the Aubusson carpets, and two million dollars' worth of securities in McCall and McGee Industries) when the company plane bearing her young husband to a board meeting crashed into a mountainside in upstate New York eleven months into the marriage. In that marrying the young heir had been considered by everyone (excepting her father, who, characteristically, had remained silent) a fantastic stroke of luck for a girl who hadn't enough on the ball to survive two semesters at college, Susan (who eventually confided to me that she really hadn't liked McCall that much) took his death very hard. Believing that her chances were all used up at twenty, she retired to her bed and lay there, mute and motionless, every single day during the month of mourning. As a result she wound up doing woodwork for six months at a fashionable "health farm" down in Bucks County known as the Institute for Better Living. Her father would have preferred that she return to the house on Mercer Street after she had completed her convalescence, but Susan's "counselor" at the Institute had long talks with her about maturity and by the end of her stay had convinced her to return to the apartment at Park and Seventy-ninth and "give it a try on her own." To be sure, she too would have preferred to return to Princeton and the father she adored—doing "research" for him in the library, lunching with him at Lahiere's, hiking with him on weekends along the canal—if only living with her father didn't entail living under the gaze of her mother, that gaze that frightened her largely because it said, "You must grow up and you must go away."

In Manhattan, the rich and busy ladies in her building who "adopted" her made it their business to keep Susan occupied —running their errands for them during the week, and on Saturdays, Sundays, and holidays accompanying schoolchildren around town to be sure they didn't lose their mufflers and were home in time for supper (to which Susan, having sung her servile little lungs out for it, would sometimes be invited). That was what she did *for eleven years*—and, of course, she "fixed up" the apartment that she and this ghost named "Jamey" had never really "finished." Every few years she enrolled in a course at the night division at Columbia. Always she would take copious notes and diligently do all the reading, until such time as she began to fear that the professor was going to call upon her to speak. She would disappear then from the class, for a time, however, keeping up with the reading at home—even giving herself tests of her own devising. Men made some use of her over these eleven years, mostly after charity dinners and dances, which she attended on the arm of a bachelor nephew or some young cousin of the chairwoman, a rising something or other in the world. That was easy enough, and after a while did not even require eight hundred milligrams of Miltown for her to be able to "cope": she just opened her legs a little way, and he who was rising in the world did what little remained to be done. Sometimes the cousins and nephews (or maybe it was just the thoughtful chairwomen) sent her flowers the next day: she saved the cards in a folder in the file cabinet that contained her lecture notes and self-administered, ungraded examinations. "Will call. Great night. Love, A." or B. or C.

Early each summer there would generally be a knock on her apartment door: a man to ask if she would have dinner with him while his wife was away in the country. These were the husbands of the women in the building for whom she went around town all day picking up swatches of fabrics and straightening out errors in charge accounts. Their wives had told them what a lovely young person Susan was, and then they would themselves have caught sight of the five foot nine inch redhead when she was getting in and out of taxis in front of the building, her arms loaded with other people's Bergdorf boxes and her dress shimmying up her slender legs. One of these men, a handsome and charming investment banker ("like a father to me," the thirty-year-old widow told me, without blinking an eye), gave her a new electric range for a present when fall came and he wanted to be sure she kept her mouth shut; she didn't need a new range (not even to keep her mouth shut), but because she did not want to hurt his feelings, she had the one she and Jamey and the decorator had bought ripped out and the new one installed. And not one of these hot-weather paramours of hers, afflicted as he might be with middle-age wife-weariness, ever wanted to run off with the rich and beautiful young woman and start a new life—and that to Susan was as damning a fact as any in the prosecution's case against her self-esteem.

I didn't want to run off with her either. Yet I came back, night after night, returned to her apartment to eat and read and sleep, which was not what young A., B., C., D., or E. had ever done. And for good reason: they obviously had too much going for them, too much confidence and vitality and hope for the future, to settle for more than a night with the likes of Susan the Submissive. I, on the other hand, at the age of thirty, with my prizes and my publication behind me, had had it. I sat at dinner in Jamey's baronial chair, Susan serving me like a geisha. I shaved in Jamey's lacquered brothel of a bathroom, my towels warming on the electrical heating stand while I discovered the luxury of his Rolls razor. I read in his gargantuan club chair, my feet up on the ottoman covered in Jamey's mother's favorite flame stitch, a gift for his twenty-second (and last) birthday. I drank those rare vintages of Jamey's wine that Susan had kept at the proper temperature in an air-conditioned pantry all these years, as though she expected that he might rise from the grave one day and ask to taste his Richebourg. When my shoes got wet in a rainstorm, I stuffed them with his wooden shoe trees and padded around in his velvet slippers from Tripler's. I borrowed stays from his shirts. I weighed myself on his scale. And was generally bored by his wife. *But she did not make a single demand.*

All Susan said to me about our arrangement was this, and being Susan, she didn't even say it aloud: "I'm yours. I'll do anything. Come and go as you like. Let me feed you. Let me sit with you at night and watch you read. You can do anything you want to my body. I'll do anything you say. Just have dinner with me sometimes and use some of these things. And I'll never utter a peep. I'll be good as gold. I won't ask what you do when you go away. You don't have to take me anywhere. Just stay here sometimes and make use of whatever you want, including me. You see, I have all these thick bath-sized towels and Belgian lace tablecloths, all this lovely crockery, three bathrooms, two televisions, and two million dollars of Jamey's money with more of my own to come, I have these breasts and this vagina, these limbs, this skin—and no life. Give me just a little bit of that, and in return whenever you want to you can come here and recover from your wife. Any hour of the day or night. You don't even have to call beforehand."

It's a deal, I said. The broken shall succor the broken.

Of course, Susan was not the first young woman that I had met in New York since I'd come East seeking asylum in June of '62. She was just the first one I'd settled in with. According to the custom of that era—it is depressing to think that it may be the custom still—I had been to parties, befriended girls (which is to say, stood exchanging ironic quips with them in the corner of someone's crowded West Side apartment), and then had gone to bed with them, either before or after taking them out to dinner a couple of times. Some were undoubtedly nice people, but I didn't have the staying power or the confidence really to find out. Oftentimes during my first year in New York I discovered that I did not really want to take off my clothes or those of my new-found acquaintance, once we had gotten back to one or another of our apartments, and so I would fall into silent fits of melancholy that must have made me seem rather freakish—or at least affected. One young knockout, I remember, took it very personally and became incensed that I should suddenly have turned lugubrious on her after having been "so ferociously charming" with my back against the wall of one of those crowded living rooms; she asked if it was true that I was trying to kick being queer, and I, dim-witted as can be, began to struggle to remove her pantyhose, an act which turned out to consume such passion as I had. She took her leave shortly thereafter, and the following morning, going down for the paper and my seeded roll, I found wedged into the frame of the door an index card that had penciled on it, "Abandon Hope, All Ye Who Enter Here." Those parties I went to, with their ongoing intersexual competition in self-defense, bred a lot of this sort of scuffling, or maybe a little bit went a long way with me then; eventually invitations from editors and writers to parties where there would be "a lot of girls" I mostly turned down; when I didn't, I generally regretted it afterward.

Only months after my arrival, it became clear to me—depressingly so—that New York City was probably the worst possible place, outside of the Vatican, for a man in my predicament to try to put an end to his old life and begin a new one. As I was discovering at these parties, I was in no shape to get much pleasure out of my status as a "single" man; and, as I discovered

in my lawyer's office, the state of New York was hardly about
to grant that status *de jure* recognition. Indeed, now that the
Peter Tarnopols were New York residents, it looked as though
they would be husband and wife forever. Too late I learned
that had we gotten separated back in Wisconsin, we could, according to the law there, have been divorced after having voluntarily lived separate and apart for five years. (Of course, had I
returned to Wisconsin in June of '62, rather than staying on at
Morris's apartment and from there launching into my career as
Spielvogel's patient, it is doubtful that I ever could have managed to set myself up in Madison separate and apart from
Maureen.) But, as things turned out, in the sanctuary that I
had taken New York to be, the only grounds for divorce was
adultery, and since Maureen did not want to divorce me on
any grounds, and I had no way of knowing whether she was an
adulteress, or proving it even if I knew, it looked in all likeli-
hood as though I would be celebrating my golden wedding
anniversary on the steps of the State House in Albany. Moreover, because my lawyer had been unable to get Maureen and
her attorney to agree to a legal separation or to any kind of
financial settlement (let alone to a Mexican or Nevada divorce
that would have required mutual consent to be incontestable),
my official marital status in New York very shortly came to be
that of the guilty party in a separation action brought by a wife
against a husband who had "abandoned" her. Though we had
lived together as husband and wife for only three years, I was
ordered by the New York court to provide maintenance for my
abandoned wife to the tune of one hundred dollars a week,
and to provide it until death did us part. And in New York State
what else could part us?

I could, of course, have moved and taken up residence in
some state with a less restrictive divorce law, and for a while,
with the aid of *The Complete Guide to Divorce* by Samuel G.
Kling—the book that became my bedside Bible in that first bewildering phase of my life as a New York resident—I seriously
investigated the possibilities. Reading Kling I found out that in
some eleven states "separation without cohabitation and without reasonable expectation of reconciliation" was grounds for
divorce, after anywhere from eighteen months to three years.
One night I got out of bed at four A.M. and sat down and

wrote letters to the state universities in each of the eleven states and asked if there might be a job open for me in their department of English; within the month I had received offers from the universities of Florida, Delaware, and Wyoming. According to Kling, in the first two states "voluntary three-year separation" provided grounds for divorce; in Wyoming, only two years' separation was necessary. My lawyer was quick to advise me of the various means by which Maureen might attempt to contest such a divorce; he also let me know that upon granting me a divorce the out-of-state judge would in all probability order me to continue to pay the alimony set by the New York court in the separation judgment; furthermore (to answer my next question), if I refused after the divorce to make the alimony payments, I could be (and with Maureen as my antagonist, no doubt would be) hauled into court under state reciprocity agreements and held in contempt by the Florida or Delaware or Wyoming judge for failing to support my former spouse in New York. A divorce, my lawyer said, I might be able to pull off—but escape the alimony? never. Nonetheless, I went ahead and accepted a job teaching American literature and creative writing the following September in Laramie, Wyoming. I went immediately to the library and took out books on the West. I went up to the Museum of Natural History and walked among the Indian artifacts and the tableau of the American bison. I decided I would try to learn to ride a horse, at least a little, before I got out there. And I thought of the money I would not be paying to Dr. Spielvogel.

Some ten weeks later I wrote to tell the chairman of the English department in Laramie that because of unforeseen circumstances I would be unable to take the job. The unforeseen circumstance was the hopelessness I had begun to feel at the prospect of a two-year exile in Wyoming. After which I might be able to ride a horse, but I would *still* have to pay through the nose. *If* the divorce even went uncontested! And would Florida be any better? Less remote, but a year longer to qualify for the divorce, and the end result just as uncertain. It was about this time that I decided that the only way out was to leave America and its marital laws and reciprocal state agreements and begin my life anew as a stranger in a foreign country. Since I understood that Maureen could always attach future royalties if they were to come through a New York publishing house, I would have to sell world rights to my next book to my English publisher and receive all payment through him. Or why not start from scratch—grow a beard and change my name? . . . And who was to say there would ever be a next book?

I spent the following few months deciding whether to return to Italy, where I still had a few friends, or to try Norway, where chances were slim that anybody would ever find me (unless of course they went looking). How about Finland? I read all about Finland in the *Encyclopaedia Britannica*. High rate of literacy, long winters, and many trees. I imagined myself in Helsinki, and, while I was at it, Istanbul, Marrakesh, Lisbon, Aberdeen, and the Shetland Islands. Very good place to disappear, the Shetland Islands. Pop. 19,343, and not that far, really, from the North Pole. Principal industries, sheep farming and fishing. Also raise famous ponies. No mention in *Britannica* of treaty agreement with New York State for extradition of marital criminals. . . .

But, oh, if I was outraged in New York over all I had lost in that marriage, imagine how I would feel when I woke up bearded in my cottage on the moors in Scalloway to discover I had lost my country as well. What "freedom" would I have won then, speaking American to the ponies? What "justice" would I have made, an ironical Jewish novelist with a crook and a pack of sheep? And what's worse, suppose she found me out and followed me there, for all that my name is now Long Tom Dumphy? Not at all unlikely, given that I couldn't shake her in this, a country of two hundred million. Oh, imagine what that would be like, me with me stick and Maureen with her rage in the middle of the roarin' North Sea, and only 19,343 others to hold us apart?

So, unhappily (and not at all, really) I accepted my fate as a male resident of the state of New York of the republic of America who no longer cared to live with a wife whose preference it was to continue to live with (and off) him. I began, as they say, to try to make the best of it. Indeed, by the time I met Susan I was actually beginning to pass out of the first stages of shell shock (or was it fallout sickness?) and had even found myself rather taken with (as opposed to "taken by," very much a preoccupation at the time) a bright and engaging girl named Nancy Miles, fresh out of college and working as a "checker" for the *New Yorker*. Nancy Miles was eventually to go off to Paris to marry an American journalist stationed there, and subsequently to publish a book of autobiographical short stories, most of them based upon her childhood as a U.S. Navy commander's daughter in postwar Japan. However, the year I met her she was free as a bird, and soaring like one, too. I hadn't been so drawn to anyone since the Wisconsin debacle, when I had thrown myself at the feet of my nineteen-year-old student Karen (for whom I intermittently continued to pine, by the way; I imagined her sometimes with me and the sheep in Scalloway), but after three consecutive evenings together of nonstop dinner conversation, the last culminating in love-making as impassioned as anything I'd known since those illicit trysts between classes in Karen's room, I decided not to call Nancy again. Two weeks passed, and she sent me this letter:

Mr. Peter Tarnopol
Institute for Unpredictable Behavior
62 West 12th Street
New York, N.Y.

Dear Mr. Tarnopol:
    With reference to our meeting of 5/6/63:
    1. What happened?
    2. Where are we?
    While I fully recognize that numerous demands of this nature must strain the limits of your patience, I nonetheless make bold to request that you fill out the above questionnaire and return it to the address below as soon as it is convenient.

I remain,<br>yours,<br>Perplexed

Perplexed perhaps, but not broken. That was the last I heard from Nancy. I chose Susan.

It goes without saying that those seeking sanctuary have ordinarily to settle for something less than a seven-room apartment on the Upper East Side of Manhattan in which to take refuge from the wolves or the cops or the cold. I for one had never lived in anything approaching Susan's place for size and grandeur. Nor had I ever eaten so well in my life. Maureen's cooking wasn't that bad, but generally dinnertime was the hour reserved at our house for settling scores with me and my sex—unsettled scores that some evenings seemed to me to have been piling up ever since the first nucleic acid molecule went ahead and reproduced itself several billion years ago; consequently, even when the food was hot and tasty, the ambience was wrong. And in the years before I took to dining in each night on Maureen's gall, there had been army chow or university cafeteria stew. But Susan was a pro, trained by masters at what she had not learned at Calpurnia's knee: during the year she had been waiting for her fiancé to be graduated from Princeton and their life of beauty and abundance to begin, she had commuted up to New York to learn how to cook French, Italian, and Chinese specialties. The course in each cuisine lasted six weeks, and Susan stayed on (as she hadn't at Wellesley) triumphantly to complete all three. To her great glee she discovered she could now at least *outcook* her mother. Oh, what a wonderful wife (she hoped and prayed) she was going to make for this fantastic stroke of luck named James McCall the Third!

During her widowhood Susan had only rarely had the opportunity to feed anyone other than herself, and so it was that I became the first dinner guest ever to appreciate in full a culinary expertise that spanned the continents. I had never tasted food so delicious. And not even my own dutiful mother had waited on me the way this upper-crust waitress did. I was under standing instructions to proceed to eat without her, so that she could scamper freely back and forth into the kitchen getting the next dish going in her wok. Good enough. We had little outside of the food to talk about anyway. I asked about her family, I asked about her analysis, I asked about Jamey and the McCalls. I asked why she had left Wellesley in her first year. She shrugged and she flushed and she averted her eyes. She replied, oh they're very nice, and he's very nice, and she's such a sweet and thoughtful person, and "Why did I leave Wellesley? Oh, I just left." For weeks I got no more information or animation than I had the night we met, when I was seated next to her at the dinner party I was invited to annually at my publisher's town house: unswerving agreeableness, boundless timidity—a frail and terrified beauty. And in the beginning that was just fine with me. Bring on the blanquette de veau.

Each morning I headed back to the desk in my West Twelfth Street sublet, off to school to practice the three Rs—reading, writing, and angrily toting up yet again the alimony and legal bills. In the elevator, as I descended from 9D, I met up with the school-children a third my age whom Susan took on weekends to the Planetarium and the puppet shows, and the successful business executives whose August recreation she had sometimes been. And what am *I* doing here, I would ask myself. With *her*! Just how debilitated can I be! My brother's recent warning would frequently come back to me as I exited past the doorman, who always courteously raised his cap to Mrs. McCall's gentleman caller, but had surmised enough about my bankroll not to make a move to hail a cab. Moe had telephoned me about Susan the night after I had come around with her to have dinner at his and Lenore's invitation. He laid it right on the line. "Another Maureen, Pep?" "She's hardly a Maureen." "The gray eyes and the 'fine' bones have got you fooled, kiddo. Another fucked-up shiksa. First the lumpenproletariat, now the aristocracy. What are you, the Malinowski of Manhattan? Enough erotic anthropology. Get rid of her, Pep. You're sticking your plug in the same socket." "Moe, hold the advice, okay?" "Not this time. I don't care to come home a year from now, Peppy, to find you shitting into your socks." "But I'm all right." "Oh, Christ, here we go again." "Moey, I happen to know what I'm doing." "With a woman you know what you're doing? Look, what the hell is Spielvogel's attitude toward this budding catastrophe—what is *he* doing to earn his twenty bucks an hour, anything?" "Moe, she is *not* Maureen!" "You're letting the legs fool you, kid, the legs and the ass." "I tell you I'm not in it for that." "If not that, what? Her deep intelligence? Her quick wit? You mean on top of being tongue-tied, the ice cube can't screw right either? Jesus! A pretty face must go an awful long way with you—that, plus a good strong dose of psychoneurosis, and a girl is in business with my little brother. You come over here tonight for dinner, Peppy, you come eat with *us* every night— I've got to talk some sense into you." But each evening I turned up at Susan's, not Moe's, carrying with me my book to be read later by the fire, envisioning, as I stepped through the door, my blanquette, my bath, and my bed.

So the first months passed. Then one night I said, "Why don't you go back to college?" "Oh, I couldn't do that." "Why couldn't you?" "I have too much to do already." "You have nothing to do." "Are you *kidding*?" "Why don't you go back to college, Susan?" "I'm too busy, really. Did you say you *did* want kirsch on your fruit?"

Some weeks later. "Look, a suggestion." "Yes?" "Why don't you move in bed?" "Haven't you enough room?" "I mean move. Underneath me." "Oh, that. I just don't, that's all." "Well, try it. It might liven things up." "I'm happy as I am, thank you. Don't you like the spinach salad?" "*Listen* to me: why don't you move your body when I fuck you, Susan?" "Oh, please, let's just finish dinner." "I want you to move when I fuck you." "I told you, I'm happy as I am." "You're miserable as you are." "I'm not, and it's none of your business." "Do you know how to move?" "Oh, why are you torturing me like this?" "Do you want me to show you what I mean by 'move'?" "Stop *this*. I am not going to talk about it! I don't have to be shown anything, certainly not by you! Your life isn't such a model of order, you know." "What about college? Why don't you go back to college?" "Peter, *stop*. Please! Why are you *doing* this to me?" "Because the way you live is awful." "It is *not*." "It's crazy, really." "If it's so crazy then what are you doing here every night? I don't force you to spend the night. I don't ask anything of you at all." "You don't ask anything of anyone, so that's neither here nor there." "That's none of your business either." "It is my business." "*Why?* Why *yours*?" "Because I *am* here—because I *do* spend the night." "Oh, please, you must stop right now. Don't make me argue, please. I hate arguments and I refuse to participate in one. If you want to argue with somebody, go argue with your wife. I thought you come here *not* to fight."

She had a point, *the* point—here I need contend with *nothing*—but it stopped me only for a while. Eventually one night some two months later she jumped up from the table and, popping her one tear, said, "I can't go back to school, and leave me alone about it—I'm too old and I'm too stupid! What school would even take me!"

It turned out to be C.C.N.Y. They gave her credit for one semester's work at Wellesley. "This is just too silly. I'm practically thirty-one. People will laugh." "Which people are those?" "People. I'm not going to do it. By the time I graduated I'd be fifty." "What are you going to do instead till you're fifty, shop?" "I help my friends." "Those friends can hire fellows pulling rickshaws to help them the way you do." "That's just being cynical about people you don't like. I have a huge apartment to take care of, besides." "What are you so frightened of?" "That's not the issue." "What is it then?" "That you won't just let me do things the way I want to. Everything I do is wrong in your eyes. You're just like my mother. She never thinks I can do anything right either." "Well, I think you can." "Only because you're embarrassed by my stupidity. It doesn't do for your 'self-image' to be seen with such a sap—so the upshot is that in order to save *your* face, *I* have to go to college! And move in bed! I don't even know where C.C.N.Y. *is*—on a map! What if I'm the only person there who's white?" "Well, you may be the only person there quite *so* white—" "Don't joke—not now!" "You're going to be fine." "Oh, Peter," she moaned, and clinging to her napkin crawled into my lap to be rocked like a child—"what if I have to talk in class? What if they call on me?" Through my shirt I could feel *ice* packs on my back—her two hands. "What do I do *then?*" she pleaded. "Speak." "But if I *can't*. Oh, why are you putting me through this misery?" "You told me why. My self-image. So I can fuck you with a clear conscience." "Oh, you, you couldn't fuck anybody with a clear conscience—dumb, smart, or in between. And be *serious*. I'm so terrified I feel *faint*." Though not too terrified to utter aloud, for the first time in her life, that most dangerous of American words. The next afternoon I had one of those mock headlines printed up in a Times Square amusement palace and presented it to her at dinner, a phony tabloid with a black three-inch banner reading: SUSAN SAYS IT!

In the kitchen one night a year later I sat on a stool near the stove sipping a glass of the last of Jamey's Mouton-Rothschild, while Susan prepared ratatouille and practiced a talk she had to give the next morning in her introductory philosophy class, a five-minute discourse on the Skeptics. "I can't remember what comes next—*I can't do it*." "Concentrate." "But I'm *cooking* something." "It will cook itself." "Nothing cooks itself that tastes any good." "Then stop a minute and let's hear what you're going to say." "But I don't care about the Skeptics. And *you* don't, Peter. And nobody in my class cares, I can assure you of that. And what if I just can't talk? What if I open my mouth and nothing comes out? That's what happened to me at Wellesley." And to me at Brooklyn College, but I didn't tell her, not on that occasion. "Something," I said confidently, "will come out." "Yes? *What?*" "Words. Concentrate on the words the way you concentrate on the eggplant there—" "Would you come with me? On the subway? Just till I get up there?" "I'll even come to the class with you." "No! You mustn't! I'd be *paralyzed* if you were there." "But I'm here." "This is a kitchen," she said, smiling, but not all that happy. And then, with some further prodding, she went ahead and delivered her philosophy report, though more to the ratatouille than to me. "Perfect." "Yes?" "Yes." "Then why," asked Susan, who was turning out to be a wittier young widow than any of us had imagined, "then why do I have to do it again tomorrow? Why can't this count?" "Because it's a kitchen." "Shit," said Susan, "that's not fair."

Am I describing two people falling in love? If so, I didn't recognize it for that at the time. Even after a year, Susan's still seemed to me my hideout, my sanctuary from Maureen, her lawyer, and the courts of the state of New York, all of whom had designated me a *defendant*. But at Susan's I needed no more defense than a king upon his throne. Where else could I go to be so revered? The answer, friends, is nowhere; it had been a long time between salaams. The least I could do in exchange was to tell her how to live right. Admittedly, A Lot I Knew, but then it did not take much to know that it is better to be a full-time student at City College than a matriculated customer at Bergdorf's and Bonwit's from nine to five, and better, I believed, to be alive and panting during the sex act than in a state of petrifaction, if you are going to bother to perform the act at all. So I, ironically enough, coached my student in remedial copulation and public speaking, and she nursed me with the tenderest tenderness and the sweetest regard. A new experience all around. So was the falling in love, if that's what our mutual education and convalescence added up to. When she made the dean's list I was as proud as any papa, bought her a bracelet and dinner; and when she tried and failed to come, I was crushed and disbelieving, like a high-school teacher whose brilliant, impoverished student has somehow been turned down for the scholarship to Harvard. How could it be, after all those study sessions we had put in together? All that dedication and hard work! Where had we gone wrong? I have suggested how unnerving it was for me to be accomplice to that defeat—the fact is that somewhere along the way Susan's effort to reach an orgasm came to stand in my mind for the full recovery of us both. And maybe this, as much as anything, helped to make it unattainable, the responsibility for my salvation as well as her own being far too burdensome for her to bear . . . You see, I am not claiming here that I went about conducting this affair in the manner of a reclamation engineer—nor was I seeking to unseat Dr. Golding, who was paid to cure the sick and heal the wounded, and whose own theory, as it sifted through to me, seemed to be that the more paternal or patriarchal my influence upon Susan, the more remote the prospect of the orgasm. I thought one could make as good an argument against this line of speculation as for it, but I didn't try. I was neither theoretician nor diagnostician, nor for that matter much of a "father figure" in my own estimation. It would have seemed to me that you hadn't to penetrate very far beneath the surface of our affair to see that I was just another patient looking for the cure himself.

In fact, it required my doctor to get me to continue to take my medicine named Susan, when, along the way, I repeatedly complained that I'd had enough, that the medicine was exacerbating the ailment more than it might be curing it. Dr. Spielvogel did not take my brother Moe's view of Susan—no, with Spielvogel I did. "She's hopeless," I would tell him, "a frightened little sparrow." "You would prefer another vulture?" "Surely there must be something in between," thinking, as I spoke, of Nancy Miles, that soaring creature, and the letter I'd never answered. "But you don't have something in between. You have this." "But all that timidity, all that fear . . . The woman is a slave, Doctor, and not just to me—to everyone." "You prefer contentiousness? You miss the scenes of high drama, do you? With Maureen, so you told me, it was the

*Götterdämmerung* at breakfast, lunch, and dinner. What's wrong with a little peace and quiet with your meals?" "But there are times when she is a *mouse*." "Good enough," said Spielvogel, "who ever heard of a little mouse doing a grown man any serious harm?" "But what happens when the mouse wants to be married—and to me?" "How can she marry you? You are married already." "But when I'm no longer married." "There will be time to worry about that then, don't you think?" "No. I don't think that at all. What if when I should want to leave her, she tries to do herself in? She is not stable, Doctor, she is not strong—you must understand that." "Which are you talking about now, Maureen or Susan?" "I can tell them apart, I assure you. But that doesn't mean that it isn't beyond Susan, just because it happens also to be a specialty of Maureen's." "Has she threatened you with suicide if you should ever leave her?" "She wouldn't threaten me with anything. That isn't her way." "But you are certain that she would do it, if at some future date, when the issue arose, you chose not to marry her. That is the reason you want to give her up now." "I don't particularly 'want' to. I'm telling you I ought to." "But you are enjoying yourself somewhat, am I right?" "Somewhat, yes. More than somewhat. But I don't want to lead her on. She is not up to it. Neither am I." "But is it leading her on, to have an affair, two young people?" "Not in your eyes, perhaps." "In whose then? Your own?" "In Susan's, Doctor, in Susan's! Look, what if after the affair is no more, she cannot accept the fact and commits suicide? Answer that, will you?" "Over the loss of you she commits suicide?" "Yes!" "You think every woman in the world is going to kill herself over you?" "Oh, please, don't distort the point I'm making. Not 'every woman'—just the two I've wound up with." "Is this why you wind up with them?" "Is it? I'll think about it. Maybe so. But then that is yet another reason to dissolve this affair right *now*. Why continue if there is anything like a chance of that coming to pass? Why would you want to encourage me to do a thing like that?" "Was I encouraging 'that'? I was only encouraging you to find some pleasure and comfort in her compliant nature. I tell you, many a man would envy you. Not everybody would be so distressed as you by a mistress who is beautiful and submissive and rich, and a Cordon Bleu cook into the bargain." "And, conceivably, a suicide." "That remains to be seen. Many things are conceivable that have little basis in reality." "I'm afraid in my position I can't afford to be so cavalier about it." "Not cavalier. Only no more convinced than is warranted, in the circumstances. And no more terrified." "Look, I am not up to any more desperate stunts. I've got a right to be terrified. I was married to Maureen. I still am!" "Well then, if you feel so strongly, if you've been burned once and don't want to take the chance—" "I am saying, to repeat, that it may not be such a 'chance'—and I don't feel I have a right to take it. It's her life that is endangered, not mine." "'Endangered'? What a narcissistic melodrama you are writing here, Mr. Tarnopol. If I may offer a literary opinion." "Yes? Is that what it is?" "Isn't it?" "I don't always know, Doctor, exactly what you mean by 'narcissism.' What I think I am talking about is responsibility. You are the one who is talking about the pleasure and comforts in staying. You are the one who is talking about what is in it for me. You are the one who is telling me not to worry about Susan's expectations or vulnerability. It would seem to me that it's *you* who are inviting *me* to take the narcissistic line." "All right, if that's what you think, then leave her before it goes any further. You have this sense of responsibility to the woman—then act upon it." "But just a second ago you were suggesting that my sense of responsibility was *misplaced.* That my fears were *delusional.* Or weren't you?" "I think they are excessive, yes."

Right now I get no advice about Susan from anyone. I am here to be free of advisers—and temptation. Susan a temptation? Susan a temptress? What a word to describe her! Yet I have never ached for anyone like this before. As the saying goes, we'd been through a lot together, and not in the way that Maureen and I had been "through it." With Maureen it was the relentless *sameness* of the struggle that nearly drove me mad; no matter how much reason or intelligence or even brute force I tried to bring to bear upon our predicament, I could not change a thing—everything I did was futile, including of course doing nothing. With Susan there was struggle all right,

but then there were rewards. Things changed. *We* changed.
There was progress, development, marvelous and touching
transformations all around. Surely the last thing you could say
was that ours was a comfortable, settled arrangement that
came to an end because our pleasures had become tiresome
and stale. No, the progress *was* the pleasure, the transformations what gave me most delight—which is what has made her
attempt at suicide so crushing . . . what makes my yearning
for her all the more bewildering. Because now it looks as
though *nothing* has changed, and we are back where we began. I have to wonder if the letters I begin to write to her and
leave unfinished, if the phone calls I break off dialing before
the last digit, if that isn't me beginning to give way to the siren
song of The Woman Who Cannot Live Without You, She
Who Would Rather Be Dead Than Unwed—if this isn't me on
the brink again of making My Mistake, contriving to continue,
after a brief intermission, what Spielvogel would call my narcissistic melodrama. . . . But then it is no less distressing for
me to think that out of fear of My Mistake, I am making
another even worse: relinquishing for no good reason the generous, gentle, good-hearted, *un*-Maureenish woman with
whom I have actually come to be in love. I think to myself,
"Take this yearning seriously. You *want* her," and I rush to the
phone to call down to Princeton—and then at the phone I ask
myself if "love" has very much to do with it, if it isn't the vulnerability and brokenness, the *neediness*, to which I am being
drawn. Suppose it is really nothing more than a helpless beauty
in a bikini bathing suit taking hold of my cock as though it
were a lifeline, suppose it is only that that inspires this longing.
Such things have been known to happen. "Sexual vanity," as
Mrs. Seabury says. "Rescue fantasies," says Dr. Spielvogel,
"boyish dreams of Oedipal glory." "Fucked-up shiksas," my
brother says, "you can't resist them, Pep."

Meanwhile Susan remains under the care of her mother in
Princeton, and I remain up here, under my own.

## 3. MARRIAGE À LA MODE

Rapunzel, Rapunzel,
Let down your hair.
—from the Grimms' fairy tale

For those young men who reached their maturity in the fifties, and who aspired to be grown-up during that decade, when as one participant has written, everyone *wanted* to be thirty, there was considerable moral prestige in taking a wife, and hardly because a wife was going to be one's maidservant or "sexual object." Decency and Maturity, a young man's "seriousness," were at issue precisely because it was thought to be the other way around: in that the great world was so obviously a man's, it was only within marriage that an ordinary woman could hope to find equality and dignity. Indeed, we were led to believe by the defenders of womankind of our era that we were exploiting and degrading the women we *didn't* marry, rather than the ones we did. Unattached and on her own, a woman was supposedly not even able to go to the movies or out to a restaurant by herself, let alone perform an appendectomy or drive a truck. It was up to us then to give them the value and the purpose that society at large withheld—by marrying them. If we didn't marry women, who would? Ours, alas, was the only sex available for the job: the draft was on.

No wonder then that a young college-educated bourgeois male of my generation who scoffed at the idea of marriage for himself, who would just as soon eat out of cans or in cafeterias, sweep his own floor, make his own bed, and come and go with no binding legal attachments, finding female friendship and sexual adventure where and when he could and for no longer than he liked, laid himself open to the charge of "immaturity," if not "latent" or blatant "homosexuality." Or he was just plain "selfish." Or he was "frightened of responsibility." Or he could not "commit himself" (nice institutional phrase, that) to "a permanent relationship." Worst of all, most shameful of all, the chances were that this person who thought he was perfectly able to take care of himself on his own was in actuality "unable to love."

An awful lot of worrying was done in the fifties about whether people were able to love or not—I venture to say, much of it by young women in behalf of the young men who didn't particularly *want* them to wash their socks and cook their meals and bear their children and then tend them for the rest of their natural days. "But aren't you capable of loving anyone? Can't you think of anyone but yourself?" when translated from desperate fifties-feminese into plain English, generally meant "I want to get married and I want you to get married to."

Now I am sure that many of the young women of that period who set themselves up as specialists in loving hadn't a very clear idea of how strong a charge their emotions got from the instinct for survival—or how much those emotions arose out of the yearning to own and be owned, rather than from a reservoir of pure and selfless love that was the special property of themselves and their gender. After all, how lovable *are* men? Particularly men "unable to love"? No, there was more to all that talk about "commitment" and "permanent relationships" than many young women (and their chosen mates) were able to talk about or able at that time fully to understand: the more was the fact of female dependence, defenselessness, and vulnerability.

This hard fact of life was of course experienced and dealt with by women in accordance with personal endowments of intelligence and sanity and character. One imagines that there were brave and genuinely self-sacrificing decisions made by women who refused to accede to those profoundest of self-delusions, the ones that come cloaked in the guise of love; likewise, there was much misery in store for those who were never able to surrender their romantic illusions about the arrangement they had made in behalf of their helplessness, until they reached the lawyer's office, and he threw their way that buoy known as alimony. It has been said that those ferocious alimony battles that have raged in the courtrooms of this country during the last few decades, the way religious wars raged throughout Europe in the seventeenth century, were really "symbolic" in nature. My guess is that rather than serving as a symbol around which to organize other grievances and heartaches, the alimony battle frequently tended to clarify what was generally obscured by the metaphors with which marital arrangements were camouflaged by the partners themselves. The extent of the panic and rage aroused by the issue of alimony, the ferocity displayed by the people who were otherwise sane and civilized enough, testifies, I think, to the shocking—and humiliating—realization that came to couples in the courtroom about the fundamental role that each may actually have played in the other's life. "So, it has descended to this," the enraged contestants might say, glaring in hatred at one another—but even that was only an attempt to continue to hide from the most humiliating fact of all: that it really *was* this, all along.

Now I realize that it is possible to dismiss these generalizations as a manifestation of my bitterness and cynicism, and unfortunate consequence of my own horrific marriage and of the affair that recently ended so unhappily. Furthermore, it can be said that, having chosen women like Maureen and Susan (or, if you prefer, having had them chosen for me by my own aberrant, if not pathological, nature), I for one should not generalize, even loosely, about what men want (and get) from women, or what women want and get out of men. Well, I grant that I do not find myself feeling very "typical" at this moment, nor am I telling this story in order to argue that my life is representative of anything; nonetheless, I am naturally interested in looking around to see how much of my experience with women has been special to me and—if you must have it that way—my pathology, and how much is symptomatic of a more extensive social malaise. And looking around, I conclude this: in Maureen and Susan I came in contact with two of the more virulent strains of a virus to which only a few women among us are immune.

Outwardly, of course, Maureen and Susan couldn't have been more dissimilar, nor could either have had a stronger antipathy for the "type" she took the other to be. However, what drew them together as women—which is to say, what drew me to them, for that is the subject here—was that in her own extreme and vivid way, each of these antipathetic originals demonstrated that sense of defenselessness and vulnerability that has come to be a mark of their sex and is often at the core of their relations with men. That I came to be bound to Maureen by *my* helplessness does not mean that either of us ever really stopped envisioning *her* as the helpless victim and myself as the victimizer who had only to desist in his brutishness for everything to be put right and sexual justice to be done. So strong was the myth of male inviolability, of male dominance and potency, not only in Maureen's mind but in mine, that even when I went so far as to dress myself in a woman's clothes and thus concede that as a man I surrendered, even *then* I could never fully assent to the idea that in our household conventional assumptions about the strong and the weak did not adequately describe the situation. Right down to the end, I still saw Maureen, and she saw herself, as the damsel in distress; and in point of fact, beneath all that tough exterior, all those claims to being "in business for herself" and nobody's patsy, Maureen was actually more of a Susan than Susan was, *and to herself no less than to me.*

There is a growing body of opinion which maintains that by and large marriages, affairs, and sexual arrangements generally are made by masters in search of slaves: there are the dominant and the submissive, the brutish and the compliant, the exploiters and the exploited. What this formula fails to explain, among a million other things, is why so many of the "masters" appear themselves to be in bondage, oftentimes to their "slaves." I do not contend—to make the point yet again—that my story furnishes anything like an explanation or a paradigm; it is only an instance, a postchivalric instance to be sure, of what might be described as the Prince Charming phenomenon. In this version of the fairy tale the part of the maiden locked in the tower is played consecutively by Maureen Johnson Tarnopol and Susan Seabury McCall. I of course play the prince. My performance, as described here, may give rise to the sardonic suggestion that I should have played his horse. But, you see, it was not as an animal that I wished to be a star—it was decidedly *not* horsiness, goatishness, foxiness, lionliness, or beastliness in any form that I aspired to. I wanted to be humanish: manly, a man.

At the time when all this began, I would never even have thought it necessary to announce that as an aspiration—I was too confident at twenty-five that success was all but at hand—nor did I foresee a career in which being married and then trying to get unmarried would become my predominant activity and obsession. I would have laughed had anyone suggested that struggling with a woman over a marriage would come to occupy me in the way that exploring the South Pole had occupied Admiral Byrd—or writing *Madame Bovary* had occupied Flaubert. Clearly the last thing I could have imagined was myself, a dissident and skeptical member of my generation, succumbing to all that moralizing rhetoric about "permanent relationships." And, in truth, it did take something more than the rhetoric to do me in. It took a Maureen, wielding it. Yet the humbling fact remains: when the dissident and skeptical member of his generation was done in, it was on the same grounds as just about everyone else.

I was fooled by appearances, largely my own.

As a young writer already publishing stories in literary quarterlies, as one who resided in a Lower East Side basement apartment between Second Avenue and the Bowery, living on army savings and a twelve-hundred-dollar publisher's advance that I doled out to myself at thirty dollars a week, I did not think of myself as an ordinary or conventional university graduate of those times. My college acquaintances were all off becoming lawyers and doctors; a few who had been friends on the Brown literary magazine were working on advanced degrees in literature—prior to my induction into the army, I had myself served a year and a half in the Ph.D. program at the University of Chicago, before falling by the wayside, a casualty of "Bibliography" and "Anglo-Saxon"; the rest—the fraternity boys, the athletes, the business majors, those with whom I'd had little association at school—were by now already married and holding down nine-to-five jobs. Of course I dressed in blue button-down oxford shirts and wore my hair clipped short, but what else was I to wear, a serape? long curls? This was 1958. Besides, there were other ways in which it seemed to me I was distinguishable from the mass of my contemporaries: I read books and I wanted to write them. My master was not Mammon or Fun or Propriety, but Art, and Art of the earnest moral variety. I was by then already well into writing a novel about a retired Jewish haberdasher from the Bronx who on a trip to Europe with his wife nearly strangles to death a rude

German housewife in his rage over "the six million." The haberdasher was modeled upon my own kindly, excitable, hardworking Jewish father who had had a similar urge on a trip he and my mother had taken to visit me in the army; the haberdasher's GI son was modeled upon myself, and his experiences closely paralleled mine in Germany during my fourteen months as a corporal in Frankfurt. I had had a German girl friend, a student nurse, large and blonde as a Valkyrie, but sweet to the core, and all the confusion that she had aroused in my parents, and in me, was to be at the heart of the novel that eventually became *A Jewish Father*.

Over my desk I did not have a photograph of a sailboat or a dream house or a diapered child or a travel poster from a distant land, but words from Flaubert, advice to a young writer that I had copied out of one of his letters: "Be regular and orderly in your life like a bourgeois, so that you may be violent and original in your work." I appreciated the wisdom in this, and coming from Flaubert, the wit, but at twenty-five, for all my dedication to the art of fiction, for all the discipline and seriousness (and *awe*) with which I approached the Flaubertian vocation, I still wanted my life to be *somewhat* original, and if not violent, at least interesting, when the day's work was done. After all, hadn't Flaubert himself, before he settled down at his round table to become the tormented anchorite of modern literature, gone off as a gentleman-vagabond to the Nile, to climb the pyramids and sow his oats with dusky dancing girls?

So: Maureen Johnson, though not exactly Egyptian, struck me as someone who might add a little outside interest to my dedicated writer's life. Did she! Eventually she *displaced* the writing, she was so interesting. To begin with, she was twenty-nine years of age, that temptingly unknown creature of a young man's eroto-heroic imaginings, *an older woman*. Moreover, she had the hash marks to prove it. Not one but two divorces: first from the husband in Rochester, a Yugoslav saloonkeeper named Mezik, whose sixteen-year-old barmaid she had been; she claimed that Mezik, a heavy drinker with a strong right hook, had once "forced" her to go down on a friend of his, the manager of an upholstery factory—later she changed the story somewhat and said that the three of them had been drunk at the time, and that the men had drawn straws to see which of them young Maureen would go off with to the bedroom; she had decided to blow Mezik's buddy, rather than have intercourse with him, because it had seemed to her, in the circumstances and in her innocence, less demeaning. "It wasn't," she added. Then the marriage and divorce from Walker, a handsome young actor with a resonant voice and a marvelous profile who turned out to be a homosexual—that is to say, he'd "promised" Maureen he'd get over it after the wedding, but only got worse. Twice then she had been "betrayed" by men—nonetheless there was plenty of the scrapper in her when we met. And plenty of tough wit. "I am Duchess of Malfi still," was a line she pulled on me our first night in bed—not bad, I thought, not bad, even if it was obviously something her actor husband had taught her. She had the kind of crisp good looks that are associated with "dark Irishmen"—only a little marred in her case by a lantern jaw—a lithe, wiry little body (the body of a tomboyish prepubescent, except for the sizable conical breasts) and terrific energy and spirit. With her quick movements and alert eyes, she was like one of nature's undersized indefatigables, the bee or the hummingbird, who are out working the flowers from sunup to sundown, sipping from a million stamens in order to meet their minimum daily nutritional requirements. She jocularly boasted of having been the fastest runner, male or female, of her era in the Elmira, New York, grade-school system, and that (of all she told me) may well have been the truth. The night we met—at a poet's party uptown—she had challenged me to a footrace from the Astor Place subway station to my apartment two blocks away on East Ninth: "Winner calls the shots!" she cried, and off we went—I triumphed, but only by the length of a brownstone, and at the apartment, breathless from the race she'd run me, I said, "Okay, the spoils: take off your clothes," which she gladly (and rapidly) proceeded to do in the hallway where we stood, panting. Hot stuff, this (thought I); very *interesting*. Oh yes, she was fast, that girl—but I was faster, was I not? . . . Also, I should mention here, Maureen had these scores to settle with my sex, and rather large delusions about her gifts, which she had come to believe lay somewhere, anywhere, in the arts.

At the age of sixteen, an eleventh-grader, she had run away from her family's home in Elmira—a runaway, that got me too. I'd never met a real one before. What did her father do? "Everything. Nothing. Handyman. Night watchman. Who remembers any more?" Her mother? "Kept house. Drank. Oh, Christ, Peter, I forgot them long ago. And they, me." She ran off from Elmira to become—of course, an actress . . . but of all places, to Rochester. "What did I know?" she said, dismissing her innocence with a wave of the hand; a dead issue, that innocence. In Rochester she met Mezik ("married the brute—and then met his buddy"), and after three years of frustration with the second-raters in the local avant-garde theater group, switched to art school to become—an abstract painter. Following her divorce, she gave up painting—and the painter whose mistress she had become during her separation from Mezik and who had broken his "promise" to help get her in with his dealer in Detroit—and took harpsichord lessons while waiting on tables in Cambridge, Massachusetts, a town she'd heard had fewer types like Mezik in residence. There, just twenty-one, she married Walker of the Brattle Theater; five long years followed, of him and his Harvard boys. By the time we met, she had already tried wood sculpture in Greenwich Village (her teacher's wife was fiercely jealous of her, so she dropped it) and was back "in the theater," temporarily "in the production end"—that is, taking tickets and ushering at an off-Broadway theater on Christopher Street.

As I say, I believed all these reversals and recoveries, all this *movement* of hers, to be evidence of a game, audacious, and determined little spirit; and it was, it was. So too did this mess of history argue for a certain instability and lack of focus in her life. On the other hand, there was so much focus to my own, and always had been, that Maureen's chaotic, daredevil background had a decidedly exotic and romantic appeal. She had been around—and around. I liked that idea; I hadn't been anywhere really, not quite yet.

She was also something of a rough customer, and that was new to me too. At the time I took up with Maureen, I had for nearly a year been having a passionate affair with a college girl named Dina Dornbusch, a senior at Sarah Lawrence and the daughter of a wealthy Jewish family from Long Island. She was an ambitious literature and language major, and we met when she came to my basement apartment, along with four other coeds and a *Mademoiselle* editor, to interview me about my work. I had just gotten out of the army, and my "work" at the time consisted only of the six short stories that had been published in the quarterlies while I had been stationed in Frankfurt; that they had been read by these awed young girls was very nice to know. I already knew of course that they had been read with interest by New York book publishers and literary agents, for their numerous letters of inquiry had reached me in Germany, and upon returning to the U.S. after my discharge, I had chosen an agent and subsequently signed a publisher's contract that provided me with a modest advance for the novel I was writing. But that I had, while serving as a draftee in Germany, achieved enough "fame" for these girls to settle on me as the young American writer they wished to interview for a feature in the magazine, well, needless to say, that opened up a fantasy or two in my head. To be sure, I talked to them about Flaubert, about Salinger, about Mann, about my experiences in Germany and how I thought I might put them to use in fiction, but nonetheless I was wondering throughout how to get the girl with the marvelous legs and the earnest questions to stay behind when the others left.

Oh, why did I forsake Dina Dornbusch—for Maureen! Shall I tell you? Because Dina was still in college writing papers on "the technical perfection" of "Lycidas." Because Dina listened to me so intently, was so much my student, taking my opinions for her own. Because Dina's father gave us front-row seats to Broadway musicals that we had to go to see for fear of offending him. Because—yes, this is true, too; incredible, but true—because when Dina came in to visit me from school, practically all we did, from the moment she stepped into the doorway, was fuck. In short, because she was rich, pretty, protected, smart, sexy, adoring, young, vibrant, clever, confident, ambitious—that's why I gave her up for Maureen! She was a girl still, who had just about everything. I, I decided at twenty-five, was beyond "that." I wanted something called "a woman."

At twenty-nine, with two unhappy marriages behind her, with no rich, doting father, no gorgeous clothes, and no future, Maureen seemed to me to have earned all that was implied by that noun; she was certainly the first person of her sex I had ever known intimately to be so completely adrift and on her own. "I've always been more or less in business for my-self," she'd told me at the party where we'd met—straight, un-sentimental talk, and I liked it. With Dina, everybody seemed always to be in business for her. Likewise with myself.

Prior to Maureen, the closest I had come to a girl who had known real upheaval in her life was Grete, the student nurse in Frankfurt, whose family had been driven from Pomerania by the advancing Russian army. I used to be fascinated by what-ever she could tell me about her experience of the war, but that turned out to be next to nothing. Only a child of eight when the war ended, all she could remember of it was living in the country with her brothers and sisters and her mother, on a farm where they had eggs to eat, animals to play with, and spelling and arithmetic to learn in the village school. She re-membered that when the family, in flight in the spring of '45, finally ran into the American army, a GI had given her an orange; and on the farm sometimes, when the children were being particularly noisy, her mother used to put her hands up to her ears and say, "Children, quiet, quiet, you sound like a bunch of Jews." But that was as much contact as she seemed to have had with the catastrophe of the century. This did not make it so simple for me as one might think, nor did I in turn make it easy for Grete. Our affair frequently bewildered her because of my moodiness, and when she then appeared to be innocent of what it was that had made me sullen or short-tempered, I became even more difficult. Of course, she *had* been only eight when the European war ended—nonetheless, I could never really believe that she was simply a big, sweet, good-natured, commonsensical eighteen-year-old girl who did not care very much that I was a dark Jew and she a blonde Aryan. This suspiciousness, and my self-conscious struggle with it, turned up in the affair between the two young lovers depicted in *A Jewish Father.*

What I liked, you see, was something taxing in my love af-fairs, something problematical and puzzling to keep the imagi-nation going even when I was away from my books; I liked most being with young women who gave me something to think about, and not necessarily because we talked together about "ideas."

So, Maureen was a rough customer—I thought about that.

I wondered if I was "up"—nice word—to someone with her history and determination. It would seem by the way I hung in there that I decided that I at least ought to be. I had been up to Grete and the problems she raised for me, had I not? Why back away from difficulties, or disorder, or even turbulence—what was there to be afraid of? I honestly didn't know.

Besides, for a very long time, the overwhelming difficulty—Maureen's helplessness—was largely obscured by the fight in her and by the way in which she cast herself as the victim always of charlatans and ingrates, rather than as a person who hadn't the faintest idea of the relationship of beginning, middle, and end. When she fought me, I was at first so busy fighting back I didn't have time to see her defiance as the measure of her ineptitude and desperation. Till Maureen I had never even fought a man in anger—with my hands, that is; but I was much more combative at twenty-five than I am now and learned quickly enough how to disarm her of her favorite weapon, the spike of a high-heeled shoe. Eventually I came to realize that not even a good shaking such as parents administer to recalcitrant children was sufficient to stop her once she was on the warpath—it required a slap in the face to do that. "Just like Mezik!" screamed Maureen, dropping dramatically to the floor to cower before my violence (and pretending as best she could that it did not give her pleasure to have uncovered the brute in the high-minded young artist).

Of course by the time I got around to hitting her I was already in over my head and looking around for a way out of an affair that grew more distressing and bewildering—and frightening—practically by the hour. It was not only the depths of acrimony between us that had me reeling, but the shocking realization of this helplessness of hers, that which *drove* her to the episodes of wild and reckless rage. As the months passed I had gradually come to see that nothing she did ever worked—or, rather, I had finally come to penetrate the obfuscating rhetoric of betrayal and victimization in order to see it *that way*: the Christopher Street producer went back on his "promise" to lift her from the ticket office into the cast; the acting teacher in the West Forties who needed an assistant turned out to be a "a psychotic"; her boss at one job was "a slave driver," at the next, "a fool," at the next, "a lecher," and invariably, whenever

she quit in disgust or was fired and came home in angry tears
—whenever yet another of those "promises" that people were
forever making to her had been broken—she would return to
my basement apartment in the middle of the day to find me
over the typewriter, pouring sweat—as happens when I'm
feeling fluent—and reeking through my button-down oxford
shirt like a man who'd been out all day with the chain gang. At
the sight of me working away feverishly at what I wanted most
to do, her rage at the world of oppressors was further stoked by
jealousy of me—even though, as it happened, she greatly admired my few published stories, defended them vehemently
against all criticism, and enjoyed vicariously the small reputation that I was coming to have. But then vicariousness was her
nemesis: what she got through men was all she got. No wonder she could neither forgive nor forget him who had wronged
her by "forcing" her at sixteen into bed with his buddy, or him
who preferred the flesh of Harvard freshmen to her own; and
if she could not relinquish the bartender Mezik or the bit player
Walker, imagine the meaning she must have found in one
whose youthful earnestness and single-minded devotion to a
high artistic calling might magically become her own if only
she could partake forever of his flesh and blood.

Our affair was over (except that Maureen wouldn't move
out, and I hadn't the sense, or the foresight, to bequeath to her
my two rooms of secondhand furniture and take flight; having
never before been defeated in my life in anything that mattered,
I simply could not recognize defeat as a possibility for me,
certainly not at the hands of someone seemingly so inept)—
our affair was over, but for the shouting, when Maureen told
me . . . Well, you can guess what she told me. Anybody could
have seen it coming a mile away. Only I didn't. Why would a
woman want to fool Peter Tarnopol? Why would a woman
want to tell me a lie in order to get me to marry her? What
chance for happiness in such a union? No, no, it just could not
be. No one would be so silly and stupid as to do a thing like
that *and certainly not to me.* I Had Just Turned Twenty-Six. I
Was Writing A Serious Novel. I Had My Whole Life Ahead Of
Me. No—the way *I* pictured it, I would tell Maureen that this
affair of ours had obviously been a mistake from the beginning
and by now had become nothing but a nightmare for both of

us. "As much my fault as yours, Maureen"—I didn't believe it, but I would say it, for the sake of getting out without further altercation; the only sensible solution, I would say, was for each now to go his own separate way. How could we be anything but better off without all this useless conflict and demeaning violence in our lives? "We just"—I would tell her, in straight, unsentimental talk such as she liked to use herself—"we just don't have any business together any more." Yes, that's what I would say, and she would listen and nod in acquiescence (she would have to—I would be so decent about it, and so sensible) and she would go, with me wishing her good luck.

It didn't work out that way. Actually it was in the midst of one of the ten or fifteen quarrels that we had per day, now that she had decided to stay at home and take up writing herself, that I told her to leave. The argument, which began with her accusing me of trying to prevent her from writing fiction because I was "frightened" of competition from a woman, ended with her sinking her teeth into my wrist—whereupon, with my free hand, I bloodied her nose. "You and Mezik! No difference *at all!*" The barkeeper, she claimed, used to draw blood from her every single day during the last year of their married life—he had turned her nose "into a faucet." For me it was a first, however—and a shock. Likewise her teeth in my flesh was like nothing I had ever known before in my stable and unbloody past. I had been raised to be fearful and contemptuous of violence as a means of settling disputes or venting anger—my idea of manliness had little to do with dishing out physical punishment or being able to absorb it. Nor was I ashamed that I could do neither. To find Maureen's blood on my hand was in fact *un*manning, as disgraceful as her teeth marks on my wrist. "Go!" I screamed, "Get out of here!" And because she had never seen me in such a state before—I was so unhinged by rage that while she packed her suitcase I stood over her tearing the shirt off my own body—she left, borrowing my spare typewriter, however, so she could write a story about "a heartless infantile son-of-a-bitch so-called artist just like you!"

"Leave that typewriter where it is!" "But what will I write on then?" "Are you kidding? Are you *crazy*? You're going to 'expose' me, and you want me to give you the weapon to do it with?" "But you have *two* of them! Oh, I'm going to tell the world, Peter, I'll tell them just what a selfish, self-important, egomaniacal baby you are!" "Just go, Maureen—and *I'll* tell them! But I won't have any more fucking screaming and arguing and *biting* around here when I am trying to do my work!" "Oh fuck your high and mighty work! What about *my life*!" "Fuck your life, it's not my affair any longer! Get out of here! Oh, take it—take it and just go!" Maybe she thought (now that my shirt was hanging off me in strips) that I might start in next tearing *her* to shreds—for all at once she backed off and was out of the apartment, taking with her, to be sure, the old gray Remington Royal portable that had been my parents' bar mitzvah present to the hotshot assistant sports editor of the *Yonkers High Broadcaster.*

Three days later she was back at the door, in blue duffel coat and knee socks, wan and scrappy looking as a street urchin. Because she could not face her top-floor room on Carmine Street alone, she had spent the three days with friends of hers, a Village couple in their early fifties whom I couldn't stand, who in turn considered me and my narratives "square." The husband (advertised by Maureen as "an old friend of Kenneth Patchen's") had been Maureen's teacher when she first came to New York and went into wood sculpture. Months back she had declared that she had been badly misled by these two "schizorenos," but never explained how.

As was her way the morning after even the most horrendous scenes, she laughed off the violent encounter of three days earlier, asking me (in wonderment at my naiveté) how I could take seriously anything she may have said or done in anger. One aspect of my squareness (according to those who worked in wood) was that I had no more tolerance for the irregular or the eccentric than George F. Babbitt of Zenith, Middle America. I was not open to experience in my basement apartment on East Ninth the way those middle-aged beatniks were in their Bleecker Street loft. I was a nice Jewish boy from Westchester who cared only about Success. I was their Dina Dornbusch.

"Luckily I am," I told her, "otherwise you'd be at the bottom of the East River." She was sitting in a chair, still in her duffel coat; I had given no sign that I had any intention of allowing her to move back in. When she had gone to peck me on the cheek in the doorway, I had—again, to her amusement—pulled my head away. "Where's the typewriter?" I asked, my way of saying that as far as I was concerned the only excuse Maureen could have to be visiting me was to return what she had borrowed. "You middle-class monster!" she cried. "You throw me out into the street. I have to go sleep on somebody's floor with sixteen cats lapping my face all night long—and all you can think about is your portable typewriter! Your *things*. It's a thing, Peter, *a thing*—and I'm a human being!" "You could have slept at your own place, Maureen." "I was *lonely*. You don't understand that because you have ice in your heart instead of feelings. And my own place isn't a 'place,' as you so blithely put it—it's a shithole of an attic and you know it! *You* wouldn't sleep there for half an hour." "Where's the typewriter?" "The typewriter is a *thing*, damn it, an inanimate object! What about *me*?" and leaping from the chair, she charged, swinging her pocketbook like a shillelagh. "CLIP ME WITH THAT, MAUREEN, AND I'LL KILL YOU!" "Do it!" was her reply. "Kill me! Some man's going to—why not a 'civilized' one like you! Why not a follower of Flaubert!" Here she collapsed against me, and with her arms around my neck, began to sob. "Oh, Peter, I don't have anything. Nothing at all. I'm really lost, baby. I didn't want to go to them—I *had* to. Please, don't make me go away again right now. I haven't even had a shower in three days. Let me just take a shower. Let me just calm down—and this time I'll go forever, I promise." She then explained that the loft on Bleecker Street had been burglarized one night when all except the cats were out eating spaghetti on Fourteenth Street; my typewriter had been stolen, along with all of her friends' wood-carving tools, their recorders, and their Blatstein, which sounded to me like an automatic rifle but was a painting.

I didn't believe a word of it. She went off to the bathroom, and when I heard the shower running, I put my hand into the pocket of her duffel coat and after just a little fishing around in the crumpled Kleenex and the small change came up with a pawn ticket. If I hadn't been living half a block from the Bowery, I don't imagine it would have occurred to me that Maureen had taken the typewriter up the street for the cash. But I was learning—though not quite fast enough.

Now an even worldlier fellow than myself—George F.

Babbitt, say, of Zenith—would have remembered the old business adage, "Cut your losses," and after finding the pawn ticket, would have dropped it back into her pocket and said nothing. Shower her, humor her, and get her the hell out, George F. Babbitt would have said to himself, and peace and quiet will reign once again. Instead I rushed into the bathroom—no Babbitt I—where we screamed at each other with such ferocity that the young married couple upstairs, whose life we made a misery during these months (the husband, an editor at a publishing house, cuts me to this day), began to pound on the floor above with a broom handle. "You petty little thief! You *crook!*" "But I did it for you!" "For me? You pawned my typewriter for *me?*" "Yes!" "What are you *talking* about?" Here, with the water still beating down on her, she slumped to the bottom of the bathtub, and sitting on her haunches, began actually to keen in her woe. Unclothed, she would sometimes make me think of an alley cat—quick, wary, at once scrawny and strong; now, as she rocked and moaned with grief under the full blast of the shower, something about the weight and pointiness of her large conical breasts, and her dark hair plastered to her head, made her look to me like some woman out of the bush, a primitive whose picture you might come upon in *National Geographic*, praying to the sun-god to roll back the waters. "Because—" she howled, "because I'm pregnant. Because—because I wasn't going to tell you. Because I was going to get the money however I could and get an abortion and never bother you again. Peter, I've been shoplifting too." "Stealing? Where?" "Altman's—a little from Klein's. I *had* to!" "But you *can't* be pregnant, Maureen—*we haven't slept together for weeks!*" "BUT I AM! TWO MONTHS PREGNANT!" "Two months?" "Yes! And I never said a word, because I didn't want to interfere with your ART!" "Well you should have, goddam it, because I would have given you the money to go out and get an abortion!" "Oh, you are so generous—! But it's too late—I've taken enough from men like you in my life! You're going to marry me or I'm going to kill myself! And I will do it!" she cried, hammering defiantly on the rim of the tub with her two little fists. "This is no empty threat, Peter—I cannot take you people any more! You selfish, spoiled, immature, irresponsible

Ivy League bastards, born with those spoons in your mouths!"
The silver spoon was somewhat hyperbolic, and even she knew
that much, but she was hysterical, and in hysteria, as she eventually made clear to me, anything goes. "With your big fat advance and your high Art—oh, you make me sick the way you
hide from life behind that *Art* of yours! I hate you and I hate
that fucking Flaubert, and you are going to marry me, Peter,
because I have had enough! I'm not going to be another
man's helpless victim! You are not going to dump me the way
you dumped that girl!"

"That girl" was how she referred to Dina, toward whom
she had never until that moment been anything but dismis-
sive; now, all at once, she invoked in her own behalf not just
Dina, but Grete *and* the Pembroke undergraduate who had
been my girl friend during my senior year at Brown. All of
them shared with Maureen the experience of being "discarded" when I had finished having my "way" with them.
"But we are not leftovers, Peter; we're not trash or scum and
we will not be treated that way! We are human beings, and we
will not be thrown into a garbage pail by *you*!" "You're not
pregnant, Maureen, and you know damn well you're not.
That's what all this 'we' business is about," I said, suddenly,
with perfect confidence. And with that, she all but collapsed—"We're not *talking* about me right now," she said,
"we're talking about *you*. Don't you know *yet* why you got rid
of your Pembroke pal? Or your German girl friend? Or that
girl who had everything? Or why you're getting rid of me?" I
said, "You're not pregnant, Maureen. That is a lie." "It is
not—and listen to me! Do you have no idea at all why it is you
are so afraid of marriage and children and a family and treat
women the way that you do? Do you know what you really
are, Peter, aside from being a heartless, selfish writing machine?" I said, "A fag." "That's right! And making light of it
doesn't make it any less true!" "I would think it makes it
more true." "It does! You are the most transparent latent homosexual I have ever run across in my life! Just like big brave
Mezik who forced me to blow his buddy—*so that he could
watch.* Because it's really what he wanted to do himself—but
he didn't even have the guts for that!" "*Forced* you? Oh, come
on, pal, you've got pointy teeth in that mouth of yours—I've

felt your fangs. Why didn't you bite it off and teach them both a lesson, if you were being *forced* to?" "I should have! Don't you think I didn't think of it! Don't you think a woman doesn't think of it every time! And don't you worry, mister, if they weren't twelve inches taller than me, I would have bitten the thing off at the root! And spit on the bleeding stump—just like I spit on you, you high and mighty Artist, for throwing me two months pregnant out into the street!" But she was weeping so, that the spittle meant for me just rolled down her lips onto her chin.

She slept in the bed that night (first bed in three days, I was reminded) and I sat at my desk in the living room, thinking about running away—not because she continued to insist she had missed two periods in a row, but because she was so tenaciously hanging on to what I was certain was a lie. I could leave right then for any number of places. I had friends up in Providence, a young faculty couple who'd gladly put me up for a while. I had an army buddy in Boston, graduate-school colleagues still out in Chicago, there was my sister Joan in California. And of course brother Morris uptown, if I should require spiritual comfort and physical refuge near at hand. He would take me in for as long as was necessary, no questions asked. Since I'd settled in New York, I had been getting phone calls from Moe every couple of weeks checking to see if there was anything I needed and reminding me to come to dinner whenever I was in the mood. At his invitation I had even taken Maureen up to their apartment one Sunday morning for bagels and the smoked fish spread. To my surprise, she had appeared rather cowed by my brother's bearish manner (Moe is a great one to cross-examine strangers), and the general intensity of the family life seemed to make her morose; she did not have much to say after we left, except that Moe and I were very different people. I agreed; Moe was very much the public man (the university, the UN commissions, political meetings and organizations ever since high school) and very much the paterfamilias . . . She said, "I meant he's a brute." "A what?" "The way he treats that wife of his. It's unspeakable." "He's nuts about her, for Christ's sake." "Oh? Is that why he walks all over her? What a little sparrow *she* is! Has she ever had an idea of her own in her life? She just sits there, eating his crumbs.

And that's her life." "Oh, that's not her life, Maureen." "Sorry, I don't like him—or her."

Moe didn't like Maureen either, but at the outset said nothing, assuming it was my affair not his, and that she was just the girl of the moment. As I had assumed myself. But when combat between Maureen and me stepped up dramatically, and I apparently began to look and sound as confused and embattled as I'd become, Moe tried on a couple of occasions to give me some brotherly advice; each time I shook him off. As I still couldn't imagine any long-range calamity befalling me, I objected strenuously to being "babied," as I thought of it—particularly by someone whose life, though admirable, was *grounded* in ways I was just too young to be concerned about. As I saw it, it was essential for me to be able to confront whatever troubles I'd made for myself without his, or anyone else's, assistance. In brief, I was as arrogant (and blind) as youth and luck and an aristocratic literary bent could make me, and so, when he invited me up to Columbia for lunch I told him, "I'll work it all out, don't worry." "But why should it be 'work'? Your *work* is your work, not this little Indian." "I take it that's some kind of euphemism. For the record, the mother's family was Irish, the father's German." "Yeah? She looks a little Apache to me, with those eyes and that hair. There's something savage there, Peppy. No? All right, don't answer. Sneer now, pay later. You weren't brought up for savagery, kid." "I know. Nice boy. Jewish." "What's so bad about that? You are a nice civilized Jewish boy, with some talent and some brains. How much remains to be seen. Why don't you attend to that and leave the lions to Hemingway." "What is that supposed to mean, Moey?" "You. You look like you've been sleeping in the jungle." "Nope. Just down on Ninth Street." "I thought girls were for fun, Pep. Not to scare the shit out of you." I was offended both by his low-mindedness and his meddling and refused to talk further about it. Afterward I looked in the mirror for the signs of fear—or doom. I saw nothing: still looked like Tarnopol the Triumphant to me.

The morning after Maureen had announced herself pregnant, I told her to take a specimen of urine to the pharmacy on Second and Ninth; that way, said I without hiding my skepticism, we could shortly learn just how pregnant she was. "In other words, you don't believe me. You want to close your eyes to the whole thing!" "Just take the urine and shut up." So she did as she was told: took a specimen of urine to the drugstore for the pregnancy test—only it wasn't her urine. I did not find this out until three years later, when she confessed to me (in the midst of a suicide attempt) that she had gone from my apartment to the drugstore by way of Tompkins Square Park, lately the hippie center of the East Village, but back in the fifties still a place for the neighborhood poor to congregate and take the sun. There she approached a pregnant Negro woman pushing a baby carriage and told her she represented a scientific organization willing to pay the woman for a sample of her urine. Negotiations ensued. Agreement reached, they retired to the hallway of a tenement building on Avenue B to complete the transaction. The pregnant woman pulled her underpants down to her knees, and squatting in a corner of the unsavory hallway—still heaped with rubbish (just as Maureen had described it) when I paid an unsentimental visit to the scene of the crime upon my return to New York only a few years later—delivered forth into Maureen's preserve jar the stream that sealed my fate. Here Maureen forked over two dollars and twenty-five cents. She drove a hard bargain, my wife.

During the four days that we had to wait—according to Maureen—for the result of the pregnancy test, she lay on my bed recalling scenes and conversations out of her wasted past: delirious (or feigning delirium—or both), she quarreled once again with Mezik, screamed her hatred at Mezik's buddy from the upholstery factory, and choked and wept with despair to discover Walker in their bathroom in Cambridge, dressed in her underwear, his own white sweat socks stuffed into the cups of the brassiere. She would not eat; she would not converse; she refused to let me telephone the psychiatrist who had once tried treating her for a couple of months; when I called her friends over on Bleecker Street, she refused to talk to them. I went ahead anyway and suggested to them that they might want to come over and see her—maybe they at least could get her to eat something—whereupon the wife grabbed the phone away from the husband and said, "We don't want to see that one again *ever*," and hung up. So, all was not well with the "schizorenos" on Bleecker Street either, after Maureen's brief visit . . . And I was afraid now to leave the apartment for fear that she would try to kill herself when I was gone. I had never lived through three such days before in my life, though I was to know a hundred more just as grim and frightening in the years to come.

The night before we were to learn the test results, Maureen abruptly stopped "hallucinating" and got up from bed to wash her face and drink some orange juice. At first she wouldn't speak directly to me, but for an hour sat perfectly still, calm and controlled, in a chair in the living room, wrapped in my bathrobe. Finally I told her that as she was up and around, I was going out to take a walk around the block. "Don't try anything," I said, "I'm just going to get some air." Her tone, in response, was mild and sardonic. "Air? Oh, where, I wonder?" "I'm taking a walk around the block." "You're about to leave me, Peter, I know that. Just the way you've left every girl you've ever known. Find 'em-fuck 'em-and-forget 'em Flaubert." "I'll be right back." When I unlatched the door to go out, she said, as though addressing a judge from the witness stand— prophetic bitch!—"And I never saw him again, Your Honor."

I went around to the drugstore and asked the pharmacist if by any chance the result of Mrs. Tarnopol's pregnancy test— so Maureen had identified herself, just a bit prematurely—due back tomorrow might have come in that night. He told me the result had come in that morning. Maureen had gotten it wrong—we hadn't to wait four days, only three. Was the error inadvertent? Just one of her "mistakes"? ("So I make mistakes!" she'd cry. "I'm not perfect, damn it! Why must everybody in this world be a perfect robot—a compulsive little middle-class success machine, like you! Some of us are *human*.") But if not a mistake, if intentional, why? Out of habit? An addiction to falsification? Or was this *her* art of fiction, "creativity" gone awry . . . ?

Harder to fathom was the result. How could Maureen be pregnant for two whole months and manage to keep it from me? It made no sense. Such restraint was beyond her— represented everything she was *not*. Why would she have let me throw her out that first time without striking back with this secret? It made no sense. *It could not be.*

Only it was. Two months pregnant, by me.

Only *how?* I could not even remember the last time we two had had intercourse. Yet she was pregnant, *somehow*, and if I didn't marry her, she would take her life rather than endure the humiliation of an abortion or an adoption or of abandoning a fatherless child. It went without saying that she, who could not hold a job for more than six months, was incapable of raising a child on her own. And it went without saying—to me, to me—that the father of this fatherless child-to-be was Peter Tarnopol. Never once did it occur to me that if indeed she were pregnant, someone other than I might have done it. Yes, I already knew what a liar she was, yet surely not so thoroughgoing as to want to deceive me about something as serious as fatherhood. *That* I couldn't believe. This woman was not a character out of a play by Strindberg or a novel by Hardy, but someone with whom I'd been living on the Lower East Side of Manhattan, sixty minutes by subway and bus from Yonkers, where I'd been born.

Now, unduly credulous as I may have been, I still needn't have married her; had I been so independent, so manly, so "up" to travail as I aspired to be in my middle twenties, she would never have become my wife, even if a laboratory test had "scientifically" proved that she was with child and even if I had been willing to accept on faith that mine was the penis responsible. I could still have said this: "You want to kill yourself, that's your business. You don't want an abortion, also up to you. But I'm not getting married to you, Maureen, under any circumstances. Marrying you would be insane."

But instead of going home to tell her just that, I walked from Ninth Street all the way up to Columbia and back, concluding on upper Broadway—only two blocks from Morris's building—that the truly manly way to face up to my predicament was to go back to the apartment, pretending that I still did not know the result of the pregnancy test, and deliver the following oration: "Maureen, what's been going on here for three days makes no sense. I don't care if you're pregnant or not. I want you to marry me, regardless of how the test comes out tomorrow. I want you to be my wife." You see, I just couldn't believe, given her behavior during the past three days, that she was bluffing about doing herself in; I was sure that if I walked out on her for good, she would kill herself. And that was unthinkable—I could not be the cause of another's death. Such a suicide was murder. So I would marry her instead. And, further, I would do my best to make it appear that in marrying her I had acted out of choice rather than necessity, for if our union were to be anything other than a nightmare of recrimination and resentment, it would have to appear to Maureen— and even, in a way, to me—that I had married her because I had decided that I wanted to, rather than because I had been blackmailed, or threatened, or terrorized into it.

But why ever would I want to? The whole thing made no sense—especially as we had not copulated in God only knew how long! And I never wanted to again! I hated her.

Yes, it was indeed one of those grim and unyielding predicaments such as I had read about in fiction, such as Thomas Mann might have had in mind when he wrote in an autobiographical sketch the sentence that I had already chosen as one of the two portentous epigraphs for *A Jewish Father*: "All actuality is deadly earnest, and it is morality itself that, one with life, forbids us to be true to the guileless unrealism of our youth."

It seemed then that I was making one of those moral decisions that I had heard so much about in college literature courses. But how different it all had been up in the Ivy League, when it was happening to Lord Jim and Kate Croy and Ivan Karamazov instead of to me. Oh, what an authority on dilemmas I had been in the senior honors seminar! Perhaps if I had not fallen so in love with these complicated fictions of moral anguish, I never would have taken that long anguished walk to the Upper West Side and back, and arrived at what seemed to me the only "honorable" decision for a young man as morally "serious" as myself. But then I do not mean to attribute my ignorance to my teachers, or my delusions to books. Teachers and books are still the best things that ever happened to me, and probably had I not been so grandiose about my honor, my integrity, and my manly duty, about "morality itself," I would never have been so susceptible to a literary education and its attendant pleasures to begin with. Nor would I have embarked upon a literary career. And it's too late now to say that I shouldn't have, that by becoming a writer I only exacerbated my debilitating obsession. Literature got me into this and literature is gonna have to get me out. My writing is all I've got now, and though it happens not to have made life easy for me either in the years since my auspicious debut, it is really all I trust.

My trouble in my middle twenties was that rich with confidence and success, I was not about to settle for complexity and depth in books alone. Stuffed to the gills with great fiction— entranced not by cheap romances, like Madame Bovary, but by *Madame Bovary*—I now expected to find in everyday experience that same sense of the difficult and the deadly earnest that informed the novels I admired most. My model of reality, deduced from reading the masters, had at its heart *intractability*. And here it was, a reality as obdurate and recalcitrant and (in addition) as awful as any I could have wished for in my most bookish dreams. You might even say that the ordeal that my daily life was shortly to become was only Dame Fortune smiling down on "the golden boy of American literature" (*New York Times Book Review*, September 1959) and dishing out to her precocious favorite whatever literary sensibility required. Want complexity? Difficulty? Intractability? Want the deadly earnest? Yours!

Of course what I also wanted was that my intractable existence should take place at an appropriately lofty moral altitude, an elevation somewhere, say, between *The Brothers Karamazov* and *The Wings of the Dove*. But then not even the golden can expect to have everything: instead of the intractability of serious fiction, I got the intractability of soap opera. Resistant enough, but the wrong genre. Though maybe not, given the leading characters in the drama, of which Maureen, I admit, was only one.

I returned to Ninth Street a little after eleven; I had been gone nearly three hours. Maureen, to my surprise, was now completely dressed and sitting at my desk in her duffel coat.

"You didn't do it," she said, and lowering her face to the desk, began to cry.

"Where were you going, Maureen?" Probably back to her room; *I* assumed to the East River, to jump in.

"I thought you were on a plane to Frankfurt."

"What were you going to do, Maureen?"

"What's the difference . . ."

"Maureen! Look up at me."

"Oh, what's the difference any more, Peter. Go, go back to that Long Island girl, with her pleated skirts and her cashmere sweaters."

"Maureen, listen to me: I want to marry you. I don't care whether you're pregnant or not. I don't care what the test says tomorrow. I want to marry you." I sounded to myself about as convincing as the romantic lead in a high-school play. I think it may have been in that moment that my face became the piece of stone I was to carry around on my neck for years thereafter. "Let's get married," I said, as if saying it yet again, another way, would fool anyone about my real feelings.

Yet it fooled Maureen. I could have proposed in Pig Latin and fooled Maureen. She could of course carry on in the most bizarre and unpredictable ways, but in all those years of surprises, I would never be so stunned by her wildest demonstration of rage, her most reckless public ravings, as I was by the statement with which she greeted this proposal so obviously delivered without heart or hope.

She erupted, "Oh, darling, we'll be happy as kings!"

That was the word—"kings," plural—uttered wholly ingenuously. I don't think she was lying this time. She believed that to be so. We would be happy as kings. Maureen Johnson and Peter Tarnopol.

She threw her arms around me, as happy as I had ever seen her—and for the first time I realized that she *was* truly mad. I had just proposed marriage to a madwoman. In deadly earnest.

"Oh, I always knew it," she said joyously.

"Knew what?"

"That you loved me. That you couldn't hold out forever against that kind of love. Not even you."

She was crazy.

And what did that make of me? A "man"? *How?*

She went on and on about the paradise that lay before us. We could move to the country and save money by growing our own vegetables. Or continue to live in the city where she could become my agent (I had an agent, but no matter). Or she could just stay home and bake bread and type my manuscripts (I typed my own, but no matter) and get back to her wood sculpture.

"You'll have to stay at home anyway," I said. "The baby."

"Oh, lovey," she said. "I'll do it—for you. Because you *do* love me. You see, that's all I had to find out—that you loved me. That you weren't Mezik, that you weren't Walker. *That I could trust you.* Don't you understand? Now that I know, I'll do anything."

"Meaning?"

"Peter, stop being suspicious—you don't *have* to be any more. I'll have an abortion. If the test comes back tomorrow saying that I'm pregnant—and it will, I've never missed two periods before in my life, never—but don't worry, I'll go off and get an abortion. Whatever you want, I'll do it. I know of a doctor. In Coney Island. And I'll go to him, if you want me to."

I wanted her to, all right. I'd wanted her to right at the out-set, and had she agreed then, I would never have made my "manly" proposal of marriage. But better now than not at all. And so the next day, after I phoned the drugstore and pre-tended to be hearing for the first time the lab report verifying Mrs. Tarnopol's pregnancy, I went to the bank and withdrew ten weeks' worth of advance and another twenty dollars for the round-trip taxi fare to Coney Island. And on Saturday morning, I put Maureen in a taxi and she went off to Coney Island by herself, which she said was the only way the abor-tionist would receive his patients. I stood out on Second Ave-nue watching the cab move south, and I thought: "Now get out. Take a plane to anywhere, but go while the going is good." But I didn't, because that isn't what a man like myself did. Or so I "reasoned."

Besides, in bed the night before, Maureen had wept in fear-ful anticipation of the illegal operation (had she had the abor-tion, it would actually have been her third, I eventually found out) and clinging to me, she begged, "You won't desert me, will you? You'll be here when I get home—won't you? Be-cause I couldn't take it if you weren't . . ." "I'll be here," said I, manfully.

And there I was when she returned at four that afternoon, my fond lover, pale and wan (the strain of sitting six hours at the movies), wearing a Kotex between her legs to absorb the blood (said she), and still in pain from the abortion she had undergone (said she) without an anesthetic. She went immediately to bed to ward off the hemorrhage that she feared was coming on, and there she lay, on into the night, teeth chattering, limbs trembling, in an old, washed-out sweatshirt of mine and a pair of my pajamas. I piled blankets on top of her, but that still didn't stop her shaking. "He just stuck his knife up there," she said, "and wouldn't give me anything for the pain but a tennis ball to squeeze. He promised he would put me out, on the phone he promised me, and then when I was on the table and said, 'Where's the anesthetic?', he said, 'What do you think, girlie, I'm out of my mind?' I said, 'But you promised. How else can I possibly stand the pain?' And you know what he told me, that smelly old bastard? 'Look, you want to get up and go, fine with me. You want me to get rid of the baby, then squeeze the magic ball and shut up. You had your fun, now you're going to have to pay.' So I stayed, I stayed and I squeezed down on the ball, and I tried to think just about you and me, but it hurt, oh, he hurt me so much."

A horrifying tale of humiliation and suffering at the hands of yet another member of my sex, and a lie from beginning to end. Only it took me a while to find out. In actuality, she had pocketed the three hundred dollars (against the day I would leave her penniless) and after disembarking from the cab when it got to Hudson Street, had gone up to Times Square by subway to see Susan Hayward in *I Want to Live*, saw it three times over, the morbid melodrama of a cocktail waitress (if I remember correctly—I had already taken her to see it once myself) who gets the death penalty in California for a crime she didn't commit: right up Maureen's alley, that exemplary little tale. Then she'd donned a Kotex in the washroom and had come on home, weak in the knees and white around the gills. As who wouldn't be, after a day in a Times Square movie house?

All this she confessed three years later in Wisconsin.

The next morning I went alone to a booth—Maureen charging, as I left the apartment, that I was running away, leaving her bleeding and in pain while I disappeared forever with "that girl"—and telephoned my parents to tell them I was getting married.

"Why?" my father demanded to know.

"Because I want to." I was not about to tell my father, in whom I had not confided anything since I was ten, what I had been through in the past week. I had loved him dearly as a child, but he was only a small-time haberdasher, and I now wrote short stories published in the high-brow magazines and had a publisher's advance on a serious novel dense with moral ambiguity. So which of us could be expected to understand the principle involved? Which was what again? Something to do with my duty, my courage, my word.

"Peppy," my mother said, after having received the news in silence, "Peppy, I'm sorry, but I have to say it—there's something wrong with that woman. Isn't there?"

"She's over thirty years old," said my father.

"She's twenty-nine."

"And you're just twenty-six, you're a babe in the woods. Son, she's kicked around too long for my money. You're mother is right—something ain't right there with her."

My parents had met my intended just once, in my apartment; on the way home from a Wednesday matinee, they had stopped off to say hello, and there was Maureen, on my sofa, reading the script of a TV serial in which someone had "promised" her a part. Ten minutes of amiable, if self-conscious talk, and then they took the train back home. What they were saying about Maureen I assumed grew out of conversations with Morris and Lenore. I was wrong. Morris had never mentioned Maureen to them. They had figured her out on their own—after only ten minutes.

I tried acting lighthearted; laughing, I said, "She's not the girl across the street, if that's what you mean."

"What does she even do for a living? Anything?"

"She told you. She's an actress."

"Where?"

"She's looking for work."

"Son, listen to me: you're a college graduate. You're a summa cum laude. You had a four-year scholarship. The army is behind you. You've traveled in Europe. The world is before you, *and it's all yours.* You can have anything, *anything*—why are you settling for this? Peter, are you listening?"

"I'm listening."

"Peppy," asked my mother, "do you—love her?"

"Of course I do." And what did I want to shout into the phone at that very moment? *I'm coming home. Take me home.*

*This isn't what I want to do. You're right, there's something wrong with her: the woman is mad. Only I gave my word!*

My father said, "Your voice don't sound right to me."

"Well, I didn't expect this kind of reaction, frankly, when I said I would be getting married."

"We want you to be happy, that's all," said my mother.

"This is going to make you happy, marrying her?" asked my father. "I'm not talking about that she's Gentile. I'm not a narrow-minded dope, I never was. I don't live in a dead world. The German girl in Germany was something else, and her I never disliked personally, you know that. But that's water under the bridge."

"I know. I agree."

"I'm talking about happiness now, with another human being."

"Yes, I follow you."

"You don't sound right," he said, his own voice getting huskier with emotion. "You want me to come down to the city? I'll come in a minute—"

"No, don't be silly. Good Christ, no. I know what I'm doing. I'm doing what I want."

"But why so sudden?" my father asked, fishing. "Can you answer me that? I'm sixty-five years old, Peppy, I'm a grown man—you can talk to me, and the truth."

"What's 'sudden' about it? I've known her nearly a year. Please, don't fight me on this."

"Peter," said my mother, teary now, "we don't fight you on anything."

"I know, I know. I appreciate that. So let's not start now. I just called to tell you. A judge is marrying us on Wednesday at City Hall."

My mother's voice was weak now, almost a whisper, when she asked, "You want us to come?" It didn't sound as though she cared to be told yes. What a shock that was!

"No, there's no need for you to be there. It's just a formality. I'll call you afterwards."

"Peppy, are you still on the outs with your brother?"

"I'm not on the outs with him. He lives his life and I live mine."

"Peter, have you spoken to him about this? Peppy, your

older brother is a brother boys dream about having. He adores you. Call him, at least."

"Look, it's not a point I want to debate with Moe. He's a great arguer—and I'm not. There's nothing to argue over."

"Maybe he wouldn't argue. Maybe at least he'd like to know, to come to whatever it is—the wedding ceremony."

"He won't want to come."

"And you won't talk to him, only for a few minutes? Or to Joan?"

"What does Joan know about my life? Dad, just let me get married, okay?"

"You make it sound like nothing, like marrying a person for the rest of your life is an everyday affair. It ain't."

"I'm summa cum laude. I know that."

"Don't joke. You left us when you were too young, that's the problem. You always had your way. The apple of your mother's eye—you could have anything. The last of her babies . . ."

"Look, look—"

"You thought you already knew everything at fifteen—remember? We should never have let you skip all those grades and get ahead of yourself—that was our first mistake."

On the edge of tears now, I said, "That may be. But I would have been out of grade school by now anyway. Look, I'm getting married. It'll be all right." And I hung up, before I lost control and told my father to come down and take back to his home his twenty-six-year-old baby boy.


## 4. DR. SPIELVOGEL

We may incite [the patient] to jealousy or inflict upon him the pain of disappointed love, but no special technical design is necessary for that purpose. These things happen spontaneously in most analyses.
          —Freud, "Analysis Terminable and Interminable"

I first met Dr. Spielvogel the year Maureen and I were married. We had moved out of my Lower East Side basement apartment to a small house in the country near New Milford, Connecticut, not far from where Spielvogel and his family were summering at Candlewood Lake. Maureen was going to grow vegetables and I was going to write the final chapters of *A Jewish Father*. As it turned out, the seeds never got in the ground (or the bread in the oven, or the preserves in the jar), but because there was a twelve-by-twelve shack at the edge of the woods back of the house *with a bolt on the door*, somehow the book got finished. I saw Spielvogel maybe three times that summer at parties given by a New York magazine editor who was living nearby. I don't remember that the doctor and I had much to say to each other. He wore a yachting cap, this New York analyst summering in rural Connecticut, but otherwise he seemed at once dignified and without airs—a tall, quiet, decorous man, growing stout in his middle forties, with a mild German accent and that anomalous yachting cap. I never even noticed which woman was his wife; I discovered later that he had noticed which was mine.

When, in June of '62, it became necessary, according to my brother, for me to remain in New York and turn myself over to a psychiatrist, I came up with Spielvogel's name; friends in Connecticut that summer had spoken well of him, and, if I remembered right, treating "creative" people was supposed to be his specialty. Not that that made much difference to me in the shape I was in. Though I continued to write every day, I had really stopped thinking of myself as capable of creating anything other than misery for myself. I was not a writer any longer, no matter how I filled the daylight hours—I was Maureen's husband, and I could not imagine how I could get to be anything else ever again.

His appearance, like mine, had changed for the worse in three years. While I had been battling with Maureen, Spielvogel had been up against cancer. *He* had survived, though the disease appeared to have shrunk him down some. I remembered him of course in the yachting cap and with a summer tan; in his office, he wore a drab suit bought to fit a man a size larger, and an unexpectedly bold striped shirt whose collar now swam around his neck. His skin was pasty, and the heavy black frames of the glasses he wore tended further to dramatize this shrinkage he had undergone—beneath them, behind them, his head looked like a skull. He also walked now with a slight dip, or list, to the left, the cancer having apparently damaged his hip or leg. In all, the doctor he reminded me of most was Dr. Roger Chillingworth in Hawthorne's *Scarlet Letter*. Appropriate enough, because I sat facing him as full of shameful secrets as the Reverend Arthur Dimmesdale.

Maureen and I had lived a year in western Connecticut, a year at the American Academy in Rome, and a year at the university in Madison, and as a result of all that moving around I had never been able to find anyone in whom I was willing to confide. By the end of three years I had convinced myself that it would be "disloyal," a "betrayal," to tell even the closest friends I had made in our wanderings what went on between Maureen and me in private, though I imagined they could guess plenty from what often took place right out on the street or in other people's houses. Mostly I didn't open up to anyone because I was so ashamed of my defenselessness before her wrath and frightened of what she might do either to herself or to me, or to the person in whom I'd confided, if she ever found out what I had said. Sitting in a chair immediately across from Spielvogel, looking in embarrassment from his shrunken skull to the framed photograph of the Acropolis that was the only picture on his cluttered desk, I realized that I still couldn't do it: indeed, to tell *this* stranger the whole sordid story of my marriage seemed to me as reprehensible as committing a serious crime.

"You remember Maureen?" I asked. "My wife?"

"I do. Quite well." His voice, in contrast to his appearance, was strong and vigorous, causing me to feel even more puny and self-conscious . . . the little stool pigeon about to sing. My impulse was to get up and leave, my shame and humiliation (and my disaster) still my own—and simultaneously to crawl into his lap. "A small, pretty, dark-haired young woman," he said. "Very determined looking."

"Very."

"A lot of spunk there, I would think."

"She's a lunatic, Doctor!" I began to cry. For fully five minutes I sobbed into my hands—until Spielvogel asked, "Are you finished?"

There are lines from my five years of psychoanalysis as memorable to me as the opening sentence of *Anna Karenina*—

"Are you finished?" is one of them. The perfect tone, the perfect tactic. I turned myself over to him, then and there, for good or bad.

Yes, yes, I was finished. "All I do these days is collapse in tears . . ." I wiped my face with a Kleenex from a box that he offered me and proceeded to "spill"—though not about Maureen (I couldn't, right off) but about Karen Oakes, the Wisconsin coed with whom I had been maniacally in love during the winter and early spring of that year. I had been watching her bicycle around the campus for months before she showed up in my undergraduate writing section in the second semester to become the smartest girl in the class. Good-natured, gentle, a beguiling mix of assertive innocence and shy adventurousness, Karen had a small lyrical gift as a poet and wrote clever, somewhat magisterial literary analyses of the fiction that we read in class; her candor and lucidity, I told Spielvogel, were as much a balm to me as her mild temperament, her slender limbs, her pretty and composed American girl's face. Oh, I went on and on about Ka-reen (the pet name for the pillow talk), growing increasingly intoxicated, as I spoke, with memories of our ardent "passion" and brimming "love"—I did not mention that in all we probably had not been alone with one another more than forty-eight hours over the course of the three months, and rarely for more than forty-five minutes at a clip; we were together either in the classroom with fifteen undergraduates for chaperones, or in her bed. Nonetheless she was, I said, "the first good thing" to happen in my private life since I'd been discharged from the army and come to New York to write. I told Spielvogel how she had called herself "Miss Demi-Womanhood of 1962"; he did not appear to be one-hundredth as charmed by the remark as I had been, but then he had not just disrobed for the first time the demiwoman who had said it. I recounted to him the agonies of doubt and longing that I had experienced before I went ahead, three weeks into the semester, and wrote "See me" across the face of one of her A+ papers. She came, as directed, to my office, and accepted my courtly, professorial invitation to be seated. In the first moments, courtliness was rampant, as a matter of fact. "You wanted to see me?" "Yes, I did, Miss Oakes." A silence ensued, long and opaquely eloquent enough to satisfy Anton Chekhov. "Where do you come from, Miss Oakes?" "Racine." "And what does your father do?" "He's a physician." And then, as though hurling myself off a bridge, I did it: reached forward and laid a hand upon her straw-colored hair. Miss Oakes swallowed and said nothing. "I'm sorry," I told her, "I couldn't help it." She said: "Professor Tarnopol, I'm not a sophisticated person." Whereupon I proceeded to apologize profusely. "Oh, please, don't worry," she said, when I wouldn't stop, "a lot of teachers do it." "Do they?" the award-winning novelist asked. "Every semester so far," said she, nodding a little wearily; "and usually it's English." "What happens then, usually?" "I tell them I'm not a sophisticated person. Because I'm not." "And then?" "That's it, generally." "They get conscience-stricken and apologize profusely." "They have second thoughts, I suppose." "Just like me." "And me," she said, without blinking; "the doctrine of *in loco parentis* works both ways." "Look, look—" "Yes?" "Look, I'm *taken* with you. Terribly." "You don't even know me, Professor Tarnopol." "I don't and I do. I've read your papers. I've read your stories and poems." "I've read yours." Oh my God, Dr. Spielvogel, how can you sit there like an Indian? Don't you appreciate the *charm* of all this? Can't you see what a conversation like that meant to me in my despair? "Look, Miss Oakes, I want to see you—I *have* to see you!" "Okay." "*Where?*" "I have a room—" "I can't go into a dormitory, you know that." "I'm a senior. I don't live in the dorm any more. I moved out." "You did?" "I have my own room in town." "Can I come to talk to you there?" "Sure."

*Sure!* Oh, what a wonderful, charming, disarming, engaging little word that one is! I went around sibilating it to myself all through the rest of the day. "What are you so bouncy about?" asked Maureen. *Shoor. Shewer. Shur.* Now just how did that beautiful and clever and willing and healthy young girl say it anyway? *Sure!* Yes, like that—crisp and to the point. *Sure!* Oh yes, sure as sure is sure, Miss Oakes is going to have an adventure, and Professor Tarnopol is going to have a breakdown . . . How many hours before I decided that when the semester was over we would run off together? Not that many. The second time we were in bed I proposed the idea to Ka-reen. We would go to Italy in June—catch the Pan Am flight from

Chicago (I'd checked on it by phone) the evening of the day she'd taken her last exam; I could send my final grades in from Rome. Wouldn't that be terrific? Oh, I would say to her, burying my face in her hair, I want to take you somewhere, Ka-reen, I want to go away with you! And she would murmur softly, "Mmmmmm, mmmmmm," which I interpreted as delicious acquiescence. I told her about all the lovely Italian piazzas in which Maureen and I had screamed bloody murder at one another: the Piazza San Marco in Venice, the Piazza della Signoria in Florence, the Piazza del Campo in Siena . . . Karen went home for spring vacation and never came back. That's how overbearing and frightening a character I had become. That murmuring was just the sound her good mind gave off as it gauged the dreadful consequences of having chosen this particular member of the conscience-stricken English faculty to begin sophisticated life with outside of a college dorm. It was one thing reading Tolstoy in class, another playing Anna and Vronsky with the professor.

After she failed to return from spring recess, I made desperate phone calls to Racine practically daily. When I call at lunchtime I am told she is "out." I refuse to believe it—where does she eat then? "Who is this, please?" I am asked. I mumble, "A friend from school . . . are you *sure* she isn't . . . ?" "Would you care to leave your name?" "No." After dinner each night I last about ten minutes in the living room with Maureen before I begin to feel myself on the brink of cracking up; rising from my reading chair, I throw down my pencil and my book—as though I am Rudolph Hess after twenty years in Spandau Prison, I cry, "I have to take a walk! I have to see some faces! I'm suffocating in here!" Once out the door, I break into a sprint, and crossing back lawns and leaping low garden fences, I head for the dormitory nearest our apartment, where there is a telephone booth on the first floor. I will catch Karen at the dinner hour and beg her at least to come back to school for the rest of this semester, even if she will not run away in June to live in Trastevere with me. She says, "Hang on a sec—let me take it on another phone." A few moments later I hear her call, "Will you hang up the downstairs phone, please, Mom?" "Karen! Karen!" "Yes, I'm back." "Ka-reen, I can't bear it—I'll meet you somewhere in Racine! I'll hitch! I can be there by nine-thirty!" But she *was* the smartest girl in my class and had no intention of letting some overwrought creative writing teacher with a bad marriage and a stalled career ruin her life. She could not save me from my wife, she said, I would have to do that myself. She had told her family she had had an unhappy love affair, but, she assured me, she had not and would not tell them with whom. "But what about your degree?" I demanded, as though I were the dean of students. "That's not important right now," said Karen, speaking as calmly from her bedroom in Racine as she did in class. "But I love you! I want you!" I shouted at the slender girl who only the week before had bicycled in sneakers and a poplin skirt to English 312, her straw-colored hair in braids and her innards still awash with semen from our lunchtime assignation in her rented room. "You just can't leave, Karen! Not now! Not after how marvelous it's been!" "But I can't save you, Peter. I'm only twenty years old." In tears I cried, "I'm only twenty-nine!" "Peter, I should never have started up. I had no idea what was at stake. That's my fault. Forgive me. I'm as sorry as I can be." "Christ, don't be 'sorry'—*just come back!*" One night Maureen followed me out of the house and across the backyards to the dormitory, and after standing out of sight for a minute with her ear to the telephone booth, threw back the door while I was pleading with Karen yet again to change her mind and come with me to Europe on the Pan Am night flight from O'Hare. "Liar!" screamed Maureen, "whoremongering liar!" and ran back to the apartment to swallow a small handful of sleeping pills. Then, on hands and knees, she crawled into the living room in her underwear and knelt there on the floor with my Gillette razor in her hand, waiting patiently for me to finish talking with my undergraduate harlot and come on home so that she could get on with the job of almost killing herself.

I told Spielvogel what Maureen had confessed to me from the living-room floor. Because this had happened only two months earlier, I found with Spielvogel, as I had that morning with Moe in the taxi back from the airport, that I could not recount the story of the false urine specimen without becoming woozy and weak, as though once the story surfaced in my mind, it was only a matter of seconds before the fires of rage had raced through me, devouring all vitality and strength. It is not that easy for me to tell it today without at least a touch of vertigo. And I have never been able to introduce the story into a work of fiction, not that I haven't repeatedly tried and failed in the five years since I received Maureen's confession. I cannot seem to make it credible—probably because I still don't entirely believe it myself. How could she? To me! No matter how I may contrive to transform low actuality into high art, that is invariably what is emblazoned across the face of the narrative, in blood: HOW COULD SHE? TO ME!

"And then," I told Spielvogel, "do you know what she said next? She was on the floor with the blade of the razor right on her wrist. In her panties and bra. And I was just standing over her. Dumbstruck. *Dumbstruck*. I could have kicked her head in. I should have!"

"And what did she say?"

"Say? She said, 'If you forgive me for the urine, I'll forgive you for your mistress. I'll forgive you for deceiving me with that girl on the bicycle and begging her to run away with you to Rome.'"

"And what did you do?" asked Spielvogel.

"Did I kick her, you mean? No. No, no, no, no, no. I didn't do anything—to her. Just stood there for a while. I couldn't right off get over the *ingenuity* of it. The *relentlessness*. That she had thought of such a thing *and then gone ahead and done it*. I actually felt *admiration*. And pity, *pity!* That's true. I thought, 'Good Christ, what *are* you? To do this thing, *and then to keep it a secret for three years!*' And then I saw my chance to get out. As though it required this, you see, nothing less, for me to feel free to go. Not that I went. Oh, I *told* her I was going, all right. I said, I'm leaving, Maureen, I can't live any more with somebody who would do such a thing, and so on. But she was crying by then and she said, 'Leave me and I'll cut my wrists. I'm full of sleeping pills already.' And I said, and this is true, I said, 'Cut them, why should I care?' And so she pressed down with the razor—and blood came out. It turned out that she had only scratched herself, but what the hell did I know? She could have gone through to the bone. I started shouting, 'Don't—don't do that!' and I began wrestling with her for the razor. I was terrified that I was going to get my own veins slashed in the rolling around, but I kept trying to get it away, grabbing at the damn thing—and I was crying. That goes without saying. All I do now is cry, you know—and she was crying, of course, and finally I got the thing away from her and she said, 'Leave me, and I'll ruin that girl of yours! I'll have that pure little face in every paper in Wisconsin!' And then she began to scream about my 'deceiving' her and how I couldn't be trusted and she always knew it—and this is just three minutes after describing in detail to me buying the urine from that Negro woman on Avenue B!"

"And what did you do then?"

"Did I slit her throat from ear to ear? No. No! I fell apart. Completely. I went into a tantrum. The two of us were smeared with blood—my left palm had been cut, up by the thumb, and her wrist was dripping, and God only knows what we looked like—like a couple of Aztecs, fucking up the sacrificial rites. I mean, it's comical when you think about it. I am the Dagwood Bumstead of fear and trembling!"

"You had a tantrum."

"That's not the *half* of it. I got down on my knees—I *begged* her to let me go. I banged my head on the floor, Doctor. I began running from room to room. Then—then I did what she told me Walker used to do. Maybe Walker never even did it; that was probably a lie too. Anyway, *I* did it. At first I was just running around looking for some place to hide the razor from her. I remember unscrewing the head and dropping the blade into the toilet and flushing and flushing and the damn thing just lying there at the bottom of the bowl. Then I ran into our bedroom—I was screaming all this time, you see, 'Let me go! Let me go!' and sobbing, and so on. And all the while I was tearing my clothes off. I'd done that before, in a rage with her, but this time I actually tore everything off me. And I put on Maureen's underwear. I pulled open her dresser and I put on a pair of her underpants—I could just get them up over my prick. Then I tried to get into one of her brassieres. I put my arms through the shoulder loops, that is. And then I just stood there like that, crying—and bleeding. Finally she came into the room—no, she just got as far as the doorway and stood there, looking at me. And, you see, that's all she was wearing, too, her underwear. She saw me and she broke into sobs again, and she cried, 'Oh, sweetheart, no, no . . .'"

"Is that all she said?" asked Spielvogel. "Just called you 'sweetheart'?"

"No. She said, 'Take that off. I'll never tell anybody. Just take that off right now.' "

"That was two months ago," said Dr. Spielvogel, when it appeared that I had nothing more to say.

"Yes."

"And?"

"It's not been good, Doctor."

"What do you mean?"

"I've done some other strange things."

"Such as?"

"Such as staying with Maureen—that's the strangest thing of all! Three years of it, and now I know what I know, and I'm still living with her! And if I don't fly back tomorrow, she says she's going to tell the world 'everything.' That's what she told my brother to tell me on the phone. And she will. *She will do it.*"

"Any other 'strange things'?"

". . . with my sperm."

"I didn't hear you. Your sperm? What about your sperm?"

"My semen—I leave it places."

"Yes?"

"I smear it places. I go to people's houses and I leave it— places."

"You break into people's houses?"

"No, no," I said sharply—what did he think I was, a madman? "I'm invited. I go to the bathroom. I leave it somewhere . . . on the tap. In the soap dish. Just a few drops . . ."

"You masturbate in their bathrooms."

"Sometimes, yes. And leave . . ."

"Your signature."

"Tarnopol's silver bullet."

He smiled at my joke; I did not. I had still more to tell. "I've done it in the university library. Smeared it on the bindings of books."

"Of books? Which books?"

"Books! Any books! Whatever books are handy!"

"Anywhere else?"

I sighed.

"Speak up, please," said the doctor.

"I sealed an envelope with it," I said in a loud voice. "My bill to the telephone company."

Again Spielvogel smiled. "Now that is an original touch, Mr. Tarnopol."

And again I broke into sobs. "What does it mean!"

"Come now," said Dr. Spielvogel, "what do you think it 'means'? You don't require a soothsayer, as far as I can see."

"That I'm completely out of control!" I said, sobbing. "That I don't know what I'm doing any more!"

"That you're angry," he said, slapping the arm of his chair. "That you are furious. You are not *out* of control—you are *under* control. Maureen's control. You spurt the anger everywhere, except where it belongs. There you spurt tears."

"But she'll ruin Karen! She will! She knows who she is—she used to check out my students like a hawk! She'll destroy that lovely innocent girl!"

"Karen sounds as if she can take care of herself."

"But you don't know Maureen once she gets going. She could *murder* somebody. She used to grab the wheel of our VW in Italy and try to run us off the side of a mountain—because I hadn't opened a door for her leaving the hotel in Sorrento! She could carry a grudge like that for days—then she would erupt with it, in the car, weeks later! You can't imagine what it's like when she goes wild!"

"Well, then, Karen should be properly warned, if that is the case."

"It *is* the case! It's hair-raising! Grabbing the wheel from my hands and spinning it the other way when we're winding down a mountain road! You must believe what I've been through—I am not exaggerating! To the contrary, I'm leaving things *out*!"

Now, with my avenger dead and her ashes scattered from a plane into the Atlantic Ocean, now with all that rage *stilled*, it seems to me that I simply could not have been so extensively unmanned by Maureen Johnson Mezik Walker Tarnopol, dropout from Elmira High, as I indicated (and demonstrated) to Spielvogel during our first hour together. I was, after all, bigger than she was, more intelligent than she was, better educated than she was, and far more accomplished. What then (I asked the doctor) had made me such a willing, or will-less, victim? Why couldn't I find the strength, or just the simple survival mechanism, to leave her once it became obvious that it was no longer she who needed rescuing from her disasters, but I from mine? Even after she had confessed to committing the urine fraud, even *then* I couldn't get up and go! Now why? Why should someone who had battled so determinedly all his life to be independent—his own child, his own adolescent, his own man—why should someone with my devotion to "seriousness" and "maturity" knuckle under like a defenseless little boy to this cornball Clytemnestra?

Dr. Spielvogel invited me to look at the nursery for the answer. The question with which he began our second session was, "Does your wife remind you of your mother?"

My heart sank. Psychoanalytic reductivism was not going to save me from the IRT tracks, or worse, from returning to Wisconsin at the end of the week to resume hostilities with Maureen. In reply to the question I said, no, she did not. My wife reminded me of no one I had ever known before, anywhere. Nobody in my entire lifetime had ever dared to deceive, insult, threaten, or blackmail me the way she did—certainly no woman I had ever known. Nor had anyone ever hollered at me like that, except perhaps the basic training cadre at Fort Dix. I suggested to Spielvogel that it wasn't because she was like my mother that I couldn't deal with her, but, if anything, because she was so *unlike* her. My mother was not aggrieved, contentious, resentful, violent, helpless, or suicidal, and she did not ever want to see me humbled—far from it. Certainly, for our purposes, the most telling difference between the two was that my mother *adored* me, worshipped me across the board, and I had basked in that adoration. Indeed, it was her enormous belief in my perfection that had very likely helped to spawn and nourish whatever gifts I had. I supposed that it could be said that I had knuckled under to my mother when I was still a little boy—but in a little boy that is not knuckling under, is it? That is just common sense and a feel for family life: childhood realpolitik. One does not expect to be treated like a thirty-year-old at five. But at fifteen I certainly did expect deferential treatment of a kind, and from my mother I got it. As I remember it, I could sweet-talk that lady into just about anything during my high-school years, without too much effort get her to agree to the fundamental soundness of my position on just about every issue arising out of my blooming sense of prerogatives; in fact, it was with demonstrable delight (as I recalled it) that she acquiesced to the young prince whom she had been leading all these years toward the throne.

It was the supernumerary father I'd had to struggle with back then. He was anxious for me in my ambitiousness and cockiness. He had seen less of me as a child—off in the store all day, and in bad times selling roofing and siding for his brother-in-law door to door at night—and understandably he had some trouble when he first discovered that the little bird's beak he'd been feeding all those years had been transformed overnight into a yapping adolescent mouth that could outtalk him, outreason him, and generally outsmart him with the aid of "logic," "analogy," and assorted techniques of condescension. But then came my four-year scholarship to Brown, and that crown of crowns, straight As in college, and gradually he too gave in and left off even trying to tell me what to think and do. By my seventeenth year it was already pretty clear that I did not mean to use my freedom from parental constraint and guidance to become a bum, and so, to his credit, he did the best an aggressive entrepreneur and indestructible breadwinner and loving father could, to let me be.

Spielvogel wouldn't see it that way. He questioned my "fairly happy childhood," suggested that people could of course delude themselves about the good old days that had never been. There might be a harsher side to it all that I was conveniently forgetting—the *threatening* aspect of my mother's competence and vigor and attentiveness, and the "castration anxiety," as he called it, that it had fostered in her baby boy, the last, and emotionally the most fragile, of her offspring. From my descriptions of Morris's life and my few vivid childhood recollections of him, Dr. Spielvogel concluded that my brother had been "constitutionally" a much tougher specimen than I to begin with, and that this biological endowment had been reinforced in his formative years when he had virtually to raise himself while my mother was off working most of each day in the store with my father. As for Joan, it was Spielvogel's educated guess that as the ugly duckling and the girl in the family she had hardly been in danger of being overwhelmed by my mother's attention; to the contrary, she had probably felt herself at the periphery of the family circle, neglected and useless as compared with the hearty older brother and the clever younger one. If so (he continued, writing his Tarnopol family history), it would not be surprising to find her in her forties still so avid to *have*—famous friends, modish beauty, exotic travels, fancy and expensive clothes: to have, in a word, the admiration and envy of the crowd. He shocked me by asking if my sister also took lovers with such avidity. "Joannie? It never occurred to me." "Much hasn't," the doctor assured the patient.

Now I for one had never denied that my mother might have been less than perfect; of course I remembered times when she seemed to have scolded me too severely or needlessly wounded my pride or hurt my feelings; of course she had said and done her share of thoughtless things while bringing me up, and at times, in anger or uncertainty, had like any parent taken the tyrannical way out. But not until I came under the influence of Dr. Spielvogel could I possibly have imagined a child any more valued or loved than Mrs. Tarnopol's little boy. Any more, in fact, and I really *would* have been in trouble. My argument with this line the doctor began to take on my past was that if I had suffered anything serious from having had a mother like my own, it was because she had nourished in me a boundless belief in my ability to *win* whatever I wanted, an optimism and innocence about my charmed life that (now that I thought about it) could very well have left me less than fortified against the realities of setback and frustration. Yes, perhaps what made me so pathetic at dealing with Maureen in her wildest moments was that I simply could not believe that anybody like her could exist in the world that had been advertised to me as Peter's oyster. It wasn't the repetition of an ancient "trauma" that rendered me so helpless with my defiant wife—it was its uniqueness. I might as well have been dealing with a Martian, for all the familiarity I had with female rage and resentment.

I admitted readily to Dr. Spielvogel that of course I had been reduced in my marriage to a bewildered and defenseless little boy, but that, I contended, was because I had never been a *bewildered* little boy before. I did not see how we could account for my downfall in my late twenties without accounting simultaneously for all those years of success and good fortune that had preceded it. Wasn't it possible that in my "case," as I willingly called it, triumph *and* failure, conquest *and* defeat derived from an indestructible boyish devotion to a woman as benefactress and celebrant, protectress and guide? Could we not conjecture that what had made me so available to the Bad Older Woman was the reawakening in me of that habit of obedience that had stood me in such good stead with the Good Older Woman of my childhood? A small boy, yes, most assuredly, no question about it—but not at all, I insisted, because the protecting, attentive, and regulating mother of my fairly happy memories had been Spielvogel's "phallic threatening mother figure" to whom I submitted out of fear and whom a part of me secretly loathed. To be sure, whoever held absolute power over a child had inevitably to inspire hatred in him at times, but weren't we standing the relationship on its head by emphasizing her fearsome aspect, real as it may have been, over the lovingness and tenderness of the mother who dominated the recollections of my first ten years? And weren't we drastically exaggerating my submissiveness as well, when all available records seemed to indicate that in fact I had been a striving, spirited little boy, nicknamed Peppy, who hardly behaved in the world like a whipped dog? Children, I told Spielvogel (who I assumed knew as much), had undergone far worse torment than I ever had for displeasing adults.

Spielvogel wouldn't buy it. It was hardly unusual, he said, to have felt loved by the "threatening mother"; what was distressing was that at this late date I should continue to depict her in this "idealized" manner. That to him was a sign that I was still very much "under her spell," unwilling so much as to utter a peep of protest for fear *yet* of reprisal. As he saw it, it was my vulnerability as a sensitive little child to the pain such a mother might so easily inflict that accounted for "the dominance of narcissism" as my "primary defense." To protect myself against the "profound anxiety" engendered by my mother —by the possibilities of rejection and separation, as well as the helplessness that I experienced in her presence—I had cultivated a strong sense of superiority, with all the implications of "guilt" and "ambivalence" over being "special."

I argued that Dr. Spielvogel had it backwards. My sense of

superiority—if he wanted to call it that—was not a "defense" against the threat of my mother, but rather my altogether willing acceptance of her estimation of me. I just agreed with her, that's all. As what little boy wouldn't? I was not pleading with Spielvogel to believe that I had ever in my life felt like an ordinary person or wished to be one; I was only trying to explain that it did not require "profound anxiety" for my mother's lastborn to come up with the idea that he was somebody to conjure with.

Now, when I say that I "argued" or "admitted," and Spielvogel "took issue," etc., I am drastically telescoping a dialectic that was hardly so neat and narrow, or so pointed, as it evolved from session to session. A summary like this tends to magnify considerably my own resistance to the archaeological reconstruction of my childhood that began to take shape over the first year or so of therapy, as well as to overdraw the subtle enough means by which the doctor communicated to me his hypotheses about the origin of my troubles. If I, in fact, had been less sophisticated about "resistance"—and he'd had less expertise—I might actually have been able to resist him more successfully. (On the basis of this paragraph, Dr. Spielvogel would undoubtedly say that my resistance, far from being overcome by my "sophistication," has triumphed over all in the end. For why do I assign to him, rather than myself, the characterization of my mother as "a phallic threatening figure," if not because I am *still* unwilling to be responsible for thinking such an unthinkable thought?) Also, had I been less desperate to be cured of whatever was ailing me, and ruining me, I probably could have held out somewhat longer—though being, as of old, the most willing of pupils, I would inevitably, I think, have seriously entertained his ideas just out of schoolboy habit. But as it was, because I so wanted to get a firm grip upon myself and to stop being so susceptible to Maureen, I found that once I got wind of Dr. Spielvogel's bias, I became increasingly willing to challenge my original version of my fairly happy childhood with rather Dickensian recollections of my mother as an overwhelming and frightening person. Sure enough, memories began to turn up of cruelty, injustice, and of offenses against my innocence and integrity, and as time passed, it was as though the anger that I felt toward Maureen had risen over its banks and was beginning to rush out across the terrain of my childhood. If I would never wholly relinquish my benign version of our past, I nonetheless so absorbed Spielvogel's that when, some ten months in analysis, I went up to Yonkers to have Passover dinner with my parents and Morris's family, I found myself crudely abrupt and cold with my mother, a performance almost as bewildering afterward to me as to this woman who so looked forward to each infrequent visit that I made to her dinner table. Peeved, and not about to hide it, my brother took me aside at one point in the meal and said, "Hey, what's going on here tonight?" I could not give him anything but a shrug for a reply. And try as I might, when I later kissed her goodbye at the door, I did not seem to have the wherewithal to feign even a little filial affection—as though my mother, who had been crestfallen the very first time she had laid eyes on Maureen, and afterward had put up with the fact of her solely to please me, was somehow an accomplice to Maureen's vindictive rage.

Somewhere along in my second year of therapy, when relations with my mother were at their coolest, it occurred to me that rather than resenting Spielvogel, as I sometimes did, for provoking this perplexing change in behavior and attitude toward her, I should see it rather as a strategy, harsh perhaps but necessary, designed to deplete the fund of maternal veneration on which Maureen had been able to draw with such phenomenal results. To be sure, it was no fault of my mother's that I had blindly transferred the allegiance she had inspired through the abundance of her love to someone who was in actuality my enemy; it could be taken, in fact, as a measure of just how gratifying a mother she had been, what a *genius* of a mother she had been, that a son of hers, decades later, had found himself unable to "wrong" a woman with whom his mother shared nothing except a common gender, and a woman whom actually he had come to *despise*. Nonetheless, if my future as a man required me to sever at long last the reverential bonds of childhood, then the brutal and bloody surgery on the emotions would have to proceed, and without blaming the physician in charge for whatever pain the operation might cause the blameless mother or for the disorientation it produced in the apron-strung idolatrous son . . . Thus did I try to rationalize the severity with which I was coming to judge my mother, and to justify and understand the rather patriarchal German-Jewish doctor, whose insistence on "the phallic threatening mother" I sometimes thought revealed more about some bête noire of his than of my own.

But that suspicion was not one that I cared, or dared, to pursue. I was far too much the needy patient to presume to be my doctor's doctor. I had to trust someone if I hoped ever to recover from my defeat, and I chose him.

I had, of course, no real idea what kind of man Dr. Spielvogel was outside of his office, or even in the office with other patients. Where exactly he had been born, raised, and educated, when and under what circumstances he had emigrated to America, what his wife was like, whether he had children— I knew no more about these simple facts of his life than I did about the man who sold me my morning paper; and I was too obedient to what I understood to be the rules of the game to ask, and too preoccupied with my own troubles to be anything more than sporadically curious about this stranger in whose presence I lay down on a couch in a dimly lit room for fifty minutes, three afternoons a week, and spoke as I had never spoken even to those who had proved themselves worthy of my trust. My attitude toward the doctor was very much like that of the first-grader who accepts on faith the wisdom, authority, and probity of his teacher, and is unable to grasp the idea that his teacher also lives in the ambiguous and uncertain world beyond the blackboard.

I had myself been just such a youngster, and experienced my first glimpse of my doctor riding a Fifth Avenue bus with the same stunned disbelief and embarrassment that I had felt at age eight when, in the company of my sister, I had passed the window of a neighborhood barbershop one day and saw the man who taught "shop" in my school getting a shine and a shave. I was four months into my analysis on the drizzly morning when I looked up from the bus stop in front of Doubleday's on Fifth Avenue and saw Spielvogel, in a rainhat and a raincoat, looking out from a seat near the front of the No. 5 bus and wearing a decidedly dismal expression on his face. Of course years before I had seen him in his yachting cap sipping a drink at a summer party, so I knew for a fact that he did not really cease to exist when he was not practicing psychoanalysis on me; I happened too to have been acquainted with several young training analysts during my year of graduate work at Chicago, people with whom I'd gotten along easily enough during evenings in the local student bar. But then Spielvogel was no casual beer-drinking acquaintance: he was the repository of my intimate history, he was to be the instrument of my psychic—my *spiritual*—recovery, and that a person entrusted with that responsibility should actually go out into the street and board a public vehicle such as carried the common herd from point A to point B—well, it was beyond my comprehension. How could I have been so stupid as to confide my darkest secrets to a person who went out in public and took a bus? How could I ever have believed that this gaunt, middle-aged man, looking so done in and defenseless beneath his olive-green rainhat, this unimpressive stranger on a *bus*, could possibly free me from my woes? And just what in God's name was I expected to do now—climb aboard, pay my fare, proceed down the aisle, tap him on the shoulder, and say—say what? "Good day, Dr. Spielvogel, it's me—you remember, the man in his wife's underwear."

I turned and walked rapidly away. When he saw me move off, the bus driver, who had been waiting patiently for me to rise from my reverie and enter the door he held open, called out, in a voice weary of ministering to the citizenry of Manhattan, "*Another* screwball," and drove off, bearing through an orange light my shaman and savior, bound (I later learned, incredulously) for an appointment with his dentist.

It was in September of 1964, at the beginning of my third year of analysis, that I had a serious falling out with Dr. Spielvogel. I considered discontinuing therapy with him, and even after I decided to stay on, found it impossible to invest in him and the process anything like the belief and hope with which I had begun. I could never actually divest myself of the idea that I had been ill-used by him, though I knew that the worst thing I could do in my "condition" was nurse feelings of victimization and betrayal. Six months ago, when I left New York, it was largely because I was so disheartened and confounded by what

Susan had done; but also it was because my dispute with Dr. Spielvogel, which never really had been settled to my satisfaction, had become again a volatile issue between us—revived, to be sure, by Susan's suicide attempt, which I had been fearing for years, but which Spielvogel had generally contended was a fear having more to do with my neurotic personality than with "reality." That I should think that Susan might try to kill herself if and when I should ever leave her, Spielvogel had chalked up to narcissistic self-dramatization. So too did he explain my demoralization after the fear had been substantiated by fact.

"I am not a fortune-teller," he said, "and neither are you. There was as much reason, if not more, to believe she would not do it as that she would. You know yourself—she knew *herself*—that this affair of yours was the most satisfying thing to happen to her in years. She had, literally, the time of her life. She began at last to become a full-grown woman. She *bloomed*, from all reports—correct? If when you left her, she did not have enough support from her doctor, from her family, from wherever, well, that is unfortunate. But what can *you* do? She did at least have what she had with you. And she could not have had it *without* you. To regret now having stayed with her all those years, because of this—well, that is not to look very carefully at the credit side of the ledger. Especially, Mr. Tarnopol, as she did not commit suicide. You act here, you know, as though that is what has happened, as though there has been a funeral, and so on. But she only *attempted* suicide, after all. And, I would think, with little intention of succeeding. The fact is that her cleaning woman was to arrive early the very next morning, and that the woman had a key with which to let herself into Susan's apartment. She knew then that she would be found in only a few hours. Correct? Of course, Susan took something of a risk to get what she wanted, but as we see, she pulled it off quite well. She did not die. You did come running. And you are running yet. Maybe only in circles, but that for her is still better than out of her life completely. It is you, you see, who is blowing this up out of all proportion. Your narcissism, again, if I may say so. Much too much overestimation of—well, of practically everything. And to use this incident, which has not ended so tragically, you know—to use this incident to break off therapy and go off into isolation again, once more the defeated man, well, I think you are making a serious mistake."

If so, I went ahead and made it. I could not continue to confide in him or to take myself seriously as his patient, and I left. The last of my attachments had been severed: no more Susan, no more Spielvogel, no more Maureen. No longer in the path of love, hate, or measured professional concern—by accident or design, for good or bad, I am not there.

Note: A letter from Spielvogel arrived here at the Colony just this week, expressing thanks for the copies of "Salad Days" and "Courting Disaster" that I mailed to him earlier in the month. I had written:

For some time now I've been debating whether to send on to you these two (postanalytic) stories I wrote during my first months here in Vermont. I do now, not because I wish to open my case up to a renewed investigation in your office (though I see how you might interpret these manuscripts in that way), but because of your interest in the processes of art (and because lately you have been on my mind). I know that your familiarity with the biographical and psychological data that furnished the raw material for such flights of fancy might give rise to theoretical speculation, and the theoretical speculation give rise in turn to the itch to communicate your findings to your fellows. Your eminent colleague Ernst Kris has noted that "the psychology of artistic style is unwritten," and my suspicion (aroused by past experience) is that you might be interested in taking a crack at it. Feel free to speculate all you want, of course, but please, nothing in print without my permission. Yes, that is still a sore subject, but not so sore (I've concluded) as to outweigh this considered impulse to pass on for your professional scrutiny these waking dreams whose "unconscious" origins (I must warn you) may not be so unconscious as a professional might like to conclude at first glance. Yours, Peter Tarnopol.

Spielvogel's reply:

It was thoughtful of you to send on to me your two new stories. I read them with great interest and enjoyment, and as ever, admiration for your skills and understanding. The two stories are so different and yet so expertly done, and to my mind balance each other perfectly. The scenes with Sharon in the first I found especially funny, and in the second the fastidious attention that the narrating voice pays to itself struck me as absolutely right, given his concerns (or "human concerns" as the

Zuckerman of "Salad Days" would have said in his undergraduate seminar). What a sad and painful story it is. Moral, too, in the best, most serious way. You appear to be doing very well. I wish you continued success with your work. Sincerely, Otto Spielvogel.

This is the doctor whose ministrations I have renounced? Even if the letter is just a contrivance to woo me back onto his couch, what a lovely and clever contrivance! I wonder whom he has been seeing about his prose style. Now why couldn't he write about *me* like that? (Or wasn't that piece he wrote about me really as bad as I thought? Or was it even worse? And did it matter either way? Surely I know what it's like having trouble writing up my case in English sentences. *I've* been trying to do it now for years. Then, was ridding myself of him wrong too? Or am I just succumbing—like a narcissist! Oh, he knows his patient, this conjurer . . . Or *am* I being too suspicious?)

So: shall I go ahead now and confuse myself further by sending copies of the stories to Susan? to my mother and father? to Dina Dornbusch? to Maureen's Group? How about to Maureen herself?

Dear Departed: It may cheer you up some to read the enclosed. Little did you know how persuasive you were. Actually had you played your cards right and been just a little less nuts we'd be miserably married yet. Even as it is, your widower thinks practically only of you. Do you think of him in Heaven, or (as I fear) have you set your sights on some big strapping neurotic angel ambivalent about his sexual role? These two stories owe much to your sense of things—you might have conceived of the self-intoxicated princeling of "Salad Days" yourself and called him me; and, allowing for artistic license of course, isn't Lydia pretty much how you saw yourself (if, that is, you could have seen yourself as you would have had others see you)? How is Eternity, by the way? In the hope that these two stories help to pass the time a little more quickly, I am, your bereaved, Peter.

Out of the whirlwind, a reply:

Dear Peter: I've read the stories and found them most amusing, particularly the one that isn't supposed to be. Your spiritual exertions (in your own behalf) are very touching. I took the liberty (I didn't imagine you would mind) of passing them on to the Lord. You will be pleased to know that "Courting Disaster" brought a smile to His lips as well. No wrath whatsoever, I'm happy to report, though He did remark (not without a touch of astonishment), "It *is* all vanity, isn't

it?" The stories are currently making the rounds of the saints, who I'm
sure will find your aspiration to their condition rather flattering. The
rumor here among the holy martyrs is that you've got a new work
under way that you say is really going "to tell it like it is." If so, I expect
that means Maureen again. How do you intend to portray me this
time? Holding your head on a plate? I think a phallus would increase
your sales. But of course you know best how to exploit my memory
for high artistic purposes. Good luck with *My Martyrdom as a Man*.
That *is* to be the title, is it not? All of us here in Heaven look forward
to the amusement it is sure to afford those who know you from on
high. Your beloved wife, Maureen. P.S. Eternity is fine. Just about long
enough to forgive a son of a bitch like you.

And now, class, will you please hand in your papers, and before
turning to Dr. Spielvogel's useful fiction, let us see what *you*
have made of the legends here contrived:

English 312
M&F 1:00–2:30
(assignations by appointment)
Professor Tarnopol

### THE USES OF THE USEFUL FICTIONS:
Or, Professor Tarnopol Withdraws
Somewhat from His Feelings

By Karen Oakes

> Certainly I do not deny when I am reading
> that the author may be impassioned, nor even
> that he might have conceived the first plan of
> his work under the sway of passion. But his
> decision to write supposes that he withdraws
> somewhat from his feelings. . . .
> —Sartre, *What Is Literature?*

> *On ne peut jamais se connaître,*
> *mais seulement se raconter.*
> —Simone de Beauvoir

"Salad Days," the shorter of the two Zuckerman stories assigned for
today, attempts by means of comic irony to contrast the glories and
triumphs of Nathan Zuckerman's golden youth with the "misfortune" of his twenties, to which the author suddenly alludes in the
closing lines. The author (Professor Tarnopol) does not elucidate in

the story the details of that misfortune; indeed, the point he makes is that, by him at least, it cannot be done. "Unfortunately, the author of this story, having himself experienced a similar misfortune at about the same age, does not have it in him, even yet, midway through his thirties, to tell it briefly or to find it funny. 'Unfortunate,'" concludes the fabricated Zuckerman, speaking in behalf of the dissembling Tarnopol, "because he wonders if that isn't more the measure of the man than of the misfortune."

In order to dilute the self-pity that (as I understand it) had poisoned his imagination in numerous previous attempts to fictionalize his unhappy marriage, Professor Tarnopol establishes at the outset here a tone of covert (and, to some small degree, self-congratulatory) self-mockery; this calculated attitude of comic detachment he maintains right on down to the last paragraph, where abruptly the shield of lightheartedness is all at once pierced by the author's pronouncement that in his estimation the true story really isn't funny at all. All of which would appear to suggest that if Professor Tarnopol has managed in "Salad Days" to make an artful narrative of his misery, he has done so largely by refusing directly to confront it.

In contrast to "Salad Days," "Courting Disaster" is marked throughout by a tone of sobriety and an air of deep concern; here is all the heartfeltness that has been suppressed in "Salad Days." A heroic quality adheres to the suffering of the major characters, and their lives are depicted as far too grave for comedy or satire. The author reports that he began this story intending that his hero should be tricked into marrying exactly as he himself had been. Why that bedeviling incident from Professor Tarnopol's personal history could not be absorbed into this fictional artifice is not difficult to understand: the Nathan Zuckerman imagined in "Courting Disaster" requires no shotgun held to his head for him to find in the needs and sorrows of Lydia Ketterer the altar upon which to offer up the sacrifice of his manhood. It is not compromising circumstances, but (in both senses) the *gravity* of his character, that determines his moral career; all the culpability is his.

In "Courting Disaster," then, Professor Tarnopol conceives of himself and Mrs. Tarnopol as characters in a struggle that, in its moral pathos, veers toward tragedy, rather than Gothic melodrama, or soap opera, or farce, which are the modes that generally obtain when Professor Tarnopol narrates the story of his marriage to me in bed. Likewise, Professor Tarnopol invents cruel misfortunes (i.e., Lydia's incestuous father, her sadistic husband, her mean little aunts, the illiterate Moonie) to validate and deepen Lydia's despair and to exacerbate Nathan's morbid sense of responsibility—this plenitude of heartache, supplying, as it were, "the objective correlative" for the emotions of shame, grief, and guilt that inform the narration.

And that informed Professor Tarnopol's marriage.

To put the matter altogether directly: if Mrs. Tarnopol had been such a Lydia, if Professor Tarnopol had been such a Nathan, and if I, Karen Oakes, had been a Moonie of a stepdaughter instead of just the star pupil of my sex in English 312 that semester, then, *then* his subsequent undoing would have made a certain poetic sense.

But as it is, he is who he is, she is who she is, and I am simply myself, the girl who would not go with him to Italy. And there is no more poetry, or tragedy, or for that matter, comedy to it than that.

Miss Oakes: As usual, A+. Prose overly magisterial in spots, but you understand the stories (and the author) remarkably well for one of your age and background. It is always something to come upon a beautiful young girl from a nice family with a theoretical turn of mind and a weakness for the grand style and the weighty epigraph. I remember you as an entirely beguiling person. On my deathbed I shall hear you calling from your room, "Will you hang up the downstairs phone, please, Mom?" That plain-spoken line spoke volumes to me too. Kareen, you were right not to run off to Italy with me. It wouldn't have been Moonie and Zuckerman, but it probably wouldn't have been any good. Still, you should know that whatever the "neurotic" reason, I was gone on you—let no man, lay or professional, say I wasn't, or ascribe my "hangup" over you simply to my having transgressed the unwritten law against copulating with those sort-of forbidden daughters known as one's students (though I admit: asking Miss Oakes, from behind my desk, to clarify further for the other students some clever answer she'd just given in class, only twenty minutes after having fallen to my knees in your room to play the supplicant beneath your belly, *was* a delicious sensation; cunnilingus aside, I don't think *teaching* has ever been so exciting, before or since, or that I've ever felt so tender or devoted to any class as I did to our English 312. Perhaps the authorities should reconsider, from a strictly pedagogical point of view, the existing taboo, being mindful of the benefits that may accrue to the class whose teacher has taken one of its members as his secret love; I'll write the AAUP about this, in good scholarly fashion of course outlining for them the tradition, from Socrates to Abelard to me—nor will I fail to mention the thanks we three received from the authorities for having thrown ourselves so conscientiously into our work. To think, I recounted to you on our very first "date" what they did to Abelard—yet, here I am still stunned at how I got mutilated by the state of New York). Ah, Miss Oakes, if only I hadn't been so overbearing! Memories of my behavior make me cringe. I told you about

Isaac Babel and about my wife with the same veins popping. My in-sistence, my doggedness, and my tears. How it must have alarmed you to hear me sobbing over the phone—your esteemed professor! If only I had taken it a little easier and suggested a couple of weeks to-gether in northern Wisconsin, some lake somewhere, rather than for-ever in tragic Europe, who knows, you might have been willing to start off that way. You were brave enough—it's just that I didn't have the wherewithal for a little at a time. At any rate, I have had enough Vivid Experience to last awhile, and am off in the bucolic woods writing my memoirs. Whether this will put the Vivid Experience to rest I don't know. Perhaps what I'll think when I'm done is that these pages add up to Maureen's final victory over Tarnopol the novelist, the culmination of my life as her man and no more. To be writing "in all candor" doesn't suggest that I've withdrawn that much from my feelings. But then why the hell should I? So maybe my animus is not wholly transformed—so maybe I am turning art into a chamberpot for hatred, as Flaubert says I shouldn't, into so much camouflage for self-vindication—so, if the other thing is what literature is, then this ain't. Ka-reen, I know I taught the class otherwise, but so what? I'll try a character like Henry Miller, or someone out-and-out bilious like Céline for my hero instead of Gustave Flaubert—and won't be such an Olympian writer as it was my ambition to be back in the days when nothing called personal experience stood between me and aesthetic detachment. Maybe it's time to revise my ideas about being an "artist," or "artiste" as my adversary's lawyer preferred to pronounce it. Maybe it was always time. Only one drawback: in that I am not a renegade bohemian or cutup of any kind (only a municipal judge could have taken me for that), I may not be well suited for the notoriety that at-tends the publication of an unabashed and unexpurgated history of one's erotic endeavors. As the history itself will testify, I happen to be no more immune to shame or built for public exposure than the next burgher with shades on his bedroom windows and a latch on the bathroom door—indeed, maybe what the whole history signifies is that I am sensitive to nothing in all the world as I am to my moral reputation. Not that I like being fleeced of my hard-earned dough either. Maybe I ought just to call this confession "The Case Against Leeches, by One Who Was Bled," and publish it as a political tract—go on Johnny Carson and angrily shake an empty billfold at America, the least I can do for all those husbands who've been robbed deaf, dumb, and blind by chorines and maureens in the courts of law. In-veigh with an upraised fist against "the system," instead of against my own stupidity for falling into the first (the first!) trap life laid for me. Or ought I to deposit these pages too into my abounding liquor car-ton, and if I must embroil myself in the battle yet again, go at it like an artist worthy of the name, without myself as the "I," without the bawling and the spleen, and whatever else unattractive that shows? What do you think, shall I give this up and go back to Zuckermanizing myself and Lydiafying Maureen and Moonieing over you? If I do take the low road of candor (and anger and so forth) and publish what I've got, will you (or your family) sue for invasion of privacy and defamation of character? And if not you, won't Susan or her family? Or will she go one better and, thoroughly humiliated, do herself in? And how will *I* take it when my photograph appears on the *Time* magazine book page, captioned "Tarnopol: stripped to his panties and bra." I can hear myself screaming already. And what about the letter in the Sunday *Times* book review section, signed by members of Maureen's Group, challenging my malicious characterization of Maureen as a pathological liar, calling *me* the liar and my *book* the fraud. How will I like it when the counterattack is launched by the opposition—will it strike me then that I have exorcised the past, or rather that now I have wed myself to it as irrevocably as ever I was wed to Maureen? How will I like reading reviews of my private life in the Toledo *Blade* and the Sacramento *Bee*? And what will *Commentary* make of this confession? I can't imagine it's good for the Jews. What about when the professional marital experts and authorities on love settle in for a marathon discussion of my personality problems on the "David Susskind Show"? Or is that just what I need to straighten me out? Maybe the best treatment possible for my excessive vulnerability and preoccupation generally with My Good Name (which is largely how I got myself into this fix to begin with) is to go forth brazenly crying, "Virtue! a fig! 'tis in ourselves that we are thus or thus." Sure, quote Iago to them—tell them, "Oh, find me self-addicted and self-deluded, find me self and nothing more! Call me a crybaby, call me a misogynist, call me a *murderer*, see if I care. 'Tis only in ourselves that we are thus or thus—bra and panties notwithstanding. Your names'll never harm me!" Only they do, Ka-reen, the names drive me wild, and always have. So where am I (to get back to literature): still too much "under the sway of passion" for Flaubertian transcendence, but too raw and touchy by far (or just too ordinary, a citizen like any other) to consider myself equal to what might, in the long run, do my sense of shame the greatest good: a full-scale unbuttoning, à la Henry Miller or Jean Genet . . . Though frankly (to use the adverb of the unbuttoned), Tarnopol, as he is called, is beginning to seem as imaginary as my Zuckermans anyway, or at least as detached from the memoirist—his revelations coming to seem like still another "useful fiction," and not because I am telling lies. I am trying to keep to the facts. Maybe all I'm saying is that words, being words, only approximate the real thing, and so no matter how close I come, I only come *close*. Or maybe I mean that as far as I can see there is no conquering or exorcising the past with words—words born either of imagination or forthrightness—as there seems to be (for me) no forgetting it. Maybe I am just learning what a past is. At any rate, all I can do with my story is tell it. And tell it. And tell it. And *that's* the truth. And you, what do you do to pass the time? And why do I care all of a sudden, and again? Perhaps because it occurs to me that you are now twenty-five, the age at which I passed out of Eden into the real unreal world—or perhaps it's just because I remember you being so uncrazy and so much your own person. Young, of course, but that to me made it all the more extraordinary. As did your face. Look, this sexual quarantine is not going to last forever, even I know that. So if you're ever passing through Vermont, give me a call. Maureen is dead (you might not have guessed from how I've gone on here) and another love affair ended recently with my friend (the Susan mentioned above) attempting to kill herself. So come on East and try your luck. See me. You always liked a little adventure. As did your esteemed professor of sublimation and high art, Peter T.

My dispute with Spielvogel arose over an article he had written for the *American Forum for Psychoanalytic Studies* and published in a special number focusing on "The Riddle of Creativity." I happened to catch sight of the magazine on his desk as I was leaving the office one evening in the third year of my analysis—noticed the symposium title on the cover and then his name among the contributors listed below. I asked if I might borrow it to read his paper. He answered, "Of course," though it seemed to me that before issuing gracious consent, a look of distress, or alarm, had crossed his face—as though anticipating (correctly) what my reaction to the piece would be . . . But if so, why had the magazine been displayed so conspicuously on the desk I passed every evening leaving his office? Since he knew that like most literary people I as a matter of course scan the titles of all printed matter lying out in the open—by now he had surely observed that reading-man's tic in me a hundred times—it would seem that either he didn't care one way or another whether I noticed the *Forum*, or that he actually wanted me to see his name on the magazine's cover and read his contribution. Why then the split second of alarm? Or was I, as he was inevitably to suggest later, merely "projecting" my own "anticipatory anxiety" onto him?

"Am I submitted in evidence?" I asked, speaking in a mild,

jesting tone, as though it was as unlikely as it was likely and didn't matter to me either way. "Yes," answered Spielvogel. "Well," said I, and pretended to be taken aback a little in order to hide just how surprised I was. "I'll read it tonight." Spielvogel's polite smile now obscured entirely whatever that might really mean to him.

As was now my custom, after the six o'clock session with Dr. Spielvogel, I walked from his office at Eighty-ninth and Park down to Susan's apartment, ten blocks to the south. It was a little more than a year since Susan had become an undergraduate at City College, and our life together had taken on a predictable and pleasant orderliness—pleasant, for me, for being so predictable. I wanted nothing more than day after day without surprises; just the sort of repetitious experience that drove other people wild with boredom was the most gratifying thing I could imagine. I was high on routine and habit.

During the day, while Susan was off at school, I went home and wrote, as best I could, in my apartment on West Twelfth Street. On Wednesdays I went off in the morning to Long Island (driving my brother's car), where I spent the day at Hofstra, teaching my two classes and in between having conferences with my writing students. Student stories were just beginning at this time to turn heavily "psychedelic"—undergraduate romantics of my own era had called their unpunctuated pages of random associations "stream-of-consciousness" writing—and to take "dope" smoking as their subject. As I happened to be largely uninterested in drug-inspired visions or the conversation that attended them, and rather impatient with writing that depended for its force upon unorthodox typographical arrangements or marginal decorations in Magic Marker, I found teaching creative writing even less rewarding than it had been back in Wisconsin, where at least there had been Karen Oakes. My other course, however, an honors reading seminar in a dozen masterpieces of my own choosing, had an unusually powerful hold on me, and I taught the class with a zealousness and vehemence that left me limp at the end of my two hours. I did not completely understand what inspired this state of manic excitement or produced my molten volubility until the course had evolved over a couple of semesters and I realized what the principle of selection was that lay behind my reading list from the masters. At the outset I had thought I was just assigning great works of fiction that I admired and wanted my fifteen senior literature students to read and admire too—only in time did I realize that a course whose core had come to be *The Brothers Karamazov*, *The Scarlet Letter*, *The Trial*, *Death in Venice*, *Anna Karenina*, and Kleist's *Michael Kohlhaas* derived of course from the professor's steadily expanding extracurricular interest in the subject of transgression and punishment.

In the city at the end of my workday I would generally walk the seventy-odd blocks to Spielvogel's office—for exercise and to unwind after yet another session at the desk trying, with little success, to make art out of my disaster, but also in the vain attempt to get myself to feel like something other than a foreigner being held against his will in a hostile and alien country. A small-city boy to begin with (growing up in Yonkers in the thirties and forties, I probably had more in common with youngsters raised in Terre Haute or Altoona than in any of the big New York boroughs), I could not see a necessary or sufficient reason for my being a resident of the busiest, most congested spot on earth, especially since what I required above all for my kind of work were solitude and quiet. My brief tenure on the Lower East Side following my discharge from the service certainly evoked no nostalgia; when, shortly after my day in court with Maureen, I hiked crosstown one morning from West Twelfth Street to Tompkins Square Park, it was not to reawaken fond memories of the old neighborhood, but to search through the scruffy little park and the rundown streets nearby for the woman from whom Maureen had bought a specimen of urine some three and a half years earlier. In a morning of hunting around, I of course saw numerous Negro women of childbearing age out in the park and in the aisles of the local supermarket and climbing on and off buses on Avenue A and B, but I did not approach a single one of them to ask if perchance back in March of 1959 she had entered into negotiations with a short, dark-haired young woman from "a scientific organization," and if so, to ask if she would now (for a consideration) come along to my lawyer's office to sign an affidavit testifying that the urine submitted to the pharmacist as Mrs. Tarnopol's had in actuality been her own. Enraged and frustrated as I was by the outcome of the separation hearing, crazed enough to spend an entire morning on this hopeless and useless undercover operation, I was never *completely* possessed.

Or is that what I am now, living here and writing this?

My point is that by and large to me Manhattan was: one, the place to which I had come in 1958 as a confident young man starting out on a promising literary career, only to wind up deceived there into marriage with a woman for whom I had lost all affection and respect; and two, the place to which I had returned in 1962, in flight and seeking refuge, only to be prevented by the local judiciary from severing the marital bond that had all but destroyed my confidence and career. To others perhaps Fun City and Gotham and the Big Apple, the Great White Way of commerce and finance and art—to me the place where I paid through the nose. The number of people with whom I shared my life in this most populous of cities could be seated comfortably around a kitchen table, and the Manhattan square footage toward which I felt an intimate attachment and considered essential to my well-being and survival would have fit, with room to spare, into the Yonkers apartment in which I'd been raised. There was my own small apartment on West Twelfth Street—rather, the few square feet holding my desk and my wastebasket; on Seventy-ninth and Park, at Susan's, there was the dining table where we ate together, the two easy chairs across from one another where we read in her living room at night, and the double bed we shared; ten blocks north of Susan's there was a psychoanalyst's couch, rich with personal associations; and up on West 107th Street, Morris's cluttered little study, where I went once a month or so, as often willingly as not, to be big-brothered—that being the northernmost pin on this runaway husband's underground railway map of New York. The remaining acreage of this city of cities was just *there*—as were those multitudes of workers and traders and executives and clerks with whom I had no connection whatsoever—and no matter which "interesting" and lively route I took to Spielvogel's office at the end of each day, whether I wandered up through the garment district, or Times Square, or the diamond center, or by way of the old bookstores on Fourth Avenue, or through the zoo in Central Park, I could never make a dent in my feeling of foreignness or alter my sense of myself as someone who had been *detained* here by the authorities, stopped in transit like that great paranoid victim and avenger of injustice in the Kleist novella that I taught with such passion out at Hofstra.

One anecdote to illustrate the dimensions of my cell and the thickness of the walls. Late one afternoon in the fall of '64, on my way up to Spielvogel's, I had stopped off at Schulte's secondhand bookstore on Fourth Avenue and descended to the vast basement where thousands of "used" novels are alphabetically arranged for sale in rows of bookshelves twelve feet high. Moving slowly through that fiction warehouse, I made my way eventually to the Ts. And there it was: my book. To one side Sterne, Styron, and Swift, to the other Thackeray, Thurber, and Trollope. In the middle (as I saw it) a secondhand copy of *A Jewish Father*, in its original blue and white jacket. I took it down and opened to the flyleaf. It had been given to "Paula" by "Jay" in April 1960. Wasn't that the very month that Maureen and I had it out amid the blooming azaleas on the Spanish Steps? I looked to see if there were markings on any of the pages, and then I placed the book back where I had found it, between *A Tale of a Tub* and *Henry Esmond*. To see out in the world, and in such company, this memento of my triumphant apprenticeship had set my emotions churning, the pride and hopelessness all at once. "That bitch!" said I, just as a teenage boy, cradling half a dozen books in his arms, and wearing a washed-out gray cotton jacket, noiselessly approached me on his sneakers. An employee, I surmised, of Schulte's lower depths. "Yes?" "Excuse me," he said, "is your name Peter Tarnopol by any chance, sir?" I colored a little. "It is." "The novelist?" I nodded my head, and then *he* turned a very rich red himself. Uncertain clearly as to what to say next, he suddenly blurted, "I mean— what ever happened to you?" I shrugged. "I don't know," I told him, "I'm waiting to find out myself." The next instant I was out into the ferment and pressing north: skirting the office workers springing from the revolving doors and past me down into the subway stations, I plunged through the scrimmage set off by the traffic light at each intersection—down the field I charged, cutting left and right through the faceless counterforce, until at last I reached Eighty-ninth Street, and dropping onto the couch, delivered over to my confidant and coach what I had carried intact all the way from Schulte's crypt—the bookboy's heartfelt question that had been blurted out at me so sweetly, and my own bemused reply. That was all I had heard through the world-famous midtown din which travelers journey halfway round the globe to behold.

So then: after paying my call on the doctor, I would head on down to Susan's for dinner and to spend the evening, the two of us most nights reading in those easy chairs on either side of the fireplace, until at midnight we went to bed, and before sleep, regularly devoted ourselves for some fifteen or twenty minutes to our mutual effort at erotic rehabilitation. In the morning Susan was up and out by seven thirty—Dr. Golding's first patient of the day—and about an hour later I departed myself, book in hand, only occasionally now getting a look from one of the residents who thought that if the young widow McCall had fallen to a gentleman caller of the Israelite persuasion in baggy corduroy trousers and scuffed suede shoes, she might at least instruct him to enter and exit by way of the service elevator. Still, if not suitably haut bourgeois for Susan's stately co-op, I was in most ways leading the "regular and orderly" life that Flaubert had recommended for him who would be "violent and original" in his work.

And the work, I thought, was beginning to show it. At least there was beginning to *be* work that I did not feel I had to consign, because it was so bad, to the liquor carton at the bottom of my closet. In the previous year I had completed three short stories: one had been published in the *New Yorker*, one in the *Kenyon Review*, and the third was to appear in *Harper's*. They constituted the first fiction of mine in print since the publication of *A Jewish Father* in 1959. The three stories, simple though they were, demonstrated a certain clarity and calm that had not been the hallmark of my writing over the previous years; inspired largely by incidents from boyhood and adolescence that I had recollected in analysis, they had nothing to do with Maureen and the urine and the marriage. *That* book, based upon my misadventures in manhood, I still, of course, spent maddening hours on every day, and I had some two thousand pages of manuscript in the liquor carton to prove it. By now the various abandoned drafts had gotten so shuffled together and interwoven, the pages so defaced with Xs and arrows of a hundred different intensities of pen and pencil, the margins so tattooed with comments, reminders, with schemes for pagination (Roman numerals, Arabic numerals, letters of the alphabet in complex combinations that even I, the cryptographer, could no longer decode) that what impressed one upon attempting to penetrate that prose was not the imaginary world it depicted, but the condition of the person who'd been doing the imagining: the manuscript was the message, and the message was Turmoil. I had, in fact, found a quotation from Flaubert appropriate to my failure, and had copied it out of my worn volume of his correspondence (a book purchased during my army stint to help tide me over to civilian life); I had Scotch-taped the quotation to the carton bearing those five hundred thousand words, not a one of them *juste*. It seemed to me it might be a fitting epitaph to that effort, when and if I was finally going to have to call it quits. Flaubert, to his mistress Louise Colet, who had published a poem maligning their contemporary, Alfred de Musset: "You wrote with a personal emotion that distorted your outlook and made it impossible to keep before your eyes the fundamental principles that must underlie any imaginative composition. It has no aesthetic. You have turned art into an outlet for passion, a kind of chamberpot to catch an overflow. It smells bad; it smells of hate!"

But if I could not leave off picking at the corpse and remove it from the autopsy room to the grave, it was because this genius, who had done so much to form my literary conscience as a student and an aspiring novelist, had also written—

Art, like the Jewish God, wallows in sacrifice.

And:

In Art . . . the creative impulse is essentially fanatic.

And:

. . . the excesses of the great masters! They pursue an idea to its furthermost limits.

These inspirational justifications for what Dr. Spielvogel might describe simply as "a fixation due to a severe traumatic experience" I also copied out on strips of paper and (with some self-irony, I must say) taped them too, like so many fortune-cookie ribbons, across the face of the box containing my novel-in-chaos.

On the evening that I arrived at Susan's with the *American Forum for Psychoanalytic Studies* in my hand, I called hello from the door, but instead of going to the kitchen, as was my habit—how I habituated myself during those years! how I coveted whatever orderliness I had been able to reestablish in my life!—to chat with her from a stool while she prepared our evening's delicacies, I went into the living room and sat on the edge of Jamey's flame-stitch ottoman, reading quickly through Spielvogel's article, entitled "Creativity: The Narcissism of the Artist." Somewhere in the middle of the piece I came upon what I'd been looking for—at least I *supposed* this was it: "A successful Italian-American poet in his forties entered into therapy because of anxiety states experienced as a result of his enormous ambivalence about leaving his wife. . . ." Up to this point in the article, the patients described by Spielvogel had been "an actor," "a painter," and "a composer"—so this *had* to be me. Only I had not been in my forties when I first became Spielvogel's patient; I'd come to him at age twenty-nine, wrecked by a mistake I'd made at twenty-six. Surely between a man in his forties and a man in his twenties there are differences of experience, expectation, and character that cannot be brushed aside so easily as this . . . And "successful"? Does that word (in my mind, I immediately began addressing Spielvogel directly), does that word describe to you the tenor of my life at that time? A "successful" apprenticeship, absolutely, but when I came to you in 1962, at age twenty-nine, I had for three years been writing fiction I couldn't stand, and I could no longer even teach a class without fear of Maureen rushing in to "expose" me to my students. Successful? His forties? And surely it goes without saying that to disguise (in my brother's words) "a nice civilized Jewish boy" as something called "an Italian-American," well, that is to be somewhat dim-witted about matters of social and cultural background that might well impinge upon a person's psychology and values. And while we're at it, Dr. Spielvogel, a poet and a novelist have about as much in common as a jockey and a diesel driver. Somebody ought to tell you that, especially since "creativity" is your subject here.

Poems and novels arise out of radically different sensibilities and resemble each other not at all, and you cannot begin to make sense about "creativity" or "the artist" or even "narcissism" if you are going to be so insensitive to fundamental distinctions having to do with age, accomplishment, background, and vocation. And if I may, sir—his *self* is to many a novelist what his own physiognomy is to a painter of portraits: the closest subject at hand demanding scrutiny, a problem for his art to solve—given the enormous obstacles to truthfulness, *the* artistic problem. He is not simply looking into the mirror because he is transfixed by what he sees. Rather, the artist's success depends as much as anything on his powers of detachment, on *de*narcissizing himself. That's where the excitement comes in. That hard *conscious* work that makes it *art*! Freud, Dr. Spielvogel, studied his own dreams not because he was a "narcissist," but because he was a student of dreams. And whose were at once the least and most accessible of dreams, if not his own?

. . . And so it went, my chagrin renewed practically with each word. I could not read a sentence in which it did not seem to me that the observation was off, the point missed, the nuance blurred—in short, the evidence rather munificently distorted so as to support a narrow and unilluminating thesis at the expense of the ambiguous and perplexing actuality. In all there were only two pages of text on the "Italian-American poet," but so angered and disappointed was I by what seemed to me the unflagging wrongness of the description of my case, that it took me ten minutes to get from the top of page 85 to the bottom of 86. ". . . enormous ambivalence about leaving his wife. . . . It soon became clear that the poet's central problem here as elsewhere was his castration anxiety vis-à-vis a phallic mother figure. . . ." Not so! His central problem here as elsewhere derives from nothing of the sort. That will not serve to explain his "enormous ambivalence" about leaving his wife any more than it describes the prevailing emotional tone of his childhood years, which was one of intensive *security*. "His father was a harassed man, ineffectual and submissive to his mother. . . ." What? Now where did you get that idea? My father was harassed, all right, but not by his wife—any child who lived in the same house with them knew that much. He was harassed by his own adamant refusal to allow his three

children or his wife to do without: he was harassed by his own
vigor, by his ambitions, by his business, by the times. By his
overpowering commitment to the idea of Family and the religion he made of Doing A Man's Job! My "ineffectual" father
happened to have worked twelve hours a day, six and seven
days a week, often simultaneously at two exhausting jobs, with
the result that not even when the store was as barren of customers as the Arctic tundra, did his loved ones lack for anything essential. Broke and overworked, no better off than a
serf or an indentured servant in the America of the thirties, he
did not take a drink, jump out of the window, or beat his wife
and kids—and by the time he sold Tarnopol's Haberdashery
and retired two years ago, he was making twenty thousand
bucks a year. Good Christ, Spielvogel, from whose example
did I come to associate virility with hard work and self-
discipline, if not from my father's? Why did I like to go down
to the store on Saturdays and spend all day in the stockroom
arranging and stacking the boxes of goods? In order to hang
around an ineffectual father? Why did I listen like Desdemona
to Othello when he used to lecture the customers on Interwoven socks and McGregor shirts—because he was *bad* at it?
Don't kid yourself—and the other psychiatrists. It was because
I was so *proud* of his affiliation with those big brand names—
because his pitch was so *convincing*. It wasn't his wife's hostil-
ity he had to struggle against, but the world's! And he did it,
with splitting headaches to be sure, *but without giving in.* I've
told you that a hundred times. Why don't you believe me?
Why, to substantiate your "ideas," do you want to create this
fiction about me and my family, when your gift obviously lies
elsewhere. Let *me* make up stories—you make sense! ". . . in
order to avoid a confrontation with his dependency needs
toward his wife the poet acted out sexually with other women
almost from the beginning of his marriage." But that just is
not so! You must be thinking of some other poet. Look, is this
supposed to be an amalgam of the ailing, or me alone? Who
was there to "act out" with other than Karen? Doctor, I had a
desperate *affair* with that girl—hopeless and ill-advised and
adolescent, that may well be, but also passionate, also painful,
also *warm-hearted*, which was what the whole thing was about
to begin with: I was dying for some *humanness* in my life,

*that's* why I reached out and touched her hair! And oh yes, I fucked a prostitute in Naples after a forty-eight hour fight with Maureen in our hotel. And another in Venice, correct—making two in all. Is that what you call "acting out" with "other women almost from the beginning of his marriage"? The marriage only lasted three years! It was *all* "almost" the beginning. And why don't you mention how it began? ". . . he once picked up a girl at a party. . . ." But that was here in New York, months and months *after* I had left Maureen in Wisconsin. The marriage was *over*, even if the state of New York refused to allow that to be so! ". . . the poet acted out his anger in his relationships with women, reducing all women to masturbatory sexual objects. . . ." Now, do you really mean to say that? All women? Is that what Karen Oakes was to me, "a masturbatory sexual object"? Is that what Susan McCall is to me now? Is that why I have encouraged and cajoled and berated her into going back to finish her schooling, because she is "a masturbatory sexual object"? Is that why I nearly give myself a stroke each night trying to help her to come? Look, let's get down to the case of cases: Maureen. Do you think that's what *she* was to me, "a masturbatory sexual object"? Good God, what a reading of my story *that* is! Rather than reducing that lying, hysterical bitch to an object of any kind, I made the grotesque mistake of *elevating* her to the status of a human being toward whom I had a *moral responsibility*. Nailed myself with my romantic morality to the cross of her desperation! Or, if you prefer, caged myself in with my cowardice! And don't tell me that was out of "guilt" for having *already* made of her "a masturbatory sexual object" because you just can't have it both ways! Had I actually been able to treat her as some goddam "object," or simply to see her for what she was, I would never have done my manly duty and married her! Did it ever occur to you, Doctor, in the course of your ruminations, that maybe *I* was the one who was made into a sexual object? You've got it all backwards, Spielvogel—inside out! And how can that be? How can you, who have done me so much good, have it all so wrong? Now *there* is something to write an article about! *That* is a subject for a symposium! Don't you see, it isn't that women mean too little to me—what's caused the trouble is that they mean so much. The testing ground, not for potency, but *virtue!* Believe me, if I'd listened to my prick instead of to my upper organs, I would never have gotten into this mess to begin with! I'd still be fucking Dina Dornbusch! And she'd have been my wife!

What I read next brought me up off the ottoman and to my feet, as though in a terrifying dream my name had finally been called—then I remembered that blessedly it was not a Jewish novelist in his late twenties or early thirties called Tarnopol, but a nameless Italian-American poet in his forties that Spielvogel claimed to be describing (and diagnosing) for his colleagues. ". . . leaving his semen on fixtures, towels, etc., so completely libidinized was his anger; on another occasion, he dressed himself in nothing but his wife's underpants, brassiere, and stockings. . . ." Stockings? Oh, I didn't put on her stockings, damn it! Can't you get anything right? And it was not at all "another occasion"! One, she had just drawn blood from her wrist with my razor; two, she had just confessed (a) to perpetrating a fraud to get me to marry her and (b) to keeping it secret from me for three wretched years of married life; three, she had just threatened to put Karen's "pure little face" in every newspaper in Wisconsin—

Then came the worst of it, what made the protective disguise of the Italian-American poet so ludicrous . . . In the very next paragraph Spielvogel recounted an incident from my childhood that I had myself narrated somewhat more extensively in the autobiographical *New Yorker* story published above my name the previous month.

It had to do with a move we had made during the war, when Moe was off in the merchant marine. To make way for the landlord's newlywed daughter and her husband, we had been dispossessed from the second-floor apartment of the two-family house where we had been living ever since the family had moved to Yonkers from the Bronx nine years earlier, when I'd been born. My parents had been able to find a new apartment very like our old one, and fortunately only a little more expensive, some six blocks away in the same neighborhood; nonetheless, they had been infuriated by the high-handed treatment they had received from the landlord, particularly given the loving, proprietary care that my mother had taken of the building, and my father of the little yard, over the years.

For me, being uprooted after a lifetime in the same house was utterly bewildering; to make matters even worse, the first night in our new apartment I had gone to bed with the room in a state of disarray that was wholly foreign to our former way of life. Would it be this way forevermore? Eviction? Confusion? Disorder? Were we on the skids? Would this somehow result in my brother's ship, off in the dangerous North Atlantic, being sunk by a German torpedo? The day after the move, when it came time to go home from school for lunch, instead of heading off for the new address, I "unthinkingly" returned to the house in which I had lived all my life in perfect safety with brother, sister, mother, and father. At the second-floor landing I was astonished to find the door to our apartment wide open and to hear men talking loudly inside. Yet standing in the hallway on that floor planed smooth over the years by my mother's scrub brush, I couldn't seem to get myself to remember that we had moved the day before and now lived elsewhere. "It's Nazis!" I thought. The Nazis had parachuted into Yonkers, made their way to our street, and taken everything away. *Taken my mother away.* So I suddenly perceived it. I was no braver than the ordinary nine-year-old, and no bigger, and so where I got the courage to peek inside I don't know. But when I did, I saw that "the Nazis" were only the housepainters sitting on a drop cloth on what used to be our living-room floor, eating their sandwiches out of wax-paper wrappings. I ran—down that old stairwell, the feel of the rubber treads on each stair as familiar to me as the teeth in my head, and through the neighborhood to our new family sanctum, and at the sight of my mother in her apron (unbeaten, unbloodied, unraped, though visibly distressed from imagining what might have happened to delay her punctual child on his way home from school), I collapsed into her arms in a fit of tears.

Now, as Spielvogel interpreted this incident, I cried in large part because of "guilt over the aggressive fantasies directed toward the mother." As I construed it—in the short story in journal form, entitled "The Diary of Anne Frank's Contemporary"—I cry with relief to find that my mother is alive and well, that the new apartment has been transformed during the morning I have been in school into a perfect replica of the old one—and that we are Jews who live in the haven of

Westchester County, rather than in our ravaged, ancestral, Jew-hating Europe.

Susan finally came in from the kitchen to see what I was doing off by myself.

"Why are you standing there like that? Peter, what's happened?"

I held the journal in the air. "Spielvogel has written an article about something he calls 'creativity.' And I'm in it."

"By *name*?"

"No, but identifiably me. *Me* coming home to the wrong house when I was nine. He *knew* I was using it. I talked about that story to him, and still he goes ahead and has some fictitious Italian-American poet—!"

"Who? I can't follow you."

"Here!" I handed her the magazine. "Here! This straw fucking patient is supposed to be me! Read it! Read this thing!"

She sat down on the ottoman and began to read. "Oh, Peter."

"Keep going."

"It says . . ."

"What?"

"It says here—you put on Maureen's underwear and stockings. Oh, he's out of his mind."

"He's not—I did. Keep reading."

Her tear appeared. "You *did*?"

"Not the stockings, *no*—that's him, writing his banal fucking fiction! *He* makes it sound like I was dressing up for the drag-queen ball! All I was doing, Susan, was saying, 'Look, I wear the panties in this family and don't you forget it!' That's all it boils down to! Keep reading! He doesn't get *anything* right. It's all perfectly *off*!"

She read a little further, then put the magazine in her lap. "Oh, sweetheart."

"What? *What?*"

"It says . . ."

"My sperm?"

"Yes."

"*I did that too.* But I don't any more! Keep reading!"

"Well," said Susan, wiping away her tear with a fingertip,

"don't shout at *me*. I think it's awful that he's written this and put it in print. It's unethical, it's reckless—and I can't even believe he would do such a thing. You tell me he's so smart. You make him sound so *wise*. But how could anybody wise do something so insensitive and uncaring as *this*?"

"Just read on. Read the whole hollow pretentious meaningless thing, right on down to the footnotes from Goethe and Baudelaire to prove a connection between 'narcissism' and 'art'! So what else is new? Oh, Jesus, what this man thinks of as *evidence*! 'As Sophocles has written,'—and that constitutes *evidence*! Oh, you ought to go through this thing, line by line, and watch the ground shift beneath you! Between every paragraph there's a hundred-foot drop!"

"What are you going to do?"

"What *can* I do? It's printed—it's out."

"Well, you just can't sit back and take it. He's betrayed your confidence!"

"I know that."

"Well, that's terrible."

"I know that!"

"Then *do* something!" she pleaded.

On the phone Spielvogel said that if I was as "distressed" as I sounded—"I am!" I assured him—he would stay after his last patient to see me for the second time that day. So, leaving Susan (who had much to be distressed about, too), I took a bus up Madison to his office and sat in the waiting room until seven thirty, constructing in my mind angry scenes that could only culminate in leaving Spielvogel forever.

The argument between us was angry, all right, and it went on unabated through my sessions for a week, but it was Spielvogel, not I, who finally suggested that I leave him. Even while reading his article, I hadn't been so shocked—so unwilling to believe in what he was doing—as when he suddenly rose from his chair (even as I continued my attack on him from the couch) and took a few listing steps around to where I could see him. Ordinarily I addressed myself to the bookcase in front of the couch, or to the ceiling overhead, or to the photograph of the Acropolis that I could see on the desk across the room. At the sight of him at my side, I sat straight up. "Look," he said, "this has gone far enough. I think either you will have now to forget this article of mine, or leave me. But we cannot proceed with treatment under these condition."

"What kind of choice is that?" I asked, my heart beginning to beat wildly. He remained in the middle of the room, supporting himself now with a hand on the back of a chair. "I have been your patient for over two years. I have an investment here—of effort, of time, of hope, of money. I don't consider myself recovered. I don't consider myself able to go at my life alone just yet. And neither do you."

"But if as a result of what I have written about you, you find me so 'untrustworthy' and so 'unethical,' so absolutely 'wrong' and, as you put it, 'off' about relations between you and your family, then why would you want to stay on as a patient any longer? It is clear that I am too flawed to be your doctor."

"Come off it, please. Don't hit me over the head with the 'narcissism' again. You know why I want to stay on."

"Why?"

"Because I'm scared to be out there alone. But also because I *am* stronger—things in my life *are* better. Because staying with you, I was finally able to leave Maureen. That was no inconsequential matter for me, you know. If I hadn't left her, I'd be dead—dead or in jail. You may think that's an exaggeration, but I happen to know that it's true. What I'm saying is that on the practical side, on the subject of my everyday life, you have been a considerable help to me. You've been with me through some bad times. You've prevented me from doing some wild and foolish things. Obviously I haven't been coming here three times a week for two years for no reason. But all that doesn't mean that this article is something I can just forget."

"But there is really nothing more to be said about it. We have discussed it now for a week. We have been over it thoroughly. There is nothing new to add."

"You could add that you were wrong."

"I have answered the charge already and more than once. I don't find anything I did 'wrong.'"

"It was wrong, it was at the very least imprudent, for you to use that incident in your article, knowing as you did that I was using it in a story."

"We were writing simultaneously, I explained that to you."

"But I told you I was using it in the Anne Frank story."

"You are not remembering correctly. I did not know you had used it until I read the story last month in the *New Yorker*. By then the article was at the printer's."

"You could have changed it then—left that incident out. And I am not remembering incorrectly."

"First you complain that by disguising your identity I misrepresent you and badly distort the reality. You're a Jew, not an Italian-American. You're a novelist, not a poet. You came to me at twenty-nine, not at forty. Then in the next breath you complain that I fail to disguise your identity enough—rather, that I have *revealed* your identity by using this particular incident. This of course is your ambivalence again about your 'specialness.'"

"It is not of course my ambivalence again! You're confusing the argument again. You're blurring important distinctions— just as you do in that piece! Let's at least take up each issue in turn."

"We have taken up each issue in turn, three and four times over."

"But you still refuse to get it. Even if your article was at the printer, once you had read the Anne Frank story you should have made every effort to protect my privacy—and my trust in you!"

"It was impossible."

"You could have withdrawn the article."

"You are asking the impossible."

"What is more important, publishing your article or keeping my trust?"

"Those were not my alternatives."

"But they *were*."

"That is the way you see it. Look here, we are clearly at an impasse, and under these conditions treatment cannot be continued. We can make no progress."

"But I did not just walk in off the street last week. *I am your patient.*"

"True. And I cannot be under attack from my patient any longer."

"Tolerate it," I said bitterly—a phrase of his that had helped me through some rough days. "Look, given that you must

certainly have had an *inkling* that I might be using that incident in a piece of fiction, since you in fact *knew* I was working
on a story to which that incident was the conclusion, mightn't
you at the very least have thought to ask my permission, ask if
it was all right with me . . ."

"Do you ask permission of the people you write about?"

"But I am not a psychoanalyst! The comparison won't work.
I write fiction—or did, once upon a time. *A Jewish Father* was
not 'about' my family, or about Grete and me, as you certainly
must realize. It may have originated there, but it was finally a
contrivance, an artifice, a *rumination* on the real. A self-
avowed work of imagination, Doctor! I do not write 'about'
people in a strict factual or historical sense."

"But then you think," he said, with a hard look, "that I
don't either."

"Dr. Spielvogel, please, that is just not a good enough answer. And you must know it. First off, you are bound by ethical considerations that happen not to be the ones that apply to
my profession. Nobody comes to me with confidences the way
they do to you, and if they tell me stories, it's not so that I can
cure what ails them. That's obvious enough. It's in the nature
of being a novelist to make private life public—that's a part of
what a novelist is up to. But certainly it is not what I thought
*you* were up to when I came here. I thought your job was to
treat me! And second, as to accuracy—you are *supposed* to be
accurate, after all, even in you haven't been as accurate as I
would want you to be in this thing here."

"Mr. Tarnopol, 'this thing here' is a scientific paper. None
of us could write such papers, none of us could share our
findings with one another, if we had to rely upon the permission or the approval of our patients in order to publish. You
are not the only patient who would want to censor out the unpleasant facts or who would find 'inaccurate' what he doesn't
like to hear about himself."

"Oh that won't wash, and you know it! I'm willing to hear
anything about myself—and always have been. My problem, as
I see it, isn't my impenetrability. As a matter of fact, I tend to
rise to the bait, Dr. Spielvogel, as Maureen, for one, can testify."

"Oh, do you? Ironically, it is the narcissistic defenses dis-

cussed here that prevent you from accepting the article as
something other than an assault upon your dignity or an attempt to embarrass or belittle you. It is precisely the blow to
your narcissism that has swollen the issue out of all proportion
for you. Simultaneously, you act as though it is about nothing
*but* you, when actually, of the fifteen pages of text, your case
takes up barely two. But then you do not like at all the idea of
yourself suffering from 'castration anxiety.' You do not like the
idea of your aggressive fantasies vis-à-vis your mother. You
never have. You do not like me to describe your father, and by
extension you, his son and heir, as 'ineffectual' and 'submissive,' though you don't like when I call you 'successful' either.
Apparently that tends to dilute a little too much your comforting sense of victimized innocence."

"Look, I'm sure there are in New York City such people as
you've just described. Only I ain't one of 'em! Either that's
some model you've got in your head, some kind of patient for
all seasons, or else it's some other patient of yours you're
thinking about; I don't know what the hell to make of it,
frankly. Maybe what it comes down to is a problem of self-
expression; maybe it's that the writing isn't very precise."

"Oh, the writing is also a problem?"

"I don't like to say it, but maybe writing isn't your strong
point."

He smiled. "Could it be, in your estimation? Could I be
precise enough to please you? I think perhaps what so disturbs
you about the incident in the Anne Frank story is not that by
using it I may have disclosed your identity, but that in your
opinion I plagiarized and abused your material. You are made
so very angry by this piece of writing that I have dared to publish. But if I am such a weak and imprecise writer as you suggest, then you should not feel so threatened by my little foray
into English prose."

"I don't feel 'threatened.' Oh, please, don't argue like Maureen, will you? That is just more of that language again, which
doesn't at all express what you mean and doesn't get anyone
anywhere."

"I assure you, unlike Maureen, I said 'threatened' because I
meant 'threatened.'"

"But maybe writing *isn't* your strong point. Maybe that is an objective statement of fact and has nothing to do with whether I am a writer or a tightrope walker."

"But why should it matter so much to you?"

"Why? Why?" That he could seriously ask this question just took the heart out of me; I felt the tears welling up. "Because, among other things, I am the subject of that writing! I am the one your imprecise language has misrepresented! Because I come here each day and turn over the day's receipts, every last item of my most personal life, and in return I expect an accurate accounting!" I had begun to cry. "You were my friend, and I told you the truth. I told you everything."

"Look, let me disabuse you of the idea that the whole world is waiting with bated breath for the newest issue of our little journal in which you claim you are misrepresented. I assure you that is not the case. It is not the *New Yorker* magazine, or even the *Kenyon Review*. If it is any comfort to you, most of my colleagues don't even bother to read it. But this is your narcissism again. Your sense that the whole world has nothing to look forward to but the latest information about the secret life of Peter Tarnopol."

The tears had stopped. "And that is your reductivism again, if I may say so, and your obfuscation. Spare me that word 'narcissism,' will you? You use it on me like a club."

"The word is purely descriptive and carries no valuation," said the doctor.

"Oh, is that so? Well, you be on the receiving end and see how little 'valuation' it carries! Look, can't we grant that there is a difference between self-esteem and vanity, between pride and megalomania? Can we grant that there actually is an ethical matter at stake here, and that my sensitivity to it, and your apparent indifference to it, cannot be explained away as a psychological aberration of *mine*? You've got a psychology too, you know. You do this with me all the time, Dr. Spielvogel. First you shrink the area of moral concern, you say that what I, for instance, call my responsibility toward Susan is so much camouflaged narcissism—and then if I consent to see it that way, and I leave off with the moral implications of my conduct, you tell me I'm a narcissist who thinks only about his own welfare. Maureen, you know, used to do something similar—only she worked the hog-tying game from the other way round. She made the kitchen *sink* into a moral issue! Everything in the whole wide world was a test of my decency and honor—and the moral ignoramus you're looking at believed her! If driving out of Rome for Frascati, I took a wrong turn, she had me pegged within half a mile as a felon, as a fiend up from Hell by way of Westchester and the Ivy League. And I believed her! . . . Look, look—let's *talk* about Maureen a minute, let's talk about the possible consequences of all this for me, 'narcissistic' as that must seem to you. Suppose Maureen were to get hold of this issue and read what you've written here. It's not unlike her, after all, to be on her toes where I'm concerned—where *alimony* is concerned. I mean it won't do, to go back a moment to what you just said—it won't do to say that nobody reads the magazine anyway. Because if you really believed that, then you wouldn't publish your paper there to begin with. What good are your findings published in a magazine that has no readers? The magazine is around, and it's read by somebody, surely here in New York it is—and if it somehow came to Maureen's attention . . . well, just imagine how happy she would be to read those pages about me to the judge in the courtroom. Just imagine a New York municipal judge taking that stuff in. Do you see what I'm saying?"

"Oh, I see very well what you're saying."

"Where you write, for instance, that I was 'acting out' sexually with other women 'almost from the beginning of the marriage.' First off, that is not accurate either. Stated like that, you make it seem as though I'm just another Italian-American who sneaks off after work each day for a quick bang on the way home from the poetry office. Do you follow me? You make me sound like somebody who is simply fucking around with women all the time. And that is not so. God knows what you write here is not a proper description of my affair with Karen. That was nothing if it wasn't earnest—and earnest in part because I was so *new* at it!"

"And the prostitutes?"

"Two prostitutes—in three years. That breaks down to about half a prostitute a year, which is probably, among miserably married men, a national record for *not* acting out. Have you forgotten? *I was miserable!* See the thing in context, will you? You seem to forget that the wife I was married to was Maureen. You seem to forget the circumstances under which we were married. You seem to forget that we had an argument in every piazza, cathedral, museum, trattoria, pensione, and hotel on the Italian peninsula. Another man would have beaten her head in! My predecessor Mezik, the Yugoslav barkeep, would have 'acted out' with a right to the jaw. I am a literary person. I went forth and did the civilized thing—I laid a three-thousand-lire whore! Ah, and that's how you came up with 'Italian-American' for me, isn't it?"

He waved a hand to show what he thought of my *aperçu*—then said, "Another man might have confronted his wife more directly, that is true, rather than libidinizing his anger."

"But the only direct way to confront that woman was *to kill her*! And you yourself have told me that killing people is against the law, crazy wives included. I was not 'sexually acting out,' whatever that means—I was trying to stay alive in all that madness. Stay *me*! 'Let me shun that,' and so on!"

"And," he was saying, "you conveniently forget once again the wife of your young English department colleague in Wisconsin."

"Good Christ, who are you, Cotton Mather? Look, I may be childish and a weakling, I may even be the narcissist of your fondest professional dreams—*but I am not a slob!* I am not a bum or a lecher or a gigolo or some kind of walking penis. Why do you want to portray me that way? Why do you want to characterize me in your writing as some sort of heartless rapist manqué? Surely, surely there is another way to describe my affair with Karen—"

"But I said nothing about Karen. I only reminded you of the wife of your colleague, whom you ran into that afternoon at the shopping center in Madison."

"You've got such a good memory, why don't you also remember that I didn't even fuck her! She blew me, in the car. So what? *So what?* I tell you, it was a surprise to the two of us. And what's it to you, anyway? I mean that! We were friends. She wasn't so happily married either. That, for Christ's sake, wasn't 'sexually acting out.' It was friendship! It was heartbrokenness! It was generosity! It was tenderness! It was despair! It was being adolescents together for ten secret minutes in the rear of a car before we both went nobly back into Adulthood! It was a sweet and harmless game of Let's Pretend! Smile, if you like, smile from your pulpit, but that's still closer to a proper description of what was going on there than what *you* call it. And we did not let it go any further, which was a possibility, you know; we let it remain a kind of happy, inconsequential accident and returned like good soldiers to the fucking front lines. Really, Your Holiness, really, Your Excellency, does that in your mind add up to 'acting out sexually with other women from the beginning of the marriage'?"

"Doesn't it?"

"Two street whores in Italy, a friend in a car in Madison . . . and Karen? No! I call it practically *monkish*, given the fact of my marriage. I call it pathetic, that's what! From the beginning of his marriage, the Italian-American poet had some crazy idea that now that he was a husband his mission in life was to be *faithful*—to whom never seemed to cross his mind. It was like *keeping his word* and *doing his duty*—what had gotten him married to this shrew in the first place! Once again the Italian-American poet did what he thought to be 'manly' and 'upright' and 'principled'—which, needless to say, was only what was cowardly and submissive. Pussy-whipped, as my brother so succinctly puts it! As a matter of fact, Dr. Spielvogel, those two Italian whores and my colleague's wife back of the shopping center, and Karen, constituted the only praiseworthy, the only manly, the only *moral* . . . oh, the hell with it."

"I think at this point we are only saying the same thing in our different vocabularies. Isn't that what you just realized?"

"No, no, no, no, no. I just realized that you are never going to admit to me that you could be mistaken in any single particular of diction, or syntax, let alone in the overriding idea of that paper. Talk about narcissism as a defense!"

He did not bristle at my tone, contemptuous as it had become. His voice throughout had been strong and even—a touch of sarcasm, some irony, but no outrage, and certainly no tears. Which was as it should be. What did he have to lose if I left?

"I am not a student any longer, Mr. Tarnopol. I do not look to my patients for literary criticism. You would prefer that I leave the professional writing to you, it would seem, and confine my activities to this room. You remember how distressed you were several years ago to discover that I occasionally went out into the streets to ride the bus."

"That was awe. Don't worry, I'm over it."

"Good. No reason for you to think I'm perfect."

"I don't."

"On the other hand, the alternative is not necessarily to think I am another Maureen, out to betray and deceive you for my own sadistic and vengeful reasons."

"I didn't say you were."

"You may nonetheless think that I am."

"If you mean do I think that I have been misused by you, the answer is yes. Maureen is not the issue—that article is."

"All right, that is your judgment. Now you must decide what you are going to do about the treatment. If you want to continue with your attack upon me, treatment will be impossible —it would be foolish even to try. If you want to return to the business at hand, then of course I am prepared to go forward. Or perhaps there is a third alternative that you may wish to consider—perhaps you will choose to take up treatment with somebody else. This is for you to decide before the next session."

Susan was enraged by the decision I did reach. I never had heard her argue about anything as she did against Spielvogel's "brutal" handling of me, nor had she ever dared to criticize me so forthrightly either. Of course her objections were in large part supplied by Dr. Golding, who, she told me, had been "appalled" by the way Spielvogel had dealt with me in the article in the *Forum*; however, she would never even have begun to communicate Golding's position to me if it were not for startling changes that were taking place in her attitude toward herself. Now, maybe reading about me walking around in Maureen's underwear did something to boost her confidence with me, but whatever had triggered it, I found myself delighted by the emergence of the vibrant and emphatic side so long suppressed in her—at the same time that I was greatly troubled by the possibility that what she and her doctor were suggesting about my decision to stay with Spielvogel constituted more of the humbling truth. Certainly in my defense I offered up to Susan what sounded even to me like the feeblest of arguments.

"You should leave him," she said.

"I can't. Not at this late date. He's done me more good than harm."

"But he's got you all wrong. How could that do anybody any good?"

"I don't know—but it did me. Maybe he's a lousy analyst and a good therapist."

"That makes no sense, Peter."

"Look, I'm not getting into bed with my worst enemy any more, am I? I am out of that, am I not?"

"But any doctor would have helped you to leave her. Any doctor who was the least bit competent would have seen you through that."

"But he happens to be the one who did it."

"Does that mean he can just get away with anything as a result? His sense of what you are is all wrong. Publishing that article without consulting you about it first was all wrong. His attitude when you confronted him with what he had done, the way he said, 'Either shut up or go'—that was as wrong as wrong can be. And you know it! Dr. Golding said that was as reprehensible as anything he had ever heard of between a doctor and his patient. Even his writing stinks—you said it was just jargon and crap."

"Look, I'm staying with him. I don't want to talk about it any more."

"If *I* answered *you* like that, you'd hit the ceiling. You'd say, 'Stop backing away! Stand up for yourself, twerp!' Oh, I don't understand why you are acting like this, when the man has so clearly abused you. Why do you let people get away with such things?"

"Which people?"

"Which people? People like Maureen. People like Spiel-vogel. People who . . ."

"What?"

"Well, walk all over you like that."

"Susan, I cannot put in any more time thinking of myself as someone who gets walked over. It gets me nowhere."

"Then don't be one! Don't let them get away with it!"

"It doesn't seem to me that in this case anybody is getting away with anything."

"Oh, Lambchop, that isn't what Dr. Golding says."

Spielvogel simply shrugged off what Dr. Golding said, when I passed it on to him. "I don't know the man," he grunted, and that was that. Settled. As though if he did know him, he could tell me Golding's motives for taking such a position—otherwise, why bother? As for Susan's anger, and her uncharacteristic vehemence about my leaving him, well, I understood that, did I not? She hated Spielvogel for what Spielvogel had written about the Peter who was to *her* so inspirational and instructive, the man she had come to adore for the changes he was helping to bring about in her life. Spielvogel had demythologized her Pygmalion—of course Galatea was furious. Who expected otherwise?

I must say, his immunity to criticism *was* sort of dazzling. Indeed, the imperviousness of this pallid doctor with the limping gait seemed to me, in those days of uncertainty and self-doubt, a condition to aspire to: *I am right and you are wrong, and even if I'm not, I'll just hold out and hold out and not give a single inch, and that will make it so.* And maybe that's why I stayed on with him—out of admiration for his armor, in the hope that some of that impregnability would rub off on me. Yes, I thought, he is teaching me by example, the arrogant German son of a bitch. Only I won't give him the satisfaction of telling him. Only who is to say he doesn't know it? Only who is to say he does, other than I?

As the weeks passed and Susan continued to grimace at the mention of Spielvogel's name, I sometimes came close to making what seemed to me the best possible defense of him—and thereby of myself, for if it turned out that I had been as deluded about Spielvogel as about Maureen, it was going to be awfully hard ever to believe in my judgment again. In order to substantiate my own claim to sanity and intelligence, and to protect my sense of trust from total collapse (or was it just to perpetuate my childish illusions? to cherish and protect my naiveté right on down to the last good drop?), I felt I had to make as strong a case as I could for him. And even if that meant accepting as valid his obfuscating defense—even if it meant looking back myself with psychoanalytic skepticism upon my own valid objections! "Look," I wanted to say to Susan, "if it weren't for Spielvogel, I wouldn't even be here. If it weren't for Spielvogel saying 'Why not stay?' every time I say 'Why not leave?' I would have been out of this affair long ago. We have him to thank for whatever exists between us—he's the one who was your advocate, not me." But that it was largely because of Spielvogel's encouragement that I had continued to visit her almost nightly during that first year, when I was so out of sympathy with her way of living, was really not her business, even if she wouldn't let up about his "reprehensible" behavior; nor would it do her fragile sense of self-esteem any good to know that even now, several years into our affair—with me her Lambchop and her my Suzie Q., with all that tender lovers' playfulness between us—that it was Spielvogel who prevented me from leaving her whenever I became distressed about those burgeoning dreams of marriage and family that I did not share. "But she wants to have children—and now, before she gets any older." "But you don't want to." "Right. And I can't allow her to nurse these expectations. That just won't do." "Then tell her not to." "I *do*. I *have*. She can't bear hearing it any more. She says, 'I know, I know, you're not going to marry me—do you have to tell me that every *hour*?'" "Well, every hour is perhaps a little more frequent than necessary." "Oh, it isn't every hour—it just sounds that way to her. You see, because I tell her where things stand doesn't mean she takes it to heart." "Yes, but what more can you do?" "Go. I should." "I wouldn't think she thinks you should." "But if I stay . . ." "You might *really* fall in love with her. Does it ever occur to you that maybe this is what you are running away from? Not the children, not the marriage . . . but the love?" "Oh, Doctor, don't start practicing psychoanalysis. No, that doesn't occur to me. I don't think it should, because I don't think it's true." "No? But you are somewhat in love already—are you not? You tell me how sweet she is, how kind she is. How gentle. You tell me how beautiful she is when she sits there reading. You tell me what a touching person she is. Sometimes you are positively lyrical about her." "Am I?" "Yes, yes, and you know that." "But there is still too much that's wrong there, *you* know *that*." "Yes, well, this I could have warned you about at the outset." "Please, the husband of Maureen Tarnopol understands that the other gender is also imperfect." "Knowing this, the husband of Maureen Tarnopol should be grateful perhaps for a woman, who despite her imperfections, happens to be tender and appreciative and absolutely devoted to him. She is all these things, am I right?" "She is all these things. She also turns out to be smart and charming and funny." "And in love with you." "And in love with me." "And a cook—such a cook. You tell me about her dishes, you make my mouth water." "You're very hung up on the pleasure principle, Dr. Spielvogel." "And you? Tell me, where are you running again? To what? To whom? Why?" "To no one, to nothing—but '*why?*' I've told you why: suppose she tries to commit suicide!" "Still with the suicide?" "But what if she does it!" "Isn't that her responsibility? And Dr. Golding's? She is in therapy after all. Are you going to run for fear of this remote possibility?" "I can't take it hanging over my head. Not after all that's gone on. Not after Maureen." "Maybe you are too thin-skinned, you know? Maybe it is time at thirty to develop a thicker hide." "No doubt. I'm sure you rhinoceroses lead a better life. But my hide is my hide. I'm afraid you can shine a flashlight through it. So give me some other advice." "What other advice is there? The choice is yours. Stay or run." "This choice that is mine you structure oddly." "All right, *you* structure it." "The point, you see, is that if I do stay, she must realize that I am marrying no one unless and until *I want to do it.* And everything conspires to make me think that *I don't want to do it.*" "Mr. Tarnopol, somehow I feel I can rely on you to put that proviso before her from time to time."

Why did I stay with Spielvogel? Let us not forget his Mosaic prohibitions and what they meant to a thin-skinned man at the edge of he knew not what intemperate act.

Thou shalt not covet thy wife's underwear.

Thou shalt not drop thy seed upon thy neighbor's bathroom floor or dab it upon the bindings of library books.

Thou shalt not be so stupid as to buy a Hoffritz hunting knife to slay your wife and her matrimonial lawyer.

"But why can't I? What's the difference any more? They're driving me crazy! They're ruining my life! First she tricked me into marrying her with that urine, now they're telling the judge I can write movies and make a fortune! She tells the court that

I 'obstinately' refuse to go out to Hollywood and do an honest day's work! Which is true! I obstinately refuse! *Because that is not my work!* My work is writing fiction! And I can't even do *that* any more! Only when I say I can't, they say, right, so just get your ass out to Hollywood where you can earn yourself a thousand bucks a day! Look! Just look at this affidavit she filed! Look what she calls me here, Doctor—'a well-known seducer of college girls'! That's how she spells 'Karen'! Read this document, will you please? I brought it so you can see with your own eyes that I am not exaggerating! Just look at *this* version of me! 'A seducer of college girls'! They're trying to hold me up, Doctor Spielvogel—this is legalized extortion!" "To be sure," said my Moses, gently, "but still you cannot buy that knife and stick it in her heart. You must not buy a knife, Mr. Tarnopol." "WHY NOT? GIVE ME ONE GOOD REASON WHY NOT!" "Because killing is against the law." "FUCK THE LAW! THE LAW IS WHAT IS KILLING ME!" "Be that as it may, kill her and they will put you in jail." "So what!" "You wouldn't like it there." "I wouldn't care—she'd be dead. *Justice* would come into this world!" "Ah, but Just as the world would become following her death, for you it still wouldn't be paradise. You did not even like the army that much, remember? Well, jail is worse. I don't believe you would be happy there." "I'm not exactly happy *here*." "I understand that. But there you would be even less happy."

So, with him to restrain me (or with him to pretend to restrain me, while I pretend to be unrestrained), I did not buy the knife in Hoffritz's Grand Central window (her lawyer's office was just across the street, twenty flights up). And a good thing too, for when I discovered that the reporter from the *Daily News* who sat in a black raincoat at the back of the courtroom throughout the separation proceedings had been alerted to the hearing by Maureen's lawyers, I lost all control of myself (no pretending now), and out in the corridor during the lunch recess, I took a swing at the dapper, white-haired attorney in his dark three-piece suit with the Phi Beta Kappa key dangling conspicuously from a chain. He was obviously a man of years (though in my state, I might even have attacked a somewhat younger man), but he was agile and easily blocked my wild blow with his briefcase. "Watch out, Egan, watch out for me!"

It was pure playgroundese I shouted at him, language dating back to the arm's-length insolence of grade-school years; my eyes were running with rage, as of old, but before I could swing out at his briefcase again, my own lawyer had grabbed me around the middle and was dragging me backward down the corridor. "You jackass," said Egan coldly, "we'll fix your wagon." "You goddam thief! You publicity hound! What more can you do, you bastard!" "Wait and see," said Egan, unruffled, and even smiling at me now, as a small crowd gathered around us in the hall. "She tricked me," I said to him, "and you know it! With that urine!" "You've got quite an imagination, son. Why don't you put it to work for you?" Here my lawyer managed to turn me completely around, and running and pushing at me from behind, shoved me a few paces farther down the courthouse corridor and into the men's room.

Where we were promptly joined by the stout, black-coated Mr. Valducci of the *Daily News*. "Get out of here, you," I said, "leave me alone." "I just want to ask you some questions. I want to ask about your wife, that's all. I'm a reader of yours. I'm a real fan." "I'll bet." "Sure. *The Jewish Merchant*. My wife read it too. Terrific ending. Ought to be a movie." "Look, I've heard enough about the movies today!" "Take it easy, Pete—I just want to ask you, for instance, what did the missus do before you were married?" "The missus was a show girl! She was in the line at the Latin Quarter! Fuck off, will you!" "Whatever you say, whatever you say," and with a bow to my attorney, who had now interposed himself between the two of us, Valducci stepped back a ways and asked, deferentially, "You don't mind if I take a leak, do you? Since I'm already here?" While Valducci voided, we looked on in silence. "Just shut up," my lawyer whispered to me. "See you, Pete," said Valducci, after meticulously washing and drying his hands, "see you, Counselor."

The next morning, over Valducci's by-line, in the lower half of page five, ran this three-column head—

PRIZE-WINNING AUTHOR TURNS
COURTROOM PRIZEFIGHTER

The story was illustrated with my book-jacket photo, dark-eyed, thin-faced innocence, circa 1959, and a photograph of

Maureen taken the day before, her lantern jaw slicing the offending air as she strides down the courthouse steps on the arm of Attorney Dan P. Egan, who, the story noted (with relish) was seventy years old and formerly middleweight boxing champion at Fordham; in his heyday, I learned, he was known as "Red," and was still a prized toastmaster at Fordham alumni functions. The tears I had shed during my contretemps with Red did not go unreported. "Oh, I should never have listened to you about that knife. I could have killed Valducci too." "You are not satisfied with page five?" "I should have done it. And that judge too. Cut his self-righteous gizzard out, sitting there pitying poor Maureen!" "Please," said Spielvogel, laughing lightly, "the pleasure would have been momentary." "Oh, no, it wouldn't." "Oh, yes, believe me. Murder four people in a courtroom, and before you know it, it's over and you're behind bars. This way, you see, you have it always to imagine when your spirit needs a lift."

So I stayed on as Spielvogel's patient, at least so long as Maureen drew breath (and breathed fire), and Susan McCall was my tender, appreciative, and devoted mistress.

## 5. FREE

> Here lies my wife: here let her lie!
> Now she's at rest, and so am I.
> —John Dryden, "Epitaph Intended for His Wife"

It was three years later, in the spring of 1966, that Maureen telephoned to say she had to talk to me "personally" as soon as possible, and "alone," no lawyers present. We had seen each other only twice since that courtroom confrontation reported in the *Daily News*, at two subsequent hearings held at Maureen's request in order to determine if she could get any more than the hundred a week that Judge Rosenzweig had originally ordered the well-known seducer of college girls to pay in alimony to his abandoned wife. Both times a court-appointed referee had examined my latest tax return, my royalty statements and bank records, and concluded that no increase was warranted. I had pleaded that what was warranted was a re-duction, since my income, rather than increasing, had fallen off by about thirty per cent since Judge Rosenzweig had first ordered me to pay Maureen five thousand dollars a year out of the ten I was then making. Rosenzweig's decision had been based on a tax return that showed me earning a salary of fifty-two hundred a year from the University of Wisconsin and another five thousand from my publisher (representing one quarter of the substantial advance I was getting for my second book). By 1964, however, the last of the publisher's four an-nual payments of five thousand dollars had been doled out to me, the book they had contracted with me for bore no resem-blance to a finished novel, and I was broke. Out of each year's ten thousand in income, five thousand had gone to Maureen for alimony, three to Spielvogel for services rendered, leaving two for food, rent, etc. At the time of the separation there had been another sixty-eight hundred in a savings account—my paperback proceeds from *A Jewish Father*—but that too had been divided equally between the estranged couple by the judge, who then laid the plaintiff's legal fees on the defendant; by our third appearance at the courthouse, the remainder of those savings had been paid out to meet my own lawyer's bills. In '65 Hofstra raised me to sixty-five hundred a year for teaching my two seminars, but my income from writing con-sisted only of what I could bring in from the short stories I was beginning to publish. To meet expenses I cut down my ses-sions with Spielvogel from three to two a week, and began to borrow money from my brother to live on. Each time I came before the referee I explained to him that I was now giving my wife somewhere between sixty-five and seventy per cent of my income, which did not strike me as fair. Mr. Egan would then point out that if Mr. Tarnopol wished to "normalize" his in-come, or even "to improve his lot in life, as most young men strive to do," he had only to write fiction for *Esquire*, the *New Yorker*, *Harper's*, the *Atlantic Monthly*, or for *Playboy* maga-zine, whose editors would pay him—here, to read the phe-nomenal figure, he donned his tortoiseshell glasses—"three thousand dollars for a single short story." As evidence in sup-port of his claim, he produced letters subpoenaed from my files, wherein the fiction editors of these magazines invited me to submit any work I had on hand or planned for the future. I explained to the referee (an attentive, gentlemanly, middle-aged Negro, who had announced, at the outset, that he was honored to meet the author of *A Jewish Father*; another admirer—God only knew what that meant) that every writer of any eminence at all receives such letters as a matter of course; they were not in the nature of bids, or bribes, or guarantees of purchase. When I finished writing a story, as I had recently, I turned it over to my agent, who, at my suggestion, submitted it to one or another of the commercial magazines Mr. Egan had named. There was nothing I could do to make the magazine purchase it for publication; in fact, over the previous few years three of these magazines, the most likely to publish my work, had repeatedly *rejected* fiction of mine (letters of rejection submitted here by my lawyer as proof of my plunging literary reputation), despite those warm invitations for submission, which of course cost them nothing to send out. Certainly, I said, I could not submit to them stories that I had not written, and I could not write stories—about here I generally lost my temper, though the referee's equanimity remained serenely intact—*on demand!* "Oh, my," sighed Egan, turning to Maureen, "the artiste bit again." "What? What did you say?" I threateningly inquired, though we sat around a conference table in a small office in the courthouse, and I, like the referee, had heard every word that Egan had whispered. "I said, sir," replied Egan, "that I wish I was an artiste and didn't have to work 'on demand' either." Here we were brought gently to order by the referee, who, if he did not give me my reduction, did not give Maureen her increase either.

I took no comfort in his "fairness," however. Money was constantly on my mind: what was being extorted from me by Maureen, in collusion (as I saw it) with the state of New York, and what I was now borrowing from Moe, who refused to take interest or to set a date for repayment. "What do you want me to do, shylock my own flesh and blood?" he said, laughing. "I hate this, Moey." "So you hate it," was his reply.

My lawyer's opinion was that actually I ought to be happy that the alimony now appeared to have been "stabilized" at a hundred a week, regardless of fluctuation in my income. I said, "Regardless of fluctuation down, you mean. What about fluctuation up?" "Well, you'd be getting more that way, too, Peter," he reminded me. "But then 'stabilized' doesn't mean stabilized at all, does it, if I should ever start to bring in some cash?" "Why don't we cross that bridge when we come to it? For the time being, the situation looks as good to me as it can."

But it was only a few days after the last of our hearings that a letter arrived from Maureen; admittedly, I should have destroyed it unread. Instead I tore open the envelope as though it contained an unknown manuscript of Dostoevsky's. She wished to inform me that if I "drove" her to "a breakdown," I would be the one responsible for her upkeep in a mental hospital. And that would come to something more than "a measly" hundred dollars a week—it would come to *three* times that. She had no intention of obliging me by being carted off to Bellevue. It was clearly Payne Whitney she was shooting for. And this, she told me, was no idle threat—her psychiatrist had warned her (which was why she was warning me) that she might very well have to be institutionalized one day if I were to continue to refuse "to be a man." And being a man, as the letter went on to explain, meant either coming back to her to resume our married life, and with it "a civilized role in society," or failing that, going out to Hollywood where, she informed me, anybody with the Prix de Rome in his hip pocket could make a fortune. Instead I had chosen to take that "wholly unrealistic" job at Hofstra, working *one day a week*, so that I could spend the rest of my time writing a vindictive novel about *her*. "I'm not made of steel," the letter informed me, "no matter what it pleases you to tell people about me. Publish a book like that and you will regret the consequences till your dying day."

As I begin to approach the conclusion of my story, I should point out that all the while Maureen and I were locked in this bruising, painful combat—indeed, almost from the moment of our first separation hearing in January 1963, some six months after my arrival in New York—the newspapers and the nightly television news began to depict an increasingly chaotic America and to bring news of bitter struggles for freedom and power which made my personal difficulties with alimony payments and inflexible divorce laws appear by comparison to be inconsequential. Unfortunately, these highly visible dramas of social

disorder and human misery did nothing whatsoever to miti-
gate my obsession; to the contrary, that the most vivid and
momentous history since World War Two was being made in
the streets around me, day by day, *hour by hour*, only caused
me to feel even more isolated by my troubles from the world at
large, more embittered by the narrow and guarded life I now
felt called upon to live—or able to live—because of my brief,
misguided foray into matrimony. For all that I may have been
attuned to the consequences of this new social and political
volatility, and like so many Americans moved to pity and fear
by the images of violence flashing nightly across the television screen, and by the stories of brutality and lawlessness appearing each morning on page one of the *New York Times*, I
simply could not stop thinking about Maureen and her hold
over me, though, to be sure, my thinking about her hold over
me was, as I well knew, the very means by which she continued
to hold me. Yet I couldn't stop—no scene of turbulence or act
of terror that I read about in the papers could get me to feel
myself any less embattled or entrapped.

In the spring of 1963, for instance, when for nights on end I
could not get to sleep because of my outrage over Judge
Rosenzweig's alimony decision, police dogs were turned loose
on the demonstrators in Birmingham; and just about the time I
began to imagine myself plunging a Hoffritz hunting knife
into Maureen's evil heart, Medgar Evers was shot to death in
his driveway in Mississippi. In August 1963, my nephew Abner
telephoned to ask me to accompany him and his family to the
civil rights demonstration in Washington; the boy, then eleven,
had recently read *A Jewish Father* and given a report on it in
school, likening me, his uncle (in a strained, if touching conclusion), to "men like John Steinbeck and Albert Camus." So
I drove down in their car to Washington with Morris, Lenore,
and the two boys, and with Abner holding my hand, listened
to Martin Luther King proclaim his "dream"—on the way
home I said, "You think we can get him to speak when I go to
alimony jail?" "Sure," said Moe, "also Sartre and Simone de
Beauvoir. They'll assemble at City Hall and sing 'Tarnopol Shall
Overcome' to the mayor." I laughed along with the kids, but
wondered who *would* protest, if I defied the court order to
continue to support Maureen for the rest of her natural days

and said I'd go to jail instead, for the rest of mine if need be. No one would protest, I realized: enlightened people everywhere would *laugh*, as though we two squabbling mates were indeed Blondie and Dagwood, or Maggie and Jiggs . . . In September, Abner was student chairman of his school's memorial service to commemorate the death of the children killed in the Birmingham church bombing—I attended, again at his invitation, but halfway through a reading by a strapping black girl of a poem by Langston Hughes, slipped out from my seat beside my sister-in-law to race over to my lawyer's office and show him the subpoena that had been served on me earlier that morning while I sat getting my teeth cleaned in the dentist's office—I had been asked to show cause why the alimony shouldn't be raised now that I was "a full-time faculty member" of Hofstra College . . . In November President Kennedy was assassinated in Dallas. I made my walk to Spielvogel's office by what must have turned out to be a ten-mile route. I wandered uptown in the most roundabout fashion, stopping wherever and whenever I saw a group of strangers clustered together on a street corner; I stood with them, shrugged and nodded at whatever they said, and then moved on. And of course I wasn't the only unattached soul wandering around like that, that day. By the time I got to Spielvogel's the waiting-room door was locked and he had gone home. Which was just as well with me: I didn't feel like "analyzing" my incredulity and shock. Shortly after I arrived at Susan's I got a phone call from my father. "I'm sorry to bother you at your friend's," he said, somewhat timidly, "I got the name and number from Morris." "That's okay," I said, "I was going to call you." "Do you remember when Roosevelt died?" I did indeed—so too had the young protagonist of *A Jewish Father*. Didn't my father remember the scene in my novel, where the hero recalls his own father's grieving for FDR? It had been drawn directly from life: Joannie and I had gone down with him to the Yonkers train station to pay our last respects as a family to the dead president, and had listened in awe (and with some trepidation) to our father's muffled, husky sobbing when the locomotive, draped in black bunting and carrying the body of FDR, chugged slowly through the local station on its way up the river to Hyde Park; that summer, when we went for a week's vacation to a hotel in South Fallsburg, we had stopped off at Hyde Park to visit the fallen president's grave. "Truman should be such a friend to the Jews," my mother had said at the graveside, and the emotion that had welled up in me when she spoke those words came forth in a stream of tears when my father added, "He should rest in peace, he loved the common man." This scene too had been recalled by the young hero of *A Jewish Father*, as he lay in bed with his German girl friend in Frankfurt, trying to explain to her in his five-hundred-word German vocabulary who he was and where he came from and why his father, a good and kindly man, hated her guts . . . Nonetheless my father had asked me on the phone that night, "Do you remember when Roosevelt died?"—for whatever he read of mine he could never really associate with our real life; just as I on the other hand could no longer have a real conversation with him that did not seem to me to be a reading from my fiction. Indeed, what he then proceeded to say to me that night struck me as something out of a book I had already written. And likewise what little I said to him—for this was a father-and-son routine that went way back and whose spirit and substance was as familiar to me as a dialogue by Abbott and Costello, . . . which isn't to say that being a partner in the act ever left me unaffected by our patter. "You're all right?" he asked, "I don't mean to interrupt you at your friend's. You understand that?" "That's okay." "But I just wanted to be sure you're all right." "I'm all right." "This is a terrible thing. I feel for the old man—he must be taking it hard. To lose another son—and like that. Thank God there's still Bobby and Ted." "That should help a little." "Ah, what can help," moaned my father, "but you're all right?" "I'm fine." "Okay, that's the most important thing. When are you going to court again?" he asked. "Next month sometime." "What does your lawyer say? What are the prospects? They can't sock you again, can they?" "We'll see." "You got enough cash?" he asked. "I'm all right." "Look, if you need cash—" "I'm fine. I don't need anything." "Okay. Stay in touch, will you, please? We're starting to feel like a couple of lepers up here, where you're concerned." "I will, I'll be in touch." "And let me know immediately how the court thing turns out. And if you need any cash." "Okay." "And don't worry about anything. I

know he's a southerner, but I got great faith in Lyndon Johnson. If it was Humphrey I'd breathe easier about Israel—but
what can we do? Anyway, look, he was close to Roosevelt all
those years, he had to learn something. He's going to be all
right. I don't think we got anything to worry about. Do you?"
"No." "I hope you're right. This is awful. And you take care of
yourself. I don't want you to be strapped, you understand?"
"I'm fine."

Susan and I stayed up to watch television until Mrs.
Kennedy had arrived back in Washington on Air Force One.
As the widow stepped from the plane onto the elevator platform, her fingers grazed the coffin, and I said, "Oh, the heroic
male fantasies being stirred up around the nation." "Yours
too?" asked Susan. "I'm only human," I said. In bed, with the
lights off, and clasped in one another's arms, we both started
to cry. "I didn't even vote for him," Susan said. "You didn't?"
"I could never tell you before. I voted for Nixon." "Jesus, but
you were fucked up." "Oh, Lambchop, Jackie Kennedy
wouldn't have voted for him if she hadn't been his wife. It's
the way we were raised."

In September 1964, the week after Spielvogel published his
findings on my case in the *American Forum for Psychoanalytic
Studies*, the Warren Commission published theirs on the assassination. Lee Harvey Oswald, alone and on his own, was
responsible for the murder of President Kennedy, the commission concluded; meanwhile Spielvogel had determined
that because of my upbringing I suffered from "castration anxiety" and employed "narcissism" as my "primary defense."
Not everyone agreed with the findings either of the eminent
jurist or of the New York analyst: so, in the great world and in
the small, debate raged about the evidence, about the conclusions, about the motives and the methods of the objective
investigators . . . And so those eventful years passed, with
reports of disaster and cataclysm continuously coming over the
wire services to remind me that I was hardly the globe's most
victimized inhabitant. I had only Maureen to contend with—
what if I were of draft age, or Indochinese, and had to contend
with LBJ? What was my Johnson beside theirs? I watched the
footage from Selma and Saigon and Santo Domingo, I told

myself that *that* was awful, suffering that could not be borne . . . all of which changed nothing between my wife and me. In October 1965, when Susan and I stood in the Sheep Meadow of Central Park, trying to make out what the Reverend Coffin was saying to the thousands assembled there to protest the war, who should I see no more than fifteen feet away, but Maureen. Wearing a button pinned to her coat: "Deliver Us Dr. Spock." She was standing on the toes of her high boots, trying to see above the crowd to the speaker's platform. The last word I'd had from her was that letter warning me about the deluxe nervous breakdown that I would soon be getting billed for because of my refusal "to be a man." How nice to see she was still ambulatory—I supposed it argued for my virility. Oh, how it burned me up to see her *here*! I tapped Susan. "Well, look who's against the war." "Who?" "Tokyo Rose over there. That's my wife, Suzie Q." "That one?" she whispered. "Right, with the big heartfelt button on her breast." "Why— she's pretty, actually." "In her driven satanic way, I suppose so. Come on, you can't hear anything anyway. Let's go." "She's shorter than I thought—from your stories." "She gets taller when she stands on your toes. The bitch. Eternal marriage at home and national liberation abroad. Look," I said, motioning up to the police helicopter circling in the air above the crowd, "they've counted heads for the papers—let's get out of here." "Oh, Peter, don't be a baby—" "Look, if anything could make me *for* bombing Hanoi, she's it. With that button yet. Deliver *me*, Dr. Spock—from *her*!"

That antiwar demonstration was to be my last contact with her until the spring of 1966, when she phoned my apartment, and in an even and matter-of-fact voice said to me, "I want to talk to you about a divorce, Peter. I am willing to talk sensibly about all the necessary arrangements, but I cannot do it through that lawyer of yours. The man is a moron and Dan simply cannot get through to him."

Could it be? Were things about to change? Was it about to be *over*?

"He is not a moron, he is a perfectly competent matrimonial lawyer."

"He *is* a moron, *and* a liar, but that isn't the point, and I'm not going to waste my time arguing about it. Do you or don't you want a divorce?"

"What kind of question is that? Of course I do."

"Then why don't the two of us sit down together and work it out?"

"I don't know that we two could, 'together.'"

"I repeat: do you or do you not want a divorce?"

"Look, Maureen—"

"If you do, then I will come to your apartment after my Group tonight and we can iron this thing out like adults. It's gone on long enough and, frankly, I'm quite sick of it. I have other things to do with my life."

"Well, that's good to hear, Maureen. But we surely can't meet to settle it in my apartment."

"Where then? The street?"

"We can meet on neutral ground. We can meet at the Algonquin."

"Really, what a baby you are. Little Lord Fauntleroy from Westchester—to this very day."

"The word 'Westchester' still gets you, doesn't it? Just like 'Ivy League.' All these years in the big city and still the night watchman's daughter from Elmira."

"Ho hum. Do you want to go on insulting me, or do you want to get on with the business at hand? Truly, I couldn't care less about you or your opinion of me at this point. I'm well over that. I have a life of my own. I have my flute."

"The flute now?"

"I have my flute," she went on, "I have Group. I'm going to the New School."

"Everything but a job," I said.

"My doctor doesn't feel I can hold a job right now. I need time to think."

"What is it you 'think' about?"

"Look, do you want to score points with your cleverness, or do you want a divorce?"

"You can't come to my apartment."

"Is that your final decision? I will not talk about a serious matter like this in the street or in some hotel bar. So if that is your final decision, I am hanging up. For God's sake, Peter, I'm *not* going to eat you up."

"Look," I said, "all right, come here, if that's all we're going to talk about."

"I assure you I have nothing else to converse about with a person like you. I'll come right from Group."

That word! "What time is 'Group' over?" I asked.

"I'll be at your place at ten," she said.

"I don't like it," said Spielvogel, when I phoned with the news of the rendezvous I'd arranged, all on my own.

"I don't either," I said. "But if she changes the subject, I'll throw her out. I'll have her go. But what else could I say? Maybe she finally means it. I can't afford to say no."

"Well, if you said yes, it's yes."

"I *could* still call her up and get out of it, of course."

"You want to do that?"

"I want to be *divorced*, that's what I want. That's why I thought I had better grab hold of the opportunity while I had it. If it means risking a scene with her, well, I'll have to risk it."

"Yes? You are up to that? You won't collapse in tears? You won't tear your clothes off your back?"

"No, no. That's over."

"Well, then," said Spielvogel, "good luck."

"Thanks."

Maureen arrived promptly at ten P.M. She was dressed in a pretty red wool suit—a demure jacket over a silk blouse, and a flared skirt—smarter than anything I'd ever seen her in before; and though drawn and creased about the eyes and at the corners of her mouth, her face was deeply tanned—nothing urchinlike or "beat" about this wife of mine any longer. It turned out that she had just come back from five days in Puerto Rico, a vacation that her Group had insisted on her taking. *On my money, you bloodsucker. And the suit too. Who paid for that but putz-o here!*

Maureen made a careful survey of the living room that Susan had helped me to furnish for a few hundred dollars. It was simple enough, but through Susan's efforts, cozy and comfortable: rush matting on the floor, a round oak country table, some unpainted dining chairs, a desk and a lamp, bookcases, a daybed covered with an India print, a secondhand easy chair with a navy-blue slipcover made by Susan, along with navy-blue curtains she'd sewn together on her machine. "Very quaint," said Maureen superciliously, eyeing the basket of logs by the fireplace, "and very *House and Garden*, your color scheme."

"It'll do."

From supercilious to envious in the twinkling of an eye— "Oh, I would think it would do quite nicely. You ought to see what I live in. It's half this size."

"The proverbial shoe box. I might have known."

"Peter," she said, drawing a breath that seemed to catch a little in her chest, "I've come here to tell you something." She sat down in the easy chair, making herself right at home.

"To tell—?"

"I'm not going to divorce you. I'm never going to divorce you."

She paused and waited for my response; so did I.

"Get out," I said.

"I have a few more things to say to you."

"I told you to get out."

"I just got here. I have no intention of—"

"You lied. You lied *again*. You told me on the phone less than three hours ago that you wanted to talk—"

"I've written a story about you. I want to read it to you. I've brought it with me in my purse. I read it to my class at the New School. The instructor has promised to try to get it published, that's how good he thinks it is. I'm sure you won't agree—you have those high Flaubertian standards, of course— but I want you to hear it. I think you have a right to before I go ahead and put it in print."

"Maureen, either get up and go, under your own steam, or I am going to throw you out."

"Lay one finger on me and I will have you put in jail. Dan Egan knows I'm here. He knows you invited me here. He didn't want me to come. He's seen you in action, Peter. He said if you laid a finger on me I was to call him immediately. And in case you think it's on your lousy hundred dollars that I went to Puerto Rico, it wasn't. It was Dan who gave me the money, when the Group said I had to get away."

"Is that a 'Group' you go to or a travel agency?"

"Ha ha."

"And the chic outfit. Therapist buy you that, or did your fellow patients pass the cup?"

"No one 'bought' it for me. Mary Egan gave it to me—the suit used to be hers. She bought it in Ireland. Don't worry, I'm not exactly living the high life on the money you earn through the sweat of your brow four hours a week at Hofstra. The Egans are my friends, the best friends I've ever had."

"Fine. You need 'em. Now scram. *Get out.*"

"I want you to hear this story," she said, reaching into her purse for the manuscript. "I want you to know that you're not the only one who has tales to tell the world about that marriage. The story—" she said, removing the folded pages from a manila envelope—"the story is called 'Dressing Up in Mommy's Clothes.'"

"Look, I'm going to call the police and have *them* throw you out of here. How will that suit Mr. Egan?"

"You call the police and I'll call Sal Valducci."

"You won't call anybody."

"Why don't you telephone your Park Avenue millionairess, Peppy? Maybe she'll send her chauffeur around to rescue you from the clutches of your terrible wife. Oh, don't worry, I know all about the bee-yoo-tiful Mrs. McCall. A bee-yoo-tiful drip—a helpless, hopeless, rich little society drip! Oh, don't worry, I've had you followed, you bastard—I know what you're up to with women!"

"You've had me *what?*"

"Followed! Trailed! Damn right I have! And it cost me a fortune! But you're not getting away scot-free, you!"

"But I'll divorce you, you bitch, any day of the week! We don't *need* detectives, we don't *need*—"

"Oh, don't you tell me what I need, dealing with someone like you! I don't have a millionairess, you know, to buy me cuff links at Cartier's! I make my way in the world on my own!"

"Shit, so do we all! And what cuff links? What the hell are you talking about?"

But she was off and running again, and the story of "the Cartier cuff links" she would carry with her to her grave. "Oh just your speed, she is! Poor little rich girls, or little teenage students all gaga over this artistical teacher, like our friend with the braids in Wisconsin. Or that Jewish princess girl from Long Island. And how about the big blonde German nurse you were fucking in the army? A nurse—just perfect for you! Just perfect for our big mamma's boy with the tearful brown eyes! A *real* woman, and you're in tears, Peter. A real woman and—"

"Look, who set you up in business as a *real* woman? Who appointed you the representative of womankind? Stop trying to shove your bloody Kotex down my throat, Maureen—you're not a real *anything*, *that's* your goddam trouble! Now get out! How *dare* you have me followed!"

She didn't budge.

"I'm telling you to *go*."

"When I'm finished saying what I came here to say I will leave—and then without your assistance. Right now I'm going to read this story, because I want you to understand in no uncertain terms that two can play this writing game, two can play at this kind of slander, if it's slandering me you have in your vindictive mind. Quid pro quo, pal."

"Get—out."

"It's a short story about a writer named Paul Natapov, who unknown to the readership that takes him so *seriously*, and the highbrow judges who give him *awards*, likes to relax around the house in his wife's underwear."

"You fucking lunatic!" I cried, and pulled her up from the chair by one arm. "Now out, out, out you psychopath! *There*—there's the only thing that's *real* about you, Maureen, *your psychopathology*! It isn't the woman that drives me to tears, it's the nut! Now *out*!"

"No! No! You're only after my story," she screamed—"but tear it to shreds—I still have a carbon in Dan Egan's safe!"

Here she flung herself to the floor, where she took hold of the legs of the chair and began kicking up at me, bicycle fashion, with her high-heeled shoes.

"Get up! Cut it out! Go! Go, Maureen—or I'm going to beat your crazy head in!"

"Just you try it, mister!"

With the first crack of my hand I bloodied her delicate nose.

"Oh, my God . . ." She moaned as the blood spurted from

her nostrils and down onto the jacket of her handsome suit, blood a deeper red than the nubby wool.

"And that is only the beginning! That is only the start. I'm going to beat you to an unrecognizable *pulp*!"

"Go ahead! What do I care. The story's still in Dan's safe! Go ahead! Kill me, why don't you!"

"Okay, I *will*," and cuffed her head, first one side, then the other. "If that's what you want, I will!"

"Do it!"

"Now—" I said, striking at the back of her skull with the flat of my palm, "now—" I hit her again, same spot, "*now* when you go to court, you won't have to make it all up: now you'll have something *real* to cry about to the good Judge Rosenzweig! A real beating, Maureen! The real thing, at last!" I was on the floor, astraddle her, cuffing her head with my open hand. Her blood was smeared everywhere: over her face, my hands, the rush matting, all over the front of her suit, down her silk blouse, on her bare throat. And the pages of the story were strewn around us, most of them bloodied too. The real thing—and it was marvelous. I was loving it.

I, of course, had no intention of killing her right then and there, not so long as those jails that Spielvogel had warned me about still existed. I was not even really in a rage any longer. Just enjoying myself thoroughly. All that gave me pause—oddly—was that I was ruining the suit in which she'd looked so attractive. But overlook the suit, I managed to tell myself. "I'm going to kill you, my beloved wife, I'm going to end life for you here today at the age of thirty-six, but in my own sweet time. Oh, you should have agreed to the Algonquin, Maureen."

"Go ahead—" drooling now down her chin, "my life, my life is such shit, let me die already . . ."

"Soon, soon now, very soon now you're going to be nice and dead." I hadn't to wonder for very long where to assault her next. I rolled her onto her face and began to pound with a stiff palm at her behind. The skirt of the red suit and her half-slip were hiked up in the back, and there was her little alley cat's behind, encased in tight white underpants, perhaps the very pair about which her class at the New School had heard so much of late. I beat her ass. Ten, fifteen, twenty strokes—I counted them out for her, aloud—and then while she lay there sobbing, I stood up and went to the fireplace and picked up the black wrought-iron poker that Susan had bought for me in the Village. "And now," I announced, "I am going to kill you, as promised."

No word from the floor, just a whimper.

"I'm afraid they are going to have to publish your fiction posthumously, because I am about to beat your crazy, lying head in with this poker. I want to see your brains, Maureen. I want to see those brains of yours with my own eyes. I want to step in them with my shoes—and then I'll pass them along to Science. God only knows what they'll find. Get ready, Maureen, you're about to die horribly."

I could make out now the barely audible words she was whimpering: "Kill me," she was saying, "kill me kill me—" as oblivious as I was in the first few moments to the fact that she had begun to shit into her underwear. The smell had spread around us before I saw the turds swelling the seat of her panties. "Die me," she babbled deliriously—"die me good, die me long—"

"Oh, Christ."

All at once she screamed, "*Make me dead!*"

"Maureen. Get up, Maureen. Maureen, come on now."

She opened her eyes. I wondered if she had passed over at last into total madness. To be institutionalized forever—at my expense. Ten thousand bucks more a year! I was finished!

"Maureen! *Maureen!*"

She managed a bizarre smile.

"Look." I pointed between her legs. "Don't you see? Don't you know? Look, please. You've shit all over yourself. Do you hear me, do you understand me? *Answer me!*"

She answered. "You couldn't do it."

"*What?*"

"You couldn't do it. You coward."

"Oh, Jesus."

"Big brave man."

"Well, at least you're yourself, Maureen. Now get *up*. Use the bathroom!"

"A yellow coward."

"*Wash yourself!*"

She pushed up on her elbows and tried to bring herself

to her feet, but with an agonized groan, slumped backward. "I—I have to use your phone."

"After," I said, reaching down with a hand to help lift her.

"I have to phone *now*."

I gagged and averted my head. "Later—!"

"You beat me"—as though the news had just that moment reached her. "Look at this blood! My blood! You beat me like some Harlem whore!"

I had now to step away from the odor she gave off. Oh, this was just too much madness, too much all around. The tears started rolling out of me.

"Where is your phone!"

"Look, who are you calling?"

"Whoever I want! You *beat* me! You filthy pig, *you beat me!*" She had made it now up onto her knees. One blow with the poker—still in my right hand, by the way—and she would phone no one.

I watched her stumbling over her own feet to the bedroom. One shoe on and one shoe off. "No, the *bath*room!"

"I have to phone . . ."

"You're leaking your shit all over!"

"You beat me, you monster! Is that all you can think of? The shit on your *House and Garden* rug? Oh, you middle-class bastard, I don't believe it!"

"WASH YOURSELF!"

"NO!"

From the bedroom came the sound of the casters rolling into the worn grooves in the wooden floor. She had collapsed onto the bed, as though dropping from the George Washington Bridge.

She was dialing—and sobbing.

"Hello? Mary? It's Maureen. He beat up on me, Mary—he—hello? No? *Hello?*" With an animalish whine of frustration, she hung up. Then she was dialing again, so slowly and fitfully she might have been falling off to sleep between every other digit. "Hello? Hello, is this the Egans? Is this 201-236-2890? Isn't this Egans? Hello?" She let out another whine and threw the receiver at the hook. "I want to talk to the Egans! I want the Egans!" she cried, banging the receiver up and down now in its cradle.

I stood in the doorway to the bedroom with my poker.

"What the hell are *you* crying about?" she said, looking up at me. "You wanted to beat me, and you beat me, *so stop crying*. Why can't you be a man for a change and *do* something, instead of being such a crybaby!"

"Do what? Do *what*?"

"You can dial the Egans! You broke my fingers! *I have no feeling in my fingers!*"

"I didn't touch your fingers!"

"Then why can't I dial! DIAL FOR ME! STOP CRYING FOR FIVE SECONDS AND DIAL THE RIGHT NUMBER!"

So I did it. She told me to do it, and I did it. 201-236-2890. Ding-a-ling. Ding-a-ling.

"Hello?" a woman said.

"Hello," said I, "is this Mary Egan?"

"Yes. Who is this, please?"

"Just a moment, Maureen Tarnopol wants to talk to you." I handed my wife the phone, gagging as her aroma reached me again.

"Mary?" Maureen said. "Oh Mary," and wretchedly, she was sobbing once again. "Is, is Dan home? I have to talk to Dan, oh Mary, he, he beat me, Peter, that was him, he beat up on me, bad—"

And I, fully armed, stood by and listened. Who was I to phone for her next, the police to come and arrest me, or Valducci to write it up in the *Daily News*?

I left her to herself in the bedroom, and with a sponge and a pan of water from the kitchen began to clean the blood and feces from the rush matting on the living room floor. I kept the poker by my side—now, ridiculously, for protection.

I was on my knees, the fifteenth or twentieth wad of paper toweling in my hand, when Maureen came out of the bedroom.

"Oh, what a good little boy," she said.

"Somebody has to clean up your shit."

"Well, you're in trouble now, Peter."

I imagined that she was right—my stomach felt all at once as though *I* were the one who had just evacuated in his pants—but I pretended otherwise. "Oh, am I?"

"When Dan Egan gets home, I wouldn't want to be in your shoes."

"That remains to be seen."

"You better run, my dear. Fast and far."

"*You* better wash yourself—and then go!"

"I want a drink."

"Oh, Maureen, please. You stink!"

"I NEED A DRINK! YOU TRIED TO MURDER ME!"

"YOU'RE TRACKING SHIT EVERYWHERE!"

"Oh, that's *typical* of you!"

"DO AS I SAY! WASH YOURSELF!"

"NO!"

I brought out a bottle of bourbon and poured each of us a big drink. She took the glass and before I could say "No!" sat right down on Susan's slipcover.

"Oh, you bitch."

"Fuck it," she said, hopelessly, and threw down the drink, barroom style.

"You call me the baby, Maureen, and sit there in your diaperful, defying me. Why must you defy me like this? *Why?*"

"Why not," she said, shrugging. "What else is there to do." She held the glass out for another shot.

I closed my eyes, I didn't want to look at her. "Maureen," I pleaded, "get out of my life, will you? Will you *please*? I beg you. How much more time are we going to use up in this madness? Not only my time but *yours*."

"You had your chance. You chickened out."

"Why must it end in *murder*?"

Coldly: "I'm only trying to make a man out of you, Peppy, that's all."

"Oh, give it up then, will you? It's a lost cause. You've won, Maureen, okay? *You're the winner.*"

"Bullshit I am! Oh, don't you pull that cheap bullshit on me."

"But what more do you want?"

"What I don't have. Isn't that what people want? *What's coming to me.*"

"But *nothing* is coming to you. Nothing is coming to *anyone*."

"And that also includes you, golden boy!" And leaking through her underpants, she finally, fifteen minutes after the initial request, marched off to the bathroom—where she slammed and locked the door.

I ran up and hammered on it—"And don't you try to kill yourself in there! *Do you hear me?*"

"Oh, don't worry, mister—you ain't gettin' off that easy this time!"

It was nearly midnight when she decided on her own that she was ready to leave: I had to sit and watch her try to clean the blood from the pages of "Dressing Up in Mommy's Clothes" (by Maureen J. Tarnopol) with a damp sponge; I had to find her a large paper clip and a clean manila envelope for her manuscript; I had to give her two more drinks, and then listen to myself compared, not entirely to my advantage, with Messrs. Mezik and Walker. While I went about removing the odoriferous slipcovers and bedspread to the bedroom clothes hamper, I was berated at length for my class origins and allegiances, as she understood them; my virility she analyzed while I sprinkled the rush matting with Aqua Velva. Only when I threw all the windows open and stood there in the breeze, preferring to breathe fumes from outside rather than inside the apartment, did Maureen finally get up to go. "Am I now supposed to oblige you, Peter, by jumping?" "Just airing the place—but exit however you like." "I came in through the door and I will now go out through the door." "Always the lady." "Oh, you won't get away with this!" she said, breaking into tears as she departed.

I double-locked and chained the door behind her, and immediately telephoned Spielvogel at his home.

"Yes, Mr. Tarnopol. What can I do for you?"

"I'm sorry to wake you, Dr. Spielvogel. But I thought I'd better talk to you. Tell you what happened. She came."

"Yes?"

"And I beat her up."

"Badly?"

"She's still walking."

"Well, that's good to hear."

I began to laugh. "Literally beat the shit out of her. I'd bloodied her nose, you see, and spanked her ass, and then I told her I was going to kill her with the fireplace poker, and apparently the idea excited her so, she crapped all over the apartment."

"I see."

I couldn't stop laughing. "It's a longer story than that, but that's the gist of it. She just started to shit!"

Spielvogel said, after a moment, "Well, you sound as though you had a good time."

"I did. The place still stinks, but actually, it was terrific. In retrospect, one of the high points of my life! I thought, 'This is it, I'm going to do it. She wants a beating, I'll give it to her!' The minute she came in, you see, the minute she sat down, she virtually asked for it. Do you know what she told me? 'I'm not going to divorce you ever.'"

"I expected as much."

"Yes? Then why didn't you say something?"

"You indicated to me it was worth the risk. You assured me you wouldn't collapse, however things went."

"Well, I didn't . . . did I?"

"Did you?"

"I don't know. Before she left—after the beating—she called her lawyer. I dialed the number for her."

"You did?"

"And I cried, I'm afraid. Not torrentially, but some. I tell you, though, it wasn't for me, Doctor—believe it or not, it was for her. You should have seen that performance."

"And now what?"

"Now?"

"Now you ought to call your lawyer, yes?"

"Of course!"

"You sound a little unstrung," said Spielvogel.

"I'm really all right. I feel fine, surprisingly enough."

"Then telephone the lawyer. If you want, call me back and tell me what he said. I'll be up."

What my lawyer said was that I was to leave town immediately and stay away until he told me to come back. He informed me that for what I had done I could be placed under arrest. In my euphoria, I had neglected to think of it that way.

I called Spielvogel back to give him the news and cancel my sessions for the coming week; I said that I assumed (please no haggling, I prayed) that I wouldn't have to pay for the hours that I missed—"likewise if I get ninety days for this." "If you are incarcerated," he assured me, "I will try my best to get someone to take over your hours." Then I telephoned Susan, who had been waiting by her phone all night to learn the outcome of my meeting with Maureen—was I getting divorced? No, we were getting out of town. Pack a bag. "At this hour? How? Where?" I picked her up in a taxi and for sixty dollars (it would have gone for three sessions with Spielvogel anyway, said I to comfort myself) the driver agreed to take us down the Garden State Parkway to Atlantic City, where I had once spent two idyllic weeks as a twelve-year-old in a seaside cottage with my cousins from Camden, my father's family. There, within the first twelve hours, I had fallen in love with Sugar Wasserstrom, a sprightly curly-haired girl from New Jersey, a schoolmate of my cousin's, prematurely fitted out with breasts just that spring (April, my cousin told me from his bed that night). That I came from New York made me something like a Frenchman in Sugar's eyes; sensing this, I told lengthy stories about riding the subway, till shortly she began to fall in love with me too. Then I let her have my Gene Kelly version of "Long Ago and Far Away," crooned it right into her ear as we snuggled down the boardwalk arm in arm, and with that, I believe, I finished her off. The girl was gone. I kissed her easily a thousand times in two weeks. Atlantic City, August 1945: my kingdom by the sea. World War Two ended with Sugar in my arms—I had an erection, which she tactfully ignored, and which I did my best not to bring to her attention. Doubled-up with the pain of my unfired round, I nonetheless kept on kissing. How could I let suffering stop me at a time like this? Thus the postwar era dawned, and, at twelve, my adventures with girls had begun.

I was to stay away as long as Dan Egan remained in Chicago on business. My lawyer was waiting for Egan to get back to be absolutely certain he wasn't going to press charges for assault with intent to kill—or to attempt to persuade him not to. In the meantime, I tried to show Susan a good time. We had breakfast in bed in our boardwalk hotel. I paid ten dollars to have her profile drawn in pastels. We ate big fried scallops and visited the Steel Pier. I recalled for her the night of V-J Day, when Sugar and I and my cousins and their friends had conga-ed up and down the boardwalk (with my aunt's permission) to celebrate Japan's defeat. Was I effusive! And free with the cash! But it's my money, isn't it? Not hers—mine! I still couldn't grow appropriately serious about the grave legal consequences of my brutality, or remorseful, quite yet, about having done so coldheartedly what, as a little Jewish boy, I had been taught to despise. A man beating a woman? What was more loathsome, except a man beating a child?

The first evening I checked in on the phone with Dr. Spielvogel at the hour I ordinarily would have been arriving at his office for my appointment. "I feel like the gangster hiding out with his moll," I told him. "It sounds like it suits you," he said. "All in all it was a rewarding experience. You should have told me about barbarism a long time ago." "You seem to have taken to it very nicely on your own."

In the late afternoon of our second full day, my lawyer phoned—no, Egan wasn't back from Chicago, but his wife had called to say that Maureen had been found unconscious in her apartment and taken by ambulance to Roosevelt Hospital. She had been out for two days and there was a chance she would die.

*And covered with bruises,* I thought. *From my hands.*

"After she left me, she went home and tried to kill herself."

"That's what it sounds like."

"I better get up there then."

"Why?" asked the lawyer.

"Better that I'm there than that I'm not." Even I wasn't quite sure what I meant.

"The police might come around," he told me.

*Valducci might come around,* I thought.

"You sure you want to do this?" he asked.

"I'd better."

"Okay. But if the cops are there, call me. I'll be home all night. Don't say anything to anyone. Just call me and I'll come over."

I told Susan what had happened and that we were going back to New York. She too asked why. "She's not your business any more, Peter. She is not your concern. She's trying to drive you crazy, and you're *letting* her."

"Look, if she dies I'd better be there."

"*Why?*"

"I ought to be, that's all."

"But why? Because you're her 'husband'? Peter, what if the police *are* there? What if they arrest you—and put you in jail! Do you see what you've done—you could go to jail now. Oh, Lambchop, you wouldn't last an *hour* in jail."

"They're not going to put me in jail," I said, my heart quaking.

"You beat her, which was stupid enough—but this is even *more* stupid. You keep trying to do the 'manly' thing, and all you ever do is act like a child."

"Oh, do I?"

"There *is* no 'manly' thing with her. Don't you see that yet? There are only crazy things. Crazier and crazier! But you're like a little boy in a Superman suit, with some little boy's ideas about being big and strong. Every time she throws down the glove, *you* pick it up! If she phones, you answer! If she writes letters, you go crazy. If she does nothing, you go home and work on your novel about her! You're like—like her puppet! She yanks—you jump! It's—it's *pathetic*."

"Oh, is it?"

"Oh," said Susan, brokenhearted, "why did you have to hit her? Why did you do that?"

"Actually, I thought it pleased you."

"Did you really? *Pleased* me? I hated it. I just haven't told you in so many words because you were so pleased with *yourself*. But why on earth did you do it? The woman is a psychopath, you tell me that yourself. What is gained by beating up someone who isn't even responsible for what she says? What is the good of it?"

"I couldn't take any more, that's the good of it! She may be a psychopath, but I am the psychopath's husband *and I can't take any more*."

"But what about your will? You're the one who is always telling me about using my will. You're the one who got me back to college, hitting me over the head with my *will*—and then you, you who hate violence, who are sweet and civilized, turn around and do something totally out of control like *that*. Why did you let her come to your apartment to begin with?"

"To get a divorce!"

"But that's what your *lawyer* is for!"

"But she won't cooperate with my lawyer."

"And who will she cooperate with instead? You?"

"Look, I am trying to get out of a *trap*. I stepped into it back when I was twenty-five, and now I'm thirty-three and I'm *still* in it—"

"But the trap is *you*. You're the trap. When she phoned you, why didn't you just hang up? When she said no to the Algonquin, why didn't you realize—"

"Because I thought I saw a way out! Because this alimony is bleeding me dry! Because going back and forth into court to have my income scrutinized and my check stubs checked is driving me mad! Because I am four thousand dollars in debt to my brother! Because I have nothing left of a twenty-thousand-dollar advance on a book that I cannot write! Because when little Judge Rosenzweig hears I teach only two classes a week, he's ready to send me to Sing Sing! He has to sit on his ass all day to earn his keep, while coed seducers like me are out there abandoning their wives left and right—and teaching only two classes! They want me to get a paper route, Susan! They wouldn't care if I sold Good Humors! Abandoned her? She's with me day and night! The woman is unabandonable!"

"By *you*."

"Not by me—by *them*!"

"Peter, you're going wild."

"I *am* wild! I've *gone*!"

"But Lambchop," she pleaded, "*I* have money. You could use *my* money."

"I could *not*."

"But it's not even mine. It's no one's, really. It's Jamey's. It's my grandfather's. And they're all dead, and there's tons of it, *and why not*? You can pay back your brother, you can pay back the publisher and forget that novel, and go on to something new. And you can pay her whatever the court says, and then just *forget her*—oh, do forget her, once and for all, before you ruin everything. If you haven't already!"

Oh, I thought, would that be something. Pay them all off, and start in clean. *Clean!* Go back to Rome and start again . . . live with Susan and our pots of geraniums and our bottles of Frascati and our walls of books in a white-washed apartment on the Janiculum . . . get a new VW and go off on all those trips again, up through the mountains in a car with nobody grabbing at the wheel . . . *gelati* in peace in the Piazza Navona . . . marketing in peace in the Campo dei Fiori . . . dinner with friends in Trastevere, *in peace*: no ranting, no raving, no tears . . . and writing about something other than Maureen . . . oh, just think of all there is to write about in this world that is not Maureen . . . Oh, what luxe!

"We could arrange with the bank," Susan was saying, "to send her a check every month. You wouldn't even have to think about it. And, Lambchop, that would be that. You could just wipe the whole thing out, like that."

"That wouldn't be that, and I couldn't wipe anything out like that, and *that* is that. Besides, she's going to die anyway."

"Not her," said Susan, bitterly.

"Pack your stuff. Let's go."

"But why will you let her crucify you with money when there's no need for it!"

"Susan, it is difficult enough borrowing from my big brother."

"But I'm not your brother. I'm your—*me*."

"Let's go."

"No!" And angrier than I could ever have imagined her, she marched off into the bathroom adjoining our room.

Sitting on the edge of the bed, I closed my eyes and tried to think *clearly*. My limbs weakened as I did so. *She's black and blue. Couldn't they say I killed her? Couldn't they make the case that I stuffed the pills down her throat and left her there to croak? Can they find fingerprints on flesh? If so, they'll find mine!*

Here I experienced a cold shock on the top of the head.

Susan was standing over me, having just poured a glass of water, drawn from the tap, on my head. Violence breeds violence, as they say—for Susan, it was the most violent act she had ever dared to commit in her life.

"I hate you," she said, stamping her foot.

And on that note we packed our bags and the box of salt water taffy I had bought for Dr. Spielvogel, and in a rented car we departed the seaside resort where many and many a year ago

I had first encountered romantic love: Tarnopol Returns To Face The Music In New York.

At the hospital, blessedly, no Valducci and no police—no handcuffs, no squad car, no flashbulbs, no TV cameras grinding away at the mug of the prize-winning murderer . . . Paranoid fantasy, all that—grandiose delusions for the drive up the parkway, narcissismo, with a capital N! Guilt and ambivalence over his specialness? Oh, Spielvogel, maybe you are right in ways you do not even know—maybe this Maureen of mine is just the Miss America of a narcissist's dreams. I wonder: have I chosen this She-Wolf of a woman because I am, as you say, such a Gargantua of Self-Love? Because secretly I *sympathize* with the poor girl's plight, know it is only *right* that she should lie, steal, deceive, risk her very life to have the likes of me? Because she says with every wild shriek and desperate scheme, "Peter Tarnopol, you are the cat's meow." Is that why I can't call it quits with her, because I'm flattered so?

No, no, no, no more fancy self-lacerating reasons for how I am being destroyed. I can walk away all right—only let me!

I took the elevator to the intensive-care unit and gave my name to the young nurse at the desk there. "How," I asked softly, "is my wife?" She told me to take a seat and wait to talk to the doctor who was presently in with Mrs. Tarnopol. "She's alive," I said. "Oh, yes," the nurse answered, reaching out kindly to touch my elbow. "Good. Great," I replied; "and there's no chance of her—" The nurse said, "You'll have to ask the doctor, Mr. Tarnopol."

Good. Great. She may die yet. And I will finally be free!

And in jail!

But I didn't do it!

Someone was tapping me on the shoulder.

"Aren't you Peter?"

A short, chubby woman, with graying hair and a pert, lined face, and neatly attired in a simple dark-blue dress and "sensible" shoes, was looking at me rather shyly; as I would eventually learn, she was only a few years older than I and a fifth-grade teacher in a Manhattan parochial school (and, astonishingly, in therapy because of a recurrent drinking problem); she looked no more threatening than the helpful librarian out of my childhood, but there in that hospital waiting room all I saw looking up at me was an enemy, Maureen's avenger. I backed off a step.

"Aren't you Peter Tarnopol the writer?"

The kindly nurse had lied. Maureen was dead. I was being placed under arrest for first-degree murder. By this police-woman. "Yes," I said, "yes, I write."

"I'm Flossie."

"Who?"

"Flossie Koerner. From Maureen's Group. I've heard so much about you."

I allowed with a weak smile that that might be so.

"I'm so glad you got here," she said. "She'll want to see you as soon as she comes around . . . She has to come around, Peter—she has to!"

"Yes, yes, don't you worry now . . ."

"She loves life so," said Flossie Koerner, clutching at one of my hands. I saw now that the eyes behind the spectacles were red from weeping. With a sigh, and a sweet, an endearing smile really, she said, "She loves you so."

"Yes, well . . . we'll just have to see now . . ."

We sat down beside one another to wait for the doctor.

"I feel I practically know you," said Flossie Koerner.

"Oh, yes?"

"When I hear Maureen talk about all those places you visited in Italy, it's all so vivid, she practically makes me feel I was there, with the two of you, having lunch that day in Siena—and remember that little pensione you stayed at in Florence?"

"In Florence?"

"Across from the Boboli Gardens. That that sweet little old lady owned, the one who looked like Isak Dinesen?"

"Oh, yes."

"And the little kitty with the spaghetti sauce on its face."

"I don't remember that . . . "

"By the Trevi Fountain. In Rome."

"Don't remember . . ."

"Oh, she's so proud of you, Peter. She boasts about you like a little girl. You should hear when someone dares to criticize the tiniest thing in your book. Oh, she's like a lioness pro-tecting one of her cubs."

"She is, eh?"

"Oh, that's finally Maureen's trademark, isn't it? If I had to sum her up in one word, that would be it: loyalty."

"Fierce loyalty," I said.

"Yes, so fierce, so determined—so full of belief and passion. Everything means so *much* to her. Oh, Peter, you should have seen her up in Elmira, at her father's funeral. It was you of course that she wanted to come with her—but she was afraid you'd misunderstand, and then she's always been so ashamed of them with you, and so she never dared to call you. I went with her instead. She said, 'Flossie, I can't go up there alone—but I have to be there, I have to . . .' She had to be there, Peter, to forgive him . . . For what he did."

"I don't know about any of this. Her father died?"

"Two months ago. He had a heart attack and died right on a bus."

"And what had he done that she had to forgive?"

"I shouldn't say."

"He was a night watchman somewhere . . . wasn't he? Some plant in Elmira . . ."

She had taken my hand again— "When Maureen was eleven years old . . ."

"What happened?"

"I shouldn't be the one to tell it, to tell you."

"What happened?"

"Her father . . . forced her . . . but at the graveside, Peter, she forgave him. I heard her whisper the words myself. You can't imagine what it was like—it went right through me. 'I forgive you, Daddy,' she said."

"Don't you think it's strange she never told me this herself?"

Don't you think it might even be something she happened to read about in *Tender Is the Night?* Or Krafft-Ebing? Or in the "Hundred Neediest Cases" in the Christmas issue of the Sunday *Times?* Don't you think that maybe she's just trying to outdo the rest of you girls in the Group? Sounds to me, Flossie, like a Freudian horror story for those nights you all spend roasting marshmallows around the therapist's campfire.

"Tell *you?*" said Flossie. "She was too humiliated to tell *anyone,* her whole life long, until she found the Group. All her life she was terrified people would find out, she felt so—so polluted by it. Not even her mother knew."

"You met her mother?"

"We stayed overnight at their house. Maureen's been back twice to see her. They spend whole days talking about the past. Oh, she's trying so hard to forgive her too. To forgive, to forget."

"Forget what? Forgive what?"

"Mrs. Johnson wasn't much of a mother, Peter . . ."

Flossie volunteered no lurid details, nor did I ask.

"Maureen didn't want you, above all, ever to know any of this. We would try so hard to tell her that they weren't her fault. I mean intellectually of course she understood that . . . but emotionally it was just embedded in her from her earliest childhood, that shame. It was really a classic case history."

"Sounds that way."

"Oh, I *told* her you would understand."

"I believe I do."

"How can she die? How can a person with her will to live and to struggle against the past, someone who battles for survival the way she does, and for a future—how can she die! The last time she came down from Elmira, oh, she was so torn up. That's why we all thought Puerto Rico might lift her spirits. She's such a wonderful dancer."

"Oh?"

"But all that dancing, and all that sun, and just getting away—and then she got back and just took a nose dive. And did *this*. She's so proud. Too proud sometimes, I think. That's why she takes things so much to heart. Where you're concerned, especially. Well, you were everything to her, you know that. You see, intellectually she knows by now how sorry you are. She knows that girl was just a tramp, and one of those things men do. It's partly Mr. Egan—I shouldn't say it, but it's being in his clutches. Every time you go plead with her to come back to you, he turns around and says no, you're not to be trusted. Maybe I'm telling tales out of school—but we are talking about Maureen's *life*. But you see, he's such a devout Catholic, Mr. Egan, and Mrs. Egan even more so—and, Peter, being Jewish you may not understand what it means to them when a husband did what you did. My parents would react the same way. I grew up in that kind of atmosphere, and I know how strong it is. They don't know how the world has changed—they don't know about girls like that Karen, and they don't want to know. But I see those college girls today, the kinds of morals they have, and their disrespect for everything. I know what they're capable of. They get a beeline on an attractive man old enough to be their own father—"

The doctor appeared.

*Tell me she is dead. I'll go to jail forever. Just let that filthy psychopathic liar be dead. The world will be a better place.*

But the news was "good." Mr. Tarnopol could go in now to see his wife. She was out of danger—she had come around; the doctor had even gotten her to speak a few words, though she was so groggy she probably hadn't understood what either of them had said. Fortunately, the doctor explained, the whiskey she had taken with the pills had made her sick and she'd thrown up most of "the toxic material" that otherwise would have killed her. The doctor warned me that her face was bruised— "Yes? It is?"—as she had apparently been lying for a good deal of the time with her mouth and nose pushed into the mattress and her own vomit. But that too was fortunate, for if she had not been on her stomach while throwing up, she probably would have strangulated. There were also bruises on the buttocks and thighs. "There are?" Yes, indicating that she had spent a part of the two days on her back as well. All that movement, the doctor said, was what had kept her alive.

I was in the clear.

But so was Maureen.

"How did they find her?" I asked the doctor.

"I found her," Flossie said.

"We have Miss Koerner to thank for that," the doctor said.

"I was calling there for days," said Flossie, "and getting no answer. And then last night she missed Group. I got suspicious, even though she sometimes doesn't come, when she gets all wrapped up in her flute or something—but I just got very suspicious, because I knew she was in this depression since coming back from Puerto Rico. And this afternoon I couldn't stand worrying any more, and I told Sister Mary Rose that I had to leave and in the middle of an arithmetic class I just got in a taxi and came over to Maureen's and knocked on the door. I just kept knocking and then I heard Delilah and I was *sure* something was up."

"Heard who?"

"The cat. She was meowing away, but there was still no answer. So I got down on my hands and knees in the corridor there, and there's a little space under the door, because it doesn't fit right, which I always told Maureen was dangerous, and I called to the pussy and then I saw Maureen's hand hanging down over the side of the bed. I could see her fingertips almost touching the carpet. And so I ran to a neighbor and phoned the police and they broke in the door, and there she was, just in her underwear, her bra too I mean, and all this . . . mess, like the doctor said."

I wanted to find out from Flossie if a suicide note had been found, but the doctor was still with us, and so all I said was, "May I go in to see her now?"

"I think so," he said. "Just for a few minutes."

In the darkened room, in one of the half dozen criblike beds, Maureen lay with her eyes closed, under a sheet, hooked up by tubes and wires to various jugs and bottles and machines. Her nose was swollen badly, as though she'd been in a street brawl. Which she had been.

I looked silently down at her, perhaps for as long as a minute, before I realized that I had neglected to call Spielvogel. I wanted all at once to talk over with him whether I really ought to be here or not. I would like to ask him his opinion. I would like to know my own. What *was* I doing here? Rampant narcissismo—or, as Susan diagnosed it, just me being a boy again? Coming when called by my master Maureen! Oh, if so, tell me how I stop! How do I ever get to be what is described in the literature as *a man*? I had so wanted to be one, too— why then is it always beyond me? Or—could it be?—is this boy's life a man's life after all? Is this *it*? Oh, could be, I thought, could very well be that I have been expecting much too much from "maturity." This quicksand is *it*—adult life!

Maureen opened her eyes. She had to work to bring me into focus. I gave her time. Then I leaned over the bed's side bars, and with my face looming over hers, said, "This is Hell, Maureen. You are in Hell. You have been consigned to Hell for all eternity."

I meant for her to believe every word.

But she began to smile. A sardonic smile for her husband,

even in extremis. Faintly, she said, "Oh, delicious, if you're here too."

"This is Hell, and I am going to look down at you for all of Time and tell you what a lying bitch you are."

"Just like back in Life Itself."

I said, shaking a fist, "What if you had died!"

For a long time she didn't answer. Then she wet her lips and said, "Oh, you would have been in such hot water."

"But *you* would have been *dead*."

*That* roused her anger, *that* brought her all the way around. Yep, she was alive now. "Please, don't bullshit me. Don't give me 'Life is Sacred.' It is not sacred when you are constantly in pain." She was weeping. "My life is just pain."

*You're lying, you bitch. You're lying to me, like you lie to Flossie Koerner, like you lie to your Group, like you lie to everyone. Cry, but I won't cry with you!*

So swore he who aspired to manhood; but the little boy who will not die began to go to pieces.

"The pain, Maureen,"—the tears from my face plopped onto the sheet that covered her—"the pain comes from all this *lying* that you do. Lying is the form your pain *takes*. If only you would make an effort, if only you would give it up—"

"Oh, how can you? Oh get out of here, you, with your crocodile tears. Doctor," she cried feebly, "help."

Her head began to thrash around on the pillow— "Okay," I said "calm down, calm yourself. *Stop*." I was holding her hand.

She squeezed my fingers, clutched them and wouldn't let go. It had been a while now since we'd held hands.

"How," she whimpered, "how . . ."

"Okay, just take it easy."

"—How can you be so heartless when you see me like this?"

"I'm sorry."

"I'm only alive two minutes . . . and you're over me calling me a liar. Oh, boy," she said, just like somebody's little sister.

"I'm only trying to suggest to you how to alleviate the pain. I'm trying to tell you . . ." ah, go on with it, go on, "*the lying is the source of your self-loathing*."

"Bull*shit*," she sobbed, pulling her fingers from mine. "You're trying to get out of paying the alimony. I see right through you, Peter. Oh thank God I didn't die," she moaned.

"I forgot all about the alimony. That's how mortified and miserable you left me!"

"Oh, Maureen, this *is* fucking hell."

"Who said no?" said she, and exhausted now, closed her eyes, though not for oblivion, not quite yet. Only to sleep, and rise in a rage one last time.

When I came back into the waiting room there was a man with Flossie Koerner, a large blond fellow in gleaming square-toed boots and wearing a beautifully cut suit in the latest mode. He was so powerfully good-looking—charismatic is the word these days—that I did not immediately separate out the tan from the general overall glow. I thought momentarily that he might be a detective, but the only detectives who look like him are in the movies.

I got it: he too must just be back from vacationing in Puerto Rico!

He extended a hand, big and bronzed, for me to shake. Soft wide French cuffs; gold cuff links cast in the form of little microphones; strange animalish tufts of golden hair on the knuckles . . . Why, just from the wrists to the fingernails he was something to conjure with—now how in hell did she get *him*? Surely to catch this one would require the piss of a pregnant contessa. "I'm Bill Walker," he said. "I flew here as soon as I got the news. How is she? Is she able to talk?"

It was my predecessor, it was Walker, who had "promised" to give up boys after the marriage, and then had gone back on his word. My, what a dazzler he was! In my lean and hungry Ashkenazic way I am not a bad-looking fellow, but this was *beauty*.

"She's out of danger," I told Walker. "Oh yes, she's talking; don't worry, she's her old self."

He flashed a smile warmer and larger than the sarcasm warranted; he didn't even see it as sarcasm, I realized. He was just plain overjoyed to hear she was alive.

Flossie, also in seventh heaven, pointed appreciatively to the two of us. "You can't say she doesn't know how to pick 'em."

It was a moment before I understood that I was only being placed alongside Walker in the category of Good-Looking Six-Footers. My face flushed—not just at the thought that she who had picked Walker had picked me, but that both Walker and I had picked her.

"Look, maybe we ought to have a drink afterwards, and a little chat," Walker suggested.

"I have to run," I replied, a line that Dr. Spielvogel would have found amusing.

Here Walker removed a billfold from the side-vented jacket that nipped his waist and swelled over his torso, and handed me a business card. "If you get up to Boston," he said, "or if for any reason you want to get in touch about Maur."

Was a pass being made? Or did he actually care about "Maur"? "Thanks," I said. I saw from the card that he was with a television station up there.

"Mr. Walker," said Flossie, as he started for the nurse's desk. She was still beaming with joy at the way things had worked out. "Mr. Walker—would you?" She handed him a piece of scratch paper she had drawn hastily from her purse. "It's not for me—it's for my little nephew. He collects them."

"What's his name?"

"Oh, that's so kind. His name is Bobby."

Walker signed the paper and, smiling, handed it back to her.

"Peter, Peter." She was plainly chagrined and embarrassed, and touched my hand with her fingertips. "Would *you*? I couldn't ask earlier, not with Maureen still in danger . . . you understand . . . don't you? But, now, well, I'm just so elated . . . so relieved." With that she handed me a piece of paper. Perplexed, I signed my name to it. I thought: Now all she needs is Mezik's X and Bobby will have the set. What's going on with this signature business? A trap? Flossie and Walker in cahoots with—with whom? My signature to be used for *what*? Oh, please, relax. That's paranoid madness. More narcissismo.

Says who.

"By the way," Walker told me, "I admired *A Jewish Father* tremendously. Powerful stuff. I thought you really captured the moral dilemma of the modern American Jew. When can we expect another?"

"As soon as I can shake that bitch out of my life."

Flossie couldn't (and consequently wouldn't) believe her ears.

"She's not such a bad gal, you know," said Walker, in a low stern voice, impressive now for its restraint as well as its timbre.

"She happens to be one of the gamest people I know, as a matter of fact. She's been through a lot, that girl, and survived it all."

"So have I been through it, pal. At her hands!" A film of perspiration had formed on my forehead and beneath my nose—I was greatly enraged by this tribute to Maureen's guts, particularly coming from this guy.

"Oh," he said icily, and swelling a little as he spoke, "I understand you know how to take care of yourself, all right. You've got hands too, from what I hear." He lifted one corner of his mouth, a contemptuous smile . . . tinged slightly (unless I was imagining things) with a coquettish invitation. "If you can't stand the heat, as they say—"

"Gladly. *Gladly,*" I interrupted. "Just go in there and tell her to unlock the kitchen door!"

Flossie, a hand now on either of us, jumped in— "He's just upset, Mr. Walker, from everything that's happened."

"I should hope so," said Walker. He took three long strides to the nurse's desk, where he announced, "I'm Bill Walker. I spoke earlier to Dr. Maas."

"Oh. Yes. You can see her now. But only for a few minutes."

"Thank you."

"Mr. Walker?" The nurse, a stout, pretty twenty-year-old, till then all tact and good sense, turned shy and awkward suddenly. Flushing, she said to him, "Would you mind? I'm going off duty. Would you, please?" And she too produced a piece of paper for him to sign.

"Of course." Walker leaned over the desk toward the nurse. "What's your name?" he asked.

"Oh, that doesn't matter," she said, going even deeper scarlet. "Just say 'Jackie'—that'd be enough."

Walker signed the paper, slowly, with concentration, and then headed off into the intensive-care room.

"Who's he?" I asked Flossie.

My question confused her. "Why, Maureen's husband, between you and that Mr. Mezik."

"And that's why all the world wants his autograph?" I asked sourly.

"Don't—don't you really know?"

"Know what?"

"He's the Huntley-Brinkley of Boston. He's the anchorman of their six o'clock news. He was just on the cover of the last *TV Guide*. He's the one that used to be a Shakespearean actor."

"I see."

"Peter, I'm sure it's that Maureen just didn't want to make you jealous by mentioning him right now. He's just been helping her over the rough spots, that's really all there is to it."

"And he's the one who took her to Puerto Rico."

Flossie, out of her depth completely now, and not at all sure any longer what was to be said to smooth life over for this triumvirate with whose fate she was intimately involved, shrugged and nearly wilted. We, I realized, were her own private soap opera: she was the audience to our drama, our ode-singing chorus; this was the Fortinbras my Deep Seriousness had called forth. Fair enough, I thought—this Fortinbras for this farce!

Flossie said, "Well—"

"Well, what?"

"Well, I think so, that they were together there, yes. But, believe me, he's just somebody, well, that she could turn to . . . after you did . . . what you did . . . with Karen."

"I get it," I said, and pulled on my coat.

"Oh, *please* don't be jealous. It's a brother-sister relationship more than anything else—someone close, lending her a helping hand. She's over him, I swear to you. She knew long ago that with him it would always be career-career. He can propose from now till doomsday, she'd never go back to a man whose work and talent is his everything. That's true. Please don't jump to conclusions because of him, it's not fair. Peter, you must have faith—she *will* take you back, I'm sure of it."

I passed a phone booth on my way through the hospital lobby, but didn't stop to call anyone to ask if I was about to do the wrong thing again or the right thing at last—I saw a way out (I thought) and so I ran. This time to Maureen's apartment on West Seventy-eighth Street, only a few blocks from the hospital to which the ambulance had carried her some hours earlier. There had to be evidence against her *somewhere* in that apartment—in the diary she kept, some entry describing how she had laid this trap from which I still could not escape, a confession about the urine written in her own

hand—that we would submit in evidence in court, to Judge
Milton Rosenzweig, whose mission it was to prevent phallic
havoc from being unleashed on the innocent and defenseless
abandoned women of the county of New York of the state of
New York. Oh, little robed Rosenzweig, he would have kept
the primal horde in line! How he bent over backwards not to
show favoritism to his, the Herculean sex . . . Prior to my
own separation hearing there had been the case of Kriegel *v.*
Kriegel; it was still in session when I arrived with my lawyer at
the courthouse on Centre Street. "Your Honor," pleaded
Kriegel, a heavyset businessman of fifty, addressing himself
(when we entered the courtroom) directly to the judge; his attorney, standing beside him, made sporadic attempts to quiet
his client down, but from Kriegel's posture and tone it was
clear that he had decided to Throw Himself Upon the Mercy
of the Court. "Your Honor," he said, "I understand full well
that she lives in a walk-up. But *I* didn't tell her to get a walk-
up. That was her choice. She could get an elevator building on
what I give her a week, I assure you. But, Your Honor, *I cannot give her what I do not have.*" Judge Rosenzweig, up by his
bootstraps from Hell's Kitchen to N.Y.U. Law, and still a burly
little battler for all his sixty-odd years, flicked continually with
one index finger at an earlobe as he listened—as though over
the decades he had found this the best means to prevent the
bullshit addressed to the bench from passing down into the
Eustachian tube and poisoning his system. His humorous ban-
tering side and his stern contemptuous side were all right in
that gesture. He wore the gown of a magistrate, but the manner
(and the hide) was that of an old Marine general who had
spent a lifetime hitting the beaches in defense of Hearth and
Home. "Your Honor," said Kriegel, "I'm in the feather business, as the court knows. That's it, sir. I buy and I sell feathers.
I'm not a millionaire like she tells you." Judge Rosenzweig,
obviously pleased by the opportunity for light banter provided
him by Mr. Kriegel, said, "Still, that's a nice suit you got on
your back. That's a Hickey-Freeman suit. Unless my eyes deceive me, that's a two-hundred-dollar suit." "Your Honor—"
said Kriegel, spreading his hands deferentially before the judge,
as though he held in each palm the three or four feathers that
he passed on to the pillow people in the course of a day, "Your

Honor, please, I would not come to court in rags." "Thank you." "I mean it, Your Honor." "Look, Kriegel, I know you. You own more colored property in Harlem than Carter has little liver pills." "Me? No, not me. Your Honor. I beg to differ with Your Honor. That's my brother. That's *Louis* Kriegel. I'm Julius." "You're not in with your brother? Are you sure that's what you want to tell the court, Mr. Kriegel?" "*In* with him?" "In with him." "Well, if so, only on the side, Your Honor." Then me. I don't shilly-shally quite so long as Kriegel; no, no Judge Rosenzweig has to badger forever a man of my calling—*and* Thomas Mann's *and* Leo Tolstoy's—to get at the Truth! "What's it mean here, Mr. Tarnopol, 'a well-known seducer of college girls'? What's that mean?" "Your Honor, I think that's an exaggeration." "You mean you're not well-known for it, or you're not a seducer of college girls?" "I'm not a 'seducer' of anybody." "So what do they mean here, do you think?" "I don't know, sir." My lawyer nods approvingly at me from the defense table; I have done just as I was instructed to in the taxi down to the courthouse: ". . . just say you don't know and you have no idea . . . make no accusations . . . don't call her a liar . . . don't call her anything but Mrs. Tarnopol . . . Rosenzweig has a great feeling for abandoned women . . . he won't permit name-calling of abandoned women in his court . . . just shrug it off, Peter, and don't admit a thing—because he is a prick of the highest order under the best of circumstances. And this isn't the best of circumstances, a teacher fucking his students." "I didn't fuck my *students*." "Fine. Good. That's just what you tell him. The judge has a granddaughter at Barnard College, her picture, Peter, is all over his chambers. Friend, this old gent is the Stalin of Divorce Court Communism: 'From each according to his ability, to each according to her need.' And with a vengeance. So watch it, Peter, will you?" On the witness stand I unfortunately forgot to. "Are you telling me then," said Rosenzweig, "that Mr. Egan, in his affidavit prepared for Mrs. Tarnopol, has lied to the court? Is this an outright lie—yes or no?" "As stated, it is, yes." "Well, how would you state it to make it true? Mr. Tarnopol, I'm asking you a question. Give me an answer, please, so we can get on here!" "Look, I have nothing to hide—I have nothing to feel guilty about—" "Your Honor," interrupted my lawyer, even as I told the judge, "I had a love affair." "Yes?" said Rosenzweig, smiling, his ear-flicking finger poised now at the side of his head— "How nice. With whom?" "A girl in my class—whom I loved, Your Honor—a young woman." And that of course helped the cause enormously, that qualification.

But now we would all find out just who the guilty party was, just who had committed a crime against whom! "Judge Rosenzweig, you may remember that the last time I appeared before you, I brought no charges against Mrs. Tarnopol. I was cautioned by my attorney, and rightly so, to say nothing whatsoever about a fraud that had been perpetrated on me by my wife, because at that time, Your Honor, we had nothing in the way of evidence to support so damning an accusation. And we realized that, understandably, His Honor would not take kindly to unsubstantiated charges being brought against an 'abandoned' woman, who was here only to seek the protection that the law rightfully provides her. But now, Your Honor, we have the proof, a confession written in the 'abandoned' woman's own hand, that on March 1, 1959, she purchased, for two dollars and twenty-five cents in cash, several ounces of urine from a pregnant Negro woman with whom she made contact in Tompkins Square Park, on the Lower East Side of Manhattan. We have proof that she did then take said urine to a drugstore at the corner of Second Avenue and Ninth Street, and that she submitted it, in the name of 'Mrs. Peter Tarnopol,' to the pharmacist for a pregnancy test. We further have proof . . ." No matter that my lawyer had already told me that it was much too late for evidence of a fraud to do me any good, if ever it would have. I had to get the goods on her! Find something to restrain her, something that would make her quit and go away! Because I could not take any longer playing the role of the Archenemy, Divorcing Husband as Hooligan, Moth in the Fabric of Society and Housewrecker in the Householder's State!

And luck (I thought) was with me! The door broken in by the police late that afternoon had not yet been repaired—the door (just as I'd been hoping and praying) was ajar, freedom a footstep away! Bless the mismanagement of this megalopolis!

A light was burning in the apartment. I knocked very gently. I did not want to rouse the neighbors in the other two apartments on the landing. But no one appeared to check out the door of their hospitalized neighbor—bless too this city's vast indifference! The only one I aroused was a fluffy black Persian cat who slithered up to greet me as I slipped into the empty apartment. The recent acquisition named Delilah. Nothing subtle there, Maureen. *I never said I was,* she answers as I push the door shut behind me. *You want subtlety, read* The Golden Bowl. *This is life, bozo, not high art.*

More luck! There, right out on the dining table, the three-ring school notebook in which Maureen used to scribble her "thoughts"—generally in the hours immediately following a quarrel. Keeping "a record," she once warned me, of who it was that "started" all our arguments, the proof of what "a madman" I was. When we were living together at the Academy in Rome and later in Wisconsin, she used to keep the diary carefully hidden away—it was "private property," she told me, and if I should ever try to "steal" it, she would not hesitate to call in the local constabulary, be it Italian or middle western. This, though she herself had no compunction about opening mail that came for me when I wasn't home: "I'm your wife, aren't I? Why shouldn't I? Do you have something to hide from your own wife?" I expected then that, when I did get my hands on it, the diary would contain much that she wanted to hide from her husband. I rushed to the dining table, anticipating a gold mine.

I turned to an entry dated "8/15/58," written in the early weeks of our "courtship." "It's hard to sketch my own personality really, since personality implies the effect one has on others, and it's difficult to know truly what that effect is. However, I think I can guess some of this effort correctly. I have a moderately compelling personality." And on in that vein, describing her moderately compelling personality as though she were a freshman back in high school in Elmira. "At best I can be quite witty and bright and I think at best I can be a winning person . . ."

The next entry was dated "Thursday, October 9, 1959." We were by then already married, living in the little rented house

in the country outside New Milford. "It's almost a year—" actually it was over a year, unless she had removed a page, the
one I was looking for, describing the purchase of the urine!

—since I've written here and my life is different in every way. It's a
miracle how change of circumstances can truly change your essential
self. I still have awful depressions, but I truly have a more optimistic
outlook and only at the blackest moments do I feel hopeless.
Strangely tho', I do think more often about suicide, it seems to grow
as a possibility altho' I really wouldn't do it now, I'm certain. I feel P.
needs me more than ever now, tho' that of course is something he
would never admit to. If it weren't for me he'd still be hiding behind
his Flaubert and wouldn't know what real life was like if he fell over it.
What did he ever think he was going to write *about*, knowing and believing nothing but what he read in books? Oh, he can be such a self-
important snob and fool! Why does he fight me like this? I could be
his Muse, if only he'd let me. Instead he treats me like the enemy.
When all I've ever really wanted is for him to be the best writer in the
world. It's all too brutally ironic.

That missing page, *where was it?* Why was there no mention
made of what she had done to get P. to need her so!
    "Madison, May 24, 1962." A month after she had discovered
me in the phone booth telephoning Karen; a month after she
had taken the pills and the whiskey, put a razor to her wrist,
and then confessed about the urine. An entry that caused a wave
of nausea to come over me as I read it. I had been leaning over
the table all this time, reading on my feet; now I sat down and
read three times over her revelations of May 24, 1962: "Somehow"—somehow!—

P. has a deep hostile feeling for me and when face to face the emotion
I sense now is hatred. Somehow I've finally become despairing and
hopeless about it all and feel utterly cheerless most of the time. I love
P. and our life together—or what our life *could* be if only he weren't
so neurotic, but it seems impossible. It's so joyless. His emotional
coldness grows in leaps and bounds. His inability to love is positively
frightening. He simply does not touch, kiss, smile, etc., let alone make
love, a most unsatisfying state for me. I felt fed up with everything
this morning and ready to throw it all over. Yet I know I must not
lose heart. Life is not easy—P.'s naive expectations to the contrary.
However, I sometimes think that to think about and try to ferret out
P.'s neurosis is fruitless, for accurate as I may be, even if he were analyzed it would take years and years with a case like his, and no doubt

I'd be discarded in the process anyway, though he might at last see what a madman he is. The only satisfaction is that I know perfectly well that if he does give me up, he will inevitably marry next someone who has her own talent and ego to match, who will care for that instead of him. Would he be surprised then! I almost wish it for him except I don't wish it for myself. But he is killing my feeling so that if all this coldness from him should continue, finally my star will ascend and my heart will be stony instead of his. What a pity that would be, tho'.

"West 78th St., 3/22/66." The next-to-last entry, written just three weeks earlier. After our day in court with Judge Rosenzweig. After the two go-rounds with the court-appointed referee. After Valducci. After Egan. After alimony. Four years after I'd left her, seven years after the urine. The entry, in its entirety:

Where have I been? Why haven't I realized this? Peter doesn't *care* for me. He never did! He married me only because he thought he *had* to. My God! It seems so plain now, how could I have been mistaken before? Is this insight a product of Group? I wish I could go away. It's so degrading. I wonder if I'll ever have the luck to be in love with someone who loves me, the real me, and not some cockeyed idea of me, à la the Meziks, Walkers, and Tarnopols of this world. That seems to me now nearly all I could want, though I now know how practical I really am—or how practical it's necessary to be to survive.

And the last entry. She *had* written a suicide note, but it would seem that no one had thought to look for it in her three-ring school notebook. The handwriting, and the prose, indicated that she was already under the influence of the pills, and/or the whiskey, when she began to write her final message to herself:

Marilyn Monroe Marilyn Monroe Marilyn Monroe Marilyn Monroe why do they do these Marilyn Monroe why to use Marilyn why to use us Marilyn

That was it. Somehow she had then made it from the table back to the bed, nearly to die there like the famous movie star herself. Nearly!

A policeman had been watching me from the door for I didn't know how long. He had his pistol drawn.

"Don't shoot!" I cried.

"Why not?" he asked. "Get up, you."

"It's okay, Officer," I said. I rose on boneless legs. I rose on air. Without even being asked I put my hands over my head. The last time I'd done that I'd been eight, a holster around my sixteen-inch waist and a Lone Ranger gun, made in Japan and hollow as a chocolate bunny, poking me in the ribs—a weapon belonging to my little pal from next door, Barry Edelstein, wearing his chaps and his sombrero, and telling me, in the accent of the Cisco Kid, "Steeck 'em up, amigo." That, by and large, was my preparation for this dangerous life I now led.

"I'm Peter Tarnopol," I hurriedly explained. "I'm Maureen Tarnopol's husband. She's the one who lives here. We're separated. Legally, legally. I just came from the hospital. I came to get my wife's toothbrush and some things. She's my wife still, you see; she's in the hospital—"

"I know who's in the hospital."

"Yes, well, I'm her husband. The door was open. I thought I better stay here until I can get it fixed. Anybody could walk right in. I was sitting here. Reading. I was going to call a locksmith."

The cop just stood there, pointing his pistol. I should never have told him we were separated. I should never have told Rosenzweig I'd had "a love affair" with a student. I should never have gotten involved with Maureen. Yes, that was my biggest mistake.

I said some more words about a locksmith.

"He's on his way," the cop told me.

"Yes? He is? Good. Great. Look, if you still don't believe me, I have a driver's license."

"On you?"

"Yes, yes, in my wallet. May I reach for my wallet?"

"All right, never mind, it's okay . . . just got to be careful," he mumbled, and lowering his pistol, took a step into the room. "I just went down for a Coke. I seen she had her own, but I didn't want to take it. That ain't right."

"Oh," said I, as he dropped the pistol into his holster, "you should have."

"Fuckin' locksmith." He looked at his watch.

When he stepped all the way into the apartment I saw how very young he was: a pug-nosed kid off the subway, with a gun and a badge and dressed up in a blue uniform. Not so unlike Barry Edelstein as I'd thought while the pistol was pointed at my head. Now he wouldn't engage my eyes directly, embarrassed it seemed for having drawn the gun, movie style, or for having spoken obscenely to an innocent man, or, most likely, for having been discovered by me away from his post. Yet another member of the sex, abashed to be revealed as unequal to his task.

"Well," I said, closing the three-ring notebook and tucking it under my arm, "I'll just get those things now, and be off—"

"Hey," he said, motioning to the bedroom, "don't worry about the mattress in there. I just couldn't take the stink no more, so I washed it out. That's how come it's wet like that. Ajax and a little Mr. Clean, and that did it. Don't worry—it won't leave no mark when it dries."

"Well, thank you. That was very nice of you."

He shrugged. "I put all the stuff back in the kitchen, under the sink there."

"Fine."

"That Mr. Clean is some stuff."

"I know. I've heard them say that. I'll just get a few things and go."

We were friends now. He asked, "What is the missus anyway? An actress?"

"Well . . . yes."

"On TV?"

"No, no, just around."

"What? Broadway?"

"No, no, not yet anyway."

"Well, that takes time, don't it? She shouldn't be discouraged."

I went into Maureen's bedroom, a tiny cell just big enough for a bed and a night table with a lamp on it. Because the closet door could only be opened halfway before it banged against the foot of the bed, I had to reach blindly around inside until I came up with a nightdress that was hanging on a hook. "Ah," I said, nice and loud, "*here* it is—right . . . where . . . she said!" To complete the charade, I decided to open and then shut loudly the drawer to the little night table.

A can opener. In the drawer there was a can opener. I did not immediately deduce its function. That is, I thought it must be there to open cans.

Let me describe the instrument. The can-opening device itself is screwed to a smooth, grainy-looking wooden handle, about two and a half inches around and some five inches long, tapering slightly to its blunt end. The opening device consists of a square aluminum case, approximately the size of a cigarette lighter, housing on its underside a small metal tooth and a little ridged gear; projecting upward from the top side of the case is an inch-long shaft to which is attached a smaller wooden handle, about three inches long. Placing the can opener horizontally over the edge of the can, you press the pointed metal tooth down into the rim, and proceed to open the can by holding the longer handle in one hand, and rotating the smaller handle with the other; this causes the tooth to travel around the rim until it has severed the top of the can from the cylinder. It is a type of can opener that you can buy in practically any hardware store for between a dollar and a dollar and a quarter. I have priced them since. They are manufactured by the Eglund Co., Inc., of Burlington, Vermont—their "No. 5 Junior" model. I have Maureen's here on my desk as I write.

"How ya' doin'?" the cop called.

"Oh, fine."

I slammed the drawer shut, having first deposited the No. 5 Junior in my pocket.

"So that's it," I said, coming back around into the living room, Delilah glued to my trouser cuff.

"Mattress look okay to you?"

"Great. Perfect. Thanks again. I'll be off, you know—I'll leave the locksmith to you then, right?"

I was one flight down and flying, when the young cop appeared at the landing over my head. "Hey!"

"What!"

"Toothbrush!"

"Oh!"

"Here!"

I caught it and kept going.

The taxi I flagged down to take me crosstown to Susan's was one of those fitted out like the prison cell of an enterprising convict or the den of an adolescent boy: framed family photographs lined up on the windshield, a large round alarm clock strapped atop the meter, and some ten or fifteen sharpened Eberhard pencils jammed upright in a white plastic cup fastened by a system of thick elastic bands to the grill separating the passenger in the back seat from the driver up front. The grill was itself festooned with blue-and-white tassels, and an arrangement of gold-headed upholstery tacks stuck into the roof above the driver's head spelled out "Gary, Tina & Roz"— most likely the names of the snappily dressed children smiling out from the family photographs of wedding and bar mitzvahs. The driver, an elderly man, must have been their grandfather.

Ordinarily I suppose I would have commented, like every other passenger, on the elaborate decor. But all I could look at and think about then was the Eglund Company's No. 5 Junior can opener. Holding the aluminum end in my left hand, I passed the larger handle through a circle formed out of my thumb and index finger of my right hand; then, wrapping the other three fingers loosely around it, I moved the handle slowly down the channel.

Next I placed the handle of the can opener between my thighs and crossed one leg over the other, locking it in place. Only the square metallic opening device, with its sharp little tooth facing up, poked out from between my legs.

The cab veered sharply over to the curb.

"Get out," the driver said.

"Do what?"

He was glaring at me through the grill, a little man, with dark pouches under his eyes and bushy gray eyebrows, wearing a heavy wool sweater under a suit. His voice quivered with rage—"Get the hell out! None of that stuff in my cab!"

"None of what? I'm not *doing* anything."

"Get out, I told you! Out, you, before I use the tire iron on your head!"

"What do you think I was doing, for Christ's sake!"

But by now I was on the sidewalk.

"You filthy son of a bitch!" he cried, and drove off.

Clutching the can opener in my pocket and holding the diary in my lap, I eventually made it to Susan's—though not without further incident. As soon as I had gotten settled in the back seat of a second cab, the driver, this one a young fellow with a wispy yellow beard, fixed me in the rearview mirror and said, "Hey, Peter Tarnopol." "What's that?" "You're Peter Tarnopol—right?" "Wrong." "You look like him." "Never heard of him." "Come on, you're putting me on, man. You're him. You're really him. Wow, man. What a coincidence. I just had Jimmy Baldwin in here last night." "Who's he?" "The writer, man. You're putting me on. You know who else I had in here?" I didn't answer. "Mailer. I get all you fuckin' guys. I had another guy in here, I swear to fuck he musta weighed eighty-two pounds. This tall string bean with a crew cut. I took him out to Kennedy. You know who it was?" "Who?" "Fuckin' Beckett. You know how I know it was him? I said to him, 'You're Samuel Beckett, man.' And you know what he said? He says, 'No, I'm Vladimir Nabokov.' What do you think of that?" "Maybe it *was* Vladimir Nabokov." "No, no, I never had Nabokov. Not yet. What are you writin' these days, Tarnopol?" "Checks." We had arrived at Susan's building. "Right here," I told him, "that awning." "Hey, you live all right, Tarnopol. You guys do okay, you know that?" I paid him, while he shook his head in wonderment; as I was leaving the taxi, he said, "Watch this, I'll turn the corner and pick up fuckin' Malamud. I wouldn't put it past me."

"Good evening, sir," said Susan's elevator man, appearing out of nowhere and startling me in the lobby, just as I had made it gravely past the doorman and was removing the can opener from my pocket . . . But once inside the apartment I pulled it from my pocket again and cried out, "Wait'll you see what *I* got!"

"She's alive?" asked Susan.

"And kicking."

"—the police?"

"Weren't there. Look—look at this!"

"It's a can opener."

"It's also what she masturbates with! Look! Look at this nice sharp metal tooth. How she must love that protruding out of her—how she must love to look down at that!"

"Oh, Peter, where ever did you—"

"From her apartment—next to her bed."

Out popped the tear.

"What are you crying about? It's perfect—don't you see? Just what she thinks a man is—a torture device. A surgical instrument!"

"But where—"

"I told you. From her bedside table!"

"You stole it, from her apartment?"

"Yes!"

I described to her then in detail my adventures at the hospital and after.

When I finished she turned and went off to the kitchen. I followed her and stood by the stove as she began to brew herself a cup of Ovaltine.

"Look, you yourself tell me I shouldn't be defenseless with her."

She would not speak to me.

"I am only doing what I have to do, Susan, to get sprung from this trap."

No reply.

"I am tired, you see, of being guilty of sex crimes in the eyes of every hypocrite, lunatic, and—"

"But the only one who thinks you're guilty of *anything* is *you*."

"Yes? Is that why they've got me supporting her for the rest of my life, a woman I was married to for three years? A woman who bore me no children? Is that why they will not let me get divorced? Is that why I am being punished like this, Susan? Because *I* think I'm guilty? *I think I'm innocent!*"

"Then if you do, why do you need to steal something like *that*?"

"*Because nobody believes me!*"

"*I* believe you."

"But you are not the judge in this case! You are not the sovereign state of New York! I have got to get her fangs out of my neck! Before I drown in this rage!"

"But what good is a can opener? How do you even know it is what you say it is? You don't! Probably, Peter, she just uses it *to open cans.*"

"In her bedroom?"

"Yes! People can open cans in bedrooms."

"And they can play with themselves in the kitchen, but

usually it's the other way around. It's a dildo, Susan—whether you like that idea or not. Maureen's very own surrogate dick!"

"And so what if it is? What business is it of yours? It's not your affair!"

"Oh, isn't it? Then why is everything in my life *her* affair? And Judge Rosenzweig's affair! And the affair of her Group! And the affair of her class at the New School! I get caught with Karen and the judge has me down for Lucifer. She on the other hand, fucks household utensils—"

"But you cannot bring this thing into court—they'd think you were crazy. It *is* crazy. Don't you see that? What do you think you would accomplish by waving it around in the judge's face? *What?*"

"But I have her diary, too!"

"But you told me you read it—you said there's nothing there."

"I haven't read it *all*."

"But if you do, it's only going to make you crazier than you are now!"

"I AM NOT THE ONE WHO'S CRAZY!"

Said Susan, "You *both* are. And I can't take it. Because I'll go mad too. I cannot drink any more Ovaltine in one day! Oh, Peter, I can't take you any more like this. I can't *stand* you this way. Look at you, with that thing. Oh, throw it away!"

"No! No! This way you can't stand me is the way that I am! This is the way that I am going to be—until I win!"

"Win *what?*"

"My balls back, Susan!"

"Oh, how can you use that cheap expression? Oh, Lambchop, you're a sensible, sweet, civilized, darling man. And I love you as you are!"

"*But I don't.*"

"But you *should.* What possible use can those—"

"I don't know yet! Maybe none! Maybe some! But I'm going to find out! And if you don't like it, I'll leave. Is that what you want?"

She shrugged ". . . if this is the way you're going to be—"

"This is the way I am going to be! And *have* to be! It's too rough out there, Susan, to be *darling!*"

". . . then I think you better."

"Leave?"

". . . Yes."

"Good! Fine!" I said, utterly astonished. "Then I'll go!"

To which she made no reply.

So I left, taking Maureen's can opener and diary with me.

I spent the rest of the night back in the bedroom of my own apartment—the living room faintly redolent still of Maureen's bowel movement—reading the diary, a dreary document, as it turned out, about as interesting on the subject of a woman's life as "Dixie Dugan." The sporadic entries rambled on without focus, or stopped abruptly in the midst of a sentence or a word, and the prose owed everything to the "Dear Diary" school, the pure expression of self-delusion and unknowingness. In one so cunning, how bizarre! But then writers are forever disappointing readers by being so "different" from their work, though not usually because the work fails to be as compelling as the person. I was mildly surprised—but only mildly—by the persistence with which Maureen had secretly nursed the idea of "a writing career," or at least tantalized herself with it in her semiconscious way, throughout the years of our marriage. Entries began: "I won't apologize this time for not writing for now I see that even V. Woolf let her journal go for months at a time." And: "I must set down my strange experience in New Milford this morning which I'm sure would make a good story, if one could write it in just the right way." And: "I realized today for the first time—how naive of me!— that if I were to write a story, or a novel, that was published, P. would have awful competitive feelings. Could I do that to him? No wonder I'm so reluctant to launch upon a writing career—it all has to do with sparing his ego."

Along the way there were a dozen or so newspaper clippings stapled or Scotch-taped to the loose-leaf pages, most of them about me and my work, dating back to the publication of my novel in the first year of our marriage. Pasted neatly on one page there was an article clipped from the *Times* when Faulkner died, a reprint of his windy Nobel Prize speech. Maureen had underlined the final grandiose paragraph: "The poet's voice need not merely be the record of man, it can be one of the props, the pillars to help him endure and prevail." Beside it she had penciled a bit of marginalia to make the head swim: "P and me?"

To me the most intriguing entry recounted her visit two years earlier to Dr. Spielvogel's office. She had gone there to talk to him about "how to get Peter back," or so Spielvogel had reported it to me, following the call on him, which she had made unannounced at the end of the day. According to Spielvogel, he had told her that he did not think getting me back was possible any longer—to which she had, by his report, replied, "But I can do anything. I can play it weak or strong, whichever will work."

Maureen's version:

April 29, 1964

I must record my conversation with Spielvogel yesterday, for I don't want to forget any more than is inevitable. He said I had made one serious mistake: confessing to P. I realize that too. If I had not been so desolated by learning about him and that little student of his, I would never have made such an unforgivable error. If I had never told him we would still be together. That gave him just the sort of excuse he could use against me. Spielvogel agrees. Spielvogel said that he thinks he knows what course Peter would take if we were to come back together and remain married, and I understood him to mean that he would be constantly unfaithful to me with one student after another. S. has rather settled theories about the psyche and neuroses of the artist and it's hard to know whether he's right or not. He advised me very directly to "work through" my feelings for Peter and to find someone else. I told him I felt too old but he said not to think in terms of chronological age but how I look. He thinks I'm "charming and attractive" and "gaminlike." S.'s feeling is that it's impossible to be married to an actor or writer happily, that in other words, "they're all alike." He gave Lord Byron and Marlon Brando as examples, but is Peter really like that? I'm possessed today with these thoughts, I can hardly do anything. He emphasized that I wasn't facing the extreme narcissism of the writer, that he focuses such an enormous amount of attention on himself. I told him my own theory that I worked out in Group that P.'s unfaithfulness to me is the result of the fact that he felt me so high-powered that he felt it necessary to "practice" with his little student. That he could only really feel like a potent male with such an unthreatening nothing. S. seemed very interested in my theory. S. said that Peter goes back over and over again to the confession in order to rationalize his inability to love me, or to love anyone for that matter. S. indicates that this lovelessness is characteristic of the narcissistic type. I wonder if S. is fitting Peter into a preconceived mold, tho' it does make great sense when I think of how rejecting of me P. has been from the very beginning.

I thought, upon coming to the end of that entry, "What a thing—everybody in the world can write fiction about that marriage, except me! Oh, Maureen, you should never have spared my ego your writing career—better you should have written down everything in that head of yours and spared me all this reality! On the printed page, instead of on my hide! Oh, my one and only and eternal wife, is this what you really think? Believe? Do these words describe to you who and what you are? It's almost enough to make a person feel sorry for you. Some person, somewhere."

During the night I paused at times in reading Maureen to read Faulkner. "I believe that man will not merely endure: he will prevail. He is immortal not because he alone among creatures has an inexhaustible voice, but because he has a soul, a spirit capable of compassion and sacrifice and endurance." I read that Nobel Prize speech from beginning to end, and I thought, "And what the hell are *you* talking about? How could you write *The Sound and the Fury*, how could you write *The Hamlet*, how could you write about Temple Drake and Popeye, and write *that*?"

Intermittently I examined the No. 5 Junior can opener, Maureen's corncob. At one point I examined my own corncob. Endure? Prevail? We are lucky, sir, that we can get our shoes on in the morning. That's what *I* would have said to those Swedes! (If they'd asked.)

Oh, there was bitterness in me that night! And much hatred. But what was I to do with it? Or with the can opener? Or with the diary confessing to a "confession"? What was *I* supposed to do to prevail? Not "man," but Tarnopol!

The answer was nothing. "Tolerate it," said Spielvogel. "Lambchop," said Susan, "forget it." "Face facts," my lawyer said, "you're the man and she's the woman." "Are you still sure of that?" I said. "Piss standing up and you're the man." "I'll sit down." "It's too late," he told me.

*

Six months later, on a Sunday morning, only minutes after I had returned from breakfast and the *Times* at Susan's and was settling down at my desk to work—the liquor carton had just been dragged from the closet, and I was stirring around in that dispiriting accumulation of disconnected beginnings, middles, and endings—Flossie Koerner telephoned my apartment to tell me that Maureen was dead.

I didn't believe her. I thought it was a ruse cooked up by Maureen to get me to say something into the telephone that could be tape-recorded and used to incriminate me in court. I thought, "She's going back in again for more alimony—this is another trick." All I had to say was, "Maureen dead? Great!" or anything even *remotely* resembling that for Judge Rosenzweig or one of his lieutenants to reason that I was an incorrigible enemy of the social order still, my unbridled and barbaric male libido in need of yet stronger disciplinary action.

"Dead?"

"Yes. She was killed in Cambridge, Massachusetts. At five in the morning."

"Who killed her?"

"The car hit a tree. Bill Walker was driving. Oh, Peter," said Flossie, with a rasping sob, "she loved life so."

"And she's dead . . . ?" I had begun to tremble.

"Instantly. At least she didn't suffer . . . Oh, why didn't she have the seat belt on?"

"What happened to Walker?"

"Nothing bad. A cut. But his whole Porsche was destroyed. Her head . . . her head . . ."

"Yes, what?"

"Hit the windshield. Oh, I knew she shouldn't go up there. The Group tried to stop her, but she was just so terribly hurt."

"By what? Over what?"

"What he did with the shirt."

"What shirt?"

"Oh . . . I hate to say it . . . given who he is . . . and I'm not accusing him . . ."

"What is it, Flossie?"

"Peter, Bill Walker is a bisexual person. Maureen herself didn't even know. She—" She broke down sobbing here. I meanwhile had to clamp my mouth shut to stop my teeth from chattering. "She—" said Flossie, starting in again, "she gave him this beautiful, expensive lisle shirt, you know for a present? And it didn't fit—or so he said afterward—and instead of returning it for a bigger size, he gave it to a man he knows. And she went up to tell him what she thought of that kind of behavior, to have a frank confrontation . . . And they must have been drinking late, or something. They had been to a party . . ."

"Yes?"

"I'm not blaming anyone," said Flossie. "I'm sure it was nobody's deliberate fault."

Was it true then? Dead? Really dead? Dead in the sense of nonexistent? Dead as the dead are dead? Dead as in death? Dead as in dead men tell no tales? Maureen is *dead*? *Dead* dead? Deceased? Extinct? Called to her eternal rest, the miserable bitch? Crossed the bar?

"Where's the body?" I asked.

"In Boston. In a morgue. I guess . . . I think . . . you'll have to go get her, Peter. And take her home to Elmira. Someone will have to call her mother . . . Oh, Peter, you'll have to deal with Mrs. Johnson—I couldn't."

Peter get her? Peter take her to Elmira? Peter deal with her mother? Why, if it's true, Flossie, if this isn't the most brilliant bit of dissimulation yet staged and directed by Maureen Tarnopol, if you are not the best supporting soap-opera actress of the Psychopathic Broadcasting Network, then Peter *leave* her. Why Peter even bother with her? Peter let her lie there and rot!

As I still didn't know for sure whether our conversation was being recorded for Judge Rosenzweig's edification, I said, "Of course I'll get her, Flossie. Do you want to come with me?"

"I'll do anything at all. I loved her so. And she loved you, more than you could ever know—" But here a noise came out of Flossie that struck me as indistinguishable from the wail of animal over the carcass of its mate.

I knew then that I wasn't being had. Or probably wasn't.

I was on the phone with Flossie for five minutes more; as soon as I could get her to hang up—with the promise that I would be over at her apartment to make further plans within the hour—I telephoned my lawyer at his weekend place in the country.

"I take it that I am no longer married. Is that correct? Now tell me, is that right?"

"You are a widower, friend."

"And there's no two ways about it, is there? This is *it*."

"This is it. Dead is dead."

"In New York State?"

"In New York State."

Next I telephoned Susan, whom I had left only half an hour earlier.

"Do you want me to come down?" she asked, when she could ask anything.

"No. No. Stay where you are. I have to make some more phone calls, then I'll call you back. I have to go to Flossie Koerner's. I'll have to go up to Boston with her."

"Why?"

"To get Maureen."

"*Why?*"

"Look, I'll call you later."

"You sure you don't want me to come?"

"No, no, please. I'm fine. I'm shaking a little but aside from that everything's under control. I'm all right." But my teeth were chattering still, and there seemed nothing I could do to stop them.

Next, Spielvogel. Susan arrived in the middle of the call: had she flown from Seventy-ninth Street? Or had I just gone blank there at my desk for ten minutes? "I had to come," she whispered, touching my cheek with her hand. "I'll just sit here."

"—Dr. Spielvogel, I'm sorry to bother you at home. But something has happened. At least I am assuming that it happened because somebody told me that it happened. This is not the product of imagination, at least not mine. Flossie Koerner called, Maureen's friend from group therapy. Maureen is dead. She was killed in Boston at five in the morning. In a car crash. She's dead."

Spielvogel's voice came back loud and clear. "My goodness."

"Driving with Walker. She went through the windshield. Killed instantly. Remember what I told you, how she used to carry on in the car in Italy? How she loved grabbing that wheel? You thought I was exaggerating when I said she used to actually try to kill us both, that she would *say* as much. But I wasn't! Christ! Oh, Christ! She could go wild, like a tiger—in that little VW! I told you how she almost killed us on that mountain when we were driving from Sorrento—do you remember? Well, she finally did it. *Only this time I wasn't there.*"

"Of course," Spielvogel reminded me, "you don't know all the details quite yet."

"No, no. Just that she's dead. Unless they're lying."

"Who would be lying?"

"I don't know any more. But things like this don't happen. This is as unlikely as the way I got into it. Now the whole *thing* doesn't make any sense."

"A violent woman, she died violently."

"Oh, look, a lot of people who aren't violent die violently and a lot of violent people live long, happy lives. Don't you see—it could be a ruse, some new little fiction of hers—"

"Designed to do what?"

"For the alimony. To catch me—off guard—*again!*"

"No, I wouldn't think so. Caught you are not. Released is the word you are looking for. You have been released."

"Free," I said.

"That I don't know about," said Spielvogel, "but certainly released."

Next I dialed my brother's number. Susan hadn't yet taken off her coat. She was sitting in a straight chair by the wall with her hands folded neatly in her lap like a kindergartener. At the sight of her in that posture an alarm went off in me, but too much else was happening to pay more than peripheral attention to its meaning. *Only why hasn't she taken off her coat?*

"Morris?"

"Yes."

"Maureen's dead."

"Good," my brother said.

Oh, they will get us for that—but who, who will get us?

I have been released.

Next I got her mother's number from Elmira information.

"Mrs. Charles Johnson?"

"That's right."

"This is Peter Tarnopol calling. I'm afraid I have some bad news. Maureen is dead. She was killed in a car crash."

"Well, that's what usually comes of runnin' around. I could have predicted it. When did this happen?"

"Early this morning."

"And how many'd she take with her?"

"None. Nobody. She was the only one killed."

"And what'd you say your name was?"

"Peter Tarnopol. I was her husband."

"Oh, is that so? Which are you? Number one, two, three, four, or five?"

"Three. There were only three."

"Well, generally in this family there is only one. Good of you to call, Mr. Tarnopol."

"—What about the funeral?"

But she'd hung up.

Finally I telephoned Yonkers. The man whose son I am began to choke with emotion when he heard the news—you would have thought it was somebody he had cared for. "What an ending," he said. "Oh, what an ending for that little person."

My mother listened in silence on the extension. Her first words were, "You're all right?"

"I'm doing all right, yes. I think so."

"When's the funeral?" asked my father, recovered now, and into his domain, the practical arrangements. "Do you want us to come?"

"The funeral—I tell you, I haven't had time to think through the funeral. I think she always wanted to be cremated. I don't know yet where . . ."

"Maybe he's not even going," my mother said to my father.

"You're not going?" my father asked. "You think that's a good idea, not going?" I could envision him reaching up to squeeze his temples with his free hand, a headache having all at once boiled up in his skull.

"Dad, I haven't thought it through yet. Okay? One thing at a time."

"Be smart," my father said. "Listen to me. You go. Wear a dark suit, put in an appearance, and that'll be that."

"Let him decide," my mother told him.

"He decided to marry her without my advice—it wouldn't hurt now if he listened when I told him how to stick her in the ground!"

"He says she wanted to be cremated anyway. They put the ashes in the ground, Peter?"

"They scatter them, they scatter them—I don't know what they do with them. I'm new to this, you know."

"That's why I'm telling you," my father said, "to *listen*. You're new to *everything*. I'm seventy-two and I'm *not*. You go to the funeral, Peter. That way nobody can ever call you pisher."

"I think they'll call me pisher either way, those disposed in that direction."

"But they can never say you weren't there. Listen to me, Peter, please—I've lived a life. Stop being out there on your own, *please*. You haven't listened to anybody since you were four-and-a-half years old and went off to kindergarten to conquer the world. You were four-and-a-half years old and you thought you were the president of General Motors. What about the day there was that terrible thunderstorm? Four-and-a-half years old—"

"Look, Dad, not now—"

"Tell him," he said to my mother, "tell him how long this has been going on with him."

"Oh, not now," said my mother, beginning to cry.

But he was fired up; miraculously, I was in the clear, and so he could finally let me know just how angry he was that I had squandered my familial inheritance of industriousness and stamina and pragmatism—all those lessons learned from him on Saturdays in the store, why had I tossed them to the wind? "No, no," he would say to me from atop the ladder in the stockroom, as I handed up to him the boxes of Interwoven socks, "no, not like that, Peppy—you're making it hard for yourself. Like this! Get it right! Always do a job right. Doing it wrong, son, don't make sense at all!" All the entrepreneurial good sense, all that training in management and order, why hadn't I seen it for the wisdom that it was? Why couldn't a haberdashery store be a source of sacred knowledge too? Why, Peppy? Not profound enough to suit you? All too banal and unmomentous? Oh, yes, what are Flagg Brothers shoes and

Hickok belts and Swank tie clasps to a unique artistic spirit like yours!

"—it was a terrible thunderstorm," he was saying, "there was thunder and everything, and you were in school, Peter, in kindergarten. Four-and-a-half years old and you wouldn't let anybody even take you, after the first week, not even Joannie. No, *you* had to do it alone. You don't remember this, huh?"

"No, no."

"Well, it was raining, I'll tell you. And so your mother got your little raincoat, and your rainhat and your rubbers, and she ran to the school at the end of the day so you shouldn't have to get soaked coming home. And you don't remember what you did?"

Well, at last I was crying too. "No, no, I guess I don't."

"You *balked*. You gave her a look that could have killed."

"I did?"

"Oh, you did! And told her off. 'Go home!' you told her. Four-and-a-half years old! And would not even so much as put on the *hat*. Walked out, right past her, and home in the storm, with her chasing after you. Everything you had to do by yourself, to show what a big shot you were—and look, Peppy, look what has come of it! At least now listen to your family *once*."

"Okay, I will," I said, hanging up.

Then, eyes leaking, teeth chattering, not at all the picture of a man whose nemesis has ceased to exist and who once again is his own lord and master, I turned to Susan, still sitting there huddled up in her coat, looking, to my astonishment, as helpless as the day I had found her. Sitting there *waiting*. Oh, my God, I thought—now you. You being you! And *me*! This me who is me being me and none other!

# THE PROFESSOR OF DESIRE

*For Claire Bloom*

TEMPTATION comes to me first in the conspicuous personage of Herbie Bratasky, social director, bandleader, crooner, comic, and m.c. of my family's mountainside resort hotel. When he is not trussed up in the elasticized muscleman's swim trunks which he dons to conduct rumba lessons by the side of the pool, he is dressed to kill, generally in his two-tone crimson and cream-colored "loafer" jacket and the wide canary-yellow trousers that taper down to enchain him just above his white, perforated, sharpie's shoes. A fresh slice of Black Jack gum is at the ready in his pocket while another is being savored, with slow-motion sassiness, in what my mother derisively describes as Herbie's "yap." Below the stylishly narrow alligator belt and the gold droop of key chain, one knee works away inside his trousers, Herbie keeping time to hides he alone hears being beaten in that Congo called his brain. Our brochure (from fourth grade on composed by me, in collaboration with the owner) headlines Herbie as "our Jewish Cugat, our Jewish Krupa—all rolled into one!"; further on he is described as "a second Danny Kaye," and, in conclusion, just so that everyone understands that this 140-pound twenty-year-old is not nobody and Kepesh's Hungarian Royale is not *exactly* nowhere, as "another Tony Martin."

Our guests appear to be nearly as mesmerized by Herbie's shameless exhibitionism as I am. A newcomer will have barely settled into a varnished wicker rocker on the veranda before one of the old-timers from the hot city the previous week starts giving him the lowdown on this wonder of our tribe. "And wait till you see the tan on this kid. He's just got that kind of skin—never burns, only tans. And from the first day in the sun. This kid has got skin on him right out of the Bible times."

Because of a damaged eardrum, our drawing card—as it pleases Herbie to call himself, particularly into the teeth of my mother's disapproval—is with us throughout the Second World War. Ongoing discussion from the rocking chairs and the card tables as to whether the disability is congenital or self-inflicted.

The suggestion that something other than Mother Nature might have rendered Herbie unfit to fight Tojo, Mussolini, and Hitler—well, I am outraged, personally mortified by the very idea. Yet, how tantalizing to imagine Herbie taking a hatpin or a toothpick in his own hands—taking an ice pick!—and deliberately mutilating himself in order to outfox his draft board.

"I wouldn't put it past him," says guest A-owitz; "I wouldn't put anything past that operator. What a pistol he is!" "Come on, he did no such thing. That kid is a patriotic kid like anybody else. I'll tell you how he went half deaf like that, and ask the doctor here if I'm not right: from banging on those drums," says guest B-owitz. "Oh, can that kid play drums," says C-owitz; "you could put him on the stage of the Roxy right now—and I think the only reason he ain't is that, like you say, he doesn't hear right from the drums themselves." "Still," says D-owitz, "he don't say definitely yes or no whether he did it with some instrument or something." "But that's the showman in him, keeping you hanging by suspense. His whole stock-in-trade is that he's crazy enough for anything—that's his whole *act*." "Still, even to kid around about it don't strike me right. The Jewish people have got their hands full as it is." "Please, a kid who dresses like that right down to the key chain, and with a build like that that he works on day and night, plus those drums, you think he is gonna do himself serious physical damage just out of spite to the war effort?" "I agree, one hundred percent. Gin, by the way." "Oh, you caught me with my pants down, you s.o.b. What the hell am I holding these jacks for, will somebody tell me? Look, you know what you don't find? You don't find a kid who is good-looking like this one, who is funny like he is too. To take that kind of looks, and to be funny, and to go crazy like that with the drums, that to me is something special in the annals of show business." "And what about at the pool? How about on the diving board? If Billy Rose laid eyes on him, clowning around in the water like that, he'd be in the Aquacade tomorrow." "And what about that voice on him?" "If only he wouldn't kid *around* with it—if only he would sing *serious*." "If that kid sang serious he could be in the Metropolitan Opera." "If he sang serious, he could be a cantor, for Christ sakes, with no problem. He could break your heart. Just imagine for yourself what he would look like in a white tallis with that tan!" And here at last I am spotted, working on a model R.A.F. Spitfire down at the end of the veranda rail. "Hey, little Kepesh, come here, you little eavesdropper. Who do you want to be like when you grow up? Listen to this—stop shuffling the cards a minute. Who's your hero, Kepaleh?"

I don't have to think twice, or at all. "Herbie," I reply, much to the amusement of the men in the congregation. Only the mothers look a little dismayed.

Yet, ladies, who else could it be? Who else is so richly endowed as to be able to mimic Cugie's accent, the shofar blowing, and, at my request, a fighter plane nose-diving over Berchtesgaden—*and* the Fuehrer going crazy underneath? Herbie's enthusiasm and virtuosity are such that my father must sometimes caution him to keep certain of his imitations to himself, unique though they may be. "But," protests Herbie, "my fart is perfect." "Could be, for all I know," replies the boss, "but not in front of a mixed crowd." "But I've been working on it for months. Listen!" "Oh, spare me, Bratasky, please. It just ain't exactly what a nice tired guest wants to hear in a casino after his dinner. You can appreciate that, can't you? Or can't you? I don't get you sometimes, where your brain is. Don't you realize that these are people who keep kosher? Don't you get it about women and children? My friend, it's simple— the shofar is for the High Holidays and the other stuff is for the toilet. Period, Herbie. Finished."

So he comes to imitate for me, his awestruck acolyte, the toots and the tattoos that are forbidden him in public by my Mosaic dad. It turns out that not only can he simulate the panoply of sounds—ranging from the faintest springtime sough to the twenty-one-gun salute—with which mankind emits its gases, but he can also "do diarrhea." Not, he is quick to inform me, some poor shlimazel in its throes—that he had already mastered back in high school—but the full Wagnerian strains of fecal *Sturm und Drang*. "I could be in Ripley's," he tells me. "You read Ripley's, don't you—then judge for yourself!" I hear the rasp of a zipper being undone. Then a most enviable stream belting an enamel bowl. Next the whoosh of the flush, followed by the gargle and hiccup of a reluctant tap commencing to percolate. And all of it emanating from Herbie's mouth.

I could fall down and worship at his feet.

"And catch *this*!" This is two hands soaping one another—but seemingly in Herbie's mouth. "All winter long I would go into the toilet at the Automat and just sit there and listen." "You would?" "Sure. I listen even to my own self every single time I go to the can." "You do?" "But your old man, he's the expert, and to him it's only one thing—dirty! 'Period!'" adds Herbie, and in a voice exactly like my old man's!

*And he means every word he says.* How come, I wonder. How can Herbie know so much and care so passionately about the tintinnabulations of the can? And why do tone-deaf philistines like my father care so little?

So it seems in summer, while I am under the demon drummer's spell. Then Yom Kippur comes and Bratasky goes, and what good does it do me to have learned what someone like that has to teach a growing boy? Our -witzes, -bergs, and -steins are dispersed overnight to regions as remote to me as Babylon—Hanging Gardens called Pelham and Queens and Hackensack—and the local terrain is reclaimed by the natives who till the fields, milk the cows, keep the stores, and work year round for the county and the state. I am one of two Jewish children in a class of twenty-five, and a feel for the rules and preferences of society (as ingrained in me, it seems, as susceptibility to the feverish, the flamboyant, the bizarre) dictates that, regardless of how tempted I may be to light my fuse and show these hicks a few of Herbie's fireworks, I do not distinguish myself from my schoolmates by anything other than grades. To do otherwise, I realize—and without my father even having to remind me—will get me nowhere. And nowhere is not where I am expected to go.

So, like a boy on a calendar illustration, I trudge nearly two miles through billowing snowdrifts down our mountain road to the school where I spend my winters excelling, while far to the south, in that biggest of cities, where anything goes, Herbie (who sells linoleum for an uncle during the day and plays with a Latin American combo on weekends) strives to perfect the last of his lavatory impressions. He writes of his progress in a letter that I carry hidden away in the button-down back pocket of my knickers and reread every chance I get; aside from birthday cards and stamp "approvals," it is the only piece of mail I have ever received. Of course I am terrified that if I should drown while ice skating or break my neck while sledding, the envelope postmarked BROOKLYN, NY will be found by one of my schoolmates, and they will all stand around my corpse holding their noses. My mother and father will be shamed forever. The Hungarian Royale will lose its good name and go bankrupt. Probably I will not be allowed to be buried within the cemetery walls with the other Jews. And all because of what Herbie dares to write down on a piece of paper and then mail through a government post office to a nine-year-old child, who is imagined by his world (and thus by himself) to be pure. Does Bratasky really fail to understand how decent people feel about such things? Doesn't he know that even sending a letter like this he is probably breaking a law, and making of me an accomplice? But if so, why do I persist in carrying the incriminating document around with me all day long? It is in my pocket even while I am on my feet battling for first place in the weekly spelling bee against the other finalist, my curly-haired co-religionist and the concert-pianist-to-be, brilliant Madeline Levine; it is in my pajama pocket at night, to be read by flashlight beneath the covers, and then to sleep with, next to my heart. "I am really getting down to a science how it sounds when you pull the paper off the roller. Which about gives me the whole shmeer, kid. Herbert L. Bratasky *and nobody else in the world* can now do taking a leak, taking a crap, diarrhea—*and* unrolling the paper itself. That leaves me just one mountain to climb—wiping!"

By the time I am eighteen and a freshman at Syracuse, my penchant for mimicry very nearly equals my mentor's, only instead of imitations à la Bratasky, I do Bratasky, the guests, and the characters on the staff. I impersonate our tuxedoed Rumanian headwaiter putting on the dog in the dining room—"This way, please, Monsieur Kornfeld . . . Madame, more derma?"—then, back in the kitchen, threatening in the coarsest Yiddish to strangle the drunken chef. I impersonate our Gentiles, the gawky handyman George, shyly observing the ladies' poolside rumba class, and Big Bud, the aging muscular lifeguard (and grounds attendant) who smoothly hustles the vacationing housewife, and then, if he can, her nubile offspring sunning her new nose job. I even do a long dialogue (tragical-comical-historical-pastoral) of my exhausted parents undressing for bed the night after the close of the season. To find that the most ordinary events out of my former life are considered by others to be so *entertaining* somewhat astonishes me—also I am startled at first to discover that not everybody seems to have enjoyed formative years so densely populated with vivid types. Nor had I begun to imagine that I was quite so vivid myself.

In my first few semesters at college I am awarded leading roles in university productions of plays by Giraudoux, Sophocles, and Congreve. I appear in a musical comedy, singing, and even dancing, in my fashion. There seems to be nothing I cannot do on a stage—there would seem to be nothing that can keep me *off* the stage. At the beginning of my sophomore year, my parents visit school to see me play Tiresias—older, as I interpret the role, than the two of them together—and afterward, at the opening-night party, they watch uneasily as I respond to a request from the cast to entertain with an imitation of the princely rabbi with the perfect diction who annually comes "all the way" from Poughkeepsie to conduct High Holiday services in the casino of the hotel. The following morning I show them around the campus. On the path to the library several students compliment me on my staggering rendition of old age the night before. Impressed—but reminding me also, with a touch of her irony, that not so long ago the stage star's diapers were hers to change and wash—my mother says, "Everybody knows you already, you're famous," while my father, struggling with disappointment, asks yet again, "And medical school is out?" Whereupon I tell him for the tenth time—*telling* him it's the tenth time—"I want to act," and believe as much myself, until that day when all at once performing, in my fashion, seems to me the most pointless, ephemeral, and pathetically self-aggrandizing of pursuits. Savagely I turn upon myself for allowing everyone, indeed, to know me already, to glimpse the depths of mindless vanity that the confines of the nest and the strictures of the sticks had previously prevented me from exposing, even to myself. I am so humiliated by the nakedness of what I have been up to that I consider transferring to another school, where I can start out afresh, untainted in the eyes of others by egomaniacal cravings for spotlight and applause.

Months follow in which I adopt a penitential new goal for myself every other week. I *will* go to medical school—and train to be a surgeon. Though perhaps as a psychiatrist I can do even more good for mankind. I will become a lawyer . . . a diplomat . . . why *not* a rabbi, one who is studious, contemplative, *deep* . . . I read *I and Thou* and the Hasidic tales, and home on vacation question my parents about the family's history in the old country. But as it is over fifty years since my grandparents emigrated to America, and as they are dead and their children by and large without any but the most sentimental interest in our origins in mid-Europe, in time I give up the inquiry, and the rabbinical fantasy with it. Though not the effort to ground myself in what is substantial. It is still with the utmost self-disgust that I remember my decrepitude in *Oedipus Rex*, my impish charm in *Finian's Rainbow*—all that cloying *acting*! Enough frivolity and manic showing off! At twenty I must stop impersonating others and Become Myself, or at least begin to impersonate the self I believe I ought now to be.

He—the next me—turns out to be a sober, solitary, rather refined young man devoted to European literature and languages. My fellow actors are amused by the way in which I abandon the stage and retreat into a rooming house, taking with me as companions those great writers whom I choose to call, as an undergraduate, "the architects of my mind." "Yes, David has left the world," my drama society rival is reported to be saying, "to become a man of the cloth." Well, I have my airs, and the power, apparently, to dramatize myself and my choices, but above all it is that I am an absolutist—a *young* absolutist—and know no way to shed a skin other than by inserting the scalpel and lacerating myself from end to end. I am one thing or I am the other. Thus, at twenty, do I set out to undo the contradictions and overleap the uncertainties.

During my remaining years at college I live somewhat as I had during my boyhood winters, when the hotel was shut down and I read hundreds of library books through hundreds of snowstorms. The work of repairing and refurbishing goes on daily throughout the Arctic months—I hear the sound of the tire chains nicking at the plowed roadways, I hear planks dropping off the pickup truck into the snow, and the simple inspiring noises of the hammer and the saw. Beyond the snow-caked sill I see George driving down with Big Bud to fix the cabanas by the covered pool. I wave my arm, George blows the horn . . . and to me it is as though the Kepeshes are now three animals in cozy, fortified hibernation, Mamma, Papa, and Baby safely tucked away in Family Paradise.

Instead of the vivid guests themselves, we have with us in winter their letters, read aloud and with no deficiency of vividness or volume by my father at the dinner table. *Selling himself* is the man's specialty, as he sees it; likewise, *showing people a good time*, and, no matter how ill-mannered they themselves may be, *treating them like human beings*. In the off-season, however, the balance of power shifts a little, and it is the clientele, nostalgic for the stuffed cabbage and the sunshine and the laughs, who divest themselves of their exacting imperiousness —"They sign the register," says my mother, "and every *ballagula* and his *shtunk* of a wife is suddenly the Duke and the Duchess of Windsor"—and begin to treat my father as though he too were a paid-up member of the species, rather than the target for their discontent, and straight man for their ridiculous royal routines. When the snow is deepest, there are sometimes as many as four and five newsy letters a week—an engagement in Jackson Heights, moving to Miami because of health, opening a second store in White Plains . . . Oh, how he loves getting news of the best and the worst that is happening to them. That proves something to him about what the Hungarian Royale means to people—that proves everything, in fact, and not only about the meaning of his hotel.

After reading the letters, he clears a place at the end of the table, and beside a plate full of my mother's *rugalech*, and in his sprawling longhand, composes his replies. I correct the spelling and insert punctuation where he has drawn the dashes that separate his single run-on paragraph into irregular chunks of philosophizing, reminiscence, prophecy, sagacity, political analysis, condolence, and congratulation. Then my mother types each letter on Hungarian Royale stationery—below the inscription that reads, "*Old Country Hospitality In A Beauti-*

*ful Mountain Setting. Dietary Laws Strictly Observed. Your Proprietors, Abe and Belle Kepesh*"—and adds the P.S. confirming reservations for the summer ahead and requesting a small deposit.

Before she met my father on a vacation in these very hills—he was then twenty-one, and without a calling, spending the summer as a short-order cook—she worked for her first three years out of high school as a legal secretary. As legend has it, she had been a meticulous, conscientious young woman of astounding competence, who all but lived to serve the patrician Wall Street lawyers who employed her, men whose stature—moral *and* physical—she will in fact speak of reverentially until she dies. Her Mr. Clark, a grandson of the firm's founder, continues sending her birthday greetings by telegram even after he retires to Arizona, and every year, with the telegram in her hand, she says dreamily to my balding father and to little me, "Oh, he was such a tall and handsome man. And so dignified. I can still remember how he stood up at his desk when I came into his office to be interviewed for the job. I don't think I'll ever forget that posture of his." But, as it happened, it was a burly, hirsute man, with a strong prominent cask of a chest, Popeye's biceps, and no class credentials, who saw her leaning on a piano singing "Amapola" with a group of vacationers up from the city, and promptly said to himself, "I'm going to marry that girl." Her hair and her eyes were so dark, and her legs and bosom so round and "well developed" that he thought at first she might actually be Spanish. And the besetting passion for impeccability that had endeared her so to the junior Mr. Clark only caused her to be all the more alluring to the energetic young go-getter with not a little of the slave driver in his own driven, slavish soul.

Unfortunately, once she marries, the qualities that had made her the austere Gentile boss's treasure bring her very nearly to the brink of nervous collapse by the end of each summer—for even in a small family-run hotel like ours there is always a complaint to be investigated, an employee to be watched, linens to be counted, food to be tasted, accounts to be tallied . . . on and on and on it goes, and, alas, she can never leave a job to the person supposed to be doing it, not when she discovers that it is not being Done Right. Only in the winter, when my father and I assume the unlikely roles of Clark *père* and *fils*, and she sits in perfect typing posture at the big black Remington Noiseless precisely indenting his garrulous replies, do I get a glimpse of the demure and happy little *señorita* with whom he had fallen in love at first sight.

Sometimes after dinner she even invites me, a grade-school child, to pretend that I am an executive and to dictate a letter to her so that she can show me the magic of her shorthand. "You own a shipping company," she tells me, though in fact I have only just been allowed to buy my first penknife, "go ahead." Regularly enough she reminds me of the distinction between an ordinary office secretary and what she had been, which was a *legal* secretary. My father proudly confirms that she had indeed been the most flawless legal secretary ever to work for the firm—Mr. Clark had written as much to him in a letter of congratulation on the occasion of their engagement. Then one winter, when apparently I am of age, she teaches me to type. No one, before or since, has ever taught me anything with so much innocence and conviction.

But that is winter, the secret season. In summer, surrounded, her dark eyes dart frantically, and she yelps and yipes like a sheep dog whose survival depends upon driving his master's unruly flock to market. A single little lamb drifting a few feet away sends her full-speed down the rugged slope—a baa from elsewhere, and she is off in the opposite direction. And it does not stop until the High Holidays are over, and even then it doesn't stop. For when the last guest has departed, inventory-taking must begin—must! that minute! What has been broken, torn, stained, chipped, smashed, bent, cracked, pilfered, what is to be repaired, replaced, repainted, thrown out entirely, "a total loss." To this simple and tidy little woman who loves nothing in the world so much as the sight of a perfect, un-smudged carbon copy falls the job of going from room to room to record in her ledger the extent of the violence that has been wreaked upon our mountain stronghold by the vandal hordes my father persists in maintaining—over her vehement opposition—are only other human beings.

Just as the raging Catskill winters transform each of us back into a sweeter, saner, innocent, more sentimental sort of Kepesh, so in my room in Syracuse solitude goes to work on me and gradually I feel the lightweight and the show-off blessedly taking his leave. Not that, for all my reading, underlining, and note-taking, I become *entirely* selfless. A dictum attributed to no less notable an egotist than Lord Byron impresses me with its mellifluous wisdom and resolves in only six words what was beginning to seem a dilemma of insuperable moral proportions. With a certain strategic daring, I begin quoting it aloud to the coeds who resist me by arguing that I'm too smart for such things. "Studious by day," I inform them, "dissolute by night." For "dissolute" I soon find it best to substitute "desirous"—I am not in a palazzo in Venice, after all, but in upstate New York, on a college campus, and I can't afford to unsettle these girls any more than I apparently do already with my "vocabulary" and my growing reputation as a "loner." Reading Macaulay for English 203, I come upon his description of Addison's collaborator Steele, and, "Eureka!" I cry, for here is yet *another* bit of prestigious justification for my high grades and my base desires. "A rake among scholars, a scholar among rakes." Perfect! I tack it to my bulletin board, along with the line from Byron, and directly above the names of the girls whom I have set my mind to *seduce*, a word whose deepest resonances come to me, neither from pornography nor pulp magazines, but from my agonized reading in Kierkegaard's *Either/Or*.

I have only one male friend I see regularly, a nervous, awkward and homely philosophy major named Louis Jelinek, who in fact is my Kierkegaard mentor. Like me, Louis rents a room in a private house in town rather than live in the college dormitory with boys whose rituals of camaraderie he too considers contemptible. He is working his way through school at a hamburger joint (rather than accept money from the Scarsdale parents he despises) and carries its perfume wherever he goes. When I happen to touch him, either accidentally or simply out of high spirits or fellow feeling, he leaps away as though in fear of having his stinking rags contaminated. "Hands off," he snarls. "What are you, Kepesh, still running for some fucking office?" Am I? It hadn't occurred to me. Which one?

Oddly, whatever Louis says to me, even in pique or in a tirade, seems significant for the solemn undertaking I call "understanding myself." Because he is not interested, as far as

I can see, in pleasing anyone—family, faculty, landlady, shop-keepers, and certainly least of all, those "bourgeois barbarians," our fellow students—I imagine him to be more profoundly in touch with "reality" than I am. I am one of those tall, wavy-haired boys with a cleft in his chin who has developed winning ways in high school, and now I cannot seem to shake them, hard as I try. Especially alongside Louis do I feel pitifully banal: so neat, so clean, so *charming* when the need arises, and despite all my disclaimers to the contrary, not quite unconcerned as yet with appearances and reputation. Why can't I be more of a Jelinek, reeking of fried onions and looking down on the entire world? Behold the refuse bin wherein he dwells! Crusts and cores and peelings and wrappings—the perfect mess! Just look upon the clotted Kleenex beside his ravaged bed, Kleenex *clinging* to his tattered carpet slippers. Only seconds after orgasm, and even in the privacy of my locked room, I automatically toss into a wastebasket the telltale evidence of self-abuse, whereas Jelinek—eccentric, contemptuous, unaffiliated, and unassailable Jelinek—seems not to care at all what the world knows or thinks of his copious ejaculations.

I am stunned, can't grasp it, for weeks afterward won't believe it when a student in the philosophy program says in passing one day that "of course" my friend is a "practicing" homosexual. *My* friend? It cannot be. "Sissies," of course, I am familiar with. Each summer we would have a few famous ones at the hotel, little Jewish pashas on holiday, first brought to my attention by Herbie B. With fascination I used to watch them being carried out of the sunlight and into the shade, even as they dizzily imbibed sweet chocolate drinks through a pair of straws, and their brows and cheeks were cleansed and dried by the handkerchiefs of galley slaves called Grandma, Mamma, and Auntie. And then there were the few unfortunates at school, boys born with their arms screwed on like girls, who couldn't throw a ball right no matter how many private hours of patient instruction you gave them. But as for a practicing homosexual? Never, never, in all my nineteen years. Except, of course, that time right after my bar mitzvah, when I took a bus by myself to a stamp collectors' fair in Albany, and in the Greyhound terminal there was approached at the urinal by a middle-aged man in a business suit who whispered to me over my shoulder,

"Hey, kid, want me to blow you?" "No, no, thank you," I replied, and quickly as I could (though without giving offense, I hoped) moved out of the men's room, out of the terminal, and made for a nearby department store, where I could be gathered up in the crowd of heterosexual shoppers. In the intervening years, however, no homosexual had ever spoken to me again, at least none that I knew of.

Till Louis.

Oh, God, does this explain why I am told to keep my hands to myself when our shirtsleeves so much as brush against each other? Is it because for him being touched by a boy carries with it the most serious implications? But, if so, wouldn't a person as forthright and unconventional as Jelinek come right out and say so? Or could it be that while my shameful secret with Louis is that under it all I am altogether ordinary and respectable, a closet Joe College, his with me is that he's queer? As though to prove how very ordinary and respectable I really am, I never ask. Instead, I wait in fear for the day when something Jelinek says or does will reveal the truth about him. Or has his truth been with me all along? Of course! Those globs of Kleenex tossed about his room like so many little posies . . . are they not intended to divulge? to *invite*? . . . is it so unlikely that some night soon this brainy hawk-nosed creature, who disdains, on principle, the use of underarm deodorant and is already losing his hair, will jump forth in his ungainly way from behind the desk where he is lecturing on Dostoevsky, and try to catch me in an embrace? Will he tell me he loves me and stick his tongue in my mouth? And what will I say in response, exactly what the innocent, tempting girls say to me? "No, no, please don't! Oh, Louis, you're too smart for this! Why can't we just talk about books?"

But precisely because the idea frightens me so—because I am afraid that I may well be the "hillbilly" and "hayseed" that he delights in calling me when we disagree about the deep meaning of some masterpiece—I continue to visit him in his odoriferous room and sit across the litter from him there talking loudly for hours about the most maddening and vexatious ideas, and praying that he will not make a pass.

Before he can, Louis is dismissed from the university, first for failing to show up at a single class during an entire semester, and then for not even deigning to acknowledge the notes from his adviser asking him to come talk over the problem. Snaps Louis indignantly, sardonically, disgustedly, "*What* problem?" and darts and cranes his head as though the "problem," for all he knows, might be somewhere in the air above us. Though all agree that Louis's is an extraordinary mind, he is refused enrollment for the second semester of his junior year. Overnight he disappears from Syracuse (no goodbyes, needless to say) and almost immediately is drafted. So I learn when an F.B.I. agent with an undeflectable gaze comes around to question me after Louis deserts basic training and (as I picture it) goes to hide out from the Korean War in a slum somewhere with his Kierkegaard and his Kleenex.

Agent McCormack asks, "What about his homosexual record, Dave?" Flushing, I reply, "I don't know about that." McCormack says, "But they tell me you were his closest buddy." "They? I don't know who you mean." "The kids over on the campus." "That's a vicious rumor about him—it's totally untrue." "That you were his buddy?" "No, sir," I say, heat again rising unbidden to my forehead, "that he had a 'homosexual record.' They say those things because he was difficult to get along with. He was an unusual person, particularly for around here." "But you got along with him, didn't you?" "Yes. Why shouldn't I?" "No one said you shouldn't. Listen, they tell me you're quite the Casanova." "Oh, yes?" "Yeah. That you really go after the girls. Is that so?" "I suppose," turning from his gaze, and from the implication I sense in his remark that the girls are only a front. "That wasn't the case with Louis, though," says the agent ambiguously. "What do you mean?" "Dave, tell me something. Level with me. Where do you think he is?" "I don't know." "But you'd let me in on it, if you did, I'm sure." "Yes, sir." "Good. Here's my card, if you should happen to find out." "Yes, sir; thank you, sir." And after he leaves I am appalled by the way I have conducted myself: my terror of prison, my Lord Fauntleroy manners, my collaborationist instincts—and my shame over just about everything.

The girls that I go after.

Usually I pick them up (or at least *out*) in the reading room of the library, a place comparable to the runway of a burlesque house in its power to stimulate and focus my desire. Whatever is imperfectly suppressed in these neatly dressed, properly bred middle-class American girls is immediately apparent (or more often than not, immediately imagined) in this all-pervasive atmosphere of academic propriety. I watch transfixed the girl who plays with the ends of her hair while ostensibly she is studying her History—while I am ostensibly studying mine. Another girl, wholly bland tucked in her classroom chair just the day before, will begin to swing her leg beneath the library table where she idly leafs through a *Look* magazine, and my craving knows no bounds. A third girl leans forward over her notebook, and with a muffled groan, as though I am being impaled, I observe the breasts beneath her blouse push softly into her folded arms. How I wish I were those arms! Yes, almost nothing is necessary to set me in pursuit of a perfect stranger, nothing, say, but the knowledge that while taking notes from the encyclopedia with her right hand, she cannot keep the index finger of her left hand from tracing circles on her lips. I refuse—out of an incapacity that I elevate to a principle—to resist whatever I find irresistible, regardless of how unsubstantial and quirky, or childish and perverse, the source of the appeal might strike anyone else. Of course this leads me to seek out girls I might otherwise find commonplace or silly or dull, but I for one am convinced that dullness isn't their whole story, and that because my desire *is desire*, it is not to be belittled or despised.

"Please," they plead, "why don't you just talk and be nice? You can be so nice, if you want to be." "Yes, so they tell me." "But don't you see, this is only my body. I don't want to relate to you on that level." "You're out of luck. Nothing can be done about it. Your body is sensational." "Oh, don't start saying that again." "Your ass is sensational." "Please don't be crude. You don't talk that way in class. I love listening to you, but not when you insult me like this." "Insult? It's high praise. Your ass is marvelous. It's perfect. You should be thrilled to have it." "It's only what I sit on, David." "The hell it is. Ask a girl who doesn't own one quite that shape if she'd like to swap. That should bring you to your senses." "Please stop making fun of me and being sarcastic. *Please*." "I'm not making fun of you. I'm taking you as seriously as anybody has ever taken you in your life. Your ass is a masterpiece."

No wonder that by my senior year I have acquired a "terrible" reputation among the sorority girls whose sisters I have attempted to seduce with my brand of aggressive candor. Given the reputation, you would think that I had already reduced a hundred coeds to whoredom, when in fact in four years' time I actually succeed in achieving full penetration on but two occasions, and something vaguely resembling penetration on two more. More often than not, where physical rapture should be, there logical (and illogical) discourse is instead: I argue, if I must, that I have never tried to mislead anyone about my desire or her desirability, that far from being "exploitive," I am just one of the few honest people around. In a burst of calculated sincerity—miscalculated sincerity, it turns out—I tell one of the girls how the sight of her breasts pressing against her arms had led me to wish I were those arms. And is this so different, I ask, pushing on with the charm, from Romeo, beneath Juliet's balcony, whispering, "See! how she leans her cheek upon her hand:/ O! that I were a glove upon that hand,/ That I might touch that cheek." Apparently it is quite different. During my last year at college there are times when the phone actually goes dead at the other end after I announce who is calling, and the few nice girls who are still willing to take their chances and go out alone with me are, I am told (by the nice girls themselves), considered nearly suicidal.

I also continue to earn the amused disdain of my high-minded friends in the drama society. Now the satirists among them have it that I have given up holy orders to take on our cheerleading squad; and a far cry, that, from enacting the sexual angst of Strindberg and O'Neill. Well, so they think.

In fact, there is only one cheerleader in my life to bring to me the unadulterated agonies of a supreme frustration and render ridiculous my rakish dreams, a certain Marcella "Silky" Walsh, from Plattsburg, New York. Doomed longing begins when I attend a basketball game one night to watch her perform, having met her in the university cafeteria line that afternoon and gotten a glimpse up close of that bounteous cushion, that most irresistible of bonbons, her lower lip. There is a cheer wherein each of the girls on the squad places one fist on her hip and with the other rhythmically pumps away at the air, all the while arching farther and farther back from the waist. To the seven other girls in brief, white pleated skirts and bulky white sweaters the sequence of movements seems only so much peppy gymnastic display, to be executed with unsparing energy and at the edge of hilarity. Only in the slowly upturning belly of Marcella Walsh is there the smoldering suggestion (inescapable to me) of an offering, of an invitation, of a lust that is eager and unconscious and so clearly (to my eyes) begging to be satisfied. Yes, she alone seems (to me, to me) to sense that the tame and harnessed vehemence of this insipid cheer is but the thinnest disguise for the raw chant to be uttered while a penis propels into ecstasy that rising pelvis of hers. Oh, God, how can my coveting that pelvis thrust so provocatively toward the mouth of the howling mob, how can coveting those hard and tiny fists which speak to me of the pleasantest of all struggles, how can coveting those long and strong tomboyish legs that quiver ever so slightly as the arc is made and her silky hair (from which derives her pet name) sweeps back against the gymnasium floor—how can coveting the minutest pulsations of her being be "meaningless" or "trivial," "beneath" either me *or* her, while passionately rooting for Syracuse to win the NCAA basketball championship makes sense?

This is the line of reasoning that I take with Silky herself, and with which in time (oh, the time! the hours of debate that might have been spent cheering one another on to oceanic orgasms!) I hope to clear the way for those piercing erotic pleasures I have yet to know. Instead, I have to put aside logic, wit, candor, yes, and literary scholarship too, to put aside every reasonable attempt at persuasion—and at last all dignity as well—I have finally to turn as pitiful and craven as a waif in a famine before Silky, who has probably never seen anyone quite so miserable before, will allow me to shower kisses on her bare midriff. Since she really is the sweetest and most well-meaning of girls, hardly cruel enough or cold enough to reduce even a dirty-minded Romeo, a dean's list Bluebeard, a budding Don Giovanni and Johannes the Seducer to abject suppliance, I may kiss the belly about which I have spoken so "obsessively," but no more. "No higher and no lower," she whispers, from where I have her bent backward over a sink in the pitch-black laundry room of her dormitory basement. "David, no lower, I said. How can you even want to *do* a thing like that?"

So, between the yearnings and the myriad objects of desire, my world interposes its arguments and obstructions. My father doesn't understand me, the F.B.I. doesn't understand me, Silky Walsh doesn't understand me, neither the sorority girls nor the bohemians understand me—not even Louis Jelinek ever really understood me, and, unlikely as it sounds, this alleged homosexual (wanted by the police) has been my closest friend. No, nobody understands me, not even I myself.

I arrive in London to begin my fellowship year in literature after six days on a ship, a train ride up from Southampton, and a long ride on the Underground out to a district called Tooting Bec. Here, on an endless street of mock Tudor houses, and not in Bloomsbury, as I had requested, the King's College accommodations office has arranged lodgings for me in a private home. After I am shown to my grim little attic room by the retired army captain and his wife whose tidy, airless house this is—and with whom, I learn, I will be taking my evening meals—I look at the iron bedstead on which I am to spend the next three hundred nights or so, and in an instant am bereft of the high spirits with which I had crossed the Atlantic, the pure joy with which I had fled from all the constraining rituals of undergraduate life, and from the wearisome concern of the mother and father whom I believe have ceased to nourish me. But Tooting Bec? This tiny room? My meals across from the captain's hairline mustache? And for what, to study Arthurian legends and Icelandic sagas? Why all this punishment just for being smart!

My misery is raw and colossal. In my wallet is the phone number of a teacher of paleography at King's given me by his friend, one of my Syracuse professors. But how can I phone this distinguished scholar and tell him within an hour of my arrival that I want to hand in my Fulbright and go home? "They chose the wrong applicant—I'm not serious enough to suffer like this!" With the captain's stout and kindly wife assisting— convinced by my coloring that I am Armenian, she mumbles to me all the while something about new carpets for the parlor —I find the phone in the hallway and dial. I am only inches from tears (I am really only inches from phoning collect to the Catskills), but scared and miserable as I am, it turns out that I am even more scared of confessing to being scared and miserable, for when the professor answers, I hang up.

Four or five hours later—night having fallen over Western Europe, and my first English meal of tinned spaghetti on toast having been more or less digested—I make for a London courtyard that I had learned about during the crossing. It is called Shepherd Market, and it provides me with an experience that alters considerably my attitude toward being a Fulbright fellow. Yes, even before I attend my first lectures on the epic and the romance, I begin to understand that for an unknown lad to have traveled to an unknown land may not have been a mistake after all. Terrified I am of course of dying like Maupassant; nonetheless, only minutes after peering timidly into the notorious alleyway, I have had a prostitute—the first whore of my life, and what is more, the first of my three sexual partners to date to have been born outside the continental United States (outside the state of New York, to be exact) and in a year prior to my own birth. Indeed, when she is astride me and is suddenly gravity's to do with as it wishes, I realize with an odd, repulsive sort of thrill that this woman whose breasts collide above my head like caldrons—whom I chose from among her competitors on the basis of these behemoth breasts and a no less capacious behind—was probably born prior to the outbreak of World War I. Imagine that, before the publication of *Ulysses*, before . . . but even as I am trying to place her in the century, I find that rather more quickly than I had planned—as though, in fact, one or the other of us is racing to make a train—I am being urged on to my big finale with the unbidden assistance of a sure, swift, unsentimental hand.

I discover Soho on my own the next night. I also discover in the *Columbia Encyclopedia* that I have lugged across the sea, along with Baugh's *Literary History of England* and the three paperback volumes of Trevelyan, that the final stages of *his* venereal disease finished Maupassant off at forty-three. Nonetheless, I still cannot think of anywhere I would rather be, following my dinner with the captain and the captain's wife, than in a room with a whore who will do whatever I wish— no, not after dreaming about paying for this privilege ever since I was twelve and had my allowance of a dollar a week to save up for anything I wanted. Of course if I chose whores less whorish-looking my chances of dying of VD rather than of old age might appreciably diminish. But what sense is there in having a whore who doesn't look and talk and behave like one? I am not in search of a girl friend, after all, not quite yet. And when I am ready for her it isn't to Soho that I take myself, but to lunch on a herring at a restaurant near Harrods called the Midnight Sun.

The mythology of the Swedish girl and her sexual freedom is, during these years, in its first effulgence, and despite the natural skepticism aroused in me by the stories of insatiable appetite and odd proclivities that I hear around the college, I happily play hooky from my ancient Norse studies in order to find out for myself just how much truth there may be in all this titillating schoolboy speculation. Off then to the Midnight Sun, where the waitresses are said to be sex-crazed young Scandinavian goddesses who serve you their native dishes while dressed in colorful folk costumes, painted wooden clogs that display their golden legs to great advantage, and peasant bodices that cross-lace up the front and press into view the enticing swell of their breasts.

It is here that I meet Elisabeth Elverskog—and poor Elisabeth meets me. Elisabeth has taken a year off from the University of Lund in order to improve her English, and is living with another Swede, the daughter of friends of her family, who had left the University of Uppsala two years earlier to improve *her* English, and has not gotten around yet to going back. Birgitta, who entered England as a student and supposedly is taking courses at London University, works in Green Park collecting the penny rental for a deck chair, and, unbeknownst to Elisabeth's family, collecting such adventures as come her way. The basement flat Elisabeth shares with Birgitta is in a rooming house off Earl's Court Road inhabited mostly by students several tones darker than the girls. Elisabeth confesses to me that she is not too crazy about the place—the Indians, against whom she has no racial prejudice, distress her by cooking curried dishes in their rooms all hours of the night, and the Africans, against whom she has no racial prejudice either, sometimes reach out and touch her hair when they pass in the corridor, and though she understands why, and realizes they mean her no harm, it still makes her tremble a little each time it happens.

However, in her compliant and good-natured way, Elisabeth has decided to accept the minor indignities of the hallway—and the general squalor of the neighborhood—as part of the adventure of living abroad until June, when she will return to spend the summer with her family at their vacation house in the Stockholm archipelago.

I describe for Elisabeth my own monkish accommodations and do an imitation that amuses her enormously of the captain and his wife telling me that they do not permit cohabitation on the premises, not even between themselves. And when I do an imitation of her own singsong English, she laughs still more.

For the first few weeks, small, dark-haired, and (to my mind) fetchingly buck-toothed Birgitta pretends to be asleep when Elisabeth and I arrive in their basement room and pretend not to be making love. I don't think the excitement I experience when we three suddenly give up the pretense is any greater than it was while we all held our breath and pretended that nothing out of the ordinary was going on. I am so dizzily elated over the change that has taken place in my life since I thought to have lunch at the Midnight Sun—indeed, since I subdued my fears and stepped into Shepherd Market to seek out the whoriest of whores—I am in such an egoistical frenzy over this improbable thing that is happening to me, not just with one but with two Swedish (or, if you will, *European*) girls, that I do not see Elisabeth slowly going to pieces from the effort of being a fully participating sinner in our intercontinental ménage, half of what can only be called my harem.

Maybe I don't see it because she is in something of a frenzy of her own—a drowning frenzy, a wild thrashing about in order to stay afloat—and as a result seems often to be *enjoying* herself so much; that is, I take the excitement for pleasurable excitement, certainly so when we three go off with a picnic lunch and a tennis ball to spend a Sunday on Hampstead Heath. I teach the girls "running bases"—and could Elisabeth be more delighted by anything than to be caught in a screaming, hilarious rundown between Birgitta and myself?—and they teach me *brännboll*, bits and pieces of flycatcher-up and stick-ball, which combine into a game they played in Stockholm as schoolchildren. When it rains we play cards together, gin or canasta. The old king, Gustav V, was a passionate gin-rummy player, I am told, as are Birgitta's mother and father and brother and sister. Elisabeth, whose circle of Gymnasium friends had apparently idled away hundreds of afternoons at canasta, picks up gin rummy after just half an hour of watching a few games between Birgitta and me. She is captivated by the patter I deliver during the game, and takes immediately to using it herself—as did I at eight or so, back when I learned it all at the feet of Klotzer the Soda Water King (said by my mother to be the heaviest guest in Hungarian Royale history—when Mr. Klotzer lowered his behind onto our wicker, she had sometimes to cover her eyes—and a marathon monologuist and sufferer at the card table). Says Elisabeth, sadly arranging and rearranging the cards that Birgitta has dealt her, "I got a hand like a foot," and when she lays down her melds in triumph, it pleases her no end—it pleases *me* no end—to hear her ask her opponent, "What's the name of the game, Sport?" Oh, and when she calls the wild card in canasta the "yoker"—well, that just slays me. How on earth can she be going to pieces? *I'm* not! And what about our serious and maddening discussions of World War II, during which I try to explain—and not always in a soft voice either—to explain to these two self-righteous neutralists just what was going on in Europe when we were all growing up? Isn't it Elisabeth who is in fact more vehement (and innocently simple-minded) than Birgitta, who insists, even when I practically threaten to *slap* some sense into her, that the war was "everybody's fault"? How then can I tell that she is not only going to pieces but also thinking from morning to night about how to do herself in?

After the "accident"—so we describe in the telegram to her parents the broken arm and the mild concussion Elisabeth sustains by walking in front of a truck sixteen days after I move from Tooting Bec into the girls' basement—I continue to hang my tweed jacket in her closet and to sleep, or to try to, in her bed. And I actually believe that I am staying on there because in my state of shock I am simply *unable* to move out as yet. Night after night, under Birgitta's nose, I write letters to Stockholm in which I set out to explain myself to Elisabeth; rather, I sit down at my typewriter to begin the paper I must soon deliver in my Icelandic Saga tutorial on the decline of skaldic poetry through the overuse of the kenning, and wind up telling Elisabeth that I had not realized she was trying only to please me, but altogether innocently—"altogether unforgivably"—had believed that, like Birgitta and like myself, she had been pleasing herself first of all. Again and again—on the Underground, in the pub, during a lecture—I take her very first letter, written from her bedroom the day she had arrived back home, and uncrumple it to reread those primary-school sentences that have the Sacco and Vanzetti effect every time—what an idiot I have been, how callous, how blind! "*Älskade David!*" she begins, and then, in her English, goes on to explain that she had fallen in love with me, not with Gittan, and had gone to bed with the two of us only because I wanted her to and she would have done anything I wanted her to do . . . and, she adds in the tiniest script, she is afraid she would again if she were to return to London—

I am not a strong girl as Gittan. I am just a weak one Bettan, and I can't do anything about it. It was like being in hell. I was in love with someone and what I did had nothing to do with love. It was like I no more was human being. I am so stupid and my english is strange when I write, I am sorry for that. But I know I must never again do what we three did as long as I live. So the silly girl have learned something.

*Din Bettan*

And, below this, Bettan's forgiving afterthought: "*Tusen pussar och kramar*"—a thousand kisses and hugs.

In my own letters I confess again and again that I had been blind to the nature of her real feeling for me—blind to the depth of my feelings for *her*! I call that unforgivable too, and "sad," and "strange," and when the contemplation of this ignorance of mine brings me nearly to tears, I call it "terrifying"—and mean it. And this in turn leads me to try to give both of us some hope by telling her that I have found a room for myself (in only a matter of days I do intend to inquire about one) in a university residence hall, and that henceforth she should write to me there—if she should ever want to write to me again—rather than at the old address, in care of Birgitta . . . And in the midst of composing these earnest apologies and petitions for pardon, I am overcome with the most unruly and contradictory emotions—a sense of unworthiness, of loathsomeness, of genuine shame and remorse, and simultaneously as strong a sense that I am not guilty of anything, that it is as much the fault of those Indians cooking curried rice at 2 a.m. as it is mine that innocent, undefended Elisabeth stepped in the path of that truck. And what *about* Birgitta, who was supposed to have been Elisabeth's protector, and who now merely lies on the bed across the room from me, studying her English grammar, unmoved utterly—or so she pretends—by my drama of self-disgust? As though, since it was Elisabeth's arm, rather than neck, that was broken by the truck, *she* is entirely in the clear! As though Elisabeth's behavior with us is for Elisabeth's conscience alone to reckon with . . . and not hers . . . and not mine. But surely, *surely*, Birgitta is no less guilty than I am of misusing Elisabeth's pliable nature. Or is she? Wasn't it Birgitta rather than me to whom Elisabeth would instinctively turn for affection whenever she needed it most? When, depleted, we lay together on the threadbare rug—for it was the floor, not the bed, we used mostly as our sacrificial altar—when we would be lying there, dead limbs amid the little undergarments, groggy, sated, and confused, it was invariably Birgitta who held Elisabeth's head and gently stroked her face and whispered lullaby words like the kindest of mothers. My arms, my hands, my words didn't seem to be of any use to anyone at that point. The way it worked, my arms, hands, and words meant everything—until I came, and then the two girls huddled up together like playmates off in a tree house, or in a tent where there is just no room for another . . .

Leaving my letter half-written, I go barging out into the street and walk halfway across London (in the direction of Soho generally) to bring myself under control. I try, on these Raskolnikovian sojourns (Raskolnikov, admittedly, as played by Pudd'nhead Wilson), to "think things through." That is, I should like, if I can, to be able to deal with this unexpected turn of events the way Birgitta does. And since I don't seem able to arrive at that kind of equanimity spontaneously—or marshal that kind of strength, if strength it is—how about if I try to *reason* my way into her shoes? Yes, use my Fulbright fellow's brain—it's got to be good for something over here! Think it through, damn it! It's not that difficult. You didn't roll around on these two girls so as to set yourself up in business as a saint! Far from it! You didn't think up the things you all did so as to please the old folks at home! Far from it! Either go back and play patty-cake with Silky Walsh, or stay where you are and want what you want! Birgitta is human too, you know! Strong and clearheaded is human too (if strong and clearheaded it is), and blubbering is not becoming, over the age of four! Nor is the naughty-boy bit! Elisabeth is perfectly right: Gittan is Gittan, Bettan is Bettan, and now it is about time you were you!

Well, "thinking things through" in this manner, it is never too long before I wind up recollecting that night when Birgitta and I kept asking and asking Elisabeth—hounding and hounding Elisabeth—about what we had already cross-examined one another: what was it she secretly wanted most, what was it that she only dared to think about herself and never in her life had had the courage to do or to have done to her? "What is it you've never been able to admit to anyone, Elisabeth, not even to yourself?" Clinging with ten fingers to the blanket dragged from the bed to cover us all on the floor, Elisabeth began softly to weep, and in that charming, musical English admitted she wanted to be had from behind while bending over a chair.

I found no satisfaction in her reply. Only after I had pressed her further, only after I had demanded, "But what else—what more? That's nothing!"—only then did she at last break down and "confess" that she wanted me to do it to her like that while her hands and feet were tied down. And maybe she did and maybe she didn't . . .

Passing through Piccadilly, I compose yet another paragraph of moral speculation for the latest letter intended to educate my innocent victim—and me. In truth, I am trying with what wisdom—and what prose resources and literary models—is mine to understand if in fact I have been what the Christians call wicked and what I would call inhuman. "And even if you had *actually* wanted what you told us you wanted, what law says that whatever secret longing one is asked to satisfy must be satisfied forthwith? . . ." We had used the belt from my trousers and a strap from Birgitta's knapsack to bind Elisabeth to a straight-backed chair. Once again the tears came rolling down her face, causing Birgitta to touch her cheek and to ask her, "Bettan, you want to stop now?" But Elisabeth's long trailing locks, that child's length of amber hair, whipped across her bare back, so vehemently did she shake her head in defiance. Defiance of whom, I wonder. Of what? Why, I don't begin to know a thing about her! "No," Elisabeth whispered. The only word she spoke from start to finish. "No stop?" I asked. "Or no go on? Elisabeth, do you understand me—? Ask her in Swedish, ask her—" But "no" is all she will answer; "no," and "no," and "no" again. And so it was that I proceeded as I sort of believed I was being directed to. Elisabeth weeps, Birgitta watches, and suddenly I am so excited by it all—by the panting, dog-like sounds the three of us are making, by what the three of us are *doing*—that all traces of reluctance drop away, and I know that I could do *anything*, and that I want to, and that I will! Why not four girls, why not five—". . . who but the wicked would hold that whatever longing one is asked to satisfy must be satisfied forthwith? Yet, dearest, sweetest, precious girl, that appeared to be the very law under which we three had decided—had *agreed*—to live!" And by now I am in a hallway on Greek Street, where at last I stop thinking about what next to write to Elisabeth on the unfathomable subject of my iniquity, and thinking too about this unfathomable Birgitta—*has* she no remorse? no shame? no loyalty? no limits? —who must by now have read the half-written letter left by me in my Olivetti (and which surely will impress her with just how *deep* a sultan I am).

In a little room above a Chinese laundry, I try my luck with a thirty-shilling whore, a fading Cockney milkmaid called Terry the Tart who thinks me "a sexy bah-stard" and whose plucky lewdness had, once upon a time, a most startling effect upon the detonation of my seed. Now Terry's skills go for nought. She gives me her extraordinary collection of dirty pictures to look at; she describes, with no less imagination than Mrs. Browning, the ways in which she will love me; indeed, she praises to the skies the breadth and height of my member and its depth of penetration when last seen erect; but the fifteen minutes of hard labor she then puts in over the recumbent lump is without significant result. Taking such comfort as I can from the tender way Terry puts it—"Sorry, Yank, 'e seems a bit sleepy tonight"—I head back across London to our basement, finishing up as I go with that day's inquiry into the evil I may or may not have done.

As it turns out, I would have been better off applying all this concentration to the excessive use of the kenning in the latter half of the twelfth century in Iceland. That, in time, is something I could have made some sense of. Instead, I seem to get nowhere near the truth, or even the feel of the truth, in the prolix letters I regularly address to Stockholm, while the scholarly essay I finally read before my tutorial group prompts the tutor to invite me back to his office after class, to sit me down in a chair, and to ask, with only the faintest trace of sarcasm, "Tell me, Mr. Kepesh, are you sure you are serious about Icelandic poetry?"

A teacher taking me to task! As unimaginable, this, as my sixteen days in one room with two girls! As Elisabeth Elverskog's attempt at suicide! I am so stunned and humiliated by this chastisement (especially coming in the wake of the accusations that I have been leveling at myself in my capacity as Elisabeth's family's attorney) that I cannot find the courage to return to the tutorial ever again; like Louis Jelinek I do not even respond to the notes asking me to come talk to my tutor about my disappearance. Can it be? I am on my way to failing a course. *In God's name, what next?*

This.

One night Birgitta tells me that while I have been lying gloomily on Elisabeth's bed playing the "fallen priest" she has been doing something "a little perverse." Actually it goes back some time, to when she had first arrived in London two years ago and had gone to see a doctor about a digestive problem. The doctor had told her that to make a diagnosis he would need a vaginal smear. He asked her to disrobe and arrange herself on the examination table, and then with either his hand or an instrument—she had been so startled at the time she still wasn't sure—had begun to massage between her legs. "Please, what is it that you are doing?" she had asked him. According to Birgitta, he'd had the nerve to say in response, "Look, do you think I like this? I've a bad back, my dear, and this posture doesn't help it any. But I must have a specimen and this is the only way I can get it." "Did you let him?" "I didn't know what else to do. How do I tell him to stop? I had just arrived three days here. I was frightened a little, you know, and I wasn't sure I understood his English. And he looked like a doctor. Tall and nice-looking and kind. And very nice clothes. And I thought maybe this is the way they do it here. He kept saying, 'Are you getting cramps yet, my dear?' At first I didn't know what that means—then I got my clothes on and I left. There were people in the waiting room, there was a nurse . . . He sent a bill for two guineas." "He did? And you paid it?" I ask. "No." "And?" I ask, wavering between incredulity and excitement. "Last month," says Birgitta, her English emerging even more deliberately than usual, "I go to him again. I started to think all the time of it. That's what I think of when you are writing all your letters to Bettan." Is that true, I wonder—is any of it true? "And?" I say. "Now once a week I go to his office. For my lunch hour." "And he masturbates you? You let him masturbate you?" "Yes." "Is this the truth, Gittan?" "I close my eyes and he does it to me with his hand." "And—then?" "I get dressed. I go back to the park." I am craving for more—and more lurid even than this—but there is none. He masturbates her, and he lets her go. Can this be true? Do such things happen? "What's his name? Where is his office?" To my surprise, without any reluctance Birgitta tells me.

Some hours later, having failed to comprehend a single paragraph of *Arthurian Tradition and Chrétien de Troyes* (an invaluable source, I have been told, for the paper now due in my other tutorial), I rush out to a telephone kiosk at the end of our street and search the directory for the doctor's name—and find it, and at the Brompton Road address! Tomorrow morning first thing I will call him up—I will say (perhaps even in my Swedish accent), "Dr. Leigh, you had better watch out, you had better leave your hands off foreign young girls or you are going to get yourself in a lot of trouble." But it seems that I do not really want to reform the lascivious doctor so much as to find out (inasmuch as I can) whether Birgitta's story is true. Not that I know for sure even yet whether I want it to be true or not. Wouldn't I be better off if it weren't?

When I get back to the flat I undress her. And she submits. With what self-possession does she submit—she and submission are thick as thieves! We are both panting and greatly worked up. I am clothed and she is naked. I call her a little whore. She begs me to pull her hair. How hard she wants it pulled I am not sure—no one has ever asked such a thing of me before. God, how far I have come from kissing Silky's navel in the dormitory laundry room just last spring! "I want to know you're here," she cries—"do it more!" "Like this?" "Yes!" "Like this, my whore? my filthy little Birgitta whore!" "Ah, yes! Ah yes, yes!"

An hour earlier I had been fearful that it might be decades before I was potent again, that my punishment, if such it was, might even last *forever*. Now I spend a night overcome by a passion whose harsh energies I have never allowed myself to begin to know before; or maybe it is that I have never before known a girl of roughly my own age to whom such forcefulness would have been anything other than an outrage. I have been so stepped in cajoling and wheedling and begging my way toward pleasure that I had not known I was actually capable of such a *besiegement* of another, or that I wished to be besieged and assaulted in turn. Straddling her head with my legs, I force my member into her mouth as though it were at once the lifeline that will prevent her suffocation and the instrument upon which she will strangle. And, as though I am her saddle, she plants herself upon my face and rides and rides and rides. "Tell me things!" cries Birgitta, "I like to be told things! Tell me all kind of things!" And in the morning there is no remorse for anything said or done—far from it. "We appear to be two of a kind," I say. She laughs and says, "I know that a long time." "That's why I stayed, you know." "Yes," she replies, "I know that."

Yet I continue writing Elisabeth (though no longer in Birgitta's presence). In care of a university residence hall—an American friend has arranged to receive my mail in his box there, and forward it to me—Elisabeth sends a photograph showing that her arm is no longer in a cast. On the back of the photograph she has printed, "Me." I write immediately to thank her for the picture of herself healed and healthy again. I tell her that I am making progress in my Swedish grammar book, that I pick up a *Svenska Dagbladet* on Charing Cross Road each week and try at least to read the front-page stories with the aid of the English-Swedish pocket dictionary she gave me. And though in fact it is Birgitta's newspaper that I take a stab at translating—during the time previously reserved for sweating over my Eddas—while I am writing to Elisabeth I believe I am doing it for her, for our future, so that I can marry her and settle down in her homeland, eventually to teach American literature there. Yes, I believe I could yet fall in love with this girl who wears around her neck a locket with her father's picture in it . . . indeed, that I should have already. Her face *alone* is so lovable! Look at it, I tell myself—look, you idiot! Teeth that couldn't be whiter, the ripe curve of her cheeks, enormous blue eyes, and the reddish-amber hair that I once told her—it was the night I received the little dictionary inscribed "From me to you"—was best described in English by "tresses," a poetical word out of fairy stories. "Common" is the English word which she tells me (after looking in the dictionary) best describes her nose. "It is a farm girl's nose," she says, "it is like the thing you plant in the garden to grow tulips." "Not quite." "How do you say that?" "Tulip bulb." "Yes. When I am forty I will look horrible because of this tulip bulb." But the nose is just the nose of millions and millions, and, on Elisabeth, actually touching in its utter lack of pride or pretension. Oh, what a sweet face, so full of the happiness of her childhood! the frothiness of her laugh! her innocent heart! This is the girl who knocked me out just by saying "I got a hand like a foot!" Oh, how incredibly moving a thing it is, a person's innocence! How it catches me off guard each time, that unguarded trusting look!

Yet, work myself up as I will over her photograph, it is with slender little Birgitta, a girl a good deal less innocent and vulnerable—a girl who confronts the world with a narrow foxy face, a nose delicately pointed and an upper lip ever so slightly protruding, a mouth ready, if need be, to answer a charge or utter a challenge—that I continue to live out my year as a visiting fellow in erotic daredevilry.

Of course, strolling around Green Park renting out deck chairs to passers-by, Birgitta is tendered invitations almost daily by men visiting London as tourists, or men out prowling on their lunch hour, or men on their way home to wives and children at the end of the day. Because of the opportunities for pleasure and excitement afforded by these meetings, she had decided against returning to Uppsala after her year's leave of absence and had given up her courses in London, too. "I think I get a better English education this way," says Birgitta.

One March afternoon when suddenly the sun appears, out of the blue, over dreary London, I take the Underground to the park and, sitting under a tree, I watch her, some hundred yards away, engaged in conversation with a gentleman nearly three times my age who is reclining in one of the deck chairs. It is almost an hour before the conversation ends, the gentleman rises, makes a formal bow in her direction, and departs. Could it be somebody she knows? Somebody from home? Could it be Dr. Leigh from the Brompton Road? Without telling her, I travel to the park every afternoon for almost a week and, keeping back in the shadows of the trees, spy upon her at work. I am surprised at first to find myself so enormously excited each time I see Birgitta standing over a deck chair in which a man is seated. Of course, all they ever do is talk. That is all I ever see. Never once do I see either a man touching Birgitta or Birgitta touching a man. And I am almost certain she does not make assignations and go off with any of them after work. But what excites me is that she might, that she could . . . that if I proposed such a thing to her, she probably would do it. "What a day," she says at dinner one evening. "The whole Portuguese navy is here. Feee! What men!" But if I were to say . . .

Only a few weeks later she startles me one evening by saying, "Do you know who came to see me today? Mr. Elverskog." "Who?" "Bettan's father." I think: They have found my letters! Oh, why did I put in writing that stuff about tying her hands to the chair! It's me they're after, the *two* families!" "He came to see you here?" "He knows where I work," says Birgitta, "so he came there." Is Birgitta lying to me, is she doing something "a little perverse" again? But how can she possibly know that all along I have been terrified of Elisabeth breaking down and turning us in, and of her father coming after me, with a Scotland Yard detective, or with his whip . . . "What's he doing in London, Gittan?" "Oh, his business—I don't know. He just came to the park to say hello." *And did you go off to his hotel room with him, Gittan? Would you like to make love with Elisabeth's father? Wasn't he the tall, distinguished-looking gentleman who bowed farewell to you that sunny day in*

*March? Isn't he the old man I saw you listening to so avidly several months ago? Or was that the doctor who likes to play doctor with you in his office? What was he saying to you, that man, just what was he proposing that held your attention so?*

I don't know what to think, and so I think everything.

In bed later, when she wants to be excited by hearing "all kings of things," I come to the very brink of saying to her, "Would you do it with Mr. Elverskog? Would you do it with a sailor, if I told you to? Would you do it with him for money?" I don't, not simply for fear that she will say yes (as she might, if only for the thrill of saying it), but because I might reply, "Then go ahead, my little whore."

At the end of the term Birgitta and I take a hitchhiking trip on the Continent, looking at museums and cathedrals during the day, and then after dark, in cafés and *caves* and tavernas, training our sights on girls. About leading Birgitta back into this, I have no such scruples as I had in London about tempting her to visit Mr. Elverskog in his hotel. "Another girl" is one of those "things" with which we have aroused one another continually during the months since Elisabeth's departure. To find other girls is, in fact, one of the reasons we are on this holiday. And we are not bad at it, not at all. To be sure, alone neither Birgitta nor I is ever quite so cunning or brave, but together it seems that we strongly reenforce one another's waywardness and, as the nights go by, become more and more adroit at charming perfect strangers. Yet, no matter how skillfully, how *professionally*, we come to maneuver as a team, I still go a little weak and dizzy when it appears that we have actually succeeded in finding a willing third and all of us get up as one to go find a quieter place to talk. Birgitta reports similar symptoms in herself—though out on the street wins my admiration by daring to reach out and push away from her face the hair of the game young student who is daring to see what develops. Yes, seeing my partner so plucky and confident, I recover my faculties—and my balance—and give each of the girls an arm, and, now, without so much as a quiver in my voice, with my worldly mix of irony and bonhomie, say, "Let's go, friends—come along!" And all the while I am thinking what I have been thinking now for months: *Is this happening? This, too?* For in my wallet along with Elisabeth's picture is a photo of her family's seaside house, sent to me just before I received my lamentable grades and boarded the boat-train with Birgitta. I have been invited to visit her on tiny Trångholmen and to stay on the island as long as I wish. And why don't I? And marry her there! Her father knows nothing, and he never will. The whip, the detective, the scenes of vengeful murderous rage, the secret plot to make me pay for what I have done to his daughter—that is all my imagination running wild. Why not let my imagination run another way? Why not imagine Elisabeth and myself rowing past the rocky shore and the tall pine trees, all the way down the length of the island to where the Waxholms ferry docks each day? Why not imagine her family beaming and waving at us when we return in the boat with the milk and the mail? Why not imagine this sweet Elisabeth on the porch of the Elverskogs' pretty barn-red house, pregnant with the first of our Swedish-Jewish children? Yes, there is Elisabeth's unfathomable and wonderful love and there is Birgitta's unfathomable and wonderful daring, *and whichever I want I can have.* Now isn't *that* unfathomable! Either the furnace or the hearth! Ah, this must be what is meant by the possibilities of youth.

More youthful possibilities. In Paris, in a bar not far from the Bastille, where the infamous marquis had himself been punished for his vile and audacious crimes, a prostitute sits in a corner with us and, while she jokes with me in French about my crew cut, is busy stroking Birgitta beneath the table. In the midst of our excitement—for I also have a hand moving under the table—a man looms up, berating me for the indignities that I am making my young wife submit to. I rise with a throbbing heart to explain that we happen not to be husband and wife, that we are students, that what we do is our business—but, despite my excellent pronunciation and perfect grammatical constructions, he pulls a hammer out of his overalls, and raises it into the air. "*Salaud!*" he cries. "*Espèce de con!*" Hand in hand with Birgitta, and for the first time ever, I run for my life.

We do not discuss what will happen when the month is over. Rather, each thinks: Given what has been, what else can be? That is, I assume that I will return to America alone in order to resume my education, this time *seriously*, and Birgitta assumes that when I leave she will pack her knapsack and come with me.

Birgitta's parents have already been told that she is thinking of going to study next in America for a year, and apparently that is all right with them. Even if it weren't, Birgitta would probably still do as she pleased.

When I rehearse the difficult conversation that must take place sooner or later, I hear myself sounding very limp and whiny indeed. Nothing I can say comes out right, nothing she can say sounds wrong—and yet it is I, of course, who invent the dialogue. "I am going to Stanford. I am going back to get my degree." "So?" "I have terrible dreams about school, Gittan. Nothing like this has ever happened to me before. I fucked up my Fulbright but good." "Yes?" "And, as for the two of us—" "Yes?" "Well, I don't see that we have any future. Do *you*? I mean we would never be able to go back to ordinary sex. That can never work for us—we've upped the ante much too high. We've gone too far to go back." "We have?" "I think so, yes." "But it wasn't my idea alone, you know." "I didn't say that it was." "So then we stop going too far." "But *we* can't. Oh, come on, you know that." "But I do whatever you want." "That's not possible any longer. Or are you saying that I've had you in my power all along, that you're another Elisabeth I've corrupted?" She smiles her fetching buck-toothed smile. "Who then is the other Elisabeth?" she asks. "*You*? Oh, but that is not so. You say so yourself. You are a whoremaster by nature, you are a polygamist by nature, there is even the rapist in you—" "Well, maybe I've changed my mind about all that; maybe I was foolish to say such things." "But how can you change your mind about what is your nature?" she asks.

In reality, going home to resume my serious education hardly requires that I fight my way, a little helplessly, a little foolishly, through this thicket of flattering objections. No, no challenging debate about my "nature" is necessary for me to be free of her and our fantastical life of thrilling pleasures—at least not right then and there. We are undressing for bed in a room we have rented for the night in a town in the Seine Valley, some thirty kilometers from Rouen, where I intend the next day to visit Flaubert's birthplace, when Birgitta begins to reminisce about the silly dreams that used to be awakened in her as a teenager by the name California: convertible cars, millionaires, James Dean— I interrupt: "I'm going to California by myself. I'm going by myself—on my own."

Minutes later she is dressed again and her knapsack is ready for the road. My God, she is bolder even than I imagined! How many such girls can there be in the world? She dares to do everything, and yet she is as sane as I am. Sane, clever, courageous, self-possessed—and wildly lascivious! Just what I've always wanted. Why am I running away, then? In the name of what? More Arthurian legends and Icelandic sagas? Look, if I were to empty my pockets of Elisabeth's letters and Elisabeth's photographs—and empty my imagination of Elisabeth's father—if I were to give myself completely over to what I have, to whom I am with, to what may actually *be* my nature— "Don't be ridiculous," I say, "where can you find a room at this hour? Oh, damn it, Gittan, I *have* to go to California alone! I've got to go back to school!"

In response, no tears, no anger, and no real scorn to speak of. Though not too much admiration for me as a shameless carnal force. She says from the door, "Why did I like you so much? You are such a boy," and that is all there is to the discussion of my character, all, apparently, that her dignity requires or permits. Not the masterful young master of mistresses and whores, not the precocious dramatist of the satyric and the lewd, and something of a fledgling rapist too—no, merely "a boy." And then gently, so very gently (for despite being a girl who moans when her hair is pulled and cries for more when her flesh is made to smart with a little pain, despite her Amazonian confidence in the darkest dives and the nerves of iron that she can display in the chancy hitchhiking world, aside from the stunning sense of inalienable right with which she does whatever she likes, that total immunity from remorse or self-doubt that mesmerizes me as much as anything, she is also courteous, respectful, and friendly, the perfectly brought-up child of a Stockholm physician and his wife), she closes the door after her so as not to awaken the family from whom we have rented our room.

Yes, easily as that do young Birgitta Svanström and young David Kepesh rid themselves of each other. Ridding himself of what he is *by nature* may be a more difficult task, however, since young Kepesh does not appear to be that clear, quite yet, as to what his nature is, exactly. He is awake all night wondering what he will do if Birgitta should steal back into the room before dawn; he wonders if he oughtn't to get up and lock the door. Then when dawn arrives, when noon arrives, and she is nowhere to be found, neither in the town of Les Andelys nor in Rouen—not at the Grosse Horloge; not at the Cathedral; not at the birthplace of Flaubert or the spot where Joan of Arc went up in flames—he wonders if he will ever see the likes of her and their adventure again.

Helen Baird appears some years later, when I am in the final stretch of graduate studies in comparative literature and feeling triumphant about the determination I have mustered to complete the job. Out of boredom, restlessness, impatience, and a growing embarrassment that naggingly informs me I am too old to be sitting at a desk still being tested on what I know, I have come near to quitting the program just about every semester along the way. But now, with the end in sight, I utter my praises aloud while showering at the end of the day, thrilling myself with simple statements like "I did it" and "I stuck it out," as though it is the Matterhorn I have had to climb in order to qualify for my orals. Following the year with Birgitta, I have come to realize that in order to achieve anything lasting, I am going to have to restrain a side of myself strongly susceptible to the most bewildering and debilitating sort of temptations, temptations that as long ago as that night outside Rouen I already recognized as inimical to my overall interests. For, far as I had gone with Birgitta, I knew how very easy it would have been for me to have gone further still—more than once, I remember the thrill it had given me imagining her with men other than myself, imagining her taking money to bring home in her pocket . . . But *could* I have gone on to that so easily? Actually have become Birgitta's pimp? Well, whatever my talent may have been for that profession, graduate school has not exactly encouraged its development . . . Yes, when the battle appears to have been won, I am truly relieved by my ability to harness my good sense in behalf of a serious vocation—and not a little touched by my virtue. Then Helen appears to tell me, by example and in so many words, that I am sadly deluded and mistaken. Is it so as never to forget the charge that I marry her?

Hers is a different brand of heroism from what, at that time, I take mine to be—indeed, it strikes me as its antithesis. A year of U.S.C. at eighteen, and then she had run off with a journalist twice her age to Hong Kong, where he was already living with a wife and three children. Armed with startling good looks, a brave front, and a strongly romantic temperament, she had walked away from her homework and her boy friend and her weekly allowance and, without a word of apology or explanation to her stunned and mortified family (who thought for a week she had been kidnapped or killed), taken off after a destiny more exhilarating than sophomore year in the sorority house. A destiny that she had found—and only recently abandoned.

Just six months earlier, I learn, she had given up everyone and everything that she had gone in search of eight years before—all the pleasure and excitement of roaming among the antiquities and imbibing the exotica of gorgeous places alluringly unknown—to come back to California and begin life anew. "I hope I never again have to live through a year like this last one" is nearly the first thing she says to me the night we meet at a party given by the wealthy young sponsors of a new San Francisco magazine "of the arts." I find Helen ready to tell her story without a trace of shyness; but then I had not been shy myself, once we'd been introduced, about meandering away from the girl I'd arrived with, and hunting her down through the hundreds of people milling around in the town house. "Why?" I ask her—the first of the whys and whens and hows she will be obliged to answer for me—"What's the year been like for you? What went wrong?" "Well, for one thing, I haven't been anywhere for six months at a stretch since I did my time as a coed." "Why did you come back, then?" "Men. Love. It all got out of hand." Instantly I am ready to attribute her "candor" to a popular-magazine mentality—and a predilection for promiscuity, pure and simple. Oh, God, I think, so beautiful, and so corny. It seems from the stories she goes on to tell me that she has been in fifty passionate affairs already—aboard fifty schooners already, sailing the China Sea with men who ply her with antique jewelry and are married to

somebody else. "Look," she says, having sized up how I seem
to have sized up such an existence, "what do you have against
passion anyway? Why the studied detachment, Mr. Kepesh? You
want to know who I am—well, I'm telling you." "It's quite a
saga," I say. She asks, with a smile, "Why shouldn't it be?
Better a 'saga' than a lot of other things I can think of. Come
now, what do you have against passion anyway? What harm has
it ever done you? Or should I ask, what good?" "The question
right now is what it has or hasn't done for you." "Fine things.
Wonderful things. God knows, nothing I'm ashamed of."
"Then why are you here and not there, being impassioned?"
"Because," Helen answers, and without any irony at all for
protection—which may be what makes me begin to surrender
some of my own, and to see that she is not only stunning-
looking, she is also real, and here with me, and maybe even mine
if I should want her—"Because," she tells me, "I'm getting
on."

At twenty-six, getting on. Whereas the twenty-four-year-old
Ph.D. candidate who is my date for the evening—and who
eventually leaves the party in a huff, without me—had been
saying on the way over that, sorting her index cards in the library just that afternoon, she had been wondering if and when
her life would ever get underway.

I ask Helen what it was like to come back. We have left the
party by now and are across from one another in a nearby bar.
Less passively than I, she has given the slip to the companion
with whom she started the evening. If I want her . . . but do
I? *Should* I? Let me hear first what it had been like coming
back from running away. For me, of course, there had been far
more relief than letdown, and I had been adrift for only a year.
"Oh, I signed an armistice with my poor mother, and my kid
sisters followed me around like a movie star. The rest of the
family gaped. Nice Republican girls didn't do what I did. Except that seems to be all I ever met everywhere I went, from
Nepal to Singapore. There's a small army of us out there, you
know. I'd say half the girls who fly out to Rangoon on that crate
that goes to Mandalay are generally from Shaker Heights."
"And now what do you do?" "Well, first I have to figure out
some way to stop crying. I cried every day I was back for the
first few months. Now that seems to be over, but, frankly,

from the way I feel when I wake up in the morning I might as *well* be in tears. It's that it was all so beautiful. Living in all that loveliness—it was overwhelming. I never stopped being thrilled. I got to Angkor every single spring, and in Thailand we would fly from Bangkok up to Chiengmai with a prince who owned elephants. You should have seen him with all his elephants. A nut-colored little old man moving like a spider in a herd of the most enormous animals. You could have wrapped him twice around in one of their ears. They were all screaming at one another, but he just walked along, unfazed. You probably think seeing that is, well, seeing only that. Well, that isn't what I thought. I thought, 'This is what it is.' I used to go down in the sailboat—this is in Hong Kong—to get my friend from work at the end of the day. He sailed with the boat boy to work in the morning and then at night we sailed home together, right down between the junks and the U.S. destroyers."

"The good colonial life. It isn't for nothing they hate giving up those empires. But I still don't understand precisely why you gave up yours."

And in the weeks that follow I continue to find it hard to believe—despite the tiny ivory Buddhas, the jade carvings, and the row of rooster-shaped opium weights that are arranged by her bedside table—that this way of life ever really was hers. Chiengmai, Rangoon, Singapore, Mandalay . . . why not Jupiter, why not Mars? To be sure, I know these places exist beyond the Rand McNally map on which I trace the course of her adventures (as once I traced down an adventure of Birgitta's in the London phone directory), and the novels of Conrad where I first encountered them—and so, of course, do I know that "characters" live and breathe who choose to make their destiny in the stranger cities of the world . . . What then fails to persuade me completely that living, breathing Helen is one of them? My being with her? Is the unbelievable character Helen in her diamond-stud earrings or is it the dutiful graduate teaching assistant in his wash-and-dry seersucker suit?

I even become somewhat suspicious and critical of her serene, womanly beauty, or rather, of the regard in which she seems to hold her eyes, her nose, her throat, her breasts, her hips, her legs—why, even her feet would seem to her to have charming little glories to be extolled. How does she come by this regal bearing anyway, this aristocratic sense of herself that seems to derive almost entirely from the smoothness of skin, the length of limb, the breadth of mouth and span of eyes, and the fluting at the very tip of what she describes, without batting an eyelid (shadowed in the subtlest green), as her "Flemish" nose? I am not at all accustomed to someone who bears her beauty with such a sense of attainment and self-worth. My experience—running from the Syracuse undergraduates who did not want to "relate" to me "on that level," to Birgitta Svanström, for whom flesh was very much there to be investigated for every last thrill—has been of young women who make no great fuss about their looks, or believe at least that it is not seemly to show that they do. True, Birgitta knew well enough that her hair cut short and carelessly nicely enhanced her charming furtiveness, but otherwise how she framed her unpainted face was not a subject to which she appeared to give much thought from one morning to the next. And Elisabeth, with an abundance of hair no less praiseworthy than Helen's, simply brushed it straight down her back, letting it hang there as it had since she was six. To Helen, however, all that marvelous hair—closest in shading to the Irish setter—seems to be in the nature of a crown, or a spire, or a halo, there not simply to adorn or embellish but to express, to symbolize. Perhaps it is only a measure of how narrow and cloistered my life has become—or perhaps it is in fact the true measure of a courtesan like power that emanates from Helen's sense of herself as an idolized object that might just as well have been carved of one hundred pounds of jade—but when she twists her hair up into a soft knot at the back of her head, and draws a black line above her lashes—above eyes in themselves no larger and no bluer than Elisabeth's—when she dons a dozen bracelets and ties a fringed silk scarf around her hips like Carmen to go out to buy some oranges for breakfast, the effect is not lost upon me. Far from it. I have from the start been overcome by physical beauty in women, but by Helen I am not just intrigued and aroused, I am also alarmed, and made deeply, deeply uncertain—utterly subjugated by the authority with which she claims and confirms and makes singular her loveliness, yet as suspicious as I can be of the prerogatives, of the *place*, thereby bestowed upon her in her own imagination. Hers seems to me sometimes such a banalized conception of self and experience, and yet, all the same, enthralling and full of fascination. *For all I know, maybe she is right.*

"How come," I ask—still asking, still apparently very much hoping to express what is fiction in this fabulous character she calls herself and in the Asiatic romance she claims for a past— "how come *you* gave up the good colonial life, Helen?" "I had to." "Because the inheritance money had made you independent?" "It's six thousand lousy dollars a year, David. Why, I believe even ascetic college teachers make that much." "I only meant that you might have decided youth and beauty weren't going to get you through indefinitely." "Look, I was a kid, and school meant nothing to me, and my family was just like everyone else's—sweet and boring and proper, and living lo these many years under a sheet of ice at 18 Fern Hill Manor Road. The only excitement came at mealtime. Every night when we got to dessert my father said, 'Is that it?' and my mother burst into tears. And so at the age of eighteen I met a grown man, and he was marvelous-looking, and he knew how to talk, and he could teach me plenty, and he knew what I was all about, which nobody else seemed to know at all, and he had wonderful elegant ways, and wasn't really a brutal tyrant, as tyrants go; and I fell in love with him—yes, in two weeks; it happens and not just to schoolgirls, either—and he said, 'Why don't you come back with me?' and I said yes—and I went." "In a 'crate'?" "Not that time. Paté over the Pacific and fellatio in the first-class john. Let me tell you, the first six months weren't a picnic. I'm not in mourning over that. You see, I was just a nicely brought-up kid from Pasadena, that's all, really, in her tartan skirt and her loafers—my friend's *children* were nearly as old as I was. Oh, splendidly neurotic, but practically my age. I couldn't even learn to eat with chopsticks, I was so scared. I remember one night, my first big opium party, I somehow wound up in a limousine with four of the wildest pansies—four Englishmen, dressed in gowns and gold slippers. I couldn't stop laughing. 'It's surreal,' I kept saying, 'it's surreal,' until the plumpest of them looked down his lorgnette at me and said, 'Of course it's surreal, dear, you're nineteen.'" "But you came back. Why?" "I can't go into that." "Who was this man?" "Oh, you are becoming a *cum laude* student of real life, David." "Wrong. Learned it all at Tolstoy's feet."

I give her *Anna Karenina* to read. She says, "Not bad—only it wasn't a Vronsky, thank God. Vronskys are a dime a dozen, friend, and bore you to tears. It was a man—very much a Karenin, in fact. Though not at all pathetic, I hasten to add." *That* stops me for a moment: what an original way to see the famous triangle! "Another husband," I say. "Only the half of it." "Sounds mysterious; sounds like high drama. Maybe you ought to write it all down." "And perhaps you ought to lay off reading what all has been written down." "And do what instead with my spare time?" "Dip a foot back into the stuff itself." "And there's a book about that, you know. Called *The Ambassadors*." I think: And there's also a book about you. It's called *The Sun Also Rises* and her name is Brett and she's about as shallow. So is her whole crew—so, it seems, was yours. "I'll bet there's a book about it," says Helen, gladly rising, with her confident smile, to the bait. "I'll bet there are thousands of books about it. I used to see them all lined up in alphabetical order in the library. Look, so there is no confusion, let me only mildly overstate the case: I hate libraries, I hate books, and I hate schools. As I remember, they tend to turn everything about life into something slightly other than it is—'slightly' at best. It's those poor innocent theoretical bookworms who do the teaching who turn it all into something worse. Something ghastly, when you think about it." "What do you see in me, then?" "Oh, you really hate them a little too. For what they've done to you." "Which is?" "Turned you into something—" "Ghastly?" I say, laughing (for we are having this little duel beneath a sheet in the bed beside the little bronze opium weights). "No, not quite. Into something slightly other, slightly . . . wrong. Everything about you is just a little bit of a lie—except your eyes. They're still you. I can't even look into them very long. It's like trying to put your hand into a bowl of hot water to pull out the plug." "You put things vividly. You're a vivid creature. I've noticed your eyes too." "You're misusing yourself, David. You're hopelessly intent on being what you're not. I get the sense that you may be riding for a very bad fall. Your first mistake was to give up that spunky Swede with the knapsack. She sounds a little like a guttersnipe, and—I have to say it—from the snapshot looks to me a little squirrely around the mouth, but at least she was fun to be with. But of course that's a word you just despise, correct? Like 'crate' for beat-up airplane. Every time I say 'fun' I see you positively wincing with pain. God, they've really done a job on you. You're so damn smug, and yet I think secretly you know you lost your nerve." "Oh, don't simplify me *too* much. And don't romanticize my 'nerve' either—okay? I like to have a good time now and then. I have a good time sleeping with you by the way." "By the way, you have more than a good time sleeping with me. You have the best time you've ever had with anybody. And, dear friend," she adds, "don't simplify me either."

"Oh, God," says Helen, stretching languorously when morning comes, "fucking is such a lovely thing to do."

True, true, true, true, true. The passion is frenzied, inexhaustible, and in my experience, singularly replenishing. Looking back to Birgitta, it seems to me, from my new vantage point, that we were, among other things, helping each other at age twenty-two to turn into something faintly corrupt, each the other's slave and slaveholder, each the arsonist and the inflamed. Exercising such strong sexual power over each other, *and* over total strangers, we had created a richly hypnotic atmosphere, but one which permeated the inexperienced *mind* first of all: I was intrigued and exhilarated at least as much by the idea of what we were engaged in as by the sensations, what I felt and what I saw. Not so with Helen. To be sure, I must first accustom myself to what strikes me at the height of my skepticism as so much theatrical display; but soon, as understanding grows, as familiarity grows, and feeling with it, I begin at last to relinquish some of my suspiciousness, to lay off a little with my interrogations, and to see these passionate performances as arising out of the very fearlessness that so draws me to her, out of that determined abandon with which she will give herself to whatever strongly beckons, and regardless of how likely it is to bring in the end as much pain as pleasure. I have been dead wrong, I tell myself, trying to dismiss hers as a corny and banalized mentality deriving from *Screen Romance*—rather, she is *without* fantasy, there is no *room* for fantasy, so total is her concentration, and the ingenuity with which she sounds her desire. Now, in the aftermath of orgasm, I find myself weak with gratitude and the profoundest feelings of self-surrender. I am the least guarded, if not the simplest, organism on earth. I don't even know what to say at such moments. Helen does, however. Yes, there are the things that this girl knows and knows and knows. "I love you," she tells me. Well, if something has to be said, what makes more sense? So we begin to tell each other that we are lovers who are in love, even while my conviction that we are on widely divergent paths is revived from one conversation to the next. Convinced as I would like to be that a kinship, rare and valuable, underlies and nourishes our passionate rapport, I still cannot wash away the grand uneasiness Helen continues to arouse. Why else can't we stop—can't *I* stop—the fencing and the parrying?

Finally she agrees to tell me why she gave up all she'd had in the Far East: tells me either to address my suspiciousness directly or to enrich the mystique I cannot seem to resist.

Her lover, the last of her Karenins, had begun to talk about arranging for his wife to be killed in an "accident." "Who was he?" "A very well-known and important man" is all she is willing to say. I swallow that as best I can and ask: "Where is he now?" "Still there." "Hasn't he tried to see you?" "He came here for a week." "And did you sleep with him?" "Of course I slept with him. How could I resist sleeping with him? But in the end I sent him back. It nearly did me in. It was hideous, seeing him go for good." "Well, maybe he'll go ahead and have his wife killed anyway, as an enticement—" "Why must you make fun of him? Is it so impossible for you to understand that he's as human as you?" "Helen, there are ways of dealing with a mate you want to be rid of, short of homicide. You can just walk out the door, for one thing." "Can you, 'just'? Is that the way they do it in the Comparative Literature Department? I wonder what it will be like," she says, "when you can't have something you want." "Will I blow somebody's brains out to get it? Will I push somebody down the elevator shaft? What do you think?" "Look, *I'm* the one who gave up everything and nearly died of it—because I couldn't bear to hear the idea even *spoken*. It terrified me to know that he could even *have* such a thought. Or maybe it was so excruciatingly tempting that *that's* why I went running. Because all I had to say was yes; that's all he was waiting for. He was desperate, David, and he was serious. And do you know how easy it would have been to say what he wanted to hear? It's only a word, it takes just a split second: yes." "Only maybe he asked because he was so sure you'd say no." "He couldn't be sure. *I* wasn't sure." "But such a well-known and important man could certainly have gone ahead then and had the thing done on his own, could he not—and without your knowing he was behind it? Surely such a well-known and important man has all kinds of means at his disposal to get a measly wife out of the way: limousines that crash, boats that sink, airplanes that explode in mid-air. Had he done it on his own to begin with, what *you* thought about it all would never even have come up. If he asked your opinion, maybe it was to *hear* no." "Oh, this is interesting. Go on. I say no, and what does he gain?" "What he has: the wife *and* you. He gets to keep it all, and to cut a very grand figure into the bargain. That you ran, that the whole idea took on reality for you, had moral consequences for you—well, he probably hadn't figured on getting that kind of rise out of a beautiful, adventurous, American runaway." "Very clever, indeed. A plus, especially the part about 'moral consequences.' All that's wrong is that you haven't the faintest understanding of what there was between us. Just because he's someone with power, you think he has no feelings. But there are men, you know, who have both. We met two times a week for two years. Sometimes more—but never less. And it never changed. It was never anything but perfect. You don't believe such things happen, do you? Or even if they do, you don't want to believe they matter. But this happened, and to me and to him it mattered more than anything." "But so has coming back happened. So did sending him away happen. So did your terror happen and your revulsion. This guy's machinations are beside the point. It mattered to you, Helen, that your limit had been reached." "Maybe I was mistaken and that was only so much sentimentality about myself. Or some childish kind of hope. Maybe I should have stayed, gone beyond any limit—and learned that it wasn't beyond me at all." "You couldn't," I say, "and you didn't."

And who, oh, who is being the sentimentalist now?

It appears then that the capacity for pain-filled renunciation joined to the gift for sensual abandon is what makes her appeal inescapable. That we never entirely get along, that I am never entirely *sure*, that she somehow lacks depth, that her vanity is so enormous, well, all that is nothing—isn't it?—beside the esteem that I come to have for this beautiful and dramatic young heroine, who has risked and won and lost so much already, squarely facing up to appetite. And then there is the beauty itself. Is she not the single most desirable creature I have ever known? With a woman so physically captivating, a woman whom I cannot take my eyes from even if she is only drinking her coffee or dialing the phone, surely with someone whose smallest bodily movement has such a powerful sensuous hold upon me, I need hardly worry ever again about imagination tempting me to renewed adventures in the base and the bewildering. Is not Helen the enchantress whom I had already begun searching for in college, when Silky Walsh's lower lip stirred me to pursue her from the university cafeteria to the university gymnasium and on to the dormitory laundry room— that creature to me *so* beautiful that upon her, and her alone, I can focus all my yearning, all my adoration, all my curiosity, all my lust? If not Helen, who then? Who ever will intrigue me more? And, alas, I still so need to be intrigued.

Only if we marry . . . well, the contentious side of the affair will simply dwindle away of itself, will it not, an ever-deepening intimacy, the assurance of permanence, dissolving whatever impulse remains, on either side, for smugness and self-defense? Of course it would not be quite such a gamble if Helen were just a little more like this and a little less like that; but, as I am quick to remind myself—imagining that I am taking the *mature* position—that is not how we are bestowed upon each other in the world this side of dreams. Besides, what I call her "vanity" and her "lack of depth" is just what makes her so interesting! So then, I can only hope that mere differences of "opinion" (which, I readily admit—if that will help—I am often the first to point up and to dramatize) will come to be altogether beside the point of the passionate attachment that has, so far, remained undiminished in spite of our abrasive, rather evangelical dialogues. I can only hope that just as I have been mistaken about her motives before, I am wrong again when I suspect that what she secretly hopes to gain by marriage is an end to her love affair with that unpathetic Karenin in Hong Kong. I can only hope that it is in fact

I whom she will marry and not the barrier I may seem to be against the past whose loss had very nearly killed her. I can only hope (for I can never know) that it is I with whom she goes to bed, and not with memories of the mouth and the hands and the member of that most perfect of all lovers, he who would murder his wife in order to make his mistress his own.

Doubting and hoping then, wanting and fearing (anticipating the pleasantest sort of lively future one moment, the worst in the next), I marry Helen Baird—after, that is, nearly three full years devoted to doubting-hoping-wanting-and-fearing. There are some, like my own father, who have only to see a woman standing over a piano singing "Amapola" to decide in a flash, "There—there is my wife," and there are others who sigh, "Yes, it is she," only after an interminable drama of vacillation that has led them to the ineluctable conclusion that they ought never to see the woman again. I marry Helen when the weight of experience required to reach the monumental decision to give her up for good turns out to be so enormous and so moving that I cannot possibly imagine life without her. Only when I finally know *for sure* that *this must end now*, do I discover how deeply wed I already am by my thousand days of indecision, by all the scrutinizing appraisal of possibilities that has somehow made an affair of three years' duration seem as dense with human event as a marriage half a century long. I marry Helen then—and she marries me—at the moment of impasse and exhaustion that must finally come to all those who spend years and years and years in these clearly demarcated and maze-like arrangements that involve separate apartments and joint vacations, assumptions of devotion and designated nights apart, affairs terminated with relief every five or six months, are happily forgotten for seventy-two hours, and then resumed, oftentimes with a delicious, if effervescent, sexual frenzy, following a half-fortuitous meeting at the local supermarket; or begun anew after an evening phone call intended solely to apprise the relinquished companion of a noteworthy documentary to be rerun on television at ten; or following attendance at a dinner party to which the couple had committed themselves so long ago it would have been unseemly not to go ahead and, together, meet this last mutual social obligation. To be sure, one or the other might have answered the obligation by going off to the party alone, but alone there would have been no accomplice across the table with whom to exchange signs of boredom and amusement, nor afterward, driving home, would there have been anyone of like mind with whom to review the charms and deficiencies of the other guests; nor, undressing for bed, would there have been an eager, smiling friend lying unclothed atop the bed sheet to whom one allows that the only truly engaging person present at the table happened to have been one's own previously underrated mate manqué.

We marry, and, as I should have known and couldn't have known and probably always knew, mutual criticism and disapproval continue to poison our lives, evidence not only of the deep temperamental divide that has been there from the start, but also of the sense I continue to have that another man still holds the claim upon her deepest feelings, and that, however she may attempt to hide this sad fact and to attend to me and our life, she knows as well as I do that she is my wife only because there was no way short of homicide (or so they say) for her to be the wife of that very important and well-known lover of hers. At our best, at our bravest and most sensible and most devoted, we do try very hard to hate what divides us rather than each other. If only that past of hers weren't so vivid, so grandiose, so operatic—if somehow one or the other of us could forget it! If I could close this absurd gap of trust that exists between us still! Or ignore it! Live *beyond* it! At our best we make resolutions, we make apologies, we make amends, we make love. But at our worst . . . well, our worst is just about as bad as anybody's, I would think.

What do we struggle over mostly? In the beginning—as anyone will have guessed who, after three years of procrastination, has thrown himself headlong and half convinced into the matrimonial flames—in the beginning we struggle over the toast. Why, I wonder, can't the toast go in while the eggs are cooking, rather than before? This way we can get to eat our bread warm rather than cold. "I don't believe I am having this discussion," she says. "Life isn't toast!" she finally screams. "It is!" I hear myself maintaining. "When you sit down to eat toast, life is toast. And when you take out the garbage, life is garbage. You can't leave the garbage halfway down the stairs, Helen. It belongs in the can in the yard. Covered." "I forgot it." "How can you forget it when it's already in your hand?" "Perhaps, dear, because it's garbage—and what difference does it make anyway!" She forgets to affix her signature to the checks she writes and to stamp the letters she mails, while the letters I give her to mail for me and the household turn up with a certain regularity in the pockets of raincoats and slacks months after she has gone off to deposit them in the mailbox. "What do you think about between Here and There? What makes you so forgetful, Helen? Yearnings for old Mandalay? Memories of the 'crate' and the lagoons and the elephants, of the dawn coming up like thunder—" "I can't think about your letters, damn it, every inch of the way." "But why is it you think you've gone outside with the letter in your hand to *begin* with?" "For some air, that's why! To see some sky! To breathe!"

Soon enough, instead of pointing out her errors and oversights, or retracing her steps, or picking up the pieces, or restraining myself (and then going off to curse her out behind the bathroom door), I make the toast, I make the eggs, I take out the garbage, I pay the bills, and I mail the letters. Even when she says, graciously (trying, at *her* end, to bridge the awful gap), "I'm going out shopping, want me to drop these—" experience, if not wisdom, directs me to say "No—no, thanks." The day she loses her wallet after making a withdrawal from the savings account, I take over the transactions at the bank. The day she leaves the fish to rot under the car's front seat after going out in the morning to get the salmon steaks for dinner, I take over the marketing. The day she has the wool shirt that was to have been dry-cleaned laundered by mistake, I take over going to the cleaners. With the result that before a year is out I am occupied—and glad of it—some sixteen hours a day with teaching my classes and rewriting into a book my thesis on romantic disillusionment in the stories of Anton Chekhov (a subject I'd chosen before even meeting my wife), and Helen has taken increasingly to drink and to dope.

Her days begin in jasmine-scented waters. With olive oil in her hair to make it glossy after washing, and her face anointed with vitamin creams, she reclines in the tub for twenty minutes each morning, eyes closed and the precious skull at rest against a small inflated pillow; the woman moves only to rub gently with her pumice stone the rough skin on her feet. Three times a week the bath is followed by her facial sauna: in her midnight-blue silk kimono, embroidered with pink and red poppies and yellow birds never seen on land or sea, she sits at the counter of our tiny kitchenette, her turbaned head tilted over a bowl of steaming water sprinkled with rosemary and chamomile and elder flower. Then, steamed and painted and coiffed, she is ready to dress for her exercise class—and wherever else it is she goes while I am at school: a close-fitting Chinese dress of navy-blue silk, high at the collar and slit to the thigh; the diamond-stud earrings; bracelets of jade and of gold; her jade ring; her sandals; her straw bag.

When she returns later in the day—after Yoga, she decided to go into San Francisco "to look around": she talks (has talked for years) of plans to open a Far East antique shop there—she is already a little high, and by dinnertime she is all smiles: mellow, blotto, wry. "Life is toast," she observes, sipping four fingers of rum while I season the lamb chops. "Life is leftovers. Life is leather soles and rubber heels. Life is carrying forward the balance into the new checkbook. Life is writing the correct amount to be paid out onto each of the stubs. *And* the correct day, month, and year." "That is all true," I say. "Ah," she says, watching me as I go about setting the table, "if only his wife didn't forget what she puts in to broil and leave everything to burn; if only his wife could remember that when David had dinner in Arcadia, his mother always set the fork on the left and the spoon on the right and never never both on the same side. Oh, if only his wife could bake and butter his potato the way Mamma did in the wintertime."

By the time we are into our thirties we have so exacerbated our antipathies that each of us has been reduced to precisely what the other had been so leery of at the outset, the professorial "smugness" and "prissiness" for which Helen detests me with all her heart—"You've actually done it, David—you are a full-fledged young fogy"—no less in evidence than her "utter mindlessness," "idiotic wastefulness," "adolescent dreaminess," etc. Yet I can never leave her, nor she me, not, that is, until outright disaster makes it simply ludicrous to go on waiting for the miraculous conversion of the other. As much to our wonderment as to everyone else's, we remain married nearly as long as we had been together as lovers, perhaps because of the opportunity this marriage now provides for each of us to assault head-on what each takes to be his demon (and had seemed at first to be the other's salvation!). The months go by and we remain together, wondering if a child would somehow resolve this crazy deadlock . . . or an antique shop of her own for Helen . . . or a jewelry shop . . . or psychotherapy for us both. Again and again we hear ourselves described as a strikingly "attractive" couple: well dressed, traveled, intelligent, worldly (especially as young academic couples go), a combined income of twelve thousand dollars a year . . . and life is simply awful.

What little spirit smolders on in me during the last months of the marriage is visible only in class; otherwise, I am so affectless and withdrawn that a rumor among the junior faculty members has me "under sedation." Ever since the approval of my dissertation I have been teaching, along with the freshman course "Introduction to Fiction," two sections of the sophomore survey in "general" literature. During the weeks near the end of the term when we study Chekhov's stories, I find, while reading aloud to my students passages which I particularly want them to take note of, that each and every sentence seems to me to allude to my own plight above all, as though by now every single syllable I think or utter must first trickle down through my troubles. And then there are my classroom daydreams, as plentiful suddenly as they are irrepressible, and so obviously inspired by longings for miraculous salvation— reentry into lives I lost long ago, reincarnation as a being wholly unlike myself—that I am even somewhat grateful to be depressed and without anything like the will power to set even the mildest fantasy in motion.

"I realized that when you love you must either, in your reasoning about that love, start from what is higher, more important than happiness or unhappiness, sin or virtue in their usual meaning, or you must not reason at all." I ask my students what's meant by these lines, and while they tell me, notice that in a far corner of the room the poised, soft-spoken girl who is my most intelligent, my prettiest—and my most bored and arrogant—student is finishing off a candy bar and a Coke for lunch. "Oh, don't eat junk," I say to her, silently, and see the two of us on the terrace of the Gritti, squinting through the shimmer over the Grand Canal across to the other façade of the perfect little palazzo where we have taken a shuttered room . . . we are having our midday meal, creamy pasta followed by tender bits of lemoned veal . . . and at the very table where Birgitta and I, arrogant, nervy youngsters not much older than these boys and girls, sat down to eat on the afternoon we pooled much of our wealth to celebrate our arrival in Byron's Italy . . .

Meanwhile, my other bright student is explaining what the landowner Alyohin means at the conclusion of "About Love" when he speaks of "what is higher . . . than happiness or unhappiness, sin or virtue in their usual meaning." The boy says, "He regrets that he didn't yield to his feeling and run off with the woman he fell in love with. Now that she's going away, he's miserable for having allowed conscience and scruples, and his own timidity, to forbid him confessing his love to her just because she is already married and a mother." I nod, but clearly without comprehension, and the clever boy looks dismayed. "Am I wrong?" he asks, turning scarlet. "No, *no*," I say, but all the while I am thinking, "What are you doing, Miss Rodgers, dining on Peanut Chews? We should be sipping white wine . . ." And then it occurs to me that, as an undergraduate at U.S.C., Helen probably looked rather like my bored Miss Rodgers in the months before that older man—a man of about my age!—plucked her out of the classroom and into a life of romantic adventure . . .

Later in the hour, I look up from reading aloud out of "Lady with a Lapdog" directly into the innocent and uncorrupted gaze of the plump, earnest, tenderhearted Jewish girl from Beverly Hills who has sat in the front row all year long writing down everything I say. I read to the class the story's final paragraph, in which the adulterous couple, shaken to find how deeply they love one another, try vainly "to understand why he should have a wife and she a husband." "And it seemed to them that in only a few more minutes a solution would be found and a new, beautiful life would begin; but both of them know very well that the end was still a long, long way away and that the most complicated and difficult part was only just beginning." I hear myself speaking of the moving transparency of the ending—no false mysteries, only the harsh facts directly stated. I speak of the amount of human history that Chekhov can incorporate in fifteen pages, of how ridicule and irony gradually give way, even within so short a space, to sorrow and pathos, of his feel for the disillusioning moment and for those processes wherein actuality seemingly pounces upon even our most harmless illusions, not to mention the grand dreams of fulfillment and adventure. I speak of his pessimism about what he calls "this business of personal happiness," and all the while I want to ask the chubby girl in the front row, who is rapidly recording my words in her notebook, to become my daughter. I want to look after her and see that she is safe and happy. I want to pay for her clothes and her doctor bills and for her to come and put her arms around me when she is feeling lonely or sad. If only it were Helen and I who had raised her to be so sweet! But how could we two raise anything?

And later that day, when I happen to run into her walking toward me on the campus, I feel impelled yet again to say to someone who is probably no more than ten or twelve years my junior that I want to adopt her, want her to forget her own parents, about whom I know nothing, and let me father and protect her. "Hi, Mr. Kepesh," she says, with a little wave of the hand, and that affectionate gesture does it, apparently. I feel as though I am growing lighter and lighter, I sense an emotion coming my way that will pick me up and turn me over and deposit me I know not where. Am I going to have my nervous collapse right here on the walk in front of the library? I take one of her hands in mine—I am saying, through a throat clogged with feeling, "You're a good girl, Kathie." She ducks her head, her forehead colors. "Well," she says, "I'm glad somebody around here likes me." "You're a good girl," I repeat, and release the soft hand I am holding and go home to see if childless Helen is sober enough to prepare dinner for two.

About this time we are visited by an English investment banker named Donald Garland, the first of Helen's Hong Kong friends ever to be invited to dine with us in our apartment. To be sure, she has on occasion made herself spectacularly beautiful so as to go into San Francisco to have lunch with somebody or other out of paradise lost, but never before have I seen her approach such a meeting in this mood of happy, almost childlike anticipation. Indeed, in the past there have been times when, having spent hours getting made up for the luncheon engagement, she would emerge from the bathroom in her drabbest robe, announcing herself unable to leave the house to see anyone. "I look hideous." "You don't at all." "I do," and with that she returns to bed for the day.

Donald Garland, she tells me now, is "the kindest man" she has ever known. "I was taken to lunch at his house my first week in Hong Kong, and we were the best of friends from then on. We just adored each other. The center of the table was strewn with orchids he'd picked from his garden—in my honor, he said—and the patio where we ate looked out over the crescent of Repulse Bay. I was eighteen years old. He must have been about fifty-five. My God. Donald is probably seventy! I could never believe he was over forty; he was always happy, so youthful, so thrilled with everything. He lived with the most easygoing and good-natured American boy. Chips must have been about twenty-six or -seven then. On the phone this afternoon Donald told me the most terrible news—one morning two months ago Chips died of an aneurysm at breakfast; just keeled over dead. Donald took the body back to Wilmington, Delaware, and buried it, and then he couldn't leave. He kept booking plane tickets and canceling. Now, finally, he's on his way home."

Chips, Donald, Edgar, Brian, Colin . . . I have no response to make, no interrogations or cross-examination, nothing faintly resembling sympathy, curiosity, or interest. Or patience. I had long ago heard all I could stand about the doings of the wealthy Hong Kong circle of English homosexuals who had "adored" her. I exhibit only a churlish sort of surprise to find that I am to be a party to this very special reunion. She shuts her eyes tightly, as though she must obliterate me momentarily from sight just in order to survive. "Don't talk to me like that. Don't take that terrible tone. He was my dearest friend. He saved my life a hundred times." *And why did you risk it a hundred times?* But the interrogatory accusation, and the terrible tone that goes with it, I manage to squelch, for by now even I know that I am being diminished far more by my anger at everything she does and did than by those ways of hers I ought to have learned to disregard, or to have accepted with a certain grace, long, long ago . . . Only as the evening wears on, and Garland becomes increasingly spirited in his reminiscences, do I wonder if she has invited him to the apartment so that I might learn at first hand just how very far from the apex she has fallen by insanely joining her fate to this fogy's. Whether or not that is her intention, it is something like the result. In their company I am no easygoing good-natured Chips, but entirely the Victorian schoolmaster whose heart stirs only to the crack of the whip and the swish of the cane. In a vain attempt to force this pious, sour, censorious little prig out of my skin, I try hard to believe that Helen is simply showing this man who has meant so much to her and been so kind to her, and who has himself just suffered a terrible blow, that all is well in her life, that she and her husband live comfortably and amicably, and that her protector hasn't to worry about her any longer. Yes, Helen is only acting as would any devoted daughter who wished to spare a doting father some harsh truth . . . In short: simple as the explanation for Garland's presence might have seemed to someone else, it is wholly beyond my grasp, as though now that living with Helen has ceased to make the least bit of sense, I cannot discover the truth about anything.

At seventy, delicate, small-boned Garland still does have a youthful sort of charm, and a way about him at once worldly and boyish. His forehead is so fragile-looking it seems it could be cracked with the tap of a spoon, and his cheeks are the small, round, glazed cheeks of an alabaster Cupid. Above the open shirt a pale silk scarf is tied around his neck, almost completely hiding from view the throat whose creases are the only sign of his age. In that strangely youthful face all there is to speak of sorrow are the eyes, soft, brown, and awash with feeling even while his crisp accent refuses to betray the faintest hint of grief.

"Poor Derek was killed, you know." Helen did not know. She puts her hand to her mouth. "But *how*? Derek," she says, turning to me, "was an associate in Donald's firm. A very silly man sometimes, very muddled and so on, but such a good heart, really—" My dead expression sends her quickly back to Garland. "Yes," he says, "he was a very kind person, and I was devoted to him. Oh, he could talk and go on, but then you just had to tell him, 'Derek, that's enough now,' and he'd shut up. Well, two Chinese boys thought that he hadn't given them enough money, so they kicked him down a flight of stairs. Broke Derek's neck." "How terrible. How awful. Poor, poor man. And what," asks Helen, "has happened to all his animals?" "The birds are gone. Some sort of virus wiped them out the week after he was killed. The rest Madge adopted. Madge adopted them and Patricia looks after them. Otherwise, those two won't have anything to do with each other." "Again?" "Oh, yes. She can be a good bitch, that Madge, when she wants to be. Chips did her house over for her a year ago. She nearly drove the poor boy crazy with her upstairs bath." Helen tries yet again to bring me into the company of the living: she explains that Madge and Patricia, who own houses down along the bay from Donald, were stars of the British cinema in the forties. Donald rattles off the names of the movies they made. I nod and nod, just like an agreeable person, but the smile I make a stab at presenting him does not begin to come off. The look Helen has for me does, however, quite effectively. "And how does Madge look?" Helen asks him. "Well, when she makes up, she still looks wonderful. She ought never to wear a bikini, of course." I say, "Why?" but no one seems to hear me. The evening ends with Garland, by now a little drunk, holding Helen's hand and telling me about a famous masquerade party held in a jungle clearing on a small island in the Gulf of Siam owned by a Thai friend of his, half a mile out to sea from the southern finger of Thailand. Chips, who designed Helen's costume, had put her all in white, like Prince Ivan in *The Firebird*. "She was ravishing. A silk Cossack shirt and full silk trousers gathered into soft silver kid boots, and a silver turban with a diamond clasp. And around her waist a jeweled belt of emeralds." Emeralds? Bought by whom? Obviously by Karenin. Where's the belt now, I wonder? What do you have to return and what do you get to keep? You certainly get to keep the memories, that's for sure. "A little Thai princess burst into tears at the very sight of her. Poor little thing. She'd come wearing everything but the kitchen stove and expected people to swoon. But the one who looked like royalty that night was this dear girl. Oh, it was quite a to-do. Hasn't Helen ever shown you the photographs? Don't you have photographs, dear?" "No," she says, "not any more."

"Oh, I wish I'd brought mine. But I never thought I'd see you—I didn't even know who I was when I left home. And remember the little boys?" he says, after a long sip from his brandy glass. "Chips, of course, got all the little native boys stripped down, with just a little coconut shell around their how-dee-dos, and Christmas tinsel streaming down around their necks. What a sight they were when the wind blew! Well, the boat landed, and there were these little chaps to greet the guests and to lead us up a torch-lined path to the clearing where we had the banquet. Oh, my goodness, yes—Madge came in the dress that Derek wore for his fortieth birthday party. Never would spend money, if she could help it. Always angry about something, but mostly it's the money everyone's stealing from her. She said, 'You can't just go to one of these things, you have to have something wonderful to wear.' So I said to her, only as a joke, mind you, 'Why don't you come in Derek's dress? It's white chiffon covered with Diamonte and with a long train. And cut very low in the back. You'll look lovely in it, darling.' And Madge said, 'How could it be cut low in the back, Donald? How in the world could Derek have worn it? What about the hair on his back, and all that disgusting rubbish?' And I said, 'Oh, darling, he only shaves once every three years.' You see," Garland says to me, "Derek was rather the old Guards officer type—slim, elegant, very pink-complexioned, altogether the most extraordinarily hairless person. Oh, there's a photograph of Helen you must see, David. I must send it to you. It's Helen being led from the boat by these enchanting little native boys streaming Christmas tinsel. With her long legs and all that silk clinging to her, oh, she was absolute perfection. And her face—her face in that photograph is classic. I must send it to you; you must have it. She was the most ravishing thing. Patricia said about Helen, the first moment she laid eyes on her—that was at lunch at my house, and the darling girl still had the most ordinary little clothes—but Patricia said then she had star quality, that without a doubt she could be a film star. And she could have been. She still has it. She always will." "I know," replies the schoolmaster, silently swishing his cane.

After he leaves, Helen says, "Well, there's no need to ask what you thought of him, is there?" "It's as you said: he adores you." "Really, just what has empowered you to sit in judgment of other people's passions? Haven't you heard? It's a wide, wide world; room for everybody to do whatever he likes. Even you once did what you liked, David. Or so the legend goes." "I sit in judgment of nothing. What I sit in judgment of, you wouldn't believe." "Ah, yourself. Hardest on yourself. Momentarily I forgot." "I sat, Helen, and I listened and I don't remember saying anything about the passions or preferences or private parts of anybody from here to Nepal." "Donald Garland is probably the kindest man alive." "Fine with me." "He was always there when I needed someone. There were weeks when I went to live in his house. He protected me from some terrible people." *Why didn't you just protect yourself by staying away from them?* "Good," I say; "you were lucky and that was great." "He likes to gossip and to tell tales, and of course he got a little maudlin tonight—look what he's just been through. But he happens to know what people are, just how much and just how little—and he is devoted to his friends, even the fools. The loyalty of those kind of men is quite wonderful, and not to be disparaged by anyone. And don't you be misled. When he is feeling himself he can be like iron. He can be unmovable, and marvelous." "I am sure he was a wonderful friend to you." "He still is!" "Look, what are you trying to tell me? I don't always get the gist of things these days. Rumor has it my students are going to give *me* the final exam, to see if they've been able to get anything through my skull. What are we talking about now?" "About the fact that I am still a person of consequence to quite a few people, even if to you and the learned professors and their peppy, dowdy little wives I am beneath contempt. It's true I'm not clever enough to bake banana bread and carrot bread and raise my own bean sprouts and 'audit' seminars and 'head up' committees to outlaw war for all time, but people still look at me, David, wherever I go. I could have married the kind of men who *run* the world! I wouldn't have had to look far, either. I hate to have to say such a vulgar, trashy thing about myself, but it's what you're reduced to saying to someone who finds you repulsive." "I don't find you repulsive. I'm still awestruck that you chose me over the president of ITT. How can someone unable even to finish a little pamphlet on Anton Chekhov feel anything but gratitude to be living with the runner-up for Queen of Tibet? I'm honored to have been chosen to be your hair shirt." "It's debatable who is the hair shirt around here. I am repugnant to you, Donald is repugnant to you—" "Helen, I neither liked the man nor disliked the man. I did my level fucking best. Look, my best friend as long ago as college was practically the only queer *there*. I had a queer for a friend in 1950—before they even existed! I didn't know what one was, but I had one. I don't care *who* wears *whose* dress—oh, fuck it, forget it, I quit."

Then on a Saturday morning late in the spring, just as I have sat down at my desk to begin marking exams, I hear the front door of our apartment open and shut—and finally the dissolution of this hopeless misalliance has begun. Helen is gone. Several days pass—hideous days, involving two visits to the San Francisco morgue, one with Helen's demure, bewildered mother, who insists on flying up from Pasadena and bravely coming along with me to look at the broken body of a drowned "Caucasian" woman, age thirty to thirty-five—before I learn her whereabouts.

The first telephone call—informing me that my mate is in a Hong Kong jail—is from the State Department. The second call is from Garland, who adds certain lurid and clarifying details: she had gone from the Hong Kong airport directly by taxi to the well-known ex-lover's mansion in Kowloon. He is the English Onassis, I am told, son and heir of the founder of the MacDonald-Metcalf Line, and king of the cargo routes from the Cape of Good Hope to Manila Bay. At Jimmy Metcalf's home, she had not even been allowed past the servant posted at the door, not after her name had been announced to Metcalf's wife. And when, some hours later, she left her hotel to tell the police of the plan made some years earlier by the president of MacDonald-Metcalf to have his wife run down by a car, the officer on duty at the police station made a telephone call and subsequently a packet of cocaine was found in her purse.

"What happens now?" I ask him. "My God, Donald, now what?"

"I get her out," says Garland.

"Can that be done?"

"It can."

"How?"

"How would you think?"

Money? Blackmail? Girls? Boys? I don't know, I don't care, I won't ask again. *Whatever works, do it.*

"The question is," says Garland, "what happens when Helen is free? I can, of course, make her quite comfortable right here. I can provide her with all she needs to pull herself together again, and to go on. I want to know what you think is for the best. She cannot afford to be caught in between again."

"In between what? Donald, this is all a little confusing. I have no idea what's best, frankly. Tell me, please, why didn't she go to you when she got there?"

"Because she got it in her head to see Jimmy. She knew that if she'd come first to me I would never have let her go anywhere near him. I know the man, better than she does."

"And you knew she was coming?"

"Yes, of course."

"The night you were here for dinner."

"No, no, my dear boy. Only a week ago. But she was to have cabled. I would have been at the airport to meet her. But she did it Helen's way."

"She shouldn't have," I say dumbly.

"The question is, does she come back to you or stay with me? I'd like you to tell me which you think is best."

"You're sure she's getting out of jail, you're sure the charges will be dropped—"

"I wouldn't have phoned to say what I'm saying otherwise."

"What happens then . . . well, it's up to Helen, isn't it? That is, I'd have to talk to her."

"But you can't. I'm lucky I could. We're lucky she isn't in irons already and halfway to Malaysia. Our police chief is not the most charitable of men, except on his own behalf. And your rival is not Albert Schweitzer."

"That is apparent."

"She used to tell me, 'It's so difficult to go shopping with Jimmy. If I see something I like, he buys me twelve.' She used to say to him, 'But, Jimmy, I can only wear one at a time.' But Jimmy never understood, Mr. Kepesh. He does everything by twelves."

"Okay, I believe that."

"I don't want anything further to go wrong for Helen—ever," says Garland. "I want to know exactly where Helen stands, and I want to know now. She has been through years of hell. She was a marvelous, dazzling creature, and life has treated her hideously. I won't allow either one of you to torture her again."

But I can't tell him where she stands—I don't know where *I* stand. First, I say, I must reach Helen's family and calm their fears. He will hear from me.

Will he? Why?

As though I have just reported that her daughter has been detained by a club meeting after school, Helen's mother says, politely, "And when will she be home?"

"I don't know."

But this does not appear to faze the adventuress's mother. "I do hope you'll keep me informed," she says, brightly.

"I will."

"Well, thank you for calling, David."

What else can the mother of an adventuress do but thank people for calling and keeping her informed?

And what does the husband of an adventuress do while his wife is in jail in the Far East? Well, at dinnertime I prepare an omelette, make it very carefully, at just the right heat, and serve it to myself with a little chopped parsley, a glass of wine, and a slice of buttered toast. Then I take a long hot shower. He doesn't want me to torture her: all right, I won't torture her—but best of all, I won't torture myself. After the shower I decide to get into my pajamas and to do my night's reading in bed, all by myself. No girls, not yet. That will come in its own sweet time. Everything will. Can it be? I am back where I was six years ago, the night before I ditched my sensible date and took Hong Kong Helen home from that party. Except that now I have my job, I have my book to complete, and I seem to have this comfortable apartment, so charmingly and tastefully decorated, all to myself. What is Mauriac's phrase? "To revel in the pleasures of the unshared bed."

For some hours my happiness is complete. Have I ever heard or read of something like this happening, of a person being catapulted out of his misery *directly* into bliss? The common wisdom has it that it works the other way around. Well, I am here to say that on rare occasions it seems to work this way too. My God, I do feel good. I will not torture her, or myself, ever again. Fine with me.

Two hundred and forty minutes of this, more or less.

With a loan from Arthur Schonbrunn, a colleague who had been my thesis adviser, I buy a round-trip ticket and fly off to Asia the next day. (At the bank I discover that the entire balance in our savings account had been withdrawn by Helen the week before, for her one-way air ticket, and to start her new life.) On the plane there is time to think—and to think and to think and to think. It must be that I want her back, that I can't give her up, that I am in love with her whether I've known it or not, that she is my destiny—

Not one word of this stuff convinces me. Most are words I despise: Helen's kind of words, Helen's kind of thinking. I can't live without this, he can't live without that, my woman, my man, my destiny . . . Kid stuff! Movie stuff! *Screen Romance!*

Yet if this woman is not *my woman*, what am I doing here? If she is not *my destiny*, why was I on the phone from 2 to 5 a.m.? Is it just that pride won't permit me to abdicate in favor of her homosexual protector? No, that's not what's done it. Nor am I Acting Responsibly, or out of shame, or masochism, or vindictive glee . . .

Then that leaves love. Love! At this late date! Love! After all that's been done to destroy it! More love, suddenly, than there was anywhere along the way!

I spend the rest of my waking hours on that flight remembering every single charming, sweet, beguiling word she has ever spoken.

Accompanied by Garland—grim, courteous, impeccably now the banker and businessman—a Hong Kong police detective, and the clean-cut young man from the American consulate who is also there to meet my airplane, I am taken to a jail to see my wife. As we leave the terminal for the car, I say to Garland, "I thought she was to be out by now." "The negotiations," he says, "seem to involve more interests than we had imagined." "Hong Kong," the young consulate officer in-

forms me wryly, "is the birthplace of collective bargaining."
Everybody in the car seems to know the score, except me.

I am searched and then allowed to sit with her in a tiny room
whose door is dramatically locked behind us. The sound of
the lock catching makes her reach wildly for my hand. Her face
is blotchy, her lips are blistered, her eyes . . . her eyes I cannot look into without my innards crumbling. And Helen
smells. And as for all that I felt for her up in the air, well, I simply cannot bring myself to love her like that down here on
the ground. I have never loved her quite like that down on the
ground before, and I'm not going to start in a jail. I am not that
kind of an idiot. Which maybe makes me some other kind of
idiot . . . but that I will have to determine later.

"They planted cocaine on me." "I know." "He can't get away
with that," she says. "He won't. Donald is going to get you
out of here." "*He has to!*" "He is, he's doing it. So you don't
have to worry. You'll be out very soon now." "I have to tell
you something terrible. All our cash is gone. The police stole
it. He told them what to do to me—and they did it. They
laughed at me. They touched me." "Helen, tell me the truth
now. I have to know. We all have to know. When you get out
of here, do you want to stay on with Donald in his house? He
says he will look after you, he—" "But I can't! No! Oh, don't
leave me here, please! Jimmy will kill me!"

On the return flight Helen drinks until the stewardess says
she cannot serve her another. "I'll bet you were even faithful
to me," she says, oddly "chatty" suddenly. "Yes, I'll bet you
were," she says, serene in a dopey sort of way now that the
whiskey has somewhat dimmed the horrors of incarceration
and she is beyond the nightmare of Jimmy Metcalf's revenge.
I don't bother to answer one way or the other. Of the two
meaningless copulations of the last year there is nothing to say;
she would only laugh if I were to tell her who her rivals had
been. Nor could I expect much sympathy were I to try to explain to her how unsatisfying it had been to deceive her with
women who hadn't a hundredth of her appeal to me—who
hadn't a hundredth of her character, let alone her loveliness—
and whose faces I could have spit into when I realized how
much of *their* satisfaction derived from putting Helen Kepesh

in her place. Quickly enough—*almost* quickly enough—I had seen that deceiving a wife as disliked as Helen was by other women just wasn't going to be possible without humiliating myself in the process. I hadn't a Jimmy Metcalf's gift for coldly rearing back and delivering the grand and fatal blow to my opponent; no, vengeance was his style and contentious melancholia was mine . . . Helen's speech is badly slurred by liquor and fatigue, but now that she has had a bath, and a meal, and a change of clothes, and a chance to make up her face, she intends to have a conversation, her first in days and days. She intends now to resume her place in the world, and not as the vanquished, but as herself. "Well," she says, "you didn't have to be *such* a good boy, you know. You could have had your affairs, if that would have made you any happier. I could have taken it." "Good to know that," I say. "It's you, David, who wouldn't have survived in one piece. You see, I've been faithful to you, whether you believe it or not. The only man I've been faithful to in my life." Do I believe that? Can I? And if I should? Where does *that* leave me? I say nothing. "You don't know yet where I used to go sometimes after my exercise class." "No, I don't." "You don't know why I went out in the morning wearing my favorite dress." "I had my ideas." "Well, they were wrong. I had no lover. Never, never with you. Because it would have been too hideous. You couldn't have taken it—and so I didn't do it. You would have been crushed, you would have forgiven me, and you would never have been yourself again. You would have gone around bleeding forever." "I went around bleeding anyway. We both went around bleeding. Where did you go all dressed up?" "I went out to the airport." "And?" "And I sat in the Pan Am waiting room. I had my passport in my handbag. And my jewelry. I sat there reading the paper until somebody asked if I wanted to have a drink in the first-class lounge." "And I'll bet somebody always did." "Always—that's right. And I'd go there and have a drink. We would talk . . . and then they would ask me to go away with them. To South America, to Africa, everywhere. A man even asked me to come with him on a business trip to Hong Kong. But I never did it. Never. Instead, I came back home and you started in on me about the checkbook stubs." "You did this how often?" "Often enough," she replies. "Enough for what—to see if you still had the power?" "No, you idiot, to see if *you* still had the power." She began to sob. "Will it startle you," she asks, "to hear that I think we should have had that baby?" "I wouldn't have risked it, not with you." My words knock the wind out of her, what wind is left. "Oh, you shit, that was unnecessary, there are less cruel ways . . ." she says. "Oh, why didn't I let Jimmy kill her when he wanted to!" she cries. "Quiet down, Helen." "You should see her now—she stood there, ten feet inside the hallway, glaring out at me. You should see her—she looks like a whale! That beautiful man goes to bed with a whale." "I said quiet down." "He told them to plant cocaine on me—on me, the person he loves! He let them take my purse and steal my money! And how I loved that man! I only left him to save him from committing a murder! And now he hates me for being too decent, and you despise me for being indecent, and the truth of it is that I'm better and stronger and braver than both of you. At least I was—and I was when I was only twenty years old! *You* wouldn't risk a baby with *me*? What about someone like *you*? Did it ever occur to you that about a baby it may have been the other way around? No? Yes? Answer me! Oh, I can't wait to see the little sparrow you do take the risk with. If only you had taken it into your hands long ago, years ago—at the beginning! I should have had nothing to say about it!" "Helen, you're exhausted and you're loaded and you don't know what you're saying. A lot you cared about having a baby." "A lot I did, you fool, you dope! Oh, why did I come on this airplane with you! I could have stayed with Donald! He needs someone as much as I do. I should have stayed with him in his house, and told *you* to go on home. Oh, why did I lose my nerve in that jail!" "You lost it because of your Jimmy. You thought when you got out he'd kill you." "But he wouldn't—that was crazy! He only did what he did because he loves me so, and I loved him! Oh, I waited and I waited and I waited—I've waited for you for six years! Why didn't you take me into your world like a man!" "Maybe you mean why didn't I take you out of yours. I couldn't. The only kind to take *you* out is the kind who took you in. Sure, I know about my terrible tone, and the scornful looks I can give, but I never went and got a hit-man in about the toast, you know. Next time you want to be saved from a tyrant, find another tyrant to do the job. I admit defeat." "Oh, God, oh, Jesus God, why must they be either brutes or choirboys? Stewardess," she says, grabbing the girl's arm as she passes in the aisle, "I don't want a drink, I've had enough. I only want to ask a question of you. Don't be frightened. Why are they either brutes or choirboys, do you know?" "Who, madam?" "Don't you find that in your travels from one continent to the other? They're even afraid, you know, of a sweet little thing like you. That's why you have to go around grinning like that. Just look the bastards right in the eye and they're either at your knees or at your throat."

When at last Helen has fallen asleep—her face rolling familiarly on my shoulder—I take the final exams out of my briefcase and begin where I had had to leave off a hundred or so hours ago. Yes, I have taken my schoolwork with me—and a good thing too. I cannot imagine how I could get through the million remaining hours of the flight without these examination papers to hang on to. "Without this . . ." and see myself strangling Helen with the coil of her waist-long hair. Who strangles his lover with her hair? Isn't it somebody somewhere in Browning? Oh, who cares!

"The search for intimacy, not because it necessarily makes for happiness, but because it is necessary, is one of Chekhov's recurrent themes."

The paper I have chosen to begin with—to begin again with—is by Kathie Steiner, the girl I had dreamed of adopting. "Good," I write in the margin alongside her opening sentence; then I reread it and after "necessary" make an insertion mark and write, "for survival(?)." And all the while I am thinking, "And miles below are the beaches of Polynesia. Well, dear, dazzling creature, a lot of good that does us! Hong Kong! The whole damn thing could have taken place in Cincinnati! A hotel room, a police station, an airport. A vengeful megalomaniac and some crooked cops! And a would-be Cleopatra! Our savings gone on this trashy Grade-B thriller! Oh, this voyage is the marriage itself—traversing four thousand miles of the exotic globe twice over, and for no good reason at all!"

Struggling to fix my attention once again on the task at hand—and not on whether Helen and I should have had a child, or who is to blame because we didn't; refusing to charge myself yet again with all I could have done that I didn't do, and all I did that I shouldn't have—I return to Kathie Steiner's final exam. Jimmy Metcalf instructs the police: "Kick her ass a little, gentlemen, it'll do the whore some good," while I subdue my emotions by reading carefully through each of Kathie's pages, correcting every last comma fault, reminding her about her dangling-modifier problem, and dutifully filling the margin with my commentary and questions. Me and my "finals"; my marking pen and my paper clips. How the Emperor Metcalf would enjoy the spectacle—likewise Donald Garland and his uncharitable chief of police. I suppose I ought to laugh a little myself; but as I am a literature professor and not a policeman, as I am someone who long ago squeezed out what little of the tyrant was ever in him—from the look of things, maybe squeezed out just a bit too much—instead of laughing it all off, I come to Kathie's concluding sentence, and am undone. The hold I have had on myself since Helen's disappearance dissolves like that, and I must turn my face and press it into the darkened window of the humming airship that is carrying us back home to complete, in orderly and legal fashion, the disentanglement of our two wrecked lives. I cry for myself, I cry for Helen, and finally I seem to cry hardest of all with the realization that somehow not every last thing *has* been destroyed, that despite my consuming obsession with my marital unhappiness and my dreamy desire to call out to my young students for their help, I have somehow gotten a sweet, chubby, unharmed and as yet unhorrified daughter of Beverly Hills to end her sophomore year of college by composing this grim and beautiful lament summarizing what she calls "Anton Chekhov's overall philosophy of life." But can Professor Kepesh have taught her this? How? *How?* I am only just beginning to learn it on this flight! "We are born innocent," the girl has written, "we suffer terrible disillusionment before we can gain knowledge, and then we fear death—and we are granted only fragmentary happiness to offset the pain."

I AM finally extracted from the rubble of my divorce by a job offer from Arthur Schonbrunn, who has left Stanford to become chairman of the comparative literature program at the State University of New York on Long Island. I have already begun seeing a psychoanalyst in San Francisco—only shortly after I began seeing the lawyer—and it is he who recommends that when I return East to teach I continue therapy with a Dr. Frederick Klinger, whom he knows and can recommend as someone who is not afraid to speak up with his patients, "a solid, reasonable man," as he is described to me, "a specialist," I am told, "in common sense." But are reason and common sense what I need? Some would say that I have ruined things by far too narrow a devotion to exactly these attributes.

Frederick Klinger is solid, all right: a hearty, round-faced fellow, full of life, who, with my permission, smokes cigars throughout the sessions. I don't much like the aroma myself, but allow it because smoking seems even further to concentrate the keenness with which Klinger attends to my despair. Not many years older than me, and sporting fewer gray hairs than I have lately begun to show, he exudes the contentment and confidence of a successful man in his middle years. I gather from the phone calls which, to my distress, he takes during my hour, that he is already a key figure in psychoanalytic circles, a member of the governing bodies of schools, publications, and research institutes, not to mention the last source of hope for any number of souls in disrepair. At first I find myself somewhat put off by the sheer relish with which the doctor seems to devour his responsibilities—put off, to be truthful, by nearly everything about him: the double-breasted chalk-stripe suit and the floppy bow tie, the frayed Chesterfield coat growing tight over the plumpening middle, the *two* bursting briefcases at the coat rack, the photos of the smiling healthy children on the book-laden desk, the tennis racket in the umbrella stand—put off even by the gym bag pushed behind the big worn Eames chair from which, cigar in hand, he addresses himself to my confusion. Can this snazzy, energetic conquistador possibly understand that there are mornings when on the way from the bed to the toothbrush I have to struggle to prevent myself from dropping down and curling up on the living-room floor? I don't entirely understand the depth of this plunge myself. Having failed at being a husband to Helen—having failed at figuring out how to make Helen a wife—it seems I would rather sleep through my life now than live it.

How, for instance, have I come to be on such terrible terms with sensuality? "You," he replies, "who married a *femme fatale*?" "But only to de-fatalize her, to de-fang her, along the way. All that nagging at her, at Helen, about the garbage and the laundry and the toast. My mother couldn't have done a better job. About every last detail!" "Too divine for details, was she? Look, she isn't the Helen born of Leda and Zeus, you know. She's of the earth, Mr. Kepesh—a middle-class Gentile girl from Pasadena, California, pretty enough to get herself a free trip to Angkor Wat every year, but that's about it, in the way of supernatural achievement. And cold toast is cold toast, no matter how much jewelry the cook may have accumulated over the years from rich married men with a taste for young girls." "I was frightened of her." "Sure you were." His phone rings. No, he cannot possibly be at the hospital before noon. Yes, he has seen the husband. No, the gentleman does not seem willing to cooperate. Yes, that is most unfortunate. Now back to this uncooperative gentleman. "Sure you were frightened," he says, "you couldn't trust her." "I *wouldn't* trust her. And she *was* faithful to me. I believe that." "Neither here nor there. Some game she was playing with herself, that's all. What value did it have when the fact is that the two of you had no real business together ever? From the sound of it the only thing each of you did *totally* out of character was to marry the other." "I was frightened of Birgitta, too." "My God," he exclaims, "who wouldn't have been?" "Look, either I'm not making myself clear or you don't even want to begin to understand me. I'm saying that these were special creatures, full of daring and curiosity—and freedom. They were not ordinary young women." "Oh, I understand that." "Do you? I think sometimes that you'd prefer to assign them both to some very tawdry category of humankind. But what made them special is that they weren't tawdry, not to me, neither one of them.

They were exceptional." "Granted." The phone rings. Yes, what is it? I am in session, yes. No, no, go ahead. Yes. Yes. Of course he understands. No, no, he's pretending, pay no attention. All right, increase the dosage to four a day. But no more. And call me if he continues crying. Call me anyway. Goodbye. "Granted," he says, "but what were you supposed to do, having *married* one of these 'special creatures'? Spend days as well as nights fondling her perfect breasts? Join her opium den? The other day you said the only thing you learned from six years with Helen was how to roll a joint." "I think saying that is what is known as courting the analyst's favor. I learned plenty." "The fact remains—you had your work to do." "The work is just a habit," I say, without disguising my irritation with his dogged "demythologizing." "Perhaps," I wearily suggest, "reading books is the opiate of the educated classes." "Is it? Are you thinking of becoming a flower child?" he says, lighting up a new cigar. "Once Helen and I were sunbathing in the nude on a beach in Oregon. We were on vacation, driving north. After a while we spotted a guy watching us from off in some brush. We started to cover up, but he came toward us anyway and asked if we were nudists. When I said no he gave us a copy of his nudist newspaper in case we wanted to subscribe." Klinger laughs loudly. "Helen said to me that God Himself must have sent him because it had been, by that time, fully ninety minutes since I'd read anything." Again Klinger laughs with genuine amusement. "Look," I tell him, "you just don't know what it was like when I first met her. It's not to be so easily disparaged. You don't know what I was like, nor can you—nor can I, any more—seeing me in this shape. But I was a fearless sort of boy back in my early twenties. More daring than most, especially for that woebegone era in the history of pleasure. I actually did what the jerk-off artists dreamed about. Back when I started out on my own in the world, I was, if I may say so, something of a sexual prodigy." "And you want to be one again, in your thirties?" I don't even bother to answer, so narrow and wrongheaded does the common sense he's mastered strike me. "Why allow Helen," Klinger continues, "who has disfigured herself so in the frantic effort to be the high priestess of Eros—who very nearly destroyed you with her pronouncements and insinuations—why allow her judgment power over you still? How long do you intend to let her go on rebuking you where you feel weakest? How long do you intend to go on *feeling* weak over such utter foolishness? What was this 'daring' search of hers—?" The telephone. "Excuse me," he says. Yes, this is he. Yes, go ahead. Hello—yes, I can hear you very well. How is Madrid? What? Well, of course he's suspicious, what did you expect? But you just tell him that he is behaving stupidly and then forget it. No, of course you don't want to get into a fight. I understand. Just say it, and then try to have some courage. You can stand up to him. Go back up to the room and tell him. Come on now, you know very well you can. All right. Good luck. Have a good time. I said, then go out and have a good time. Goodbye. "What was this search of hers," he says, "but so much evasion, a childish flight from the real attainable projects of a life?" "Then, on the other hand," I say, "maybe the 'projects' are so much evasion of the search." "Please, you like to read and write about books. That, by your own testimony, gives you enormous satisfaction—did, at any rate, and will again, I assure you. Right now you're fed up with everything. But you like being a teacher, correct? And from what I gather you are not uninspired at it. I still don't know what alternative you have in mind. You want to move to the South Seas and teach great books to the girls in sarongs at the University of Tahiti? You want to have a go at a harem again? To be a fearless prodigy again, playing at Jack and Jill with your little Swedish daredevil in the working-class bars of Paris? You want a hammer over your head again—though maybe this time one that finds the mark?" "Burlesquing what I'm talking about doesn't do me any good, you know. It's obviously not going back to Birgitta that's on my mind. It's going ahead. I can't go *ahead*." "Perhaps going ahead, on that road anyway, is a delusion." "Dr. Klinger, I assure you that I am sufficiently imbued by now with the Chekhovian bias to suspect as much myself. I know what there is to know from 'The Duel' and other stories about those committed to the libidinous fallacy. I too have read and studied the great Western wisdom on the subject. I have even taught it. I have even practiced it. But, if I may, as Chekhov also had the ordinary good sense to write: in psychological matters, 'God preserve us from generalizations.'" "Thank you for the literature lesson. Tell me this, Mr.

Kepesh: can you really be in the doldrums about what has be-fallen her—over what you seem to think you have 'done' to her—or are you just trying to prove to us that you are a man of feeling and conscience? If so, don't overdo it. Because *this* Helen was bound to spend a night in jail, sooner or later. Des-tined for it long before she met you. From the sound of it, it's how she landed on you—in the hope of being saved from the hoosegow, and the other inevitable humiliations. And that you know, as well as I do."

But whatever he may say, however he may bully, burlesque, or even try a smidgen of charm in order to get me to put the marriage and divorce behind me, I am, whether he believes it or not, never altogether immune from self-recrimination when stories reach me of the ailments that are said to be trans-forming the one-time Occidental princess of the Orient into a bitter hag. I learn of a debilitating case of rhinitis that cannot seem to be checked by drugs and necessitates that she live with a tissue continuously rubbing away at her nose—at the fluted nostrils that flare as though catching the wind when she achieves her pleasure. I hear tell of extensive skin eruptions, on the cunning fingers ("You like this? . . . this? . . . oh, you do like it, my darling!"), and on her wide, lovely lips ("What do you see first in a face? The eyes or the mouth? I like that you discovered my mouth first"). But then Helen's is not the only flesh slowly taking its revenge, or doing penance, or losing heart, or removing itself from the fray. Eating hardly anything, I have dropped since the divorce to scarecrow weight, and for the second time in my life I am bereft of my potency, even for an entertainment as unambitious as self-love. "I should never have come home from Europe," I tell Klinger, who has at my request put me on an anti-depressant drug, which pries me out of bed in the morning but then leaves me for the rest of the day with vague, other-worldly feelings of encapsulation, of vast unpassable reaches between myself and the flourishing hordes. "I should have gone all the way and become Birgitta's pimp. I'd be a happier, healthier member of society. Somebody else could teach the great masterworks of disillusionment and re-nunciation." "Yes? You would rather be a pimp than an associ-ate professor?" "That's one way of putting it." "Put it your own way." "This something in me that I turned against," I say in a fit of hopelessness, "before I even understood it, or let it have a life . . . I throttled it to death . . . killed it, practically overnight. And why? Why on earth was *murder* required?"

In the weeks that follow I attempt, between phone calls, to describe and chronicle the history of this something that, in my hopeless and de-energized state, I continue to think of as "murdered." I speak at length now not just of Helen but of Birgitta as well. I go back to Louis Jelinek, even to Herbie Bratasky, speak of all that each meant to me, what each excited and alarmed, and of how each was dealt with, in my way. "Your rogues' gallery," Klinger calls them one day in the twentieth or thirtieth week of our debate. "Moral delinquency," he observes, "has its fascination for you." "Also," I say, "for the authors of *Macbeth* and *Crime and Punishment*. Sorry to have mentioned the names of two works of art, Doctor." "Quite all right. I hear all sorts of things here. I'm used to it." "I do seem to get the feeling that it's somehow against house rules for me to call upon my literary reserves in these skirmishes of ours, but the only point I'm trying to make is that 'moral delinquency' has been on the minds of serious people for a long time now. And why 'delinquents,' anyway? Won't 'independent spirits' do? It's no *less* accurate." "I only mean to suggest that they aren't wholly harmless types." "Wholly harmless types probably lead rather constricted lives, don't you think?" "On the other hand, one oughtn't to underestimate the pain, the isolation, the uncertainty, and everything else unpleasant that may accompany 'independence' of this kind. Look at Helen now." "Please, look at me now." "I am. I do. I suspect that she is worse off. You at least haven't put *all* your eggs in that basket." "I cannot maintain an erection, Dr. Klinger. I cannot maintain a smile, for that matter." Whereupon his phone rings.

Fastened to no one and to nothing, drifting, drifting, sometimes, frighteningly, sinking; and, with the relentlessly clever and commonsensical doctor, quarreling, bickering, and debating, arguing yet again the subject which had been the source of so much martial bitterness—only when I am supine it is generally I who wind up taking Helen's part, while he who sits up takes mine.

\*

Each winter my parents come down to New York City to spend three or four days visiting family, friends, and favorite guests. In times gone by, we all used to stay on West End Avenue with my father's younger brother, Larry, a successful kosher caterer, and his wife, Sylvia, the Benvenuto Cellini of strudel, and, in childhood, my favorite aunt. Until I was fourteen, I would, to my astonished delight, be put to bed there in the same room with my cousin Lorraine. Sleeping beside a bed with a live girl in it—a "developing" girl, at that—going out to dine at Moskowitz and Lupowitz (on food described by my father as *nearly* as good as what is prepared in the kitchen of the Hungarian Royale), waiting in subfreezing temperatures to get in to see the Rockettes, sipping cocoa amid the thick draperies and the imposing furniture sets of haberdashery wholesalers and produce merchants whom I have known only in their voluminous half-sleeve shirts and their drooping swim trunks, and who are called by my father the Apple King and the Herring King and the Pajama King—everything about these New York visits holds a secret thrill for me, and invariably from "overexcitement" I develop a "strep throat" on the drive home, and back on our mountaintop have to spend at least two or three days in bed recovering. "We didn't visit Herbie," I say sullenly, only seconds before our departure—to which my mother invariably responds, "A summer isn't enough with him? We have to travel to Brooklyn to make a special trip?" "Belle, he's teasing you," my father says, but on the sly shakes a fist in my direction, as though for mentioning the Fart King to my mother I deserve no less than a blow to the head.

Now that I am back East and my uncle and aunt live in Cedarhurst, Long Island, I respond by phone to a letter from my father and invite my parents to stay in my apartment rather than at a hotel when they come down for their annual winter visit. The two rooms on West Seventy-fifth Street are not actually mine but, through an ad in the *Times*, have been sublet, furnished, from a young actor who has gone to try his luck in Hollywood. There is a crimson damask on the bedroom walls, perfumes lined up on a bathroom shelf, and, in boxes that I discover at the rear of the linen closet, a half-dozen wigs. The night I find them I indulge my curiosity and try a couple on. I look like my mother's sister.

Near the beginning of my occupancy, the phone rings one night and a man asks, "Where's Mark?" "He's in California. He'll be there for two years." "Yeah, sure. Look, you just tell him Wally's in town." "But he's not here. I have an address for him out there." I begin to recite it, but the voice, grown gruff and agitated now, interrupts: "Then who are you?" "His tenant." "Is that what they call it in the thee-yater? What do you look like, sweetpants? You got big blue eyes too?" When the calls persist, I have the telephone number changed, but then it is through the intercom that connects my apartment to the downstairs hallway of the brownstone that the repartee continues. "You just tell your little pal—" "Mark is in California, you can reach him out there." "Ha ha—that's a good one. What's your name, honey? Come to the doorway and we'll see whether I can reach you." "Come on, Wally, leave me alone. He's gone. Go away." "You like the rough stuff too?" "Oh, take off, will you?" "Take what off, sweetpants? What do you want me to take off?" So the flirtation goes.

Nights when I am at my loneliest, nights when I start talking to myself and to people who are not present, I sometimes have to suppress a powerful urge to call for help into the intercom. What holds me back isn't that it makes no sense but, rather, the fear that one of my neighbors or, what is worse, Patient Wally will be standing in the entryway just as my strident cry comes through; what I fear is the kind of help I might get—if not my homosexual suitor, the Bellevue emergency squad. So I go into the bathroom instead, close the door behind me, and leaning over the mirror to look at my own drawn face, I let it out. "I want somebody! I want somebody! I want somebody!" Sometimes I can go on like this for minutes at a time in an attempt to bring on a fit of weeping that will leave me limp and, for a while at least, empty of longing for another. I of course am not *so* far gone as to believe that screaming aloud in a closed-off room will make the somebody I want appear. Besides, who is it? If I knew I wouldn't have to holler into the mirror—I could write or phone. *I want somebody*, I cry—and it is my parents who arrive.

I carry their suitcases upstairs while my father lugs the Scotch cooler in which are packed some two-dozen round plastic containers of cabbage soup, matzoh-ball soup, kugel, and flanken, all frozen and neatly labeled. Inside the apartment my mother takes an envelope from her purse—"DAVID" is typed exactly at the center and underlined in red. The envelope contains instructions for me typewritten on hotel stationery: time required for the defrosting and heating of each dish, details as to seasoning. "Read it," she says, "and see if you have any questions." My father says, "How about if he reads it after you get out of your coat and sit down?" "I'm fine," she says. "You're tired," he tells her. "David, you have enough room in your freezer? I didn't know how big a freezer you had here." "Mamma, room to spare," I say lightly. But when I open the refrigerator she groans as though her throat has just been slit. "One this and one that, and that's it?" she cries. "Loot at that lemon, it looks older than I do. How do you eat?" "Out, mostly." "And your father told me I was overdoing it." "You've been tired," he says to her, "and you *were* overdoing." "I knew he wasn't taking care of himself," she says. "You're the one who has to take care of herself," he says. "What is it?" I ask, "what's the matter with you, Ma?" "I had a little pleurisy, and your father is making it into a production. I get a little pain when I knit for too long. That's the whole outcome of all the money thrown away on doctors and tests."

She does not know—nor do I, until my father comes with me the next morning to buy a paper and some things for breakfast and then to walk me gravely up toward where Larry and Sylvia used to put us all up on West End Avenue—that she is dying of cancer that has spread from the pancreas. This then explains his letter saying, "Maybe if we could stay with you this one time . . ." Does it also explain her request to visit landmarks she has not been to in decades? I almost believe she knows just what is happening and this display of exuberance is to spare *him* from knowing she knows. Each protecting the other from the horrible truth—my parents like two brave and helpless children . . . And what can I do about it? "But dying—*when*?" I ask him as we turn back, the two of us in tears, to my apartment. For several moments he cannot answer. "That's the worst of it," he manages finally to say. "Five weeks, five months, five years—five *minutes.* Every doctor tells me something different!"

And back at the apartment she asks me again, "Will you take us to Greenwich Village? Will you take us to the Metropolitan Museum of Art? When I worked for Mr. Clark one of the girls used to eat the most delicious green noodles at an Italian restaurant in Greenwich Village. I wish I could remember the name. It couldn't be Tony's, could it, Abe?" "Honeybunch," my father says, his voice already tinged with grief, "it wouldn't even be there after all this time." "We could look—and what if it was!" she says, turning with excitement to me. "Oh, David, how Mr. Clark loved the Museum of Art! Every Sunday when his sons were growing up he took them there to see the paintings."

I accompany them everywhere, to see the famous Rembrandts at the Metropolitan, to look for a Tony's that serves green noodles, to visit their oldest and dearest friends, some of whom I haven't seen in over fifteen years but who kiss and embrace me as though I were still a child, and then, because I am a professor, ask me serious questions about the world situation; we go, as of old, to the zoo and to the planetarium, and finally on a pilgrimage to the building where she was once a legal secretary. Following lunch in Chinatown, we stand at the corner of Broad and Wall Streets on a chilly Sunday afternoon, and, as always, with perfect innocence, she reminisces about her days with the firm. And how different for her it would have been, I think, had she stayed on to be one of Mr. Clark's girls for life, one of those virgin spinsters who adore the fatherly boss and play auntie on holidays to the boss's children. Without the interminable demands of a family-run resort hotel, she might actually have known some serenity, have lived in accordance with her simple gifts for tidiness and order rather than at their mercy. On the other hand, she would never have known my father and me—*we* would never have been. If only, if only . . . If only what? She has cancer.

They sleep in the double bed in the bedroom while I lie awake under a blanket on the living-room sofa. My mother is about to vanish—that's what it comes down to. And her last memory of her only child will be of his meager, rootless existence—her last memory will be of this lemon I live with!

Oh, with what disgust and remorse do I recall the series of mistakes—no, the one habitual and recurrent mistake—that has made these two rooms my home. Instead of being enemies, of providing one another with the *ideal* enemy, why couldn't Helen and I have put that effort into satisfying each other, into steady, dedicated living? Would that have been so hard for two such strong-willed people? *Should* I have said at the very outset, "Look, we're having a child"? Lying there listening to my mother breathing her last, I try to infuse myself with new resolve: I must, I *will*, end this purposeless, pointless . . . and into my thoughts comes Elisabeth, of all people, with the locket around her neck and her broken arm healed. How sweet, how welcoming she would be to my widowed father! But without an Elisabeth, what can I do for him? How ever will he survive up there on his own? Oh, why must it be Helen and Birgitta at one extreme or life with a lemon at the other?

As the sleepless minutes pass—or, rather, do not seem to pass at all—all the thoughts that can possibly distress me seem to coalesce into an unidentifiable nonsense word that will not let me be. To free myself from its insipid thralldom, I begin to toss angrily from one side of the couch to the other. I feel half in, half out of deep anesthesia—immersed back in the claustrophobic agonies of the recovery room, which I last saw at the age of twelve, following my appendectomy—until the word resolves itself at last into nothing other than the line of keys, read from left to right, on which my mother taught me to rest the tips of my fingers when I learned typing from her on the hotel's Remington Noiseless. But now that I know the origin of this commonplace alphabetical scrambling, it is worse even than before. As though it *is* a word after all, and the one that holds within its unutterable syllables all the pain of her baffled energies and her frenetic life. And the pain of my own. I suddenly see myself struggling with my father over her epitaph, the two of us are hurling each other against enormous pieces of rock, while I insist to the stonecutter that ASDFGHJKL be carved beneath her name on the tombstone.

I cannot sleep. I wonder if it is possible that I will never be able to sleep again. All my thoughts are either simple or crazy, and after a while I cannot distinguish which is which. I want to go into the bedroom and get into their bed. I rehearse in my mind how I will do it. To ease them out of their initial timidity, I will just sit first at the edge of the bed and quietly talk to them about the best of the past. Looking down at their familiar faces side by side on the fresh pillowcases, at their two faces peering out at me from above the sheet drawn up to their chins, I will remind them of how very long it's been since last we all snuggled up together under a single blanket. Wasn't it in a tourist cabin just outside Lake Placid? Remember that little box of a room? Was it 1940 or '41? And, am I right, didn't it cost Dad just one dollar for the night? Mother thought that it would be good for me to see the Thousand Islands and Niagara Falls during my Easter vacation. That's where we were headed, in the Dodge. Remember, you told us how Mr. Clark took his little boys each summer to see the sights of Europe; remember all those things you told me that I had never heard before; God, remember me and the two of you and the little Dodge back before the war . . . and then, when they are smiling, I will take off my robe and crawl into the bed between them. And before she dies, we will all hold each other through one last night and morning. Who will ever know, aside from Klinger, and why should I care what he or anyone makes of it?

Near midnight the doorbell rings. At the intercom in the kitchenette I depress the lever and ask, "Who is it?"

"The plumber, sweetpants. Last time you were out. How's your leak, fixed yet?"

I don't respond. My father has come into the living room in his robe. "Somebody you know? At this hour?"

"Just some clown," I say, as the bell rings now to the rhythm of "Shave and a Haircut."

"What is it?" my mother calls from the bedroom.

"Nothing, Ma. Go to sleep."

I decide to speak into the intercom one more time. "Cut it out or I'm going to call the cops."

"Call 'em. Nothing I'm doing is actionable, kiddo. Why don't you just let me up? I'm not half bad, you know. I'm all bad."

My father, standing now at my elbow and listening, has gone a little white.

"Dad," I say, "go back to bed. It's just one of those things that happen in New York. It's nothing."

"He knows you?"

"No."

"Then how does he know to come here? Why does he talk like that?"

A pause, and the bell is ringing again.

Thoroughly irritated now, I say, "Because the fellow I sublet from is a homosexual—and, as best I can gather, this was a friend of his."

"A Jewish fellow?"

"Who I rented from? Yes."

"Jesus," snaps my father, "what the hell is the *matter* with a guy like that?"

"I think I'm going to have to go downstairs."

"By yourself?"

"I'll be all right."

"Don't be crazy—two is better than one. I'll come with you."

"Dad, that's not necessary."

From the bedroom my mother calls, "Now what?"

"Nothing," my father says. "The bell is stuck. We're going downstairs to fix it."

"At this hour?" she calls.

"We'll be right back," my father says to her. "Stay in bed." To me he whispers, "You got some kind of stick, a bat or something?"

"No, no—"

"What if he's armed? You got an umbrella, at least?"

In the meantime, the ringing has stopped. "Maybe he's gone," I say.

My father listens.

"He's gone," I say. "He left."

My father, however, has no intention of going back to bed now. Closing the door to the bedroom—"Shhhh," he whispers to my mother, "everything's fine, go to sleep"—he comes to sit across from the sofa. I can hear how heavily he is breathing as he prepares himself to speak. I am not all that relaxed myself. Propped stiffly up against the pillow, I wait for the bell to start ringing again.

"You're not involved"—he clears his throat—"with something you want to tell me about . . ."

"Don't be silly."

"Because you left us, Davey, when you were seventeen years old and since then there has been no interfering with the kind of influences you let yourself under."

"Dad, I'm not under any 'influences.'"

"I want to ask you a question. Outright."

"Go ahead."

"It's not about Helen. I never asked you about that, and I don't want to start now. I always treated her like a daughter-in-law. Didn't I, didn't your mother, always with respect—?"

"Yes, absolutely."

"I held my tongue. We didn't want her to turn against us. She can have nothing against us to this day. All things considered, I think we did excellent. I am a liberal person, son—and in my politics even more than liberal. Do you know that in 1924 I voted for Norman Thomas for the governor of New York with the first vote I ever cast? And in '48 I voted for Henry Wallace—which maybe was meaningless and a mistake, but the point is that I was probably the only hotel owner in the whole country who voted for somebody that everybody was calling a Communist. Which he wasn't—but the point is, I have never been a narrow man, never. You know—and if you don't, you should—it was never that the woman was a shiksa that bothered me. Shiksas are a fact of life and they are not going to go away just because Jewish parents might like it better that way. And why should they? I am a believer in all the races and religions living together in harmony, and that you married a Gentile girl was never the point to your mother and me. I think we did excellent on that score. But that doesn't mean I could stomach the rest of her and her attitudes. The truth of the matter, if you want to know, is that I didn't have a good night's sleep in the three years you were married."

"Well, neither did I."

"Is that true? Then why the hell didn't you get out right off the bat? Why did you get in that damn mess to begin with?"

"You want me to go over that territory, do you?"

"No, no—you're right—the hell with it. As far as I'm concerned, if I never hear her name again, that won't be too soon. You are all I care about."

"What do you want to ask?"

"David, what is Tofranil, that I see it in the medicine chest, a big bottle full? What are you taking this drug for?"

"It's an anti-depressant. Tofranil."

He hisses. Disgust, frustration, disbelief, contempt. I must first have heard that sound out of him a hundred years ago, when he had to fire a waiter who wet his bed and stank up the attic where the help slept. "And *why* do you need that? Who told you to take a thing like that and put it in your bloodstream?"

"A psychiatrist."

"You go to a psychiatrist?"

"Yes."

"*Why?*" he cries.

"To keep me afloat. To figure things out. To have someone to talk to . . . confidentially."

"Why not a *wife* to talk to? That's what a wife is for! I mean this time a *real* wife, not somebody who it must have cost you your whole school salary just to pay the beauty parlors. All this is all *wrong*, son. It is no way to live! A psychiatrist, and being on strong drugs, and people showing up at all hours—people who aren't even people—"

"There is nothing to get worked up about."

"There is *everything* to get worked up about."

"No, no," I say, lowering my voice. "Dad, there is only Mother . . ."

He puts a hand over his eyes and quickly begins to cry. With his other hand he makes a fist which he waves at me. "This is what I have had to be all my life! *Without* psychiatrists, *without* happy pills! I am a man who has never said die!"

And once again, the downstairs doorbell.

"Forget it. Let it ring. Dad, he'll go away."

"And then come back? I'll crack his head open, and, believe me, then he'll go away for good!"

Here the bedroom door opens and my mother appears in her nightgown. "Who are you cracking in the head?"

"Some lousy stinking fairy who won't leave him alone!"

The bell again: two shorts, a long; two shorts, a long. Wally is drunk.

*Her* eyes tearful now, my tiny mother says, "And how often does this go on?"

"Not often."

"But—why don't you report him?"

"Because by the time the police come he'd be gone. You don't want the police for something like this."

"And you swear to me," says my father, "this is nobody you know?"

"I swear to you."

My mother comes into the living room and sits beside me. She takes my hand and clutches it. The three of us listen to the bell—mother, father, and son.

"You know what would fix the son of a bitch once and for all?" my father says. "Boiling water."

"*Abe!*" cries my mother.

"But it would teach him where he don't belong!"

"Dad, you mustn't make too much of it."

"And don't you make so little! Why do you hang *around* with such people?"

"But I don't."

"Then why do you live in a place like this, where they show up and make trouble for you? Do you need more trouble still?"

"Calm down, please," says my mother. "It isn't *his* fault some maniac rings his doorbell. This is New York. He told you. This is what happens."

"That doesn't mean you leave yourself unprotected, Belle!" Jumping up from his chair, he rushes to the intercom. "Hey! You!" He shouts, "Cut it out! This is David's father—!"

Stroking her arm—already skeletal—I whisper, "It's okay, it's all right, he's not working the thing right anyway. Don't worry, Ma, please—the fellow can't even hear him."

"—you want third-degree burns, we'll give them to you! Do what you want to do in some gutter somewhere, but if you know what's good for you, don't come near my son!"

Two months later, in the hospital in Kingston, my mother dies. After the funeral guests have all left, my father urges me to take the food she has frozen for me only the month before, the last things cooked by her on this earth. I say, "And what are *you* going to eat?" "I was a short-order man before you were even born. Take it. Take what she made for you." "Dad, how are you going to live here by yourself? How are you possibly going to manage the season? Why did you shoo everybody away? Don't be so brave. You can't stay up here alone." "I can look after myself fine. Her going is not something we didn't expect. Please, take it. Take it all. She wanted you to. She said whenever she remembered the inside of your refrigerator, she saw red. She cooked for you," he says, his voice trembling, "and then she went away." He begins to sob. I put my arms around him. "Nobody understood her," he says, "the guests, never, *never*. She was a good person, Davey. When she was young, everything thrilled her, the littlest things even. She had a nervous nature only when the summer got hectic and out of control. So they made fun of her. But do you remember the winter? The peace and quiet? The fun we had? Remember the letters at night?" Those words do it: for the first time since her death the morning before, I break down completely. "Of course I do, sure I do." "Oh, sonny, that's when she was herself. Only who knew it?" "We did," I tell him, but he repeats, with an angry sob, "And who knew it!"

He carries the frozen food in a shopping bag out to my car. "Here, please, in her memory." And so I return to New York with the half-dozen containers each bearing the same typewritten label: "Tongue with Grandma's famous raisin sauce— 2 portions."

Within a week, I am driving back up to the country again, this time with my Uncle Larry, to take my father to Cedarhurst, where he will move in with his brother and sister-in-law. Though only temporarily, he says while we pack his suitcase in the car; just till he is over the shock. In a few days he is sure he will be himself. He has to be, that's all there is to it. "I've been working since I was fourteen years old. You don't give in to a thing like this," he says. "You tighten your belt and you go on." Besides, it is winter, and there is always the risk up there of fire. Yes, the handyman and his wife will be living on the grounds, but that is no guarantee against the possibility of the hotel burning down in his absence.

It is true, of course, that dozens of mysterious fires have broken out in abandoned hotels and boardinghouses ever since the region began to pass out of fashion as a Jewish summer resort at about the time I was going off to college, but as he and my mother have been able, even in recent years, to hang on to a remnant of their aging clientele and to keep the main house open and the grounds respectable-looking, the arsonists had never before seemed to him a real threat. But now on the drive down the Thruway they are all he can think about. He names for my uncle and me the local hoodlums—"Men, thirty- and forty-year-old men!"—whom he has always suspected of setting the fires. "No, no," he says to my uncle, who has offered his standard analysis as to where the trouble begins, "not even anti-Semites. Too stupid even for that! Just plain de- mented no-good idiots, fit for the lunatic asylum. Just people who like to see flames! And when it is in ashes, you know who they will accuse? I've seen it a dozen times. Me! That I did it for the insurance money! Because my wife is gone and I want to get out! The blame will fall on my good name! And half the time you know who else I sometimes think that does it? The volunteer fire fighters themselves! Yes—so they can rush out in the fire engines in the middle of the night and ride up and down the mountain in their helmets and boots!"

Even after he is comfortably installed in what used to be Lorraine's bedroom, there is no calming his fears for the em- pire built of his sweat and his blood. Every night I call him on the phone and he tells me he cannot get to sleep for worrying about a fire. And he has other things to worry about now as well. "That fairy never came back, did he?" "No," I say, knowing it best to lie. "See—it paid to threaten him. Unfortu- nately that's all some people understand, is the fist," says my father, who has never struck another person in his life. "And how are Uncle Larry and Aunt Sylvia?" I ask. "Wonderful. They couldn't be kinder. Every other word is 'Stay.'" "Well, that sounds reassuring," I say. But no, another ten days, he tells me, and the worst of being without her will be over. Has to be. He has to get back up there while the damn place is still in one piece!

And then it is another five days, and then another, until at last, following an emotional Sunday car ride alone with me, he agrees to put the Hungarian Royale up for sale. His face in his hands, he says, "But I never said die in my life." "There's no shame in it, Dad. Things have just changed." "But I don't *give* up," he cries. "Nobody is going to see it that way," I say, and drive him back to his brother's.

And during this time hardly a night passes when I do not

think about the girl I knew for barely two months back when I was a twenty-two-year-old sexual prodigy, the girl who wore a locket around her neck with her father's picture in it. I even think of writing to her, in care of her parents. I even get up out of bed and search through my papers, looking for the Stockholm address. But by now Elisabeth must certainly be married and a mother two or three times over, and assuredly she does not think of me. No woman alive thinks of me, certainly not with love.

Though my department chairman Arthur Schonbrunn is a handsome and exquisitely groomed middle-aged man of unflagging charm and punctiliousness—as adroit and gracious a social being as I have ever seen in action—his wife, Deborah, is someone for whom I have never been able to work up much enthusiasm, even when I was Arthur's favorite graduate student and she was frequently my affectionate and hospitable hostess. In those first years at Stanford, I used to spend a certain amount of my time, in fact, trying to figure out what bound a man so scrupulous about the amenities, so tirelessly concerned to oppose, from the highest principles, the burgeoning political assaults upon university curriculum—what bound such a man of conscience to a woman whose very favorite public performance was in the role of the dizzy dame whose beguiling charm is her reckless and impudent "candor"? The very first time I was invited by Arthur to have dinner with the two of them, I remember thinking at the end of the evening's conversation—conversation consisting largely of Deborah's coquettishly "outrageous" chatter—"This is surely the loneliest man alive." How pained and disenchanted I was at twenty-three by this first look into my fatherly professor's domestic life . . . only to be told by Arthur the following day about his wife's "wonderful powers of observation" and her "gift" for "getting right to the heart of the problem." And, along these lines, I remember another night, years later, when Arthur and I were working late in our offices—that is, Arthur was at work, while I was immobile at my desk, hopeless as usual about the loveless impasse Helen and I had reached and hadn't the strength or the courage to resolve. When Arthur saw me apparently looking even more benumbed than usual, he came in and, until 3 a.m., tried his best to protect me from the crazier sort of solutions that might enter the head of a dreadfully unhappy husband having trouble getting himself to go home. Time and again he reminded me of the fine piece of work my thesis had been. The important thing now was to get back to revising it for book publication. Indeed, much that Arthur said to me that night sounded very like what Dr. Klinger was eventually to say to me about me, my work, and Helen. And I, in turn, poured out my grievances, and at one point lowered my face to my desk and wept. "I figured it was that bad," said Arthur. "We both did. But much as we care for you, we never felt it was our business to say anything. We've had enough experience by now to know that always comes between friends, sooner or later. But still there were days when I wanted to shake you for being such a fool. You don't know how many times I talked to Debbie about what could be done to get you to save yourself from all this unhappiness. Nothing was more upsetting for us than remembering what you'd been like when you first got here, and then seeing what was happening to you with her. But I couldn't do a thing, David, unless you came to me—and that's not how you go about things. You're someone who goes so far with people, and no further, and the result is that you're rather more alone with yourself than many people are. I'm not so unlike that myself."

Near the end of his vigil—and for the first time ever—Arthur spoke about his own personal life almost as though we were men of the same age and rank. In his twenties, when he was an instructor at Minnesota, he too had been involved with "a wildly neurotic and destructive woman." Scandalous public quarrels, two harrowing abortions, despair so enormous that he had actually come to think that suicide was the only way he might ever be able to extricate himself from his confusion and pain. He showed me a small scar on his hand, where this mad, pathetic little librarian, whom he could not stand and yet could not leave, had once stabbed him with a table fork at breakfast . . . And while Arthur tried to give me hope (and guidance) by associating his own early misfortune—and subsequent recovery—with what I was going through, I only wanted to say, "But how dare you? What do you call what you have now? Debbie is so *common*; her spontaneity so much guile-filled play-acting; her candor so much tactless showing-off; capricious for the company; devilish for Daddy—Arthur, none of it means a thing, audacious behavior with nothing at stake! While Helen—my God, Helen is a hundred times, Helen is a thousand times . . ." But of course I rose to no such heights of virtuous indignation, uttered no words so foolish as these about the falsity and shallowness of his wife as against the integrity, intelligence, charm, beauty, and bravery of mine—uxoriousness, after all, being his line, and certainly that night, dreams of uxoricide being somewhat more like mine.

Is this chivalry of Arthur's to be pitied or envied? Is my former mentor and current benefactor a little bit of a liar, a little bit of a masochist, or is he just in love? Or is it that Debbie, with her slightly shrill kittenishness and vaguely slatternly good looks, is the touch of the disreputable that makes bearable an otherwise stiflingly decorous life?

"Vizzied" is the diagnosis rendered by our resident poet, Ralph Baumgarten: "vizzied" or "vizzified"—both adjectives deriving from "vizzy," an uncommon noun of Baumgarten's strewn throughout his verse, rhyming with "fizzy" and "tizzy," closely related to "fuzzy" and "buzz," and referring, of course, to the pudenda. The vizz-ridden—to this class of husbands is Arthur Schonbrunn consigned by the unmarried poet—are those who slavishly conform to standards of propriety and respectability which, as Baumgarten sees it, have been laid down by generations of women to disarm and domesticate men. Of which domestication the poet himself is clearly having none. I tend to agree with Baumgarten that it is in part because of his own decidedly undeferential attitude toward the other gender—and his sexual predilections generally—that the young literary roughneck is not to be reappointed when his contract here runs out. However, if he has, by his manner, earned the disdain of certain of our colleagues and their wives, it has not caused him to be any less flagrant about what he likes and how he likes it. For him flagrancy appears to be much of the fun. "Picked up a girl at the Modern Museum, and on our way out we ran into your pals, Kepesh. Debbie hustled the girl off to the ladies' room to get the latest lowdown on me, and Arthur, in the course of his pleasantries, asked how long Rita and I had been friends. I told him about an hour and a half. I said we were leaving because the museum seemed to afford no comfortable corner where we might go down on each other. But what, I wondered, did Arthur make of her plump little behind? Well, he wouldn't tell me. Gave me a lecture on compassion, instead."

No arguing that Baumgarten throws a rather large net out to catch his little minnows in. When the two of us are walking on the streets of Manhattan, hardly a woman under fifty or a girl over fifteen passes by from whom he does not attempt to extract information that he manages to intimate is absolutely vital to his survival. "Gee, what a nice coat!" he says, flashing his grin at a young woman in a ratty fur pushing a baby carriage. "Oh, thanks." "May I ask what it's made of? What kind of an animal was that? I never saw a coat quite like that before." "This? It's a fake." "*Really?*" Within minutes he is barely this side of stupefaction (not all of it feigned, either) at learning that this young woman in the fake fur is already divorced, the mother of three small children, and a dropout from the University of Two Thousand Miles Away. To me, standing self-consciously off to the side, he calls, "Did you hear that, Dave? This is Alice. Alice was born in Montana—yet here she is wheeling a baby carriage in New York." And no less than Baumgarten, the young mother herself now seems a little wonderstruck to have been transported such a distance in a mere twenty-four years.

Success with strangers, Baumgarten informs me, resides in never asking a question of them that can't be answered without thinking, and then being wholly attentive to the reply, no matter how pedestrian. "You remember your James, Kepesh—'Dramatize, dramatize.' Get these people to understand that who they are and where they're from and what they wear is *interesting*. In a manner of speaking, *momentous. That's* compassion. And, please, display no irony, will you? Your problem is you scare 'em off with your wonderful feel for the complexity of things. My experience is that the ordinary woman in the streets doesn't cotton to irony, really. It's irony, really, that pisses her off. She wants attention. She wants appreciation. She surely doesn't want to match wits with you, boy. Save all that subtlety for your critical article. When you get out there on the street, *open up.* That's what streets are *for*."

During my first months at the university I discover that when Baumgarten's name comes up at faculty gatherings there is always someone around who cannot stand the sight of him, and is more than willing to say why. Debbie Schonbrunn holds that the "abomination-in-residence" would be comical were he not so—the word is a favorite of hers and Arthur's—"destructive." Of course in response I need say nothing: just drink my drink and start back to New York. "Oh, he's not so bad," I tell her. "In fact," I add, "I sort of like him." "And what is there to 'like' so?" Go home, Kepesh. That empty apartment is where you belong; between this predictable discussion and that faggy apartment, there is no doubt where you will be better off. "What is there to *dislike* so?" I reply. "Where do I begin?" asks Deborah; "his contempt for women, for one thing. He is a murderous, conscienceless womanizer. He hates women." "Looks to me as though he rather likes them." "David, you are being contrary and disingenuous, and just a little hostile, and I'm really not sure why. Ralph Baumgarten is an abomination and so is his poetry. I have never read anything so dehumanized in my life. Read that first book of his and see for yourself just how much he likes girls." "Well, I haven't read him yet"—a lie—"but we've had lunch a few times. He isn't so reprehensible, as far as I can see. Could be, Deborah, that the poetry isn't exactly the man." "Ah, but it *is*: mean and smug and overbearing and actually quite stupid. And what *about* 'the man'? That walk of his, that *glide*; those army clothes; that face—well, actually he hasn't got a face, has he? Just mean, flat eyes and that surly grin. The mystery is how any girl can even go near him." "Well, he must have something." "Or *they* lack something. Really, you have such innate elegance and he is a carrion vulture right down to his claws, and why you would want even to associate with him . . ." "I get along with him," I say, shrugging my shoulders, and *now* put down my drink and go on home.

Soon enough, news reaches me as to what Debbie's powers of observation have uncovered in our conversation. It is what I should have expected, certainly, and probably what I deserve. The only surprise, really, is my surprise—that, and the vulnerability.

It seems that at a dinner party at the Schonbrunns' the hostess had announced to all in attendance that Baumgarten has become David Kepesh's "alter ego," "acting out fantasies of aggression against women" David harbors as a consequence of his marriage and its "mortifying" ending. The mortifying ending in Hong Kong—the cocaine, the cops, the works—as well as mortifying tidbits from the beginning and the middle were then narrated for the edification of all. I am given these details by a nice enough man, a guest at the Schonbrunns', who is no part of this story, and who thought he was doing me a good turn.

A correspondence ensues. Initiated by me and, alas, perpetuated by me too.

Dear Debbie:

Word has reached me that at a dinner party last week you were talking a little freely about my private affairs—namely, my marriage, my "mortifications," and what you are said to have described as my "aggressive fantasies against women." How would you know about my fantasies, if I may ask? And why should Helen and I be the subject for dinner conversation among people most of whom I have never even met? For the sake of a friendship with Arthur which goes back some time now, and which we have only just had the chance to rekindle, I hope that you will refrain in the future from discussing with perfect strangers my aggressive fantasies and my mortifying history. Otherwise, it is going to be difficult for me to be myself with Arthur, and, of course, with you.

> Sincerely,
> David

Dear David:

I do apologize for blabbing to people who don't know you, and won't do it again. Although I would do anything if you'll tell me the name of the s.o.b. who spilled his and/or her guts. Just so they don't set their teeth in my rack of lamb again!

To salve your wounds, I want to add, first, that your name only came up in passing—alas, you weren't the subject of a whole night's conversation—and, second, I think you have every justification for resenting Helen as much as you do, and, third, it isn't really so strange or shameful that your anger with Helen should take the form for now of an association with a young man who punishes women the way that vulture does. But, if you view your friendship with him one way, and I see it another, that's certainly all right with me—as I think it should be with you.

Lastly, if I spoke thoughtlessly about Helen to my dinner guests, it is probably because back at Stanford she was, as you well know, rather ostentatious about herself, and consequently a prime topic of conversation among any number of people, including your friends. And you yourself were not averse to talking about her with us, whenever you came home with Arthur.

But, dear David, enough of this is enough. Will you come to have dinner with us—how is this Friday night? Come, by yourself or with somebody (other than the Visigoth) if you like. If you bring a girl I promise I won't breathe a word about your misogyny all the time you're here.

Love,<br>Debbie

P.S. I'd give anything to know the name of the skunk who turned me in.

Dear Debbie:

I can't say that your reply strikes me as satisfactory. You seem not at all to grasp how indiscreet you were with what you know, and think you know, about me. Surely that I shared certain confidences with Arthur, and he in turn shared them with you, cannot be offered to me as a mitigating factor. Do you understand why? Nor do I see how you can fail to realize that my marriage is still painful to me, and the pain is not lessened when I learn that it is being discussed like so much soap opera by people to whom I once unburdened myself of some of my troubles.

The spirit in which your letter was written only seems to have worsened the situation for me, and I don't see any way to accept your invitation.

David

Dear David:

I'm sorry you found my note unsatisfactory. Actually it was purposely superficial in tone—I rather thought it suited what you considered my crime.

Do you really see me as some harridan hell-bent on sullying your spotless reputation or invading your privacy by vicious, hurtful innuendo? Obviously you do, and that's monstrous, of course, but simply because you believe it to be so, doesn't make it so.

I apologized for speaking carelessly about you to strangers, because I know I do that sometimes. I assumed that what came back to you was just that—foolish and careless. I know I never said anything so awful it would cause you any pain. Remembering back to your own judgments of yourself with the ladies—stories of your student days, remember?—I never dreamt you saw yourself as being beyond reproach. I will admit I never saw you as a perfect angel in relation to women, but neither did it think that summed you up as a person. I did enjoy you and care for you as a friend.

I must say I would be very sorry to hear that you had flailed out at any of those others who were your friends in California just because they were "indiscreet" enough to mention you in conversation. And to mention you not out of unkindness, or viciousness or malice, but only because they happen to know all you have been through.

I am afraid that your letter tells me more about you than I care to know.

Debbie

Dear David:

Debbie is replying to your last letter, but now I feel compelled to mix in too.

It seems to me that Debbie made an effort, stopping short of abject prostration before you, to apologize for what she considered a just complaint. At the same time she tried to indicate by her joking tone that what she did was not as serious as you seem to feel. I agree with her from what I know about the situation, and it strikes me that your last letter, with its aggressive, exasperated, self-righteous tone, is more seriously hurtful than anything Deborah may have been guilty of. I have no idea, by the way, what you think Deborah may have said about you (a little documentation would have helped here), but I can assure you that it was little more than dinner-table conversation that lasted a few minutes and maligned you in no way. I suspect that you may have said a lot worse about her in passing conversations (though presumably not before strangers). It seems to me that friends ought to be more willing to forgive each other their occasional frailties.

Sincerely,<br>Arthur

Dear Arthur:

You can't have it both ways: that Debbie took "a joking tone" or, as she put it, a "purposely superficial . . . tone" because that best expressed her attitude toward what was bothering me, and that simultaneously she "made an effort short of abject prostration" before me. Debbie's indiscretion was of course forgivable, and I indicated as much in my first letter. But that she should continue, not only to be so obtuse, but to be so casual about all this, leads me to view her lapse as something other than an example of "occasional frailty" displayed by a friend.

David

Dear David:

I have hesitated about replying to your last letter because it left me with very little to say. I find it incredible you could even imagine Deborah ever meant you any harm. It is also somewhat incredible that you fail to see that in blowing up this situation as you have, you are arguing only too well for the truth of Deborah's observation about the aggressive nature of your attitude toward women these days. Rather than pressing on with the attack, why don't you stop and think for a moment why it was you refused to accept the apology she made for her tactlessness at the outset—why did you prefer instead to jeopardize our friendship in order to beat her over the head with her alleged misconduct?

Short of divorcing Debbie and sending her out in the street in rags, I don't know what I can do that would prove sufficient to restore friendly relations between you. I'd be grateful to hear any suggestions.

Sincerely,
Arthur

It is Klinger who mercifully utters the magic formula that puts an end to all this. I tell him what I intend to say in my next message to Arthur—already half typed in a second draft—about the Freudian noose that he would now like to tighten around my neck. And I am still a little wild about his request, two letters back (and tucked between parentheses), for "a little documentation." What does he think we are, student and teacher, still Ph.D. candidate and dissertation adviser? Those letters weren't sent him for a grade! I don't care how beholden I am supposed to be—I won't have them saying I am something I am not! I will not be maligned and belittled by her reckless neurotic slander! Nor will I let Helen be slandered either! "Aggressive fantasies"! All that means is I can't stand *her*! And why the hell *doesn't* he throw her out into the street in rags? It's a marvelous idea! I'd *respect* him for it! The whole community would!

When my day's tirade has run its course, Klinger says, "So she gossips about you—who the hell pays any attention?"

Eleven words, but all at once I am, yes, mortified, and see *myself* for the neurotic fool. So peevish! So purposeless still! Without focus, without meaning—without a single friend! And making only enemies! My angry letters to the Devoted Couple constitute the whole of my critical writing since my return to the East, all I have been able to marshal sufficient concentration, stamina, and wisdom to get down on paper. Why, I spend entire evenings rewriting them for brevity and tone . . . while my Chekhov book has all but been abandoned. Imagine —drafts and drafts, and of what? Nothing! Oh, something about the drift of things doesn't look right to me, Doctor. Fending off Wally, fighting with Debbie, hanging on for dear life to your apron strings—oh, where is the way of living that will make all this nothingness *truly* nothing, instead of being all I have and all I do?

Strangely, my run-in with the Schonbrunns serves to enliven a friendship with Baumgarten that hadn't really amounted to much before—or, not so strangely at all, given those old vested interests contending for a say in my new and barely lived-in life. Following what I take to be the doctor's orders, I abandon the Schonbrunn correspondence—though indignant rejoinders, *clinching* rejoinders, continue to provide lively company as I drive along the Expressway to school each morning—and then late one afternoon, acting on what I assume at the time to be a harmless impulse, I stop at Baumgarten's office and ask him to join me for coffee. And the following Sunday evening, when I return from a visit to my father and find that back in my apartment I am, on the scale of loneliness, hovering near a hundred—right up there with my own dad—I turn down the flame under the soup I am warming in my little spinster's sauce-pan, and telephone Baumgarten to invite him to come share the very last container of food prepared and frozen by my mother.

Soon we are meeting once a week for dinner at a small Hun-garian restaurant on upper Broadway, not far from where each of us lives. No more than Wally is Baumgarten the someone for whom I used to cry out before the bathroom mirror during my first months of mourning in New York (the mourning that preceded the mourning for the only one of us who actually died). But then that longed-for someone may very likely never turn up—because in fact she already did: was here, was mine, and has been lost, destroyed because of some terrible mecha-nism that causes me to challenge and challenge—finally to chal-lenge to the death—what once I thought I wanted most. Yes, I miss Helen! Suddenly I *want* Helen! How meaningless and ridiculous all those arguments seem now! What a gorgeous, lively, passionate creature! Bright, funny, mysterious—and gone! Oh, why on earth did I do what I did? It all should have been so different! And when, if ever, will there be another?

So—little more than a decade of adult life behind me, and already I have the sense that all my chances have been used up; indeed, pondering my past over that pathetic little enameled saucepan, I invariably feel as though I have not simply been through a bad marriage but in fact through all the female sex, and that I am so constructed as to live harmoniously with no one.

Over cucumber salad and stuffed cabbage (not bad, but nothing to compare, I inform Baumgarten—and sounding not so unlike my father—to the Hungarian Royale in its heyday), I show him an old picture of Helen, as inviting and seductive a passport photo as may ever have passed through customs. I have unstapled it from her International Driver's License, which turned up only recently—to each his own discordances and incongruities—in a carton of Stanford papers, among my lecture notes on François Mauriac. I bring Helen's photograph to dinner with me, then wonder for half the meal whether to take it out of my wallet or, rather, wonder why I would. Some ten days earlier I had brought the picture to his office to show to Klinger, intending to prove to him that, blind as I may have been to certain dire consequences, I was by no means blind to everything.

"A real beauty," says Baumgarten when, with some of the anxiety of a student handing in a plagiarized paper, I pass the picture across the table. And then I am hanging on to his every word! "A queen bee, all right," he says. "Yes, sir, and followed aloft by the drones." He is a long time savoring it. Too long. "Makes me jealous," he informs me, and not to be polite either. He is reporting a genuine emotion.

Well, I think, at least *he* won't disparage her, or me . . . yet I am reluctant to go ahead now and try to puzzle out anything truly personal in Baumgarten's presence, as though any challenge he might offer to Klinger's perspective—and the willingness with which I now try to yield to it—might actually send me reeling, perhaps even all the way back to where I was when I would start off the day on my knees. It hardly pleases me, of course, to feel so susceptible still to this sort of confusion, or to feel so very thinly protected from the elements by my therapy, or to find that, at this moment, I seem to share Debbie Schonbrunn's sense of Baumgarten as a source of contamination. The fact is that I *do* look forward to our evening out together, that I *am* interested in listening to the stories he tells, stories, as with Helen, of someone on the friendliest of terms with the sources of his excitement, and confidently opposed to—in fact, rather amused by—all that stands in opposition. Yet it is also a fact that my attachment to Baumgarten is increasingly marked by uncertainty, by what amount at times almost to seizures of doubt, the stronger our friendship grows.

Baumgarten's family story is pretty much a story of pain and little else. The father, a baker, died only recently, destitute and alone on the ward of a V.A. hospital—he had deserted his family sometime during Baumgarten's adolescence ("later rather than sooner"), and only after years of horrific depressions that had all but turned family life into one long tearful wake. Baumgarten's mother had worked for thirty years stitching gloves in a loft near Penn Station, fearful of her boss, of the shop steward, of the subway platform and the third rail, then at home afraid of the cellar stairs, the gas oven, the fuse box, even of a hammer and a nail. She had suffered a disabling stroke when Ralph was at college, and since has been staring at the wall in a Jewish home for the aged and infirm in Woodside. Every Sunday morning when her youngest child pays his visit—wearing that cocky grin on his face, bearing the *Sunday News* under his arm, and in his hand carrying a little paper bag from the delicatessen with her bagel in it—the nurse precedes him into the room with a perky introduction intended to give a lift to the frail little woman sitting like a sack in her chair, safe at last from all the world's weaponry: "Guess who's here with the goodies, Mildred. Your professor!"

Aside from those expenses of the mother's care which are not covered by the government and which Baumgarten pays out of his university salary, there has also fallen to him a father's responsibilities to his older sister, who lives in New Jersey with three children and a husband who haplessly runs a dry-cleaning store there. The three kids Uncle Baumgarten describes as "dummies"; the sister he describes as "lost," raised from infancy on the mother's terrors and the father's gloom, and now, at about my age, alive to nothing but a welter of superstitions which, says Baumgarten, have come through untouched from the shtetl. Because of her looks, and her clothes, and the odd things she says to her children's schoolmates, she is known as the "gypsy lady" in the Paramus housing development where the family lives.

It surprises me, hearing tales of this mercilessly beaten-down clan from its inextinguishable survivor, that Baumgarten has never, to my knowledge, written a single line about the way in which his unhappy family is unlike any other, or about why he cannot turn his back on the wreckage, despite the disgust aroused in him by memories of his upbringing in this household of the dead. No, not a single word on that subject in his two books of verse, the first impudently titled, at twenty-four, *Baumgarten's Anatomy*, and the most recent, called after a line from an erotic poem of Donne's, *Behind, Before, Above, Between, Below*. I must admit to myself—if not to a Schonbrunn —that after a week of Baumgarten as bedtime reading, the interest I have long had in the fittings and fixtures of the other sex seems to me just about sated. Yet, narrow as his subject strikes me—or, rather, his means of exploration—I find in the blend of shameless erotomania, microscopic fetishism, and rather dazzling imperiousness a character at work whose unswerving sense of his own imperatives cannot but arouse my curiosity. But then at first even watching him eat his dinner arouses my curiosity—it is as hard at times for me to watch as it is to look away. Is it really the untamed animal in him that causes this carnivore to tear at the meat between his teeth with such stupendous muscle power, or does he not masticate his food genteelly simply because the rest of us agree to do it that way? Where *did* he first eat flesh, in Queens or in a cave? One night the sight of Baumgarten's incisors severing the meat from the bone of his breaded veal chop sends me home later to my bookshelves to take down the collection of Kafka's stories and to reread the final paragraph of "A Hunger Artist," the description of the young panther who is put into the sideshow cage to replace the professional abstinent after he expires of starvation. "The food he liked was brought without hesitation by the attendants, he seemed not even to miss his freedom;

his noble body, furnished almost to the bursting point with all that it needed, seemed to carry freedom around with it too; somewhere in its jaws it seemed to lurk . . ."

Yes, and what "it" lurks in these strong jaws? Freedom also? Or something more like the rapacity of one once very nearly buried alive? Are his the jaws of the noble panther or of the starved rat?

I ask him, "How come you've never written about your family, Ralph?" "Them?" he says, giving me his indulgent look. "Them," I say, "and you." "Why? So I can read to a full house at the Y? Oh, Kepesh"—five years my junior, he nonetheless enjoys talking to me as though I am the kid and, too, something of an unredeemable square—"spare me the subject of the Jewish family and its travails. Can you actually get worked up over another son and another daughter and another mother and another father driving each other nuts? All that loving; all that hating; all those meals. And don't forget the *menschlichkeit*. And the baffled quest for dignity. Oh, and the *goodness*. You can't write that stuff and leave out the goodness. I understand somebody has just published a whole book on our Jewish literature of goodness. I expect any day to read that an Irish critic has come out with a work on conviviality in Joyce, Yeats, and Synge. Or an article by some good old boy from Vanderbilt on hospitality in the Southern novel: 'Make Yourself at Home: The Theme of Hospitality in Faulkner's "A Rose for Emily.""""

"I just wondered if it might not give you access to other feelings."

He smiles. "Let the other guys have the other feelings, okay? They're used to having them. They *like* having them. But virtue isn't my bag. Too bo-ring." A favorite word, sung by Baumgarten with the interval of a third between the two syllables. "Look," he says, "I can't even take that much of Chekhov, that holy of holies. Why isn't he ever implicated in the shit? You're an authority. Why is the brute never Anton but some other slob?"

"That's a strange way to go at Chekhov, you know, expecting Céline. Or Genet. Or you. But then maybe the brute isn't always Baumgarten, either. It doesn't sound that way when you tell me about those visits to Paramus, or to the old-age home. Sounds more like Chekhov, actually. The family serf."

"Don't be too sure. Besides, besides, why bother to write that kind of stuff down? Has it not been done—and done? Do they need me too to scratch my name on the Wailing Wall? For me the books count—my own included—where the writer incriminates *himself.* Otherwise, why bother? To incriminate the other guy? Best leave that to our betters, don't you think, and that cunning Yiddish theater they've evolved, called Literary Criticism. Ah, those noble middle-aged Jewish sons, with their rituals of rebellion and atonement! Ever read them on the front of the Sunday *Times?* All the closet cunt hunters coming on like old man Tolstoy. All that sympathy for the humble of the earth, all that guarding of the sacred flame, which, by the way, don't cost them a fucking dime. Look, all those deeply suffering Jewish culture-bearers *need* a fallen Jewish ass to atone for their sins on in public—so why not mine? Keeps their wives in the dark; gives their girl friends someone sensitive to suffering to suck off; and goes a very long way with the Brandeis Kollege of Musical Knowledge. Every year I read in the papers about the powers-that-be up there awarding them merit badges for their neckerchiefs. Virtue, virtue, who's got the virtue? Biggest Jewish racket since Meyer Lansky in his prime."

Yes, he is steamed up now, and with no regard for the loudness of his voice or the windmilling of his arms—and not without pleasure in his broadside biliousness—he goes on about the lasciviousness (well known to all Manhattan, Baumgarten claims) of the "esteemed professor" who demolished his second book of poems in an omnibus review in the *Times.* "No 'culture,' no 'heart,' and what is worse, no 'historical perspective.' As if the esteemed professor has historical perspective when he is sticking it into some graduate assistant! No, they don't like it too much when you get down in there and burrow away just for the sake of the fishy little vizzy in your face. No, no, if you're a real man of letters in the humanist tradition you have historical perspective while you're doing it."

Not till we down our tea and strudel does he finish (for the night) with his investigation into the hypocrisies, pieties, and boring-ness generally of the literary world and the humanist tradition (largely as it is embodied in the reviewers of his books and the members of his department), and begin to speak, with a different sort of relish, of his other chosen arena of assertion. Like so many of his stories of the pleasant surprises that the hunt turns up, what he narrates over the dregs of dessert touches upon certain old but vivid recollections of my own. Indeed, there are times when, listening to him speak with such shamelessness of the wide range of his satisfactions, I feel that I am in the presence of a parodied projection of myself. A parody—a possibility. Maybe Baumgarten feels somewhat the same about me, and *this* explains the curiosity at either end. I am a Baumgarten locked in the Big House, caged in the kennels, a Baumgarten Klingered and Schonbrunned into submission—while he is a Kepesh, oh, what a Kepesh! with his mouth frothing and his long tongue lolling, leash slipped and running wild.

Why am I here with him? Passing time, sure, sure—and meanwhile, what is passing in and out of me? In the presence of the appetitious Baumgarten, am I looking to be exposed ever so mildly to the virulent strain, and thereby immunized for good? Or am I half hoping to be reinfected? Have I taken the healing of myself into my own hands at last, or is it rather that the convalescence is over, and I am just about ready to begin to conspire *against* the doctor and his bo-ring admonitions?

"One night last winter," he says, eyeing the round rear end of the largish Hungarian waitress who is trundling in carpet slippers back to the kitchen to make us some tea, "I was browsing in Marboro's—" And I can see him browsing already; I *have* seen it, a dozen times at least. BAUMGARTEN: Hardy? GIRL: Why—yes. BAUMGARTEN: *Tess of the d'Urbervilles*, is that what you've got there? GIRL (*looking at the book jacket*): That's right, it is—"—and I started talking to this nice red-cheeked girl who told me she had just come down on the train from visiting her family in Westchester. Sitting a couple of seats in front of her there'd been a fellow in a suit and tie and an overcoat who kept looking back at her over his shoulder and jacking off under the coat. I asked her what she did about it. 'What do you think I did?' she said. 'I looked him right in the eye, and when we got into Grand Central, I went up to him, and I said, "Hey, I think we should meet, I'd like to meet you."' Well, he took off, started running out of the station, but the girl kept right on him, trying to explain to him that she was *se-rious*—she liked the way he looked, she admired his courage, she was terrifically flattered by what he had done, but the guy disappeared into a taxi before she could convince him that he was in for a good time. Anyway, we struck it off, you might say, and went back to her apartment. It was over on the East River, in one of those hi-rise villages. When we got there she showed me the view up the river, and the kitchen with all the cookbooks, and then she wanted me to take off her clothes and tie her to the bed. Well, I haven't played with a rope since Troop 35, but I managed. Did it with dental floss, Kepesh, twelve yards of it—got her spread-eagled, arms and legs, just the way she wanted. Took me forty-five minutes. And you should have heard the sounds coming out of that girl. You should have seen what she looked like, excited like that. Very stirring image. Makes you understand the creeps more. Any-way, she told me to go and get the poppers out of the medi-cine chest. Well, there weren't any, they were all gone. It seems one of her friends had stolen them. So I told her I had some coke at home, and I'd get it if she wanted me to. 'Go, get it, get it,' she said. So I went. But when I came downstairs from my place and got a taxi to start back to hers, I realized that I didn't know her name—and for the life of me I couldn't re-member which of those fucking buildings she lived in. Kepesh, I was stymied," he says, and reaching across the table with a thumb and forefinger to get the strudel crumbs off my plate, manages to sweep my water glass into my lap with the cuff of his army coat. For some reason Baumgarten always eats in his coat. Maybe Jesse James did, too. "Oops," he cries, seeing the glass go down, but of course this isn't the first time; indeed, "oops" may be the four-letter word that most frequently falls from Baumgarten's lips, certainly while he is turning the table into his trough. "Sorry," he says; "you all right?" "It'll dry," I say, "it always does. Go on. What did you do?" "What *could* I do? Nothing. I started wandering from one building to the next, looking at the names on the directories. Jane was her first name, or so she said, so whenever I saw a 'J,' like a schmuck I rang the buzzer. Couldn't find her, of course, though I had several promising conversations. Anyway, a guard came up and asked me what I was looking for. I told him I must be in the wrong building, but when I went out he followed me into the portico area there, and so I hung around for about a minute or two, looking up and admiring the moon. And then I went home. And after that I bought the *Daily News* on the way to school every day. I looked in there for weeks to see if the cops had found a skeleton tied to a bed with dental floss over on the decadent East Side. Finally I just gave up. Then this summer I was coming out of a movie down on Eighth Street, and there standing in line to get in for the next show is the same girl. Plain Jane. And you know what she says? She spots me, and a smile spreads across her face, and she says, 'Far out, man.' "

Skeptical, but laughing, I say. "That all happened, huh?"

"Dave, just walk the streets and say hello to the folks. *Everything* happens."

And then, after Baumgarten has asked the waitress—new to our restaurant, and whose aging, peasanty overflow he had decided he must get to know—whether she can recommend someone to give him Hungarian lessons; after he has taken her name and number—"Live alone there, do you, Eva?"—he excuses himself and goes to the back of the restaurant, where there is a pay phone. In order to write down Eva's telephone number, he has emptied his coat pocket of a handful of papers and envelopes, on which, I see, he already has recorded the names and whereabouts of those others of her sex who have crossed his path during the day. The number of whomever he is calling now he has carried off with him to the phone, leaving the little mess of personal papers for me to contemplate at my leisure, the papers and the life that goes with them.

With a fingernail, I am able to flick into view the last paragraph of a letter neatly typewritten on heavy cream-colored stationery.

. . . I've gotten you your fifteen-year-old (eighteen, actually, but fleshwise I'll swear you'd never know the difference, and anyway, fifteen is *jail*)—a succulent sophomore, and not just young but a real beauty besides, a sweet girl and worldly both, and altogether I can't see how you could improve on her. I found her for you all by myself, her name is Rona and we are having lunch next week, so if you meant it (assuming you do remember mentioning this fancy), I will open negotiations at this time. I feel reasonably confident of success. Kindly semaphore your intentions next time you're in the office, one blink for yes, two for no, if I should go ahead. So there's my half of the bargain —I'm procuring for you, as desired and with my heart somewhere up near my mouth—now *please* put me in touch with the orgiasts. The only good reasons for no that I can think of are (a) you are involved there yourself—and in that case I would simply abstain from those soirees, if you prefer—or (b) you're afraid of being compromised by somebody at the heart of the Kremlin—then just give me the name and I'll say I heard about it elsewhere than you. Otherwise, why not give your (slightly atrophied) faculty of human sympathy a little workout (I've read somewhere it was once believed to be an essential quality for a poet) as long as it won't cost you anything, and bring a little ray of sunshine into the dim life of a (rapidly) fading spinster.

Your chum,
T.

And who is "T," I wonder, in the "Kremlin"? The assistant to the provost or the director of student health? And who—on another piece of paper—is "L"? Her words crossed out and rewritten on every line; her felt-tipped pen on the brink of anemia—what does *she* want of the poet with the slightly atrophied heart? Is "L"'s the pleading voice Baumgarten is so patiently listening to in the telephone booth? Or is that "M," or "N" or "O" or "P"—?

Ralph, I refuse to be sorry about last night unless you can point out in a *believable* way there was something twisted or mean about my wanting to see you. I had thought that if I could only sit in the same room with a man who wasn't trying to push me or convince me or confuse me, someone whom I liked and respected, that I might get closer to something in myself that matters and is real. I was under the impression that you didn't live in a dream world, and have sometimes wondered since the baby whether I do. I didn't want to make love. Sometimes you act like someone who is adept at removing a lady's drawers and that's all. I certainly won't make any more spontaneous visits after 10 p.m. It is just that wanting and needing to talk to someone with whom I am *not* involved, I chose you, when, I admit, in some way I want to be involved, some part wanting to be in your arms, when the other part insists that what I really need is your friendship, your advice—*and* distance. I guess I don't quite want to admit that you move me. But that doesn't mean I don't think there is something crazy about you—

Inside the booth, Baumgarten hangs up the phone and so I stop reading his fan mail. We pay Eva, Baumgarten collects his property, and together—his "pal" on the phone is best left to herself this evening, he informs me—we head toward the nearest Bookmasters, where, as usual, one or the other of us will lay out five dollars for five remaindered books he most likely will never get around to reading. "Inebriate of cunt and print!" as my secret sharer exclaims somewhere in the song of himself behind, before, above, between, below.

It takes two full weeks, six whole sessions, before I am able to tell the psychoanalyst to whom I am supposed to tell everything that only a little later that evening we had met a high school girl shopping for a paperback for her English class. (BAUMGARTEN: Emily or Charlotte? GIRL: Charlotte. BAUMGARTEN: *Villette* or *Jane Eyre*? GIRL: I never heard of the first one. *Jane Eyre*.) Breezy, streetwise, and just a little terrified, she had accompanied us back to Baumgarten's one room, and there, on his Mexican rug, amid several piles of his own two erotic books of verse, she had auditioned for a modeling job for the new erotic picture magazine being started on the West Coast by our bosses, the Schonbrunns. Magazine to be called *Cunt*. "The Schonbrunns," he explains, "are sick and tired of pulling their punches."

A lanky strawberry blonde in fringed leather jacket and jeans, the girl had told us straight out, while being interviewed in the bookstore, that she would not be at all shy about taking off her clothes for a photographer—so, at Baumgarten's, she is given one of his Danish magazines to look at, for the inspiration in it.

"Could you do this, Wendy?" he asks her earnestly as she sits on the sofa leafing through the magazines with one hand and, with the other, holding the Baskin-Robbins ice cream cone that Baumgarten (the impeccable scenarist) couldn't resist buying for her on the way home. ("What's your favorite flavor, Wendy? Go ahead, please, have a double dip, have sprinkles, have everything. How about you, Dave? Want some Chocolate Ribbon, too?") Clearing her throat, she closes the magazine in her lap, bites into what remains of the cone, and casually as she can manage, says, "That's a little far for me." "What isn't?" he asks her; "just tell me what isn't." "Maybe something more along the lines of *Playboy*," she says.

Working together then, something like teammates moving the ball across the midcourt line against a tight defense, something like two methodical day laborers driving a post into the ground with alternating blows of their mallets—something like Birgitta and myself back on the continent of Europe during the Age of Exploration—we manage, by bringing her through a series of provocative postures in progressive stages of undress, to get her flat on her back in her bikini underpants and her boots. And that, says the seventeen-year-old senior from Washington Irving High—trembling ever so slightly as she gazes up at our four eyes looking down—that is as far as she will go.

What next? That her limit is to be *the* limit is understood by Baumgarten and myself without any consultation. I make that clear to Klinger—also point out that no tears were shed, no force used, not so much as a fingertip touched her flesh.

"And this happened when?" Klinger asks me.

"Two weeks ago," I say, and rise from the couch to get my coat.

And leave. I have withheld my confession for two full weeks, and even now, until the end of the hour. Consequently, I am able just to walk out the door, and do not have to add—and never will—that it was not a recidivist's shame that deterred me from narrating the incident earlier, but rather the small color snapshot of Klinger's teenage daughter, in faded dungarees and school T-shirt, taken on a beach somewhere and displayed in a triptych frame on his desk between photographs of his two sons.

A<small>ND</small> then the summer after I return East I meet a young woman altogether unlike this small band of consolers, counselors, tempters, and provocateurs—the "influences," as my father would have it—off whom my benumbed and unsexed carcass has been careening since I've been a womanless, pleasureless, passionless man on his own.

I am invited for a weekend on Cape Cod by a faculty couple I have just gotten to know, and there I am introduced to Claire Ovington, their young neighbor, who is renting a tiny shingled bungalow in a wild-rose patch near the Orleans beach for herself and her golden Labrador. Some ten days after the morning we spend talking together on the beach—after I have sent her a painfully charming letter from New York, and consulted for several clammy hours with Klinger—I take the impulse by the horns and return to Orleans, where I move into the local inn. I am drawn at first by the same look of soft voluptuousness that had (against all seemingly reasonable reservations) done so much to draw me to Helen, and which has touched off, for the first time in over a year, a spontaneous surge of warm feeling. Back in New York after my brief weekend visit, I had thought only about her. Do I sense the renewal of desire, of confidence, of capacity? Not quite yet. During my week at the inn, I cannot stop behaving like an overzealous child at dancing class, unable to go through a door or to raise a fork without the starchiest display of good manners. And after the *self*-display of that letter, that bravura show of wit and self-assurance! Why did I listen to Klinger? "Of course, go—what can you lose?" But what does *he* have to lose if I fail? Where's his tragic view of life, damn it? Impotence is no joke—it's a plague! People kill themselves! And alone in my bed at the inn, after yet another evening of keeping my distance from Claire, I can understand why. In the morning, just before I am to leave for New York once again, I arrive at her bungalow for an early breakfast, and midway through the fresh blueberry pancakes try to redeem myself a little by admitting to my shame. I don't know how else to get out of this with at least some self-esteem intact, though why I will ever have to care about self-esteem again I cannot imagine. "I seem to have come all the way up here—after writing to you like that, and then arriving out of nowhere—well, after all that fanfare, I seem to have come upon the scene and . . . disappeared." And now moving over me—moving right up to the roots of my hair—I feel something very like the shame that I must have imagined I could avoid *by* disappearing. "I must seem odd to you. At this point I seem odd to myself. I've seemed odd to myself for some time now. I'm only trying to say that it's nothing you've done or said that's made me behave so coldly." "But," she says, before I can begin another round of apology about this "oddity" that I am, "it's been so pleasant. In a way it's been the sweetest thing." "It has?" I say, fearful that I am about to be humbled in some unforeseen way. "*What* has?" "Seeing somebody shy for a change. It's nice to know it still exists in the Age of Utter Abandon."

God, as tender within as without! The tact! The calm! The *wisdom*! As physically alluring to me as Helen—but there the resemblance ends. Poise and confidence and determination, but, in Claire, all of it marshaled in behalf of something more than high sybaritic adventure. At twenty-four, she has earned a degree from Cornell in experimental psychology, a master's from Columbia in education, and is on the faculty of a private school in Manhattan, where she teaches eleven- and twelve-year-olds, and, as of the coming semester, will be in charge of the curriculum-review committee. Yet, for someone who, as I come to learn, emanates in her professional role a strong aura of reserve, a placid, coolheaded, and seemingly unassailable presence, she is surprisingly innocent and guileless about the personal side of her life, and, as regards her friends, her plants, her herb garden, her dog, her cooking, her sister Olivia, who summers on Martha's Vineyard, and Olivia's three children, she has about as much reserve as a healthy ten-year-old girl. In all, this translucent mix of sober social aplomb and domestic enthusiasms and youthful susceptibility is simply irresistible. What I mean is *no resistance is necessary*. A tempter of a kind to whom I can at last succumb.

Now it is as if a gong has been struck in my stomach when I recall—and I do, daily—that I had written Claire my clever, flirtatious letter, and then had very nearly been content to leave it at that. Had even told Klinger that writing out of the blue to a voluptuous young woman I had spoken with casually on a beach for two hours was a measure of just how hopeless my prospects had become. I had almost decided against showing up for breakfast that last morning on the Cape, so fearful was I of what my convalescent desire might have in store for me were I, with a suitcase in one hand and my plane ticket in the other, to try to put it to a crazy last-minute test. How ever *did* I manage to make it past my shameful secret? Do I owe it to sheer luck, to ebullient, optimistic Klinger, or do I owe everything I now have to those breasts of hers in that bathing suit? Oh, if so, then bless each breast a thousand times! For now, now I am positively exultant, thrilled, astonished— grateful for everything about her, for the executive dispatch with which she orders her life as for the patience that she brings to our lovemaking, that canniness of hers that seems to sense exactly how much raw carnality and how much tender solicitude it is going to require to subdue my tenacious anxiety and renew my faith in coupling and all that may come in its wake. All the pedagogic expertise bestowed upon those sixth-graders is now bestowed upon *me* after school—such a gentle, tactful tutor comes to my apartment each day, and yet always the hungry woman with her! And those breasts, those breasts— large and soft and vulnerable, each as heavy as an udder upon my face, as warm and heavy in my hand as some fat little animal fast asleep. Oh, the look of this large girl above me when she is still half stripped! And, mind you, an assiduous keeper of records as well! Yes, the history of each passing day in calendar books going back through college, her life's history in the photographs she has been taking since childhood, first with a Brownie, now with the best equipment from Japan. And those lists! Those wonderful, orderly lists! I too write out on a yellow pad what I plan to accomplish each day, but by bedtime I seem never to find a soothing little check mark beside each item, confirming that the letter has been dispatched, the money withdrawn, the article xeroxed, the call made. Despite my own strong penchant for orderliness, passed along through the maternal chromosomes, there are still mornings when I can't even locate the list I drew up the night before, and, usually, what I don't feel like doing one day, I am able to put off to the next without too many qualms. Not so with Mistress Ovington—to every task that presents itself, regardless of how difficult or dreary, she gives her complete attention, taking each up in its turn and steadfastly following it through to its conclusion. And, to my great good luck, reconstituting my life is apparently just such a task. It is as though at the top of one of her yellow pads she has spelled out my name and then, beneath, in her own spherical hand, written instructions to herself, as follows: "Provide DK with—1. Loving kindness. 2. Impassioned embraces. 3. Sane surroundings." For within a year the job is somehow done, a big check mark beside each life-saving item. I give up the anti-depressants, and no abyss opens beneath me. I sublet the sublet apartment, and, without being wracked too much by memories of the handsome rugs, tables, dishes, and chairs once jointly owned by Helen and me and now hers alone, I furnish a new place of my own. I even accept an invitation to a dinner party at the Schonbrunns', and at the end of the evening politely kiss Debbie's cheek while Arthur paternally kisses Claire's. Easy as that. Meaningless as that. At the door, while Arthur and Claire conclude the conversation they'd been having at dinner—about the curriculum that Claire is now devising for the upper grades—Debbie and I have a moment to chat privately. For some reason—alcoholic intake on both sides, I think—we are holding hands! "Another of your tall blondes," says Debbie, "but this one seems a bit more sympathetic. We both find her very sweet. And very bright. Where did you meet?" "In a brothel in Marrakesh. Look, Debbie, isn't it about time you got off my ass? What does that mean, my 'tall blondes'?" "It's a fact." "No, it is not even a fact. Helen's hair was auburn. But suppose it was cut from the same bolt as Claire's—the fact is that 'blondes,' in that context, and that tone, is, as you may even know, a derogatory term used by intellectuals and other serious people to put down pretty women. I also believe it is dense with unsavory implication when addressed to men of my origin and complexion. I remember how fond you used to be at Stanford of pointing out to people the anomaly of a literate chap like myself coming from the 'Borscht Belt.' That too used to strike me as a bit reductive." "Oh, you take yourself too seriously. Why don't you just admit you have a penchant for these big blondes and leave it at that? It's nothing to be ashamed of. They do look lovely up on water skis with all that hair streaming. I bet they look lovely everywhere." "Debbie, I'll make a deal with you. I'll admit I know nothing about you, if you'll admit you know nothing about me. I'm sure you have a whole wondrous being and inner life that I know nothing about." "Nope," she says, "this is it. This is the whole thing. Take it or leave it." Both of us begin to laugh. I say, "Tell me, what does Arthur see in you? It's really one of the mysteries of life. What do you have that I'm blind to?" "Everything," she replies. Out in the car, I give Claire an abridged version of the conversation. "The woman is warped," I say. "Oh, no," says Claire, "just silly, that's all." "She tricked you, Clarissa. Silly is the cover—assassination is the game." "Ah, sweetie," says Claire, "it's *you* she's tricked!"

So much for my rehabilitation back into society. As for my father and his awesome loneliness, well, now he takes the train from Cedarhurst to have dinner in Manhattan once a month; he can't be coaxed in any more often, but in truth, before there was the new apartment, and Claire to help with the conversation and the cooking, I didn't work at coaxing him that hard, no, not so each of us could sit and peer sadly at the other picking at his spareribs, two orphans in Chinatown . . . not so I could wait to hear him ask over the lichee nuts, "And that guy, he hasn't come back to bother you, has he?"

And, to be sure, from the maw of that maelstrom called Baumgarten I withdrew my toes a little. We still have lunch together from time to time, but the grander feasts I leave him to partake of on his own. And I do not introduce him to Claire.

My, how easy life is when it's easy, and how hard when it's hard!

One night, after dinner at my apartment, while Claire is preparing her next day's lessons at the cleared dining table, I finally get up the nerve, or no longer seem to need "nerve," to reread what there is of my Chekhov book, shelved now for more than two years. In the midst of the laborious and deadly competence of those fragmentary chapters intended to focus upon the subject of romantic disillusionment, I find five pages that are somewhat readable—reflections growing out of

Chekhov's comic little story, "Man in a Shell," about the tyrannical rise and celebrated fall—"I confess," says the good-hearted narrator after the tyrant's funeral, "it is a great pleasure to bury people like Belikov"—the rise and fall of a provincial high school official whose love of prohibitions and hatred of all deviations from the rules manages to hold a whole town of "thoughtful, decent people" under his thumb for fifteen years. I go back to reread the story, then to reread "Gooseberries" and "About Love," written in sequence with it and forming a series of anecdotal ruminations upon the varieties of pain engendered by spiritual imprisonment—by petty despotism, by ordinary human complacency, and finally, even by the inhibitions upon feeling necessary to support a scrupulous man's sense of decency. For the next month, with a notebook on my lap, and some tentative observations in mind, I return to Chekhov's fiction nightly, listening for the anguished cry of the trapped and miserable socialized being, the well-bred wives who during dinner with the guests wonder "Why do I smile and lie?", and the husbands, seemingly settled and secure, who are "full of conventional truth and conventional deception." Simultaneously I am watching how Chekhov, simply and clearly, though not quite so pitilessly as Flaubert, reveals the humiliations and failures—worst of all, the destructive power—of those who seek a way *out* of the shell of restrictions and convention, out of the pervasive boredom and the stifling despair, out of the painful marital situations and the endemic social falsity, into what they take to be a vibrant and desirable life. There is the agitated young wife in "Misfortune" who looks for "a bit of excitement" against the grain of her own offended respectability; there is the lovesick landowner in "Ariadne," confessing with Herzogian helplessness to a romantic misadventure with a vulgar trampy tigress who gradually transforms him into a hopeless misogynist, but whom he nonetheless waits on hand and foot; there is the young actress in "A Boring Story," whose bright, hopeful enthusiasm for a life on the stage, and a life with men, turns bitter with her first experiences of the stage and of men, and of her own lack of talent—"I have no talent, you see, I have no talent and . . . and lots of vanity." And there is "The Duel." Every night for a week (with Claire only footsteps away) I reread Chekhov's masterpiece about the weaseling, slovenly, intelligent, literary-minded seducer Layevsky, immersed in his lies and his self-pity, and Layevsky's antagonist, the ruthless punitive conscience who all but murders him, the voluble scientist Von Koren. Or so it is that I come to view the story: with Von Koren as the ferociously rational and merciless prosecutor called forth to challenge the sense of shame and sinfulness that is nearly all that Layevsky has become, and from which, alas, he no longer can flee. It is this immersion in "The Duel" that finally gets me writing, and within four months the five pages extracted from the old unfinished rehash of my thesis on romantic disillusionment are transformed into some forty thousand words entitled *Man in a Shell*, an essay on license and restraint in Chekhov's world—longings fulfilled, pleasures denied, and the pain occasioned by both; a study, at bottom, of what makes for Chekhov's pervasive pessimism about the methods—scrupulous, odious, noble, dubious—by which the men and women of his time try in vain to achieve "that sense of personal freedom" to which Chekhov himself is so devoted. My first book! With a dedication page that reads "To C.O."

"She is to steadiness," I tell Klinger (and Kepesh, who must never, never, never forget), "what Helen was to impetuosity. She is to common sense what Birgitta was to indiscretion. I have never seen such devotion to the ordinary business of daily life. It's awesome, really, the way she deals with each day as it comes, the attention she pays minute by minute. There's no dreaming going on there—just steady, dedicated *living*. I trust her, that's the point I'm making. That's what's done it," I announce triumphantly, "trust."

To all of which Klinger eventually replies goodbye then and good luck. At the door of his office on the spring afternoon of our parting, I have to wonder if it can really be that I no longer need bucking up and holding down and hearing out, warning, encouragement, consent, consolation, applause, and opposition—in short, professional doses of mothering and fathering and simple friendship three times a week for an hour. *Can* it be that I've come through? Just like that? Just because of Claire? What if I awaken tomorrow morning once again a man with a crater instead of a heart, once again without a man's capacity and appetite and strength and judgment, without the least bit of mastery over my flesh or my intelligence or my feelings . . .

"Stay in touch," says Klinger, shaking my hand. Just as I could not look squarely at him the day I neglected to mention the impact on my conscience of his daughter's snapshot—as though suppressing that fact I might be spared his unuttered judgment, or my own—so I cannot let his eyes engage mine when we say farewell. But now it is because I would prefer not to give vent to my feelings of elation and indebtedness in an outburst of tears. Sniffing all sentiment back up my nose—and firmly, for the moment, suppressing all doubt—I say, "Let's hope I don't have to," but once out on the street by myself, I repeat the incredible words aloud, only now to the accompaniment of the appropriate emotions: "I've come through!"

The following June, when the teaching year is over for the two of us, Claire and I fly to the north of Italy, my first time back in Europe since I'd gone prowling there with Birgitta a decade earlier. In Venice we spend five days at a quiet pensione near the Accademia. Each morning we eat breakfast in the pensione's aromatic garden and then, in our walking shoes, weave back and forth across the bridges and alleyways that lead to the landmarks Claire has marked on the map for us to visit that day. Whenever she takes her pictures of these palazzos and piazzas and churches and fountains I wander off a ways, but always looking back to get a picture of her and her unadorned beauty.

Each evening after dinner under the arbor in the garden, we treat ourselves to a little gondola ride. With Claire beside me in the armchair that Mann describes as "the softest, most luxurious, most relaxing seat in the world," I ask myself yet again if this serenity truly exists, if this contentment, this wonderful accord is real. *Is* the worst over? Have I no more terrible mistakes to make? And no more to pay on those behind me? Was all that only so much Getting Started, a longish and misguided youth out of which I have finally aged? "Are you sure we didn't die," I say, "and go to heaven?" "I wouldn't know," she replies; "you'll have to ask the gondolier."

Our last afternoon I blow us to lunch at the Gritti. On the

terrace I tip the headwaiter and point to the very table where I had imagined myself sitting with the pretty student who used to lunch on Peanut Chews in my classroom; I order exactly what I ate that day back in Palo Alto when we were studying Chekhov's stories about love and I felt myself on the edge of a nervous collapse—only this time I am not imagining the delicious meal with the fresh, untainted mate, this time both are real and I am well. Settling back—I with a cold glass of wine; Claire, the teetotaling daughter of parents who overimbibed, with her *acqua minerale*—I look out across the gleaming waters of this indescribably beautiful toy town and I say to her, "Do you think Venice is really sinking? The place seems in vaguely the same position as last time I was here."

"Who were you with then? Your wife?"

"No. It was my Fulbright year. I was with a girl."

"Who was that?"

Now, how endangered or troubled would she feel, what, if anything, do I risk awakening if I go ahead and tell her all? Oh, how dramatically put! What did "all" consist of—any more, really, than a young sailor goes out to find in his first foreign port? A sailor's taste for a little of the lurid, but, as things turned out, neither a sailor's stomach nor strength . . . Still, to someone so measured and orderly, someone who has turned all her considerable energy to making normal and ordinary what had for her been heartbreakingly irregular in her childhood home, I think it best to answer, "Oh, nobody, really," and let the matter drop.

Whereupon the nobody who has been no part of my life for over ten years is all I can think of. In that Chekhov class the mismatched husband had recalled sunnier days on the terrace of the Gritti, an unbruised, audacious, young Kepesh still running around Europe scot-free; now on the terrace of the Gritti, where I have come to celebrate the triumphant foundation of a sweet and stable new life, to celebrate the astonishing renewal of health and happiness, I am recalling the earliest, headiest hours of my sheikdom, the night in our London basement when it is my turn to ask Birgitta what it is *she* most wants. What I most want the two girls have given me; what Elisabeth most wants we are leaving for last—she does not know . . . for in her heart, as we are to discover when the truck knocks her down, she wants none of it. But Birgitta has desires about which she is not afraid to speak, and which we proceed to satisfy. Yes, sitting across from Claire, who has said that my semen filling her mouth makes her feel that she is drowning, that this is something she just doesn't care to do, I am remembering the sight of Birgitta kneeling before me, her face upturned to receive the strands of flowing semen that fall upon her hair, her forehead, her nose. "*Här!*" she cries, "*här!*", while Elisabeth, wearing her pink woolen robe, and reclining on the bed, looks on in frozen fascination at the naked masturbator and his half-clothed suppliant.

As if such a thing matters! As if Claire is withholding anything that *matters*! But admonish myself as I will for amnesia, stupidity, ingratitude, callowness, for a lunatic and suicidal loss of all perspective, the rush of greedy lust I feel is not for this lovely young woman with whom I have only recently emerged into a life promising the most profound sort of fulfillment, but for the smallish buck-toothed comrade I last saw leaving my room at midnight some thirty kilometers outside Rouen over ten years ago, desire for my own lewd, lost soul mate, who, back before my sense of the permissible began its inward collapse, welcomed as feverishly and gamely as did I the uncommon act and the alien thought. Oh Birgitta, go away! But this time we are in our room right here in Venice, a hotel on a narrow alleyway off the Zattere, not very far from the little bridge where Claire had taken my picture earlier in the day. I tie a kerchief around her eyes, careful to knot it tightly at the back, and then I am standing over the blindfolded girl and—ever so lightly to begin with—whipping her between her parted legs. I watch as she strains upward with her hips to catch the bite of each stroke of my belt on her genital crease. I watch this as I have never watched anything before in my life. "Say all the things," Birgitta whispers, and I do, in a low, subdued growl such as I have never used before to address anyone or anything.

For Birgitta then—for what I would now prefer to dismiss as a "longish and misguided youth"—a surging sense of lascivious kinship . . . and for Claire, for this truly passionate and loving rescuer of mine? Anger; disappointment; disgust—contempt for all she does so marvelously, resentment over that little thing she will not deign to do. I see how very easily I could have no use for her. The snapshots. The lists. The mouth that will not drink my come. The curriculum-review committee. Everything.

The impulse to fly up from the table and telephone Dr. Klinger I suppress. I will not be one of those hysterical patients at the other end of the overseas line. No, not that. I eat the meal when it is served, and sure enough, by the time the desert is to be ordered, yearnings for Birgitta begging me and Birgitta beneath me and Birgitta below me, all such yearnings have begun to subside, as left to themselves those yearnings will. And the anger disappears too, to be replaced by shame-filled sadness. If Claire senses the rising and ebbing of all this distress—and how can she not? how else understand my silent, icy gloom?—she decides to pretend ignorance, to talk on about her plans for the curriculum-review committee until whatever has cast us apart has simply passed away.

From Venice we drive a rented car to Padua to look at the Giottos. Claire takes more pictures. She will have them developed when we get home and then, sitting cross-legged on the floor—the posture of tranquillity, of concentration, the posture of a very good girl indeed—paste them, in their proper sequence, into the album for this year. Now northern Italy will be in the bookcase at the foot of the bed where her volumes of photographs are stored, now northern Italy will be forever *hers*, along with Schenectady, where she was born and raised, Ithaca, where she went to college, and New York City, where she lives and works and lately has fallen in love. And I will be there at the foot of the bed, along with her places, her family, and her friends.

Though so many of her twenty-five years have been blighted by the squabbling of contentious parents—arguments abetted, as often as not, by too many tumblers of Scotch—she regards the past as worth recording and remembering, if only because she has outlasted the pain and disorder to establish a decent life of her own. As she likes to say, it is the only past she has got to remember, hard as it may have been when the bombs were bursting around her and she was trying her best to grow up in one piece. And then, of course, that Mr. and Mrs. Ovington put more energy into being adversaries than into being the comforters of their children does not mean that their daughter must deny *herself* the ordinary pleasures that ordinary families (if such there be) take as a matter of course. To all the pleasant amenities of family life—the exchanging of photographs, the giving of gifts, the celebration of holidays, the regular phone calls—both Claire and her older sister are passionately devoted, as though in fact she and Olivia are the thoughtful parents and their parents are the callow offspring.

From a hotel in a small mountain town where we find a room with a terrace and a bed and an Arcadian view, we make day trips to Verona and Vicenza. Pictures, pictures, pictures. What is the opposite of a nail being driven into a coffin? Well, that is what I hear as Claire's camera clicks away. Once again I feel I am being sealed up into something wonderful. One day we just walk with a picnic lunch up along the cowpaths and through the flowering fields, whole nations of minute bluets and lacquered little buttercups and unreal poppies. I can walk silently with Claire for hours on end. I am content just to lie on the ground propped up on one elbow and watch her pick wild flowers to take back to our room and arrange in a water glass to place beside my pillow. I feel no need for anything more. "More" has no meaning. Nor does Birgitta appear to have meaning any longer, as though "Birgitta" and "more" are just different ways of saying the same thing. Following the performance at the Gritti, she has failed to put in anything like such a sensational appearance again. For the next few nights she does come by to pay me a visit each time Claire and I make love—kneeling, always kneeling, and begging for what thrills her most—but then she is gone, and I am above the body I am above, and with that alone partake of all the "more" I now could want, or want to want. Yes, I just hold tight to Claire and the unbeckoned visitor eventually drifts away, leaving me to enjoy once again the awesome fact of my great good luck.

On our last afternoon, we carry our lunch to the crest of a field that looks across high green hills to the splendid white tips of the Dolomites. Claire lies stretched out beside where I am sitting, her ample figure gently swelling and subsiding with each breath she draws. Looking steadily down at this large, green-eyed girl in her thin summer clothes, at her pale, smallish, oval, unmarred face, her scrubbed, unworldly prettiness— the beauty, I realize, of a young Amish or Shaker woman—I say to myself, "Claire is enough. Yes, 'Claire' and 'enough'—they, too, are one word."

From Venice we fly by way of Vienna—and the house of Sigmund Freud—to Prague. During this last year I have been teaching the Kafka course at the university—the paper that I am to read a few days from now in Bruges has Kafka's preoccupation with spiritual starvation as its subject—but I have not as yet seen his city, other than in books of photographs. Just prior to our departure I had graded the final examinations written by my fifteen students in the seminar, who had read all of the fiction, Max Brod's biography, and Kafka's diaries and his letters to Milena and to his father. One of the questions I had asked on the examination was this—

In his "Letter to His Father" Kafka writes, "My writing is all about you; all I did there, after all, was to bemoan what I could not bemoan upon your breast. It was an intentionally long-drawn-out leave-taking from you, yet, although it was enforced by you, it did take its course in the direction determined by me . . ." What does Kafka mean when he says to his father, "My writing is all about you," and adds, "yet it did take its course in the direction determined by me"? If you like, imagine yourself to be Max Brod writing a letter of your own to Kafka's father, explaining what it is your friend has in mind . . .

I had been pleased by the number of students who had taken my suggestion and decided to pretend to be the writer's friend and biographer—and, in describing the inner workings of a most unusual son to a most conventional father, had demonstrated a mature sensitivity to Kafka's moral isolation, to his peculiarities of perspective and temperament, and to those imaginative processes by which a fantasist as entangled as Kafka was in daily existence transforms into fable his everyday struggles. Hardly a single benighted literature major straying into ingenious metaphysical exegesis! Oh, I am pleased, all right, with the Kafka seminar and with myself for what I've done there. But these first months with Claire, what hasn't been a source of pleasure?

Before leaving home I had been given the name and telephone number of an American spending the year teaching in Prague, and, happily, as it turns out (and what doesn't these days?), he and a Czech friend of his, another literature professor, have the afternoon free and are able to give us a tour of old Prague. From a bench in the Old Town Square we gaze across at the palatial building where Franz Kafka attended Gymnasium. To the right of the columned entry way is the ground-floor site of Hermann Kafka's business. "He couldn't even get away from him at school," I say. "All the worse for him," the Czech professor replies, "and all the better for the fiction." In the imposing Gothic church nearby, high on one wall of the nave, a small square window faces an apartment next door where, I am informed, Kafka's family had once lived. So Kafka, I say, could have sat there furtively looking down on the sinner confessing and the faithful at prayer . . . and the interior of this church, might it not have furnished, if not every last detail, at least the atmosphere for the Cathedral of *The Trial?* And those steep angular streets across the river leading circuitously to the sprawling Hapsburg castle, surely they must have served as inspiration for him too . . . Perhaps so, says the Czech professor, but a small castle village in northern Bohemia that Kafka knew from his visits to his grandfather is thought to have been the principal model for the topography of *The Castle*. Then there is the little country village where his sister had spent a year managing a farm and where Kafka had gone to stay with her during a spell of illness. Had we time, says the Czech professor, Claire and I might benefit from an overnight visit to the countryside. "Visit one of those xenophobic little towns, with its smoky taverna and its buxom barmaid, and you will see what a thoroughgoing realist this Kafka was."

For the first time I sense something other than geniality in this smallish, bespectacled, neatly attired academic—I sense all that the geniality is working to suppress.

Near the wall of the castle, on cobbled Alchemist Street— and looking like a dwelling out of a child's bedtime story, the fit habitation for a gnome or elf—is the tiny house that his youngest sister had rented one winter for Kafka to live in, another of her efforts to help separate the bachelor son from father and family. The little place is now a souvenir shop. Picture postcards and Prague mementos are being sold on the spot where Kafka had meticulously scribbled variants of the same paragraph ten times over in his diary, and where he had drawn his sardonic stick figures of himself, the "private ideograms" he hid, along with practically everything else, in a drawer. Claire takes a picture of the three literature professors in front of the perfectionist writer's torture chamber. Soon it will be in its place in one of the albums at the foot of her bed.

While Claire goes off with the American professor, and her camera, for a tour of the castle grounds, I sit over tea with Professor Soska, our Czech guide. When the Russians invaded Czechoslovakia and put an end to the Prague Spring reform movement, Soska was fired from his university post and at age thirty-nine placed in "retirement" on a minuscule pension. His wife, a research scientist, also was relieved of her position for political reasons and, in order to support the family of four, has been working for a year now as a typist in a meat-packing plant. How has the retired professor managed to keep up his morale, I wonder. His three-piece suit is impeccable, his gait quick, his speech snappy and precise—how does he do it? What gets him up in the morning and to sleep at night? What gets him through each day?

"Kafka, of course," he says, showing me that smile again. "Yes, this is true; many of us survive almost solely on Kafka. Including people in the street who have never read a word of his. They look at one another when something happens, and they say, 'It's Kafka.' Meaning, 'That's the way it goes here now.' Meaning, 'What else did you expect?' "

"And anger? Is it abated any when you shrug your shoulders and say, 'It's Kafka'?"

"For the first six months after the Russians came to stay with us I was myself in a continuous state of agitation. I went every night to secret meetings with my friends. Every other day at least I circulated another illegal petition. And in the time remaining I wrote, in my most precise and lucid prose, in my most elegant and thoughtful sentences, encyclopedic analyses of the situation which then circulated in *samizdat* among my colleagues. Then one day I keeled over and they sent me to the hospital with bleeding ulcers. I thought at first, all right, I will lie here on my back for a month, I will take my medicine and eat my slops, and then—well, then *what*? What will I do when I stop bleeding? Return to playing K. to their Castle and their Court? This can all go on interminably, as Kafka and his readers so well know. Those pathetic, hopeful, striving K.'s of his, running madly up and down all those stairwells looking for their solution, feverishly traversing the city contemplating the new development that will lead to, of all things, their success. Beginnings, middles, and, most fantastical of all, endings— that is how they believe they can force events to unfold."

"But, Kafka and his readers aside, will things change if there is no opposition?"

The smile, disguising God only knows the kind of expression he would *like* to show to the world. "Sir, I have made my position known. The entire country has made its position known. This way we live now is not what we had in mind. For myself, I cannot burn away what remains of my digestive tract by continuing to make this clear to our authorities seven days a week."

"And so what do you do instead?"

"I translate *Moby Dick* into Czech. Of course, a translation happens already to exist, a very fine one indeed. There is absolutely no need for another. But it is something I have always thought about, and now that I have nothing else pressing to be accomplished, well, why not?"

"Why that book? Why Melville?" I ask him.

"In the fifties I spent a year on an exchange program, living in New York City. Walking the streets, it looked to me as if the place was aswarm with the crew of Ahab's ship. And at the helm of everything, big or small, I saw yet another roaring Ahab. The appetite to set things right, to emerge at the top, to be declared a 'champ.' And by dint, not just of energy and will, but of enormous rage. And *that*, the rage, that is what I should like to translate into Czech . . . if"—smiling—"that *can* be translated into Czech.

"Now, as you might imagine, this ambitious project, when completed, will be utterly useless for two reasons. First, there is no need for another translation, particularly one likely to be inferior to the distinguished translation we already have; and second, no translation of mine can be published in this country. In this way, you see, I am able to undertake what I would not otherwise have dared to do, without having to bother myself any longer worrying whether it is sensible or not. Indeed, some nights when I am working late, the futility of what I am doing would appear to be my deepest source of satisfaction.

To you perhaps this may appear to be nothing but a pretentious form of capitulation, of self-mockery. It may even appear that way to me on occasion. Nonetheless, it remains the most serious thing I can think to do in my retirement. And you," he asks, so very genially, "what draws you so to Kafka?"

"It's a long story too."

"Dealing with?"

"Not with political hopelessness."

"I would think not."

"Rather," I say, "in large part, with sexual despair, with vows of chastity that seem somehow to have been taken by me behind my back, and which I lived with against my will. Either I turned against my flesh, or it turned against me—I still don't know quite how to put it."

"From the look of things, you don't seem to have suppressed its urgings entirely. That is a very attractive young woman you are traveling with."

"Well, the worst is over. *May* be over. At least is over for *now*. But while it lasted, while I couldn't be what I had always just assumed I was, well, it wasn't quite like anything I had ever known before. Of course you are the one on intimate terms with totalitarianism—but if you'll permit me, I can only compare the body's utter single-mindedness, its cold indifference and absolute contempt for the well-being of the spirit, to some underlying, authoritarian regime. And you can petition it all you like, offer up the most heartfelt and dignified and logical sort of appeal—and get no response at all. If anything, a kind of laugh is what you get. I submitted my petitions through a psychoanalyst; went to his office every other day for an hour to make my case for the restoration of a robust libido. And, I tell you, with arguments and perorations no less involuted and tedious and cunning and abstruse than the kind of thing you find in *The Castle*. You think poor K. is clever—you should have heard me trying to outfox impotence."

"I can imagine. That's not a pleasant business."

"Of course, measured against what you—"

"Please, you needn't say things like that. It is *not* a pleasant business, and the right to vote provides, in this matter, little in the way of compensation."

"That is true. I did vote during this period, and found it

made me no happier. What I started to say about Kafka, about reading Kafka, is that stories of obstructed, thwarted K.'s banging their heads against invisible walls, well, they suddenly had a disturbing new resonance for me. It was all a little less remote, suddenly, than the Kafka I'd read in college. In my own way, you see, I had come to know that sense of having been summoned—or of imagining yourself summoned—to a calling that turns out to be beyond you, yet in the face of every compromising or farcical consequence, being unable to wise up and relinquish the goal. You see, I once went about living as though sex were sacred ground."

"So to be 'chaste' . . ." he says, sympathetically. "Most unpleasant."

"I sometimes wonder if *The Castle* isn't in fact linked to Kafka's own erotic blockage—a book engaged at every level with not reaching a climax."

He laughs at my speculation, but as before, gently and with that unrelenting amiability. Yes, just so profoundly compromised is the retired professor, caught, as in a mangle, between conscience and the regime—between conscience and searing abdominal pain. "Well," he says, putting a hand on my arm in a kind and fatherly way, "to each obstructed citizen his own Kafka."

"And to each angry man his own Melville," I reply. "But then what are bookish people to do with all the great prose they read—"

"—but sink their teeth into it. Exactly. Into the books, instead of into the hand that throttles them."

Late that afternoon, we board the streetcar whose number Professor Soska had written in pencil on the back of a packet of postcards ceremoniously presented to Claire at the door of our hotel. The postcards are illustrated with photographs of Kafka, his family, the Prague landmarks associated with his life and his work. The handsome little set is no longer in circulation, Soska explained to us, now that the Russians occupy Czechoslovakia and Kafka is an outlawed writer, *the* outlawed writer. "But you do have another set, I hope," said Claire, "for yourself—?" "Miss Ovington," he said, with a courtly bow, "I have Prague. Please, permit me. I am sure that everyone who meets you wants to give you a gift." And here he suggested the visit to

Kafka's grave, to which it would not, however, be advisable for him to accompany us . . . and motioning with his hand, he drew our attention to a man standing with his back to a parked taxicab some fifty feet up the boulevard from the door of the hotel: the plainclothesman, he informs us, who used to follow him and Mrs. Soska around in the months after the Russian invasion, back when the professor was helping to organize the clandestine opposition to the new puppet regime and his duodenum was still intact. "Are you sure that's him, here?" I had asked. "Sufficiently sure," said Soska, and stooping quickly to kiss Claire's hand, he moved with a rapid, comic stride, rather like a man in a walking race, into the crowd descending the wide stairs of the passageway to the underground. "My God," said Claire, "it's too awful. All that terrible smiling. And that getaway!"

We are both a little stunned, not least of all, in my case, for feeling myself so safe and inviolable, what with the passport in my jacket and the young woman at my side.

The streetcar carries us from the center of Prague to the outlying district where Kafka is buried. Enclosed within a high wall, the Jewish graveyard is bounded on one side by a more extensive Christian cemetery—through the fence we see visitors tending the graves there, kneeling and weeding like patient gardeners—and on the other by a wide bleak thoroughfare bearing truck traffic to and from the city. The gate to the Jewish cemetery is chained shut. I rattle the chain and call toward what seems a watchman's house. In time a woman with a little boy appears from somewhere inside. I say in German that we have flown all the way from New York to visit Franz Kafka's grave. She appears to understand, but says no, not today. Come back Tuesday, she says. But I am a professor of literature and a Jew, I explain, and pass a handful of crowns across to her between the bars. A key appears, the gate is opened, and inside the little boy is assigned to accompany us as we follow the sign that points the way. The sign is in five different tongues—so many peoples fascinated by the fearful inventions of this tormented ascetic, so many fearful millions: Khrobu/К могиле/Zum Grabe/To the Grave of/à la tombe de/FRANZE KAFKY.

Of all things, marking Kafka's remains—and unlike anything else in sight—a stout, elongated, whitish rock, tapering upward to its pointed glans, a tombstone phallus. That is the first surprise. The second is that the family-haunted son is buried forever—still!—between the mother and the father who outlived him. I take a pebble from the gravel walk and place it on one of the little mounds of pebbles piled there by the pilgrims who've preceded me. I have never done so much for my own grandparents, buried with ten thousand others alongside an expressway twenty minutes from my New York apartment, nor have I made such a visit to my mother's tree-shaded Catskill grave site since I accompanied my father to the unveiling of her stone. The dark rectangular slabs beyond Kafka's grave bear familiar Jewish names. I might be thumbing through my own address book, or at the front desk looking over my mother's shoulder at the roster of registered guests at the Hungarian Royale: Levy, Goldschmidt, Schneider, Hirsch . . . The graves go on and on, but only Kafka's appears to be properly looked after. The other dead are without survivors hereabouts to chop away the undergrowth and to cut back the ivy that twists through the limbs of the trees and forms a heavy canopy joining the plot of one extinct Jew to the next. Only the childless bachelor appears to have living progeny. Where better for irony to abound than à la tombe de Franze Kafky?

Set into the wall facing Kafka's grave is a stone inscribed with the name of his great friend Brod. Here too I place a small pebble. Then for the first time I notice the plaques affixed to the length of cemetery wall, inscribed to the memory of Jewish citizens of Prague exterminated in Terezin, Auschwitz, Belsen, and Dachau. There are not pebbles enough to go around.

With the silent child trailing behind, Claire and I head back to the gate. When we get there Claire snaps a picture of the shy little boy and, using sign language, instructs him to write down his name and address on a piece of paper. Pantomiming with broad gestures and stagy facial expressions that make me wonder suddenly just how childish a young woman she is— just how childlike and needy a man I have become—she is able to inform the little boy that when the photograph is ready she will send a copy to him. In two or three weeks Professor Soska is also to receive a photograph from Claire, this one taken earlier in the day outside the souvenir shop where Kafka had once spent a winter.

Now why do I want to call what joins me to her childish? Why do I want to call this happiness names? Let it happen! Let it be! Stop the challenging before it even starts! You need what you need! Make peace with it!

The woman has come from the house to open the gate. Again we exchange some remarks in German.

"There are many visitors to Kafka's grave?" I ask.

"Not so many. But always distinguished people, Professor, like yourself. Or serious young students. He was a very great man. We had many great Jewish writers in Prague. Franz Werfel. Max Brod. Oskar Baum. Franz Kafka. But now," she says, casting her first glance, and a sidelong, abbreviated one at that, toward my companion, "they are all gone."

"Maybe your little boy will grow up to be a great Jewish writer."

She repeats my words in Czech. Then she translates the reply the boy has given while looking down at his shoes. "He wants to be an aviator."

"Tell him people don't always come from all over the world to visit an aviator's grave."

Again words are exchanged with the boy, and, smiling pleasantly at me—yes, it is only to the Jewish professor that she will address herself with a gracious smile—she says, "He doesn't mind that so much. And, sir, what is the name of your university?"

I tell her.

"If you would like, I will take you to the grave of the man who was Dr. Kafka's barber. He is buried here too."

"Thank you, that is very kind."

"He was also the barber of Dr. Kafka's father."

I explain to Claire what the woman has offered. Claire says, "If you want, go ahead."

"Better not to," I say. "Start with Kafka's barber, and by midnight we may end up by the grave of his candlestick maker."

To the graveyard attendant I say, "I'm afraid that's not possible right now."

"Of course your wife may come too," she starchily informs me.

"Thank you. But we have to get back to our hotel."

Now she looks me over with undisguised suspiciousness, as

though it well may be that I am not from a distinguished American university at all. She has gone out of her way to unlock the gate on a day other than the one prescribed for tourists, and I have turned out to be less than serious, probably nothing but a curiosity seeker, a Jew perhaps, but in the company of a woman quite clearly Aryan.

At the streetcar stop I say to Claire, "Do you know what Kafka said to the man he shared an office with at the insurance company? At lunchtime he saw the fellow eating his sausage and Kafka is supposed to have shuddered and said, 'The only fit food for a man is half a lemon.'"

She sighs, and says, sadly, "Poor dope," finding in the great writer's dietary injunction a disdain for harmless appetites that is just plain silly to a healthy girl from Schenectady, New York.

That is all—yet, when we board the streetcar and sit down beside each other, I take her hand and feel suddenly purged of yet another ghost, as de-Kafkafied by my pilgrimage to the cemetery as I would appear to have been de-Birgittized once and for all by that visitation on the terrace restaurant in Venice. My obstructed days are behind me—along with the *un*obstructed ones: no more "more," and no more nothing, either!

"Oh, Clarissa," I say, bringing her hand to my lips, "it's as though the past can't do me any more harm. I just don't have any more regrets. And my fears are gone, too. And it's all from finding you. I'd thought the god of women, who doles them out to you, had looked down on me and said, 'Impossible to please—the hell with him.' And then he sends me Claire."

That evening, after dinner in our hotel, we go up to the room to prepare for our early departure the next day. While I pack a suitcase with my clothes and with the books I have been reading on the airplanes and in bed at night, Claire falls asleep amid the clothing she has laid out on the comforter. Aside from the Kafka diaries and Brod's biography—my supplemental guidebooks to old Prague—I have with me paperbacks by Mishima, Gombrowicz, and Genet, novels for next year's comparative literature class. I have decided to organize the first semester's reading around the subject of erotic desire, beginning with these disquieting contemporary novels dealing with prurient and iniquitous sexuality (disquieting to students because they are the sort of books admired most by a reader like Baumgarten, novels in which the author is himself pointedly implicated in what is morally most alarming) and ending the term's work with three masterworks concerned with illicit and ungovernable passions, whose assault is made by other means: *Madame Bovary*, *Anna Karenina*, and "Death in Venice."

Without awakening her, I pick Claire's clothes off the bed and pack them in her suitcase. Handling her things, I feel overwhelmingly in love. Then I leave her a note saying that I have gone for a walk and will be back in an hour. Passing through the lobby I notice that there are now some fifteen or twenty pretty young prostitutes seated singly, and in pairs, beyond the glass doorway of the hotel's spacious café. Earlier in the day there had been just three of them, at a single table, gaily chatting together. When I asked Professor Soska how all this is organized under socialism, he had explained that most of Prague's whores are secretaries and shopgirls moonlighting with tacit government approval; a few are employed full-time by the Ministry of the Interior to get what information they can out of the various delegations from East and West that pass through the big hotels. The covey of miniskirted girls I see seated in the café are probably there to greet the members of the Bulgarian trade mission who occupy most of the floor beneath ours. One of them, who is stroking the belly of a brown dachshund puppy that lies cuddled in her arms, smiles my way. I smile back (costs nothing) and then am off to the Old Town Square, where Kafka and Brod used to take their evening stroll. When I get there it is after nine and the spacious melancholy plaza is empty of everything except the shadows of the aged façades enclosing it. Where the tourist buses had been parked earlier in the day there is now only the smooth, worn, cobblestone basin. The place is empty—of all, that is, except mystery and enigma. I sit alone on a bench beneath a street lamp and, through the thin film of mist, look past the looming figure of Jan Hus to the church whose most sequestered proceedings the Jewish author could observe by peering through his secret aperture.

It is here that I begin to compose in my head what at first strikes me as no more than a bit of whimsy, the first lines of an introductory lecture to my comparative literature class inspired by Kafka's "Report to an Academy," the story in which an ape addresses a scientific gathering. It is only a little story of a few thousand words, but one that I love, particularly its opening, which seems to me one of the most enchanting and startling in literature: "Honored Members of the Academy! You have done me the honor of inviting me to give your Academy an account of the life I formerly led as an ape."

"Honored Members of Literature 341," I begin . . . but by the time I am back at the hotel and have seated myself, with pen in hand, at an empty table in a corner of the café, I have penetrated the veneer of donnish satire with which I began, and on hotel stationery am writing out in longhand a formal introductory lecture (not uninfluenced by the ape's impeccable, professorial prose) that I want with all my heart to deliver—and to deliver not in September but at this very moment!

Seated two tables away is the prostitute with the little dachshund; she has been joined by a friend, whose favorite pet seems to be her own hair. She strokes away at it as though it is somebody else's. Looking up from my work, I tell the waiter to bring a cognac to each of these petite and pretty working girls, neither of them as old as Claire, and order a cognac for myself.

"Cheers," says the prostitute pleasing her puppy, and after the three of us smile at one another for a brief, enticing moment, I go back to writing what seem to me then and there somehow to be sentences of the most enormous consequence for my happy new life.

Rather than spend the first day of class talking about the reading list and the general idea behind this course, I would like to tell you some things about myself that I have never before divulged to any of my students. I have no business doing this, and until I came into the room and took my seat I wasn't sure I would go through with it. And I may change my mind yet. For how do I justify disclosing to you the most intimate facts of my personal life? True, we will be meeting to discuss books for three hours a week during the coming two semesters, and from experience I know, as you do, that under such conditions a strong bond of affection can develop. However, we also know that this does not give me license to indulge what may only be so much impertinence and bad taste.

As you may already have surmised—by my style of dress, as easily as from the style of my opening remarks—the conventions traditionally governing the relationship between student and teacher are more or less those by which I have always operated, even during the turbulence of recent years. I have been told that I am one of the few remaining professors who address students in the classroom as "Mr." and "Miss," rather than by their given names. And however you may choose to attire yourselves—in the getup of garage mechanic, panhandler, tearoom gypsy, or cattle rustler—I still prefer to appear before you to teach wearing a jacket and a tie . . . though, as the observant will record, generally it will be the same jacket and the same tie. And when women students come to my office to confer, they will see, if they should even bother to look, that throughout the meeting I will dutifully leave open to the outside corridor the door to the room where we sit side by side. Some of you may be further amused when I remove my watch from my wrist, as I did only a moment ago, and place it beside my notes at the beginning of each class session. By now I no longer remember which of my own professors used to keep careful track of the passing hour in this way, but it would seem to have made its impression on me, signaling a professionalism with which I like still to associate myself.

All of which is not to say that I shall try to keep hidden from you the fact that I am flesh and blood—or that I understand that you are. By the end of the year you may even have grown a little weary of my insistence upon the connections between the novels you read for this class, even the most eccentric and off-putting of novels, and what you know so far of life. You will discover (and not all will approve) that I do not hold with certain of my colleagues who tell us that literature, in its most valuable and intriguing moments, is "fundamentally non-referential." I may come before you in my jacket and my tie, I may address you as madam and sir, but I am going to request nonetheless that you restrain yourselves from talking about "structure," "form," and "symbols" in my presence. It seems to me that many of you have been intimidated sufficiently by your junior year of college and should be allowed to recover and restore to respectability those interests and enthusiasms that more than likely drew you to reading fiction to begin with and which you oughtn't to be ashamed of now. As an experiment you might even want during the course of this year to try living without any classroom terminology at all, to relinquish "plot" and "character" right along with those very exalted words with which not a few of you like to solemnize your observations, such as "epiphany," "persona," and, of course, "existential" as a modifier of everything existing under the sun. I suggest this in the hope that if you talk about *Madame Bovary* in more or less the same tongue you use with the grocer, or your lover, you may be placed in a more intimate, a more interesting, in what might even be called a more *referential* relationship with Flaubert and his heroine.

In fact, one reason the novels to be read during the first semester are all concerned, to a greater or lesser degree of obsessiveness, with erotic desire is that I thought that readings organized around a subject with which you all have some sort of familiarity might help you even better to locate these books in the world of experience, and further to discourage the temptation to consign them to that manageable netherworld of narrative devices, metaphorical motifs, and mythical archetypes. Above all, I hope that by reading these books you will come to learn something of value about life in one its most puzzling and maddening aspects. I hope to learn something myself.

All right. This much said by way of stalling, the time has come to begin to disclose the undisclosable—the story of the *professor's* desire. Only I can't, not quite yet, not until I have explained to my own satisfaction, if not to your parents', why I would even think to cast you as my voyeurs and my jurors and my confidants, why I would expose my secrets to people half my age, almost all of whom I have never previously known even as students. Why for me an audience, when most men and women prefer either to keep such matters entirely to themselves or to reveal them only to their most trusted confessors, secular or devout? What makes it compellingly necessary, or at all appropriate, that I present myself to you young strangers in the guise not of your teacher but as the first of this semester's texts?

Permit me to reply with an appeal to the heart.

I love teaching literature. I am rarely ever so contented as when I am here with my pages of notes, and my marked-up texts, and with people like yourselves. To my mind there is nothing quite like the classroom in all of life. Sometimes when we are in the midst of talking— when one of you, say, has pierced with a single phrase right to the heart of the book at hand—I want to cry out, "Dear friends, cherish this!" Why? Because once you have left here people are rarely, if ever, going to talk to you or listen to you the way you talk and listen to one another and to me in this bright and barren little room. Nor is it likely that you will easily find opportunities elsewhere to speak without embarrassment about what has mattered most to men as attuned to life's struggles as were Tolstoy, Mann, and Flaubert. I doubt that you know how very affecting it is to hear you speak thoughtfully and in all earnestness about solitude, illness, longing, loss, suffering, delusion, hope, passion, love, terror, corruption, calamity, and death . . . moving because you are nineteen and twenty years old, from comfortable middle-class homes most of you, and without much debilitating experience in your dossiers yet—but also because, oddly and sadly, this may be the last occasion you will ever have to reflect in any sustained and serious way upon the unrelenting forces with which in time you will all contend, like it or not.

Have I made any clearer why I should find our classroom to be, in fact, the *most* suitable setting for me to make an accounting of my erotic history? Does what I have just said render any more legitimate the claim I should like to make upon your time and patience and tuition? To put it as straight as I can—what a church is to the true believer, a classroom is to me. Some kneel at Sunday prayer, others don phylacteries each dawn . . . and I appear three times each week, my tie around my neck and my watch on my desk, to teach the great stories to you.

Class, oh, students, I have been riding the swell of a very large emotion this year. I'll get to that too. In the meantime, if possible, bear with my mood of capaciousness. Really, I only wish to present you with my credentials for teaching Literature 341. Indiscreet, unprofessional, unsavory as portions of these disclosures will surely strike some of you, I nonetheless would like, with your permission, to go ahead now and give an open account to you of the life I formerly led as a human being. I am devoted to fiction, and I assure you that in time I will tell you whatever I may know about it, but in truth nothing lives in me like my life.

The two pretty young prostitutes are still unattended, still sitting across from me in their white angora sweaters, pastel miniskirts, dark net stockings, and elevating high-heel shoes—rather like children who have ransacked Mamma's closet to dress as usherettes for a pornographic movie house—when I rise with my sheaf of stationery to leave the café.

"A letter to your wife?" says the one who strokes the dog and speaks some English.

I cannot resist the slow curve she has thrown me. "To the children," I say.

She nods to the friend who is stroking her hair: yes, they know my type. At eighteen they know all the types.

Her friend says something in Czech and they have a good laugh.

"Goodbye, sir; nighty-night," says the knowing one, offering a harmless enough smirk for me to carry away from the encounter. I am thought to have gotten my kick by buying two whores a drink. Maybe I did. Fair enough.

In our room I find that Claire has changed into her night-dress and is sleeping now beneath the blankets. A note for me on the pillow: "Dear One—I loved you so much today. I *will* make you happy. C."

Oh, I *have* come through—on my pillow is the proof!

And the sentences in my hands? They hardly seem now to be so laden with implication for my future as they did when I was hurrying back to the hotel from the Old Town Square, dying to get my hands on a piece of paper so as to make *my* report to *my* academy. Folding the pages in two, I put them with the paperbacks at the bottom of my suitcase, there along with Claire's note that promises to make her dear one happy. I feel absolutely triumphant: capacious indeed.

When I am awakened in the early morning by a door slamming beneath our room—down where the Bulgarians are sleeping, one of them no doubt with a little Czech whore and a dachshund puppy—I find I cannot begin to reconstruct the meandering maze of dreams that had so challenged and agitated me throughout the night. I had expected I would sleep marvelously, yet I awaken perspiring and, for those first timeless seconds, with no sense at all of where I am in bed or with whom. Then, blessedly, I find Claire, a big warm animal of my own species, my very own mate of the other gender, and encircling her with my arms—drawing her sheer creatureliness up against the length of my body—I begin to recall the long, abusive episode that had unfolded more or less along these lines:

I am met at the train by a Czech guide. He is called X, "as in the alphabet," he explains. I am sure he is really Herbie Bratasky, our master of ceremonies, but I do nothing to tip my hand. "And what have you seen so far?" asks X as I disembark.

"Why, nothing. I am just arriving."

"Then I have just the thing to start you off. How would you like to meet the whore Kafka used to visit?"

"There is such a person? And she is still alive?"

"How would you like to be taken to talk with her?"

I speak only after I have looked to be sure that no one is eavesdropping. "It is everything I ever hoped for."

"And how was Venice without the Swede?" X asks as we step aboard the cemetery streetcar.

"Dead."

The apartment is four flights up, in a decrepit building by the river. The woman we have come to see is nearly eighty: arthritic hands, slack jowls, white hair, clear and sweet blue eyes. Lives in a rocking chair on the pension of her late husband, an anarchist. I ask myself, "An anarchist's widow receiving a government pension?"

"Was he an anarchist all his life?" I ask.

"From the time he was twelve," X replies. "That was when his father died. He once explained to me how it happened. He saw his father's dead body, and he thought, 'This man who smiles at me and loves me is no more. Never again will any man smile at me and love me as he did. Wherever I go I will be a stranger and an enemy all my life.' That's how anarchists are made, apparently. I take it you are not an anarchist."

"No. My father and I love each other to this day. I believe in the rule of law."

From the window of the apartment I can see the gliding force of the famous Moldau. "Why, there, boys and girls, at the edge of the river"—I am addressing my class—"is the *piscine* where Kafka and Brod would go swimming together. See, it is as I told you: Franz Kafka was real, Brod was not making him up. And so am I real, nobody is making me up, other than myself."

X and the old woman converse in Czech. X says to me, "I told her that you are a distinguished American authority on the works of the great Kafka. You can ask her whatever you want."

"What did she make of him?" I ask. "How old was he when she knew him? How old was she? When exactly was all this taking place?"

X (interpreting): "She says, 'He came to me and I took a look at him and I thought, "What is this Jewish boy so depressed about?"' She thinks it was in 1916. She says she was twenty-five. Kafka was in his thirties."

"Thirty-three," I say. "Born, class, in 1883. And as we know from all our years of schooling, three from six is three, eight from one doesn't go, so we must borrow one from the preceding digit; eight from eleven is three, eight from eight is zero, and one from one is zero—and that is why thirty-three is the correct answer to the question: How old was Kafka when he paid his visits to this whore? Next question: What, if any, is the relationship between Kafka's whore and today's story, 'A Hunger Artist'?"

X says, "And what else would you like to know?"

"Was he regularly able to have an erection? Could he usually reach orgasm? I find the diaries inconclusive."

Her eyes are expressive when she answers, though the crippled hands lie inert in her lap. In the midst of the indecipherable Czech I catch a word that makes my flesh run: Franz!

X nods gravely. "She says that was no problem. She knew what to do with a boy like him."

Shall I ask? Why not? I have come not just from America, after all, but out of oblivion, to which I shall shortly return. "What was that?"

Matter-of-fact, still, she tells X what she did to arouse the author of—"Name Kafka's major works in the order of their composition. Grades will be posted on the department bulletin board. All those who wish recommendations for advanced literary studies will please line up outside my office to be whipped to within an inch of their lives."

X says, "She wants money. American money, not crowns. Give her ten dollars."

I give over the money. What use will it be in oblivion? "No, that will not be on the final."

X waits until she is finished, then translates: "She blew him."

Probably for less than it cost me to find out. There is such a thing as oblivion, and there is such a thing as fraud, which I am also against. Of course! This woman is nobody, and Bratasky gets half.

"And what did Kafka talk about?" I ask, and yawn to show just how seriously I now take these proceedings.

X translates the old woman's reply word for word: "I don't remember any more. I didn't remember the next day probably. Look, these Jewish boys would sometimes say nothing at all. Like little birds, not even a squeak. I'll tell you one thing, though—they never hit me. And they were clean boys. Clean underwear. Clean collars. They would never dream to come here with so much as a soiled handkerchief. Of course everybody I always would wash with a rag. I was always hygienic.

But they didn't even need it. They were clean and they were gentlemen. As God is my witness, they never beat on my backside. Even in bed they had manners."

"But is there anything about Kafka in particular that she remembers? I didn't come here, to her, to Prague, to talk about nice Jewish boys."

She gives some thought to the question; or, more likely, no thought. Just sits there trying out being dead.

"You see, he wasn't so special," she finally says. "I don't mean he wasn't a gentleman. They were all gentlemen."

I say to Herbie (refusing to pretend any longer that he is some Czech named X), "Well, I don't really know what to ask next, Herb. I have the feeling she may have Kafka confused with somebody else."

"The woman's mind is razor-sharp," Herbie replies.

"Still, she's not exactly Brod on the subject."

The aged whore, sensing perhaps that I have had it, speaks again.

Herbie says, "She wants to know if you would like to inspect her pussy."

"To what possible end?" I reply.

"Shall I inquire?"

"Oh, please do."

Eva (for this, Herbie claims, is the lady's name) replies at length. "She submits that it might hold some literary interest for you. Others like yourself, who have come to her because of her relationship with Kafka, have been most anxious to see it, and, providing of course that their credentials established them as serious, she has been willing to show it to them. She says that because you are here on my recommendation she would be delighted to allow you to have a quick look."

"I thought she only blew him. Really, Herb, of what possible interest could her pussy be to me? You know I am not in Prague alone."

Translation: "Again, she frankly admits she doesn't know of what interest anything about her is to anyone. She says she is grateful for the little money she is able to make from her friendship with young Franz, and she is flattered that her callers are themselves distinguished and learned men. Of course, if the gentleman does not care to examine it—"

But why not? Why come to the battered heart of Europe if not to examine just this? Why come into the world at all? "Students of literature, you must conquer your squeamishness once and for all! You must face the unseemly thing itself! You must come off your high horse! There, *there* is your final exam."

It would cost me five more American dollars. "This is a flourishing business, this Kafka business," I say.

"First of all, given your field of interest, the money is tax-deductible. Second, for only a fiver, you are striking a decisive blow against the Bolsheviks. She is one of the last in Prague still in business for herself. Third, you are helping preserve a national literary monument—you are doing a service for our suffering writers. And last but not least, think of the money you have given to Klinger. What's five more to the cause?"

"I beg your pardon. What cause?"

"Your happiness. We only want to make you happy, to make you finally you, David dear. You have denied yourself too much as it is."

Despite her arthritic hands Eva is able on her own to tug her dress up until it is bunched in her lap. Herbie, however, has to hold her around with one arm, shift her on her buttocks, and draw down her underpants for her. I reluctantly help by steadying the rocking chair.

Accordioned kidskin belly, bare ruined shanks, and, astonishingly, a triangular black patch, pasted on like a mustache. I find myself rather doubting the authenticity of the pubic hair.

"She would like to know," says Herbie, "if the gentleman would care to touch it."

"And how much does that go for?"

Herbie repeats my question in Czech. Then to me, with a courtly bow, "Her treat."

"Thanks, no."

But again she assures the gentleman that it will cost him nothing. Again the gentleman courteously declines.

Now Eva smiles—between her parted lips, her tongue, still red. The pulp of the fruit, still red!

"Herb, what did she say just then?"

"Don't think I ought to repeat it, not to you."

"What was it, Herbie? I demand to know!"

"Something indecent," he says, chuckling, "about what Kafka liked the most. His big thrill."

"*What was it?*"

"Oh, I don't think your dad would want you to hear that, Dave. Or your dad's dad, and so on, all the way back to the Father of the Faithful and the Friend of God. Besides, it may just have been a malicious remark, gratuitously made, with no foundation in fact. She may only have said it because you insulted her. You see, by refusing to touch a finger to her famous vizz you have cast doubt—perhaps not entirely inadvertently either—on the very meaning of her life. Moreover, she is afraid you will go back to America now and tell your colleagues that she is a fraud. And then serious scholars will no longer come to pay their respects—which, of course, would mark the end for her, and if I may say so, the end too for private enterprise in our country. It would constitute nothing less than the final victory of the Bolsheviks over free men."

"Well, except for this new Czech routine of yours—which, I have to admit, could have fooled just about anybody but me—you haven't changed, Bratasky, not a bit."

"Too bad I can't say the same about you."

Here Herbie approaches the old woman, her face now sadly tear-streaked, and cupping his fingers as though to catch the trickle of a stream, he places his hands between her bare legs.

"Coo," she gurgles. "Coo. Coo." And closing her blue eyes, she rubs her cheek against Herbie's shoulder. The tip of her tongue I see protruding from her mouth. The pulp of the fruit, still red.

UPON returning from our travels through the beautiful cities—after I dreamed in Prague of visiting Kafka's whore, we flew the next morning to Paris, and three days later to Bruges, where at a conference on modern European literature I read the paper entitled "Hunger Art"—we decide to split the rent on a small house in the country for July and August. How better to spend the summer? But once the decision is made, all I can think about is the time I last lived in daily proximity to a woman, the tomb-like months just before the Hong Kong fiasco, when neither of us could so much as bear the sight of the other's shoes on the floor of the closet. Consequently, before I sign the lease for the perfect little house that we've found, I suggest that probably it would be best not to sublet either of our apartments in the city for the two months—a small financial sacrifice, true, but this way there will always be a place to retreat to if anything untoward should happen. I actually say "untoward." Claire—prudent, patient, tender Claire—understands well enough what I mean as I jabber on in this vein, the pen in my hand, and the agent who drew up the lease casting unamused glances from the other end of his office. Raised by heavyweight battlers from the day she was born until she was able to leave for school and a life of her own, an independent young woman now since the age of seventeen, she has no argument against having a nest to fly off to, as well as the nest that is to be shared, for so long as the sharing is good. No, we won't rent our apartments, she agrees. Whereupon, with the solemnity of the Japanese Commander-in-Chief sitting down aboard MacArthur's battleship to surrender an empire, I affix my signature to the lease.

A small, two-storied white clapboard farmhouse, then, set halfway up a hillside of dandelions and daisies from a silent, untraveled rural road, and twenty miles north of the Catskill village where I was raised. I have chosen Sullivan County over Cape Cod, and that too is fine with Claire—proximity to the Vineyard and to Olivia seems not to matter to her quite the way it did just the year before. And for me the gentle green hills and distant green mountains beyond the dormer windows take me back to the bedroom vista of my childhood—exactly my view from the room at the top of the "Annex"—and augment the sense I already have with her that I am living at last in accordance with my true spirit, that, indeed, I am "home."

And for the spirit what a summer it is! From the daily regimen of swimming in the morning and hiking in the afternoon we each grow more and more fit, while within, day to day, we grow fat as our farmer neighbor's hogs. How the spirit feasts on just getting up in the morning! on coming to in a white-washed sunlit room with my arms encircling her large, substantial form. Oh, how I do love the size of her in bed! That *tangibility* of hers! And the weight of those breasts in my hands! Oh, very different, this, from all the months and months of waking up with nothing to hold on to but my pillow!

Later—is it not yet eleven? *really?* we have eaten our cinnamon toast, taken our dip, stopped in town to buy food for dinner, brooded over the newspaper's front page, and it is only ten-fifteen?—later, from the rocker on the porch where I do my morning writing, I watch her toil in the garden. Two spiral notebooks are arranged beside me. In one I work at planning the projected book on Kafka, to be called, after my Bruges lecture, *Hunger Art*, while in the other, whose pages I approach with far greater eagerness—and where I am having somewhat more success—I move on to the substance of the lecture whose prologue I had begun composing in the hotel café in Prague, the story of *my* life in its most puzzling and maddening aspects, *my* chronicle of the iniquitous, the ungovernable and the thrilling . . . or (by way of a working title), "How David Kepesh comes to be sitting in a wicker rocker on a screened-in porch in the Catskill Mountains, watching with contentment while a teetotaling twenty-five-year-old sixth-grade teacher from Schenectady, New York, creeps about her flower garden in what appear to be overalls handed down from Tom Sawyer himself, her hair tied back with a snip of green twister seal cut from the coil with which she stakes the swooning begonias, her delicate, innocent Mennonite face, small and intelligent as a raccoon's, and soil-smudged as though in preparation for Indian night at the Girl Scout jamboree—and his happiness in her hands."

"Why don't you come out and help with the weeds?" she calls—"Tolstoy would have." "He was a big-time novelist," I say; "they have to do that sort of thing, to gain Experience. Not me. For me it's enough to see you crawling on your knees." "Well, whatever pleases," she says.

Ah, Clarissa, let me tell you, all that *is* pleases. The pond where we swim. Our apple orchard. The thunderstorms. The barbecue. The music playing. Talking in bed. Your grandmother's iced tea. Deliberating on which walk to take in the morning and which at dusk. Watching you lower your head to peel peaches and shuck corn . . . Oh, nothing, really, is what pleases. But what nothing! Nations go to war for this kind of nothing, and in the absence of such nothing, people shrivel up and die.

Of course by now the passion between us is no longer quite what it was on those Sundays when we would cling together in my bed until three in the afternoon—"the primrose path to madness," as Claire once described those rapacious exertions which end finally with the two of us rising on the legs of weary travelers to change the bed linens, to stand embracing beneath the shower, and then to go out of doors to get some air before the winter sun goes down. That, once begun, our lovemaking should have continued with undiminished intensity for almost a year—that two industrious, responsible, idealistic schoolteachers should have adhered to one another like dumb sea creatures, and, at the moment of overbrimming, have come to the very brink of tearing flesh with cannibalized jaws—well, that is somewhat more than I ever would have dared predict for myself, having already served beyond the call of duty—having already staked so much and lost so much—under the tattered scarlet standard of His Royal Highness, my lust.

Leveling off. Overheated frenzy subsiding into quiet physical affection. That is how I choose to describe what is happening to our passion during this blissful summer. Can I think otherwise—can I possibly believe that, rather than coming to rest on some warm plateau of sweet coziness and intimacy, I am being eased down a precipitous incline and as yet am nowhere near the cold and lonely cavern where I finally will touch down? To be sure, the faintly brutal element has taken it on the lam; gone is the admixture of the merciless with the tender, those intimations of utter subjugation that one sees in the purplish bruise, the wantonness one thrills to in the coarse word breathed at the peak of pleasure. We no longer *succumb* to desire, nor do we touch each other everywhere, paw and knead and handle with that unquenchable lunacy so alien to what and who we otherwise are. True, I am no longer a little bit of a beast, she is no longer a little bit of a tramp, neither any longer is quite the greedy lunatic, the depraved child, the steely violator, the helplessly impaled. Teeth, once blades and pincers, the pain-inflicting teeth of little cats and dogs, are simply teeth again, and tongues are tongues, and limbs are limbs. Which is, as we all know, how it must be.

And I for one will not quarrel, or sulk, or yearn, or despair. I will not make a religion of what is fading away—of my craving for that bowl into which I dip my face as though to extract the last dram of a syrup I cannot guzzle down fast enough . . . of the harsh excitement of that pumping grip so strong, so rapid, so unyielding, that if I do not moan that there is nothing left of me, that I am stupefied and numb, she will, in that stirring state of fervor bordering on heartlessness, continue until she has milked the very life from my body. I will not make a religion of that marvelous sight of her half-stripped. No, I intend to nurse no illusions about the chance for a great revival of the drama we would seem very nearly to have played out, this clandestine, uncensored, underground theater of four furtive selves—the two who pant in performance, the two who pantingly watch—wherein regard for the hygienic, the temperate, and the time of day or night is all so much ridiculous intrusion. I tell you, I am a new man—that is, I am a *new* man no longer—and I know when my number is up: now just stroking the soft, long hair will do, just resting side by side in our bed each morning will do, awakening folded together, mated, in love. Yes, I am willing to settle on these terms. This will suffice. No more *more*.

And before whom am I on my knees trying to strike such a bargain? Who is to decide how far from Claire I am going to slide? Honored members of Literature 341, you would think, as I do, that it would, it should, it must, be me.

*

Late in the afternoon of one of the loveliest days of August, with nearly fifty such days already away in memory and the deep contentment of knowing that there are still a couple dozen more to come, on an afternoon when my feeling of well-being is boundless and I cannot imagine anyone happier or luckier than myself, I receive a visit from my former wife. I will think about it for days afterward, imagining each time the phone rings or I hear the sound of a car turning up the steep drive to the house that it is Helen returning. I will expect to find a letter from her every morning, or rather a letter about her, informing me that she has run off again to Hong Kong, or that she is dead. When I awaken in the middle of the night to remember how once I lived and how I live now—and this still happens to me, too regularly—I will cling to my sleeping partner as though it is she who is ten years my senior—twenty, thirty years my senior—rather than the other way around.

I am out by the orchard in a canvas lounge chair, my legs in the sun and my head in the shade, when I hear the phone ringing inside the house, where Claire is getting ready to go swimming. I have not yet decided—of such decisions are my days composed—whether I'll go along with her to the pond, or just stay on quietly doing my work until it is time to water the marigolds and open the wine. Since lunch I have been out here—just myself, the bumblebees, and the butterflies, and, from time to time, Claire's old Labrador, Dazzle—reading Colette and taking notes for the course known by now around the house as Desire 341. Leafing through a pile of her books, I have been wondering if there has ever been in America a novelist with a point of view toward the taking and giving of pleasure even vaguely resembling Colette's, an American writer, man or woman, stirred as deeply as she is by scent and warmth and color, someone as sympathetic to the range of the body's urgings, as attuned to the world's every sensuous offering, a connoisseur of the finest gradations of amorous feeling, who is nonetheless immune to fanaticism of any sort, except, as with Colette, a fanatical devotion to the self's honorable survival. Hers seems to have been a nature exquisitely susceptible to all that desire longs for and promises—"these pleasures which are lightly called physical"—yet wholly untainted by puritan conscience, or murderous impulse, or megalomania, or sinister ambitions, or the score-settling rage of class or social grievance. One thinks of her as egotistic, in the sharpest, crispest sense of the word, the most pragmatic of sensualists, her capacity for protective self-scrutiny in perfect balance with the capacity to be carried away—

The top sheet of my yellow pad is spattered and crisscrossed with the fragmentary beginnings of a lecture outline—running down one margin is a long list of modern novelists, European as well as American, among whom Colette's decent, robust, bourgeois paganism still seems to me unique—when Claire comes out of the kitchen's screen door, wearing her bathing suit and carrying her white terry-cloth robe over her arm.

The book in her hand is Musil's *Young Törless,* the copy I'd just finished marking up the night before. How delighted I am with her curiosity about these books I will be teaching! And to look up at the swell of her breasts above the bikini's halter, well, that is yet another of this wonderful day's satisfactions.

"Tell me," I say, taking hold of the calf of her nearest leg, "why is there no American Colette? Or could it be Updike who comes the closest? It's surely not Henry Miller. It's surely not Hawthorne."

"A phone call for you," she says. "Helen Kepesh."

"My God." I look at my watch, for all the help that will give. "What time would it be in California? What can she want? How did she find me?"

"It's a local call."

"*Is* it?"

"I think so, yes."

I haven't yet moved from the chair. "And that's what she said, Helen *Kepesh*?"

"Yes."

"But I thought she'd taken her own name back."

Claire shrugs.

"You told her I was here?"

"Do you want me to tell her you aren't?"

"What can she *want*?"

"You'll have to ask her," says Claire. "Or maybe you won't."

"Would it be so very wrong of me just to go in there and put the phone back on the hook?"

"Not wrong," says Claire. "Only unduly anxious."

"But I *feel* unduly anxious. I feel unduly *happy*. This is all so perfect." I spread ten fingers across the soft swell of flesh above her halter. "Oh, my dear, dear pal."

"I'll wait out here," she says.

"And I *will* go swimming with you."

"Okay. Good."

"So wait!"

It would be neither cruel nor cowardly, I tell myself, looking down at the phone on the kitchen table—it would just be the most sensible thing I could do. Except, of the half-dozen people closest to my life, Helen happens still to be one. "Hello," I say.

"Hello. Oh, hello. Look, I feel odd about phoning you, David. I almost didn't. Except I seem to be in your town. We're at the Texaco station; across from a real-estate office."

"I see."

"I'm afraid it was just too hard driving off without even calling. How are you?"

"How did you know I was staying here?"

"I tried you in New York a few days ago. I called the college, and the department secretary said she wasn't authorized to give out your summer address. I said I was a former student and I was sure you wouldn't mind. But she was adamant about Professor Kepesh's privacy. Quite a moat, that lady."

"So how did you find me?"

"I called the Schonbrunns."

"My, my."

"But stopping off here for gas is really just accidental. Strange, I know, but true. And not as strange, after all, as the truly strange things that happen."

She is lying and I'm not charmed. Through the window I can see Claire holding the unopened book in her hand. We could already be in the car on the way down to the pond.

"What do you want, Helen?"

"You mean from you? Nothing; nothing at all. I'm married now."

"I didn't know."

"That's what I was doing in New York. We were visiting my husband's family. We're on our way to Vermont. They have a summer house there." She laughs; a very appealing laugh. It makes me remember her in bed. "Can you believe I've never been to New England?"

"Well," I say, "it's not exactly Rangoon."

"Neither is Rangoon any more."

"How is your health? I heard that you were pretty sick."

"I'm better now. I had a hard time for a while. But it's over. How are *you*?"

"My hard time is over too."

"I'd like to see you, if I could. Are we that far from your house? I'd like to talk to you, just for a little—"

"About what?"

"I owe you some explanations."

"You don't. No more than I owe you any. I think we'd both be better off at this late date without the explanations."

"I was mad, David, I was going crazy— David, these are difficult things to say surrounded by cans of motor oil."

"Then don't say them."

"I have to."

Out on my chair, Claire is now leafing through the *Times*.

"You better go swimming without me," I say. "Helen's coming here; with her husband."

"She's married?"

"So she says."

"Why *was* it Helen 'Kepesh' then?"

"Probably to identify herself to you. To me."

"Or to herself," says Claire. "Would you rather I weren't here?"

"Of course not. I meant I thought you'd *prefer* going swimming."

"Only if *you* prefer—"

"No, absolutely not."

"Where are they now?"

"Down in town."

"She came all this way—? I don't understand. What if we hadn't been at home?"

"She says they're on their way to his family's house in Vermont."

"They didn't take the Thruway?"

"Honey, what's happened to you? No, they didn't take the

Thruway. Maybe they're taking the back roads for the scenery. What's the difference? They'll come and they'll go. You were the one who told *me* not to be unduly anxious."

"But I wouldn't want you to be hurt."

"Don't worry. If that's why you're staying—"

Here suddenly she stands, and at the edge of tears (where I have never before seen her!) she says, "Look, you so *obviously* want me out of the way—" Quickly she starts toward where our car is parked on the other side of the house, in the dust bowl by the old collapsing barn. And I run after her, just behind the dog, who thinks it is all a game.

Consequently we are beside the barn, waiting together, when the Lowerys arrive. As their car makes its way up the long dirt drive to the house, Claire slips her terry-cloth robe on over her bathing suit. I am wearing a pair of corduroy shorts, a faded old T-shirt, battered sneakers, an outfit I've probably had since Syracuse. Helen will have no trouble recognizing me. But will I recognize her? Can I explain to Claire—should I have?—that really, all I want is to *see* . . .

I had heard that, on top of all her debilitating ailments, she had gained some twenty pounds. If so, she has by now lost all that weight, and a bit more. She emerges from the car looking exactly like herself. She is paler-complexioned than I remember —or rather, she is not pale in the cleansed, Quakerish way to which I am now accustomed. Helen's pallor is luminous, transparent. Only in the thinness of her arms and neck is there any indication that she has been through a bad time with her health, and, what is more, is now a woman in her mid-thirties. Otherwise, she is the Stunning Creature once again.

Her husband shakes my hand. I had been expecting someone taller and older—I suppose one usually does. Lowery has a close-cropped black beard, round tortoise-shell glasses, and a compact, powerful, athletic build. Both are dressed in jeans and sandals and colored polo shirts and have their hair cut in the Prince Valiant style. The only jewelry either wears is a wedding ring. All of which tells me practically nothing. Maybe the emeralds are home in the vault.

We walk around as though they are prospective buyers who have been sent up by the real-estate agent to look at the house; as though they are the new couple from down the road who have stopped by to introduce themselves; as though they are what they are—ex-wife with new husband, someone now meaning nothing, artifact of relatively little remaining historical interest uncovered during an ordinary day's archaeological excavation. Yes, giving her the directions to our so perfect lair turns out to have been neither a foolish nor, God knows, a *dangerous* mistake. Otherwise, how would I have known that I have been wholly de-Helenized too, that the woman can neither harm me nor charm me, that I am un-bewitchable by all but the most loving and benign of feminine spirits. How right Claire was to caution me against being unduly anxious; before, of course, she went ahead and—doubtless because of my own confusion upon hanging up the phone—became unduly anxious herself.

Claire is up ahead now with Les Lowery. They are headed toward the blackened, ruined oak tree at the edge of the woods. Early in the summer, during a dramatic daylong storm, the tree was struck by lightning and severed in two. While we all walked together around the house and through the garden, Claire had been talking, just a little feverishly, about the wild thunderstorms of early July; a little feverishly, and a little childishly. I had not imagined beforehand just how ominous Helen would seem to her, given the tales of her troublemaking that I have told; I suppose I had not realized how often I must have told them to her in the first months we were together. No wonder she has latched on to the quiet husband, who does in fact seem closer to her in age and spirit, and who, it turns out, is also a subscriber to *Natural History* and the *Audubon Magazine*. Some minutes earlier, on the porch, she had identified for the Lowerys the unusual Cape Cod seashells arranged in a wicker tray in the center of the dining table, between the antique pewter candlesticks that were her grandmother's gift upon her graduation from college.

While my mate and her mate are examining the burned-out trunk of the oak tree, Helen and I drift back to the porch. She is telling me all about him, still. He is a lawyer, a mountain climber, a skier, he is divorced, has two adolescent daughters; in partnership with an architect he has already made a small fortune as a housing developer; lately he has been in the news for the work he has been doing as investigating counsel for a

California State Legislature committee unraveling connections between organized crime and the Marin County Police . . . Outside I see that Lowery has moved past the oak tree and onto the path that cuts up through the woods to the steep rock formations that Claire has been photographing all summer. Claire and Dazzle appear to be headed back down to the house.

I say to Helen, "He looks a bit young to be *such* a Karenin."

"I'm sure I'd be sardonic too," she replies, "if I were you and thought I was still me. I was surprised you even came to the phone. But that's because you are a nice man. You always were, actually."

"Oh, Helen, what's going on here? Save the 'nice man' stuff for my tombstone. You may have a new life, but this lingo . . ."

"I had a lot of time to think when I was sick. I thought about—"

But I don't want to know. "Tell me," I say, interrupting her, "how was your conversation with the Schonbrunns?"

"I spoke to Arthur. She wasn't home."

"And how did he take hearing from you after all this time?"

"Oh, he took it quite well."

"Frankly I'm surprised he offered assistance. I'm surprised you asked him for it. As I remember, he was never a great fan of yours—nor you of theirs."

"Arthur and I have changed our minds about each other."

"Since when? You used to be very funny about him."

"I'm not any more. I don't ridicule people who admit what they want. Or at least admit to what they don't have."

"And what does Arthur want? Are you telling me that all along Arthur wanted *you*?"

"I don't know about all along."

"Oh, Helen, I find this hard to believe."

"I never heard anything easier to believe."

"And what exactly is it I'm supposed to be believing, again?"

"When we two got back from Hong Kong, when you moved out and I was alone, he telephoned one night and asked if he could come over to talk. He was very concerned about you. So he came from his office—it was about nine—and he talked about your unhappiness for nearly an hour. I said finally that I didn't know what any of it had to do with me any more, and then he asked if he and I might meet in San Francisco for lunch one day. I said I didn't know, I was feeling pretty miserable myself, and he kissed me. And then he made me sit down and he sat down and he explained to me in detail that he hadn't expected to do that, and that it didn't mean what I thought it meant. He was happily married still, and after all these years he still had a strong physical relationship with Debbie, and in fact he owed her his whole life. And then he told me a harrowing story about some crazy girl, some librarian he had almost married in Minnesota, and how she had once gone after him with a fork at breakfast and stabbed his hand. He'd never gotten over what might have happened to him if he had caved in and married her—he thinks it actually might have ended in a murder. He showed me the scar from the fork. He said his salvation was meeting Debbie, and that he owes everything he's accomplished to her devotion and love. Then he tried to kiss me again, and when I said I didn't think it was a good idea, he told me I was perfectly right and that he had misjudged me completely and he still wanted to have lunch with me. I really couldn't take any more confusion, so I said yes. He arranged for us to eat at a place in Chinatown where, I assure you, nobody he knew or I knew or *anybody* knew could possibly see us together. And that was it. But then that summer, when they moved East, he began writing letters. I still get them, every few months or so."

"Go on. What do they say?"

"Oh, they're awfully well-written," she says, smiling. "He must write some of those sentences ten times over before he's completely satisfied. I think they may be the kind of letters the poetry editor of the college magazine writes late at night to his girl friend at Smith. 'The weather, as clear and as sharp as a fish spine,' and so on. And sometimes he includes lines from great poems about Venus, Cleopatra, and Helen of Troy."

" 'Lo, this is she that was the world's desire.' "

"That's right—that's one of them. I thought it was a bit insulting, actually. Except I suppose it can't be because it's so 'great.' Anyway, he always somehow or other lets me know that I don't have to answer; so I don't. Why are you smiling? It's really rather sweet. Well, it's *something*. Who'da thunk it?"

"I smile," I say, "because I've had my own Schonbrunn letters—from her."

"Now, *that's* hard to believe."

"No, not if you saw them. No great lines of poetry for me."

Claire is still some fifty or so feet away, yet both of us stop speaking as she makes her way back to the house. Why? Who knows why!

And if only we hadn't! Why didn't I just talk nonsense, tell a joke, *recite* a poem, *anything* so that Claire hadn't come through the screen door into this conspiratorial silence. Hadn't to come in to see me sitting across from Helen, charmed in spite of myself.

Immediately she becomes stony—and reaches a decision. "I'm going swimming."

"What's happened to Les?" asks Helen.

"Took a walk."

"You sure you don't want some iced tea?" I ask Claire. "Why don't we all have some iced tea?"

"No. Bye." That single adolescent syllable of farewell for the guest, then she's gone.

From where I am sitting I am able to watch our car pass down the hill to the road. What does Claire think we are plotting? What *are* we plotting?

Says Helen, when the car is out of sight, "She's terribly sweet."

"And I'm a 'nice man,'" I say.

"I'm sorry if I upset your friend by coming here. I didn't mean to."

"She'll be all right. She's a strong girl."

"And I mean you no harm. That isn't why I wanted to see you."

I am silent.

"I did mean you harm once, that's true," she says.

"You weren't solely responsible for the misery."

"What you did to me you did without wanting to; you did because you were provoked. But I think now that I actually set out to torture you."

"You're rewriting history, Helen. It's not necessary. We tormented each other, all right, but it wasn't out of malice. It was confusion, and it was ignorance, and it was other things too, but had it been malice, we wouldn't have been together for very long."

"I used to burn that fucking toast on purpose."

"As I remember, it was the fucking eggs that were burned. The fucking toast never got put in."

"I used to not mail your letters on purpose."

"Why are you saying these things? To castigate yourself, to somehow absolve yourself, or just to try to get a rise out of me? Even if it's true, I don't want to know it. That's all dead."

"I just always hated so the ways that people killed their time. I had this grand life all planned out, you see."

"I remember."

"Well, that's all dead too. Now I take what I can get, and I'm grateful to have it."

"Oh, don't overdo the 'chastened' bit, if that's what this is. Mr. Lowery doesn't sound like the scrapings to me. He doesn't look it, either. He looks like a very forceful person who knows what he's about. He sounds like somebody to conjure with, taking on the Mafia *and* the police. He sounds like a rather courageous man of the world. Just right for you. It certainly looks like he agrees with you."

"Does it?"

"You look terrific," I say—and am sorry I said it. So why then do I add, "You look marvelous."

For the first time since Claire came onto the porch, we fall silent again. We look unflinchingly at one another, as though we are strangers who dare, finally, to stare openly and unambiguously—the prelude to leaping precipitously into the most shameless and exciting copulation. I suppose there is no way we can avoid a little—if not a little more than a little— flirtation. Maybe I ought to say that. And then again, maybe I ought not. Maybe I ought just to look away.

"What were you sick with?" I ask.

"Sick with? It seemed like everything. I must have seen fifty doctors. All I did was sit in waiting rooms and have X-rays taken and blood taken and have cortisone injections and wait around drugstores to have prescriptions filled, and then bolt down the pills, hoping they'd save me on the spot. You should have seen my medicine chest. Instead of Countess Olga's lovely creams and lotions, vials and vials of hideous little pills— and none of them did a thing, except to ruin my stomach. My nose wouldn't stop running for over a year. I sneezed for hours on end, I couldn't breathe, my face puffed up, my eyes itched all the time, and then I began breaking out in horrible rashes. I'd pray when I went to sleep that they'd just go away the way they came, that they'd be gone for good in the morning. One allergist told me to move to Arizona, another told me it wouldn't help because it was all in my head, and another explained in great detail to me how I was allergic to myself, or something very like that, and so I went home and got into bed and pulled the covers over my face and daydreamed about having all the blood drawn out of me and replaced by somebody else's blood, blood I could get through the rest of my life with. I nearly went crazy. Some mornings I wanted to throw myself out the window."

"But you did get better."

"I began seeing Les," Helen says. "That's how it seems to have happened. The ailments all began to subside, one by one. I didn't know how he could bear me. I was hideous."

"Probably not so hideous as you thought. It sounds as though he fell in love with you."

"After I got well I got frightened. I thought that without him I'd start getting sick again. And start drinking again—because somehow he even got me to stop that. I said to him the night he first came to pick me up, looking so strong and cocky and butch, I said, 'Look, Mr. Lowery, I'm thirty-four years old, and I'm sick as a dog, and I don't like to be buggered.' And he said, 'I know how old you are, and everybody gets sick some time, and buggering doesn't interest me.' And so we went out, and he was so marvelously sure of himself, and he fell in love with me—and of course in love with rescuing me. But I didn't love him. And I wanted time and again to be finished with him. Only when it was over, when it should have been over, I got so frightened . . . So we were married."

I don't reply. I look away.

"I'm going to have a baby," she says.

"Congratulations. When?"

"Soon as I can. You see, I don't care any more about being happy. I've given that up. All I care about is not being tortured. I'll do anything. I'll have ten babies, I'll have twenty if he wants them. And he might. There is a man, David, who has no doubts about himself at all. He had a wife and two children even while he was in law school—he was already in the housing business in law school—and now he wants a second family, with me. And I'll do it. What else *can* she do, who was once the world's desire? Own a smart little antique shop? Take a degree and go out and run something? Be one of those fading beauties?"

"If you can't be twenty years old and sailing past the junks at sunset . . . But we have had that discussion. It's no longer my business."

"What about your business? Will you marry Miss Ovington?"

"I might."

"What holds you back?"

I don't answer.

"She's young, she's pretty, she's intelligent, she's educated, and under that robe she seemed quite lovely. And as a bonus there's something childlike and innocent that I certainly never had. Something that knows how to be content, I would think. How do they get that way, do you know? How do they get so *good*? I wondered if she wouldn't be like that. Bright and pretty and good. Leslie is bright and pretty and good. Oh, David, how do you stand it?"

"Because I'm bright and pretty and good myself."

"No, my dear old comrade, not the way they are. They come by it naturally, naïvely. Resist as you will, it's not quite the same, not even for a master repressive like yourself. You're not one of them, and you're not poor Arthur Schonbrunn, either."

I don't reply.

"Doesn't she drive you even a little crazy being so bright and pretty and good?" asks Helen. "With her seashells and her flower bed and her doggie, and her recipes tacked up over the sink?"

"Is this what you came here to tell me, Helen?"

"No. It isn't. Of course it isn't. I didn't come here to say *any* of these things. You're a bright fellow—you know very well why I came. To show you my husband. To show you how I've changed, for the better, of course; and . . . and other assorted lies. I thought I might even fool myself. David, I came here because I wanted to talk to a friend, strange as that may sound right now. I sometimes think of you as the only friend

I've got left. I did when I was sick. Isn't that odd? I almost called you one night—but I knew I was none of your business now. You see, I'm pregnant. I want you to tell me something. Tell me what you think I should do. Somebody has to. I'm two months pregnant, and if I wait any longer, well, then I'll have to go ahead and have it. And I can't stand him any more. But then I can't stand anyone. Everything everyone says is somehow wrong and drives me crazy. I don't mean I argue with people. I wouldn't dare. I listen and I nod and I smile. You should see how I please people these days. I listen to Les, and I nod and I smile, and I think I'll die of boredom. There's nothing he does now that doesn't irritate me nearly to death. But I can't be sick alone like that ever again. I couldn't take it. I can take loneliness, and I can take physical misery too, but I can't take them together like that ever again. It was too horrid and too relentless, and I haven't courage any more. I seem to have used it all up; inside me I feel there's no courage left. I have to have this baby. I have to tell him I'm pregnant—and have it. Because if I don't, I don't know what will happen to me. I can't leave him. I'm too terrified to be sick again like that, itching to death, unable to breathe—and it doesn't help to be told it's all in one's head, because that doesn't make it go away. Only he does. Yes, *he* made it all go away! Oh, this is all so crazy. None of this had to be! Because if that wife of Jimmy's had been run down when he had it all arranged, that would have been it. I would have had what I wanted. And I wouldn't have thought twice about her, either. Like it or not, that's the truth about me. I wouldn't have had a moment's stinking guilt. I would have been happy. And she would have gotten what she deserved. But instead I was good—and she's made them *both* miserable. I refused to be terrible, and the result is this terrible unhappiness. Each night I toss in my bed with the nightmare of how much I don't love *anybody.*"

At last, at long last, I see Lowery coming out of the woods and descending the hill toward the house. He has removed his shirt and is carrying it in his hand. He is a strong and handsome young man, he is a great success in the world, and his presence in her life has somehow restored her to health . . . Only it is Helen's bad luck that she cannot stand him. Still

Jimmy—still those dreams of what might and should have been, if only moral repugnance had not intervened.

"Maybe I'll love the baby," she says.

"Maybe you will," I say. "That happens sometimes."

"Then again, I may despise my baby," says Helen, sternly rising to greet her husband. "I would imagine that happens sometimes too."

After they leave—just like the new couple from down the road, with smiles and good wishes all around—I get into my bathing suit and walk the mile along our road to the pond. I have no thoughts and no feelings, I am numb, like someone at the perimeter of a terrible accident or explosion, who gets a brief, startling glimpse of a pool of blood, and then goes on his way, unharmed, to continue with the ordinary activities of the day.

Some small children are playing with shovels and pails at the edge of the pond, overseen by Claire's dog and by a mother's helper, who looks up and says "Hi." The girl is reading, of all things, *Jane Eyre*. Claire's terry-cloth robe is on the rock where we always put our things, and then I locate Claire, sunning herself out on the raft.

When I pull myself up beside her I see that she has been crying.

"I'm sorry I acted like that," she says.

"Don't be, don't be. We were both thrown way off. I don't believe those things can ever work out very well."

She begins to cry again, as noiselessly as it is possible to cry. The first of her tears that I've seen.

"What is it, lovely, what?"

"I feel so lucky. I feel so privileged. I love you. You've become my whole life."

"I have?"

This makes her laugh. "It frightens you a little to hear it. I guess it would. I didn't think it was true, till today. But I've never been happy like this before."

"Clarissa, why are you still so upset? There's no reason to be, is there?"

Turning her face into the raft, she mumbles something about her mother and father.

"I can't hear you, Claire."

"I wanted them to visit."

I'm surprised, but say, "Then invite them."

"I did."

"When was that?"

"It doesn't matter. It's just that I thought—well, I didn't think."

"You wrote them? Explain yourself, please. I'd like to know what's wrong."

"I don't want to go into it. It was foolish and dreamy. I lost my head a little."

"You telephoned them."

"Yes."

"When?"

"Before."

"You mean after you left the house? Before you came down here?"

"Down in town, yes."

"And?"

"I should never phone them without warning. I never do. It never works and it never will. But at night when we're having dinner, when we're so content and everything is so peaceful and lovely, I always start to think about them. I put on a record, and start cooking dinner, and there they are."

I hadn't known. She never speaks of what she does not have, never lingers for so much as a moment upon loss, misfortune, or disappointment. You'd have to torture her to get her to complain. She is the most extraordinary ordinary person I have ever known.

"Oh," she says, pushing up to a sitting position, "oh, this day will be fine when it's over. Do you have any idea when that will be?"

"Claire, do you want to stay out here with me, or do you want to be alone, or do you want to swim, or do you want to come home and have some iced tea and a little rest?"

"They're gone?"

"Oh, they're gone."

"And you're all right?"

"I'm intact. An hour or so older, but intact."

"How was it?"

"Not all that pleasant. You didn't take to her, I know, but the woman is in a bad way . . . Look, we don't have to talk about this now. We don't have to talk about it ever. Do you want to go home?"

"Not just yet," says Claire. She dives off the edge of the raft, remains out of sight for a long count of ten, and then surfaces by the ladder. When she sits back down beside me, she says, "There's one thing we'd better talk about now. One more thing I had better say. I was pregnant. I wasn't going to tell you, but I will."

"Pregnant by whom? When?"

A wan smile. "In Europe, love. By you. I found out for sure when we got home. I had an abortion. Those meetings I went to—well, I went to the hospital for the day."

"And the 'infection'?"

"I didn't have an infection."

Helen is two months pregnant, and I am the only person who knows. Claire has been pregnant, by me, and I've known nothing. I sense something very sad, all right, at the bottom of this day's confidences and secrets, but what it is I am too weak right now to fathom. Indeed, worn down more than I had thought from all that has surrounded Helen's visit, I am ready to think it is something about me that makes for the sadness; about how I have always failed to be what people want or expect; how I have never quite pleased anyone, including myself; how, hard as I have tried, I have seemed never quite able to be one thing or the other, and probably never will be . . . "Why did you do this alone?" I ask her. "Why didn't you tell me?"

"Well, it was just at the moment you were letting yourself go, and I thought that had to happen by itself. You were surrendering to something, and it always had to be clear to both of us exactly what it was. Is *that* clear?"

"But you did want to have it."

"The abortion?"

"No, the child."

"I want to have a child, of course. I want to have one with you—I can't imagine having anyone else's. But not until you're ready to with me."

"And when did you do all this, Claire? How could I *not* know it?"

"Oh, I managed," she says. "David, the point is that I wouldn't even *want* you to want it until you know for certain that it's me and my ways and this life that you can be content with. I don't want to make anybody unhappy. I don't want to cause anyone pain. I never want to be anyone's prison. That is the worst fate I can imagine. Please, let me just say what I have to—you don't have to say anything about what you would have said or wouldn't have said had I told you what I was doing. I didn't want any of the responsibility to be yours; and it isn't; it can't be. If a mistake was made, then I made it. Right now I just want to say certain things to you, and I want you to hear them, and then we'll go home and I'll start supper."

"I'm listening to you."

"Sweetheart, I wasn't jealous of her; far from it. I'm pretty enough, and I'm young, and thank God, I'm not 'tough' or 'worldly,' if that's what that's called. Truly, I wasn't afraid of anything she could do. If I were that uncertain I wouldn't be living here. I did get confused a little when you wanted to shoo me out of the way, but I came back to the house only to get my camera. I was going to take some pictures of the two of them together. All in all, I thought it was as good a way to get through that visit as any. But when I saw you sitting alone with her, I suddenly thought, 'I can't make him happy, I won't be able to.' And I wondered suddenly if anyone could. And that stunned me so, I just had to go. I don't know if what I thought was true or not. Maybe you don't either. But maybe you do. It would be agony leaving you right now, but I'm prepared to do it, if it makes sense. And better now than three or four years down the line, when you're absolutely in every breath I draw. It's not what I want, David; it's not anything I am even remotely proposing. Saying these kinds of things you take a terrible risk of being misunderstood, and, please, please, don't misunderstand me. I'm proposing nothing. But if you do think you know the answer to my question, I'd like to be told sometime soon, because if you can't be truly content with me, then let me just go to the Vineyard. I know I could get through up there with Olivia until school begins. And after that I can manage on my own. But I don't want to give myself any further to something that isn't going to evolve someday into a family. I never had one that made the least bit of sense, and I want one that does. I have to have that. I'm not saying tomorrow, or even the day after tomorrow. But in time that's what I want. Otherwise, I'd just as soon tear the roots up now, before the job requires a hacksaw. I'd like us both to get away, if we can, without a bloody amputation."

Here, though the bright sun has baked her body dry, she shudders from head to foot. "I think that's everything I have the energy left to say. And you don't have to say a word. I wish you wouldn't, not just now. Otherwise, this will sound like an ultimatum, and it isn't. It's a clarification, that's all. I didn't even want to make it, I thought *time* would make it. But then it's time that just might do me in. But, please, it doesn't require reassuring sounds to be made in response. It's just that suddenly everything seemed as though it might be a terrible delusion. It was so frightening. Please, don't speak—unless there's something you know that I should know."

"No, there isn't."

"Then let's go home."

And last, my father's visit.

In the letter profusely thanking us for the Labor Day weekend invitation extended to him on the phone, my father asks if he may bring a friend along, another widower whom he has grown close to in recent months and whom he says he wants me in particular to meet. He must by now have discarded or used up the paper and envelopes bearing the name of the hotel, for the request is written on the back of stationery imprinted at the top with the words JEWISH FEDERATION OF NASSAU COUNTY. Imprinted beneath is a brief, pointed epistle to the Jews whose style is as easily recognizable to me as Hemingway's or Faulkner's.

Dear

I am enclosing your pledge card from the Jewish Federation of Nassau County. I, as a Jew, am making a personal appeal. There is no need to recite our commitment to maintain a Jewish homeland. We need the financial aid of every Jew.

Never again must we allow a holocaust! No Jew can be apathetic!
I beg of you, please help. *Give before it hurts.*

> Sincerely,
> Abe Kepesh
> Garfield Garden Apartments
> Co-Chairman

On the reverse side is his letter to Claire and myself, written
with a ball-point pen and in his oversized scrawl, though no
less revealing than the printed message calling for Jewish solidarity (in those childlike hieroglyphics, all the more revealing)
of the fanatically lavish loyalties that, now, in his old age, cause
him to be afflicted throughout the waking day with the dull
ache and shooting pain of wild sentiment ensnared.

The morning we get his letter I telephone him at my Uncle
Larry's office to tell him that if he does not mind sharing our
smallish guest room with his friend Mr. Barbatnik, he is of
course welcome to bring him along.

"I hate like hell to leave him here alone on a holiday, Davey,
that's the only thing. Otherwise I wouldn't bother you. See, I
just didn't think it through," he explains, "when I rushed to
say yes so quick like that. Only it's got to be no inconvenience
for Claire, if he comes. I don't want to burden her, not with
school starting up, not with all the work she must have to do
to get ready."

"Oh, she's ready, don't worry about that," and I hand the
phone over to Claire, who assures him that her school preparations were finished long ago and that it will be a pleasure to
entertain the two of them for the weekend.

"He's a wonderful, wonderful man," my father quickly assures her, as though we actually have reason to suspect that a
friend of his might turn out to be a rummy or a bum, "somebody who has been through things you wouldn't believe. He
works with me when I go collecting for the UJA. And, I tell
you, I need him. I need a hand grenade. Try to get money out
of people. Try to get *feelings* out of people and see where you
wind up. You tell them that what happened to the Jews must
never happen again, and they look at you like they never heard
of it. Like Hitler and pogroms are something I am making up
in order to fleece them out of their municipal bonds. We got

one guy in the building across the way, a brand-new widower three years older than me, who already made himself his bundle years ago in the bootleg business and God only knows what else, and you should get a load of him since his wife passed away—a new chippie on his arm every month. Dresses them up in expensive clothes, takes them in to see Broadway shows, wouldn't be caught dead driving them to the beauty parlor in anything but a Fleetwood Caddie, but just try to ask him for a hundred dollars for the UJA and he is practically in tears telling you how bad he has been hit on the market. It's a good thing I can control my temper. And between you and me, half the time I can't, and it is Mr. Barbatnik who has to call me off before I tell this s.o.b. just what I think of him. Oh, this one guy, he really gets my goat. Every time I leave him I have to go get a phenobarb from my sister-in-law. And I'm somebody who don't even believe in an aspirin."

"Mr. Kepesh," Claire says, "please feel free to bring Mr. Barbatnik with you."

But he will not say yes until he has extracted a promise that if they both come she will not think that she has to cook them three meals a day. "I want a guarantee that you are going to pretend that we're not even there."

"But what fun would that be? Suppose instead I take the easy way out and just pretend that you are."

"Hey, listen," he says to her, "you sound like a happy girl."

"I am. My cup runneth over."

Even though Claire is holding the phone to her ear across the kitchen table from me, I clearly hear what comes next. This results from the fact that my father approaches long-distance communication in much the way that he approaches so many of the riddles that elude his understanding—with the belief that the electrical waves transmitting his voice may not make it without his wholehearted and unstinting support. Without *hard work*.

"God bless you," he calls out to her, "for what you are doing for my son!"

"Well—" beneath her tan, she has reddened—"well, he's doing some nice things for me."

"I wouldn't doubt that," my father says. "I'm delighted to hear it. But still and all he has practically gone out of his way to bring trouble into his life. Tell me, does he realize how good he has got it with you? He is thirty-four years old, a grown man already, he can't afford any longer to go around wet behind the ears. Claire, does he know enough by now to appreciate what he's got?"

She tries laughing the question off, but he insists on an answer, even if finally he must give it himself. "Losing your bearings no one needs—life is confusing enough. You don't stick a knife in your own gut. But that is just what he did to himself with marrying that glamour girl, all dressed up like Suzie Wong. Oh, about her and those outfits of hers the less said the better. And those French perfumes. Pardon my language, but she smelled like a God damn barber shop. And what was he up to living in that sublet apartment with red walls made out of cloth, and with whatever else went on there, that I will never be able to fathom. I don't even want to think about it. Claire dear, listen to me, you at last are somebody worthwhile. If only you can get him to settle into a real life."

"Oh, my," she says, not a little flustered by all the emotion that is flowing her way, "if it were any more settled around here . . ."

Before she can quite figure out, at the age of twenty-five, how to conclude that sentence, my father is roaring, "Wonderful, wonderful, that is the most wonderful news about him since he finished that fellowship to be a gypsy in Europe and came back on that boat in one piece!"

In the lot behind the general store in town, he steps cautiously down from the high front step of the New York bus, but then, despite the scalding heat—despite his advanced age—*surges* forward, and not toward me, but on the wings of impulse, to the person who is no relation of his quite yet. There were those few evenings when she served him a meal in my new apartment, and then, when I gave my public lecture from *Man in a Shell* in the Scholar Series at the university, it was Claire who escorted him and my aunt and uncle into the library and sat beside him in the little auditorium there, identifying at his request which gentleman was the department chairman and which the dean. Nonetheless, now when he reaches out to embrace her, it is as though she is already pregnant with the first of his grandchildren, as though she is in fact *the* genetrix of all that is most estimable in that elite breed of creatures to which he is joined by blood and for which his admiration is overbrimming . . . if and when, that is, the membership does not go around shamelessly showing its fangs and its claws and leaving my father fit to be tied.

Seeing Claire swallowed up by this stranger, Dazzle begins leaping crazily around in the dust at his mistress's sandals—and, though my father has never had all that much trust, or found much to admire, in members of the animal kingdom who breed out of wedlock and defecate on the ground, I am surprised to see that Dazzle's display of unabashed dogginess in no way seems to deflect his attention from the girl he is holding in his arms.

At first I do not have to wonder if what we are witnessing is not designed in part at least to put Mr. Barbatnik at ease about visiting a human couple who are not legally wed—if perhaps my father intends, by the very intensity with which he squeezes her body to his, to put his own not entirely unexpected misgivings on that score to rest. I cannot remember seeing him so forceful and so animated since before my mother's illness. In fact, he strikes me as a little nuts today. But that is still better than what I expected. Usually when I call each week there is, in just about every upbeat thing he says, a melancholy strain so transparent that I wonder how he finds the wherewithal to keep going on, as he will, about how all is well, wonderful, couldn't be better. The somber "Yeah, hello?" with which he answers the phone is quite enough to inform me of what underlies his "active" days—the mornings helping my uncle in his office where my uncle needs no help; the afternoons at the Jewish Center arguing politics with the "fascists" in the steam room, men whom he refers to as Von Epstein, and Von Haberman, and Von Lipschitz—the local Goering, Goebbels, and Streicher, apparently, who give him palpitations of the heart; and then those interminable evenings soliciting at his neighbors' doors for his various philanthropies and causes, reading again column by column through *Newsday*, the *Post*, and the *Times*, watching the CBS News for the second time in four hours, and finally, in bed and unable to sleep, spreading the letters from his cardboard file box over the blanket and reviewing his correspondence with his vanished, cherished guests.

In some cases more cherished, it seems to me, now that they have vanished, than when they were around and there was too little barley in the soup, too much chlorine in the pool, and never enough waiters in the dining room.

His letter writing. With each passing month it is getting harder for him to keep track of who among the hundreds and hundreds of old-timers is retired and in Florida, and thus capable still of writing him back, and who is dead. And it isn't a matter of losing his faculties, either—it's losing all those friends, "non-stop," as he graphically describes the decimation that occurred in the ranks of his former clientele during just this last year. "I wrote five full pages of news to that dear and lovely prince of a man, Julius Lowenthal. I even put in a clipping that I've been saving up from the *Times* about how they ruined the river over in Paterson where he had his law practice. I figured it would be interesting to him down there—this pollution business was made to order for the kind of man he was. I tell you"—pointing a finger—"Julius Lowenthal was one of the most civic-minded people you could ever want to meet. The synagogue, orphans, sports, the handicapped, colored people —he gave of his time to everything. That man was the genuine article, the *best*. Well, you know what's coming. I stamp and seal the envelope and put it by my hat to take to mail in the morning, and not until I brush my teeth and get into bed and turn out the light does it dawn on me that my dear old friend is gone now since last fall. I have been thinking about him playing cards alongside a swimming pool in Miami—playing pinochle the way only he could play with that legal mind of his—and in actuality he is underground. What is even left of him by now?" That last thought is too much, even for him, especially for him, and he moves his hand angrily past his face, as though to shoo away, like a mosquito that is driving him crazy, this terrible, startling image of Julius Lowenthal decomposing. "And, unbelievable as it may sound to a young person," he says, recovering most of his equilibrium, "this is actually becoming a weekly occurrence, right down to licking the envelope and pasting on the stamp."

It will be hours before Claire and I are finally alone together, and she is able at last to unburden herself of the enigmatic decree issued by him into her ear while we four stood grouped in the fumy wake of the departed bus. The sun is softening us like so much macadam; poor confused Dazzle (barely grown accustomed to this rival) continues carrying on in the air around my father's feet; and Mr. Barbatnik—a short leprechaunish gentleman, with a large, long-eared Asian face, and astonishing scoop-like hands suspended from powerful forearms mapped with a body builder's veins—Mr. Barbatnik hangs back, as shy as a schoolgirl, his jacket folded neatly over his arm, waiting for this living, throbbing valentine, my father, to make the introductions. But my father has urgent business to settle first—like the messenger in a classical tragedy, immediately as he comes upon the stage he blurts out what he has traveled all this way to say. "Young woman," he whispers to Claire, for so it would seem he has been envisioning her, allegorically, as all that and only that, "young woman," commands my father out of the power vested in him by his daydreams— "don't let—don't let—please!"

These, she tells me at bedtime, were the only words that she could hear, pinned as she was against his massive chest; most likely, I say, because these are the only words he uttered. For him, at this point, they say it all.

And having thus ordained the future, if only for the moment, he is ready now to move on to the next event in the arrival ceremonies he must have been planning now for weeks. He reaches into the pocket of the nubby linen jacket slung across *his* arm—and apparently finds nothing. Suddenly he is slapping at the lining of the jacket as though performing resuscitation upon it. "Oh Christ," he moans, "it's lost. My God, it's on the bus!" Whereupon Mr. Barbatnik edges forward and, as discreetly as a best man to a half-dazed bridegroom, says in a soft voice, "Your pants, Abe." "Of course," my father snaps back, and reaching (still with a little desperation in the eyes) into the pocket of his houndstooth trousers—he is dressed, as they say, to the nines—extracts a small packet that he places in Claire's palm. And now he is beaming.

"I didn't tell you on the phone," he says to her, "so it would come as a total surprise. Every year you hold on to it I guarantee it will go up in value ten percent at least. Probably fifteen, and maybe more. It's better than money. And wait till you see the wonderful skill that goes into it. It's fantastic. Go ahead. Open it up."

So, while we all continue to cook away in the parking lot, my affable mate, who knows how to please, and loves pleasing, deftly unties the ribbon and removes the shiny yellow wrapping paper, not failing to remark upon its prettiness. "I picked that out too," my father tells her. "I thought that color would be up your alley—didn't I, Sol," he says, turning to his companion, "didn't I say I'll bet she's a girl who likes yellow?"

Claire takes from its velvet-lined case a small sterling-silver paperweight engraved with a bouquet of roses.

"David told me how hard you work in the garden you made, and the way you love all the flowers. Take it, please. You can use it on your desk at school. Wait till your pupils see it."

"It's beautiful," she says, and calming Dazzle with just a glance, kisses my father on the cheek.

"Look at the handiwork," he says. "You can even see the little thorns. Some person actually did that, by hand. An artist."

"It's lovely, it's a lovely gift," she says.

And only now does he turn and embrace me. "I got you something too," he says. "It's in my bag."

"You hope," I say.

"Wise guy," and *we* kiss.

At last he is ready to introduce his companion, dressed, I now realize, in the same spanking-new, color-coordinated outfit, except where my father is in shades of tan and brown, Mr. Barbatnik wears silver and blue.

"Thank God for this man," my father says as we drive slowly out of town behind a farmer's pickup truck bearing a bumper sticker informing the other motorists that ONLY LOVE BEATS MILK. The bumper sticker on our car, affixed by Claire in sympathy with the local ecologists, reads DIRT ROADS ARE DOWN TO EARTH.

Excited and garrulous as a small boy—much as *I* used to be when *he* was doing the driving around these roads—my father cannot stop talking now about Mr. Barbatnik: one in a million, the finest person he has ever known . . . Mr. Barbatnik, meanwhile, sits quietly beside him, looking into his lap, as humbled, I think, by Claire's buoyant, summery fullness as by the fact that my father is selling him to us much the way, in the good old days, he used to sell the life-lengthening benefits of a summer in our hotel.

"Mr. Barbatnik is the guy who I tell you about from the Center. If it wasn't for him, I would absolutely be a voice in the wilderness there about that son of a bitch George Wallace. Claire, pardon me, please, but I hate that lousy cockroach with a passion. You shouldn't have to ever hear the kinds of things so-called decent people think in their private thoughts. It's a disgrace. Only Mr. Barbatnik and me, we make a team, and we give it to them, but good."

"Not," says Mr. Barbatnik philosophically, in heavily accented English, "that it makes much difference."

"And, tell me, what could make a difference with those ignorant bigots? At least let them hear what someone else thinks of them! Jewish people so full of hatred that they go out and vote for a George Wallace—it's beyond me. *Why?* People who have lived and seen a whole lifetime as a minority, and the suggestion that they make in all seriousness is that they ought to line up the colored in front of machine guns and let them have it. Take actual people and mow them down."

"This of course isn't everybody that says that," Mr. Barbatnik puts in. "This is just one particular person, of course."

"I tell them, look at Mr. Barbatnik—ask him if that isn't the same thing that Hitler did with the Jews. And you know what their answer is, grown men who have raised families and run successful businesses and live in retirement now in condominiums like supposed civilized people? They say, 'How can you compare niggers with Jews?'"

"What's eating this particular person, and the group that he is the leader of—"

"And who appointed him leader, by the way? Of anything? Himself! Go ahead, Sol, I'm sorry. I just wanted to make clear to them what kind of a little dictator we're dealing with."

"What's eating them," Mr. Barbatnik says, "is that they owned homes, some of them, and businesses, and then came the colored, and when they tried to get out what they put in, they took a licking."

"Of course it's all economics when you get down to it. It always is. Wasn't it the same with the Germans? Wasn't it the same in Poland?" Here, abruptly, he breaks off his historical analysis to say to Claire and me, "Mr. Barbatnik only got here after the war." Dramatically, and yes, with pride, he adds, "He is a victim of the Nazis."

When we turn in the drive and I point out the house halfway up the hillside, Mr. Barbatnik says, "No wonder you look so happy, you two."

"They rent it," my father says. "I told him, he likes it so much, why don't he buy it? Make the guy an offer. Tell him you'll pay him cash. At least see if you get a nibble."

"Well," I say, "we're happy enough renting for now."

"Renting is throwing money down the drain. Find out from him, will you? What can it hurt? Cash on the barrelhead, see if he bites. I can help you out, Uncle Larry can help you out, as far as that goes, if it's a straight money deal that he's after. But definitely you ought to own a little piece of property at your stage of the game. And up here, you can't miss, that's for sure. You never could. In my time, Claire, you could buy a little place like this for under five thousand. Today that little house and—and how far does the property go? To the tree line? All right, say four, say five acres—"

Up the dirt drive and in through the kitchen door—and right past the blooming garden he has heard so much about—he continues with his realtor's spiel, so delighted is the man to be back home in Sullivan County, and with his only living loved one, who by all outward appearances seems finally to have been plucked from his furnace and plunked down before the hearth.

Inside the house, before we can even offer a cold drink, or show them to their room or to the toilet, my father begins to unpack his bag on the kitchen table. "*Your* present," he announces to me.

We wait. His shoes come out. His freshly laundered shirts. His shiny new shaving kit.

My present is an album bound in black leather containing thirty-two medallions the size of silver dollars, each in its own circular cavity and protected on both sides by a transparent acetate window. He calls them "Shakespeare Medals"—a scene from one of the plays is depicted on the face side, and on the other, in tiny script, a quotation from the play is inscribed. The medals are accompanied by instructions for placing them in the album. The first instruction begins, "Put on a pair of lint-free gloves . . ." My father hands me the gloves last of all. "Always wear the gloves when you handle the medals," he tells me. "They come with the set. Otherwise, they say that there can be harmful chemical effects to the medals from being touched by human skin."

"Oh, this is nice of you," I say. "Though I don't quite know why now, such an elaborate gift—"

"Why? Because it's time," he answers, with a laugh, and, too, with a wide gesture that encompasses all the kitchen appliances. "Look, Davey, what they engrave for you. Claire, look at the outside."

Centered within the arabesque design that is embossed in silver and serves as a border to the album's funereal cover are three lines, which my father points out to us, word by word, with his index finger. We all read the words in silence—all except him.

FIRST EDITION STERLING SILVER PROOF SET
MINTED FOR THE PERSONAL COLLECTION OF
PROFESSOR DAVID KEPESH

I don't know what to say. I say, "This must have cost an awful lot. It's really something."

"Isn't it? But, no, the cost don't hurt, not the way they set it up. You just collect one medal a month, to begin with. You start off with *Romeo and Juliet*—wait'll I show Claire *Romeo and Juliet*—and you work your way up from there, till you've got them all. I've been saving for you all this time. The only one who knew was Mr. Barbatnik. Look, Claire, come here, you gotta look up close—"

It is a while before they can locate the medallion depicting *Romeo and Juliet*, for in its designated slot in the lower left-hand corner of the page labeled "Tragedies" it seems he has placed *Two Gentlemen from Verona*. "Where the hell is *Romeo and Juliet*?" he asks. The four of us are able to discover it finally under "Histories" in the slot marked *The Life and Death of King John*. "But then where did I put *The Life and Death of King John*?" he asks. "I thought I got 'em all in right, Sol," he says to Mr. Barbatnik, frowning. "I thought we checked." Mr.

Barbatnik nods—they did. "Anyway," says my father, "the point is—what was the point? Oh, the *back*. Here, I want Claire to read what it says on the back, so everyone can hear. Read this, dear."

Claire reads aloud the inscription: "'. . . and a rose by any other name would smell as sweet.' *Romeo and Juliet*, Act Two, Scene Two."

"Isn't that something?" he says to her.

"Yes."

"And he can take it to school, too, you see. That's what's so useful. It's something not just for the home, but that he can have ten and twenty years from now to show his classes. And just like yours, it is sterling silver, and something that I guarantee will keep abreast of the inflation, and long after paper money is as good as worthless. Where will you put it?" This last asked of Claire, not me.

"For now," she says, "on the coffee table, so people can see. Come into the living room, everybody; we'll put it there."

"Wonderful," says my father. "Only remember, don't let your company take the medals out, unless they put on the gloves."

Lunch is served on the screened-in porch. The recipe for the cold beet soup Claire found in *Russian Cooking*, one of her dozen or so manuals in a Time-Life series on "Foods of the World" shelved neatly between the radio—whose dial seems set to play only Bach—and the wall hung with two of her sister's calm watercolors of the ocean and the dunes. The cucumber and yogurt salad, heavily flavored with crushed garlic and fresh mint from the herb garden just beyond the screen door, is out of the same set, the volume on the cuisine of the Middle East. The cold roast chicken seasoned with rosemary is a long-standing recipe of her own.

"My God," says my father, "what a spread!" "Excellent," says Mr. Barbatnik. "Gentlemen, thank you," says Claire, "but I'll bet you've had better." "Not even in Lvov, when my mother was cooking," says Mr. Barbatnik, "have I tasted such a wonderful borscht." Says Claire, smiling, "I suspect that's a little extravagant, but thank you, again." "Listen, my dear girl," says my father, "if I had you in the kitchen, I'd still be in my old line. And you'd get more than you get being a schoolteacher, believe me. A good chef, even in the old days, even in the middle of the Depression—"

But in the end Claire's biggest hit is not the exotic Eastern dishes which, in her Clairish way, she has tried today for the first time in the hope of making everybody—herself included —feel instantaneously at home together, but the hearty iced tea she brews with mint leaves and orange rinds according to her grandmother's recipe. My father cannot seem to get enough, cannot stop praising it to the skies, not after he has learned over the blueberries that Claire takes the bus to Schenectady every month to visit this ninety-year-old woman from whom she learned everything she knows about preparing a meal and growing a garden, and probably about raising a child too. Yes, it looks from the girl as though his renegade son has decided to go straight, and in a very big way.

After lunch I suggest to the two men that they might like to rest until the heat has abated somewhat and we can go for a little walk along the road. Absolutely not. What am I even talking about? As soon as we digest our food, my father says, we must drive over to the hotel. This surprises me, as it surprised me a little at lunch to hear him speak so easily about his "old line." Since moving to Long Island a year and a half ago, he has shown no interest whatsoever in seeing what two successive owners have made of his hotel, barely hanging on now as the Royal Ski and Summer Lodge. I had thought he would be just as happy staying away, but in fact he is boiling over again with enthusiasm, and after a visit to the toilet, is pacing the porch, waiting for Mr. Barbatnik to awaken from the little snooze he is enjoying in my wicker easy chair.

What if he should drop dead from all this fervor in his heart? And before I have married the devoted girl, bought the cozy house, raised the handsome children . . .

Then what am I waiting for? If later, why not now, so he too can be happy and count his life a success?

What am I waiting for?

Down the main drag and through every last store still there and open for business my father leads the three of us, he alone seemingly oblivious to the terrific heat. "I can remember when there were four butchers, three barbershops, a bowling alley, three produce markets, two bakeries, an A&P, three doctors,

and three dentists. And now, look," he says—and without chagrin; rather with the proud sagacity of one who imagines he
actually knew to get out when the getting was good—"no
butchers, no barbers, no bowling alley, just one bakery, no
A&P, and unless things have changed since I left, no dentists
and only one doctor. Yes," he announces, avuncular now, taking
the overview, sounding a little like his friend Walter Cronkite,
"the old, opulent hotel era is over—but it was something! You
should have seen this place in summertime! You know who
used to vacation here? You name it! The Herring King! The
Apple King!—" And to Mr. Barbatnik and to Claire (who does
not let on that she already made this same sentimental journey
some weeks ago at the side of his son, who had explained at
the time just what a herring king *was*) he begins a rapid-fire
anecdotal history of his life's major boulevard, foot by foot,
year by year, from Roosevelt's inauguration right on up
through L.B.J. Putting an arm around his sopping half-sleeve
shirt, I say, "I bet if you set your mind to it you could go back
before the Flood." He likes that—yes, he likes just about everything today. "Oh, could I! This is some treat! This is *really*
Memory Lane!" "It's awfully hot, Dad," I warn him. "It's
nearly ninety degrees. Maybe if we slow down—" "Slow
*down?*" he cries, and showing off, pulls Claire along on his arm
as he breaks into a crazy little trot down the street. Mr. Barbatnik smiles, and mopping his brow with his handkerchief,
says to me, "He's been hoping a long time."

"Labor Day weekend!" my father announces brightly as I
swing into the lot next to the service entrance of the "main
building." Aside from the parking lot, which has been resur-
faced, and the tumescent pink the buildings have all been
painted, little else seems to have been changed as yet, except of
course for the hotel's name. In charge now are a worried fellow only a little older than myself and his youngish, charmless
second wife. I met them briefly on the afternoon in June when
I came down with Claire to conduct my own nostalgic tour.
But there is no nostalgia for the good old days in these two, no
more than those clutching at the debris in a swollen stream are
able to feel for the golden age of the birch-bark canoe. When
my father, having sized up the situation, asks how come no full
house for the holiday—a phenomenon utterly unknown to

him, as he quickly makes only too clear—the wife goes more bull-doggish even than before, and the husband, a hefty boyish type with pale eyes and pocked skin and a dazed, friendly expression—a nice, well-meaning fellow whose creditors, however, are probably not that impressed by plans extending into the twenty-first century—explains that they have not as yet been able to fix an "image" in the public mind. "You see," he says uncertainly, "right now we're still modernizing the kitchen—"

The wife interrupts to set the record straight: young people are put off because they think it is a hotel for the older generation (for which, it would seem from her tone, my father is to blame), and the family crowd is frightened away because the fellow to whom my father sold out—and who couldn't pay his bills by August of his first and only summer as proprietor—was nothing but a "two-bit Hugh Hefner" who tried to build a clientele out of "riffraff, and worse."

"Number one," says my father before I can grab an arm and steer him away, "the biggest mistake was to change the name, to take thirty years of good will and wipe it right off the map. Paint outside whatever color you want, though what was wrong with a nice clean white I don't understand—but if that's your taste, that's your taste. But the point is, does Niagara Falls change its name? Not if they want the tourist trade they don't." The wife has to laugh in his face, or so she says: "I have to laugh in your face." "You what? *Why?*" my outraged father replies. "Because you can't call a hotel the Hungarian Royale in this day and age and expect the line to form on the right, you know." "No, no," says the husband, trying to soften her words, and meanwhile working two Maalox tablets out of their silver wrapping, "the problem is, Janet, we are caught between life-styles, and that is what we have to iron out. I'm sure, as soon as we finish up with the kitchen—" "My friend, forget about the kitchen," says my father, turning noticeably away from the wife and toward someone with whom a human being can at least have a decent conversation; "do yourself a favor and change back the name. That is half of what you paid for. Why do you want to use in the name a word like 'ski' anyway? Stay open all winter if you think there's something in it—but why use a word that can only scare away the kind of people who make a place like this a going proposition?" The wife: "I have news for you. Nobody wants today to take a vacation in a place that sounds like a mausoleum." Period. "Oh," says my father, revving up his sarcasm, "oh, the past dies these days, does it?" And launches into a solemn, disjointed philosophical monologue about the integral relationship of past, present, and future, as though a man who has survived to sixty-six *must* know whereof he speaks, is *obliged* to be sagacious with those who follow after—especially when they seem to look upon him as the begetter of their woes.

I wait to intercede, or call an ambulance. From seeing his life's work mismanaged so by this deadbeat husband and his dour little wife, will my overwrought father burst into tears, or keel over, a corpse? The one—once again—seems no les possible to me than the other.

Why am I convinced that during the course of this weekend he is going to die, that by Monday I will be a parentless son?

He is still going strong—still going a little crazy—when we climb into the car to head home. "How did I know he was going to turn out to be a hippie?" "Who's that?" I ask. "That guy who bought us out after we lost Mother. You think I would have sold to a hippie, out of my own free will? The man was a fifty-year-old man. So what if he had long hair? What am I, a hard-hat, that I hold something like that against him? And what the hell did she mean by 'riffraff' anyway? She didn't mean what I think she meant, did she? Or did she?" I say, "She only meant that they are going under fast and it hurts. Look, she is obviously a sour little pain in the ass, but failing is still failing." "Yeah, but why blame *me*? I gave these people the last of the golden geese, I gave them a good solid tradition and a loyal clientele that all they had to do was stick to what was *there*. That was *all*, Davey! 'Ski!' That's all my customers have to hear, and they run like hell. Ah, some people, they can start a hotel in the Sahara and make a go of it, and others can start in the best of circumstances and they lose everything." "That's true," I say. "Now I look back in wonder that I myself could ever accomplish so much. A nobody like me, from nowhere! I started out, Claire, I was a short-order cook. My hair was black then, like his, and thick too, if you can believe it—"

Beside him Mr. Barbatnik's sleeping head is twisted to one

side, as though he has been garrotted. Claire, however—amiable, tolerant, generous, and willing Claire—continues to smile and to nod yes-yes-yes as she follows the story of our inn and how it flourished under the loving care of this industrious, gracious, shrewd, slave-driving, and dynamic nobody. Is there a man alive, I wonder, who has led a more exemplary life? Is there an ounce of anything that he has withheld in the performance of his duties? Of what then does he believe himself to be so culpable? My derelictions, my sins? Oh, if only he would cut the summation short, the jury would announce "Innocent as a babe!" without even retiring from the courtroom.

Only he can't. Into the early evening his plea streams forth unabated. First he follows Claire around the kitchen while she prepares the salad and the dessert. When she retires to shower and to change for dinner—and to rally her forces—he comes out to where I am preparing to cook the steak on the grill behind the house. "Hey, did I tell you who I got an invitation to his daughter's wedding? You won't guess in a million years. I had to go over to Hempstead to get her blender fixed for your aunt—you know, the jar there, the top—and who do you think owns the appliance store that services now for Waring? You'll never guess, if you even remember him." But I do. It is my conjurer. "Herbie Bratasky," I say. "That's right! Did I tell you already?" "No." "But that's who it was—and can you believe it, that skinny *paskudnyak* grew up into a person and he is doing terrific. He's got Waring, he's got G.E., and now, he tells me, he is getting himself in with some Japanese company, bigger even than Sony, to be the sole Long Island distributor. And the daughter is a little doll. He showed me her picture—and then out of the blue two days ago I get this beautiful invitation in the mail. I meant to bring it, damn it, but I guess I forget because I was already packed." Already packed two days ago. "I'll send it," he says; "you'll get a real kick out of it. Look, I was thinking, it's just a thought, but how would you and Claire like to come with me—to the wedding? That would be some surprise for Herbie." "Well, let's think about it. What does Herbie look like these days? What is he now, in his forties?" "Oh, he's gotta be forty-five, forty-six, easy. But still a dynamo—and as sharp and good-looking as he was when he was a kid. He ain't got a pound on him, and still with all his hair—in fact, so much, I thought maybe it was a rug. Maybe it was, come to think of it. And still with that tan. What do you think of that? Must use a lamp. And, Davey, he's got a little boy, just like him, who plays *drums*! I told him about you, of course, and he says he already knew. He read about when you gave your speech at the school; he saw it in the *Newsday* calendar of what's happening around the area. He said he told all his customers. So how do you like that? Herbie Bratasky. How did you know?" "I took a guess." "Well, you were right. You're psychic, kiddo. Whew, that's some beautiful piece of meat. What are you paying up here by the pound? Years ago, a sirloin cut like that—" And I want to enfold him in my arms, bring his unstoppable mouth to my chest, and say, "It's okay, you're here for good, you never have to leave." But in fact we all must depart in something less than a hundred hours. And— until death do us part—the tremendous closeness and the tremendous distance between my father and myself will have to continue in the same perplexing proportions as have existed all our lives.

When Claire comes back down to the kitchen, he leaves me to watch the coals heat up, and goes into the house "to see how beautiful she looks." "Calm down . . ." I call after him, but I might as well be asking a kid to calm down the first time he walks into Yankee Stadium.

My Yankee puts him to work shucking the corn. But of course you can shuck corn and still talk. On the cork bulletin board she has hung over the sink, Claire has tacked up, along with recipes out of the *Times*, some photographs just sent her from Martha's Vineyard by Olivia. I hear them through the kitchen's screen door discussing Olivia's children.

Alone again, and with time yet before the steak goes on, I at last get around to opening the envelope forwarded to me from my box at the university, and carried around in my back pocket since we went into town hours ago to pick up the mail and our guests. I hadn't bothered to open it, since it wasn't the letter I have been expecting daily now, from the university press to which I submitted *Man in a Shell*, in its final revised version, upon our return from Europe. No, it is a letter from the Department of English at Texas Christian University, and it provides the first truly light moment of the day. Oh, Baumgarten, you are a droll and devilish fellow, all right.

Dear Professor Kepesh:

Mr. Ralph Baumgarten, a candidate for the position of Writer in Residence at Texas Christian University, has submitted your name as an individual who is familiar with his work. I am reluctant to impose on your busy schedule, but would be most grateful if you would send me, at your earliest convenience, a letter in which you set forth your views on his writing, his teaching, and on his moral character. You may be assured that your comments will be held in the very strictest confidence.

I am most grateful for your help.

Cordially yours,
John Fairbairn
Chairman

*Dear Professor Fairbairn, Perhaps you would like my opinion of the wind as well, whose work I am also familiar with* . . . I stick the letter back into my pocket and put on the steak. *Dear Professor Fairbairn, I cannot help but believe that your students' horizons will be enormously enlarged and their sense of life's possibilities vastly enriched* . . . And who next, I wonder. When I sit down at my place for dinner, will there be an extra plate at the table for Birgitta, or will she prefer to eat beside me, on her knees?

I hear from the kitchen that Claire and my father have got around finally to discussing her parents. "But *why?*" I hear him ask. From his tone I can tell that whatever the question, the answer is not unknown to him, but rather, wholly incompatible with his own passionate meliorism. Claire replies, "Because they probably never belonged together in the first place." "But two beautiful daughters; they themselves college-educated people; the two of them with excellent executive positions. I don't get it. And the drinking: *why?* Where does it get you? With all due respect, it seems to me stupid. I myself of course never had the advantages of an education. If I had—but I didn't, and that was that. But my mother, let me tell you, I just have to remember her to get a good feeling about the whole world. What a woman! Ma, I would say to her, what are you doing on the floor again? Larry and I will give you the money, you'll get somebody else in to wash the floors. But no—"

It is during dinner that, at last, in Chekhov's phrase, the angel of silence passes over him. But only to be followed quickly by the shade of melancholia. Is he teetering now at the brink of tears, having spoken and spoken and spoken and still not having *quite* said it? Is he at last about to break down and cry—or am I ascribing to him the mood claiming me? Why should I feel as though I have lost a bloody battle when clearly I have won?

We eat again on the screened-in porch, where, during the days previous, I have been making every effort, with pen and pad, to speak *my* it. Beeswax candles are burning invisibly down in the antique pewter holders; the bayberry candles, arrived by mail from the Vineyard, drip wax threads onto the table. Candles burn everywhere you look—Claire has a passion for them on the porch at night; they are probably her only extravagance. Earlier, when she went around from holder to holder with a book of matches, my father—already at the table with the napkin drawn through his belt—had begun to recite for her the names of the Catskill hotels that had tragically burned to the ground in the last twenty years. Whereupon she had assured him that she would be careful. Still, when a breeze moves lightly over the porch, and the flames all flicker, he looks around to check that nothing has caught fire.

Now we hear the first of the ripe apples dropping onto the grass in the orchard just beyond the house. We hear the hoot of "our" owl—so Claire identifies for our guests this creature we have never seen, and whose home is up in "our" woods. If we are all silent long enough, she tells the two old men—as though they are two children—the deer may come down from the woods to graze around the apple trees. Dazzle has been cautioned about barking and scaring them away. The dog pants a little at the sound of his name from her lips. He is eleven and has been hers since she was a fourteen-year-old high school girl, her dearest pal ever since the year Olivia went off to college, the closest thing to her, until me. Within a few seconds Dazzle is peacefully asleep, and once again there is only the spirited September finale by the tree toads and the crickets, most popular of all the soft summer songs ever heard.

I cannot take my eyes from her face tonight. Between the Old Master etchings of the two pouched and creased and candlelit old men, Claire's face seems, more than ever, so apple-smooth, apple-small, apple-shiny, apple-plain, apple-fresh . . . never more artless and untainted . . . never before *so* . . . Yes, and to what am I willfully blinding myself that in time must set us apart? Why continue to cast this spell over myself, wherein nothing is permitted to sift through except what pleases me? Is there not something a little dubious and dreamy about all this gentle, tender adoration? What will happen when the *rest* of Claire obtrudes? What happens if no "rest of her" is there! And what of the rest of me? How long will *that* be sold a bill of goods? How much longer before I've had a bellyful of wholesome innocence—how long before the lovely blandness of a life with Claire begins to cloy, to pall, and I am out there once again, mourning what I've lost and looking for my way!

And with doubts so long suppressed voiced at last—and in deafening unison—the emotions under whose somber portentousness I have been living out this day forge themselves into something as palpable and awful as a spike. *Only an interim,* I think, and as though I have in fact been stabbed and the strength is gushing out of me, I feel myself about to tumble from my chair. Only an interim. Never to know anything durable. Nothing except my unrelinquishable memories of the discontinuous and the provisional; nothing except this ever-lengthening saga of all that did not work . . .

To be sure, to be sure, Claire is still with me, directly across the table, saying something to my father and Mr. Barbatnik about the planets she will show them later, brilliant tonight among the distant constellations. With her hair pinned up, exposing the vulnerable vertebrae that support the stalk of her slender neck, and in her pale caftan, with its embroidered edging, sewn together early in the summer on the machine, and lending a tiny regal air to her overpowering simplicity, she looks to me more precious than ever, more than ever before like my true wife, my unborn offspring's mother . . . yet I am already bereft of my strength and my hope and my contentment. Though we will go ahead, as planned, and rent the house to use on weekends and school vacations, I am certain that in only a matter of time—that's all it seems to take, just time—what we have together will gradually disappear, and the man now holding in his hand a spoonful of her orange custard will give way to Herbie's pupil, Birgitta's accomplice, Helen's suitor, yes, to Baumgarten's sidekick and defender, to the would-be wayward son and all he hungers for. Or, if not that, the would-be *what*? When this too is gone in its turn, what then?

I can't, for the sake of us all, fall out of a chair at dinner. Yet once again I am overcome by a terrible physical weakness. I am afraid to reach for my wineglass for fear that I will not have sufficient strength to carry it the distance to my mouth.

"How about a record?" I say to Claire.

"That new Bach?"

A record of trio sonatas. We have been listening to it all week. The week before, it had been a Mozart quartet; the week before that, the Elgar cello concerto. We just keep turning over one record again and again and again until finally we have had enough. It is all one hears coming and going through the house, music that almost seems by now to be the by-product of our comings and goings, compositions exuded by our sense of well-being. All we ever hear is the most exquisite music.

Seemingly with a good reason, I manage to leave the table before something frightening happens.

The phonograph and speakers in the living room are Claire's, carried up from the city in the back seat of the car. So are most of the records hers. So are the curtains sewed together for the windows, and the corduroy spread she made to cover the battered daybed, and the two china dogs by the fireplace, which once belonged to her grandmother and became hers on her twenty-fifth birthday. As a child on her way home from school she used to stop and have tea and toast with her grandmother, and practice on the piano there; then, armed at least with that, she could continue to the battlefield of her house. On her own she decided to have that abortion. So I would not be burdened by a duty? So I could choose her just for herself? But is the notion of duty so utterly horrendous? Why didn't she tell me she was pregnant? Is there not a point on life's way when one yields to duty, *welcomes* duty as once one yielded to pleasure, to passion, to adventure—a time when duty is the pleasure, rather than pleasure the duty . . .

The exquisite music begins. I return to the porch, not quite so pale as when I left. I sit back down at the table and sip my wine. Yes, I can raise and lower a glass. I can focus my thoughts on another subject. I had better.

"Mr. Barbatnik," I say, "my father told us you survived the concentration camps. How did you do it? Do you mind my asking?"

"Professor, please let me say first how much I appreciate your hospitality to a total stranger. This is the happiest day for me in a very long time. I thought maybe I even forgot how to be happy with people. I thank you all. I thank my new and dear friend, your wonderful father. It was a beautiful day, and, Miss Ovington—"

"Please call me Claire," she says.

"Claire, you are beyond your years and young and adorable as well. And—and all day I have wanted to give you my deep gratitude. For all the lovely things you think to do for people."

The two elders have been seated to either side of her, the lover directly across: with all the love he can muster, he looks upon the fullness of her saucy body and the smallness of her face above the little vase of asters he plucked for her on his morning walk; with all the love at his command, he watches this munificent female creature, now in the moment of her fullest bloom, offer a hand to their shy guest, who takes it, grasps and squeezes it, and without relinquishing it begins to speak for the first time with ease and self-assurance, at last at home (just as she had planned it, just as she has made it come to pass). And amid all this, the lover does, in fact, feel more deeply implicated in his own life than at any moment in memory—the true self at its truest, moored by every feeling to its own true home! And yet he continues to imagine that he is being drawn away by a force as incontrovertible as gravity, which is no lie either. As though he is a falling body, helpless as any little apple in the orchard which has broken free and is descending toward the alluring earth.

But instead of crying, either in his mother tongue or with some rudimentary animalish howl, "Don't leave me! Don't go! I'll miss you bitterly! This moment, and we four together —this is what should be!" he spoons out the last of his custard and attends to the survival story that he has asked to hear.

"There was a beginning," Mr. Barbatnik is saying, "there has to be an ending. I am going to live to see this monstrosity come to an end. This is what I told myself every single morning and night."

"But how was it they didn't send you to the ovens?"

How do you come to be here, with us? Why is Claire here? Why not Helen and our child? Why not my mother? And in ten years' time . . . who then? To build an intimate life anew, out of nothing, when I am forty-five? To start over again with everything at fifty? To be forever a beweeper of my outcast state? I can't! I won't!

"They couldn't kill everybody," says Mr. Barbatnik. "This I knew. Somebody has to be left, if only one person. And so I would tell myself, this one person will be me. I worked for them in the coal mines where they sent me. With the Poles. I was a young man then, and strong. I worked like it was my own coal mine inherited from my father. I told myself that this was what I wanted to do. I told myself that this work I was doing was for my child. I told myself different things every single day to make it just that I could last till that night. And that's how I lasted. Only when the Russians started coming so quick all of a sudden, the Germans took us and at three in the morning started us off on a march. Days and days and days, until I stopped keeping track. It went on and on, and people dropping every place you looked, and sure, I told myself again that if one is left it is going to be me. But by then I knew somehow that even if I made it to the destination where we were going, when I got there they would shoot whoever of us was left. So this is how come I ran away after weeks and weeks of marching without a stop to wherever in God's name it was. I hid in the woods and at night I came out and the German farmers fed me. Yes, that's true," he says, as he stares down at his large hand, in the candlelight looking very nearly as wide as a spade and as heavy as a crowbar, and enfolding within it Claire's thin, fine fingers with their delicate bones and knuckles. "The individual German, he isn't so bad, you know. But put three Germans together in a room and you can kiss the good world goodbye."

"And then what happened?" I ask, but he continues looking down, as though to contemplate the riddle of this one hand in the other. "How were you saved, Mr. Barbatnik?"

"One night a German farm woman said to me that the Americans are here. I thought she must be lying. I figured, don't come back here to her, she's up to something no good. But the next day I saw a tank through the trees, rolling down the road, with a white star, and I ran out, screaming at the top of my lungs."

Claire says, "You must have looked so strange by then. How did they know who you were?"

"They knew. I wasn't the first one. We were all coming out of our holes. What was left of us. I lost a wife and two parents, my brother, two sisters, and a three-year-old daughter."

Claire groans, "*Oh*," as though she has just been pierced by a needle. "Mr. Barbatnik, we are asking you too many questions, we shouldn't . . ."

He shakes his head. "Darling, you live, you ask questions. Maybe it's why we live. It seems that way."

"I tell him," says my father, "that he should make a book out of all he went through. I can think of some people I'd like to give it to read. If they could read it, maybe they would shake their heads that they can be the way they are, and this man can be so kind and good."

"And before the war started?" I ask him. "You were a young man then. What did you want to be?"

Probably because of the strength of his arms and the size of his hands I expect to hear him say a carpenter or a mason. In America he drove a taxi for over twenty years.

"A human being," he answers, "someone that could see and understand how we lived, and what was real, and not to flatter myself with lies. This was always my ambition from when I was a small child. In the beginning I was like everybody, a good cheder boy. But I personally, with my own hands, liberated myself from all that at sixteen years. My father could have killed me, but I absolutely did not want to be a fanatic. To believe in what doesn't exist, no, that wasn't for me. These are just the people who hate the Jews, these fanatics. And there are Jews who are fanatics too," he tells Claire, "and also walk around in a dream. But not me. Not for a second since I was sixteen years old and told my father what I refuse to pretend."

"If he wrote a book," says my father, "it should be called 'The Man Who Never Said Die.'"

"And here you married again?" I ask.

"Yes. She had been in a concentration camp also. Three years ago next month she passed away—like your own mother, from cancer. She wasn't even sick. One night after dinner she is washing the dishes. I go in to turn on the TV, and suddenly I hear a crash from the kitchen. 'Help me, I'm in trouble.' When I run into the kitchen she is on the floor. 'I couldn't hold on to the ditch,' she says. She says 'ditch' instead of 'dish.' The word alone gave me the willies. And her eyes. It was awful. I knew then and there that she was done for. Two days later they tell us that cancer is already in her brain. And it happened out of nowhere." Without a trace of animus—just to keep the record straight—he adds, "How else?"

"Too terrible," Claire says.

After my father has gone around to each candle to snuff out the flame—blowing even at those already expired, just to be sure—we step into the garden for Claire to show them the other planets visible from the earth tonight. Talking toward their upturned eyeglasses she explains about the Milky Way, answers questions about shooting stars, points out, as she does to her sixth-graders—as she did with me on our first night here—that mere speck of a star adjacent to the handle of the Little Dipper which the Greek soldiers had to discern to qualify for battle. Then she accompanies them back into the house; if they should awaken in the morning before we do, she wants them to know where there is coffee and juice. I remain in the garden with Dazzle. I don't know what to think. I don't want to know. I want only to climb by myself to the top of the hill. I remember our gondola rides in Venice. "Are you sure we didn't die and go to heaven?" "You'll have to ask the gondolier."

Through the living-room window I see the three of them standing around the coffee table. Claire has turned the record over and put it back on the turntable to play. My father is holding the album of Shakespeare medals in his hands. It appears that he is reading aloud from the backs of the medallions.

Some minutes later she joins me on the weathered wooden bench at the top of the hill. Side by side, without speaking, we look up again at the familiar stars. We do this nearly every night. Everything we have done this summer we have done nearly every night, afternoon, and morning. Every day calling out from the kitchen to the porch, from the bedroom to the bath, "Clarissa, come see, the sun is setting," "Claire, there's a hummingbird," "Sweetheart, what's the name of that star?"

For the first time all day she gives in to exhaustion. "Oh, my," she says, and lays her head on my shoulder. I can feel the air she breathes slowly filling, then slowly leaving her body.

After inventing a constellation of my own of the sky's brightest lights, I say to her, "It's a simple Chekhov story, isn't it?"

"Isn't what?"

"This. Today. The summer. Some nine or ten pages, that's all. Called 'The Life I Formerly Led.' Two old men come to the country to visit a healthy, handsome young couple, brimming over with contentment. The young man is in his middle thirties, having recovered finally from the mistakes of his twenties. The young woman is in her twenties, the survivor of a painful youth and adolescence. They have every reason to believe they have come through. It looks and feels to both of them as though they have been saved, and in large part by one another. They are in love. But after dinner by candlelight, one of the old men tells of his life, about the utter ruination of a world, and about the blows that keep on coming. And that's it. The story ends just like this: her pretty head on his shoulder; his hand stroking her hair; their owl hooting; their constellations all in order—their medallions all in order; their guests in their freshly made beds; and their summer cottage, so cozy and inviting, just down the hill from where they sit together wondering about what they have to fear. Music is playing in the house. The most lovely music there is. 'And both of them knew that the most complicated and difficult part was only just beginning.' That's the last line of 'Lady with a Lapdog.' "

"Are you really frightened of something?"

"I seem to be saying I am, don't I?"

"But of what?"

Her soft, clever, trusting green eyes are on me now. All that conscientious, schoolroom attention of hers is focused upon me—and what I will answer. After a moment I tell her, "I don't know really. Yesterday at the drugstore I saw that they had portable oxygen units up on the shelf. The kid there showed me how they work, and I bought one. I put it in the bathroom closet. It's back of the beach towels. In case anything should happen to anyone tonight."

"Oh, but nothing is going to happen. Why should it?"

"No reason. Only when he was going on like that about the past with that couple who own the hotel, I wished I had brought it along in the car."

"David, he isn't going to die just from getting heated up about the past. Oh, sweetheart," she says, kissing my hand and holding it to her cheek, "you're worn down, that's all. He gets so worked up, he *can* wear you to a frazzle—but he means so well. And he's obviously still in the best of health. He's fine. You're just exhausted. It's time for bed, that's all."

*It's time for bed, that's all.* Oh, innocent beloved, you fail to understand and I can't tell you. I can't say it, not tonight, but within a year my passion will be dead. Already it is dying and I am afraid that there is nothing I can do to save it. And nothing that you can do. Intimately bound—bound to you as to no one else!—and I will not be able to raise a hand to so much as touch you . . . unless first I remind myself that I must. Toward the flesh upon which I have been grafted and nurtured back toward something like mastery over my life, I will be without desire. Oh, it's stupid! Idiotic! Unfair! To be robbed like this of you! And of this life I love and have hardly gotten to know! And robbed by whom? It always comes down to myself!

And so it is I see myself back in Klinger's waiting room; and despite the presence there of all those *Newsweeks* and *New Yorkers*, I am no sympathetic, unspectacular sufferer out of a muted Chekhov tale of ordinary human affliction. No, more hideous by far, more like Gogol's berserk and mortified amputee, who rushes to the newspaper office to place a maniacal classified ad seeking the return of the nose that has decided to take leave of his face. Yes, the butt of a ridiculous, vicious, inexplicable joke! Here, you therapeutic con man, I'm back, and even worse than before! Did all you said, followed every instruction, unswervingly pursued the healthiest of regimens— even took it on myself to study the passions in my classroom, to submit to scrutiny those who have scrutinized the subject most pitilessly . . . and here is the result! I know and I know and I know, I imagine and I imagine and I imagine, and when the worst happens, I might as well know nothing! You might as well know nothing! And feed me not the consolations of the reality principle! Just find it for me before it's too late! The perfect young woman is waiting! That dream of a girl and the most livable of lives! And here I hand to the dapper, portly, clever physician the advertisement headed "LOST," describing what it looked like when last seen, its real and sentimental worth, and the reward that I will offer anyone giving information leading to its recovery: "My desire for Miss Claire Ovington—a Manhattan private-school teacher, five feet ten inches tall, one hundred and thirty-eight pounds, fair hair, silverygreen eyes, the kindest, most loving, and loyal nature—has mysteriously vanished . . ."

And the doctor's reply? That perhaps it was never in my possession to begin with? Or that, obviously, what has disappeared I must learn to live without . . .

All night long, bad dreams sweep through me like water through a fish's gills. Near dawn I awaken to discover that the house is not in ashes nor have I been abandoned in my bed as an incurable. My willing Clarissa is with me still! I raise her nightgown up along the length of her unconscious body, and with my lips begin to press and tug her nipples until the pale, velvety, childlike areolae erupt in tiny granules and her moan begins. But even while I suck in a desperate frenzy at the choicest morsel of her flesh, even as I pit all my accumulated happiness, and all my hope, against my fear of transformations yet to come, I wait to hear the most dreadful sound imaginable emerge from the room where Mr. Barbatnik and my father lie alone and insensate, each in his freshly made bed.

CHRONOLOGY

NOTE ON THE TEXTS

NOTES

# Chronology

Born Philip Roth on March 19 in Newark, New Jersey, second child of Herman Roth and Bess Finkel. (Bess Finkel, the second child of five, was born in 1904 in Elizabeth, New Jersey, to Philip and Dora Finkel, Jewish immigrants from near Kiev. Herman Roth was born in 1901 in Newark, New Jersey, the middle child of seven born to Sender and Bertha Roth, Jewish immigrants from Polish Galicia. They were married in Newark on February 21, 1926, and shortly afterward opened a small family-run shoe store. Their son Sanford ["Sandy"] was born December 26, 1927. Following the bankruptcy of the shoe store and a briefly held position as city marshal, Herman Roth took a job as agent with the Newark district office of the Metropolitan Life Insurance Company, and would remain with the company until his retirement as district manager in 1966.) Family moves into second-floor flat of two-and-a-half-family house (with five-room apartments on each of the first two floors and a three-room apartment on the top floor) at 81 Summit Avenue in Newark. Summit Avenue was a lower-middle-class residential street in the Weequahic section, a twenty-minute bus ride from commercial downtown Newark and less than a block from Chancellor Avenue School and from Weequahic High School, then considered the state's best academic public high school. These were the two schools that Sandy and Philip attended. Between 1910 and 1920, Weequahic had been developed as a new city neighborhood at the southwest corner of Newark, some three miles from the edge of industrial Newark and from the international shipping facilities at Port Newark on Newark Bay. In the first half of the twentieth century Newark was a prosperous working-class city of approximately 420,000, the majority of its citizens of German, Italian, Slavic, and Irish extraction. Blacks and Jews composed two of the smallest groups in the city. From the 1930s to the 1950s, the Jews lived mainly in the predominantly Jewish Weequahic section.

1938        Philip enters kindergarten at Chancellor Avenue School in January.

1942        Roth family moves to second-floor flat of two-and-a-half-family house at 359 Leslie Street, three blocks west of Summit Avenue, still within the Weequahic neighborhood but nearer to semi-industrial boundary with Irvington.

1946        Philip graduates from elementary school in January, having skipped a year. Brother graduates from high school and chooses to enter U.S. Navy for two years rather than be drafted into the peacetime army.

1947        Family moves to first-floor flat of two-and-a-half-family house at 385 Leslie Street, just a few doors from commercial Chancellor Avenue, the neighborhood's main artery. Philip turns from reading sports fiction by John R. Tunis and adventure fiction by Howard Pease to reading the left-leaning historical novels of Howard Fast.

1948        Brother is discharged from navy and, with the aid of G.I. Bill, enrolls as commercial art student at Pratt Institute, Brooklyn. Philip takes strong interest in politics during the four-way U.S. presidential election in which the Republican Dewey loses to the Democrat Truman despite a segregationist Dixiecrat Party and a left-wing Progressive Party drawing away traditionally Democratic voters.

1950        Graduates from high school in January. Works as stock clerk at S. Klein department store in downtown Newark. Reads Thomas Wolfe; discovers Sherwood Anderson, Ring Lardner, Erskine Caldwell, and Theodore Dreiser. In September enters Newark College of Rutgers as pre-law student while continuing to live at home. (Newark Rutgers was at this time a newly formed college housed in two small converted downtown buildings, one formerly a bank, the other formerly a brewery.)

1951        Still a pre-law student, transfers in September to Bucknell University in Lewisburg, Pennsylvania. Brother graduates from Pratt Institute and moves to New York City to work for advertising agency. Parents move to Moorestown, New Jersey, approximately seventy miles southwest of Newark; father takes job as manager of Metropolitan Life's south Jersey district after having previously managed several north Jersey district offices.

1952        Roth decides to study English literature. With two friends, founds Bucknell literary magazine, *Et Cetera*, and becomes its first editor. Writes first short stories. Strongly influenced in his literary studies by English professor Mildred Martin, under whose tutelage he reads extensively, and with whom he will maintain lifelong friendship.

1954        Is elected to Phi Beta Kappa and graduates from Bucknell magna cum laude in English. Accepts scholarship to study English at the University of Chicago graduate school, beginning in September. Reads Saul Bellow's *The Adventures of Augie March*, and under its influence explores Chicago.

1955        In June receives M.A. with Honors in English. In September, rather than wait to be drafted, enlists in U.S. Army for two years. Suffers spinal injury during basic training at Fort Dix. In November, is assigned to Public Information Office at Walter Reed Army Hospital, Washington, D.C. Begins to write short stories "The Conversion of the Jews" and "Epstein." *Epoch*, a Cornell University literary quarterly, publishes "The Contest for Aaron Gold," which is reprinted in Martha Foley's *Best American Short Stories 1956*.

1956        Is hospitalized in June for complications from spinal injury. After two-month hospital stay receives honorable discharge for medical reasons and a disability pension. In September returns to University of Chicago as instructor in the liberal arts college, teaching freshman composition. Begins course work for Ph.D. but drops out after one term. Meets Ted Solotaroff, who is also a graduate student, and they become friends.

1957        Publishes in *Commentary* "You Can't Tell a Man by the Song He Sings." Writes novella "Goodbye, Columbus." Meets Saul Bellow at University of Chicago when Bellow is a classroom guest of Roth's friend and colleague, the writer Richard Stern. Begins to review movies and television for *The New Republic* after magazine publishes "Positive Thinking on Pennsylvania Avenue," a humor piece satirizing President Eisenhower's religious beliefs.

1958        Publishes "The Conversion of the Jews" and "Epstein" in *The Paris Review*; "Epstein" wins *Paris Review* Aga Khan Prize, presented to Roth in Paris in July. Spends first summer abroad, mainly in Paris. Houghton Mifflin awards Roth the Houghton Mifflin Literary Fellowship to publish the novella and five stories in one volume; George Starbuck, a poet and friend from Chicago, is his editor. Resigns from teaching position at University of Chicago. Moves to two-room basement apartment on Manhattan's Lower East Side. Becomes friendly with *Paris Review* editors George Plimpton and Robert Silvers and *Commentary* editor Martin Greenberg.

1959     Marries Margaret Martinson Williams. Publishes "Defender of the Faith" in *The New Yorker*, causing consternation among Jewish organizations and rabbis who attack magazine and condemn author as anti-Semitic; story collected in *Goodbye, Columbus* and included in *Best American Short Stories 1960* and *Prize Stories 1960: The O. Henry Awards*, where it wins second prize. *Goodbye, Columbus* is published in May. Roth receives Guggenheim fellowship and award from the American Academy of Arts and Letters. *Goodbye, Columbus* gains highly favorable reviews from Bellow, Alfred Kazin, Leslie Fiedler, and Irving Howe; influential rabbis denounce Roth in their sermons as "a self-hating Jew." Roth and wife leave U.S. to spend seven months in Italy, where he works on his first novel, *Letting Go*; he meets William Styron, who is living in Rome and who becomes a lifelong friend. Styron introduces Roth to his publisher, Donald Klopfer of Random House; when George Starbuck leaves Houghton Mifflin, Roth moves to Random House.

1960     *Goodbye, Columbus and Five Short Stories* wins National Book Award. The collection also wins Daroff Award of the Jewish Book Council of America. Roth returns to America to teach at the Writers' Workshop of the University of Iowa, Iowa City. Meets drama professor Howard Stein (later dean of the Columbia University Drama School), who becomes lifelong friend. Continues working on *Letting Go*. Travels in Midwest. Participates in *Esquire* magazine symposium at Stanford University; his speech "Writing American Fiction," published in *Commentary* in March 1961, is widely discussed. After a speaking engagement in Oregon, meets Bernard Malamud, whose fiction he admires.

1962    After two years at Iowa, accepts two-year position as writer-in-residence at Princeton. Separates from Margaret Roth. Moves to New York City and commutes to Princeton classes. (Lives at various Manhattan locations until 1970.) Meets Princeton sociologist Melvin Tumin, a Newark native who becomes a friend. Random House publishes *Letting Go*.

1963    Receives Ford Foundation grant to write plays in affiliation with American Place Theater in New York. Is legally separated from Margaret Roth. Becomes close friend of Aaron Asher, a University of Chicago graduate and editor at Meridian Books, original paperback publisher of *Goodbye, Columbus*. In June takes part in American Jewish Congress symposium in Tel Aviv, Israel, along with American writers Leslie Fiedler, Max Lerner, and literary critic David Boroff. Travels in Israel for a month.

1964    Teaches at State University of New York at Stony Brook, Long Island. Reviews plays by James Baldwin, LeRoi Jones, and Edward Albee for newly founded *New York Review of Books*. Spends a month at Yaddo, writers' retreat in Saratoga Springs, New York, that provides free room and board. (Will work at Yaddo for several months at a time throughout the 1960s.) Meets and establishes friendships there with novelist Alison Lurie and painter Julius Goldstein.

1965    Begins to teach comparative literature at University of Pennsylvania one semester each year more or less annually until the mid-1970s. Meets professor Joel Conarroe, who becomes a close friend. Begins work on *When She Was Good* after abandoning another novel, begun in 1962.

1966    Publishes section of *When She Was Good* in *Harper's*. Is increasingly troubled by Vietnam War and in ensuing years takes part in marches and demonstrations against it.

1967    Publishes *When She Was Good*. Begins work on *Portnoy's Complaint*, of which he publishes excerpts in *Esquire, Partisan Review*, and *New American Review*, where Ted Solotaroff is editor.

1968    Margaret Roth dies in an automobile accident. Roth spends two months at Yaddo completing *Portnoy's Complaint*.

1969    *Portnoy's Complaint* published in February. Within weeks becomes number-one fiction best-seller and a widely discussed cultural phenomenon. Roth makes no public appearances and retreats for several months to Yaddo. Rents house in Woodstock, New York, and meets the painter Philip Guston, who lives nearby. They remain close friends and see each other regularly until Guston's death in 1980. Renews friendship with Bernard Malamud, who like Roth is serving as a member of The Corporation of Yaddo.

1970    Spends March traveling in Thailand, Burma, Cambodia, and Hong Kong. Begins work on *My Life as a Man* and publishes excerpt in *Modern Occasions*. Is elected to National Institute of Arts and Letters and is its youngest member. Commutes to his classes at University of Pennsylvania and lives mainly in Woodstock until 1972.

1971    Excerpts of *Our Gang*, satire of the Nixon administration, appear in *New York Review of Books* and *Modern Occasions*; the book is published by Random House in the fall. Continues work on *My Life as a Man*; writes *The Breast* and *The Great American Novel*. Begins teaching a Kafka course at University of Pennsylvania.

1972    *The Breast*, first book of three featuring protagonist David Kepesh, published by Holt, Rinehart, Winston, where Aaron Asher is his editor. Roth buys old farmhouse and forty acres in northwest Connecticut, one hundred miles from New York City, and moves there from Woodstock. In May travels to Venice, Vienna, and, for the first time, Prague. Meets his translators there, Luba and Rudolph Pilar, and they describe to him the impact of the political situation on Czech writers. In U.S., arranges to meet exiled Czech editor Antonin Liehm in New York; attends Liehm's weekly classes in Czech history, literature, and film at College of Staten Island, City University of New York. Through friendship with Liehm meets numerous Czech exiles, including film directors Ivan Passer and Jiří Weiss, who become friends. Is elected to the American Academy of Arts and Sciences.

1973    Publishes *The Great American Novel* and the essay "Looking at Kafka" in *New American Review*. Returns to Prague and meets novelists Milan Kundera, Ivan Klíma, Ludvik Vaculik, the poet Miroslav Holub, and other

writers blacklisted and persecuted by the Soviet-backed
Communist regime; becomes friendly with Rita Klímová,
a blacklisted translator and academic, who will serve as
Czechoslovakia's first ambassador to U.S. following the
1989 "Velvet Revolution." (Will make annual spring trips
to Prague to visit his writer friends until he is denied an
entry visa in 1977.) Writes "Country Report" on Czechoslovakia for American PEN. Proposes paperback series,
"Writers from the Other Europe," to Penguin Books
USA; becomes general editor of the series, selecting titles,
commissioning introductions, and overseeing publication
of Eastern European writers relatively unknown to American readers. Beginning in 1974, series publishes fiction by
Polish writers Jerzy Andrzejewski, Tadeusz Borowski,
Tadeusz Konwicki, Witold Gombrowicz, and Bruno
Schulz; Hungarian writers György Konrád and Géza
Csáth; Yugoslav writer Danilo Kiš; and Czech writers Bo-
humil Hrabal, Milan Kundera, and Ludvik Vaculik; series
ends in 1989. "Watergate Edition" of *Our Gang* published,
which includes a new preface by Roth.

1974  Roth publishes *My Life as a Man*. Visits Budapest as well
as Prague and meets Budapest writers through Hungarian
PEN and the *Hungarian Quarterly*. In Prague meets Va-
clav Havel. Through friend Professor Zdenek Strybyrny,
visits and becomes friend of the niece of Franz Kafka,
Vera Saudkova, who shows him Kafka family photographs
and family belongings; subsequently becomes friendly in
London with Marianne Steiner, daughter of Kafka's sister
Valli. Also through Strybyrny meets the widow of Jiří
Weil; upon his return to America arranges for translation
and publication of Weil's novel *Life with a Star* as well as
publication of several Weil short stories in *American
Poetry Review*, for which he provides an introduction. In
Princeton meets Joanna Rostropowicz Clark, wife of
friend Blair Clark; she becomes close friend and introduces Roth to contemporary Polish writing and to Polish
writers visiting America, including Konwicki and Kazi-
mierz Brandys. Publishes "Imagining Jews" in *New York
Review of Books*; essay prompts letter from university
professor, editor, writer, and former Jesuit Jack Miles.
Correspondence ensues and the two establish a lasting intellectual friendship.

1975        Aaron Asher leaves Holt and becomes editor in chief at
            Farrar, Straus and Giroux; Roth moves to FSG with Asher
            for publication of *Reading Myself and Others*, a collection
            of interviews and critical essays. Meets British actress
            Claire Bloom.

1976        Interviews Isaac Bashevis Singer about Bruno Schulz for
            *New York Times Book Review* article to coincide with pub-
            lication of Schulz's *Street of Crocodiles* in "Writers from
            the Other Europe" series. Moves with Claire Bloom to
            London, where they live six to seven months a year for
            the next twelve years. Spends the remaining months in
            Connecticut, where Bloom joins him when she is not act-
            ing in films, television, or stage productions. In London
            resumes an old friendship with British critic A. Alvarez
            and, a few years later, begins a friendship with American
            writer Michael Herr (author of *Dispatches*, which Roth
            admires) and with the American painter R. B. Kitaj. Also
            meets critic and biographer Hermione Lee, who becomes
            a friend, as does novelist Edna O'Brien. Begins regular
            visits to France to see Milan Kundera and another new
            friend, French writer-critic Alain Finkielkraut. Visits Israel
            for the first time since 1963 and returns there regularly,
            keeping a journal that eventually provides ideas and ma-
            terial for novels *The Counterlife* and *Operation Shylock*.
            Meets the writer Aharon Appelfeld in Jerusalem and they
            become close friends.

1977        Publishes *The Professor of Desire*, second book of Kepesh
            trilogy. Beginning in 1977 and continuing over the next
            few years, writes series of TV dramas for Claire Bloom:
            adaptations of *The Name-Day Party*, a short story by
            Chekhov; *Journey into the Whirlwind*, the gulag autobi-
            ography of Eugenia Ginzburg; and, with David Plante,
            *It Isn't Fair*, Plante's memoir of Jean Rhys. At request
            of Chichester Festival director, modernizes the David
            Magarshack translation of Chekhov's *The Cherry Orchard*
            for Claire Bloom's 1981 performance at the festival as
            Madame Ranyevskaya.

1979        *The Ghost Writer*, first novel featuring novelist Nathan
            Zuckerman as protagonist, is published in its entirety in
            *The New Yorker*, then published by Farrar, Straus and

Giroux. Bucknell awards Roth his first honorary degree; eventually receives honorary degrees from Amherst, Brown, Columbia, Dartmouth, Harvard, Pennsylvania, and Rutgers, among others.

1980    *A Philip Roth Reader* published, edited by Martin Green. Milan and Vera Kundera visit Connecticut on first trip to U.S.; Roth introduces Kundera to friend and *New Yorker* editor Veronica Geng, who also becomes Kundera's editor at the magazine. Conversation with Milan Kundera, in London and Connecticut, published in *New York Times Book Review*.

1981    Mother dies of a sudden heart attack in Elizabeth, New Jersey. *Zuckerman Unbound* published.

1982    Corresponds with Judith Thurman after reading her biography of Isak Dinesen, and they begin a friendship.

1983    Roth's physician and Litchfield County neighbor, Dr. C. H. Huvelle, retires from his Connecticut practice and the two become close friends.

1984    *The Anatomy Lesson* published. Aaron Asher leaves FSG and David Rieff becomes Roth's editor; the two soon become close friends. Conversation with Edna O'Brien in London published in *New York Times Book Review*. With BBC director Tristram Powell, adapts *The Ghost Writer* for television drama, featuring Claire Bloom; program is aired in U.S. and U.K. Meets University of Connecticut professor Ross Miller and the two forge strong literary friendship.

1985    *Zuckerman Bound*, a compilation of *The Ghost Writer*, *Zuckerman Unbound*, *The Anatomy Lesson*, with epilogue *The Prague Orgy*, published.

1986    Spends several days in Turin with Primo Levi. Conversation with Levi published in *New York Times Book Review*, which also asks that Roth write a memoir about Bernard Malamud upon Malamud's death at age 72.

1987    *The Counterlife* published; wins National Book Critics Circle Award for fiction. Corresponds with exiled Romanian writer Norman Manea, who is living in Berlin, and encourages him to come to live in U.S; Manea arrives the next year, and the two become close friends.

1988        *The Facts* published. Travels to Jerusalem for Aharon Ap-
            pelfeld interview, which is published in *New York Times
            Book Review.* In Jerusalem, attends daily the trial of Ivan
            Demjanjuk, the alleged Treblinka guard "Ivan the Terri-
            ble." Returns to America to live year-round. Becomes
            Distinguished Professor of Literature at Hunter College
            of the City University of New York, where he will teach
            one semester each year until 1991.

1989        Father dies of brain tumor after yearlong illness. David
            Reiff leaves Farrar, Straus. For the first time since 1970,
            acquires a literary agent, Andrew Wylie of Wylie, Aitken,
            and Stone. Leaves FSG for Simon and Schuster. Writes a
            memoir of Philip Guston which is published in *Vanity
            Fair* and subsequently reprinted in Guston catalogs.

1990        *Deception* published by Simon and Schuster. Roth marries
            Claire Bloom in New York.

1991        Travels to post-Communist Prague for conversation with
            Ivan Klíma, published in *New York Review of Books.*

1991        *Patrimony* published; wins National Book Critics Circle
            Award for biography. Renews strong friendship with Saul
            Bellow.

1992        Reads from *Patrimony* for nationwide reading tour, ex-
            tending into 1993. Publishes brief profile of Norman
            Manea in *New York Times Book Review.*

1993        *Operation Shylock* published; wins PEN/Faulkner Award
            for fiction. Separates from Claire Bloom. Writes *Dr. Hu-
            velle: A Biographical Sketch,* which he publishes privately
            as a 34-page booklet for local distribution.

1994        Divorces Claire Bloom.

1995        Returns to Houghton Mifflin, where John Sterling is his
            editor. *Sabbath's Theater* is published and wins National
            Book Award for fiction.

1997        John Sterling leaves Houghton Mifflin and Wendy Stroth-
            man becomes Roth's editor. *American Pastoral,* first
            book of the "American trilogy," is published and wins
            Pulitzer Prize for fiction.

1998        *I Married a Communist,* the second book of the trilogy,
            is published and wins Ambassador Book Award of the
            English-Speaking Union. In October Roth attends three-

day international literary program honoring his work in Aix-en-Provence. In November receives National Medal of Arts at the White House.

2000    Publishes *The Human Stain*, final book of American trilogy, which wins PEN/Faulkner Award in U.S., the W. H. Smith Award in the U.K., and the Prix Medicis for the best foreign book of the year in France. Publishes "Rereading Saul Bellow" in *The New Yorker*.

2001    Publishes *The Dying Animal*, final book of the Kepesh trilogy, and *Shop Talk*, a collection of interviews with and essays on Primo Levi, Aharon Appelfeld, I. B. Singer, Edna O'Brien, Milan Kundera, Ivan Klíma, Philip Guston, Bernard Malamud, and Saul Bellow, and an exchange with Mary McCarthy. Receives highest award of the American Academy of Arts and Letters, the Gold Medal in fiction, given every six years "for the entire work of the recipient," previously awarded to Willa Cather, Edith Wharton, John Dos Passos, William Faulkner, Saul Bellow, and Isaac Bashevis Singer, among others.

2002    Wins the National Book Foundation's Medal for Distinguished Contribution to American Letters.

2003    Receives honorary degrees at Harvard University and University of Pennsylvania. Roth's work now appears in 31 languages.

2004    Publishes novel *The Plot Against America*, which becomes a best-seller and wins the W. H. Smith Award for best book of the year in the U.K.; Roth is the first writer in the 46-year history of the prize to win it twice.

2005    *The Plot Against America* wins the Society of American Historians' James Fenimore Cooper Prize as the outstanding historical novel on an American theme for 2003–04. On October 23, Roth's childhood home at 81 Summit Avenue in Newark is marked with a plaque as a historic landmark and the nearby intersection is named Philip Roth Plaza.

2006    Publishes *Everyman* in May. Becomes fourth recipient of PEN's highest writing honor, the PEN/Nabokov Award. Receives Power of the Press Award from the New Jersey Library Association for Newark *Star-Ledger* eulogy to his close friend, Newark librarian and city historian, Charles Cummings.

# Note on the Texts

This volume contains Philip Roth's novels *The Great American Novel* (1973), *My Life as a Man* (1974), and *The Professor of Desire* (1977).

*The Great American Novel* was published in New York by Holt, Rinehart and Winston and in England by Jonathan Cape in 1973. Before its publication excerpts appeared in *Sports Illustrated* ("The Great American Rookie," March 1973) and *Esquire* ("Every Inch a Man," May 1973). The text in this volume is taken from the 1973 Holt, Rinehart and Winston edition of *The Great American Novel*.

*My Life as a Man* was excerpted in *Modern Occasions* 1 ("Salad Days," 1970) and *Esquire* ("Courting Disaster [or Serious in the Fifties]," May 1971; "Susan," June 1974). In addition, the excerpt "Marriage à la Mode" was published in 1973 in *American Review* (vol. 18), with abbreviated versions appearing in *The New York Times* ("Marriage in the Fifties," October 3, 1973) and *The San Francisco Chronicle* ("Loving or Not in the Fifties," October 14, 1973). *My Life as a Man* was published by Holt, Rinehart and Winston in New York and by Jonathan Cape in England in 1974; the 1974 Holt, Rinehart and Winston edition of *My Life as a Man* contains the text printed here.

*The Professor of Desire* was published by Farrar, Straus and Giroux in 1977. Excerpts were published in *The New York Times Book Review* ("Overnight Guests," August 21, 1977), *Harper's* ("The Professor of Desire," August 1977), *American Poetry Review* ("After School," September–October 1977), and *Penthouse* ("The Professor of Desire," September 1977). Jonathan Cape brought out the novel in England in 1978. The text in this volume is taken from the 1977 Farrar, Straus and Giroux edition of *The Professor of Desire*.

This volume presents the texts of the original printings chosen for inclusion here, but it does not attempt to reproduce nontextual features of their typographic design. The texts are presented without change, except for the correction of typographical errors. The following is a list of typographical errors corrected, cited by page and line number: 27.36, Charley; 39.1, anymore; 39.9 Writers'; 63.34, anymore; 66.35–36, to, it; 69.21, you're out!; 78.1, shouting,; 110.18, Stree-*ike!*; 124.37, tropies; 158.10, me,; 201.33, 43]; 250.31, bits; 271.6, per second per second; 342.39, How expect;; 344.8, Mundy; 391.22, Lenny; 488.36, and,; 558.32, desert,; 567.28, Hess, twenty; 600.14, stockings. . . . ?"; 613.39, I gets; 655.40, A confession; 696.32, "silky"; 754.20, hold; 816.4, The Hunger.

# Notes

In the notes below, the reference numbers denote page and line of this volume (the line count includes chapter headings). No note is made for material included in standard desk references. Quotations from Shakespeare are keyed to *The Riverside Shakespeare*, ed. G. Blakemore Evans (Boston: Houghton Mifflin, 1974).

THE GREAT AMERICAN NOVEL

7.2    Call me Smitty.] Cf. the opening of Melville's *Moby-Dick* (1851), Chapter 1: "Call me Ishmael."

7.5    Hem] Ernest Hemingway.

7.14–15    one Bulkington] See "The Lee Shore," chapter 23 of *Moby-Dick*: "Some chapters back, one Bulkington was spoken of, a tall, new-landed mariner, encountered in New Bedford at the inn." The chapter tells of Bulkington's death at sea and reflects upon his fate.

8.5    Catalonia (with Orwell)] George Orwell's *Homage to Catalonia* (1938) is an account of his experience fighting on the Republican side in the Spanish Civil War.

8.6    knaidlach . . . kreplach] Knaidlach, more commonly known as matzo balls; kreplach, a beef dumpling. Both are served in chicken soup on Jewish holidays.

8.7    Jennie G.] Jennie Grossinger (1892–1972), hostess and main promoter of the renowned resort hotel Grossinger's in the Catskill Mountains in New York, which she co-founded with her husband.

8.38    N.W.] Noah Webster.

12.4    "I'd rather . . . President."] Play on "I'd rather be right than president," remark by Henry Clay (1777–1852) after his third unsuccessful campaign to be president in 1844.

14.23    Decoration Day] The former name of Memorial Day.

17.29    whaning-that-Aprille] See the opening of the General Prologue to Geoffrey Chaucer's *The Canterbury Tales*: "Whan that Aprill with his shoures soote / The droghte of March hath perced to the roote."

17.32    slits] "Slit" was a harsh synonym for "woman" favored by Hall of Famer Ty Cobb and other ballplayers of his era.

18.4     that one]  Nathaniel Hawthorne's *The Scarlet Letter* (1850).

20.25    Diogenes . . . Truth:]  The Greek philosopher (412?–323 BCE) was reputed to wander the streets in search of an honest man.

22.19    Luke Appling,]  Shortstop (1907–1991) who spent his entire major-league career with the Chicago White Sox, playing well into his forties.

22.23    Luke 'Hot Potato' Hamlin.]  Right-handed pitcher (1904–1978) who, with the exception of one season in which he won 20 games, had a largely undistinguished career, pitching for the Brooklyn Dodgers, Pittsburgh Pirates, and other teams.

22.32    Mr. Bowie Kuhn,]  Bowie Kuhn (b. 1926) served as Commissioner of Baseball from 1968 to 1984.

23.15–18  "Kiner! . . . "Wynn!"]  Except for New York Yankees out-fielder Charlie Keller (1916–1990), front-runners in the 1971 voting for new in-ductees into the Hall of Fame (though no player received enough votes for induction): Ralph Kiner (b. 1922), home-run-hitting outfielder for the Pitts-burgh Pirates; Yogi Berra (b. 1925), long-time catcher for the Yankees and manager of the New York Mets (1971–1975) and Yankees (1984), known for his folksy one-liners and malapropisms; Early Wynn (1920–1999), right-handed pitcher notorious for intimidating batters with his fastball, and who won more than 300 games in a long career pitching with the Washington Senators, Cleveland Indians, and Chicago White Sox.

23.24    Five points . . . Cobb.]  Ty Cobb's batting average over 24 major-league seasons was .367, the highest ever recorded. Known as "the Georgia Peach," Cobb (1886–1961) was the first inductee into the Baseball Hall of Fame; Babe Ruth was the second.

24.2–3   first-sacker . . . 1939.]  New York Yankees first baseman Lou Gehrig (1903–1941), stricken with amyotrophic lateral sclerosis (now known as Lou Gehrig's disease), had to retire from baseball because of his deterio-rating health. In December 1939, with Gehrig's health rapidly worsening, the Baseball Writers Association of America elected him to the Hall of Fame after waiving the rule that eligible players must be retired for at least one year.

24.6–7   Gehringer . . . Goslin,]  Detroit Tigers second baseman Char-lie Gehringer (1903–1993); Goose Goslin (1900–1971), clutch-hitting out-fielder for the Washington Senators, St. Louis Browns, and the Detroit Tigers in the 1920s and 1930s.

24.17–18  Neal Ball . . . 1909.]  On July 19, 1909, with runners on first and second and no outs, Cleveland Indians shortstop Neal Ball caught a line drive from Amby McConnell of the Boston Red Sox, stepped on second base, and tagged out the baserunner coming from first to end the inning by means of one of baseball's rarest feats, the unassisted triple play.

26.19–20      Life . . . pace,]   Cf. Shakespeare, *Macbeth*, V.v.20.

26.31      mewling and puking,]   Cf. Shakespeare, *As You Like It*, II.vii.144.

27.12      list of players]   The list gives the actual results of the Hall of Fame voting for 1971.

28.7      Gabby Hartnett]   Catcher (1900–1972) for the Chicago Cubs during the 1920s and 1930s, whose lifetime batting average was .297 and who set records for catchers in home runs, doubles, hits, and RBIs.

28.9      Early Wynn:]   See note 23.15–18.

28.11–12      Dazzy . . . hundred.]   Right-handed pitcher Dazzy Vance (1891–1961) won 197 games in a relatively short major-league career (he was 31 when he pitched his first full season in the majors); among his many impressive career statistics is his leading the National League in strikeouts for seven consecutive years.

28.13–14      Koufax . . . eligible!]   Baseball pitching greats Sandy Koufax (b. 1935) and Warren Spahn (1921–2003) were both inducted into the Hall of Fame in the first year of eligibility (1972 and 1973, respectively).

28.14–15      six years . . . .358!]   The lifetime batting average of second baseman Rogers Hornsby (1896–1963) is second only to Ty Cobb's; he was inducted into the Hall of Fame in 1942, five years after his final season with the St. Louis Browns in 1937.

28.15–16      Bill . . . *apiece*!]   New York Giants first baseman and manager Bill Terry (1898–1989), who retired from baseball in 1941, was inducted into the Hall of Fame in 1954; first baseman and outfielder Harry Heilmann (1894–1951), who retired due to arthritis in 1932 after playing most of his career with the Detroit Tigers, was inducted in 1952.

28.17      Marion and Reese]   Shortstop and manager Marty Marion (b. 1917), who spent most of his career in St. Louis (with the Cardinals and the Browns); Pee Wee Reese (1918–1999), shortstop for the Dodgers (Brooklyn and Los Angeles) inducted into the Hall of Fame in 1984.

28.19      Rabbit Maranville]   Shortstop (1891–1954) best known for playing 23 consecutive seasons in the National League, a record that stood until 1986.

28.24      Billy . . . Moon!]   Billy Bruton (1929–1995), centerfielder for the Milwaukee Braves and Detroit Tigers; Jackie Jensen (1927–1982), rightfielder for the New York Yankees, Washington Senators, and Boston Red Sox; Wally Moon (b. 1930), outfielder for the St. Louis Cardinals and Los Angeles Dodgers.

29.8–9 "The fact . . . institution."] From Kuhn's remarks to reporters about the 1971 voting.

29.16 "After fighting] In the passage that follows Smitty borrows elements of Ernest Hemingway's prose style and draws on the enthusiasm for deep-sea fishing expressed in the novel *The Old Man and the Sea* (1952) and other writings.

29.20 Hillerich and Bradsby] Since 1884, Hillerich and Bradsby has been manufacturing the official baseball bat of Major League Baseball, the "Louisville Slugger."

31.4–5 a barber . . . House] The passage that follows borrows from Hemingway's style in the 1926 story "The Killers."

31.34 Henry Armstrong] Henry Jackson, Jr. (1912–1988), boxer who fought under the name Henry Armstrong. He is the only boxer to hold three world championships simultaneously (featherweight, welterweight, and lightweight).

33.12 Adventure . . . kids."] In *Green Hills of Africa* (1935), chapter 1, Hemingway wrote, "All modern American literature comes from one book by Mark Twain called *Huckleberry Finn*."

34.7 Clytemnestra] In Greek myth, Clytemnestra commits adultery while her husband, Agamemnon, king of Mycenae, is at the siege of Troy, and upon his return murders him.

34.39–40 Stanley Ketchel . . . down] Middleweight champion boxer Ketchel (1886–1910) was knocked out in the twelfth round of a match with heavyweight champion Jack Johnson in 1909. Hemingway was an amateur boxer and boxing enthusiast.

35.10–12 "*The Ambassadors! . . . do!*] In the late novels *The Ambassadors* (1903) and *The Golden Bowl* (1904), James wrote extremely complex sentences to explore nuanced psychological states.

35.15–18 *Red Badge . . . Ground!*] A litany of classic American novels: Stephen Crane's *The Red Badge of Courage* (1895); Sherwood Anderson's *Winesburg, Ohio* (1919); James Fenimore Cooper's *The Last of the Mohicans* (1826); Theodore Dreiser's *Sister Carrie* (1900); Frank Norris's *McTeague* (1899); Willa Cather's *My Antonia* (1918); William Dean Howells' *The Rise of Silas Lapham* (1885); Richard Henry Dana's *Two Years Before the Mast* (1840); Edith Wharton's *Ethan Frome* (1911); and Ellen Glasgow's *Barren Ground* (1925).

35.19 Booth Tarkington] Novelist (1869–1946), author of *The Magnificent Ambersons* (1918), *Alice Adams* (1921), and numerous other novels.

35.19    Sarah Orne Jewett] Author (1849–1909) best known for her novella *The Country of the Pointed Firs* (1896).

35.20–21    Francis Scott Fitzwhat'shisname?] I.e., F. Scott Fitzgerald.

35.21    Wolfe and Dos] Novelists Thomas Wolfe (1900–1938), author of *Look Homeward, Angel* (1929) and *Of Time and the River* (1935), and John Dos Passos (1896–1970), author of the trilogy *U.S.A.* (1930–1936).

35.22–23    *The Sound . . . nothing*] Faulkner's *The Sound and the Fury* (1929) takes its title from Shakespeare's *Macbeth*, V.v.26–28: "it is a tale / Told by an idiot, full of sound and fury, / Signifying nothing."

35.34    "*Nevermore!*"] Cf. Edgar Allan Poe's poem, "The Raven" (1845), in which the refrain "Nevermore!" is repeated 11 times.

36.9–37    it is a mild . . . arm?] Cf. Ahab's address to first mate Starbuck in Melville's *Moby-Dick*, chapter 132, "The Symphony."

37.7    "Wouldn't . . . so?"] Last line of Hemingway's novel *The Sun Also Rises* (1926).

38.18–19    smart Roman punk . . . rolls.] In the account of the Crucifixion in the Gospel of John, Roman soldiers cast lots to decide who kept one of Jesus' garments; in Smitty's version, the soldiers are shooting craps.

39.9–10    Famous Writers School] In 1961, in Westport, Connecticut, illustrator Albert Dorne founded the Famous Writers School, which offered correspondence courses teaching writing on the model of his successful school for artists.

39.28    bright boy?"] In "The Killers," two thugs come into a diner looking for a Swede named Ole Andreson, whom they plan to kill; they taunt the counterman George and the recurring Hemingway character Nick Adams with the repeated epithet "bright boy."

40.37–38    the guy Hem killed . . . himself.] On July 2, 1961, at his home in Ketchum, Idaho, Hemingway shot himself after a long battle with depression.

41.1    MY KINSMEN] A reference to Nathaniel Hawthorne's early short story, "My Kinsman, Major Molineux" (1831).

41.25    lengthy intro] *The Scarlet Letter* begins with a semi-autobiographical introduction, "The Custom House," set in the writer's own time.

41.32–35    based upon real life . . . attic.] The conceit of the discovered documents is, of course, a fiction.

41.35    Prynne-Dimmesdale scandal]    As the result of her affair with the Reverend Arthur Dimmesdale, Hester Prynne becomes pregnant and, refusing to reveal the identity of her lover, is made to wear a scarlet letter ("A" for adulteress) on her clothing. Though wracked with guilt, particularly after Hester's husband, Roger Chillingworth, returns to Salem, Dimmesdale conceals his part in the affair for most of the novel.

42.19–20    Shoeless Joe's . . . Cicotte]    "Shoeless Joe" Jackson (1889–1951), star outfielder for the Chicago White Sox, and his teammate pitcher Eddie Cicotte (1884–1951) were caught throwing the 1919 World Series. The ensuing "Black Sox Scandal" earned them and six teammates lifetime banishment from baseball.

43.30–31    Pitching . . . truthful]    Pitching in a Pinch (1912) is the ghost-written autobiography of New York Giants pitcher Christy Mathewson (1880–1925).

44.2–5    first Negro leaguer . . . Paige]    Belatedly recognizing baseball's pre-1947 policy of segregation and the achievements of black players in the Negro Leagues, the Hall of Fame elected Satchel Paige for enshrinement in 1971 but assigned him a different status than other Hall of Famers because he hadn't played for ten years in the major leagues, a requirement for induction. His plaque was placed in a separate section to be devoted to Negro League players (of which he was the first elected). When pressed by reporters at a reception announcing Paige's election, Bowie Kuhn said, "Technically, you'd have to say he's not in the Hall of Fame."

45.29–30    yearning . . . Watson.]    Cf. Emma Lazarus' "The New Colossus" (1883), the poem affixed to the pedestal of the Statue of Liberty: "Give me your tired, your poor, / Your huddled masses yearning to breathe free." Miss Watson is the owner of Jim in Adventures of Huckleberry Finn.

46.8–9    today . . . whirlwind.]    The phrase echoes Hitler's slogan "Today Europe, tomorrow the world."

46.16    terrifying Ty Cobb]    In addition to his formidable talents as a player, Cobb was known for his vicious personality and aggressive behavior on the field, which included "spiking" players with upturned cleats when sliding and an incident in which he assaulted a spectator in the stands.

46.17–18    unappeasable . . . Durocher]    Leo Durocher (1905–1991) had a legendary fiery temper and irrepressible tongue.

46.18    steadfast . . . McGraw]    Managing the Giants for three decades, John McGraw (1873–1934) led the team to ten pennants and three World Series victories; his teams rarely posted a losing record.

46.20     Tinkers, Evers, and Chance] Chicago Cubs infield for the first few years of the twentieth century: shortstop Joe Tinker (1880–1948), second baseman Johnny Evers (1881–1947), and first baseman Frank Chance (1877–1924). Their great double-play combination was made famous by Franklin P. Adams' poem "Baseball's Sad Lexicon" (1910).

46.23     Astarte] Ancient Middle Eastern goddess, associated with fertility and war.

46.23     Baal] Hebrew for "Lord," name given to false gods in the Bible (see for example Numbers 25, when "Israel joined himself unto Baal–peor: and the anger of the LORD was kindled against Israel").

46.28     "the great shroud of the sea."] From the conclusion of *Moby-Dick*: "then all collapsed, and the great shroud of the sea rolled on as it rolled five thousand years ago."

46.30     Gil Gamesh] A name derived from that of the hero of the ancient Mesopotamian *Epic of Gilgamesh*.

46.30–31     survive . . . tell] The epilogue to *Moby-Dick* contains an epitaph from the Book of Job: "And I only am escaped alone to tell thee." Ishmael is the sole survivor of the destruction of the *Pequod* by Moby Dick.

46.33–48.19     Gentle . . . whale.] Several chapters in *Moby-Dick*—for example, chapter 32, "Cetology"—interrupt the narrative and present highly detailed discussions about whales and whaling. This long sentence proposing an analogous treatment of baseball imitates Melville's style.

47.16     "The Tightness of the Stitching,"] Cf. the chapter "The Whiteness of the Whale" in *Moby-Dick*.

47.23     flattened . . . designed] Retired Hall of Fame ballplayer George Wright (1847–1937) founded a sporting-goods company and developed a bat flattened on one side, which he claimed would help batters to bunt.

47.24–25     the curved-barrel . . . Kinst] Chicago inventor Emile Kinst designed a "banana bat" that he said would spin a batted ball in unpredictable ways.

47.33     Heinie . . . bat,"] Bat with an extra-wide barrel used by third baseman Heinie Groh (1889–1968), who played for the New York Giants and Cincinnati Reds.

47.33–34     Ed . . . Betsy] Favorite bat of Big Ed Delehanty (1867–1903), rightfielder who spent most of his career in Philadelphia.

47.36     Queequeg, Tashtego, and Dagoo] Harpooners of the *Pequod* in *Moby-Dick*.

48.34    "wild and distant sea."]   Cf. the penultimate paragraph of *Moby-Dick*, chapter 1, in which Ishmael refers to the "wild and distant seas" where the "great whale . . . rolled his island bulk."

49.21–22    Will Walter . . . Mars?]   Dodgers president Walter O'Malley (1903–1979), the chief architect of the plan that moved the team from Brooklyn to Los Angeles in 1957, was widely vilified as abandoning Brooklyn, then in a period of decline, for Southern California.

53.21–22    "to help . . . democracy."]   Asking for a declaration of war to enter World War I in 1917, Woodrow Wilson told Congress, "The world must be made safe for democracy."

54.18    playing fields of Eton]   Eton is the largest of England's public schools; the Duke of Wellington remarked that "the battle of Waterloo was won on the playing fields of Eton."

55.13–14    Hindenburg . . . 1918]   The Hindenburg Line, German fortifications stretching nearly 100 miles in northwestern France, were breached by Allied forces led by the British in September 1918.

57.17–18    Judge Kenesaw Mountain Landis]   Landis (1866–1944) was a federal judge who was named the first Commissioner of Baseball on November 12, 1920, and held the post until his death.

58.12    Teapot Dome]   Corruption scandal during Warren G. Harding's presidency.

59.19–20    Hubbell . . . American]   Hall of Fame players Carl Hubbell (1903–1988), left-handed pitcher for the New York Giants in the National League, and Lefty Grove (1900–1975), left-handed pitcher for the Philadelphia Athletics in the American League.

59.36    Walter Johnson,]   Hall of Fame pitcher Walter "Big Train" Johnson (1887–1946), right-hander for the Washington Senators, one of the dominant pitchers of his era who won 417 games over 21 seasons. He said of his fastball, "You can't hit what you can't see."

59.37    Georgia Peach]   Ty Cobb (see note 23.24).

73.9–10    Man o'War]   Among the greatest of American thoroughbred racehorses, Man O'War won 20 of 21 races in his competitive years, 1919–1920.

75.14–17    Waddell . . . Leonard]   Hall of Fame pitchers Rube Waddell (1876–1914), left-handed pitcher for the Philadelphia Athletics and St. Louis Browns, and Grover Cleveland Alexander (1887–1950), right-handed pitcher for the Philadelphia Phillies. Left-hander Dutch Leonard (1892–1952) pitched for the Boston Red Sox and the Detroit Tigers.

85.21     GLORIOUS MUNDY]   Play on Latin maxim *Sic transit gloria mundi* ("So passes away the glory of this world").

93.37     'wander in the wilderness.']   See Exodus 14:33: "And your children shall wander in the wilderness forty years."

96.14     let my players go."]   Cf. Exodus 5:1, when Moses tells the Egyptian pharaoh, "Let my people go."

98.2–26     Frenchy . . . Kronos]   The surnames given the members of the 1943 Ruppert Mundys are all drawn from mythology and religion; their given names are drawn almost entirely from the names of players in organized baseball's National and American leagues.

113.39     Wagner Act!]   A key part of Roosevelt's New Deal, the National Labor Relations Act (1935) known as the Wagner Act, was legislation designed to protect the rights of workers to unionize.

113.40     Carter . . . Coal!]   The Bituminous Coal Conservation Act (the "Guffey Act," 1935) authorized federal regulation of pricing and labor practices in the mining industry. In *Carter* v. *Carter Coal* (1936) the Supreme Court ruled 5–4 that Congress had exceeded its authority under the Commerce Clause and declared the law unconstitutional.

113.40     Gompers . . . Stove!]   When the American Federation of Labor (AFL), led by Samuel Gompers (1850–1924), initiated a boycott against Buck's Stove and Range Company, Gompers and the AFL were charged with contempt. The rulings were challenged but upheld by the Supreme Court in *Gompers* v. *Buck's Stove & Range Co.* (1911).

114.1     Federal Reserve Act,]   Act (1913) authorizing the creation of the Federal Reserve as the central bank of the United States.

114.1     Dred Scott]   In *Dred Scott* v. *Sandford* (1857), the Supreme Court ruled that blacks, even if free, could not become citizens of the United States and "had no rights," in the words of Chief Justice Roger B. Taney, "that a white man was bound to respect."

120.40–121.1     Pete Gray . . . Browns]   With many players serving in the military, Pete Gray (1915–2002), who had lost his right arm in an accident as a child, was called up to the major leagues and played 77 games for the St. Louis Browns in 1945.

123.23–24     spectacular . . . Joe.]   In his rookie season, 1936, Joe Di-Maggio posted impressive statistics: 29 home runs, 125 RBIs, and a .323 batting average.

165.9     Maginot Line.]   Vast stretch of fortifications built by France along its border with Germany, constructed in the 1930s.

191.26 a midget] Loosely inspired by Eddie Gaedel, a 3′7″ stage performer hired by St. Louis Browns owner Bill Veeck to bat in a game against the Detroit Tigers on August 19, 1951.

195.27 Victory Garden] To build patriotism and encourage conservation during World War II, Americans were encouraged to plant "Gardens for Victory."

195.29 Topsy!"] The mischievous child Topsy in Harriet Beecher Stowe's *Uncle Tom's Cabin* (1852), who says of herself, "I 'spect I growed."

211.39 Waner . . . National] The Waner brothers, Paul (1903–1965) and Lloyd (1906–1982), played together in the Pittsburgh Pirates outfield for 17 years. Together they had 5,611 hits, 753 more than the three major-league DiMaggios (Joe, Dom, and Vince). Both Waners are in the Hall of Fame.

222.38 Tokyo Rose] Name applied to various women who broadcast in English on behalf of the Japanese government during World War II.

228.8–9 *happiest . . . earth*] Cf. the farewell address by the terminally ill Yankee first baseman Lou Gehrig (1903–1941), delivered in front of more than 61,000 fans at Yankee Stadium, July 4, 1939 (see note 24.2–3). Gehrig told the crowd that despite his illness, "Today, I consider myself the luckiest man on the face of the earth."

241.27 Musial . . . Cooper] Stan "the Man" Musial (b. 1920), hard-hitting Hall of Fame Cardinal outfielder; Mort Cooper (1913–1958) Cardinal right-handed pitcher.

246.6 Meusel . . . Ruth] Bob Meusel (1896–1977), Earle Combs (1899–1976), and Babe Ruth (1895–1948), outfielders for the 1927 New York Yankee team known as "Murderers' Row." Meusel and Ruth were known for their great hitting. Combs was famous for getting on base by drawing walks.

263.31 Bill McKechnie's boys] Former player and longtime manager Bill McKechnie (1886–1965) managed the Cincinnati Reds during World War II.

263.34–35 Johnny Vander Meer] Left-handed pitcher (1914–1997) for the Reds.

266.8 Frick, or Harridge] Ford Frick (1895–1978), third Commissioner of Baseball, 1951–1965. William Harridge (1885–1971), president of the American League, 1931–1958.

267.18 thrown the World Series] See note 42.19–20.

269.11 Wee Willie Keeler] Outfielder for the Brooklyn Dodgers, with 2,932 hits and a lifetime batting average of .341.

281.24 *shvartze.*"] Yiddish term for blacks.

284.6    Fred Waring's]  Popular bandleader (1900–1984) whose orchestra often played at war-bond rallies during World War II and performed patriotic songs.

294.34    Walter Johnson,]  See note 59.36.

298.27–28    "Father, . . . says."]  Cf. Jesus' words on the cross, "Father, forgive them; for they know not what they do" (Luke 23:34).

299.34    "*Omoo!*]  Title of Herman Melville's second novel; *Omoo* (1847), like his first novel, *Typee* (1846), is an adventure story set in the South Seas.

304.16    "The . . . horror!"]  Cf. the final words of Kurtz in Joseph Conrad's novel *Heart of Darkness* (1902).

304.40    "Mistah . . . dead."]  Cf. the words that announce Kurtz's death in *Heart of Darkness*: "Mistah Kurtz—he dead."

307.15–16    "In victory," . . . gentleman.]  Cf. Winston Churchill in volume 1 of *The Second World War* (1948): "In Defeat: Defiance. In Victory: Magnanimity."

307.34–35    "Many . . . first.]  Cf. Jesus' words, "Many that are first shall be last; and the last shall be first" (Matthew 19:30).

309.24    pack of Bicycles,]  "Bicycle" is a popular brand of playing cards.

313.4–5    third strike . . . Series,]  The Brooklyn Dodgers lost the fourth game of the 1941 World Series to the Yankees after Dodger catcher Mickey Owen (1916–2005) dropped what would have been a game-ending third strike.

313.5–6    error . . . Merkle]  The "Merkle Boner": on first base when a teammate drove in what would have been a game- and pennant-winning run, Frederick Merkle (1888–1956) left the field without touching second base. The opposing Chicago Cubs tagged second, Merkle was ruled out on a technicality, and the game declared a tie.

317.4    MISSION FROM MOSCOW]  The popular book *Mission to Moscow* was a pro-Soviet film (1943) based on the book (1941) written by Joseph Davies, a former ambassador to the Soviet Union.

323.31    *yafka,*]  Soviet secret-police parlance for "safe house" or secret rendezvous.

327.40    Chichikov.]  His name derives from that of the protagonist of Gogol's *Dead Souls* (1842).

328.17–18    'From . . . greed.']  Cf. Karl Marx, *Critique of the Gotha Programme* (1875): "From each according to his abilities, to each according to his needs."

329.10     Smerdyakov,] His name derives from that of Pavel Fyodorovich Smerdyakov in Dostoevsky's *The Brothers Karamazov* (1880), the epileptic, mean-spirited, illegitimate son of Fyodor Pavlovich Karamazov, whom he murders.

330.30     Colonel Raskolnikov] His name derives from that of the protagonist of Dostoevsky's *Crime and Punishment* (1866).

331.21     *Congressman Martin Dies*] Martin Dies (1901–1972), Texas congressman who served as the first chairman of the House Un-American Activities Committee from 1938 to 1945.

337.30     Winesburg, Ohio,] Fictional small town that provides the setting and title of a story collection (1919) by Sherwood Anderson (1876–1941).

338.7–9     Black Hawk . . . Massachusetts] Real and fictional place names that figure in the works of American writers: Black Hawk, Nebraska (Willa Cather); Zenith, city in the state of "Winnemac" (invented by Minnesota-born Sinclair Lewis); Michigan (Ernest Hemingway); Jefferson, Mississippi (William Faulkner); Lycurgus, New York (Theodore Dreiser); Walden (Henry David Thoreau).

340.20     *Hellzapoppin'*!] Enormously popular Broadway musical comedy revue starring the team of Ole Olsen and Chic Johnson, which ran from 1938 to 1941.

345.26     Stavrogin,] The name derives from a character in Dostoevsky's *The Possessed* (1872).

348.26–27     no man . . . himself] From Meditation XVII, by English poet John Donne (1572–1631).

350.20     CHANSON DE ROLAND] Medieval French poem that culminates with its hero, Roland, dying at the battle of Roncevaux.

350.28–29     Mugsy . . . Lip?"] John McGraw (see note 46.18) and Leo Durocher (see note 46.17–18).

352.36     THE SHOT . . . LEAGUE] Play on Emerson's phrase "the shot heard round the world" describing the battle of Concord in "Hymn Sung at the Completion of the Battle Monument, Concord, Massachusetts" (1837).

353.26     "you *can't* . . . again.] Without emphasis, title of posthumously published novel (1940) by Thomas Wolfe.

358.14     *Leopold and Loeb.*"] Nathan Leopold and Richard Loeb, two 19-year-old University of Chicago students, were convicted of the 1924 murder of 14-year-old Bobby Franks.

360.1     THE ENEMY WITHIN] Book (1960) by Robert F. Kennedy.

364.39     Max Lanier] Right-handed pitcher (b. 1915) taught to throw "lefty." He was a star in the Mexican League and pitched for the St. Louis Cardinals.

365.33–34     "Say . . . O.K.!"] An echo of "Say it ain't so, Joe," reputed to be said by a young boy who wanted the disgraced baseball legend "Shoeless Joe" Jackson to say that he hadn't helped fix the 1919 World Series.

373.17–18     *The Price Is Right!*] Popular television game show.

375.12     undiscovered country . . . returns] Cf. Hamlet's soliloquy in *Hamlet,* III.i.79–80.

375.33–34     the recent publication . . . novel] *August 1914,* a novel by Alexander Solzhenitsyn (b. 1918), was published in English translation in September 1972. At the time Solzhenitsyn was a dissident writer living in the Soviet Union; he had been awarded the Nobel Prize for Literature in 1970 but did not go to Stockholm to accept the award for fear he would not be permitted to return home. Seven Soviet publishing houses had been sent the manuscript of *August 1914* but none acknowledged receiving it. The novel circulated in *samizdat* in the Soviet Union and was first published by a Russian-language publishing house in Paris in June 1971. Attacks against Solzhenitsyn and his work were mounted in the Soviet press, including a letter-writing campaign initiated by the Soviet Writers Union, which had expelled him in 1969.

MY LIFE AS A MAN

385.6     Dale Carnegie] Popular writer and public speaker (1888–1955), author of the bestselling *How to Win Friends and Influence People* (1936).

387.15–18     "The Donkey Serenade" . . . Jones."] Singer and movie actor Allan Jones (1907–1992) sang the popular song "Donkey Serenade" in *The Firefly* (1937).

387.26     that Senator Ford.] Vaudeville comedian "Senator" Ed Ford (1887–1970) created and starred in the radio show "Can You Top This?" (1940–1954).

389.22     Madame Chiang Kai-shek.] Soong May-ling (1898–2003), the American-educated wife of Republic of China President Chiang Kai-shek, was widely admired for her public affiliation with numerous philanthropic efforts.

389.25–26     Pearl Buck] Nobel Prize–winning author (1892–1973) who wrote novels such as *The Good Earth* (1931) about China, where she lived and served as a missionary as a young woman.

389.26     Emily Post] Popular writer and arbiter of etiquette (1873–1960).

390.10–13      "Mamselle" . . . Lamplighter,"]    "Mamselle" and "The Old Lamplighter" ("He made the night a little brighter wherever he would go . . . ") were sentimental songs popular in 1947 in versions by the vocal group The Pied Pipers and Kay Kyser, respectively.

391.22      Lennie Tristano]    Jazz pianist (1919–1978), considered one of the great white be-bop improvisers.

391.27      Bojangles Robinson]    Bill "Bojangles" Robinson (1878–1949), tap dancer and vaudeville performer.

391.30      pro kits]    Prophylactic kits issued to GIs to prevent venereal disease.

391.40      Stan Kenton]    Bandleader, pianist, and arranger on (1911–1979) who led an orchestra associated with "progressive jazz."

392.8      June Christie,]    June Christy (1925–1990) sang with the Stan Kenton Orchestra from 1945 to 1952.

392.16      Bala-Cynwyd]    Philadelphia suburb.

393.26      *Of Time and the River*]    Novel (1935) by Thomas Wolfe (1900–1938).

395.16      Yehudi?]    The first name of violinist and conductor Yehudi Menuhin (1916–1999) became a comic catchphrase in the mid-1940s.

396.7–8      Like Dilsey . . . he endured.]    Dilsey Gibson, long-suffering servant of the Compson family in Faulkner's novel *The Sound and the Fury* (1929). In an appendix to the novel written in 1945, Faulkner's two-word entry on Dilsey read: "They endured."

396.24–25      *Sir Gawain and the Green Knight*.]    Fourteenth-century romance written in Middle English.

401.5      Poets' Corner]    A section of the south transept of Westminster Abbey is dedicated to tombs and commemorative monuments to poets and writers, including Chaucer, Dryden, Dickens, and Tennyson.

401.6      Lake District,]    Region in northwestern England that was home to Wordsworth, Coleridge, and other English Romantic poets, and the setting for poems such as Wordsworth's "Tintern Abbey."

401.7      *Persuasion*]    Jane Austen's last completed novel, published posthumously in 1818.

401.8      Abbey Theatre,]    The National Theatre of Ireland, co-founded by W. B. Yeats in 1904.

401.8      River Liffey]    River that runs through Dublin; it plays an important role in Joyce's *Finnegans Wake* (1939)

402.30    "objective correlative"]  Aesthetic concept formulated by T. S. Eliot in his essay "Hamlet and His Problems" (1919): "The only way of expressing emotion in the form of art is by finding an 'objective correlative'; in other words, a set of objects, a situation, a chain of events which shall be the formula of that *particular* emotion."

403.35    the New Criticism,]  Type of literary criticism that dominated English departments in American universities in the postwar era through the 1980s; careful study of texts and authorial style ("close reading") is its interpretive foundation.

403.39    Lawrence]  Sexuality was a constant of D. H. Lawrence's work, notably in the long-banned novel *Lady Chatterley's Lover* (1928).

404.5–12    absence . . . *Ambassadors*]  Virginia Woolf's modernist novels *Mrs. Dalloway* (1925) and *To the Lighthouse* (1927) employ nonstandard usage in grammar, capitalization, and punctuation; Gustave Flaubert and Henry James, authors of *Madame Bovary* (1857) and *The Ambassadors* (1903), respectively, were exacting prose stylists.

407.23–24    H. L. Mencken]  Journalist, satirist, and literary critic (1880–1956).

409.24–25    Bloomsbury group,]  Early twentieth-century English artistic circle that included writers such as Virginia Woolf, E. M. Forster, Vita Sackville-West, and Lytton Strachey.

410.21    Pigalle]  Red-light district of Paris.

412.7–8    senator Bilbo . . . Smith]  Theodore G. Bilbo (1877–1947) served terms as Mississippi governor and U.S. senator and advocated white supremacy. Charles Coughlin (1891–1979), a Catholic priest and popular radio broadcaster during the 1930s who made anti-Semitic and pro-fascist statements in his broadcasts. Gerald Lyman Kenneth Smith (1898–1976), Christian fundamentalist preacher and supporter of extreme right-wing organizations.

416.16    *Song of Norway*]  1944 musical based on Edvard Grieg's life and works.

416.16    *The Student Prince*]  1924 musical adaptation of Wilhelm Meyer-Förster's play *Old Heidelberg*.

416.19    "Because"]  Recorded by Perry Como, "Because" (words by Edward Teschemacher, music by Guy d'Hardelot) was a hit single in 1948.

416.24    Jerry Vale]  Stage name of Bronx-born singer Genaro Louis Vitaliano (b. 1932).

417.5    Lily Pons . . . Galli-Curci]  French-born American coloratura soprano Lily Pons (1904–1976), a principal soprano at New York's Metropolitan

Opera from 1931 to 1961; Italian coloratura soprano Amelita Galli-Curci (1882–1963), who after achieving stardom in Europe sang for the Chicago Opera and New York's Metropolitan Opera.

417.12    Tate . . . Leavis] American poet Allen Tate (1899–1979); influential critic and teacher F. R. Leavis (1895–1978) stressed the importance of moral seriousness in literature.

425.2    stories . . . Party"] The story collection *The Garden Party* (1922) established New Zealand–born author Katherine Mansfield (1888–1923) as a major writer.

425.10    Sir Thomas Browne.] English writer and physician (1605–1682), noted for the baroque elaborateness of his prose.

425.34    *Seven Types of Ambiguity*] Influential work of literary criticism (1930) by English critic and poet William Empson (1906–1984).

427.21    Babel's experience] Russian Jewish writer Isaac Babel (1894–1941) rode into Poland with the Cossacks in 1920 and later published the *Red Cavalry* cycle of stories about his experiences.

428.20–22    Bartleby . . . not to.] Bartleby the Scrivener is the eponymous hero of Melville's short story (1853) about a law clerk whose recurring dictum is, "I would prefer not to."

430.38–39    illnesses . . . Dimmesdale,] In Henry James' *The Wings of the Dove* (1902), the young heiress Milly Theale is terminally ill; in Thomas Mann's *The Magic Mountain* (1924), Hans Castorp undergoes treatment for tuberculosis at a sanatorium; Arthur Dimmesdale's illness in *The Scarlet Letter* (see note 41.35) is related to his guilt in concealing his affair with Hester Prynne.

430.39–40    transformation of Gregor Samsa] In Franz Kafka's novella *The Metamorphosis* (1915).

432.34–36    unable . . . cholera] For *The Magic Mountain*, see note 430.38–39. *Death in Venice* (1912) is set during a cholera outbreak in Venice.

433.22    Norman Vincent Peale,] Reformed Church minister (1898–1993) and popular author, best known for his inspirational book *The Power of Positive Thinking* (1952).

434.4    Hyde Park neighborhood] Home of the University of Chicago.

436.15    Louise Colet] French poet (1810–1876) who was Flaubert's mistress and correspondent.

438.39    the O. Henry ending] An unexpected, often ironic ending, named after popular short-story writer O. Henry (pen name of William Sydney Porter, 1862–1910).

439.5    "Max" . . . "Tom"]   Maxwell Perkins (1884–1947) was Thomas Wolfe's editor at Charles Scribner's Sons.

440.11    Father Coughlin]   See note 412.7–8.

440.19    *Mansfield Park.*]   Novel (1814) by Jane Austen.

440.33    Spillane]   Mickey Spillane (b. 1918), author of bestselling crime novels.

443.34–36    Nabokov's . . . daughter.]   Humbert Humbert, the protagonist of Nabokov's *Lolita* (1955), marries Charlotte Haze to be near the real object of his desire, her daughter Dolores (Lolita).

445.28    Pappagallos]   A brand of popular women's shoes.

450.5    action takes place]   The plot described is that of the Léo Delibes' opera *Lakmé* (1883), adapted from Pierre Loti's novel *Le Mariage de Loti* originally published as *Rarahu* (1880).

451.18    an Ingres odalisque]   A reclining woman, partially or fully nude, as painted by French artist Jean Auguste Dominique Ingres (1780–1867).

453.14    Bristol Old Vic]   Theater company named after the theater complex in Bristol, England, which is its home; founded in 1946, it is an offshoot of the London Old Vic Theatre.

453.14–15    Marcel Marceau]   French mime (b. 1923).

454.2    "Mr. Interlocutor" . . . Bones,"]   Stock blackface characters in nineteenth-century American minstrelsy.

454.6    "motiveless malignity."]   In the essay "Notes on Othello" (collected in *Literary Remains*, volume 2), Coleridge describes Iago's scheming as "motiveless malignity."

455.37–38    Aschenbach . . . Tadzio.]   In Mann's *Death in Venice*, the aging novelist Gustave von Aschenbach becomes obsessed with a beautiful young boy named Tadzio.

457.6    Katherine Mansfield's]   See note 425.2.

459.5    *The Trial*]   Novel by Franz Kafka, posthumously published in 1925.

464.8–9    *The Possessed* or *The Brothers Karamazov*]   Novels by Dostoevsky, published in 1872 and 1879–80, respectively.

464.9    Henry . . . Hardy]   Henry Aldrich was an enterprising boy in The Aldrich Family radio program, first aired on NBC in 1939. Andy Hardy (played by Mickey Rooney) had a similar role in a successful series of movie comedies that included *You're Only Young Once* (1937) and *Love Finds Andy Hardy* (1938).

464.35    nineteenth-century Lemberg,]   Now L'viv in Ukraine, Lemberg was the site of pogroms against Jews.

464.35–36    fifteenth-century Madrid,]   The Jews were expelled from Spain in 1492.

466.11    shagitz . . . shiksa]   Yiddish words for male and female Gentiles.

471.34    *Dr. Otto Spielvogel*]   Fictional psychoanalyst who hears Alexander Portnoy's book-length monologue in Roth's *Portnoy's Complaint* (1969).

475.33–34    figure . . . Calais,"]   Auguste Rodin's monumental sculpture *The Burghers of Calais* (1888) depicted the six men who offered themselves as martyrs if the English would lift their siege of Calais during the Hundred Years' War.

478.2–3    Aristocrats . . . 'em."]   In the last years of the ancien régime in France there was a vogue for nobility and royalty to dress in idealized rustic costume. Fragonard: Jean-Honoré Fragonard (1732–1806), French painter.

478.34    Billy Rose's]   Rose (1899–1966) was a successful producer and entrepreneur whose ventures included the New York nightclub Diamond Horseshoe.

478.38    Black Beauty]   The horse whose story is told in *Black Beauty: The Autobiography of a Horse* (1877), novel by Anna Sewell.

480.3    Ernie Pyle]   Journalist and war correspondent (1900–1945) whose books include *Here Is Your War* (1943) and *Brave Men* (1944).

481.14    *Uncle Vanya.*]   Drama (1899) set on a provincial country estate in Russia.

485.8    Kitty and a Levin]   Couple with a loving marriage in Tolstoy's *Anna Karenina* (1877).

486.1    Abraham . . . overtones,]   Kierkegaard's *Fear and Trembling* (1843) is a study of the biblical story of Abraham's near-sacrifice of his son Isaac.

486.10    Terry Southern.]   American novelist and screenwriter (1924–1995) whose satiric works (notably *Candy*, 1955, written with Mason Hoffenberg) are often sexually outrageous and provocative.

487.29–30    Madeleine . . . *Fall*,]   Wife who cuckolds the eponymous protagonist of Saul Bellow's novel *Herzog* (1964); monstrous wife murdered by her husband in Norman Mailer's novel *An American Dream* (1965); Maggie, dead wife who haunts protagonist Quentin in Arthur Miller's play *After the Fall* (1964).

487.33–34    Chicken . . . garage.]   Cf. Herbert Hoover's 1928 presidential campaign slogan, "A chicken in every pot and a car in every garage."

Fyodor and Dmitri Karamazov are both attracted to the bewitching peasant girl Grushenka in Dostoevsky's *The Brothers Karamazov* (1879–80).

487.34     Dark Ladies] Twenty-five of Shakespeare's sonnets (Sonnets 127–152) are addressed to a woman commonly referred to as the "Dark Lady."

487.35     luftmenschen] "Men of air": dreamy, impractical men without gainful employment.

487.36     Dead End Kid?] Byword for roughneck teenage boys invariably in trouble, named for a group of young actors who appeared in Sidney Kingsley's Broadway play *Dead End* (1935).

490.30     "the culture of poverty"] Phrase popularized by anthropologist Oscar Lewis (1914–1970) and writer and activist Michael Harrington (1928–1989).

491.20     Martin Dies] See note 331.21.

491.22     Uncle Remus,] Animal tales of African-American folklore, popularized by Joel Chandler Harris in *Uncle Remus: His Songs and Sayings* (1881) and other books.

491.22     Paul Robeson] African-American singer and political activist (1898–1976).

491.27–28     Norman Thomas . . . Gompers,] Norman Thomas (1884–1968), six-time presidential candidate of the Socialist Party of America; Dwight Macdonald (1906–1982), leftist writer and social critic, editor of *Politics* from 1943 to 1949; Harry Bridges (1901–1990), Australian-born American labor leader; Samuel Gompers (1850–1924), leader of the American Federation of Labor (AFL).

492.1–2     Alger Hiss . . . spy] Alger Hiss (1904–1996) held several positions in the administration of Franklin D. Roosevelt and began working for the State Department in 1936. He was accused by Whittaker Chambers, a former communist, of having been a communist infiltrator. Hiss sued Chambers for slander, and in grand jury testimony denied Chambers' charges that he had transmitted secret documents to the Soviet Union; he was then indicted for perjury, and after two trials was convicted, serving 44 months of a five-year sentence. Hiss continued to maintain that the charges against him were false.

492.4     Roy Cohn] New York attorney (1927–1986) known for his zealous anti-communism. He served as counsel for the U.S. Senate committee headed by Senator Joseph McCarthy that in 1954 investigated alleged communist infiltration of the Army.

494.27      gribben]   An Americanization of *gribenes* (Yiddish): deep-fried chicken or goose skin.

519.28      "Abandon . . . Here."]   Inscription over the entrance to hell in Dante's *Inferno*.

525.22   Malinowski]   Bronislaw Malinowski, Polish-born anthropologist (1884–1942).

537.4–6      that exploring . . . Flaubert.]   Richard Byrd (1888–1957) made five expeditions to Antarctica; it took Flaubert five years to write *Madame Bovary*.

538.15–17      "Be regular . . . work."]   From Flaubert's letter to Gertrude Tennant, December 25, 1876.

538.25      gone off . . . the Nile,]   Flaubert traveled to Egypt with his friend Maxime du Camp in 1849.

539.11–12      "I am . . . still,"]   Defiant line spoken by the imprisoned duchess in John Webster's play *The Duchess of Malfi* (1614).

541.24      "Lycidas."]   Elegy (1638) by John Milton.

546.20–21      Kenneth Patchen's"]   American poet (1911–1972) whose works include *First Will and Testament* (1939) and *The Journal of Albion Moonlight* (1941).

546.31      George F. Babbitt of Zenith]   Conformist businessman who is the title character of Sinclair Lewis's novel *Babbitt* (1922), set in the fictional city of Zenith.

551.29      lions to Hemingway."]   Hemingway described hunting lions on an East African safari in *Green Hills of Africa* (1935).

554.14      a play . . . Hardy,]   In Strindberg's play *The Father* (1887), the wife of a cavalry captain is tormented by doubts about the paternity of his child; in Hardy's novel *The Mayor of Casterbridge* (1886), the title character learns that the woman he thought was his biological daughter was in fact fathered by another man.

555.14–19      Thomas Mann . . . our youth."]   From Mann's *A Sketch of My Life* (1930). The same passage serves as the epigraph for Roth's novel *Letting Go* (1962).

555.23–24      Lord Jim . . . Karamazov]   Central characters in Joseph Conrad's *Lord Jim* (1900), Henry James' *The Wings of the Dove* (1902), and Fyodor Dostoevsky's *The Brothers Karamazov* (1879–80).

559.24    *I Want to Live,*] Film (1958) directed by Robert Wise, based on the life of Barbara Graham, a woman convicted of murder and executed in 1955.

564.2–5    Dr. Roger Chillingworth . . . Dimmesdale.] See note 41.35.

564.40    opening sentence of *Anna Karenina*] "Happy families are all alike; every unhappy family is unhappy in its own way."

567.28–29    Rudolph Hess . . . Spandau Prison,] One of Hitler's chief deputies, Rudolph Hess (1894–1987) was convicted of war crimes at Nuremberg in 1947 and spent the remainder of his life in Berlin's Spandau Prison, after 1966 its lone inmate.

570.17    Dagwood . . . trembling!"] Dagwood Bumstead is a character in the *Blondie* comic strip. Søren Kierkegaard's philosophical tract *Fear and Trembling* (1843) is a series of meditations on the biblical story of Isaac's near-sacrifice by Abraham.

573.10    Clytemnestra?] See note 34.7.

582.24    Ernst Kris] Psychoanalyst and art historian (1900–1957), author of *Psychoanalytic Explorations in Art* (1952).

584.31–32    *On ne . . . se raconter.*] "One can never know oneself, only tell about oneself." From de Beauvoir's autobiography *La Force de l'âge* (1960), published in English translation as *The Prime of Life* in 1965.

586.1    "the objective correlative"] See note 402.30.

586.36    AAUP] American Association of University Professors.

586.40–41    what they did to Abelard] The French theologian Pierre Abélard (1079–1142) fell in love with his pupil Héloïse, and the couple conceived a child together. At the instigation of Héloïse's uncle, Abélard was castrated.

587.16–17    maybe I'm . . . shouldn't,] In a letter to Louise Colet, April 22, 1854.

587.20–21    Henry Miller . . . Céline] Henry Miller (1891–1980), author of sexually explicit books such as *Tropic of Cancer* (1934) and *Tropic of Capricorn* (1939); Louis-Ferdinand Céline (1894–1961), French novelist, author of *Journey to the End of the Night* (1932).

587.38    Johnny Carson] Host of the NBC television program "The Tonight Show" beginning in 1962.

588.19    *Commentary*] Monthly magazine published by the American Jewish Committee.

588.23 "David Susskind Show"?] Syndicated television talk show that ran from 1958 (when it was called "Open End") to 1986.

588.27 "Virtue! . . . thus."] Cf. Iago in Shakespeare's *Othello*, I.iii.48.

588.38 unbuttoning . . . Genet] French novelist, playwright, and activist (1910–1986) whose early career as a petty criminal and prostitute was the basis for books such as *The Miracle of the Rose* (1946) and *The Thief's Journal* (1949).

591.6–7 Kleist's *Michael Kohlhaas*] Novella (1810) by German writer Heinrich von Kleist, recounting a horse trader's campaign of violence against a local nobleman after his horses are confiscated.

593.21–22 *A Tale of a Tub . . . Henry Esmond.*] Works by Jonathan Swift and William Makepeace Thackeray.

595.15 not one of them *juste.*] Flaubert's dictum as a writer was to find "le mot juste" (the precise word).

598.19–20 like Desdemona to Othello] See *Othello*, I.iii.140–182, in which Othello tells of how Desdemona would "with a greedy ear / Devour up" the stories of his travels and adventures.

610.18 'Let me shun that,'] *King Lear*, III.iv.21.

614.14 Pygmalion . . . Galatea] In Ovid's *Metamorphoses*, Pygmalion creates an ivory sculpture of a beautiful woman known as Galatea, who comes to life.

623.22–23 police dogs . . . demonstrators] Widely publicized nonviolent protests in Alabama organized by Martin Luther King's Southern Christian Leadership Conference (SCLC) were disrupted by vicious police tactics, including the use of water cannons and attacks by police dogs.

623.25 Medgar Evers] Civil-rights activist Medgar Evers (1925–1963) was murdered outside his home by a white supremacist on June 11, 1963.

624.4 Blondie . . . Jiggs] Comic-strip characters: Blondie and Dagwood from *Blondie*, and Maggie and Jiggs from *Bringing Up Father*.

624.7 Birmingham Church bombing] On September 15, 1963, a bomb exploded during Sunday school hour at the Sixteenth Street Baptist Church in Birmingham, Alabama; four girls were killed and 14 other persons wounded by the blast. The church had been a gathering place for schoolchildren participating in nonviolent civil-rights demonstrations that spring.

626.2 Humphrey . . . Israel.] Minnesota senator Hubert Humphrey (1911–1978), who ran for the Democratic nomination in 1960, was a strong supporter of Israel.

626.39    Santo Domingo,]  After an attempted coup in the Dominican Republic in April 1965, President Johnson sent troops to evacuate Americans and other foreigners, and to intervene in the fighting that continued through the summer.

627.4    Reverend Coffin]  William Sloane Coffin (1924–2006), chaplain of Yale University from 1958 to 1975, was a frequent speaker at antiwar rallies during the Vietnam War.

627.8    Dr. Spock."]  American pediatrician and political activist Benjamin Spock (1903–1998), author of the bestselling *Baby and Child Care* (1946), was an outspoken opponent of the Vietnam War.

627.15    Tokyo Rose]  See note 222.38.

628.19    Little Lord Fauntleroy]  Hero of Frances Hodgson Burnett's children's book (1886) about an American boy who discovers he is the heir to an earldom in England; the character became a byword for coddled, over-privileged boys.

640.20–21    Gene Kelly . . . Away,"]  In the movie *Cover Girl* (1944), Rita Hayworth and Gene Kelly sing the song "Long Ago (and Far Away)," with music by Jerome Kern and lyrics by Ira Gershwin.

640.24–25    my kingdom by the sea.]  Repeated phrase in Edgar Allan Poe's poem "Annabel Lee" (1849)

646.30    Isak Dinesen?]  Pen name of Karen Blixen, Danish writer (1885–1962).

647.31    *Tender Is the Night*?]  Novel (1934) by F. Scott Fitzgerald.

647.31    Krafft-Ebing?]  German psychiatrist (1840–1902), best known for his book *Psychopathia Sexualis* (1886), a study of sexual perversity.

655.1    Huntley-Brinkley]  *The Huntley-Brinkley Report*, NBC television's national news program, which ran from 1956 to 1970.

655.14    Fortinbras]  Norwegian prince in Shakespeare's *Hamlet*, who assumes the throne of Denmark at the end of the play.

657.31–32    'From each . . . need.']  See note 328.17–18.

659.9–10    The Golden Bowl.]  See note 35.10–12.

662.8    Cisco Kid,]  Mexican bandit featured in comic strips, on the radio, and in movies such as *In Old Arizona* (1928) and *The Gay Caballero* (1940).

669.11    "Dixie Dugan."]  Long-running comic strip by J. P. McEvoy and John H. Striebel.

671.24–27    Temple . . . corncob.]  In William Faulkner's novel *Sanctuary* (1931), the impotent criminal Popeye rapes Temple Drake, the daughter of a prominent judge, with a corncob.

THE PROFESSOR OF DESIRE

681.18    Cugat . . . Krupa]  Xavier Cugat (1900–1990), Spanish-born bandleader who helped popularize Cuban dance music in the United States. Big-band drummer Gene Krupa (1909–1973) played with the Benny Goodman Orchestra from 1934 to 1938 and then founded his own band.

681.19    Danny Kaye,"]  Jewish comedian and entertainer (1913–1987), born David Daniel Kaminsky.

681.22    Tony Martin."]  Stage name of Jewish singer and actor Alvin Morris (b. 1912).

682.35    Aquacade]  "Aquacade," staged for the 1939 World's Fair, featured former Olympic swimmer Eleanor Holm as well as actors Johnny Weismuller and Esther Williams.

683.2    tallis]  Hebrew: Jewish prayer shawl.

683.14    Berchtesgaden]  Adolf Hitler's Bavarian mountain villa.

683.34    shlimazel]  Yiddish: An extremely unlucky person.

683.36    Ripley's,"]  *Ripley's Believe It or Not*, syndicated newspaper comic feature concerned with unusual and bizarre facts.

686.4    tragical-comical-historical-pastoral]  Phrase of Polonius in *Hamlet*, II.ii.365.

686.18    Tiresias]  Blind seer in Sophocles' *Oedipus Rex*.

687.10    *I and Thou* . . . tales,]  Martin Buber (1878–1965) popularized Hasidism in *Tales of Rabbi Nachman of Breslov* (1906) and *Legends of the Bal Shem Tov* (1908). In 1923, the philosophical work *I and Thou* established his international reputation.

687.19    *Finian's Rainbow*]  1947 Broadway musical with music by Burton Land and lyrics by E. Y. Harburg; a film version was released in 1968.

688.19–20    *ballagula*]  Yiddish: Wagon-driver; thus, a person of low social standing.

688.20    *shtunk*]  Yiddish: A stinker, an unpleasant person.

688.33    *rugalech*,]  Yiddish: a small rolled pastry generally made with a cream-cheese dough and filled with raisins, nuts, poppy-seed paste, or jam.

691.15–16    his description . . . Steele,] From an 1843 review of Lucy Aikin's *Life and Writings of Addison* by the English historian Thomas Babington, Lord Macaulay (1800–1859).

691.21–24    seduce . . . *Either/Or.*] One of the sections of Søren Kierkegaard's *Either/Or: A Fragment of Life* (1843) is the fictional "The Diary of a Seducer."

694.35    Lord Fauntleroy] See note 628.19.

696.17–19    "See! . . . cheek."] *Romeo and Juliet*, II.ii.23–25.

697.35    Johannes the Seducer] Kierkegaard's pseudonym in "The Diary of a Seducer," in which he writes: "To poeticize oneself into a young girl is an art; to poeticize oneself out of her is a masterpiece."

699.12–13    dying like Maupassant] The French writer Guy de Maupassant (1853–1893) went mad and died as the result of the syphilis he contracted as a young man.

699.24–25    before . . . *Ulysses*,] James Joyce's novel was published in 1922.

699.33    paperback . . . Trevelyan] English historian George Macauley Trevelyan (1876–1962) was the author of a history of England, published in three paperback volumes by Anchor Books.

702.40    kenning,] A conventional figurative expression used in place of a simple term.

704.30    Raskolnikovian sojourns] In Dostoevsky's *Crime and Punishment* (1866), a feverish Raskolnikov takes long walks through St. Petersburg.

704.31    Pudd'nhead Wilson] In Mark Twain's novel *The Tragedy of Pudd'nhead Wilson and the Comedy of Those Extraordinary Twins* (1894), the lawyer who reveals a long-concealed crime.

706.32–33    Mrs. Browning,] In Elizabeth Barrett Browning's *Sonnets from the Portuguese* (1850), sonnet 49, "How do I love thee? Let me count the ways."

708.25    *Arthurian . . . Troyes*] Study (1949) by medievalist Roger Sherman Loomis (1887–1966).

710.3    Eddas] Icelandic sagas.

713.23–24    Bastille . . . punished] The Marquis de Sade was imprisoned at the Bastille in Paris from February 1784 to July 4, 1789.

713.34    *"Salaud!" . . . con!"*] "Bastard!" . . . "Bitch!"

714.12    Fulbright]   Federal program awarding grants for Americans to study abroad and for foreign nationals to study in the United States, named for Arkansas senator J. William Fulbright (1905–1995).

722.4    Vronsky,]   Anna's lover in Tolstoy's *Anna Karenina* (1875).

722.6    Karenin,]   The aristocratic husband in *Anna Karenina.*

722.13–14    *The Ambassadors,"*]   See note 35.10–12.

722.15    Brett]   Lady Brett Ashley in Ernest Hemingway's *The Sun Also Rises* (1926).

729.10–11    the dawn . . . thunder—"]   See Rudyard Kipling, "Mandalay" (1892): "On the Road to Mandalay / Where the flyin' fishes play, / An' the dawn comes up like thunder outer China 'crost the Bay!"

736.28    Prince Ivan . . . *Firebird*]   Hero of ballet (1910) performed by Diaghilev's Ballets Russes, with music by Igor Stravinsky.

740.34    Albert Schweitzer."]   Physician, theologian, and musician Albert Schweitzer (1875–1965) founded a hospital in Lambaréné (in present-day Gabon, Africa) and spent most of his life working there. He was awarded the Nobel Peace Prize in 1952. He became an emblem of humanitarian values.

746.20–21    somebody . . . Browning?]   See Robert Browning's poem "Porphyria's Lover" (1836).

750.15    the opiate . . . classes."]   Cf. Karl Marx in *Critique of the Hegelian Philosophy of Right* (1844): "Religion . . . is the opium of the people."

761.16    Norman Thomas]   See note 491.27–28.

761.17–18    Henry Wallace]   Henry A. Wallace (1888–1965) served as Secretary of Agriculture (1933–49) in Roosevelt's cabinet and as Vice-President (1941–45). He was the Progressive candidate for President in 1948.

769.29–30    James . . . dramatize.']   In a preface written for the New York Edition of his novels, James recalls having written "Dramatize, dramatize" in a note to himself when he first heard the anecdote that he would transform into the novella *Daisy Miller*, first published in 1878.

776.20    François Mauriac.]   French novelist, playwright, and essayist (1885–1970), winner of the Nobel Prize in Literature in 1952.

778.17–18    poem . . . *Below*.]   See John Donne's "Elegy XIX: To His Mistress Going to Bed": "License my roving hands, and let them go, / Before, behind, between, above, below."

779.18    *menschlichkeit*.]   Humanity.

779.23      Synge.]   Irish playwright J. M. Synge (1871–1909), author of *The Playboy of the Western World* (1907).

779.25–26      "A Rose for Emily."]   William Faulkner's short story (1930) about a woman who sleeps with her lover's corpse.

779.38      Céline. Or Genet.]   See notes 587.20–21 and 588.38.

780.19–22      Brandeis . . . neckerchiefs."]   Brandeis University, which bestows an annual Creative Arts Award, is here sarcastically conflated with the comic NBC radio and television game show "Kollege of Musical Knowledge," hosted by bandleader Kay Kyser.

780.23      Meyer Lansky]   Russian-born American gangster who organized a national crime syndicate in the 1930s.

782.6–7      East River . . . villages.]   Kips Bay Plaza, completed in 1963, designed by architect I. M. Pei (b. 1917).

792.31      Herzogian helplessness]   Saul Bellow's *Herzog* (1964) tells the story of a man whose life is plunged into a crisis after he is cuckolded by his best friend.

794.29–30      softest . . . world,"]   From *Death in Venice* (1912), as von Aschenbach reflects on the "coffin-black" gondola that evokes "visions of death itself, the bier and solemn rites and last soundless voyage."

799.11      Max Brod's biography,]   Writer Max Brod (1884–1968), Kafka's close friend and literary executor, wrote the biography *Franz Kafka: A Life* (1937).

799.12      Milena]   Czech writer Milena Jesenská (1896–1944), who began corresponding with Kafka after asking if she could translate a story of his from German to Czech. Their relationship was almost entirely epistolary, and ended when she refused to leave her husband for him.

801.33      ˙samizdat]   Clandestine publication and circulation of manuscripts in the Soviet Union and Soviet-bloc countries.

801.38      K. to their Castle]   The protagonist of Kafka's novel *The Castle* (1926) is known only as "K." Joseph K., protagonist of *The Trial* (1925), is also usually referred to simply as "K."

807.10–11      Franz Werfel.]   Novelist, poet, and playwright (1890–1945), best known for his novel *The Song of Bernadette* (1941).

807.11      Oskar Baum.]   Novelist, critic, and musician (1883–1943), author of the novel *Life in Darkness* (1908). A friend of Kafka and Max Brod, he lived in Prague from 1902 to 1940.

808.35      Mishima,]   Japanese writer Yukio Mishima (1925–1970).

808.35    Gombrowicz,]   Polish writer Witold Gombrowicz (1904–1969) whose novels include *Ferdydurke* (1937).

809.35    Jan Hus]   Czech religious reformer (1369?–1415) condemned to death as a heretic and burned at the stake.

814.34    whore . . . visit?"]   Kafka is commonly believed to have been extremely fastidious in sexual matters and to have had little, if any, experience with prostitutes.

815.20    *piscine*]   French: pool.

820.27–29    Japanese . . . empire,]   General Douglas MacArthur presided over the formal Japanese surrender on the U.S.S. *Missouri* on September 2, 1945.

824.38–39    "these pleasures . . . physical"]   From Colette's *Ces Plaisirs* (*Those Pleasures,* 1932), published in English translation as *The Pure and the Impure.*

825.14    Musil's *Young Törless,*]   The first novel (1906) by the Austrian writer Robert Musil (1880–1942).

831.33    'Lo, this . . . desire.']   See Algernon Charles Swinburne's poem to Venus, "Laus Veneris" (1866), line 9: "Lo, this is she that was the world's delight."

844.10–11    Suzie Wong.]   In the film *The World of Suzie Wong* (1960), a beautiful young Chinese woman (played by Nancy Kwan) falls in love with an American (played by William Holden) in Hong Kong.

849.6    George Wallace.]   Segregationist politician (1919–1998), longtime governor of Alabama and four-time presidential candidate.

854.7    Walter Cronkite,]   Journalist (b. 1916), anchorman of the *CBS Evening News* from 1962 to 1981.

855.16    Hugh Hefner"]   Founder and editor-in-chief (b. 1926) of *Playboy* magazine.

857.25    *paskudnyak*]   Yiddish: a nasty, mean, or odious person.

860.3–4    Chekhov's . . . him.]   Cf. *The Seagull* (1896), Act I, when Dr. Dorn announces, "An angel of silence is flying over our heads."

*Library of Congress Cataloging-in-Publication Data*

Roth, Philip.
  [Selections. 2006]
  Novels, 1973–1977 / Philip Roth.
      p. cm. — (The Library of America ; 165)
  Includes bibliographical references.
  Contents: The great American novel—My life as a man—The
professor of desire.
    ISBN 978-1-931082-96-9
    ISBN 1-931082-96-0 (alk. paper)
    I. Title: Novels, 1973–1977. II. The great American novel.
III. My life as a man. IV. The professor of desire. V. Series.

PS3568.O855A6   2006
813'.54—dc22                                    2006041030

# THE LIBRARY OF AMERICA SERIES

The Library of America fosters appreciation and pride in America's literary heritage by publishing, and keeping permanently in print, authoritative editions of America's best and most significant writing. An independent nonprofit organization, it was founded in 1979 with seed money from the National Endowment for the Humanities and the Ford Foundation.

*This book is set in 10 point Linotron Galliard,*
*a face designed for photocomposition by Matthew Carter*
*and based on the sixteenth-century face Granjon. The paper*
*is acid-free Domtar Literary Opaque and meets the requirements*
*for permanence of the American National Standards Institute. The*
*binding material is Brillianta, a woven rayon cloth made by*
*Van Heek-Scholco Textielfabrieken, Holland. Compo-*
*sition by Dedicated Business Services. Printing by*
*Malloy Incorporated. Binding by Dekker Book-*
*binding. Designed by Bruce Campbell.*

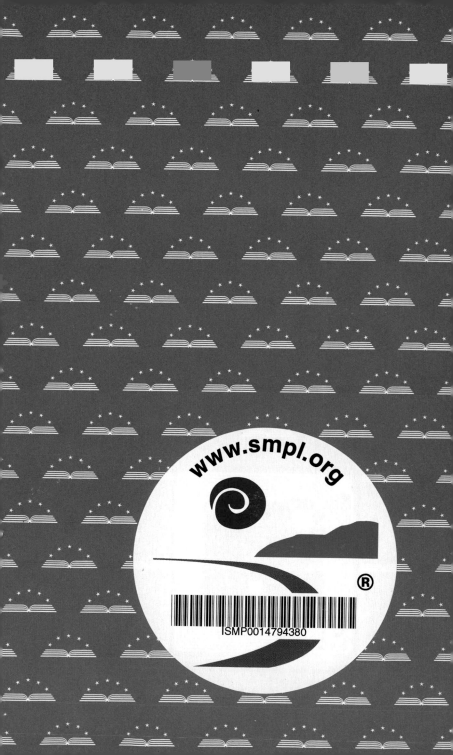